"No one will have █████████████ said. "Would you?"

"Francie, I am almost old enough to be your father," Jamie said.

"No," she answered. "It's not that. You won't have me. I'm only beautiful. But that's a dime a dozen. I have nothing to offer." She wished to please him, but she knew what she was about, and stuck to her point. "Oh, I'm a good 'lay.' You would agree with that, wouldn't you?" She laughed nervously. "Only I am what I am, and that doesn't seem to be marriageable." She said this with a grim straightness, as she let the robe that had been wrapped around her slide toward the floor. Now she stood before him naked, her whole body delicately rounded and luminous in the dawn light. She looked at him with a soft, lustful glance that acknowledged the passion that had grown between them. It was she who moved toward him lifting her mouth up to be kissed.

He kissed her then, his two hands on her breasts; and she felt the fury of his spirit run through her. She thought for a second that what she wanted to do was escape—escape his hands. His mouth. She was breathless with fear and desire, and she surrendered her will to his, sinking into a dreamlike oblivion of pleasure.

Darling, No Regrets

Davidyne Saxon Mayleas

WARNER BOOKS

A Warner Communications Company

What follows is a work of fiction. All of the characters are make-believe. Any resemblance to the Leo Burnett advertising agency is purely coincidental, and intended with loving pride. But I would particularly like to extend my thanks to the Green Giant, Snap, Crackle, Pop and the Marlboro Man, all of whom contributed so much to my education. And my deepest thanks to the many ghosts, who, on nights before presentations, still haunt the art department and the offices of copywriters, waiting for the campaign to shape-up.

I would also like to thank my editor, Bernard Shir-Cliff, a man of taste and wit. His sense of style and structure, his skills as an editor, taught me how invaluable the contribution of an editor can be.

to those I love. . . .
alive and otherwise

Your memory I buy at any price,
A wild heart never forgets
The heat of remembered kisses
. . . darling, no regrets.

—ALISON COCKBURN
(1712–1794)

Contents

Darling, No Regrets

PART I
A Daughter of Lillith
(1954—1959)

Of Adam's first wife, Lillith,
  It is told
Her enchanted hair was
  Earth's first gold.

—Dante Gabriel Rossetti

1

Where was she going to sleep? That was the question.

She stood outside the bus terminal, dazed; a nonviolent summer hung over the city. On the streets, human beings surged around her; the crowds gushed and spurted with laughter and spite and passions of all kinds.

Well, it certainly wasn't Davenport, thank heavens. Though here and there the streets did have some people who looked distantly related to Iowa. You could see silos and corn land in their faces. But there were other faces. Different shapes and sizes holding histories she couldn't decipher. In her life she'd never seen so many people as jostled and pushed and shoved each other on Eighth Avenue. The idea of that much humanity hit her like a blow to the head.

Franciejean Stewart is my name; she felt like saying it in protest. But to whom? She didn't know a soul. Not then. Not that hot August night a thousand years ago, 1954, when she got off the Greyhound bus at the midtown terminal. It had been a long ride. A fateful ride. By God and by grace she had not gotten carsick or whoopsed on her dress. She had had only one bad dream; on balance, she was pleased with herself. She had made the right decision. No matter what her friend Claire said about the soot and the dirt, the rape and the thieving that goes on in New York, she was glad she had come.

But where was she going to sleep? "Hello doll," a bald man mumbled in her ear. But she gave him a severe look. She was used to that, and besides he looked too old. Now if it had been that cute young guy over there with the gold telephone.

17

In between looking for a cab, he'd been staring at her. What did he want with that old-fashioned telephone? Pure foolishness, even in gold. Aunt Gert had one just like it in her kitchen back home. In black. There he was staring at her again. She would stare back and smile a little. That was how you did it. But her smile came too late. Unexpectedly Mr. Gold Telephone hurtled past her, racing for a cab. Just as well, she told herself comfortingly. He wasn't really that good-looking. And when you don't know a man, you're always taking a chance. No telling what men were like in New York. Where was she going to sleep?

Where tonight? And where tomorrow night? And all summer if the company was congenial. She half smiled at her own bravado. The question was, would anyone have her—anyone at all—now that it was time to ask that question.

And what about Momma? What would Momma say? What a dope I am, she thought, a damn fool. She studied the man's house? If she happened to end up with a man? She didn't think Momma would like it that much. But then it was quite possible Momma hadn't followed her to New York. She hadn't noticed her on the bus.

Francie rummaged around in her purse and pulled out the list of names and telephone numbers she'd started exactly two years ago for exactly this historic moment. Now where was it? Had she left the damn thing in Davenport? Or lost it when she took out the money to buy a coke? She started to perspire. She stooped down to dump the contents of the purse on the terminal floor when her frightened fingers found the precious crumpled paper wedged into her sunglass case. She breathed in carefully, straightened up and looked around. What a dope I am, she thought, a damn fool. She studied the list with fear and hope. The names had been collected in a haphazard fashion over the last two years, just in case. But she never said, in case what? In case she decided to write someone. Fat chance! In case she decided to visit—hmmm—getting warmer. Finally last week she knew what for—it was in case she decided to leave Davenport and never come back. Never. Never for the rest of her life. Aunt Gert wouldn't mind at all, no ma'am. Not at all. Not even a little smidgen of a bit of minding. It might even take her a month or two to notice that Francie was gone.

Now who first should she risk telephoning? Well, why not start being disappointed at the top? So she dialed Ronnie Jackson, that beautiful man whom she'd met two summers ago when he visited his folks in Davenport. He was an actor, and from her small experience of actors, she was willing to generalize: when they were not absolute rats, they were a hell of a lot nicer than ordinary folk. But after sixteen rings she finally gave up on Ronnie.

Then she called Angie Hertwig, her girl friend. If there was such a thing as a girl friend, Angie could qualify. They used to make cold cream in the basement of Angie's home and sell it to the local drugstore. The girl who answered the phone said Angie was in Texas. Then fat Barry Blue with the dentures in a glass who commuted around the Midwest. He owned a chain of laundromats and had given Francie a free pass to all of them. Which she had never used or mentioned to Aunt Gert because she did not want to hear Aunt Gert's opinion of Barry. But Barry's message service said he was out of town till the eighth. Probably in Davenport—poor Barry. And Leo Flynn's phone was disconnected. And Monroe Perl had a busy signal . . . oh! Monroe was home.

Francie slammed the receiver down and stood there trembling. A busy signal meant he was home. Okay, if he was home and she telephoned him, he could always say "no," couldn't he? He could. But if she got over there . . . She dashed out of the station, lugging her heavy white Samsonite luggage looking for a cab. This would be the fifth time in her life she'd taken a cab. As soon as she'd taken ten, she'd stop counting. Getting into the cab gave her the feeling of being a visiting French actress. Her mother was German but her father had French blood. Besides Scottish. She would rather be French than Italian. Unless she was a man. That was a different matter.

She had the impression that the cab driver thought she looked spiffy; if he had picked her up at an airport instead of a bus terminal, he might have thought she was "somebody." She hoped she looked that nice. Nice enough for Monroe to put her up at least one night. Maybe longer.

The ride up to Monroe's home was a big swallow. The city was intimidating. Tall buildings flanked taller buildings. And then bango! Seamy, slumlike buildings with garbage and

19

people spilling out all over. It should have looked ugly, but it didn't. The lights and the cars and the garbage and the people gave the city an air of tipsy carnival.

Monroe's building on East Eighty-third Street and Third Avenue was another gasp. After getting out of her fifth cab and tipping the driver, Francie thought about getting back into the cab. There must be a drugstore where she could make another telephone call. But the cab was gone. And what would she do if nobody was home after she made her last telephone call? Where would she go? Even the YWCA cost money.

That decided it. She went into Monroe's building and instantly became ice-cold with goose bumps all over. Was she that scared? Then she realized it was the air conditioning that numbed you. The lobby had a fat doorman and a big circular couch that looked as if nobody ever sat on it. Some kind of naked metal woman was sleeping on the sand behind the couch. The shiny self-service elevator zoomed to Monroe on the fifteenth floor while luxury oozed from its aluminum pores, and Francie's confidence in her Frenchiness faded with every passing floor. By the time she reached fifteen it was entirely gone.

Monroe's apartment was at the end of a long corridor of matching doors that made Francie think of a comfortable Death Row. More comfortable certainly than the one Uncle Jack had settled into. Monroe's door, according to the doorman, was 15 K. K for "Kid, you'll wear diamonds." Francie rang the bell three times. At the end of ring number three the door was opened by a woman. Not a girl. Not an old woman. Or a middle-aged woman. A young woman. But not a girl. At least thirty years old. Maybe older. In a silky-looking green thing to the floor. Francie had the wobbly feeling of slipping on ice. She had not been quite able to powder out the faint blue love bite on her throat that Wesley had given her as a farewell token, and she was sure this not-a-girl could see it. She looked like she could see everything—the safety pin holding Francie's slip to its strap; the garter belt and no panties; everything. Jesus!

"Is this where Monroe Perl lives?" she finally asked.

"Must be. My key worked." Francie stared at the woman. She could have kicked herself for letting Monroe fool her. He had sworn up and down and crossed his heart that being married was not the case with him. It simply proved again, as if she had ever doubted it, that men lie. As much as lay. So here she was in Monroe's doorway with his wife looking at her as though she was on sale in a junk shop.

"Well, what is it?" asked Mrs. Perl impatiently.

Francie fidgeted. She hated getting trapped mucking around with a married man. It was not morality. It was her idea of rank amateurism. Married men were okay for a meal and sex. A bottle of perfume. Or money for a new dress. But that was it. If the wife found out, you could get yourself killed. She knew one girl who was suspiciously hit by a car.

"What do you want?" Mrs. Perl pressed.

Yes, what do I want? Francie fidgeted some more. Fine. What do I say now? How do you do, Mrs. Perl. It's a pleasure to meet you. Your husband is a pretty fancy fucker, isn't he? He can do it every which way, and four times a night when he gets himself lathered up. So I thought maybe we'd do a little shacking up tonight since I'm in the mood, and I happen to be in town. "I believe I have the wrong apartment."

"If you're looking for Monroe Perl, you have the right apartment."

"Oh. Is he in then?"

"No." A question mark hovered in her voice.

"Well, then I'm sorry to bother you, Mrs. Perl." Francie started to turn.

"I'm not Mrs. Perl. I'm Mrs. Ring."

"Oh, Mrs. Ring." Well that changed things a bit. "How do you do." Francie turned back.

"How do you do." Isabelle Ring studied Francie in her white French starlet dress with her white starlet suitcase. If she had not learned from her psychiatrist that snobbery was insecurity turned inside out, she might have felt snobbish. But since she had passed that infantile stage of immaturity, she decided to be courteous. Then too, she was unnerved at finding the vividly pretty half child in Monroe's life. "I'll tell Monroe you stopped by. What's your name?" She asked the question with the air of authority women of money assume with the obviously indigent.

"Elloweise Schmerhorn."

"Elloweise Schmerhorn? That's a very interesting name."

"Elloweise was my grandmother's name. On my moth-

21

er's side. They named me after her so that she'd put me in her will. She did. She left me her sewing machine."

"Did she? I'm glad you got the sewing machine." Isabelle could no longer contain herself: "Monroe never mentioned you. Are you a secret side of his life?"

Francie didn't understand the secret idea so she answered matter of factly. "I'm a friend from Davenport. In Iowa."

"It's still there? I'm glad some things don't change." Isabelle Ring smoothed her hair that was shorter and less seductive than Francie's. And patted her robe that cost more money than one could get for selling Francie on the slave block in Morocco.

"Well, I guess I better be going."

"I think so." Isabelle's voice was precise and unmarked by any range of emphasis showing suspicion or interest. Nevertheless she was shaken.

Wearily Francie picked up the white starlet suitcase that was far heavier than she remembered and turned to go down the corridor. As she did, the elevator door opened; and out stepped Monroe Perl, halloing both of them and lugging his satchel of tennis things: "Hey, Isabelle! I've been trying to reach you all day. Glad you got here first. Who's your friend?" Then as he drew nearer his face dropped the fifteen floors to the ground. "Good God! Franciejean! What are you doing in New York?" He looked around distractedly like a man searching for a fire exit. Then realizing there was no escape, he decided to try to luck his way through. "Isabelle, this is Franciejean Stewart. We met in Davenport."

"I know. We introduced ourselves. She told me her name was Elloweise Schmerhorn." Her voice was full of contempt.

Francie stood wary. All women were her enemies, and she disliked being caught by one in a lie. "I don't know you. Why should I tell you my real name?"

"She's younger than Sybil Hoffman. She's young enough to be your daughter." Isabelle's voice carried more moral indignation than she actually felt. What she felt was surprise at her own jealousy. Sybil Hoffman was a joke she liked to torture Monroe with. But this girl with her cloud of white-Saxon blond hair was something else. The color of the hair was natural. And there was a vitality in the young slender body that shone through the ridiculous clothes and the clumsy

22

makeup. The girl was beautiful in spite of her amateur efforts to make herself more so.

"How old are you Elloweise/Francie?" she asked.

"Eighteen. Today's my birthday."

"Monroe, you're turning into a dirty old man. At least Dad doesn't collect teenagers."

"Isabelle, not now! Let's keep all name-calling for our private entertainments." Monroe was outraged by the accusation, which was both accurate and below the belt.

"Elloweise/Francie, did you come to New York to spend your birthday with Monroe?"

"No." Francie was poised for flight, fight or compromise. "I came because my whole future is in New York. That is, it is for a girl who expects to make a career as a model. Which I do."

"And Monroe's going to subsidize your schooling?"

"I am not! She's a kid I met on one of my Midwest trips. To see the Cowles people. You're deliberately misreading this situation in order to pick a fight."

"A girl arrives from Davenport, Iowa, with a suitcase. And she comes straight here to wash up. As a lawyer, wouldn't you say she knows where her friends are?"

"I didn't know she was coming. I had no idea."

No, he didn't know she was coming, but infected with a desire to see them really go at each other, Francie decided to say nothing. She enjoyed the taste of blood—since it wasn't yet her own.

"Did he or didn't he know you were coming?" Isabelle asked.

"When I got to the bus terminal in New York, I had to get some advice on where to stay, so I came here."

"Where to stay?" Isabelle forgot her original question. "You mean besides here with Monroe? Glorious. Let's go inside and have a birthday drink and decide where you should stay. Besides here with Monroe." Isabelle hated this minor personage who, by a simple trick of biologic composition—hair, skin, bones—had shaken all Isabelle's entrenched feelings of superiority. Isabelle's adored father had once said, in that casual tone that concealed his most significant opinions, that great beauty in a woman was a merciless asset. He said it with the frank implication that Isabelle did not have it. At the time this only mildly troubled Isabelle, who, after all, was

23

her father's daughter and as such needed no further accomplishments. But now she understood the warning. Looking at Francie and matching herself against her, woman to woman, Isabelle knew that in open contest she didn't have a chance.

"Monroe, take her suitcase. We can't stand here in the hall and discuss your sex life."

Monroe did as he was told, feeling a mixture of shameful guilt and sheepish pride at this visible evidence of his sexual prowess—even at forty.

Francie followed Monroe and Isabelle into the apartment, played upon by a feverish curiosity to begin her sight-seeing tour of how New Yorkers lived. How they ate, slept, made love, brushed their teeth, washed their hair. She was an insatiable voyeur.

Once inside the big room with the bigger view of the traffic, the muggings, the Con Ed drills of New York, she entered a state akin to religious ecstasy. Sodden with dreams of New York life, a mishmash of magazine photos, movie sets and improvised fantasies, she moved now like a happy sleepwalker among the proof of her own dreams. Forgetting completely that she had warned herself not to gawk like a ninny country kid, here she was staring, gaping, gawking at everything. She reverently admired a zebra-striped couch. Just like the one she had seen in a love magazine with the two half-naked girls sitting on it. She wondered how she'd look sitting on it half-naked. Spiffy as any of those girls, even if she wasn't that busty. Yes, sir, that's my baby. And there was a glass chair—crazy daisy! Glass was to drink beer out of, not to sit on. She heard Monroe's voice far away and distorted as though it was a bad telephone connection.

"Sit down, Francie, for God's sake! What do you want to drink?"

"Beer? Or Pepsi, please. Is this a chair? Can I sit on it?"

"Of course. It's plastic. Sit on it," said Isabelle. "It's nouveau Jewish. As opposed to oldveau Jewish. One is vulgar, the other drab. But one has to sit on something."

"You never said you didn't like my chair. You were there when I bought it!" Monroe felt a sudden protesting knot in his stomach at Isabelle's scorn.

"Since I don't have to live with that chair, I don't have

to save you from your mistakes. You have to make them, it's the only way to learn." She could not contain her fury with this girl in the room. Something had to happen. "Now excuse me. I have to slip into something less comfortable."

Left alone, the dignified social distance maintained by Francie and Monroe was abruptly canceled by a truer-textured intimacy forged in another place.

"What did you tell her about us?" hissed Monroe.

"I said you were the father of my two darling children. A boy who was the spitting image of you and a girl who looked exactly like me."

"You didn't! I'll kill you!" He did look ready to strangle her.

"I wish I had said it. I didn't think of it in time."

"You sure you said nothing?" He wanted to believe her with the desperation of a man on the verge of bankruptcy trying to collect hopeless debts.

"Oh, come on," Franciejean whispered. "What would I say? What I should have done is show her the pictures."

"What pictures?" Monroe paled and his eyes widened.

"Oh, for God's sake! It's a joke!" She realized she'd gone too far. "Who is she anyway? Why are you afraid of her?"

"I'm not afraid. We're going to be married. She has every right to be irritated at your appearance."

"Married? Does she live with you?"

"Of course not."

"Will she stay overnight tonight?"

"I don't know." Then he read her mind. "No, you can't stay here tonight."

"Why not? Please. I'll go way and come back after she's gone. We used to have lovely times together. This will be our last time." She was bargaining with the wheedling shrewdness of the fabled Armenian rug dealer. "Tomorrow I'll go away, and you'll never see me again. I swear on Saint Theresa. She's my favorite saint."

"Don't be melodramatic. You can't stay. That's final. Why the hell didn't you call first?"

"I did. The line was busy. Please! Just tonight."

Isabelle came back into the room looking casual and cool in a crisp, vine-patterned, summer dress. "You haven't been in Davenport for months. You two must have a lot to say to each other. But I wish you wouldn't whisper. It makes it harder to listen."

"We weren't whispering!" Monroe shouted.

"Yes, you were. I listened. It's these new buildings. It's impossible to have a tête-à-tête. The walls are paper thin. You mustn't think I mind your hanky-panky—whatever happened between you happened. I'm not a Scarsdale matron. Conventions have changed. If a man goes on an overnight business trip, why should he be expected to sleep alone?"

"Isabelle, please quit it!"

"Excuse me, Franciejean. You have delicate sensibilities. Well, suffice it to say you found each other." Against her will Isabelle was flooded with a swarm of jealous pictures. What she had always managed best were her own emotions. At least their outward appearance. And here she was behaving like that cliché of ordinariness, the jealous woman. "But this is no business trip," she continued. "She can't stay here. So where shall we send her?" Her tone implied that they might send Francie to the ASPCA.

A fragile silence ensued full of no suggestions and everyone's private turmoil. Finally Isabelle said, "I have a thought. How about the Barbizon Plaza for Women? I'll take Francie downstairs and put her in a cab."

Monoroe almost collapsed with relief. "That's a wonderful idea. Wonderful. I'll take her suitcase. It's too heavy for you." He finally put down his tennis satchel, which he'd been hanging on to as though for dear life all through the interlude, and now picked up Francie's suitcase.

"Why should you go down and have to come up again? I'll put her in a cab," Isabelle said.

"We'll do it together."

"Oh—I forgot. It's been so hectic here tonight I forgot to tell you. I can't spend the evening with you as we planned. I just came over to have a wee drinkie. I didn't know we were having guests. Dad's back from Paris. He called while I was dressing to meet you and asked me to have dinner with him tonight."

"You can't do that! You're seeing me tonight."

"I'm seeing Dad."

"You're seeing me!"

"Please, Monroe, try to understand."

"No. No *No*. I've had enough of that."

Originally the news of the change of plans had been meant to be another of Isabelle's many small, sadistic triumphs over Monroe. He was her natural prey, and she enjoyed on occasion the sight of him on the rack. But fate runs a frivolous lottery, and the freak appearance of Francie had undercut Isabelle's swagger. "Look, I do want to spend this evening with you. But I said yes to Dad, and I have to keep my word."

"What does your psychiatrist say about this?" Monroe was too dazed with anger to realize how far ahead he was.

"He said that Dad is a brilliant, unusual, dynamic man, so of course I like spending time with him."

"I don't understand a psychiatrist who takes your money and lets you walk around with the worst father complex in the history of Freud!"

"You can't accept the fact that my father is an exceptional man, can you?"

"You've been going to the doctor three times a week for two years, and your father still runs your life!"

"That's true. I have an Electra complex. I know it, Dr. Nadler knows it, Dad knows it. I'm a classic case. With this difference: my father *is* unique. It's practically normal to have a complex about him."

"Crap!" Monroe let out a low snarl. "Then marry him, why don't you? You'll never meet a man to equal him."

"I wish I could. But it would be incest. And we do not practice incest. We're Jews, not Egyptians!" Her face darkened. Her lips compressed.

Monroe retreated before her fury. In the rat-ta-tat-tat of quarrel he had completely forgotten Francie. But not so Isabelle.

Now she said, "Come with me, Francie. I'll put you in a cab."

Suddenly a shutter rolled back across Monroe's mind. Francie—of course! It was like playing a card which had been there but which he had been too distraught to notice.

"Francie is staying," he said quietly.

His eyes locked with Isabelle's; for perhaps ten seconds they stared at each other, the intensity in each of them running like a current into the eyes of the other. Then Isabelle looked away. For the first time in the choreography of their

27

love dance, the roles had altered. She was still the fair princess, but he was no longer the humble stableboy. Instead, he was brash. Nor would he apologize for the odor of the stable. It was a blow to Isabelle's organized opinion of him.

"You're making a mistake, Monroe."

"So are you." He held his ground and was surprised that he could.

Without a glance at Francie, Isabelle picked up her gleaming beaded purse from the foyer table and left.

Monroe clenched and unclenched his fists. "Damn! Damn! Damn!" It had not been a pleasant victory, costing too much in terms of his own self-esteem. He was a lawyer. A moderate man. He believed in due process of law. He did not like power plays. Yet that was exactly what he had done. He had taken advantage of Isabelle's abnormally high-pitched jealousy. A jealousy that had such a ring of truth, he realized sadly all others had been merely reasonable facsimiles; counterfeits of the honest coin of female possessiveness. Before tonight she had never cared.

Then Francie sneezed, and sneezed. She'd been standing still, like a deaf and dumb prisoner waiting sentence. But now nerves and a body unaccustomed to the air-conditioned summer womb in which so many New Yorkers lived, could no longer stand it. She sneezed again. Monroe looked at her with impatience and offered his handkerchief.

"Francie, I understand your predicament. Being alone in a strange city is not pleasant. It's easier if you know someone. But I wish you'd telephoned first."

"I did telephone." She sneezed again and blew her nose.

"I mean I wish you'd waited until the line was clear. Then Isabelle would have answered, and you could have hung up. And called tomorrow."

But it would not have occurred to Francie to hang up and she said so. "But if Isabelle said I wasn't home, wouldn't that have ended it? Then you'd have hung up, wouldn't you?"

"I don't know."

"Well, why did you come here? To make trouble? If you want to blackmail me, this isn't how it's done."

"For heavens sake, don't be silly."

"Then what got into you? You arrive here with a

28

suitcase, prepared to move in. Where's your sense? People have lives going. You don't go around disrupting people's lives. Isabelle and I were talking about setting the date for our marriage. And introducing me to her father. I stop being her closet stud. Now I don't know what will happen.''

Francie felt a genuine regret at having caused this bruised triangle. And a generous self-pitying resentment at the way her first night in New York—her birthday night—had blown out like an overloaded fuse.

"I have one more telephone number I can call. A friend of a friend."

"Suppose they don't want you, either?"

Francie looked bleak and obstinate. "I could sleep at the bus station, then."

Monroe stared at her. He didn't know it, and she didn't know it, but she'd set a trap for him. The trap was compassion, and he'd walked straight into it.

"Did it ever occur to you to stay at a hotel?"

"Uhm . . . I'd like not to. I don't have much money for a hotel."

"How much do you have?"

"Fifty-five dollars. And some change."

"You came to New York with fifty-five dollars? What do you plan to do for food and rent money?"

"Get a job. I'm a very good steno. And seventy words a minute typing."

"If you get the job tomorrow, you won't get paid for a week. Or suppose the job doesn't start till the first? What then?"

"That's what the fifty-five dollars is for. The dry spell."

"A most original conviction. You believe in the freedom to starve. How long do you think fifty-five dollars will last in this city?"

"As long as it has to. I know how to manage."

"I have a client who confessed to me hysterically that she can't live on a penny less than five-hundred-a-week alimony. And you're preparing the siege of New York on fifty-five dollars?"

"Five hundred a week alimony! Wow!" Francie squirreled this information in her new mental file system on New York. The one ex-wife she'd known had nothing but babies and black-and-blue marks. So it was amazing that an ex-wife, a discard from the male world, could make that much money by simply getting a divorce. Clearly life was different here.

Her respect for the unknown divorcée was so clear it made Monroe smile. "You see the kind of talent you're up against? You sure you want to stay in New York?"

"Of course I'll stay." She signed her life to the words. How could it be otherwise? Some choices are not a matter of choice. In exactly the blind, mindless way that salmon swim upstream and pigeons fly homeward, the necessities of Francie's nature formed a logic that was too powerful and too deliberate to oppose. Once she knew about the city, she was forever caught in its gravitational field.

Monroe sighed for himself and mankind. He was not unacquainted with passionate longings. "Okay, I'm hooked. Stay here tonight. Tomorrow I'll cash a check and give you some money. Then you're on your own. Find a place. I'm not your father!"

"Monroe Perl, you're a peach. A Jewish peach! You are Jewish, aren't you?"

"Yes, yes, I'm Jewish. What has that got to do with it?"

"You're the first Jewish person I've ever known. And I love you." And she danced around the room.

This was the Monroe she knew. He was always thoughtful. Not like she was sleeping with him, but like she was his sister or something. Some men wanted to get into bed with her before they knew her name. Once, he'd even given her money to go to the dentist. Then he'd sermonized for an hour about keeping her teeth in good condition. He was so serious about it he even went out and bought her an electric toothbrush. Naturally Aunt Gert made a fuss, because she claimed the brush used up too much electricity. But that didn't take from its being a kindly thing to do.

Monroe went to a closet off the living room and took out sheets, a pillow case, a pillow. These he dumped on the zebra-striped couch and started to make it up as a bed.

"It's not a hide-a-bed, but it's comfortable. My brother sleeps on it when he's in town."

Franciejean stared at him curiously. This was a change. After the spoony time in Davenport, why was she sleeping on a couch? A laugh a minute in New York. Nonetheless, she sensibly decided to help him make up the couch.

"I never expected you to have such a smash apartment."

"It ought to be. I spent enough money on it. Things cost money these days." He was pleased with her genuine enthusiasm. But it wasn't enough. "Isabelle hates the place."

"Don't let that bother you. She's a nice-looking girl, but she's not all that special. She'll be back before you have time to miss her. My Aunt Gert used to say it's a man's world. And it is."

"It depends on who the man is."

Franciejean had to think about this. One never knew about other people's sufferings. She studied Monroe with the patient stare of some long-gone farm ancestor who, every season, staked his family's existence on his own good judgment of the skies. Then she made one of her straight-to-the-mark connections that had nothing to do with intelligence. "She's richer than you?"

"Richer than most people."

"Is she the one who's getting all that alimony?"

"No. She's the one who pays alimony."

"To a man?" This was too much.

"Why not?"

"I never thought about it."

"He's not a bad sort," Monroe shrugged. "A painter. She wanted to pay it. So he could paint as he chose. Without having to dirty his art trying to be commercial." Monroe grimaced. "But it's a mistake to think such a woman is generous. No, just listen for the small, crunching sound when the cat reaches the back bone of the mouse."

"Monroe!"

"It's my mood." Abruptly he stopped making up the couch and walked into the other room. He came back carrying a brief case. "Francie, I'm going to the office to finish up a brief. There's some food in the refrigerator. Liquor in the cabinet. TV is there. Take what you need." He had forgotten the dazzling quality of Francie's skin, and he wanted to keep a safe distance. Anything with Francie was self-indulgence. Nothing plus nothing. Isabelle was his girl though sometimes she made him heartsick. "I'll be quiet when I come in and won't wake you. I'll see you in the morning." Before Francie had a chance to say thank you, he'd left.

2

The minute the door closed, Francie stopped making up the couch, kicked off her shoes, stretched her arms triumphantly, and whirled like a mad child Dervish, until she collapsed in dizzy happiness on the floor. She had made it to here, wherever here was. Now that the squeeze was over, at least for the moment, she allowed herself to know how downright frightened and tired she was. And how hungry. She headed for the kitchen.

The kitchen was smaller than she expected, but clean, compact and clearly related to the new generation of kitchens inhabited by frozen foods and packaged breakfast cereals. It struck Francie that it might be sacrilege to peel a potato in this kitchen. Or let a kid loose in it. But surely one could scramble eggs. She thought how pretty she'd look in the morning scrambling eggs for Monroe. Or frying them. Eggs were the one thing she felt she did well. She opened the cabinets to check the supplies and found a military order among the dishes, the glasses, the small grouping of canned goods, and the bottom shelves stocked with shining, brand-new, unused, copper-bottomed pots and pans. Some with their labels still adhering intact. This was an unlived-in kitchen.

When she opened the refrigerator door, her suspicions were confirmed. She wouldn't scramble eggs in the morning. There were no eggs. Or anything else that needed cooking. Inside was a grab bag of little things to eat on the run. Cherry tomatoes. Salami. Swiss cheese. Cheddar cheese. More cheese, with strange names and wrappings. One with black beads like

32

ants clinging to its sides. Peculiar. Bottles of wine. A jar of herring. Small slices of rye bread. Apples. So forth.

The refrigerator, that trustworthy spy on human nature, had told its tale. Rich New York men like Monroe did not eat hearty, home-cooked meals. At home they ate what they could peel, or slice, or open in a jar. Perhaps she wouldn't have to learn to cook, despite what Aunt Gert said. Perhaps in New York, everyone who could afford to ate in restaurants. No archaeologist ever puzzled with more diligence over the artifacts of a lost civilization than did Franciejean, studying the live culture of Manhattan.

In the bedroom the furniture was as modern as she could wish. The bed was big enough for two, even three, with a gleaming brass headboard. The one discordant note was a heavy, old-fashioned, mahogany desk with a glass top. Next to it was a worn leather chair. The desk was strewn with papers, books; things that reminded Francie of Dr. Jess back home. It told of hard work and long hours and satisfactions that were not gaudy enough or frequent enough. It flawed her vision of New York glamour to hint that life here too might have a grinding core.

To reassure herself, she went to the window and was greeted by an incredible landscape of light. A dense stream of car lights hurtled up Third Avenue bound for the edge of the earth. In the dark and all around, a million more lights seemed suspended in midair, gleaming over every variety of human happening. The city was as beautiful as it was stupefying. Fear mixed with delight possessed her: awe and happiness at once. She stared a long, hard while at the lights, wondering what they would mean to her. But the lights made no answer, and the frail human world went its way, repeating endlessly its gestures of love and despair, heedless of her appetites and her doubts.

With an air of defeat, she turned back to reconnoiter the bedroom. She inspected the closets carefully. Business suits, slacks, jackets, sweaters; and among all this male splendor, Isabelle's solitary green robe. That was all there was to prove her presence in Monroe's life. The robe gave off the odor of condescension. Usually women leave clothes where they make love, perhaps as a witching act to insure their return. Isabelle needed no enchantments. Francie wondered what it was like to be an Isabelle, released from the bondage of the

33

male world. Affecting an elaborate carelessness, Francie slipped on the expensive robe. But it was too big. She felt depressed, as though this were an omen.

In defiance she threw the robe on the bed, took off all her clothes and walked around naked. What a nice apartment, she thought. She could be happy here. She'd keep out of Monroe's way. Be quiet as a mouse. Affectionate, if he felt that way. He could do as he pleased. Go or stay. No, she didn't want to be free of men. Why should she? She examined herself in the closet-door mirror. What she saw satisfied her. She could do as well as Isabelle. In fact she might do a hell of a lot better.

She started to yawn in spite of her wide-awake curiosity. Francie didn't like going to sleep because she never knew what she might dream. She had had some lulus. But the trip and the excitement had made her even too drowsy to eat. She must go to sleep. But she knew she could not sleep on the couch. Not on her first night in New York. She had slept on a couch or a cot all her life. So, ignoring all Monroe's instructions, she climbed into his private bed with the magnificent mattress and the blue-striped sheets. She'd surprise him. She'd have the bed all cozy for him when he got home. Then maybe he'd let her stay with him. A few days anyway. She would keep out of Isabelle's way.

She lay there in limbo, feeling elegant and exotic as the sounds of the city came up from the evening streets. Maybe some rich New Yorker would fall in love with her and give her a place like this. Once, during the night, she woke up and stretched out her hand for Monroe. But he wasn't there, the dirty stay-out. She went back to sleep.

Some uncertain time later, Francie emerged from a dreamless sleep to the clamor of the telephone at her head. Oh my God, it was Momma! She'd followed her after all.

"Hello," she said into the beige receiver, her heart pounding in her ears. There was no answer. Nothing. Only the quiet, menacing click that informs a city dweller someone has been listening. This particular symptom of big-city lunacy had never happened to Francie before. "Hello," she said again. "Momma? Are you there?" Silent seconds passed. A receiver was picked up. "Hello, Momma?" she said for the second time.

A voice that sounded like a man said, "Hello? Hello?"

"Who is it?" asked Francie.

"Is that you, Francie?"

"I'm Francie. Who are you?"

"This is Monroe. Who the hell did you think it was?" The receiver was slammed down. A figure appeared in the bedroom door and switched on the overhead light. It was Monroe in silk striped pajamas and a fury. "What the hell business did you have answering the telephone?"

Francie had barely replaced the beige receiver in the beige cradle. "Was that you on the telephone?"

"It was not. I picked it up in the living room. Who the hell were you talking to?"

"I thought it might be my mother telephoning."

"Your mother—for God's sake!"

"Well, I'm not sure."

"How old are you? Are you really eighteen?"

"I told you so. Tonight was my birthday."

"Oh boy, oh boy. All I need is to land in court for abducting a minor. And listen, Francie, you crossed the state line yourself. I had nothing to do with it. I don't care what your mother thinks. It's a lie."

"Listen, I'm not at all sure it was her."

"For Christ's sake, I hope not! I could be disbarred if she brought charges."

"How could she bring charges? She doesn't know where I am. And where could she have gotten this telephone number?" But Francie knew better. Her mother could do anything. Her stomach was pinching; but she buried her fear because he was even more frightened. "I'm sure it wasn't my Momma. She's not even in New York. And she would never hang up on me. And whoever it was hung up."

"Oh God. It was Isabelle. She always hangs up. She'll think you were in bed with me."

"Then she has a dirty mind."

"Why don't you tell her you raped me? That's more plausible. Did you have to answer the telephone?"

"I'm sorry, Monroe. But it was ringing. I always answer ringing telephones."

"You have no sense. When you're sleeping in a man's house, you don't answer his telephone."

"Believe me I'll never do it again," she said with conviction. "But I didn't know you were home. You weren't in bed."

"You shouldn't answer it anyway! And I am home. I'm sleeping on the couch where I thought we agreed you would sleep. As a result of my hospitality, you are sleeping in my bed, answering my telephone, and defaming my character to my fiancée! Her psychiatrist will say I'm revealing a latent Don Juan personality and am not capable of relating to a woman on a deep emotional level. Or some horseshit like that! Francie, you infuriate me!" He raced out of the room.

Francie scrambled naked out of bed to follow him. She knew she was in grave danger of being thrown out then and there into the starry, indifferent night. She decided not to put on Isabelle's green robe. Instinctively she counted on her body to accomplish what apologies and tears might not.

"Monroe, please don't be mad at me. I didn't mean to answer the telephone." She trailed after him, sleep gone, in the middle of a bad fright. "It didn't have to be Isabelle. Other people must call you."

"It was Isabelle."

"Maybe she didn't hear my voice. Monroe, why should she call now? It's so late. I'm sure it wasn't her." She put out her hand to take his arm, but he drew away like a suspicious animal.

"It was her." He went toward the telephone. Dialing the number, he was painfully aware of Francie's physical presence. She had placed herself directly in front of him, with a remorseless desire to attract his attention, making all kinds of verbal arguments while her naked body made other kinds of appeals.

Finally he slammed down the receiver. "Either she's not home. Or she is home. Either way she's turned off the telephone. Damn you, Francie, you've made a mess!" But at the moment he didn't mean it. While his words were full of righteous indignation, his mind was busy with sex. Francie—why shouldn't he fuck her? Isabelle was behaving like a bitch. His eyes focused on Francie slowly as a chessman to be moved. He remembered all the potentialities for pleasure in that lovely, pleading body. Francie kept her eyes resolutely on him and had a moment of sheer feminine satisfaction as she recognized his thoughts. She put out her hand again to touch

36

him, and this time he did not draw away. He was far too feeble to resist the sort of pressure her nakedness was putting on him. For a moment they both simply looked at each other. The matter was sealed. Neither of them heard the key in the lock of the door.

"Hello, everybody," Isabelle remarked cheerily, "I just dropped in for a nightcap." Her voice was calm. Francie's nudity was no more than she had anticipated. But even when reality lives up to our worst expectations, we are still confounded at how much sharper the real pain is than the one we imagined.

Monroe whirled. "Isabelle, for God's sake!"

"Don't let me disturb you. Go right ahead. I see you started without me." She pretended to laugh at the old joke as she tossed her beaded bag onto the chair. But the blood rushed to her head. She had to sit down for a minute. Immediately she stood up. Imagine having a rival!

"It's not what you think! Francie was sleeping in my bed. I was sleeping on the couch and the telephone rang."

"Don't be embarrassed. It's the host who sets the tone of an orgy." In total jealousy Isabelle walked to the bar and poured herself a scotch. "What did you say her name was? I never remember a body on less than six introductions."

Francie, wishing she could dissolve in smoke, tried to get past Isabelle and out of the room. Isabelle nodded regal approval. "Yes, go put something on. You make me feel overdressed. Oh, I remember: your name is Elloweise/Francie. From Davenport."

In the bedroom Francie picked up her clothes from the floor and dressed as rapidly as possible. She listened to the rise and fall of voices in the other room and wished there were some way of getting out without going through the living room and passing Monroe and Isabelle. Maybe she would climb out on a window ledge, slide into the window of the next apartment, meet a fascinating stranger, and leave with him for some glittering adventure, never to see Isabelle or Monroe again. But there was no ledge around the fifteenth floor; and even if there was one, she knew she wouldn't have the guts to get out on it. So she might as well go into the living room and get her luggage and let Monroe despise her while she kept a sharp eye on Isabelle, who might have a bread knife stashed somewhere. If she got out alive, she would go downstairs, get a cab, and maybe sleep in the bus terminal tonight, as though she was waiting for an early morning bus.

In the living room Monroe was shouting at Isabelle, while Isabelle sat on the sheet-covered couch, completely unruffled. She smoked a cigarette and sipped her scotch in a satisfied manner. Monroe's violent protestations, though blatantly false, were soothing to her pride. It gave her an opening to be patronizing. "Please, Monroe. I am not judging you. This is not a law court. I really don't care what the two of you did. There is nothing extraordinary about infidelity. It comes from the Bible. And is continued on television. In the movies. And in almost every piece of gossip. It's as routine a part of our daily life as a hangover. I don't take it seriously. How can I?"

Something had changed in Isabelle. Something had been discovered. Though she was furious, she still knew, with the canniness of her father's blood, that outrage was now a blunted weapon. What she believed Monroe was like, could possibly be like, was not related to the Monroe who knew this girl and let her stay in his apartment under Isabelle's very nose. She turned to Francie, who had come quietly into the room.

"Was he any good in bed? Sometimes he falls asleep too quickly when he's played a lot of tennis before."

Francie knew she was facing an enemy. She had no idea what the right response to this moment might be so she experimented with the truth. "'Mrs. Ring, we weren't in bed together. He was working in the office all night. I don't know when he came home. I was asleep."

"I like that your stories tally. It shows forethought."

"It's all true! He let me stay here because he felt sorry for me. Because he's kind. Tomorrow I'm moving into the YMCA. I mean the YW. Monroe was sleeping on the couch!" Francie was now on the verge of tears. Her courage had all been used up.

"That's exactly what I said!" Monroe shouted, and then swore vehemently to make the point more emphatic.

Isabelle stared at Monroe curiously. He'd never excited her the way some previous lovers had. She'd always found him too considerate, too predictable. But now the sight of him sent quivers through her. "When he makes love to you," she asked Francie, "is he respectful or does he treat you like a whore?"

"Isabelle, shut up! Nothing happened!"

Isabelle was impressed by the new bully she saw emerging in Monroe's nature. She also respected his steadfast lying. "Quite so. Nothing happened. So let's go back to the original problem that brought us all together. Where does Francie sleep?" Isabelle had begun a rearguard action. Great generals do this after they know they have blundered. To keep up appearances with history. And themselves. "Since it's a little crowded here for the three of us, I asked Dad what to do. He's conversant with these matters, and he suggested Randy Taylor."

"Randy Taylor! She's a model! I read about her in *Teen Screen*. They gave her a movie test." Francie gasped.

"Don't take that too seriously. But she is a model. Of sorts. And in addition she's a friend of one of Dad's partners. She's looking for a girl to share her apartment."

"No!"

"Exactly my idea. You want to be a model. She is a model. Truly a roommate made in heaven." She gazed at Francie coolly. "Since you're up and dressed and still packed, we can send you over immediately."

Monroe was hesitant to break the chain of these blissful events; but he had to. "What about Miss Taylor? It's 3:00 A.M."

"Randy is expecting Francie. All the arrangements were made earlier this evening. Including Francie's share of a month's rent. That should be enough, considering her skills, to get her on her feet, and out of my life. Now let's go downstairs and put her in a cab."

Francie stared at Isabelle with sudden affection, accepting the favor with the innocent lust of a child. It was no more than she expected. It simply proved her magical destiny. That, contrary to all prior experiences, life for her could be a game in which she might never get hurt.

"Let me get on a raincoat," Monroe hastily said.

Which he did. And the oddly assorted trio went silently down the corridor, and then rode the elevator in continuing silence to the ground floor. The night doorman, blank-faced, hailed a cruising cab.

"This is the address," said Isabelle. She handed Francie a matchbook from the Brussels with a number scribbled on it. "The telephone number is on there, too. You should have no trouble."

As the cab door slammed, Francie heard Isabelle's remark to the shivering Monroe: "I've made an appointment for you and me to have brunch with Dad on Sunday. He wants to meet you."

Anyone watching the cab speeding Francie onward through the night might well wonder what was the launching pad from which one climbed to success? Was it work, sweat, the right place at the right time? Talent? Connections? Or none of these, but simply luck—a fortuitous combination of circumstances. Whatever it was, Francie, like any other striving, climbing grass-roots American, firmly believed in her ability to control the outcome of her life. And realize her dreams. After all, didn't the Declaration of Independence promise her an inalienable right to the pursuit of happiness. And wasn't she pursuing it?

3

In later years Francie would remember her first encounters with the city only in fragments. A conversation here. A face there. Something round. Something jagged. Then the kaleidoscope of memory would tilt, and the scene would sink out of sight like a vanished chip of colored glass.

She remembered uneasily that 3:30 A.M. arrival at 455 East Fifty-fifth Street. Tattered canopy. Dirty brick. No doorman. Buzzer system. Randy Taylor, 6A. An automatic elevator. Inked into the wood of the elevator walls were a variety of neighborly tips like "up yours" or "F you G." Even at 3:30 A.M. the hallway was still alive with the fragrant reminders of fish fry and beef stew. It was as good a place as any to start one's life work. But after Monroe Perl's apartment, this was a letdown. Francie felt as if a pail of slops had been poured over her head.

"This will be your room," said Randy Taylor of the glowing black hair and the soft lax figure; more overblown than *Vogue* would like. "That's your bed."

"The one near the window?"

"Yes. It has a spring mattress."

"Who sleeps in the other bed?"

"Susannah Meeker. She's away on tour with the ballet."

"It's a better bed." Francie had the hard professional eye of the orphan who was regularly shuffled around among relatives to sleep in unfamiliar beds on the aunt–cousin circuit.

"Sorry, old girl. Susannah gets mucho miffed if anyone sleeps in her beddy-bye. Fee-fi-fo-fum, who has been sleeping

41

in my yum yum yum!'' Randy's voice had become deep and
groaning like a bass saxophone. "And when she finishes
hollering on you, she eats you up!''

"It's a better bed.''

"Only in the eye of the beholder.'' Randy had resumed
her normal tone. "There's a bedboard under the mattress.
That bed is hard as a rock. You'd wake up black and blue
with broken bones.''

The next day Francie thought she'd dress up and go walk
around Times Square, which she considered the heart of the
city. She had no set plan, but she thought if she walked
around long enough somebody important would see her, and
offer her a modeling job. Randy was exasperated.

"That's a noodle-headed idea. All that happens is some
sex pervert grabs you.''

"On Times Square?''

"In fact if you swing your bag you might do some
business. Or you might not. There's so much free stuff these
days.''

"If that's not a good idea, what do I do to get started?''

"You go through the Yellow Pages and make a list of the
modeling agencies in New York City and go see everyone of
them.''

"Model agencies?''

"Yes, you ninny. You can't do modeling work without
an agency.''

"Oh, that's how it's done!''

"That's how it's done.''

Francie did as she was told, but when she asked Randy
for further advice, the dark-haired girl had lost interest. She
was vague, she was indifferent, she was busy teasing her hair.
She had long ago given up on her own career; and after the
first brief spurt of attention, she was bored by Francie's
enthusiasm. Her thinking was elsewhere. She wanted to be
respectable. The soul of a P.T.A. matron had blossomed
within her curving body, and she longed to find her niche in
the suburbs. Now she thought she had a chance. Her new
boyfriend Sam, a Central Park South dentist, was picking up
quite a bit of her expenses. With the upshot being that she
only took modeling jobs that were convenient and kept her in

the game. Sam was keen on the idea of his girlfriend being a model.

"He's recapping my front teeth and building a bridge for the back ones."

"Your teeth look fine. Why is he doing that?"

"Why not? You have to have a man do things for you if you want him to marry you. Then if he doesn't marry me, at the least he will have corrected my bite. That's better than nothing."

"I suppose so. By the way, when are you getting a screen test?"

"Me? For God's sake!"

"I saw your picture in *Teen Screen*. It said so."

"Bull!"

"I'm sorry."

"Don't mention it. I got paid for the booking."

"By the way, I'm not the kind of person who likes to intrude; but could I go to your agency?"

"You could if I had one. But I don't have a contract with one agency. I free-lance."

"Do you think I could do that?"

"Don't be silly. With no experience? And no Sam, by the way."

"Is this the Perkins Model Agency?"

"Yes."

"I'm Franciejean Stewart. I'd like to see Mr. Perkins, please."

"There is no Mr. Perkins. Is it about modeling?"

"Yes."

"Well, please sit outside and I'll call you when Miss Claire is free."

"Yes?"

"I'm Franciejean Stewart. I've been waiting outside for an hour. You said you'd call me."

"What is it about?"

"I told you what it was about. I'd like to talk to somebody about being a model."

"Oh, that's right. You're a new girl. Honestly I am embarrassed. But it gets so crazy around here that I'd forget

43

my head if it weren't zippered on. It's a shame I kept you waiting out there for a whole hour for nothing. New models are handled by Madeline Casey, and she only sees new people on Tuesdays between two and five. You could call her for an appointment except that she told me last week she was booked solid on Tuesdays until December. Why don't you call for an appointment at the end of October?"

"You have very good features, Miss Stewart. A good figure too, but your walk is heavy. Your posture needs work. You don't know how to make up to your best advantage. Otherwise, you are definitely top model material. For someone like yourself, who is obviously an investment for the Des Artes Model Agency and Charm School, we have a specially reduced charm course: ten lessons for only one hundred and seventy-five dollars followed by a model trainee course . . ."

"Francie, I don't have the money to lend. But if I did, I wouldn't. That course is crap! They won't get you a job. They'll just take your money. It's a mug's game!"

"My name is Franciejean Stewart. I have an appointment to see Donna Adams."
"I am she. When were you born, Miss Stewart?"
"August 23rd, 1946."
"Oh, that is too bad."
"Why?"
"You are Leo."
"I am?"
"Yes. Leo. I am Pisces. February 28th. According to my horoscope, I must not take on currently any new clients having the Leo sign. It is too bad. You are quite pretty. We must wait until Jupiter is in a more favorable conjunction with Pluto."

She was eighteen, and she had never asked a question. She had taken for granted that her dreams would come true as soon as she came to New York. Now she was in New York, and she stared around like a tourist. She never looked at anyone or anything except with intention, as if she didn't mean to waste a look. She was fascinated with the sights and sounds, but it was a survivor's fascination. For the city she met was not the one she had imagined. It was a dirty trick dressed up as a favor. She stood in a reception room drenched in fear.

"I'm Franciejean Stewart. I made an appointment to see Adele Collins."

"I'm sorry, Miss Stewart. She's still at the dentist. Perhaps I can help you?"

"I wanted to talk to her about my career—modeling. Is there anyone else I could see?"

"Jean Frank is on vacation. And Greta Anderson is getting married. It's a slow season right now. And there's no call for the young look at all. You're about twenty?"

"Eighteen."

"Do you have a sample book?"

"Sample book?"

"Of the ads you've been in?"

"I haven't been in any ads yet. That's why I'm here."

"Oh. Then why don't you leave your composite, and I'll have Miss Collins look at it when she gets in later."

"Composite?"

"Pictures. How green are you?"

"Oh, I take wonderful pictures. Back home everybody says so. Here are some snapshots."

"Miss Collings needs your composite."

"Honestly, they're good. See? That's me in a bathing suit. Me in pants. Me in a cocktail dress at my friend's graduation party. . . ."

Walking down the streets of the summer city, her step was quick, her smile brilliant. But the insolence of glass and steel threatened and diminished her. She felt she must give battle to the city or become submerged in it. And she felt submerged already by its hugeness and arrogance.

"Picker Associates."

"Can I speak to Mr. Picker, please?"

"No. Dick is in Paris. Who's calling?"

"I'm Franciejean Stewart. Has he moved to Paris?"

"No. He's on location. Shooting. What can I do for you?"

"I've seen his name in *Vogue* magazine. Under his

photographs. He's grand. I wondered if he'd take pictures of me. I'd pay him, of course. Maybe we could arrange it so I paid him something every week.''

"Are you kidding?''

"No, I'm serious. I'm going to be a model, and I need composites to be in my career. You know—a bunch of pictures by a professional photographer. And I thought if anyone was going to take pictures of me, I'd like Mr. Picker to do it, because he's so great.''

"He'll be delighted to hear your opinion. How many photographs would you like?''

"Gee—seven or eight. In different dresses. I guess that would be enough.''

"Let's make it a round figure. Let's say ten.''

"Okay, ten.''

"Hmm. Well, Miss Stewart, ten pictures by Richard Picker...will cost you...mmm. I'll make you a non-commercial price because it's your own personal investment. And Dick might find your face imaginative. Or your movements electric. I'd say ten thousand dollars would be about right.''

"Ten thousand dollars!''

"You said ten finished prints. That's merely one thousand dollars apiece. Of course, you'll have to wait until January. Dick is tied up solidly with commercial work until then.''

Eventually, Francie put two and two together.

"Randy, what'll I do?''

"Lend me your suitcase, the white one. Will you?''

"Yes. But what do I do? Nothing's happening. Everything's wrong.''

"You can sleep in my bed while I'm away. It's a Seely mattress.''

"Thanks. But what about when I'm awake? What do I do about composites?''

"You want my honest to God opinion?''

"I do.''

"Stop acting like Miss Flour Sack of the modeling business. You ought to know better than to call Richard Picker for composites. It's a laugh a minute. If you'll pardon a simple unglamorous suggestion, what you need is a

46

cold-water-flat photographer. Who wears sandals. Is full of genius. But has no credits. He's got a new secondhand Rollei; and he's on the make. He's looking for a gratis type model to practice on. Like you for instance."

"I don't know any photographers at all."

"I don't know any hungry ones—yes, I do! Ernest Hamilton. Lives in the Village. Met him at a party. Nice, underprivileged colored boy climbing the ladder of success. Loaded with talent, they say. Call him. He's in the book."

"I never worked with a colored photographer."

"You never worked with a white one."

"Is he all right?"

"You mean, if I understand you correctly, will he rape you?"

"I've heard all kinds of things about colored men."

"Have you got something against rape? Or is it just black rape?"

"I'm sorry. I'm not as sophisticated about things as you are."

"I suppose it's because you come from the Midwest that you're prejudiced."

"I'm not prejudiced. I'm only asking if he's—well, safe?"

"My, my, we *are* prejudiced. And underneath that prejudice is more prejudice. Well, don't worry honey. This boy is not only black. He's gay."

"Mr. Hamilton?"

"Yassuh honey chile?"

"I'm Franciejean Stewart. I'm a model."

"Good for you, darlin'. But I am not shooting any freebies no mo'. No sir. I got myself a page in *Harper's Bazaar* last month, and a Sunnybrook ad in *Glamour.* I'm arrivé, chile. If you want to partake of my extraordinary black talent, it will cost you two hundred dollars."

"Two hundred dollars?"

"Yes, but I am no Simon Legree in black face. For this trifling sum I will shoot eight rolls. Almost one hundred shots. Out of this abundance you will assuredly get four spectacular glossies."

"It's a lot of money."

"Your profile will launch a thousand cakes of soap."

47

"I don't have two hundred dollars."

"Okay, you twisted my arm. For you baby, one fifty."

"I'll call you back."

The noise of the city was too loud. There was the continued shriek and clang of cars and the deafening roar of buildings going up and buildings coming down. At night, the air conditioners hummed around her tired ears like a swarm of bees. More and more she was afraid of the city.

"It isn't going so well?"

"No, it isn't."

"I don't understand it."

"I don't either."

"A girl as pretty as you are—"

"It doesn't help."

"Why not?"

"It's complicated. You can't work without an agent. Even Sara Thom has an agent. But nobody will be my agent. I need composites first. And to get composites I need a photographer."

"That's enough. It is complicated. I'll put a check in the mail for you."

"Monroe, you're a lifesaver!"

"Three hundred dollars will hardly save your life in this city. Get a secretarial job."

"I did. With Metropolitan. But I don't get paid till the fifteenth. I make the rounds during lunch hour. Monroe, in case you're not seeing Mrs. Ring some night, I'd be pleased to have dinner with you."

"I'd like to do it, Francie, but Isabelle and I get married next month. So I'm private property."

"Oh . . . I guess you are."

"Aren't you going to congratulate me?"

"Oh, yes. Congratulations!"

"Not a bad face, Miss Stewart, but you should lose about seven pounds. And I believe one nostril flairs slightly to the left. I know a good plastics man who could straighten it out."

"My nose?"

"Yes. You didn't know? Well, the human eye, unless trained, probably would not detect the warping, but the camera most certainly will."

"Oh dear."

"Your front left molar needs capping. It's discolored."

"It is?"

"You don't study your face very carefully, do you? You need a magnifying mirror. And I think we'll have to change your hair color."

"My hair! But I'm a natural blond."

"My dear, we have three natural blonds on file right now. We hardly need another one. And you'd make a striking redhead."

"I won't do it!"

Francie was sleeping no better on Randy's Seely mattress when someone switched on the bedroom lights. She saw a girl, short and spare, upright as a pole, with long legs that made her seem taller than she was. Her features were good but not pretty. Her clothes neither intended to nor did they attract notice. She had beautiful hands and moved with the traditional duckfootedness of ballet dancers.

"Hello."

"Hello?"

"Who are you?"

"Franciejean Stewart. Who are you?"

"Susannah Meeker. Randy wrote me that you were a blond."

"I am. I had to dye my hair red for the Hightower Agency. Now they say it's wrong, so I have to bleach it back to my natural color."

"It was ever thus. Where's Randy?"

"Puerto Rico."

"In August?"

"She's on vacation. Be back tomorrow."

"Is she having another abortion?"

"She never said that."

"Forget I mentioned it."

"Golly, I'd die if that happened to me."

"Not if it were done properly."

"But it's awful!"

"An illegitimate child is funsie?"

"I hope I am not so old that I've forgotten what it means to be a young girl. I realize a young girl has many things to

49

do during her lunch hour besides eat a tuna fish sandwich. And I've had excellent reports on your work. You misspell only occasionally. And you file intelligently. But I can't allow you to take two-hour lunches. Lunch is from twelve to one. I make exceptions in the case of unusual circumstances. Otherwise . . ."

"Well, it's dumb to have to worry, when it's safe as aspirin. Plié two . . . three . . . four . . ."

"I don't feel right about it. My father was Catholic."

"But your mother was Lutheran . . . . two . . . three . . . four."

"She's right, Francie," said Randy. "You know there's no such thing as being half Catholic. It's like being half pregnant."

"And the half of you that's nonsectarian should take the pill . . . two . . . three . . . four. My gynecologist says . . . two . . . three . . . four . . . that they've made movies during intercourse . . . two . . . three . . . four . . . using a mechanical penis . . . two . . . three . . . four . . . and according to the movies . . . relevé . . . two . . . three . . . four . . . the diaphragm does not stay in place during intercourse . . . two . . . three . . . four."

"During fucking?" asked Randy.

"Yes. The medical profession no longer understands . . . three . . . four . . . how the diaphragm works . . . two . . . three . . . four."

"During fucking?"

"I said that . . . . three . . . four."

"Susannah, you said intercourse. Say fucking."

"That's gutter talk . . . . two . . . three . . . four."

A restless sea of human beings poured through the streets of the city; the streets pushed and shoved with giggles, greed and pride. During one lunch hour, Francie might see hundreds of people; but she knew no one.

"Cheese sandwich. And a glass of milk."

"Coffee. Regular. And a wheat donut. Excuse me, miss, but are you a model?"

"Oh, yes. That's my chosen career. But how did you know?"

"You're so pretty."

"Oh . . . that." She looked at him carefully and saw a man with an unfinished face and a conceited expression. She was quick to diagnose conceit, having, despite her beauty, almost none of her own.

"And we came down in the elevator together. I know the Hightower Modeling Agency is in the building we were in. I see the girls everyday. I've a client in that building."

"I didn't see you."

"I know. Let me introduce myself. My name is Harvey Evins. I'm in buttons. I own Beaux Arts Buttons. We're always using models."

"Why, Mr. Evins." Now she looked at him differently; as though she were a squirrel and he were holding out a nut. "You do?"

"Yes. Harvey Evins is the name. What's yours?"

"Randy! I've got a job lead!"

"Francie! He gave me a ring! It's two carats. And see? It's nestled, but exquisitely, in these delicate baguettes—"

"My first job!"

"My second ring. I had a sapphire last time. This is a diamond."

"I'm so excited."

"We're going to Europe on our honeymoon."

"You're getting married?"

"I am fulfilling my destiny as a woman."

"But he's so old."

"Forty-eight? He's in the prime of life."

"He's old."

"I'm thirty-one."

"You're that old?"

"It happens. But life isn't over at thirty-one. Unless of course, you're unlucky enough to be an unmarried female who is working for a living. Sam has a very comfortable income. He's going to teach me to golf. I may do an occasional booking to remind him I'm still a challenge."

"But Susannah said—"

"Oh Susannah! She said I had an abortion?"

"Yes."

"I didn't. I didn't intend to."

"But Puerto Rico in August? Susannah said—"

"Susannah doesn't understand men. She knows a lot about intercourse and nothing about fucking. Sam is a very sentimental man. His accountant tried to talk him out of it.

51

His lawyer, his daughter. Some junk about her inheritance. But when it came to the crunch, there in San Juan airport, he couldn't let me go through with it. Not with his baby. So we stayed and played blackjack, went swimming, and came home. Happy ending."

"Then you are pregnant?"

"Madonna and child. Three months going."

"But you're not married!"

"Well, I will admit that until the ring showed up, I was having a continual morning sickness. But it cleared up. First thing I do tomorrow is pick out my silver pattern."

"Golly! I guess I should say congratulations. It's a beautiful ring."

"Thanks. Congrats to you too. Whose your job bite with?"

"I met this man in Chock Full O' Nuts. He owns Beaux Arts Buttons—"

"And his name is Harvey Evins?"

"How'd you know?"

"I am gifted with extrasensory perception. And he's planning a button brochure."

"Yes, a mailing piece. And he needs a model—"

"He always needs a model. It's like a vitamin deficiency. When is he taking you to dinner?"

"Thursday. Did you ever go out with him?"

"Years ago. When I was well under thirty. I think every new model in New York has dated him. He meets the planes."

"He isn't nice?"

"He's nice enough. He's a fringe benefit of the modeling business. Listen, you better take what's left of my pills. I won't be using them again for a while."

"Oh no! I don't think they're dependable. Look what happened to you. And I don't want to get pregnant."

"Little girl, you ought to learn from Mama. I am a shining example of planned parenthood."

4

It should have been easy. Franciejean was one of the most beautiful girls one was ever likely to meet. There was color and mobility in her face; a continual impression of intense passionate life, balanced only by the deep sadness of her eyes. It should have been easy. It wasn't. And after over three years of making the rounds, she was a legend with the bush-league advertising boys. According to her rate card, it was one lay free with every job. For of all her assets, her physical beauty was the most extravagantly used and wasted. As though she despised it, sensing that it had been bestowed on her only to disgrace her by painful degrees. A man telephoned at midnight.

"Hello, Francie. Remember me?"

"Of course. Your name is Victor."

"Nope; my name is Harry."

"Well, I was close. Victor, Harry. I knew there were two syllables. You're with Maiden Form Girdles."

"No. I'm Kenmore Refrigerators. Anyway, I'd like to talk to you about an ad promotion we're planning. Wanna have a quick drink?"

"Now?"

"Why not?"

Francie had a drink. Many drinks. It actually made no difference to her whom she slept with, as long as she could tell herself it was furthering her career. But somehow she was never invited into the big time. All she did was catalogue pages, package inserts, industrials. At $20 an hour. Once, a photographer who liked her gave it to her straight: "Francie, you give yourself away too cheap. We all know the business—models are considered a client's perk. But not all the time. You ought to be more choosey."

Francie slapped his face gently and kissed him on the nose. "You're jealous."

"That's nuts. First of all I'm married with three children, and I couldn't afford you. Second of all, you never gave me a chance to get romantic—you were too easy. Now I feel like your big brother. You oughta see a shrink."

"Maybe I like sex. It's good for me."

"Who doesn't like it? And I like scotch, too. But that doesn't mean I have to be an alcoholic. But you're that way about sex. You've got this thing—and because you're a model, you kid yourself that it isn't sex; it's getting ahead. It isn't—it's sex. Or, if it isn't sex, it's something I don't understand."

"I don't understand you, Chester. Are you angry at me for something?"

"No, I'm not angry, I like you. That's why I am lecturing you."

"I wish you wouldn't," she said it with surprising dignity.

"All right, all right, little girl. I won't tell your Momma."

"That's not funny."

"Christ, she must be a whopper. You're so afraid of her."

"She's all right." Francie was staring straight ahead. "And I don't want you to talk about her anymore."

"I'm not talking about her. I'm talking about you. And you mind what I said. Get on the wagon."

There is an opinion abroad among certain types of parapsychology buffs that luck is a basic energy of nature, like heat and light; and that for some people at some time, it becomes a resource they are able to tap, almost at will. In her time in the city, Francie had come more and more to the conclusion that she was not one of the lucky people. However, that is the essence of luck. Unlike light and heat, it is an uncontrollable energy. Not predictable, not always available, but not always in short supply. One day Lady Luck smiled on Franciejean Stewart. She got her first break—a TV commercial assignment for a soft drink. The break should have made her happier. It didn't. Then in the summer of the same year, she was invited to a bash in East Hampton.

A sometime friend, elegant Josie Van Ness, invited Francie to the party she and her husband Warren were giving on Further Lane. Francie was floored and delighted at this unexpected show of hospitality. She had admired Josie from a polite distance for a long time, and it awed her that Josie did modeling not for money, but for fun. She had spent a few evenings on the town with Josie and Warren. Now she knew that both Josie and her husband belonged to that class of New Yorkers who grew up in fine houses, went to private schools, had their teeth artfully straightened and were seen at parties covered by the newspapers. These people were almost sacred; to be asked to one of their parties was the privilege of the anointed.

In the crazy disorder of her bedroom, strewn with formal dresses, slacks, coats, shoes and makeup jars, standing barefoot, her nakedness wrapped in a towel, she stared at the sleeping form outlined under a bedsheet. She had a fit of rebellion against the fate which had persuaded her to give Warren Van Ness the honor of seducing her. It occurred to her that the best thing about him was his wife Josie, and his last name, Van Ness. Very classy. In bed he wasn't half as interesting as Greg, an electrician at Filmways.

"Warren, wake up." She poked him severely in the ribs and then repeated the words loudly in his ear: *"Wake up!"* When he covered his head with the sheet, she picked up his shirt, socks, underwear from the floor, rolled them into a hard little ball and started swatting him with them.

Abruptly he rolled over and stuck his head out of the sheet. "Cut it out! Stop it." His eyes now were wide open.

"We shoulda' left hours ago instead of foolin' around. It takes two hours at least to get to Amagansett. And we'll be caught in the traffic, and I hate it. C'mon. Josie's waiting."

Warren reluctantly sorted out his clothes. "Why the hell are you so worried about Josie? She'll wait."

Francie looked at him impatiently. "She's my friend." She explained it precisely, as though giving street directions to a foreigner. "She's my friend, and I don't like to keep a friend waiting. And it's no fun here with you snoring away.

The sun is shining and everybody's on the beach and here we are stuck in the hot city in bed.''

"Things could be worse," Warren remarked, grabbing for her naked leg.

"Let go of me, you bastard! For Pete's sake, *quit it!*" she screamed and somehow yanked her leg free, dashing for the bathroom, where she locked herself in. "Warren, get dressed! Your wife is waiting."

Some hours later, Warren's black Mercedes 300 Cabriolet roared to a stop in front of a large, rambling, ten-room house, a short walking distance from the Amagansett beach, shared by Francie and eight other girls. On alternate weekends, five males took over the house. Usually there was a mix-up, and both groups showed up at the same weekend. As a result, if you came in late on a Saturday night, you were apt to stumble on a couple of strange bodies locked in embrace, asleep on a mattress on the floor, on a davenport in the living room, or tucked away in your own bed. The house was furnished in nondescript Grand Rapids; but since there were so many people continuously hanging around, you rarely saw the furniture. Often the driveway approach to the house was as crowded with cars as Spring Close restaurant. Most of the girls who shared the house were junior executives, secretaries, models. Francie shared a crowded bedroom with two other girls, and sometimes three, at which time a cot was moved into the bedroom and moving around became almost impossible.

After inexpertly parking the car, Warren extricated himself from his seat, went to the trunk and took Francie's suitcase out of the compartment. Then, with ostentatious gallantry, he carried her bag up the path to the steps of the house. As he walked, Francie followed, calling out hellos to men and women wandering up from the beach or seated on the porch. A girl in a bikini reached the entrance of the house at the same time as Warren and Francie. She greeted them and waved to Josie.

"I thought you were coming this morning, Francie. 'Lo Warren, you gorgeous thing-a-ling."

"We waited for Josie," Francie invented. "She's doing the new Gleemadent series. The girl with the young gums or some dumb thing like that."

"Listen, young gums"—Warren poked Francie in the

ribs—"Bingo boy is picking you up at nine-thirty. Be ready. The party starts at ten." He dropped her bag on the sand in front of the house and turned back toward the car, pinching Miss Bikini as he passed. Miss Bikini wagged her tail appreciatively.

"He's so cute," she said to Francie in a whisper intended for Warren to hear. "I wish he were mine."

Francie shrugged. "See if Josie will give you a visitor's pass."

By now Warren was gunning his Merce and roaring off down the road, Josie's head on his shoulder fast asleep.

"How'd she get him?" Miss Bikini persisted, while Francie struggled with her overpacked valise. "She's pretty, but the beach is full of pretty girls. He's prettier. And rich, I hear."

"His mother is rich."

"Same thing. And she's gotta die sometime. How long have he and Josie been married?"

Francie gave the girl a look of scorn. "They were engaged in their cradles, dope. You and me—we're from the wrong side of the tracks. Didn't anybody ever tell you?"

Miss Bikini stared after the receding car speculatively, thinking about this un-American sociological insight. "There's no such thing anymore," she insisted.

The main entrance to the Van Ness house was a long winding driveway that was, this evening, lined with glowing flares waving wildly in the sea breeze. Cars were parked bumper to bumper along this driveway, and the overflow spilled onto Further Lane. The house at the end of the driveway, overlooking the ocean, was as old and opulent as Francie's place was nondescript and drab. The aging house was the summer home of Warren's divorced mother, and she had graciously consented to let him use it for a party while she spent a few weeks in the south of France. The guests were arriving continuously, in twos, threes, fours, and singles. Outside on the huge lawn a mammoth platform had been set up under a striped tent for dancing. Two bars on the large patio were doing a thriving business. People of all sexes, ages, and dress were milling around the patio, the lawn, in and out of the house, drinking, talking, flirting, and dancing. Curiously, nothing could have been more inappropriate and yet somehow fitting in this old, sea-loving mansion, jammed with assorted peacocks and crazy rhythms, than the magnificent crystal Victorian chandelier that hung in the huge living room.

In a corridor, a cross section of party girls of all ages waited impatiently to comb and preen and powder their noses. They were dressed for the party in the variety of ways that reflected the different shades of life in East Hampton. There were summer formals—one all spangles and shine, another plain as a dish towel, and five times as expensive. One girl, just out of the pool, wore a wraparound towel sarong and was scolded for dripping by a pouter pigeon woman who then knocked impatiently on the door of the powder room. Before an actual riot started, Francie finally exited to a barrage of dirty looks, wearing a white dress that clung to her body like a wet glove. Naturally she wore no underthings. She inched her way toward the living room, here and there recognizing a face from the beach, from the city, from modeling.

Suddenly a tall, perspiring young man in white slacks and navy jacket loomed in her way. He was thirty years old, but there was a cherubic innocence in his face that suggested either saintliness or a low IQ.

"Where have you been? I've been looking all over for you."

"Fucking on the beach."

"Oh, come on—"

"Honestly, Bingo, you're like a police dog. Get me a scotch."

Bingo drifted off, reluctantly obeying orders as a heavyset man, sunburned and showered, pushed over to Francie.

"I've been calling you for a week. Didn't you get my messages?"

"Sure I got them."

"Then why didn't you call back?"

"Because I had nothing to say."

"Are you angry at me?" His voice was unnaturally humble. "Why are you avoiding me?"

Francie started to fidget and then stared around the room as though looking for something of interest. Impatiently the man passed his head along the curves of her body, thoroughly familiar with it, trying to arouse her, but he only aroused himself; Francie was unmoved. In exasperation he reached

58

roughly for her arm and pulled her close to himself, rubbing his body against hers. "Let's go down to the beach," he said.

Francie, much stronger than she looked, put both hands flat against his shoulders and pushed him away. "No!" she said, looking at him with cool anger, breathing deeply; and though her mouth was open as though parted for kissing, it was not meant for him.

"Then let's go for a walk and talk."

"Same answer."

"I've missed you badly, I don't sleep at all any-more. . . . Please, let's go outside." He put his finger again on her bare shoulder.

"Stop that!" She took his hand off her shoulder.

"Sorry, I didn't realize I was doing anything. I just wanted to touch you."

"I don't want you to touch me."

"You used to like it."

"Arthur, go find another girl. I'm booked for weeks." Francie moved quickly into the crowd, joining a line of people doing the hully-gully. A young man, looking for a twist partner, pulled her out of the line and into the living room where a twist was going on to the music of a record player. Francie, moving swiftly over the floor, tripped suddenly over the long legs of a youngish man seated on the steps that led to the upstairs quarters of the house. Fortunately she landed in his lap.

"Wow! Pleased to meet you."

"Enchanté." He helped Francie to her feet. "It's my big feet."

Francie looked at him interestedly. "I read somewhere that big feet and thin ankles were aristocratic."

Francie's dancing partner joined them. "Come on, girl." Then he noticed the man on the steps. "Hey, Peter, how's the boy? What are you doing at a Warren party? Slumming?"

"There were no vacant johns on Egypt Lane."

"Well, we've got plenty of toilets here. And booze. And girls. And boys. A swingin' party. Swings both ways." He pulled Francie into the center of the room.

"I'll think of you often when we're apart." She threw Peter a kiss as she moved off.

"Who was the pretty thing?" asked a man coming down the steps to sit beside Peter, a man a few years older who seemed, in some indefinable manner which was not a matter of age or dress, not of a piece with the other guests.

Peter shrugged. "I've no idea. But she is a beauty."

"I wouldn't overdo it," remarked the older man.

In the long, old-fashioned kitchen adjacent to the living room, two black maids and a white butler were busily at work, setting out new dishes of hors d'oeuvres and washing glasses. Warren and a beautiful gay boy named Gilbert were doing tricks with Gilbert's French poodle at the far end of the kitchen. Josie was checking food, sampling as she went. Francie sat on a kitchen chair kibitzing.

"He never leaves me alone. You'd think he was a teenager. And he's always wanting me to pose in the nude. Once, when I was young and dumb, I posed in the mall in Central Park at 6:00 A.M. He had me prancing around with not a stitch on but this crazy, gauzy thing . . . ugh . . . and he paid me beans. Beans."

"Francie, Arthur is a real artist with the camera. He has a showing at the Museum of Modern Art right now. It's practically an honor to pose for him. Like being a model for Picasso."

"Terrific. *You* be honored. *You* can afford his price. He's a pest and—oh boy, speak of the devil."

The heavyset man with the shock of gray hair who looked more like a successful corporate executive than a top fashion photographer pushed his way into the kitchen. He made a beeline toward Francie. "You disappeared. Please, let's dance."

Thoroughly irritated, Francie got up out of her chair and walked over to Warren. "Sorry, Arthur. Warren asked me first. Didn't you, Warren?"

Puzzled but pleased, Warren stopped playing with the dog and put his arms around Francie. "Sure, girl, sure. Come on, let's dance."

As they danced toward the dance floor in the living room, over Warren's shoulder Francie watched Josie watching Arthur. Unexpectedly, Josie put her arms around Arthur's neck and coaxed him into dancing. How could Josie bother with that creep, Francie wondered?

"You sure feel good, girl." Warren held her more tightly.

"Quit it. Josie will see you. And furthermore, I can't breathe."

"Sometimes I think you care more about Josie than me."

"I do. I like her, I don't like you."

"What are you—a lesbian?"

"Nope, just a good judge of character."

"Thanks, kid."

"Welcome."

Francie talked lightly with many men, let quite a few kiss her, let Warren caress her too intimately. Husbands, she thought scornfully, slipping out of his hands. "I guess I'm a sex goddess." She giggled to herself nervously.

The party seemed to go on for days: the musicians never stopped playing; the record player was loaded with records; the liquor never ran out. Francie felt she was the only one who ate the wonderful shrimp and oysters and franks. People were phantoms in the colorful shifting play of lights under the huge tent. They were beautiful and gracious. Or they were ugly and crazy. And all kinds of things happened—funny things, ugly things.

A young man in wet swim trunks and a young woman in a bikini came up out of the ocean, walked up the sea steps toward the house, elbowed their way into the center of the tent, and interrupted the dancing. The young man held up his hand for silence.

"All right, campers—no more decadent body contact—it's time for the event of the evening: a nice, wholesome moonlight swim."

"What's he talking about?" a dancing girl asked.

There was a general burst of confusion and excitement within the tent as people reacted to the swimming announcement, some with apprehension, some with delight.

"Come on, come on," said the wet-haired girl. "The water's perfect. It's warm as a bathtub."

"I've already taken a bath," remarked a carefully gowned woman.

"I didn't bring a swim suit," said a man.

"I don't have a suit either," wailed a girl.

"You don't need a suit."

"Do you dare me?"

"He doesn't have to, Pat, he knows you. Anyway there are suits at the bathhouse. Courtesy of the management."

"Everybody who's going swimming, pick a buddy. And remember, you are responsible for your buddy's welfare."

The people under the tent milled around arguing over who would be whose partner. Groups of people moved toward the bathhouse. Others went down toward the beach in evening clothes. Girls kicked off their shoes, a man pulled at his tie and opened his shirt. There was a general impulse to disrobe. Only a few die-hard waterproof souls kept on dancing while the band continued to play uncertainly.

Standing on the sand, silhouetted in the light streaming out of the main house, stood a group of people already in bathing suits, in the middle of a heated argument. Francie, in a bikini, sipping a martini, was leaning against Max Plummer, a plump, perspiring, bald-headed lawyer who led the argument. Through it all, Francie listened quietly, an odd look on her face.

"It's not possible," said Max flatly.

"I agree completely. It's impossible," said Mary, a tall, leggy girl with a wonderful figure.

"You're both nuts," said Jack, short, chunky, and wearing glasses.

"Yes, you are. Men are stronger than women," said Martha.

"That has nothing to do with it," remarked Tony reasonably. "It has to do with the way we're constructed."

"Exactly," said Max. "Here's this old bag—no man ever went near her when she was a young bag—and here she is, fifty years old, screamin' about how this kid raped her. It's incredible."

"Maybe he likes them old, has a mother complex," remarked Martha.

"That's crazy," said a clean-cut young man.

"He didn't rape her. She had no body bruises. Nothing. If anything happened—which I sincerely doubt—she raped him. And the jury agreed with me," said Max, shaking his head vehemently.

"I do, too. It can't be done," said the clean-cut young man.

"Sure it can," insisted Jack. "Just a little persuasion."

"That's not what we're talking about. That's seduction. That's not rape."

"It's very possible. I've heard stories."

"Sure it is—"

"You're just romantic. I'd like to see anyone try it with me," said Mary.

"I'll tell you—I'll put my money where my mouth is. I say it's impossible. It's possible to rape a woman—oh sure, if you beat her up or knock her unconscious you can do it. But not otherwise."

"I agree," said Mary.

"Here's one hundred dollars. Anybody wanna make a bet?" Max took a fat wallet out of his beach robe and pulled out a hundred dollar bill. There was silence in the crowd. People weren't quite sure what to do. In the midst of this uncertainty Bingo hurried to Francie.

"I've been looking for you all over. Gosh, you've got your suit on already. How can I go swimming? I just ate." Francie nodded her head in exaggerated sympathy. "Are you gonna swim?"

"I might," she teased. "As soon as I change into something more comfortable."

"Bingo, how'd you like to take a chance on winning $100?" asked Mary, pinching him in his small paunch.

The group of people stared at Bingo and then broke into nervous laughter. Bingo was obviously not the man for the job. He stared at all of them in bewilderment and Mary patted him fondly. At which point Jack made his offer.

"Mary, old chum, somehow you and I never got past being pen pals. But I'll put my money where my prick is. I'll bet my hundred against Max's hundred that I can move us into a more intimate relationship, as they call it. And you'll stay conscious. What do you say? Game?" He looked at Mary with a strange mixture of arrogance, anger and lust.

Mary stared at Jack thoughtfully, a look of hurt surprise on her face. Then she shrugged, and giving him a brief coy smile said, "It will be my pleasure, lover boy. Winner take all."

About ten minutes later the group huddled in a circle on the sand tripled in number, augmented by men and women in bathing suits who had stopped to watch on their way to and from the ocean. Those in the front circle were squatting or seated on the sand. Latecomers, who constituted the second and third ring of the concentric circles, were standing on tiptoe to get a better view of the action. What everyone was watching with a kind of hypnotic intensity was Mary and Jack struggling with each other on the sand, competing for the $200. They both laughed as they tussled, and bystanders alternately applauded and cheered one or the other. Max, Francie and Bingo, a little off to the side of the contestants, were watching attentively.

"See what I mean?" said Max. "He can't even keep her still."

"Mary's a dancer," said Tony. "Most women aren't that strong. Or agile."

"Makes no difference. When a woman's afraid, her adrenalin works. She gets plenty strong. I tell you it can't be done unless you knock her out."

The group, which had begun by cheering and catcalling enthusiastically, was growing more and more edgy as they watched the struggle.

"Jack, you fink," shrilled a blond girl. "You're a washout as a cave man."

"Come on, Jack, old man! If you make it you get to kiss her," shouted a boy.

"Kick him in the stomach, Mary!" called a girl.

"That's not where it counts," remarked another.

"She knows what I mean."

The struggle between Jack and Mary on the sand was quickly becoming more serious. An ugly note of reality had crept into the contest.

"Say—let's break it up. It's getting too real," said Bingo.

"How would you know that, Bingo? Who you raped lately?" asked Tony.

"Nobody." Bingo was pained. "But this looks awful."

"It's not supposed to be fun. They've got a two-hundred-dollar bet on. Winner takes all."

"See? He can't even hold her still. That was the whole point of my closing to the jury," said Max. "That housepainter couldn't've raped that woman unless she cooperated. It's impossible. Unless you knock her out. Or kill her. Or scare her."

"He may do that yet. He'll end up winning that damn money, damn it," said a girl.

The struggle was now dead serious. The cheering had stopped. There was no talk. All that could be heard was the sound of the boy and girl locked in their desperate embrace; the gasps of their heavy breathing; the thrashing around of their bodies as they rolled around on the sand. The people who were watching showed strained, fascinated, frightened faces. Everyone knew it had gone too far; but like people in a trance, no one seemed able to interfere with the horrid course of fate.

Francie's face was cold with rage. Every muscle in her body responded in synchrony with Mary's strenuous efforts to rid herself of Jack. And as Mary's strength waned, Francie's rage grew. When Jack suddenly managed to wedge his knee between Mary's flailing legs, Francie's body exploded into violence. She lunged forward into the struggle and started pounding on Jack's head with both fists: "You goddamn bastard! At least tell her you love her!"

Stunned, the crowd stared at Francie in confusion, dazed and angry at the interruption of their sadomasochistic dream. But the spell was broken. Sanity had returned; and with embarrassed relief, they erupted into feverish laughter and giggles. The boy and girl who had been struggling so fiercely together fell apart and rolled on the sand, rocking too with laughter and relief. The terror was over.

Francie, staring around her, looked like someone awakened sharply from a night fright. Without clearly knowing what she had said, she started to giggle nervously. She moved backward from the group and toward the ocean. Her steps were uneven as if she were recovering from a drunken stupor. "Hey! This is a nothing swim meet," she yelled. "Come on! Last one in is a rotten egg!"

And she whirled, running off down the beach toward the ocean, to splash feverishly and stare at the moon.

Jack and Mary, who had just been struggling in mortal combat with each other, got up shakily from the sand. Jack helped Mary to get her bearings. Then he took her hand shyly, and together they started running down the beach after Francie. The crowd followed, shouting and laughing, half hysterically, while Max, standing alone with Bingo, watched them shaking his head in disgust.

*   *   *

The party was thinning out; but Francie, now back in her dress, was reluctant to leave with Bingo. She'd been searching for something all evening; some amorphous connection that she herself did not understand. Enough men had asked for her telephone number, to take her home, to have a date the following week. So all in all the party for her was a success. But something—what?—that she had expected and hoped would happen had not happened. She was circling the grounds and the house, trying to lose herself in the people still there, avoiding Bingo, when she again saw the man she had tripped over earlier sitting in the enclosed patio, sipping a drink and talking to a man and woman. He had the kind of male good looks Francie had learned to respond to from her careful study of fashion magazines: strikingly handsome, casual and easy, one of the golden people of the world whose presence in a room somehow made the light perceptibly brighter. Men as well as women would feel the fascination of his physical being.

Francie wandered up to him. "You have romantic eyes."

He smiled appreciatively. "You're a very observant, very pretty girl."

"I think you're the most attractive man I've seen here tonight. I believe we met before. I was sitting in your lap."

"You were indeed. Let me introduce my lap. My name is Peter Devlin."

"I'm Franciejean Stewart. You're almost the most attractive man I've seen anywhere. You ought to give me a chance."

"A chance?" Peter looked at her with something like embarrassment, and then turned to the two people beside him. "This is Vera Busch and this is Jamison Welsh. Vera, Jamie, meet Franciejean Stewart."

Vera nodded courteously and told Peter she needed another drink, but Jamie answered kindly, "Hello, Miss Stewart."

Francie glanced at the man briefly, uninterested, then abruptly turned back to meet his steady gaze. He was a few years older than the golden Peter Devlin, and he was hardly handsome by the same standards. He had a face, she thought, that looked as if it had been carved out of stone, that gave the impression of his belonging to an older, more developed race.

To his friends, Jamison Welsh was sometimes affectionately known as "Mount Rushmore." His forehead protruded while his cheeks were sunken. He had a thin beaked nose, and a heavy jaw. His eyes were cold and brilliant, his best feature; and they rested on her in a detached enjoyment of her beauty as though she were some kind of rare, superfine human merchandise. But there was neither sexual desire nor pleading in his glance. For a moment Francie had the sensation of stepping into the bright sunlight of day.

Jamison Welsh did not seem to have what Scott Fitzgerald once described as the second two most important attributes in the world; namely good looks and intelligence. He had the first two: animal magnetism and money. Under the circumstances his extraordinary intelligence was often overlooked. And without any sense of the fatefulness of her decision, and contrary to all her prior romantic notions about men, Francie decided that Jamison, not Peter, was the man she most wanted to know.

"How do you do, Mr. Welsh." She smiled engagingly, and then put her face quietly up to be kissed. Jamie looked at her for a moment, not understanding, then he kissed her without enjoying it. She clung nearer, almost desperately; he kissed her again and a soft hum of passion started within him.

Even on Jamison, a man totally civilized and unsentimental, Francie had impact. She was the most direct, unambiguous woman with whom he had ever come in contact. What Francie wanted, Francie went after. There was no jockeying for position, no premeditation, no calculation to her seductiveness. Francie simply made a man conscious of the high degree of her physical beauty. And her availability.

"You're better than beautiful," Jamison said. "Everything you do comes across. Even kissing." He turned to Peter, but Peter and Vera were no longer seated at the table. They had wandered off toward the bar.

"Especially kissing." Francie smiled.

Jamison watched her with mild amusement. He found, in her talk and manner, the aesthetic pleasure which a brilliant, vigorous man is apt to find in a passing flirtation with a vividly pretty young woman. Everything about her was at once exquisite, strong, fine. Of course, he had the cynical impression that the qualities that distinguished her from the rest of her sex were chiefly physical, as though a fine glaze of beauty had been applied to quite ordinary clay. But perhaps the analogy did not hold. Perhaps this was material that originally had been fine, but the circumstances of her life had made the qualities of her mind ordinary. Still, the answer to that question was meant for another day, and abruptly he stood up. "I think it's time I was going too. It's enough party."

"Did you come with anyone?" Her smile was provocative.

"No . . ." Jamison doubted the spontaneity of her liking him, but still he admired the effort she was making.

"How nice. The man I came with is dead drunk somewhere on the beach. Maybe he drowned. It would be lovely if you would take me home."

"Where is home?" The invitation in her eyes increased his amusement.

"In a house in Amagansett."

On an impulse of curiosity, and to play the game properly, he suggested, "Why don't we go to my house? For a nightcap. I live on the Highway Behind the Pond."

"The Pond? Are there swans?"

"There are swans."

"I like swans." Her color deepened. Evidently she could still blush, but she accepted the suggestion as lightly as the tone in which it was made.

5

Jamison Welsh's house in East Hampton looked much larger than it actually was. It had the deceptive simplicity of a sixteenth-century English country cottage. There was nothing pretentious about it, as in the splendor of the Van Ness house; but to the properly schooled eye, the presence of a lavish bank account was clearly evident. To find the house, a visitor had to follow careful directions; first in discovering the right private road and then in locating the twisting dirt lane, leading off the private road, that finally led to the front door of the pale beige wood-and-stucco structure. The house was hidden from its neighbors by an acre of uncultivated woodland, but closer in were two acres of lawn and garden surrounding it that looked as if they'd been there for generations. Inside the house, an ambiance of informality—a sunny dining room with flowers everywhere, the living room filled with large overstuffed furniture, giving the guest a feeling that one could sit down anywhere—neutralized the sheer elegance of the decor. In the entrance hall, an Aubusson rug covered a scrubbed chestnut floor; in the dining room a Biedermeier maple table and a Queen Anne walnut chest stood on the original square, stone-tiled floor. Beyond the tall, graceful glass doors of the living room lay a terrace and a well-trimmed lawn sloping down to the pond.

It was to this house, rather than to the ramshackle rental where Francie was camping, that Jamison brought her that evening. It was in this house that Franciejean's education began.

It was a measure of Francie's intelligence, that, without

the slightest knowledge of furniture, of paintings, of objects d'art, she knew on entering that this house was the most beautiful home she'd ever seen. As she wandered around, staring at small pieces of sculpture, paintings, books, she felt clumsy and somehow gaudy. She felt her dress didn't fit. She didn't fit. To cover this humility she asked, "Is this all yours?"

Jamison, who was busy fixing himself a Campari, nodded, preoccupied, so Francie continued. "You must be rich. Warren's place is bigger, but this is really something. Warren's place really belongs to his mother. She supports him. Poor little rich boy. Who supports you?"

"I bought this with green stamps," Jamison remarked dryly. "What would you like to drink?"

"Anything you want to give me! And what a view. That pond! And those swans. How can you ever go to sleep at night?"

"I don't. I stay up and brood. I'm giving you Campari and soda."

"What is that?"

"You'll see."

"I like scotch too."

"I can give you that."

"No, no. I like new things too." She smiled at him slyly. "You said there was a swan on that pond—and there is."

"Occasionally there are many swans. Whole families." He handed her the drink.

"Thank you for the Cam—What is it? Campari?"

"Yes."

Francie tasted it. "Tastes like licorice sticks. Now let's go swan watching."

"All right." He sounded as if he were humoring a sleepy child. "But it's getting very late."

"I know. Are you married?" She put it to him on the simplest ground. She wanted him to understand that she already liked him so much it wouldn't matter.

Quite without any explanation, he seemed to understand that this was not a coy question. "No, I am not. Are you?"

She knew he was not asking because he cared one way or another. It was almost a gesture of politeness. "You knew I wasn't married." She laughed. It wasn't simply her lack of a wedding ring that cued him. Other wives often left off their rings at strategic moments. She knew a model who wore hers around her neck on a chain. What he knew, he knew because he knew her. "You never for one minute thought I was married. I'm not the kind who marries."

"One can never be certain. I've heard of lots of girls marrying. It's becoming quite common."

Francie made a flamboyant gesture with her arm, waving aside the mere notion. "You know I've never thought of myself as a wife. Maybe a mistress. But a wife?" She stared into the glass of Campari. "Do you live here alone—in this house? Aren't you afraid?"

"Of what? Burglars? The house is quite secluded. And protected. My houseman, who lives in the wing over the garage, is an ex-FBI agent. There's rarely any trouble out here anyway. It's a quiet community."

"I see." Francie nodded as though she were listening, but there were gaps in her attention; she missed whole sequences of words. "I didn't mean burglars. I meant—"

"Yes?" He was attracted by her long blond hair swinging loosely about her shoulders and her pale, questioning face; but at the same time, he was beginning to be bored and wondered what he would do with her and why he had agreed to bring her here.

"Well, I guess I mean ghosts, or things out of the sea. Silkies—you know."

Jamison thought, women are very strange. Even very young women are very strange. "You have a splendid imagination. I don't." He didn't feel like humoring her anymore, pretty though she was; and he sat down heavily on the couch.

The silence between them grew; and Francie saw in his eyes a certain contempt, a laxness in his mouth, an abandonment in his expression, the look of someone even more experienced than she. He was remembering other scenes; and if she did not awaken his desire shortly, she would lose her hold on him entirely. She sat down at his side putting her drink on the floor beside her, her whole body feeling warm and almost feverish. "Have you ever been married?" she asked, making up sentences to distract him.

"You do have a preoccupation with marriage." He put his hands on her shoulders in a halfhearted caress.

"Have you?" she persisted, puzzled by herself.

"No. . . ." He put one hand under her chin and raised her face to his. She thought then that he was going to kiss her, and her body started to quiver. But all he did was to study her face.

"Do you think I'm pretty?" she stammered, hoping he would not see the rash of very tiny pimples just over her ear, covered by makeup and her hairline.

"Quite pretty. Do you have many boyfriends?"

"I've lots of guys hanging around if that's what you mean. But I don't think of boys as friends."

"You don't think men and women can be friends?"

"Just once in a while. Anyway, I like you." His presence blurred her speech. "I don't think we'll ever be friends."

Jamison pulled Francie's body against him, his hands moving beneath her dress, exploring, circling, stroking. Francie's eyes began to shine in an extraordinary way. Her nipples grew hard, the hairs on her skin stood straight up; and it was as if she became hypersensitive, seeming to quiver under his fingers. A shiver passed along her spine rippling down her neck, touching every nerve. But the whole performance, though highly expert, had for him a faintly mechanical quality. He paused in the middle of his caress and held her away from him. He stared at her face; her eyes were half closed, her lips parted, so aroused that she was totally unaware of this cold scrutiny.

"What will we be?"

"I don't know. Don't stop." She was irritated by the question, the way a sleeper is bothered by noise. "What difference does it make what we'll be? Lovers with luck."

"Do you like me to touch you?" Her desire was contagious, and it further excited him that she was wearing no panties. Her body was moist and her pubic hair soft as a baby's.

"Yes."

"You're a sensualist. A born sensualist." He moved his hands between her legs, and she trembled with pleasure.

Francie raised her eyes in a disquieting stare. She laughed as she unbuttoned his shirt, opened it, rubbing her breasts against his chest, her tongue searching for his ears, for the tongue in his mouth. Then she leaned back slightly, her fingers first circling his nipples and afterward running expertly down to his waist to unfasten his belt. But he caught her

72

hands at the wrists and placed them behind his neck while he unfastened his belt himself and took out his erect penis. Unable to restrain herself, Francie dropped her hands to his penis, feeling the rush of dense blood swelling it; but now her legs trembled, her lower body opened, begging for attention. Jamie looked at her and shivered; and before her lips could touch him, he gripped her by the shoulders and pulled her down onto the carpet beside him. He took her there in a pitch of sensual frenzy, bending her as if she were a rag doll, twisting her into every position, taking whatever part of her he wanted—her mouth, her belly, her nipples—her ass—biting and kissing her at the same time. Francie was stunned at the ruthlessness of this man who had seemed so detached, so cool. His violence made her want to retaliate with fury, for she had never before allowed herself to feel; she hated this over her like some animal over its prey, pinning her down under him, plunging himself into her again and again, filling her to the very core of her vagina. A volcano of passion exploded inside her but it brought neither joy nor relief. Sensing this, he incited her to surrender to her most violent appetites.

"Go ahead, go ahead. Now try to kill me," he whispered.

She was hardly aware of biting his neck or of his teeth buried in her shoulder. She was only aware of a savage fever she had never allowed herself to feel before; she hated this man but she could not get enough of him; of his penis, of his mouth, of his body. She would kill him if she could, but it was no use—the approach of the orgasm was too much. It started in her lower legs, flowing upward along her thighs; her back and then her whole body arched upward and she shuddered convulsively. Afterward she lay back on the carpet, exhausted and only semiconscious.

Hours later—Francie did not know how many hours—she awakened in a large bed in a dawn-lit bedroom, alone. There was no man sleeping under the sheets beside her. For a few minutes Francie could recall neither who nor where she was. She had to get away—where were her clothes? Under the sheets she was naked. She scrambled hurriedly out of bed, breaking into a cold sweat as she looked around at the beautiful but unfamiliar surroundings. There was a bathrobe, a man's navy bathrobe neatly folded on a chair near the bed. She grabbed for it, slipped it on, and found it yards too large; she was swimming in it. So she took it off and instead put it over her shoulders holding it closed with one hand. But the bathrobe kept slipping off her shoulder, so she had to wrap it around her like a sarong. This done, she tiptoed out of the bedroom down a slowly brightening corridor that ultimately led into the calm early morning of the living room. The living room looked civilized and comfortable. Who would have believed what had gone on there, only a few hours earlier? Francie wondered where her clothes were; she wondered where Jamie was sleeping; she wondered and then stopped still and stared out the glass door, transfixed by the beauty of the mirrorlike pond, a solitary swan resting on the water.

"What are you doing up so early?" a quiet voice behind her asked, and she whirled in a panic to see Jamison in a silk kimono watching her. He had evidently come out of a room that she saw now must be a library.

"Nothing, I wanted to get up."

Jamison watched her thoughtfully; and as he stared, a slow emphatic flame which had started in her body, hidden by the robe, spread upward over her breasts and throat and face, to the very roots of her hair, as if she had been standing in the glow of a particularly gorgeous sunset. She was young, but far from naive. She was hardly a virgin, and he wondered what forces lay within this beautiful child, making her blood rise unwilled at the sight of him. He hoped it was a compliment. "Are you a sleepwalker? Or a dawn-walker?" he asked.

"Both. Sometimes," she said, wrapping the robe around her again.

They stood looking at each other, she with a conscious stillness, as if each waited for the other to strike the note or set the pitch. He had the advantage of experience and self-knowledge, while her face told him immediately of her embarrassment. How could she know that it was her capacity for anarchy and destruction that attracted him to her? Sexually she was capable of anything, as was he. But she hardly knew that, since she hardly knew herself. And while he could step back from his sexual deliriums, she became the thing itself.

"What is the matter?" he asked, trying to soothe her.

"Nothing—nothing. I was looking at the swans. They're so beautiful."

74

Jamison nodded. The connection between them was already established; he knew her intimately. In the early morning light her young figure wrapped in his bathrobe was so childlike, and yet what could be seen was heart-piercing by reason of its perfection and vulnerability. He saw again that her hair was like golden flax; and he saw her narrow wrists that certain Italian sculptors in the great years had loved, her long hands and fingers and the shape and color of her fingernails. He knew the fine workings of her body as though lovingly made by a great artisan for show or for a prize. Those hinges gave her a special, untutored grace of movement. If she lifted her arm to smooth her hair, it could make him stare. The gesture was so flawless. Yet he doubted that anyone but himself noticed it. She was young; she was, he gathered, broke. Her beauty was taken for granted, most of all by herself; and she herself had put it up for sale. If she went down, she would go down with a unique swiftness. She reminded him of a great three-year-old his father had once owned who had broken her leg on the backstretch at Churchill Downs and had to be destroyed.

"Francie, why are you afraid? I am not going to hurt you. I didn't really hurt you last night, did I?" He wanted to be kind.

She shook her head emphatically. "Oh no, you didn't." A flood of memories of the night before raced through her body warming her like brandy. Now her desire for him was returning; and her sense of his skin, of his odor, of the strength of his body was abnormally acute. She had never been so easily aroused, and she wanted to hide it. "No, no, it isn't you. It wasn't the sex. But I've never really slept overnight with a man. Not in his house or a hotel room. I mean not overnight. I always go home. Or he does."

Jamison shook his head in wonder and some curiosity. "Why? Is sex sinful?"

"Oh, it has nothing to do with sex. I just can't sleep in bed with a man. I hate it. It frightens me."

The remarkable thing—and remarkable was what it came down to—was the casual way he carried out the business of making her odd remarks sound natural enough. "Oh, of course. You'd rather sleep in your own bed."

"Yes. You see my mother is always watching me. She loves me a lot." She was remembering her first night in New

75

York when she almost slept over at Monroe's house. But that was before she knew that Momma had followed her.

"Aaaah; of course." The way she said it, his sense of what she was telling him, seemed to clear the air, seemed to comfort her. She knew now she could trust him to give her the right cue—as though he gave her a spoonful of medicine—except that his cue would be easy to swallow.

"I always go home afterward. I always sleep alone afterward. But this time I didn't." It did wonders for her to tell him the truth. "So I wanted to see if she was outside."

"Your mother?"

Francie nodded. "Yes, my mother. I've never really told anyone about her before. She watches over me."

The effect of her words left him with a view of what he was now facing; the truth that was truest about Franciejean. "And was she outside?"

Francie shook her head. "No, she wasn't."

It was just because he knew life, because he knew what mattered and what didn't, what was real and what wasn't, that he could ask without making anything of it. "And how long has she been dead?"

"Oh, a hundred years I guess. She died when I was ten. Maybe eleven."

"Has she ever been outside a room?"

"No! But you know, sometimes I can feel her presence."

Jamison accepted this; but it would have taken a far keener observer than Franciejean to see the inward use he made of her information. For what had come out for him with the reality of her terror was the recognition that he must move with great care. "What about your father?" he asked offhandedly.

"I think he must have been very nice. But he's not very clear. He died before my mother. I was what they left."

"Who raised you?"

"My father's sisters. My aunts."

"Ah, the family."

"Well, not 'family' the way you say it." She had the distinct impression that he was trying to reassure her—or more precisely, reassure himself about her situation. He was trying to tell himself that she had family, relatives, connections; and in telling himself, tell it to her and comfort her. But it was no use, he must accept that. She had it on the highest authority—that of her own experience—that she was alone, really alone. This she could tell him, if she could tell him anything at all. "You see, they are okay people. Good enough, I guess. But they have their own children to raise and worry about. And children cost money. And there's never been enough money. It's a good thing I grew up quickly, because I was wearing out my welcome. Even with Aunt Gert, and she was the nicest. I think she was really glad for me to go to New York."

"From where?"

"Davenport, Iowa. But I was born in Evanston." She had told him this because his manner seemed to give her the chance to talk. And it showed him, in spite of himself, how influences outside of the rational could delicately weigh with him; showed him, too, how interested he was becoming in her.

"Then you've really no relations or friends—that is, who you can count on?"

"Oh, I know tons of people. Hordes. And packs of relatives. But count on them? It wouldn't make the slightest difference to anyone if I were to die this minute." She said this without a hint of complaint. It was as it was. "Sometimes things are like that, you know." What she most wanted him to see was that she wasn't afraid.

He understood this and he nodded. "Well, you haven't had it easy. But that doesn't mean it has to be difficult forever."

"Of course not," she said. "Look—now I have you for a friend."

This brief exchange did something to him. It gave him a vivid sense of her reality. "Yes, now you have me for a friend. And mothers usually like me." The incongruity of the remark was the result of his seeing much more: seeing how little rationality mattered when someone was in her state. And her state was now, by some subtle twist of honor, his own, once he recognized her hungry dependence on him. It was as though whatever he did now, or didn't do, would resound directly in her life, so that a false note might precipitate disaster.

But what sealed the bargain finally was Franciejean herself, Francie who made the relationship viable. It was

Francie's manner, her bravery, her gaiety, and perhaps above all, her imagination that simplified his dealing with her. "I know mothers like you," she said. "I'm sure mine would. That's just why I picked you among thousands, last night." She giggled as she said it.

"I thought it was I who picked you." He was chivalrous in the best sense, if chivalry means to defend the honor of your partner as you would your own.

Reality had so often before met her in a more ugly shape than this that she felt a deep gratitude to him for the generosity of his words. But she was too world-wise to be fooled. "You're being nice," she said. "And it's nice of you to be nice. But I know who conned who. I asked you to take me home. I said I liked swans."

"I could have said 'no' if I hadn't already decided otherwise. I am old enough to take very good care of myself."

She gave him the ghost of a grateful smile. She was still so young that she could be beguiled by the idea of a miracle, and could feel this at last as another justification of her faith in her own star; a proof of her being a favorite of the gods. She had never been a favorite among human beings. She looked at him a moment with full eyes, and something came up out of her depths. "You don't mind then about my mother?" She was careless now about holding the robe around her.

"No, why should I?"

His tone gave her no clue, and she paused waiting for one; but he only let her wait and at last she had to say something. "She doesn't do any harm."

"No, she doesn't." The words came out clumsily, sounding hurriedly sewn together when he wished to sound firm.

"I guess you could say I have a mother complex."

His pity for her quickened. "I guess you could say so."

"Well, it's harmless enough." Face to face as they were, something had to pass between them. "And it isn't at the moment fatal."

"It certainly isn't." He studied her with the care he might have given a rare art object. She was indeed an odd product—her extreme youngness. She looked, if possible, even younger than her years. And then there was her beauty, her homelessness, her lack of friends, and obvious lack of means. Everything about her confirmed his initial judgment. If she weren't picked up, while still on the surface, by someone who would value her beauty and oddness, she would someday be found at the bottom. This thought determined for him a remark that would have been, a few minutes earlier, a definite risk. But the openness with which she had been speaking made the difference. "Your mother would like you to marry, I'm sure. Modeling is all well and good, but there are other things. A husband, a home, children."

"Oh, I'm sure she would. Modeling isn't at all what I thought it would be like. But it's a living." She looked at him with curiosity, and he thought for an instant he might have overstepped. "Anyway, who would I marry?"

"Some pleasant, ambitious young man who would like an extremely pretty wife. And wants to raise a family."

"You think so?"

"Don't you?"

She gave him a smile that said she knew a world he never would. "Well, I'll tell you. I have tried. But no one will have me." Then she seemed to regret his having to feel sorry for her. "But you know, life isn't only a matter of getting married. These days there are more things for women to do."

"I can't believe no one will have you."

"Would you?" She asked the question without guile or malice.

"Francie, I am almost old enough to be your father. Considering that I was always sexually precocious."

"No, it's not that. You won't have me. I'm only beautiful. But that's a dime a dozen. I have nothing to offer." She wished to please him, but she knew what she was about, and stuck to her point. "Oh yes. I'm a good lay, or a piece of tail—I hate that expression—or whatever you want to call it. You would agree to that, wouldn't you?" She laughed nervously. "Only I am what I am. And what I am doesn't seem to be marriageable." She said this with a grim straightness, as she let the robe that had been wrapped around her slide toward the floor. She stood before him naked now, her whole body delicately rounded and smooth, luminous in the dawn light. She looked at him with a soft, lustful glance that acknowledged the passion that had grown between them. It was she who moved toward him lifting her mouth up to be kissed.

He kissed her then, his hands on her breasts; and she felt the fury of his spirit run through her. She thought for a second that what she wanted to do was escape—escape his hands, his mouth. She was breathless with fear and desire. Yet some unknown girl within her wanted the feel of his skin, his hardness, to caress him with her mouth and her hands. Her whole body rubbed against him begging him to take her.

As though in a dream, she felt his hands everywhere at once upon her, following the fullness of her breasts, curving with the curve of her waist, the roundness of her buttocks, his fingers seeking the softness between the center of her legs, the wetness. In silence their eyes met, and he picked her up and carried her into the bedroom where she had been sleeping. Her hair was wild, and her mind was drugged by his caresses, a bewildering mix of fierceness and gentleness. His hands roamed everywhere, his lips and tongue following his hands. There was something animal-like about the way he made love and yet she knew she had come back for more. She felt him, a column of flesh enter her with restless fury; and her body shuddered with responsive fury and exultation. Every nerve, every cell in her vagina was newly aroused; and she seemed to dissolve into a thousand inner mouths, sucking, swallowing, melting into him, becoming him. Her fever for him rose, and she felt a great change happening within her, and she was afraid she would die of it. And then without realizing it she moaned, as deep within her soul, her womb, the shining little death-joy began to grow and grow; and she surrendered her will to his, sinking into a dreamlike oblivion of pleasure.

Sometime later, when Francie slowly opened her eyes, the sun had risen and the room was golden. From somewhere in the house she could smell the odor of coffee; and when she turned, she saw Jamie sitting beside her on the bed, this time in tennis shorts and shirt, his hands gently stroking the curves of her body beneath the sheet. Francie lay there half awake, and then, so warmed by his sight and touch that she almost reached orgasm, she turned and stretched out her arms to embrace him. But Jamison stopped his caresses, smiled and moved back, shaking his head.

"Much as I'd like to, we can't stay in bed all day. I have a tennis appointment at ten and it's nine o'clock now. Here, put this on." And he handed her a blue silk kimono much like the brown one he'd worn earlier.

"Oh," was all she said, obediently slipping into the robe.

But her tone was one of dry despair, and it represented in that sunlit room a bleak acceptance of her place in the world. For her, the party was over. Now she was to be dismissed. Don't call us, we'll call you. Jamison heard the hurt in her tone, and it moved him that she did not judge him in any way; if anything it showed him her own cold self-appraisal.

"Would you like some coffee? Some breakfast?" he asked.

"Whatever you think," she answered absently, for now her thoughts were elsewhere, preoccupied. She was circling the room restlessly like a cat. Finally she stopped beside the French doors and gently pulled a curtain aside to peep out into the garden.

Watching her movements, Jamison saw her afresh; saw her beauty, her history, her wild sensuality, her stoic acceptance of the losing game; and it all appealed again sharply to his sense of the tragic. He followed her and looked over her shoulder out the glass window at the huge old trees, the carefully tended green shrubbery, the small elegant English garden; all bathed in the hot, still, sunny morning. There was not a shadow anywhere. "You see? There is no one here."

Slowly Francie turned to him. "I know there is no one there. Who did you think I would see?"

Momentarily Jamison had the rare experience of being acutely embarrassed, so that all he could do was stare at the challenge in Francie's face. "The gardener," he answered lamely.

Francie was silently looking at him; and when she spoke again, her face testified to the queerness of her question. "Are your parents alive?"

"No."

"Ah, then you're an orphan, too."

With intelligent compassion Jamison grasped the child-like logic of her notion. It was a principle of pride. She was putting them on an equal footing. "Well, yes. Like you. But we are all orphans sooner or later. Aren't we?"

Ignoring his glibness, Francie continued with some effort, "Anyway, you think I lied to you before?"

"A white lie."

"You think I see her—Momma—sometimes?" She reduced the situation to its most awkward element.

Jamison pretended this was some kind of joke. "I think you have a vivid imagination."

She gave him a warning smile. "Well, I don't. Don't see her, that is. And you don't have to be sorry for me. I'm quite fine. And I am sorry I ever mentioned Momma to you."

Her look and her words told him that she had made a discrimination against him never before made—that he was not brave enough to bear her reality. So she would spare him the horror of her dusk; the grimness of her expectations. Strange, strange girl with her wonderful mixture of strength and weakness, of pride and self-abasement. It would have been easy for him to show pity, but that would only have eased him. For Francie it would have been an insult, contradicting her bravado.

"Who could be sorry for you?" he asked. "With your beauty? Your life ahead?"

"That's it," she agreed. "One day I shall own the world."

"That's exactly what I see. Now why don't you have some breakfast?"

"Oh, don't bother. I'll get it back at the house."

"It's no bother. Fritz—he's my houseman—can make it very quickly."

"But you have to get to a tennis court. Is it very far?"

"No, as a matter of fact it's very near. It's out back."

At this Francie stared. "You have your own private tennis court?"

Jamison's reply was completely incongruous. "Do you know how to play tennis?"

She thought about this, and he could see the relief she was taking from the implication. Maybe she wouldn't have to leave immediately. "No, but I could learn." She gave him a hopeful look.

"Not in time for today."

"I suppose not." She accepted this. "Someday I'll know how." At this point Francie had something novel to think about. "Are you that rich?"

Jamie half smiled. "How rich is that rich?"

"I don't know. Rich enough to have your own private tennis court?"

"That doesn't require one to be that rich. But I am that rich." It was then that Jamison made up his mind. "You brought your bathing suit along didn't you?"

"Oh, yes. It's in my bag."

"Well, let's get you some breakfast, and then put on your bathing suit. You can watch Williard and me play tennis. Your presence will at least make his game interesting."

"You want me to stay?" Francie's face suddenly blazed with light.

It brought Jamison straight up to the fact. "I want you to stay."

"Oh—oh—oh!" She whirled around madly, the kimono spinning out like large wings and revealing her slender body. "I can stay today?" she gasped with dizzyness, flinging her arms around him the way a child would.

He settled it once and for all. "You can stay today, tomorrow, all summer. We'll work it out for our mutual convenience." He thought "Tomorrow and tomorrow and tomorrow . . ."

ENTR'ACTE

Franciejean's mother had been born in Evanston, Illinois. She was a decidedly less affluent, quite distant relation of the Pabst family of Milwaukee. Still, this connection to those well-fed and prosperous beer barons showed itself in everything she did, everything she believed. She would never forget that she was at least a bloodline equal—if not a financial one—of that class of Midwestern German-Americans who always lived in large, overfurnished houses, overate regularly, overdressed expensively, went to family gatherings in New York and Europe and did little else in between. To those would-be inherited obligations, Eugenia Hess was eminently fitted and religiously devoted. Unfortunately for Eugenia, she had poor business judgment; and she mistakenly chose to elope romantically with Francie's father, Charles Stewart, a Chicagoan, a commodity broker who was more interested in the arts than in wheat and corn futures. As a partner in a small commodities firm on Jackson Street in Chicago, he never seemed to have enough money to satisfy his wife's expectations; and their life was frequently overcast by a cloud of unpaid bills. To Francie's high-handed mother, there was even something courageous in living as though one were as rich as one's relatives. Francie's earliest memories were of a house in which a series of Polish and German maids gave notice; quarrels in the kitchen, the dining room, the bedroom; spring discussions of whether they should summer in Minnesota or Wisconsin, hopefully with her mother's relatives. Why couldn't they afford Europe, why must they save and stay home in Evanston? Drab intervals of economy were punctuated by explosive escapades of spending. Either way, Franciejean could not recall the time when her mother thought that there was enough money.

But as a child, if her taste for the vulgarly expensive was fostered by her mother, who taught her to believe that no matter what, her accessories must match; from her father she acquired a respect for things other than clothes and jewels. It was he who, now and then, on weekends, took her to afternoon concerts at Symphony Hall and on rambling tours of the Institute of Art to stare reverently at some touring exhibition of French paintings. Meanwhile her mother lunched on Wiener schnitzel and discussed hats with a cousin who lived on Lake Shore Drive.

Then one morning in her ninth year, Francie's father returned home from the office shortly after leaving the house and told his wife and daughter, who were still at breakfast, that he was ruined. That he was bankrupt. Not too long afterward, he died suddenly. Francie mourned him silently because her mother never allowed her to show her grief or to mention his name. Her mother never forgave him his failure. To her, to be poor amounted to a fatal disease; and all Charles Stewart had left her was a small insurance annuity—just enough to keep them living within the border of modest respectability, but far too close to the poverty line for comfort.

To remedy their failing fortunes, Francie's mother tried to remarry, paying court desperately to all her wealthy relatives in the hope that somebody would turn up an acceptable suitor. But she had little to offer a prospective husband except fading prettiness and a head full of pretensions, and the opportunities that were presented were few and far between. What was available was never quite good enough, and the men she wanted had little taste for her. Now and then she would have a caller; and from those gentlemen, at first, she tried to keep Francie hidden, assuming that without a child they would then think her younger and less burdensome. But once by chance, a gentleman did meet Francie; and he was so taken with her prettiness and whimsicality that Eugenia decided the child might be an asset. From then on she wore her like a charm on a bracelet and dangled her almost seductively before any eligible visitor's eyes.

One in particular, a lawyer, Paul Norton, came to be a

more or less regular visitor; and on occasion the unspoken question in Eugenia's mind was whether it was the mother or daughter he was courting. He took to insisting that Francie accompany them on all their outings—to theater, to restaurants, on picnics. This only partially irritated Eugenia, since she found Paul a bore; but she was determined to marry him and that required agreeing to be agreeable.

Francie, on her side, intensely disliked Uncle Paul, as he fondly insisted she call him. He was certainly kind enough; if anything too kind. But when she did not respond to the candy or the dolls or the ice skates he brought her with sufficiently affectionate kisses, then he would speak to her mother in a whisper; and her mother would fly into a rage at her.

No, Francie did not like sitting on Uncle Paul's knees and kissing Uncle Paul's wet lips. She especially did not like having his hands run up and down her arms and legs and back. Young as she was, she knew—for there was no mistaking the intention in his eyes. And she came, in a relatively short space of time, to thoroughly despise Uncle Paul, his presents, his hands, his look.

But to question his manner openly was to risk offending him. And the one time she mentioned to her mother the confused wretchedness she felt when Uncle Paul was overly affectionate, her mother slapped her mouth, insisted she was lying and was mainly interested in spoiling Eugenia's chance for marriage. So with the necessary wisdom of a child who knows she lives on the slopes of a volcano, Francie tried to keep her distance from Uncle Paul and live within her own thoughts.

Then came the time of reckoning. Eugenia was forced to bed with the flu, and Francie was instructed to entertain Uncle Paul on his Saturday evening visit. That evening Paul's kindness overflowed all prior limits. It would be his dearest pleasure, he claimed, to give young Francie her first taste of the high life of Chicago. After all, one late evening would not hurt a child. They'd go to dinner, they'd go to theater. They'd have a wonderful, wonderful time—they'd be like two young lovers. And Eugenia knew exactly which dress Francie should wear—the one that matched the blue velvet ribbon Uncle Paul had given her.

That evening Francie came home quite late—later than even Eugenia expected. When Eugenia asked her daughter for a full report on her wonderful evening, Francie had nothing to say. Not a word. She continued to say nothing while she undressed, and she ran the water in the tub for a bath. When she was stripped down to her slip and bare feet, she stepped into the bathroom and closed the door on her mother's querulous voice. It was the only time Francie had ever been rude to her mother, but something warned Eugenia not to make an issue of the matter. Francie stayed in the bath a long time; and when she came out in her pajamas, she went straight to her room again and closed the door. So ended the evening with Uncle Paul.

Eugenia waited all day Sunday for Paul to telephone. He didn't. And he didn't telephone on Monday either. When she telephoned his office on Tuesday, his secretary said he'd been called to California unexpectedly. Eugenia waited a week for him to return her call, and then telephoned again. He was still out of town. Indefinitely. In another week Eugenia realized that she and Francie had seen the last of Uncle Paul, though occasionally Francie would have nightmares about him which she never bothered to describe to her mother.

Eugenia blamed Francie for Paul's disappearance, though how the child managed it she couldn't imagine. But with Paul gone, Eugenia felt that her last chance at a comfortable life had vanished; and in no time her flu became pneumonia. She could not bear the dinginess of the years that stretched before her, and she died of disgust and despair.

Later, Francie always remembered how, toward the end, her mother would sit up in bed and scrutinize her meticulously with a kind of savage intensity. "It's up to you now. If you turn out the way you should, you'll have everything you want. You'll have the face for it. And the body. If you were older, you could've wrapped Paul around your pinky. I think you probably did anyway."

Eugenia died when Francie was eleven; and after that, her life changed drastically. The small trust her father left had been used up; and Francie went to live with a series of first and second cousins and aunts, Midwestern relatives of her father. Though neither wealthy nor loving, they saw their duty as Christians to try to provide a home for the now homeless child. It supplied them too with a mean satisfaction that this waif, this daughter of the arrogant and snobbish Eugenia Stewart, was dependent now on their tender mercies; to be dealt with as they chose. It was distinctly to their credit that they were not worse than they might have been; that they did not too often choose to make Francie pay for the snubs her mother had given them; that for Charles's sake they wished to be kind; but they had their own children to think about. And after all, they didn't really care.

Of course, nothing was ever heard from Eugenia's more illustrious relatives on Lake Shore Drive or in Milwaukee. Nothing beyond formal notes of condolence. Otherwise, there was not the merest hint that help with the child could ever be expected from that quarter.

After her mother's death, after the silence that settled, Francie had years to think about it all. Sometimes she wondered if her parents had died just to spite her, to make her life miserable, lonely and lost. Sometimes she wondered how she was ever going to get back to living. What do you do if you've once had a mother and father, and now all you have are cousins and aunts and uncles who wouldn't notice if you happened to drop dead? Except of course that funerals cost money. What do you do if you once had your own bedroom with flowered wallpaper and a bed with a ruffled bedspread, and now you sleep on a couch? Or on a cot in the basement or on a hammock in the attic? What do you do if you once went to dancing school, and now you sell ribbons on Saturdays in the Five and Dime. If you once had a bicycle and now you know you stole your roller skates? What do you do in this seductive, terrifying world if you are finally seventeen and you've been taught nothing and trained for nothing? And there is no one on hand who wants to marry you? Except the Hansen boy, and you won't be a farmer's wife—what would Momma say?

In fact, as the years went along, she would often ask herself what would Momma say about this—or about that? And the older she grew so did the feeling grow that Momma was watching her, judging her, keeping a sharp eye on her every move to make sure she lived up to expectations. After all, hadn't Momma said that it was Francie's fault that Momma had lost Uncle Paul? But who was Uncle Paul, anyway? Try as she would, she could not remember who he was. She couldn't remember a face, a voice, not a single memory. Only a name that for some reason she hated—Uncle Paul.

What do you do? That's what Francie asked herself as she stood staring at her naked body in the mirror of her Aunt Gert's bedroom, where she'd been living for the last three years. Do you commit suicide? But suppose you don't have the nerve? And you don't really like the idea. That's the trouble with suicide. It's not as easy as it sounds. Maybe you sell your soul to the devil? But the devil has made no offer. Well, if you can't sell your soul, maybe you can sell your body. Francie remarked this to her image. And her image smiled back—yes, sell your body. It was then that she decided to go to New York; her mother had always wanted to go there anyway. Maybe there was something gorgeous destined to happen to her in New York. She might even try to become a model. She surely wasn't going to sell ribbons all her life.

New York might not be a great improvement over Davenport, Iowa, but it could never be worse.

She also had the feeling that Momma might not be able to find her in New York. It was supposed to be such a big city.

Of course, after she arrived, she had to admit to herself that Momma could find her anywhere. Even in New York. Sometimes she saw her disappearing into crowds, sometimes she felt her at the other end of the subway station. But when she glanced around, she saw nothing—just more strange faces. Of course, she knew her Momma was always following her because her Momma loved her so much. But Francie wished she could tell her that she could take care of herself, that she did not want to be loved, that she never wanted to be loved—anyway, not by Momma.

Jamison Welsh was an aristocrat by race and conviction; born in 1920 before the whole concept of aristocracy had come to an end, and Jackie O. replaced Jacqueline Bouvier.

Like others of his class, he came from people of property; but his position was not dependent upon wealth. The blood ran as blue in the veins of the indigent Welsh cousins as it did in the nine-figure fortune of Jamison Welsh.

Jamison Welsh was the second son of Francis Lennox Cecil Welsh II; and as things turned out, with the death of his older brother Francis, Jamison became the major heir to the Welsh holdings.

At an earlier period in their history, the Welsh family

must have conformed to a tough-minded acquisitive cast; and more than one Welsh had certainly been involved in those ruthless hard-nosed maneuvers in mining, land, or oil that built the great American fortunes. But in matters not connected with money-making, the family grew up to be cultivated gentlemen of wide education. They drank ale but also claret. They were interested in the sciences and in politics; they appreciated and often funded those aspects of the arts that increase the graciousness of living—opera, painting, the theater. They were fascinated with abstract thought and also with practical thinking. They were drawn to new theories of medicine as well as those of law and government. They could play tennis and musical instruments well, and one became a fine mathematician and was a friend of Gauss. In their time, several had performed astronomical experiments; and Jamison's grandfather had been intrigued with the possibilities of aeronautics. Physics held no frights for them; and the laws of the universe, like gravity, or the quantum theory of light, were ideas a man might deal with pleasantly and quietly over a glass of brandy in his library. Though they were rich, the Welshs were uncommonly distinguished, listing among their bloodline two governors, one president of Yale, three senators, and one Supreme Court Justice; to say nothing of an older, dimmer connection to Scottish noblemen, one of whom claimed direct descent from King Henry of Scotland, second husband to the unwise Mary Stuart.

Though an unequivocally Catholic family, none entered the Church; and quite a few were free thinkers. They tended to marry distant cousins and daughters of friends. They also married ladies from Paris and Edinburgh. Good looks were of prime importance, yet not once within the recorded memory of their choices had they married outside the Catholic Church. When Jamison was born, the languages spoken in the family were English, French, German, and some Celtic.

Jamison's tone was set early. His mother died when he was in his early teens. His father did not remarry; and though still quite animated, he was given to sudden, silent pauses. No female relative was invited in to supervise the boys and add the warming touch of a mother and a hostess; but the house was always filled with guests—scientists and politicians, opera singers and art collectors who had definite ideas. And there was always a welcome for an energetic ward heeler, a juggling empire builder, a ballet dancer. When Francis III, his older brother, died in World War Two, Jamison's father grew more polite and somewhat more silent. As did the house.

But the early period of Jamison's life, until the death of his brother, left an abiding impression. Something of the vitality of the atmosphere came through forever in his taste for ideas, for people, for the great world, for living. Jamison Welsh was civilized. And in him civilization was properly expressed. For civilization, that much misused word, stands for more than watching television, driving sport cars, or having central air conditioning. It is truly a matter of the spirit, of delight in the things of the mind, a love of beauty, of honor, grace, courtesy, elegance of mind and body. On the surface, it might seem that a man so involved in these refinements would have no sense of what is practically important, must be a dreamer, somewhat out of touch. Nothing could be less true. The temper of Jamison's mind that had trained him to be keenly aware of the beauty of life had made him equally conscious of its brevity. He was never tempted to evade facts. Most people are sentimental. They take refuge in fantasizing, in longing for the future, or romanticizing a past that never existed. Not so Jamison. An ordinary man might think it heroic to die for an "impossible dream." Jamison never thought it was sweet to die for anything. Though he fully accepted that one would have to die anyway. Jamison Welsh had no vital self-deceits.

Accordingly he recognized that his life to date had been child's play. If he were to die that day, he would have done nothing more than make money. Enough of an accomplishment for many men, but hardly enough for a man of Jamison's reach.

For many years, as head of the private banking firm of Welsh Brothers & Gardiner, Jamison had turned his mind to the conservation and further formation of the family wealth. Brilliant, canny, and highly inventive in the art of money manipulation, he had increased the bank's holdings by one half in the years of his stewardship.

But the time had come for a change. Compared with the capabilities of most men, Jamison was light-years ahead. Compared with himself, he was now for the first time to come into man's estate, to confront the full force of what

Shakespeare called "the wind and the rain." Just over the horizon line lay Washington and a testing of his mettle on the wider stage of public life, in the world of international economics.

As a consequence of a decision that had been forming for many years, he had chosen to leave all policy-making involving the family bank in the hands of Raymond Gardiner III and devote himself as much as possible to the "dismal science" of economics. It was at this turning point in his life that he met Franciejean Stewart.

6

"I know where I'm going
And I know who's going with me.
I know who I love
But the Lord knows who I'll marry."

Often when they were together Francie would half sing,
half hum, the old Scottish ballad, over and over to herself,
unconscious that she was doing it. It was one of the meager
mementos she carried with her from the early morning of her
life when her father was alive. Jamison learned to take her
humming as a signal of her happiness; and though it made
him mildly impatient that she never had the words quite right,
he took pleasure in her happiness and refrained from correcting
her.

Over the summer he began his instructions in tennis and
politics, poetry and music, wine and manners. They went
beachcombing and clamming and sailing together. Having
grown up on the water, it never occurred to Jamie that the
ocean was an exotic monster to Francie. On a hot bright day
in late July, with high winds filling the sails and the boat
skimming the water like some outsized dragonfly, suddenly
Francie stopped singing. Rounding Plumb Gut, Jamison,
absorbed in the rare feeling of freedom that the wind and sea
gave him, decided to try for even greater speed. "Duck!" he
yelled to Francie, as he tacked with the wind, knowing the
boom would sweep across the deck. It took him a few
minutes to grow aware of the silence, and he looked around

to ask if she was feeling woozy. Then it was he saw her clinging to the boom, laughing and gasping for breath, but her eyes terrified. She hung there for an instant like wash on a line, a bad joke on sailing life, and then dropped with a crazy yell—"I know where I'm going"—into the ocean. The water closed over her head. A moment later she rose to surface, splashing and sputtering, and flailing about with her arms. It dawned on Jamie then that Francie did not know how to swim. By now she was too far behind the boat to be reached by a lifesaver; and with a mix of disgust and fright, he dropped the mainsail and dived in after her, leaving the boat to drift by itself.

He reached her within a few seconds, grabbed her professionally, and held her until she stopped her thrashing. After she quieted down, he used a standard lifesaver's grip and towed the puttering, half-drowned girl back to the drifting boat. Leaving her to hang onto a line, he swung himself onto the deck and tossed a swimmer's ladder overboard. Exhausted, out of breath, and thoroughly unnerved, she climbed aboard and stretched out on the deck, retching up water. Jamison went into the hold, got out a blanket, and wrapped it around Francie, who was trying to control her shudders.

"Why the devil didn't you tell me you couldn't swim?"

"You never asked me."

"Do you know you might have drowned?"

"Then I would have drowned. It would have served me right for being so stupid."

Jamie made a vague gesture with his hand. It was difficult for him to know who he was more angry at—Francie for not knowing how to swim, or himself for negligently allowing her on the boat without a life jacket. She might have drowned if he had not looked to see where she was; and that thought made him rise and pace the deck, the consequences of a sudden wish that she not see his face until he had time to compose it.

"But why didn't you tell me?" he persisted, coming back finally to stare down at the slender figure now stretched out and limp.

Francie had kept her eyes steadily on Jamie, but now they too wandered to the deck, to the sky, to the sea, as a slow flush mounted in her face. "I was ashamed of it. I was afraid you'd stop taking me sailing with you if you knew. And you know how much you like sailing."

When by a turn of her head she did look at him, there occurred between them an unprecedented exchange. For the first time in their connection she was struck by the recognition of how much he needed her. Yes, he wanted her; he enjoyed her; but this was different. She was humble enough about herself—she knew her own merciless need of him. But it came as a shock that she might affect him in the same way—as a compelling necessity. A necessity that he might have recognized only a few moments earlier. She felt such happiness; the risk of drowning was as nothing compared to this unforeseen gain.

"You thought I'd stop taking you because you couldn't swim?" He was saying this more to himself than to her.

"Yes. It's such a dumb thing not to be able to do. But there's not much swimming around where I grew up. And anyway water scares me. A little."

"All right. Now we shall look into swimming lessons. You'll get over the fear. There are pools, and there are swimming lessons all over the Hamptons. By the summer's end you can join the Olympic team."

"But suppose I can't learn how?"

"Of course you can learn. It's not like playing the violin. Anyone can learn. It's American to swim. It's like baseball."

"But if it takes a long time? And I don't want to stop sailing with you just because I can't swim."

"But you're afraid of the water. You just said so."

"I'm not afraid when I'm with you. You'll see. I'll be super-careful from now on."

"You could still slip in again, and the next time I might not be there in time to get you."

"I won't drown. Please say yes." Her eyes might have been trying to hypnotize him into giving a 'yes' answer.

The depth of her pleading made Jamison wince. She was like some beautiful, accommodating, sacrificial lamb, begging, "Take me, use me, drown me if you have to." Why he wondered, did she insist so on jeopardizing herself? And why, he asked himself further, had he felt so little concern for her welfare on the boat? It was not like him. He could not then have explained how he knew; but he knew beyond question that by some subtle affinity of their natures, he had responded to her innermost desire. She lived her life as though almost everything she did entailed a risk. She was a child looking for dares. She had dared him to risk her life, and he had done so. The idea left him for a moment stilled.

"Yes, of course I'll take you. Of course. But next time you'll wear a life jacket. I should not have let you aboard without one. I know better than that. It's a commonsense rule. Your near drowning is as much my fault as yours." He meant deliberately to incriminate himself, to give her grounds for judging him, for taking precautions against him—and against herself.

"I'll wear it, I'll wear it!" Her voice rose with pleasure, and shrugging off the blanket, she pushed herself shakily to her feet to throw her arms around his neck. "I'll be good, beautiful, wonderful. You're an angel."

He drew her shivering body close, feeling relief that she'd let him off completely. Feeling too a pale foreboding at the extravagance of her heart. For he knew that this was not the end of it. If she would not judge him and would not be afraid for herself, it might mean that she had once been so wretched that the worst that could happen now could hardly compare with the past. Whatever fate invented, she'd accept the price. If the piper came to collect too soon, she'd try to strike a bargain. If she failed, well that too she'd learned; how often God can say "No."

Francie was twenty-one and Jamison thirty-eight when they met at the Van Ness party in East Hampton. Once their affair began and she went to live in his house, Francie found herself in love. Having never loved before, Jamison became her north, south, east, and west; her noon and midnight. She loved him innocently and completely as a plant turns to the sun. When Jamie entered a room, she saw only him. In the beginning she seldom paused to wonder about the truth of this man; she knew little about his thoughts, his moods, his life before she knew him. All she did know was that his continued presence in her life was like the long, warming light of summer.

As for Jamison, happiness was something he had rarely thought about. And love even less. It had always seemed to him that the world was committed to shallow betrayals, self-deceptions and here and there, random loyalties. Experience, he had found, seldom approached the level of the great novels. Life made promises only fools would believe, and it was wiser to cut your losses early. Now with this young girl in his life, the world seemed hallowed and harmonious. Often he would have the impression of how lovely a day was, how it overflowed with brightness and softness. Sometimes it seemed to him his vision had cleared suddenly. Iron gates had opened to reveal a sunlit landscape, and the wonder and sight of it made his heart stand still.

He was an enigma to himself those days, and thinking back to how he felt before he knew Francie, he considered somewhat ruefully that she had the power to wake the dead.

Sometimes they would ride together under the full moon; and when they raced over the sand, she was as likely to win as he. Her figure, poised and graceful on a horse, was a continual source of surprise and pride to him. Light as a feather in the saddle, she carried herself like a born rider; the horse was merely an extension of her own body. To Jamison's classical turn of mind, she could evoke the image of a female centaur. But when they lay side by side on the dune, dusted by a sea breeze and making love, it seemed more likely that she was Aphrodite.

She was beautiful and pagan and fantastical; and she could inspire in him, almost by contagion, a great wild happiness at being alive. When it overwhelmed her, every single thing included in daily human living—breathing, waking, falling asleep, eating food, drinking wine, making love—called forth in her a rapture and a wonder that echoed in him. She would also weep at the sight of a dead bird—her laughter and her storms of sudden tears were like the skyrocketing moods of the very young. She had not yet found herself a fixed perch in the universe. Life was wonderful. Life was misery. But happy or anguished, she radiated an extraordinary energy that inspired in Jamison feelings he never realized he possessed. He saw her as his own creation; and as such, he took an inordinate pride in her developing mind and arts. Was it love, he sometimes wondered, this blind groping of his blood toward hers? Whatever it was, the fact remained that her nearness produced in him a quickened sense of life.

In September, returning to New York, he moved Francie out of her apartment and into his own home on East Seventy-fourth Street. There was a wealthy happy sun glittering on Fifth Avenue the day he guided her to her first Balenciaga suit. Her first pair of Fiorintina shoes. And after shopping they went to tea at the Palm Court at the Plaza. Francie, with her animal instincts for survival, learned quickly the manners and customs of Jamison's world, without losing the special attraction of her almost theatrical American wholesomeness. She talked less; her diction was precise; her manners with everyone were perfect—actually too perfect. And she watched Jamie constantly for cues on what to say, whom to say it to, when to say it.

When they were in New York, Jamison entertained or was entertained regularly—by politicians, artists, journalists, finanaciers, theatrical people, academia, the old and new of "society." As the year passed, the arena of Jamie's life became more and more crowded with the distinguished toys of his developing professional career—conferences, international conventions, speeches, official dinners, work on a book, article-writing, opinion-giving. And Jamison had to travel, to live abroad for short and long periods; and whenever he traveled, Franciejean went with him.

They were together as much as he could manage, while he tried not to give short shrift to his work, to the meetings, the conferences, the reading, the hard long hours that the "Discipline" entailed. It was a continuing source of astonishment to Jamie that he desired to be with her so much. What had begun in bed as a ravenous sexuality grew into an intimacy previously unknown to him. As time went along, he found, somewhat to his own dismay, that life without Francie seemed stale and flat.

In London, in Paris, in Rome, he would steal time from his work to dine with her in little inns or grand hotels. He would accept the invitations of princes in palazzos, of millionaires in fabled mansions, enjoying Francie's enchantment with the spectacle of huge ballrooms, marble columns, damask-covered chairs, men in white tie, women in jewels and rich clothes recently arrived from couture houses.

In Rome, in particular, he began her classical education while she struggled heroically with the language. When he should have been in his office in Geneva, they wandered together in the grassy shadow of aqueducts and tombs. They made regular pilgrimages to see altars, statues and paintings.

"How is it you can find your way around in so many strange cities?" she asked him in wonder.

"I grew up in all of them. I go by memory."

Leaning on a lofty stone parapet that faced the glory of the Colosseum, she stood with her hand opened and her eyes closed. "I go only by you."

He shook himself as though to shrug off a momentary enchantment. "Well then, let us go see the Moses."

"Ah yes, Moses."

The late afternoon sun spread its gold on the Seven Hills. Jamie pointed to a cathedral. "That's one of the best."

"But the Victor Emmanuel monument is wedding cake."

"You are learning."

"I have a great teacher."

"I wouldn't overdo it. You are what your profession calls 'a quick study.' "

"No, I'm not. It's not the way you think it is. I'm not learning facts—what I've learned is to read your mind. I can feel what you feel five miles away. What's the word for it—you told it to me—doppelgänger?"

He smiled at her. "Yes. I was afraid of that. How will I ever be able to keep a secret from you?"

"You mean someday when you might want to?"

"Yes, I might want to."

"Well, if there are things that you don't want me to know, then I really wouldn't want to know them. Then I will be as dumb as when you first met me."

"That shows real discretion."

"I go by you."

"Can you read my mind now?"

Something in the long look she gave him, the quietness of her smile, showed that she knew him indeed. Her instinct for him was, in fact, remarkable; she knew they both wanted not to go visiting another church, not even for Moses, not now. Now she wanted to go back to the hotel. They were conscious of the same sudden need for each other at the same time; but it was generally Francie who made the first gesture. His hand on hers tightened; and while the moment lasted, the suspended happiness in his face seemed waiting to brim over. "Come, we'll go back to the Grand for a siesta."

"Vengo, vengo," she answered, smiling.

*   *   *

The first time Francie did not travel with him was by chance. One evening, having returned to Jamison's house in Mayfair and preparing to go to an Embassy dinner, Jamie told Francie that he would be flying to Washington the next morning. The President was struggling with Congress over new tariff legislation; and as one of the experts on international trade, he had been asked to attend a top-level conference. He'd be back at the end of the week. Francie nodded her head, only half listening and asked, "What will we be doing at night? Do I need formal clothes?"

Jamie shook his head smiling. "Darling, why don't you stay here? Why uproot yourself? I'll be back Saturday night. Then we can go to Scotland. And London, even without me, can be a great pleasure."

"Oh, but I'd rather be with you."

"You can survive for a week alone."

Francie turned from her boudoir table where she'd been delicately applying mascara and stared at Jamison. Though she had not moved a muscle, he had the impression her hand had flown to her mouth to stifle a moan. For a minute they remained face to face; then she rose from her seat and walked to her closet. This time Jamison was clearly aware of the intensity of self-control being exercised. As she chose her dress she murmured in a tone that matched her bright smile, "But I can pack in a jiffy."

"I know you can. But I'll be working constantly. No time for play, no parties, nothing."

"You'll just work, work, work?"

"That's right. Work, work, work."

"You like that?"

He thought about the question. "Yes, I do. I like my work."

"Okay—sold. I'm at your service. Free. You know how good I am at organizing your notes. You said yourself I was the best secretary you ever had. I type expertly. And we both know I can read your mind, as well as your handwriting. I see the things you meant to write but didn't."

He smiled inwardly to himself, for it was quite true. When she sometimes did do work for him, she showed an uncanny grasp of the way his mind worked; and because she did, she seemed to intuit the intricacies of complex discussions in economics that she had no education for understanding. She'd listened so intently to his conversations about his work, to his conversations at official dinner parties, that in almost no time she had managed to master the necessary rudiments for deciphering international finance. Had she had the proper education she would have made a first-class assistant. And God only knows what later, for she had a natural gift for mathematics and a way of analyzing arguments that belied her years and lack of training. Truly an *enfant terrible*. Yet she seemed to have no taste for abstract thought, unless it involved something he was interested in.

"Francie, you are not only the best secretary, you are the second-best assistant I've ever had. The first was a Fulbright scholar. But I still think it would be best if you stayed here and enjoyed London. The kind of work I'm going to be involved in will not require your matchless talent. Any secretary will do."

"But won't you miss me?"

"Of course I'll miss you." He had begun with easy confidence; but as he continued, he felt the effort he was making to hold the note. "But there will be very little free time for feeling sorry for myself. Or for even kissing you, if you were there to kiss."

"But I'll miss you."

"I would hope so." The look on Francie's face reminded Jamie of something he had tried long ago to shut out of consciousness. But with that portion of his mind that never rested, even in moments of stress, he had watched it for some time with growing concern. Now it was here at last, fully defined; and he drew back from it momentarily, as though backing off from a chasm.

"I mean I'll hate being alone without you," she said.

"But this is London. Not Paris. Not Rome. This is my house, not a hotel. The servants have been with me for years. You know the language. It's London. We know many people here. Even Americans." His memory had begun to fling up images as he recognized an identity of behavior, of expression and tone that he had seen in Francie before; seen in her whenever he suggested going somewhere without her. He had granted her her reluctance in Paris, in Rome, in Geneva, in Berlin, where the language barrier might present a difficulty to a young untutored American like Francie; one to whom visiting Rome was the equivalent of visiting the moon. But London was another matter; London was English and stocked with Americans. "If necessary, you can dine with the Baldwins. The MacKenzies. They'd be delighted to have you. You can go to theater. Ballet. Have Eleanore and Robin to dinner. I'll admit Emily's cooking is simply adequate. But then our friends here are not exactly gourmets. It is typically English to enjoy dull cooking."

"But I'll be alone. I've grown so accustomed to you." She was acting from some pressing motive; and the way she expressed it was to go to Jamison and put her arms around his neck, pressing her half-naked body against him. "Are you sure you don't want to take me along?"

"Dear, it's only a week. Don't be afraid."

She paused like some hard-pressed defendant on a witness stand, searching for a proper response. "I am not afraid. I am fearless, in fact. But even lion tamers have their bad moments. Mine are at night. I won't sleep. I'll lie awake and think."

"Of what will you think?"

"Of you, of course."

"I'd rather you slept."

"But you'll be a million miles away. And if I do sleep I'll have bad dreams and wake up scared stiff."

"Of whom? Your mother?"

Her face showed self-scorn. "I know it's absurd. But she can be all around and everywhere when you leave me alone." A look of compassion passed over Jamison's face, and she realized she'd gone too far. She could not stand his pity so she continued in a matter-of-fact tone. "Well, forget it. I don't know why I brought her up. I do know she's just nonsense in my head. Like baby teeth I haven't outgrown. Look—you want me to stay put, I'll stay put. After all," she continued lightly, "who would give a ghost a passport?"

He knew what the words cost her, that offhand bravado with which she dealt with her most intimate terror; and however little he could understand its workings, it tended to strengthen her hold on him. "She'll never get through the English customs," he said, forcing a smile.

"Never. I'll stay." She finger counted. "There are the Baldwins. The MacKenzies. The Tate. The Crown Jewels to see."

She was responding intuitively to his cue. The cue given her by his insistence on going alone to Washington. It was enough for her to recognize a shade of change in his desire to prompt her, even against her will, to rise to meet the difference. He pulled her to him closely, his hands roaming over her body. "I'll be back long before you're driven to drink. I promise."

"I've been acting like a child."

"With a very active imagination. I've been thinking, darling," he said, holding her away from him and studying her face. "Perhaps it would be useful if you were to speak to a psychoanalyst? About this obsession of yours with your mother."

Her face grew quiet and withdrawn. "You don't think very much of psychoanalysis. I've heard your opinion on the subject in a number of discussions."

"By and large, you're right. It's the vice of the affluent who can afford having their torments massaged."

"You said you never heard of anyone who was 'cured.' Or even of anyone who thought of themselves as 'cured.' They keep going for years and years."

"That has been my observation." He gave a deep sigh. "It has led to my belief that analysis may not be the way to deal with personality disorders. I suppose my attitude stems from my essential faith in the survival drive. People change, internally or externally, when they have to in order to survive. Not a minute before. What analysis seems to do is provide a sympathetic ear for airing anxieties and agonies. But it doesn't force one to fight one's fears or make changes in unprofitable behavior. But my opinions are open to new information. You could be the exception. And a certain amount of therapy might prove useful."

Her face was set. "But I agree with you. People fight their fears when they have to. And now I have to. Momma's becoming excess baggage."

"Well, she has been dead for many years. There's very little to be gained these days in being concerned with her opinions."

"I know that. And I don't need a psychiatrist to prove it to me. Especially since I'm not that sure I agreed with most of her opinions."

"You really prefer to handle it yourself?"

"I really do. And I also know these days that psychiatry doesn't have a chance of 'taking' unless the patient is willing. I'm not. I can handle it myself. I have a very strong survival drive. If I have to grow up, I will. Watch."

"Not too fast please. Look—we'll talk later. After we get home tonight. Perhaps you could come with me."

"No, it's settled. I'll amuse myself. Like any other adult."

"We will talk," he insisted; and saying the words, he tasted again his fear of the weakness his need of her could produce in him.

That evening at the dinner party, Jamison's eyes ranging the table seating forty people, noted Francie in rapt conversation with a handsome English type of indeterminate age; a young man who looked old or an older man who looked young. Either way, what impressed Jamison was that the two were looking at each other intently and for a longer time than small talk required. That could mean nothing if he hadn't sensed something else. What provided him with an uneasy proof that there was some subtle new element at work with Francie was that no sign of their usually close communion passed between them. It was Francie's habit to signal Jamie, when they were separated at parties, with a smile or an intimate look. But this time she did not once as much as glance his way. Her entire attention was focused on her new acquaintance. She had never before behaved in this manner; and he was about to turn in mild puzzlement to talk to the wife of the Swedish Ambassador on his right when unexpectedly Francie's eyes met his; held; and he felt again her instinct for touching his deepest self.

It was part of Francie's genius for sensuality that at home that evening, after the dinner, no taint of their earlier, half-quarrel diminished the intensity of their lovemaking. If anything, it served to heighten her senses; and she abandoned herself to an orgy of kisses and caresses.

Later, lying side by side, spent and entangled, Jamie was aware of a process going on within her, deeper than their differences should have required. A process of weighing, considering, deciding. After a while he heard her breathing change to the even rhythm of sleep, and an immense weariness possessed him.

He was not aware of having fallen asleep, but he must

have because the light was breaking when he woke with a start some hours later, unable to recall his dream or what idea it was that had abruptly stirred him. He stared at Francie's sleeping form and thought curious thoughts. Who was she really? By choice or by chance, Josie had not spared him any of the choicer details of her recent history. And in the same joking vein Warren had added a few tidbits. And what Francie herself had told him was only enough to confirm her fantastical quality; but it told him nothing about what she might become; nothing about her potential or lack of potential for change, for growth, for maturity. Physically, he believed, she loved him; he satisfied her completely. But was it not also likely that she might feel the same physical love for another man? If he were not always available to meet her needs. If that, after all, was all there was. Was she a woman on whom a man could stake his life? Or was she quicksilver—Lilith not Eve? It took him a much longer time to get back to sleep and then it was only for an hour.

In the morning the reality of having to pack his bag and take a plane without her required a great effort of will. She sat on the huge bed and watched him, looking forlorn and childlike. But the decision had been arrived at by default, because Francie made no move to pack and no protest. It was tacitly agreed between them. For such a short stint, he'd be better off without her.

"It's only a week, and I won't be around to distract you. You can think about your work entirely and forget about me."

The possibility flared like a match in a dark room that she really might mean it. She might understand.

"I have been neglecting it," he agreed. "More than I realized until this telephone call came in, and I knew I wasn't as prepared as I should be."

"You really do like all that heavy stuff, don't you?"

"Yes, I do."

"Do you like those reports and things as much as me?"

In spite of his smothered concern he smiled. "Francie, there is no report to equal you."

"Yes, in bed. But out of bed?"

"Darling, you and my work are two separate entities. It's not a matter of in or out of bed. They are different things."

"But what if you had to choose?"

"Why should I have to choose?"

"Well, I know I distract you. I don't mean to, but I do get impatient. You read so much. If it weren't for me, you'd never have any fun."

"And that's what I have you for."

"Only for fun?"

"No. For many things, very valuable things. Now let's stop this. It's a childish conversation."

"But I am a child. I've only voted once."

Jamison laughed in spite of himself. Her unexpected statistic seemed to clarify his perception. "I keep forgetting. You're quite right. You need time to grow up." For a moment it seemed possible that his misgivings were groundless. To compensate he continued with excessive optimism. "And I do think it would be good for you to have a vacation from me."

"I don't need a vacation from you. But your work needs a vacation from me."

So she accepted his idea with a bittersweet accommodation to his wishes. But as he listened to the faint resentment in her words, the match seemed to flicker and go out. Where would she be when he returned?

Later, on the plane to Washington, he thought about Francie again and again; brooded over her compulsively, as a more physically nervous man might have tapped his fingers or chain-smoked cigarettes. Originally it had seemed to him that when he took Francie into his life, from that one act had flowered a richness on all sides, a multiplicity of color and melody in the world. But as time passed he had become aware of a growing anxiety. Strange and inexplicable, he had come to realize that, in some not-yet-specified way, Francie's avid caresses represented a threat to his work. If he had given in this time, it would have been the beginning of giving up other things of value forever. He was forced now to recognize in her a compulsive policy directed at limiting his freedom of movement; the kind of freedom that his commitment to his work demanded.

The truth, he suspected, was that he'd fallen in love with a changeling who might be totally unfitted for his real life; and the idea filled him with wonder and anxiety. To be heart whole, to be on the crest of a great career, to be not yet forty and free and clear of disabling entanglements—and now to have this. It was a stroke of bad luck he didn't deserve.

If required, she would go without sleep for a week, travel thousands of miles, knock about in strange cities among strange people, attend endless boring official dinners, and wake ready to go again after a few hours rest. Her body that looked so fragile and elegant hid an iron constitution. It was secure against weather and wine. She would use it in any way he required to do anything in the world to please him—except agree willingly to be separated from him for even a short period of time. And the question that arose after long thought was, why should such clinging, such dependence, be necessary?

Because she was afraid of losing him to another woman? He strongly doubted it. She knew his history, his disposition for the solitary life; and she knew too her surprising and rare power over him. Was it possible that she was simply afraid? But of what? Yes, her fantasies were frightening; but Jamie had a sharp intimation that Francie had something far more concrete to fear than phantoms. Their disagreement over the trip left him more than a little concerned. Though why so simple a matter as a business trip without her should cause her so much apprehension was a question he was not yet prepared to face. For the question, if there was one, suggested choices to come—and the long, lonely days that might lie in wait if the eventual choice required that there be no Francie in his life.

On his return to London, he detected in Francie a new, feverish note of diplomacy, just barely discernible below the surface. It showed itself in an intensity of watching him in order to be sure she was pleasing him. But what had struck him as natural before now conveyed an undercurrent of fear.

"How was it?" he asked over dinner. "Not as bad as you thought, I'll wager."

"Not bad. Not as good either as when you're here, but better than I expected."

"Who did you see? Who was amusing?"

"Well, the Baldwins, as you suggested. And the MacKenzies. And Eleanore—and, oh yes, Edward Tripp. He took me to the theater."

"And who is Edward Tripp?"

"Oh, you remember him—he's with the Canadian Embassy. We met him at that dinner party just before you left."

"Ah, yes." And so at last he knew what he had feared and why. God damn it, he said to himself. Why couldn't she stay without a man for a week? And the more he thought about it, the more he knew she couldn't. It wasn't a matter of choice.

When they returned to the States in August, he caught himself too often wondering what Francie did with her days; what she did when she was not going for modeling interviews or to galleries with Vera, or antiquing with Peter or shopping with Josie or learning French, or— He found himself watching her suspiciously, and something in him went hard with self-contempt as he realized it. Once, at a large noisy party, he saw her in a side corridor kissing some man with more passion than sociability. Jamison was not by nature a jealous man, but the sight of the stranger's hand on Francie's bare back embarrassed and discomforted him. He had never been jealous before. ·

Unexpectedly, one afternoon he came home from Wall Street earlier than usual and found Francie engrossed on the telephone. Surprised at the sight of him and unreasonably flustered, she hung up in nervous haste. It did not occur to him to ask who she was speaking to, but she felt compelled to explain that it was Vera. In the same way that she had explained Edward Tripp. She'd called Vera to ask where she could have the Chinese ancestor portrait hanging in his study rebacked. Showing nothing, he noted to himself that she was lying. Vera had telephoned him only that morning from Rome to ask if he was interested in bidding on a Perigino that had come up for sale.

In October, he was invited to give a series of lectures at the London School of Economics; but he couldn't make up his mind about going. In recent months he'd watched the disintegration of Francie's commitment in little random slippages. She'd stare at a stranger in a restaurant, and he'd sense her control of an impulse to flirt. Now this incident on the telephone decided him. He would go to London. He had to.

Lying in bed that night, staring into nothingness, he felt the darkness inside himself. The pain of what he suspected was almost too much. Superficially he thought of his trip to come, of the topics he would lecture on, of what he hoped to accomplish; but underneath it all, his being was racked with sobs. He was suffering as much as he had ever suffered in his life. He had not wanted to part from her, but now it would have to be. It was no use trying to deny he loved her. But if he were right, if his intuitions were accurate, it was better to know it now than later. Given that his suspicions had reality, if they were permanently bonded together, they would end by destroying each other. On this point he was quite certain. Thinking of her in the darkness beside him, he seemed to see her as though surrounded by a gallant glow. She had a pact with life itself in which as much as could be had she would have. But she was doomed. The Goddess Nemesis stood behind her, watching and waiting. It was this he had seen when he first met her. It was this he had seen that afternoon, so long ago it seemed, when she almost drowned.

By morning the pain had died down, and his body felt bruised and beaten as though he had somehow survived a tidal wave; and now he had no energy left for everyday pursuits. But his mind was clear. He went through the business of preparing for the day with his standard meticulousness; and when Francie woke in a rush, so as not to miss having breakfast with him, warm waves of blood raced through his body. She laughed as she came toward him and seated herself at the breakfast table.

"Oh, you silly thing; you silly. Why didn't you wake me? You tried to get away from me. I know."

"Well, if I'd succeeded you know where to find me. I'll be at the bank today."

She came over to him and put her arms around his neck. "I love you, love you, love you," she canted singsong. "And next you'll be in London; and if I want to reach you, I will have to fly away to London. So I will, won't I? You gave me the ticket—yes, you did. What fun! I really do love London." She started toward him. "I know where I'm going. . . ."

He gathered his strength. The thought of leaving her this time appalled him. But it would have to be. "Francie," he said, "I think you should stay in New York. For the sake of your own work. It's going too well to let it slide. I think this time I should bear London alone."

She stopped humming and there was an edge of panic in her voice as she asked, "You mean you don't want me to come with you? Again?"

"Of course I want you to come with me. But it's pointless. I'll be busy. Very busy. We'll have very little time together. And what will you do with yourself while I'm working? Or preparing for my lectures? You'll be bored out of your mind. Here you have friends. Here you have your own work. And it's a city you're familiar with."

She stared at him meekly. "I'll do what I did when you went to Washington—the Baldwins, the ballet, Edward Tripp. I'll find things to do."

"That was a week. This is four weeks, and I'll be working very hard, with very little time for you. If you stay in New York, it will give you some time to focus on your own career. And brush up on your French. You said you wanted to. We've been together constantly for months. You'll have some freedom, freedom from me."

"I don't want to be free of you."

"Of course not. And I don't mean it in any serious sense. But you do have your modeling career to think about. And I am not talking about forever. I'll only be gone a month." He was silent for a moment. "Think about it, anyway. You still have a week to decide."

She nodded her head wonderingly. "All right. Maybe you're right. I'll think about it. Yes, I will." She sat with her chin in her hands, her elbows resting on the table, brooding over the idea and biting her underlip. His whole heart went out to her, for he recognized that she was in a funk. Something in the humble, stoic look of her made him feel like a bully; but he was facing the inexorable. Their own separate natures were pulling them apart, and there was nothing he could do to stop it. He could not put her under lock and key.

So Francie thought about it and thought he might be right. After all it was only four weeks. And now high-fashion editors knew her name and face. High-fashion magazines were using her. Name companies asked for her composites. Name companies booked her for shootings. Dreem-Sheen, Revlon, Ban. The day before Jamison left for London, her decision was made when her agent told her to go to the Barnett Company to audition for a multimillion-dollar TV commercial series. They were looking for a girl to be the symbol of a gourmet line of frozen foods—to do for the line what the Hathaway Man did for Hathaway shirts. The girl who got the job would make $25,000 for perhaps a week's work. . . .

When Francie arrived at the agency reception room, it was full of frank, blank, beautiful faces; thoughtless, avid and familiar; and Francie felt herself tense with the desire to make the television big time that these faces represented. By the time she left the agency with Pat Heyman, another model, she was confident she had the television producer hooked.

In a mood for celebrating she went with Pat to a working girl's party, sponsored by Pat's agent, in a penthouse on East Fifty-seventh Street. The party was for TV producers, account men, casting directors, clients, models.

Francie drifted into the party full of noise, food, drinks, and people. A man with a beard and plaid vest moved over to her.

"What's my line?"

"You sell soap, cereals and cigarettes. Also gourmet foods. You're Mel Harris with the Barnett Agency."

"Right. But the name's Matt Harris."

"I knew it began with M."

"You looked great in the control room," Matt breathed into her ear.

She smelled whiskey on his breath. Francie liked that. When men drank they were easier to handle.

"I bet Heidi Berger looked great too. Really! She does everything."

Matt put his arm around Franciejean, and she felt it tighten spasmodically; felt his hand on her back with his fingers spread.

"Not like you. You've got real style."

For a minute there was silence, and she had an odd feeling of longing as he looked her over completely. His smile was soft, yet there was a glitter in his eyes. He wanted her. And she considered a surrender. This was the way. This could swing the series. But deep within her was a feeling of numbness such as one might feel on discovering one has a fatal illness. For that was exactly the case. She did; and knowing it, she looked at her watch. "I have to go home now. We have guests for dinner."

"What about lunch sometime?"

She held out her hand. "Why not?"

"Give me a blast. Any day I'll make time for you."

Francie nodded, squeezed his hand, turned and moved out of the milling crowd.

"My God! What a looker!" Matt remarked to no one in particular.

At home that evening Jamie was in the bedroom packing for his trip to London. The room, once essentially neat and masculine, was now sprinkled with Francie's flimsy, feminine, untidy things; and these familiar tokens of intimacy reached out and hurt him as he went about his packing in the midst of his love for her. When Francie came in, she was breathless and excited; her eyes shone with triumph, yet with an eager appeal too. She put her arms around him. "Will you miss me?" she asked. "Will you?"

There was a small pause before he said it. "I gather you've decided to stay in town."

"Yes, everyone's hot for my body." She giggled. "Dreem-Sheen wants to use me for a magazine series. And guess what?"

"What?" He said it as he selected a tie.

"I auditioned today for the La Petite Maison series. It's a gourmet frozen-food line that Beatrice Food is going to do. I might get to be the La Petite girl." Francie began to whirl around the room. "I'll be rich. Famous. Sought after. The TV producer thinks I am peachy keen." Then she stopped dead-still in front of Jamie. "What do you think of them apples?"

"I can well believe it. You are quite beautiful."

There was a half-perverse, half-wistful look on her face. "I am gorgeous beyond gorgeous. But do you believe that I am peachy keen? Answer yes or no."

"I believe you are peachy keen."

"Then kiss me."

He bent to kiss her, his mouth meeting hers firmly, deeply, kissing her as he'd always kissed her. But it told her nothing—would he really miss her? More and more, in recent months she had felt herself shut out from communion with Jamie. The recognition of the distance between them brought Francie up short, brought back suddenly her old sense of isolating loneliness.

"Now, kiss me again." She lifted her lips and compulsively started to fiddle with his belt, but he took her hands away.

"Please dear, I'm packing."

"You know when the last time was?"

"Francie, do we have to—"

"It was three nights ago. Before the Baker party."

"Francie, does it ever occur to you that a man gets tired? And that sometimes I have other things to think about. Besides sex."

"But it means so much to me," she whispered.

"And to me too. But enjoyable as it is, we cannot spend our entire life in bed. I have work to do." He paused tentatively. "And men have lapses. . . . It's not unusual. My trip is on my mind. The lectures—"

But she wasn't listening. "I'm always having to fling myself at you." She was suddenly very tired. In a way, she hated him; but still she wanted to rub up against him. "And now you're going to London without me."

"You agreed yourself that you wanted to stay in New York."

"But it was your idea, not mine."

That was true, and a sick feeling rose in Jamison as he considered his motives. "But you did make a free choice."

"I only agreed to please you." She sounded like a fretful naughty child. "You know you'll miss me. Why do you want to be without me?" She put her arms around his waist under his jacket, drawing him to her again.

"I don't want to. But right now it's the sensible way to handle our lives." He said this woodenly, holding himself tensely apart from her.

"It isn't sensible. It's inhuman. How will I live all the time you're gone? I'm frightened when you're away, I'm frightened all the time. I don't know where I am, I don't feel safe unless I know we can make love and be close. I have to make love to feel all right with myself."

"You sound like Catherine the Great. Are you telling me you need a stand-in regiment in order to keep you satisfied and sane?"

"Don't be nasty to me," she said rubbing her face in his chest.

"Francie, I am not being nasty."

"You are trying to pretend you don't want me." Jamie stayed quite still. "But you do, you do. Even now I can feel it." She gave a little laugh of victory. "But you'll be sorry. You'll be sorry if you dump me." Abruptly she stepped back and wagged her finger at him. "These days I have more options than I can count. James Rockwell of Dreem-Sheen perspires at the sight of me. Matt Harris of Barnett has already made an improper offer." She looked up at him laughing, childish, angry.

"Has he indeed?"

"Yes, he has indeed. If I make myself available—you of course know what that means—well, if I make myself available, I will undoubtedly be the Queen of Hearts. And that's worth $25,000, the way the contract works. For what amounts to a few days work in a TV studio. That's almost as good as you do."

Jamison was furious at her unrelenting reliance on her body as a trading card, demeaning the value of everything that went on between them. But all he said was, "Francie, what kind of fool would hand out a $25,000 job on the basis of bed talent. The man could lose his job if he picked the wrong girl. And the right girl isn't necessarily the available one." The words comforted him hugely, and he spoke them with real relief even though a part of him doubted their truth. "Why jeopardize his career when he can have one of the city's finest for a mere $100 and take it off the expense account too."

She looked at him undecided. "You don't believe he's made a pass at me?"

This produced in Jamison a curious premonition. "Did he?" he asked.

"Yes," she said smugly. They stared at each other a moment, and Francie grew a little pale. "No," she said.

But she had showed him the glow of his own obsessive idea. "Well, did he or didn't he?"

The question forced her to keep looking at him, and he saw by one of those inexplicable reactions that reminded him of her emotional fragility that her eyes were filled with tears; that she was suffering too from an invisible hurt. "No, he didn't. Jamie I am sorry I said all that rubbish. Please take me." She opened her arms to him. "Help me. Love me. Keep me."

Her tone came home to him with such appeal that for an instant he felt the numbness draining out of his body. He reached for her, and held her hard against him, comforting her, comforting himself. "Would you really like to come to London with me?" He asked this almost abjectly.

"Oh, I love you so much." She buried her face in his chest. She had this pang like a hunger to make him part of herself, to blot out everything and everybody else.

"I know it may not be interesting for you." He hesitated. "Well, what do you think?"

Waiting for her answer, he did a mental decision free of alternatives and ended by knowing it was useless. There would still be only one way to go, sordid though it was, that would ultimately tell them where they were.

Her confused answer proved how bitterly accurate his calculations had been. "Of course," she said tearfully. "Of course I want to go. But you won't have any time for me."

"Yes. I will be busy. And you'll be alone a good deal."

"And at night you'll still want to do your work—not be with me?"

The pressure that for a short space had ebbed now built up again within him. "Yes, that's true. I'll be busy most of the days. And probably most of the nights. I've a lot of preparatory work to do for my lectures. You'll have to amuse yourself a bit."

"I might as well be here then."

"Yes, you might as well." He knew that he had to face the truth directly, make an adjustment to it then and there, so he could stand it. "There's more for you to do here." He did not add, "You know more men." It was all before him now, and he was weary with the thought that he had known the truth all along and simply not looked at it. He thought perhaps he should be disgusted with her, but what was the sense. She was what she was. Yes, she loved him; perhaps even deeply. But the fidelity, the goodwill she was trying to maintain in their relationship, seemed to be part of a desperate bargain with the gods and possible for her only after a repeated and exhausting struggle. And then not always possible.

He felt her body pressing warmly against him, her face burrowing into his chest, her hands caressing him. He stroked her shining hair; and then, aroused perhaps by his own wild jealousy, he kissed her passionately, handling her body almost brutally, beside himself with desire and hate. Francie fought back with an erotic fury that only incited him further, and together they slid to the bed panting and perspiring in a frenzy of lust and anger. He took her so quickly he came before she did, leaving her wild with excitement. When he tried to push her away she became all mouth, tongue and fingers, all stinging bites, until he responded savagely—if he could kill her this way, he would.

Afterward, out of sheer exhaustion, they fell asleep. Much later Francie woke to see Jamie standing by the window looking through the curtain out onto the darkened street. She studied the outline of his body with longing. She was beset with an intense curiosity to know what he was thinking. In spite of herself, she asked, "A penny for your thoughts. I'm not as good a mind reader as I used to be."

What was he thinking? Of the gilded Adam's wall mirror hanging in the foyer? What was he thinking? Staring out into the winter night, Jamie saw the facts with black-and-white precision, unsoftened by shadings or color. Francie had opened windows from which no sky would ever be visible. Put plainly, she could be called a whore; or as he had once thought, in a pre-Christian world, a pagan. He smiled to himself without hope, remembering the image. But labels were meaningless. The real question to ask was what was her price, and would he pay it? Was it money, or love, or marriage? Or indifference and laissez-faire? Hers was a price he could never afford. One day they must part: she must find a man who could afford her. What was he thinking? That probably no woman would ever mean as much to him again. Out loud he said, "I am thinking that it's wise that you are taking your modeling work seriously. You can use modeling as a stepping-stone to a real career. Perhaps in advertising. Because you certainly cannot be a model forever. And you have more talents than your beauty." He said this without irony.

That wasn't the answer she wanted. But she took it, saying only, "You're right, you can't be anything forever. In fact, most things you can't ever be." And she thought to herself of the proud and beautiful things she would never be. She would like to be faithful and true. But it was hard. She would like to be a wife, too, if it were possible. She remembered a story Jamie had once told her about a martyr's kisses. Was it Heloise? She wondered if it was worth dying for what you wanted. What was he really thinking?

The next morning, while Patrick was putting Jamie's luggage into the car trunk, Agnes came to tell Francie that there was a Mr. Harris on the telephone who wanted to talk to her. Jamison listened and drew a long breath as if a special danger for him had now arrived. When Francie returned she was excited and flustered.

"He wanted me to meet him and Lawrence Buckman at the Brussels for lunch. Buckman saw my composites and liked them. I said I'd call them back."

"Lawrence Buckman? I believe he's the new Chairman of La Petite Maison Foods. I noticed his name the other day in the *Wall Street Journal*. Very good. They must be quite serious."

"But if I go to lunch I can't go with you to the airport."

The straightness in her voice was all he could ask for in loyalty. But it was difficult enough. He knew, as she did not, that this parting was a real one, symbolically marking the point beyond which their relationship could not go. He felt a spading up of their intertwined roots, and he knew without consciously knowing that his whole being strained against the disengagement. What was going wrong between them would be accelerated by his absence—she would soon enough find someone to fill the void—and he saw no purpose in interfering with inevitables. "I think the luncheon is more important than your going to the airport."

"You do?" she said, earnest and distressed. "I'd rather go with you."

"But it makes no sense."

"It doesn't?"

"No."

Her eyes, wide and candid, accepted this judgment, a little surprised that he wanted her to do what she really preferred to do. "But if I don't go to the airport will you keep on loving me?" She was still child enough to show she wanted to have her cake and eat it too.

"That's something I am not able to stop."

She lifted her arms toward him gleefully. "Good! Good! If you kiss me, then I'll stay."

117

He understood her all too well; and between her appeal and her menace, he was trapped. Stooping toward her face, almost unaware of what he was doing, his mouth met hers, hard and passionately. But this woman gave him anguish; his whole body ached as from a blow; and he drew back abruptly in what amounted to self-protection. "I must go," he said. "I'll telephone you tonight."

Francie watched from the doorway as Patrick maneuvered the great old Rolls skillfully down the street toward Park Avenue. Quite unconsciously she was singing to herself:

"Some say he's dour
But I say he's bonnie.
Fairest of them all
Is my handsome, winsome Johnny."

When the car turned the corner into Park Avenue she went back into the house and dialed Matt Harris, still singing softly to herself:

"Feather beds are soft
And painted rooms are bonnie.
I would give them all
Just to go with my boy Johnny."

"The Abraham Barnett Company. Whom do you wish to speak to?" asked the switchboard girl.

Francie stopped singing. "Matt Harris, please." But while she waited, she continued:

"I know where I'm going
And I know who's going with me.
I know who I love,
But the Lord knows who I'll marry."

After she hung up the telephone, Francie stared into the middle distance, her eyes misting with tears she scarcely understood, still humming to herself to ease the pain. It was then that it happened. It came to her with a warm rush—the words, the right words came back. She seemed to be walking down some childhood street; and practically within touching distance, she could see her father and hear his voice. He was singing softly as they walked together to church, down a shaded street on a Sunday morning when the sun was just over the top of the trees and the future seemed to float before her in the soft golden air, full of the promise of happiness and love.

"I know where I'm going
And I know who's going with me.
I know my true love,
But the Deare knows who I'll marry.
But the Deare knows who I'll marry."

Of course. . . .It was Jamie's business, the Deare, not hers. Jamie would work it out for them. He'd take care of everything. He understood so much. She hoped Jamie forgave her for singing the wrong words. She was sure he knew they were the wrong words. She was also sure he forgave her, and this made her laugh and cry at the same time. Everything would work out.

7

A hotel would have been more fun. Francie wondered why so many girls hated going to hotels. Personally she'd rather. Hotels were kind of kicky. If you went to a hotel nobody would know you, and nobody cared. Though, of course, everybody actually knew everything. But as long as you registered properly and the bill was paid, nobody gave a damn. And then, the nicest thing about it was you could always have champagne sent up—or at least martinis. And food. It was like a party.

But most girls she knew liked to kid themselves. If they were going to bed and they were married or otherwise taken as she was, then they had to do it in somebody's apartment. And if neither party had a place—well you just had to find one. God! What a lot of craziness! What made an apartment more respectable than a hotel? Actually it was much worse. Somebody's clothes and messy ashtrays and last Sunday's newspapers were all over the place. It was practically like having them stand there watching you do it. And it wasn't even an orgy.

But a lady can't get laid in a hotel, no a lady can't. She certainly can't, can't, can't! That could be a jingle. No, she certainly can't. Anyway, Matt didn't think a lady could. And he was an authority on the subject of ladies, wasn't he? After all, he'd picked her.

Francie's mind turned aside from these preoccupations. She stared out the window between the long, slender slits of blinds. There was no one on the sunlit street below. It was tree-lined, empty and elegant; exactly as East Seventy-fourth off Fifth Avenue should be. Such a rich, respectable street. Francie smiled a vague, tender smile—the smile of a girl reading an unexpected love letter.

The room within was dark and cool, the silence dense as dust around her. Somewhere down the street a doorman whistled for a cab. But that was all. Here she was alone with only the swollen sound of Matt's sleeping breath.

For a second, she closed her eyes and saw again in her mind, like a scene played on a TV screen, the whole luncheon bit with Matt. It was a barrel of laughs. So gay, so gossipy, so nowhere. Surprise, surprise—Buckman couldn't come. He had meetings, meetings, meetings. And for a while, Francie thought Matt had asked her to lunch just to have lunch. To be polite. That would have been a switch.

Then when the conversation had almost reached the suffocation point, suddenly it veered out of control; and like a runaway car down a hill, raced to the implicit destination of their lunch. Francie was never sure which of them took the brakes off. At any rate, they arrived, shaken but unbruised, at an acceptable understanding. And Matt went off masterfully to make the "arrangements."

Three telephone calls later there were still no arrangements, and Matt was feeling foolish. All the possibly available apartments were in use. What a statistic that would make, Francie thought. She would have laughed if Matt weren't so serious. And with the instinct of the born rope walker, she sensed the peril to her goals if the lunch should end when the check arrived. So with a purely formal reluctance, she went to the telephone and found them a place. She giggled softly. If she knew the kind of man he was, he'd flip. Absolutely flip.

Suddenly remembering, she looked at her watch. She hadn't taken it off, all through their lovemaking. Whenever she fooled around like this, she left it on. She knew men who did the same thing. Never took their watches off. Some even left their socks on. Business was business. She had a feeling it was their way of being faithful to their wives. Ha!

God! It was three o'clock. The Dreem-Sheen commercial would be on. She hurried through the dimly lit bedroom to her dressing room at the other end of the room where she kept the TV set. She switched it on, tuning it down so as not to disturb Matt. Then, wrapping the towel she wore more securely around her body, Francie plopped down cross-legged on the floor to watch the screen with hypnotic attention. The show had just ended and the commercial came on. The announcer's voice was tenderly persuasive as a beautiful girl demonstrated the magic of Dreem-Sheen Shampoo:

"Your hair is ever young . . . ever alive . . . shining in the sunlight . . . radiant in the moonlight . . . sparkling . . . sparkling . . . hair he'll love to kiss . . . and it's yours when you shampoo your hair with Princess Pat's Dreem-Sheen . . . the shampoo made with suds that bubble like champagne . . . to add a thousand fine sparkles to your hair."

Watching the commercial, she became excited and nervous.

"They sprayed gold dust on my hair. That's why it's so shiny."

Matt Harris did not answer and Francie glanced at him scornfully. Still sound asleep. Men always go to sleep afterward. Except if they have to catch a train or a plane or call their wives. But let them alone, and off they go. Of course, with Jamie it was different; but that was a different thing anyway.

The commercial came to an end, and Francie got up from the floor and moved to a Regency desk in a corner of the bedroom. It was her special desk and she loved it. From a secret compartment she took out a sheaf of bills and examined them. A bill from Bergdorf scented with My Sin, a white one from Sulka for the ties she bought Jamie, another one from Helene Arpels for the shoes they'd made for her . . . very high-class bills.

Unconsciously she fingered the heirloom ring on her finger that Jamie had given her. Now she could feel her body played upon by currents of hysteria and fear rising like smoke in shining spirals.

Returning the bills to their compartments, she closed the door quietly and moved to the TV set. Gravely, almost sadly, she studied Matt asleep on the bed: jerksville. But she knew the word was crude; and as if to apologize, she had one of those typical switches of mood, like a sparrow turning midair, and pitied him; his blatant admiration of her. Oh well, he could have been worse. In fact considering his age, and that potbelly, he wasn't half bad.

Then calmly, deliberately, she turned the sound on the

TV set up full blast for ten seconds. After that she switched it off.

The man on the bed stirred uneasily at the explosion of sound.

"Matt, Matt! Wake up!"

Dazed with sleep, Matt opened his eyes. In the half-light, his face looked young and more buoyant than the original. "Hmmm, musta dozed off. . . ."

"Well, wake up, it's three o'clock."

"What time?"

"After three. Come on." She tried to keep her irritation from erupting into her tone.

"O.K., one cigarette, please."

Francie almost laughed out loud. That was another thing. In this kind of situation this kind of man always wanted a cigarette afterward. Boy, could I write a book. Some cigarette company ought to get the message.

A discreet ad campaign just showing a naked couple relaxing after the number. And the slogan would be, "Where there's smoke, there's fucking—and brand X." Or some damn-fool thing like that.

"All right. One." She handed him a cigarette from the box inside the bedside table.

"You sure know your way around this place. And what a layout!" he added, awed a bit. "Good friends of yours?"

"Very good. I live here."

"This is your home?" He stared at her dumbfounded.

"Mine. All mine."

Just as she'd figured, his good WASP soul was mortified.

"Christ! How could you bring me here? Suppose your husband—"

"Walked in? He won't. He's on the way to London right now."

"What about the maid?"

"I gave the housekeeper and the cook the afternoon off. That's what the telephone call was about."

She watched him squirm uneasily, peering around the dim room suspiciously. Naturally, he assumes I'm married, she thought. Naturally.

"I feel like I'm having a bad dream. And I've been caught burglarizing a neighbor's house," he said.

"Don't worry—you won't be caught."

"I don't like it. This is your home. A home is sacred."

Francie watched him with a wry reflective air of amusement.

"A home is furniture." She fumbled around in the drawer of the bedside table, and her fingers found the matches. She paused, then pushed them deeper into the drawer. She turned to Matt. "Sorry, Mister. No smoke. I can't find matches."

But Matt needed a smoke. Or a drink. Or something.

"My lighter's in my jacket pocket." He started to get up, but Francie pushed him back.

"Be my guest." She rose and walked to the chair where an hour before, Matt had dropped his clothes, helter-skelter, in a fury to get them off. Separating the jacket from the disordered pile, she rummaged in the pockets looking for the lighter.

Propped on his elbow, Matt watched her with candid animal greed.

"God, you're beautiful." Francie tossed the lighter to him. "And not an extra ounce of flesh on you. Irene's had three kids and—well, it shows." He thought about this a moment. "But if I ever catch her fooling around, I'll knock her block off. And if she does it in my house—that I work my tail off to pay for—I'll kill her!"

"Smoke your cigarette," Francie remarked, involved with the hours ahead. She was meeting Monroe who she hadn't seen in ages, and she moved back to the chair where Matt's clothes lay scattered and gathered them up in her arms.

"You'll have to start dressing. I've things to do. I'm meeting an old college friend for dinner."

"Francie."

"Hmmm?" She dumped Matt's things on the bed beside his shirt, socks, underwear, pants.

"Why do you want the series so much?"

"I want it." Her face and voice would give him no clues. They were blank as an unlabeled bottle.

"But why?" Matt was trying to understand her. "A girl like you. With your life. A house like this. You've got everything."

"There are your clothes, Matt. Please start."

"Money troubles?"

She looked at him in scorn, but she said, "A little extra never hurts. Now get dressed."

"I suppose not." He examined a small iron horse on the bedside table. "I bet that's an antique."

"Han Dynasty," she noted with artful indifference. One of her favorite roles—the born-to-the-purple bit. If there'd been more time, she'd have developed it more. As it was, she only said, "It's eighteen hundred years old. Rather rare."

Matt studied the horse with reverence. "Musta cost a fortune."

Then, nodding toward the desk in the corner of the bedroom, "You know I went to an auction once at the Parke Bernet. They were selling out somebody's estate. Beautiful things. I almost spent a month's salary on a desk like that. Then I got lucky—an old lady outbid me."

"What's the desk?"

"Victorian. Jack Le Vien designed it."

"That name should mean something to me?"

"Not if it doesn't."

Francie was warmed by a feeling of condescension. "Now please, Matt. Get dressed."

"O.K." But he didn't move. "A layout like this must cost plenty—just keeping it vacuumed must cost. But it fits you, Francie. You look like you live in this kind of place." He stared at her with admiration. She repaid his compliment with a gracious smile recalling the way she'd taken his kisses; even as a diva takes applause.

He grew even more enthusiastic.

"The minute we auditioned you, I knew you were right for La Petite. You're not merely beautiful. You look like a lady. Not one of those standard dolls who live in a cheesy studio just to be in the right neighborhood. You folks live in this whole house?"

"Yes." She was feeling much better. Matt was really a nice guy.

He sighed contentedly. "That's why I picked you. What we want for La Petite is the real thing. A lady. A quality image for a quality product. You can't fake quality on a TV screen. And these commercials gotta be quality commercials."

Francie peacocked a little. "You're so right. After all, it's a gourmet food line."

"It sure is. Well, I guess I oughta tell you—" He hesitated, his face taking on the look of an inexperienced poker player about to take a big risk. "You're practically the La Petite Girl. It was decided at an agency meeting this morning. My secretary may have called your agent by now."

Francie had the sensation of some dark thing exploding noiselessly inside her.

"What do you mean?"

"You're in the finals. You, Darleen Franc, Coco Finly, Ellen Davis."

For a second, his voice seemed to fade. "You knew all the time?"

"Yes."

"You're a louse." But she said it calmly.

"I am. You didn't have to sleep with me to make the finals."

"All right. Now, get dressed, please."

"Oh well, sweetheart, what the hell? It wasn't so bad. In fact it was great—"

"Matt, shut up!" Again her tone was quiet. Only the edges were frayed with hysteria. A thousand expressions struggled beneath the surface of her features but were erased quickly before Matt could decipher their meaning.

She walked slowly to her boudoir table, that somehow looked like a Valentine box, sat down and stared in the mirror.

Matt's voice at a distance took on a begging note. What he didn't know was that it had a familiar ring. Men used it with Francie all the time. Sometimes just to say hello.

"Listen, it may sound crazy, but I like you. And I want you to like me. I was plugging for you before I met you. You're really good. Those Dreem-Sheen commercials sold me. You've got 'natural' class."

"But you tried anyway." She answered listlessly.

"You helped."

"O.K." The words were spoken with humility and weariness.

"I am a rat. Sorry."

"All right. Get dressed, please." She was desperately trying to keep her voice polite.

"O.K., but you're a beautiful girl. Why should a guy pass up a good thing? If there's a chance he can make out." His tone was hurt and fragmented.

"Please shut up." Again her words were matter-of-fact, unemphasized.

She knew he was grateful to her for behaving so calmly. For not making him feel even more guilty. She even forgave his darn fool impulse to tell her the truth. There was no sense to it. Sex just always made some men talkative.

He felt good. Like a goddamn big shot. Probably he didn't know he had that much left in him. That's how it was with married men—the same woman week after week for years. Francie knew the symptoms. That's why he was so easy. It was like she'd dropped a spark into a barn full of hay. And now he knew he wasn't dead. She realized that in some confused way he was trying to thank her for bringing him back to life. But she was tired.

Matt smoked in silence for a moment, then started to dress. But it took him a long time to get his clothes on. He seemed to stop to think after each garment, concentrating with an intensity disproportionate to the effort involved.

Finally he said, "Well, it's only an afternoon's work. And now, far as I'm concerned, you get the job. You've got my vote all the way. And that's worth something—about twenty five thousand dollars for just three days' shooting."

"Thanks. For everything." She smiled wryly, watching him talk with a scornful alertness, as if she were waiting for him to mispronounce a word.

"All right, so I got lucky for a change. I never really expected it. . . . a girl like you, with your looks, your background . . . a life like this."

"A life like this." She said it to herself. There was a stubborn reserve in her eyes. "Matt, you mustn't talk about me."

" 'Course not."

"If my husband found out—"

"He won't. I swear."

"We'd be through. I don't think I could stand that." This was the bare case without orchestration.

"Francie, I really like you. Don't you understand that?"

"Thanks again."

"You're a basically sweet woman. In spite of the way I've acted, I feel very protective toward you." With a terrifying honesty he made the matter worse. "In so many words, you remind me of my wife."

127

She almost laughed. "What about knocking her block off if you caught her?" The question contained mockery as well as anger.

"Well, I would. But that's different. Irene and you are not the same kind of people. The rules are different for you."

His tangled loyalties amused Francie.

He continued stubbornly, like a clock that couldn't stop ticking. "You can do as you please, and get away with it. Just because you're you."

His unqualified admiration reached and relieved her. Some unresolved inner knot loosened within her. She sighed exhaustedly.

"All right. Tie your tie."

"You've got nothing to worry about. Look—we got a mutual blackmail pact. I don't want Irene to know either."

"You love her?"

"Sure. It's got nothing to do with anything else."

"She loves you?"

"I hope so." He picked up the cigarette lighter which he'd placed on the bedside table. He flicked it on, then off.

"Look—she gave it to me for Christmas. It's eighteen carat gold. She bought it with the money she saved out of the household budget. So how could I talk? If it got out it would break up my marriage too."

"Let's drop it." She wished he would stop talking. He was getting all wound up again.

"You've nothing to worry about."

"O.K."

"Absolutely nothing."

Almost unaware of what he was doing, he let the cigarette lighter drop to the floor, put his hands on her shoulders and pulled her into a standing position, holding her tightly against him. His suddenness surprised her and she tried to pull away. But he held her closely, awkwardly trying to caress her.

"Francie."

"Let me go, Matt."

"Francie, darling." The new alive sweetness was flowing again rapidly through his body.

She struggled; but it was uncertain, indefinite—his cue to continue.

"Don't." She tried to break free, but the pull of her own body was like an undertow dragging her closer to him.

"Darling, please. You feel so wonderful."

"No."

He was taking too long. They both knew it. She would have no excuse for giving in. She gathered her energies, resistance stiffening her in a desperate attempt to escape the message of her body.

"Why? What difference does it make now?" What a damn fool thing to say—she pushed at him harder.

"No . . . . No. . . ."

"Please," he begged without letting her go. He had to do something, so he kissed her, a long kiss. With a sense of despair, she felt her body lean toward his. But she still struggled. If nothing else, she would force him away out of sheer perversity. Suddenly he began to talk rapidly.

"Darling, you've got my vote, I promise. And what I say goes." He swaggered emphatically. "La Petite is yours. I swear." He had found an argument.

"Oh, Matt." Her struggles grew more feeble, and she let him kiss her. A wild unstable laughter rose inside her. Then his kiss was harder, longer, and the laughing stopped. She slipped to the floor beside him, accepting the betrayal of her body, sadly, taking pleasure almost as a puritan would.

8

Jamie stayed in London longer than Francie expected; and when he returned, their life went on more or less as before. But it was during their first week together that Francie knew, with a full measure of humiliation, how completely she'd misjudged her man. One evening, after the brief greeting, after Jamison had changed into at-home clothes, after the first glass of golden, flavorful, cooled Russian vodka by himself, he joined Francie in the library. She wore a patterned costume that showed her slender shoulders and her long, beautiful neck; the throat of Nefertiti. Her hair was loose, her profile deep in concentration as she sat on the window seat leafing through *Vogue*. But her eyes were glazed, seeing nothing. Her body was poised and waiting for Jamie.

Jamison glanced around the room, enjoying its repose, pleased with the familiarity of the graceful, highly waxed furniture, the color and depth of the rug, the flowers, the old books lining the wall, the curving fantasy world of a nineteenth-century globe; enjoying Francie as another carefully chosen object in its place. As usual, she asked him how his day had gone, as usual he told her reluctantly.

"I had lunch with Joshua Singleton."

"The pipeline man? Who wants an equity placement?"

For an instnt his eyes flickered with pride—how quickly she remembered the points. "Yes. At a strike price of twenty-six and three-quarters."

"What is the stock selling for?"

"Twenty-seven. Réynolds says the Street won't buy it."

"Your marketing director?" Jamison nodded. "I bet he thinks it's too high."

"Reynolds is a conservative."

"Reynolds runs scared."

"He's a conservative. But unfortunately, he doesn't have Joshua's brains. I think he may be wrong, we may be able to shove it down the Street's throat. Joshua has sound instincts."

"And so do you." She glowed at him.

Jamie's eyes rested on her briefly. He felt a visceral attraction without any of the former tenderness and a detached appreciation of the stunning physical elegance of the girl. He also felt a vague resentment that she had any meaning at all and he showed it in a mild impatience.

"Why are you always reading *Vogue?* Why don't you read books?"

"I finished *The Great Gatsby.*" She lifted earnest, injured eyes to his face.

"Did you like it?"

"Yes," she said in a small voice. "I felt sorry for him." She gave Jamie an uncertain glance, afraid if she said more she would say something wrong. Since his return from London a month ago, she'd found him more than proof against her femaleness. Beneath the warmth in his manner toward her, in his ardent lovemaking, there was something hard and self-contained. As time passed, she sensed she had lost some kind of power over him.

He shrugged impatiently. "Well, try another book. There are 5,000 books in this house. Should I pick one for you?" He searched through the shelves lining the wall. "Here, try this."

Francie accepted the book gingerly as though she thought it might be too hot to handle. Then seeing the title she giggled sheepishly. "I read it—*Growing Up in Samoa.* I thought it would be about young love."

He smiled at that. "I suppose it is."

"But very different from here. I liked it very much."

"If you liked that, try *The Golden Bough.* There's an abridged version on the shelf."

"I read that too."

"You thought it would be a love story?"

She laughed, trying to maintain an air of lightness. "I

hoped so. But I suspected otherwise. It wasn't where you keep fiction.''

''Were you disappointed?''

''No. I liked reading about 'The King of the Wood.' And the 'Corn Mother.' All that. It's fascinating.''

''Then you like anthropology?''

''Is that what it is?''

''Yes. The study of the origin and development of human culture. What did you read when you were fifteen?''

''I didn't like to read then. I've just begun to like it. Now I like it very much.''

''You read movie magazines.'' Again impatience swept him.

Francie's fine hands curled tightly around the magazine. ''Nobody told me what to read after Daddy died.''

''And you had no impulse to experiment? There were no libraries in Davenport?''

She hated to admit it but she did. ''I guess I was afraid to go into them.''

''Afraid to go into a library?''

''Yes.''

''I've rarely seen such an extravagant waste of a good mind. For no good reason.''

''I am trying.''

''I know you are.''

He saw a flash of unhappiness on her mouth, so brief that he could pretend not to see it at all. She was brave enough, much more than many far more stable women. He knew she was constantly fighting off her own fears. She was intelligent enough; and living with him, her education had begun to approach that of a Vassar freshman. Still, he was continuously surprised at the bottomless well of her ignorance. About history, literature, music, art. To Francie, twelve fifteen was time for lunch. It was not a major date in English history.

That night they dined at home. The dinner, light and tasteful, was prepared by Angelique, the superb French cook. There was cold salmon, warm rolls, a dish of lemons, salad under a few drops of limpid oil. The china was nineteenth-century Stratford and the wine stood cool and decanted in a glowing Steuben bottle. Jamie poured a delicate sampling into a glass.

"Cellar temperature. Perfect."

"Yes," agreed Francie.

"The French do have a special gift."

"I set the table," said Francie with a sudden lightness of heart. Without allowing either Anglique or Agnas to guide her, she had done a graceful setting for two. It had taken her weeks to learn which forks were for what and which glasses were for what. Once, early in their affair, she brought out sherry glasses instead of red wineglasses. The look of amusement in Jamie's eyes, as he explained the mistake, had shamed and worried her. After telephoning Vera for advice, she had gone immediately to Bloomingdale's to buy a book on fine glasses. Then she went to Tiffany's to study table settings. And spent hours in Doubleday, ignoring clerks and customers, reading Emily Post's *How to Set a Table*. Finally, she decided she ought to have the book; and so she bought it, forgetting the blouse she meant to buy at Bonwit's. She spent the following weeks memorizing the shapes of glasses, cutlery and place settings; and by the end of the month, she would have made a superior butler's assistant.

Before dinner ended, between the Chablis with the salmon and the Kirsch with the berries, it occurred to Francie it was not Jamie's work alone that had kept him longer in London than planned; that he had chosen to stay the extra weeks. This new idea jolted her; and to blot out the sudden anxiety, she reminded Jamie again of the packages that had arrived that week and were sitting waiting to be opened. "From London. And Spain. And Paris. How can you wait?" She looked at him with a child's searching wonder.

"I can wait." And Jamie continued savoring the fresh berries in Kirsch. He did not want to talk. He wanted to be alone so that his thoughts about his work and the future would ease the pressure of his thoughts about Francie.

Francie forced herself to eat more slowly, to curb her impatience, to sit quietly. She was trying very hard to be easy for him, unobtrusive, easy to have about. How easy he did not realize, having never lived with a woman for more than short periods.

At last they moved into the study, and Jamie started opening packages.

"Jamie, the one from London?"

"Only shoes. See?"

"Oh, my. And Spain?"

"Shirts."

"But we have shirts here."

"I have a particular *chemisier*. In Madrid. He's almost a member of the family."

"In Spain, in Spain." Francie was singsonging. "The rain in Spain falls mainly on the plain—the plain. And Paris? What's Paris?"

"A chiffon thing. For you."

"Me?" She was startled.

"Well, I can't wear it."

She looked at the chiffon thing in its box, and her hand stroked it reverently. "Dior," she said.

"I'm indulging you."

"Thank you." She tried not to fling her arms around him. She tried not to seem overawed. She even resisted undressing then and there to waltz around in the chiffon thing.

"You can try it on later," he said, smiling at her self-restraint.

She glowed her appreciation at him. "What's in the crate?"

"Andirons. And dueling sabers. For the country."

"Oh, they're beautiful." Francie watched him, sensitive to every sign, sensitive as the savage is to weather. She knew enough not to mind that he ignored her opinions, but she did like to have her share if simply by agreeing with his taste.

"They're Scottish." She remembered her father's stories.

"Yes."

"Mary Stuart."

"Very warm. The Earl of Murray. You get A minus."

Francie was delighted with the compliment and with herself for making the connections. So pleased that she could think of nothing more to say for the moment.

When the unpacking was done and the andirons and sabers properly repacked to take to the country, Jamison sat down at his desk and began going over a miscellany of reports from the bank. It was a routine he disliked, preferring to work on the computer printouts that would form the basis for his book on the GNP dollar. But he had been back now over a month; and even though simply the titular managing partner, it was best he keep himself informed.

Francie curled up in a Chippendale wing chair, turned

the pages of *The Golden Bough*, trying to concentrate, but all the while she watched Jamison with her body. She had a sense of the plausible turned upside down. Jamison, so distinguished, so rich, so rich he seemed to own half the world—why was he always working so hard? She knew that Johnny, Aunt Gert's husband, who was always scrambling to make his mortgage payments, never worked half as hard as Jamie and would have considered it an imposition if his boss had ever suggested he take work home.

"Do you have a lot of work?" Francie asked.

"Yes." He was only half hearing her.

"You always have a lot of work."

"I subscribe to the work ethic."

"You what?"

"Never mind."

"My uncle John isn't the least bit rich, and he would never consider working one tenth as hard as you do."

"I am not sure I understand your point."

"I mean what is the point of being as rich as you are if you have to work so hard?"

Jamison looked up and smiled. "It's a valid question. There are many different schools of thought on what is the point of amassed wealth."

Francie thought of Evanston long ago, of her mother in the kitchen sitting at the table, with dishes not yet cleared away, paying bills at midnight. Explaining to ten-year-old Francie exactly where they stood. What was what. Questions. Answers. Then she looked around the library at the eighteenth-century mahogany pedestal writing desk; at the Bokhara rug with the elephant footprint pattern that Agnas once told her cost $15,000. Her mother would have been impressed that anyone could spend as much as Jamison did on tables and rugs. Her mother would have been enchanted if she knew how little thought Jamison gave to cost. Yet he worked so hard.

"Were the andirons expensive?"

"I suppose so."

"My mother would never spend as much as you do on andirons. She'd spend it on earrings."

"Matre sempre certa est."

"What?"

"Never mind."

135

"Is that French?"

"Latin."

"What does it mean?"

"One always knows the mother."

"I don't understand."

"I know dear."

"Jamison, why do you work so hard?"

"I have to."

"But you have so much money. Don't you?"

"There are other reasons for work beyond money. For one thing, I enjoy what I am doing. For another, I have to work. I would hope that I might be able to do more with my life than simply be a rich man. At the risk of sounding pompous, I feel I owe something to the human race. Everyone does. And I'd like to pay my debts my way."

"Do I owe something?"

He smiled. "Yes, I would say so."

"I wonder what it is?" This was such a novel idea that Francie could hardly grasp it. If anything, it had been her tentative opinion that it was she who was owed. It was far easier to think about Jamison owing, so she continued. "Well, if you feel that way, why don't you give away your money to people who don't have any money? Wouldn't that be paying the debt?"

"Francie, that question will get us into an entire philosophical discussion of the issues involving capitalism versus socialism. It also leads to questions concerning the fundamental nature of man. And though I am quite willing to have this talk, you are not at the moment ready to understand what I'd be saying. Or to have an informed reason for either agreeing or disagreeing with my viewpoint."

"You mean I am too dumb."

"No, you are not at all dumb. You are uneducated in these matters. You are not dumb because you can't read music. You were just never trained."

Francie felt better and laughed. "Well, I'll bet you're not going to give away your money."

"That is quite correct."

"And there are families in Davenport that could live six months on what Angelique spends on our food in one week." She stood her ground stubbornly. "So you don't have to work quite that hard."

"What would you suggest I do instead of work?"

"We could go out and have more fun."

"I have fun as I told you. Working." He raised his eyes with an expression of controlled despair. "What you need is something to fully occupy that active mind of yours. Besides clothes and cosmetics. But right now, it is my impression that you are a model; and models need eight hours sleep every night. So go to bed."

Once alone, a leaden feeling settled over Jamison as he stared at the reports. In front of Francie he'd felt a need to maintain his detachment but it had become increasingly difficult. He remembered the evening after his return from London, when Francie had told him, with hope, that she was carrying his child. She reminded him that he had once said that the Welsh family believed in marriage and a family. Well, now seemed like a good time to start, didn't it?

Jamison had paused just long enough to draw a deep breath and then remarked that yes, the Welsh family believed in marriage and family—but only when they were quite ready. And only with good reasons. After that he suggested a highly competent Park Avenue physician who could perform the abortion safely and discreetly. The very harshness of his tone might have told a wiser Francie how much the words cost him.

Thinking it over afterward, his contempt for the crudity of her ploy had been boundless. He did not believe that the pregnancy was accidental; and he was bitterly uncertain as to who the father of the baby actually was. The only thing the baby accomplished was to harden his defenses against her.

But there was no use discussing it with her. The absence of a sympathetic response to her appeal had resulted in turning her hurt pride into firm resistance. If Jamie would not marry her, she would have the child anyway. With or without a legitimate father. Anyway, it was somewhat too late in the day for an abortion to be safe. She had deliberately waited too long to tell him she was pregnant.

He took a cigarette out of a jade box and sat smoking quietly. He realized he had become obsessed with the idea of the baby. It filled the whole world of feeling for him. He was constantly aware of its presence within Francie's body; although he would never acknowledge this feeling to her. But still the baby dominated their relationship, and he felt a mingled horror and love for the anonymous creature.

He squashed the cigarette, drank two ounces of gin with a glass of water and went in search of Francie.

She was in the bedroom, sitting at her dressing table, brushing her hair, wrapped in a mist of Chanel No. 5. From somewhere outside came the far off spiral of sound of a woman's voice.

"Jamie, listen."

"The dangerous hours. It's still too cool to keep that window open."

"Listen, I think she's singing."

"Drunk. Or stoned."

"Happy."

"And now go to bed. I'm going out."

"Out?"

"For a walk."

She pressed down her anxiety and turned to Jamie with a smile that bore no trace of strain or intimacy. These days she was very near hating him. Yet the tone of his voice, the way he wore his clothes—all those trivial details were so involved with her deepest self that the passion she had for him overcame her resentments.

"I'll go with you. I love walking in the city at night."

"No. You need your beauty sleep."

"I'll be the best company. I won't talk."

He stroked her hair, not at all aware he was doing it, and she thought he might change his mind. Then he said "no" with finality. "Go to sleep. I'll see that everything is shut before I leave."

"Jamie," Francie breathed deeply trying to inhale his mood. "Where are you going?"

"To the zoo."

"The zoo?"

"To see the monkeys. I feel the need for nonhuman company."

She wanted to stretch out her hand to him, but she knew as sure as if she'd been warned that she must not touch him. So she said, "I am sorry about the baby."

He sighed. "So am I, Francie."

"I wish I'd known sooner how you felt. I would have

138

had the abortion right away." She said this in reluctant apology.

Jamie's face was noncommittal. "I wish we'd both known sooner how we felt."

Francie's eyes were wary, and she was starting to perspire. Quite unaware of her own agitation, she drew a deep breath and remarked softly, "But it isn't as if we can't afford the baby."

Now that they'd started talking about the baby, Francie had the fatalistic feeling of being drawn from one wrong turning to another, without ever perceiving the right road until it was too late. "It's our baby. How can you let it go?"

Jamison listened in silence, his face withdrawn, guarded against any involuntary change of expression. It was time he decided to give her his reasons. "It is not our baby, Francie. It's yours." A slow flush darkened his face. "It's yours," he repeated. "Knowing your history. And your proclivities."

Something twisted inside Francie, and she felt a startled fear of what he might say next. She became aware of a need for caution. "What are you saying?" she asked.

Jamie treated the question politely as though it concerned the weather. "And even if this baby is ours—which I do not believe—I can't be sure whose the next one will be," he sighed. "Under the circumstances, our way of life is not suitable for children."

Francie shook her head violently. "I know what you're thinking and it's not true. Not true!" Her voice grew shrill. "The baby is our baby. Yours and mine. There's been no one—no one but you since we've been living together. All right, all right, I wasn't a virgin before. But you knew that. Nobody is a virgin anymore." She gave him a pleading look. "But since you—there's been no one else. No one but you. I love you."

"Of course. And when we met I had no illusions. Virginity, as you say, is out of fashion. Although I must admit your reputation was impressive, even in the stylish Hamptons." His eyes were mocking. "But I was a good sport. Times are changing. I went to church and lit candles. I prayed that life with me would have a beneficent influence. You would change."

"I did." Francie stood facing him stiff with apprehension. "I've been faithful."

"Please—"

"It's true."

"Oh, what's the use."

Jamie's words threw Francie into a sweat. When she had first found herself pregnant she had been terror-struck; afraid before God and man. Her heart hurt in her body when she thought of the baby sleeping within her, and she suffered an anguish of love and fear for it. She had counted on Jamie to soothe her fright, and the strength of his resistance terrified and mystified her. Now she understood, to her dismay, its source; and she wept with anger at his accusation. "I haven't done anything, I haven't. I love you. But if ever I did do something, it would be because I feel so lonely. I want someone to hold me. You hardly come near me anymore." He did not answer immediately; and then she could feel the influence of his mind over hers, often exercised without intention, but always possessing that substrata of truth which intimidated her. So she fought him while she still could; fought him with her beauty and her knowledge of his passion for her. "You were in London ten weeks. It was awful. I was so lonely. And I need love, Jamie. Why don't you love me anymore?" She moved close to him quickly and put her hand on his cheek.

"Love you?" The scar tissue over old memories started to pain him. "Remember when we first met?"

"Yes, you were different then." She looked up at him; her eyes shining, inviting him closer with her lips.

"Yes, I was. Remember Nantucket? The weekend we stayed with Josie and Warren." He spoke softly but with effort.

"I remember."

"We went sailing in the moonlight, we made love under the stars."

"I remember." The memory for Francie danced an inward dance.

"You were happy then? You were satisfied? You felt loved?" His glance fell square on Francie—grave and pitiless.

"If it had only gone on—"

"Then why did you sleep with Warren the next afternoon?"

"Warren?" The name rang in her ears like the whistle of a bullet. "I didn't."

"Because you needed love?"

"He told you!" she gasped. "The bastard! He swore he wouldn't."

Jamison studied her with a face that held no hope. "No dear. He didn't tell me. You did. I was only guessing."

There was a long time without sound, though neither of them noticed it. Jamison looked at her; he knew her clear forehead, her curving eyebrows. There she was, his young first love with whom it seemed, as though in a dream, he had spent his youth. Her hand wandered involuntarily over his sleeve; but her face, drawn with love and misery was turned away from his. "Take off your coat, Jamie. Please." She said it coaxingly, helplessly.

Her nearness seemed to cast a spell over his mind but that did not alter his intention. "No, dear, I'm going out. Tomorrow I'll call John Drew and tell him to go ahead." He put his hand on her slender wrist and took it off his sleeve. "Time is running out. We must consider the child's future. After you have the baby, John will have an appropriate couple waiting. Respectable. Comfortable. Who want a baby. Of good stock." He paused to smile sardonically. "I trust your good taste in eugenics. Now go to sleep, dear. When I come home, I'll be quiet. Good night."

She watched him leave the room. His step was light. His jacket hung precisely. His back was neutral. In some twilight region of her spirit, Francie knew that the psychological moment had passed for them.

9

The Battenberg Gallery was doing something definitely new for them: a showing of the photographs of Vincent Richards who, though by no means Henry Cartier-Bresson or Alfred Stieglitz, still had something to say with a lens that brought an animated horde in all varieties of dress to the gallery. There were men in business suits, men in standard black tie, and men in black tie and levis, with ladies in sable and silk satin and ladies in lurid metal clingings—all there to see what they could see, which was mainly each other.

A man in a rumpled, badly fitted business suit and thinning dark hair was talking to a young Brooks-Brothers type while he squinted at a huge photograph hanging on one of the walls.

"But nobody will know whose string beans those are. If it just had the La Petite name somewhere in the picture," said Charles Kreiger, the client's brand manager.

"Vincent said, 'No!' He was fairly indignant. In fact Charlie, he was so red-faced, I thought he might explode. Or hit me. He said if he puts a logo in the photograph, it becomes an advertisement and no longer art. And this is an art showing," said Bob Hale, the account man, a conciliatory note in his voice.

Jammed in so tightly that they could hardly move, the two men continued their conversation regarding the photograph, as indifferent to the noise as if they were alone in the Gobi desert.

"But we're paying Vincent good money—big money," insisted Charlie.

"Ah, fella. What's money to Vincent? He's a millionaire already. Do you know who his wife is? Inland Steel. We're lucky he decided to exhibit that photograph at all."

"That's your idea of lucky?"

"Well, think of the public relations—for free!"

A few hardy souls turned to stare at the photograph under discussion. A waiter, holding a tray of champagne-filled glasses well above the average head, passed through the crowd. Charlie's hand reached up swiftly and plucked a glass from the tray, swallowing the liquid in one huge gulp. Though the decibel count in the gallery could now have produced deafness, once he cleared his throat, Charlie was ready for another go-around. "I'd still like to talk to that Vincent fella about the logo."

"Charlie, please don't hassle him. Anyway, not tonight. He just might take the photograph out of the exhibition entirely."

"And leave a blank space on the wall."

"He has a million other photos to hang there."

"Pretty temperamental character."

"Yes, temperamental."

"Make a lousy executive."

"Make a lousy executive. But a great photographer."

Plowing through the mob toward Kreiger and Hale like a small out-of-control tank was a short, plump, curly-haired man in his early forties, wearing horn-rimmed glasses and a petulant frown. Trying to keep up with the tank were Matt Harris and Bettie Conners, a tiny, big-busted blond-haired young woman wearing a Best & Co. version of a dinner dress. She was the copywriter on the La Petite account; and what she did not know about fashion, she did know about food—as the measurements of her figure might testify.

"W-w-where the h-h-h-hell is she?" stuttered the plump, short man. "F-F-Franciejean Stewart. Isn't th-that h-h-her n-n-name? Y-Y-You said she'd b-b-be he-h-here w-w-with the ph-ph-photo-gr-gráph. Standing b-b-beside it."

"That's where I told her we'd meet her," said Matt, looking pained.

"Sh-She di-di-didn't h-hear you! Now g-get her!"

"What's her telephone number?" asked Bob Hale.

"Oh Christ! I always reach her through her agency, Eileen Ford. Her number's unlisted."

"Unlisted? Who does she think she is—Marilyn? Call Eileen. Get that doll's number. What a fuck-up!" The big, strapping Brooks-Brothers Hale turned deferentially to the small irritated hornet panting beside him. "I'm sorry, Abe. This isn't my department. But we'll have her here in fifteen minutes, if I have to call the police to find her."

"Oh, Lord. Mr. Buckman expects to meet her," moaned Charlie.

"We-we-we kn-know that, Ch-Charlie. D-don't worry."

"He's flying in from the Coast to see the show."

"Don't worry, Charlie. Worrying's our job. We'll find her," said Bob Hale firmly. "Come on, Matt. Call Eileen. Excuse us, Abe, Charlie. We'll be back in a minute." And he grabbed Matt's arm and started pulling him through the crowd.

"Where are we going to find a telephone? Does this place have one?" asked Matt.

"Of course they have one. It's probably in the back where they hide the money. Lord knows why Buckman is coming. Naturally he has to be an art lover. He couldn't be a rose nut or a stamp collector. No—*he's* an art buff. And all we have are two measly shots of string beans with almonds and green peas with onions and that doll, Franciejean. No jar, no name, nothing. Kreiger spent the last fifteen minutes chewing on my ear about it."

"That's what you get paid for. And Kreiger is a fool. Buckman is a brilliant man."

"I know, I know. They can be the worst."

"Look, Bob, he collects paintings. That's why we were able to get Kreiger to pick up the chit for Vincent. You and I both know it wasn't cheap. Buckman knows there are a lot of cheapo shutterbugs around who would die to get the La Petite assignment. He also knows Vincent won't die. As a matter of fact what he did was squeeze us in. He's not only a big-time commercial name, but he's also classy. He's in the art world. I don't think for one minute Buckman expects to see the damn fool logo. It represents a couple of million dollars of an advertising budget."

"You're right and I am wrong. I'll pray for forgiveness."

When they arrived at the back of the gallery, a very pretty, fresh-faced teenager barred their way into the office.

"I'm sorry, you can't come in here. It's Mr. Battenberg's office." She then stepped out, pulled the knob, and slammed the door short behind her.

"We know," argued Matt. "We will absolutely not steal a thing. We only want to use the telephone. It's an emergency. Life and death. My death."

"I am sorry. I really am. But it is not a public telephone. Mr. Battenberg never allows strangers into his office. Especially during openings."

"I swear we are not thieves. We are perfectly respectable advertising agency representatives. As a matter of fact, Vincent is exhibiting two of the photographs he did for us. And for a very fancy sum I might add. We simply want to call the model who appears in one of the photographs. And get her over here. You can come in with us and listen to our conversation. We won't use a single dirty word."

"I'm sorry. I can't. Something like this always comes up during openings. If it isn't a model, it's a housekeeper, or an airport, or a piano tuner. So it's become a house rule. No one is ever allowed into the office during an opening."

Bob Hale was in a rage. "Listen, kid. Find me old Battenberg, and I will talk to him."

"I'm sorry, sir, but Mr. Battenberg is somewhere in the gallery with guests, and I am not allowed to disturb him when he is in the gallery showing work. Why don't you look for him? He's quite tall, graying hair, wearing a black tie and dinner jacket—"

"Why don't you tell me your name so that I can tell him how rude you've been?"

"My name is Anya Battenberg. I'm Mr. Battenberg's middle daughter. Named after my mother, his first wife."

In some lives, deep changes take effect as imperceptibly as the first workings of autumn. So it was with Francie and Jamison. On the surface their day-to-day life seemed unchanged. Except that in the last two months, the demands of work had kept Jamie out of town as much as in, attending meetings in Washington and abroad. In his absence Francie would often sit at her dressing table, brushing her hair and studying her face obsessively, trying to see herself as Jamie saw her. But the white oval of her face, looking back at her serenely, would tell her nothing. She sometimes thought to herself, the rhyme going over and over in her head: "There's nought that's good and nought that's fair that's worth its weight in smoke. To me that's grown so free of care since my heart broke."

In this empty new place in which she found herself, the face staring back at her seemed that of a stranger. Or rather, there were two selves in her: the one she'd always thought she'd known; and a second, horrid being which was the one she suspected Jamison saw. Deep in her eyes, hushed and waiting, lurked the menacing shadow of that other self.

She could not understand who she was or what it was in her nature that caused her to behave as she did. She only knew that by some dreadful flick of an inner switch she could be set emotionally adrift, lured unwillingly by Warren or Matt or God knows who into the very action that had collapsed her world. Oh, she had tried. But living for her was a sexual trap.

When Jamie was out of town, except for seeing Peter, Francie fought hard to sustain an almost religious solitude. Left alone, she would wander aimlessly through her days, trying to adapt to her misery; to grow accustomed to the silence and loneliness that seemed to her to symbolize her future. Sometimes with that part of her mind that was young and buoyant, she kept thinking he might one day forgive her, one day really come back to her. When he was away, all her anger at his coldness would dissolve in her recollection of their times together. These memories in turn set free a horde of numbing sensations—regrets, shame, fear—and her mind would shrink back from the glare of the truth. He had loved her, and she had spoiled it, spoiled it for both of them. And yet, she kept hoping there was something she might say to him that would explain everything. If she could think what it was. Something that would make him understand that it was only he who mattered, only he whom she loved. All of her that was worth having was always his.

Sometimes she drew comfort from the thought that Jamie must no longer love her; and because he didn't love her, it aroused in her an instinct of self-defense. She could greet him when he returned home with an impersonal gaiety.

Often when he was at home, the house was filled with dinner guests, so there was no necessity for any extended personal exchange. Or if there were no guests, he was

146

frequently preoccupied with work or detained downtown at late meetings at the bank. Then Francie would go to the theater or ballet or a concert or the movies with Peter Devlin or Vera Busch or Josie and Warren or Monroe or Matt or anybody at all.

When they were together in bed and he wanted to make love, they made love as wildly, as passionately as ever. But when it was over, it was over. It was not that he was unkind. If anything she could tell he was trying to be as kind as possible. But in some vital way she had simply ceased to exist for him.

And it was often true that Francie's presence no longer pained Jamie, no longer caused in him a need to avoid her. Francie's beautiful bright being, through which all the currents of life once had seemed to flow so proudly, now was like the ghost of a long-dead beloved, decreed by some malevolent god to haunt him.

The evening of the Vincent Richards opening Francie came home from a Salem-cigarette audition to change into evening clothes, and found, to her surprise, Jamison sitting in the library, reading and smoking. The sight of him sitting there, when she thought him in Geneva, caused a catch in her breath, a gasp of joy and relief. Then remembering in a rush that though they still lived together, made love together, their relation now was actually at arm's length, the bare bones of what it once had been, the familiar depression possessed her.

Still, she had never been sorry to see him, and his presence in the room revived her feel for possibilities.

"Hello," she said, trying to sound light, and going forward eagerly to place her hands on his shoulders. "I am so glad to see you again. I couldn't be more glad. Or is it gladder? Or should I say 'so pleased'? It's a multiple-choice question. I give you 'A' before you answer because I know full well that you are an authority on grammar." And she bent forward spontaneously to brush his forehead with a kiss.

Then she stood back and gazed at him in solemn delight. There was such deep pleasure in her face that, despite himself, Jamie was seized afresh with her poignant appeal. There was no mistaking the welcome in her eyes—the helpless fidelity of her spirit, if not of her body.

"I finished up at the Fund earlier than I expected. I took

147

the first flight open—I'm tired of Geneva. Would you like to have dinner with me tonight?"

She nodded her head vehemently. "Yes. But let's stay at home. Angelique can make us something." She stumbled awkwardly, trying to organize her thoughts, to say the right words, so that he would understand her feelings. "It will be like old times, don't you see?" As soon as she said it, she knew she'd struck the wrong note and took a deep breath to hold back the tears. "I mean, of course, not old times. You can't go home again, and so forth. I did read that book, you know," she added in confusion.

"I see you've done a lot of reading." He said it with kindness. "The books have been moved around."

"Oh. You noticed."

"I noticed."

"I meant to put them back where I found them, but I never seem to be able to remember where I found them."

"It's quite all right. Agnas keeps a file of where books belong. I'll talk to her. And as long as you leave the economics and history in place, it makes no difference." He said this with a faint smile.

"I'm nowhere's near up to that yet. Economics and history. No, I have to get smarter."

"You're smart enough. It takes time, that's all."

"I'm trying very hard."

"I know you are, dear." Jamison felt a startled discomfort as though her love were a forgotten enemy. "Just go a little easier on yourself."

"How can I?" Then she broke off distractedly, trying to think what she could say to thank him for noticing her efforts and to apologize for everything else. But it was no use, no use at all; and a mingling of gratitude and shame poured out of her in a smothered sob: "How do you stand me? How do you stand my being around?" She put her face in her hands.

"Francie, Francie, stop that." He rose and stepped forward impulsively, putting his arms around her. Just below the surface, Jamison had been aware for months, from day to day, even minute to minute, what a desperate battle she was fighting. He was aware too of her inventions of good humor, her defiance of doubt, the fireworks of entertainment she put on for his benefit to make up to him for a forfeit of honesty. It was just this effort that he relied upon when he wished

148

to justify the hard core of the love that he still felt for her.

The telephone was ringing at the other end of the house, and after four rings someone picked it up.

"That's your telephone isn't it, Francie?"

"I think so."

"Were you expecting a call?"

Francie shook her head uncertainly. "No, who would be calling now?"

At that moment Agnas came to the door of the library. "Madam," she said, "there's a man on the telephone who insists on talking to you."

"Who could it be? No one but our friends have that number."

"Madam, he says it's urgent."

"Has to talk to me?" Francie grew hot with embarrassment. "What man? What is his name?"

"Matt Harris."

"Matt Harris—oh, my God, I forgot." Francie's embarrassment vanished as she realized the legitimacy of the telephone call. "Oh, Jamie, I forgot. It's the Battenberg opening. I'm supposed to be there. Vincent Richards is having a showing, and he used some of the shots he did of the La Petite vegetables—they actually look edible. And I'm in one of the shots. They want me there. Excuse me a minute, will you?" Her whole manner conveyed her intense desire not to leave him. "I have to talk to him and excuse myself."

"Won't you have to go to the opening?"

"No. I'll beg off."

"Francie, if it's work, you ought to go."

"But I don't want to go." Her voice was on the edge of tears. "I want to stay here and have dinner with you."

"You may not be able to—"

"Yes I will." She forced herself to speak with steadiness. "I'll be right back."

When Francie picked up the telephone in her dressing room, her capacity for rapid transitions made it possible for her to say charmingly, "Ah, Matt. Hello."

"Damn it, Francie, where the hell are you?"

"I'm at home, Matt. As you can tell by the fact that I've answered the telephone."

His affection for her was being drained off by his fear and anger. "Listen, Francie, you'd better get over here *toute suite* or some other chick could end up being the La Petite girl.''

"I don't see why I'm so important, Matt. You have that wonderful photograph."

"Don't argue with me, Francie."

"I'm not arguing, Matt." She kept her tone easy, equable. "Only something has come up here at home, and I have to stay in tonight."

"Listen to me, Francie. If you don't show up here in the next fifteen minutes, I will be personally responsible for recommending a change of girls in midstream. The commercial hasn't been scheduled yet. We could redo the whole thing with Coco Finly. Including the print ads."

"Matt, I don't understand the fuss. What's the brouha-ha? It's only an art gallery opening."

"It's only an art gallery opening that Lawrence Buckman has decided to fly three thousand miles to attend. Get it? Buckman—the chairman of La Petite. The big boss. You better get over here. He's going to want to meet the La Petite Girl."

"Oh—"

"Yes—oh! Get your ass over here. *Now!*" And he slammed the receiver down so hard the sound hurt her ear.

She returned to the library where Jamison was sitting silently in an armchair, waiting for her. She had been distracted by Matt's temper, but her purpose was unshaken. "I'm not going."

The intensity of her statement signaled to Jamie her need, though he knew there was nothing he could do for it anymore. So he proceeded as rationally as possible. "How can you not go? It's your work."

"I don't give a damn. I want to stay here with you, and have a quiet dinner."

He followed at his own pace. "It's a fine thought—we'll have dinner tomorrow evening. In." He paused and then went on. "Patrick tells me that Peter is downstairs in the sitting room waiting for you."

"Oh—Peter." The name broke from Francie in a smothered wail of distress. "I forgot about him."

"It seems you did. Well, there are too many people involved. You can't disappoint everyone."

Francie's eyes rested on the carpet then she looked up at Jamison, her eyes pleading. "Do I have to go?"

"I think so."

"No way out?" she asked fitfully.

He shook his head.

"Ah—the forms. The forms must be observed." She stood for a moment caught by the idea that fate had played an elaborate practical joke on her. "If you wait up, I'll come home early. I swear it by the moon."

He laughed. "Don't swear it. I've been on a plane for hours, and I may go to bed early. We'll have dinner tomorrow evening."

"But you may not?"

"May not what?"

"Go to bed early?"

"I may not. We'll see. Dear, go get dressed. I'll have Patrick bring Peter up. I'll keep him company until you are ready."

Francie had wondered how much she would have to bear, and now she was starting to see. She had been watching Jamie for some sign that she might still have some special meaning for him. But his sober impartiality, his refusal to interfere in her comings and goings, made her feel even more keenly how little she knew anymore what he was feeling. These last months of practice had taught her to improvise from moment to moment. Her rule of thumb was to keep within bounds, not to lose her head, not to let him see she was afraid. With this in view, she decided to go dress immediately. "Well, the sooner I go, the sooner I'll be home," she said, and giving him a swift backward smile disappeared from the room.

Vera Busch in a long, severely elegant, deep brown evening dress, accompanied by John Ott, fifteen years her junior, in black tie and dinner jacket, perspired their way as best they could through the carnival of people in the Battenberg Gallery. Ott paused in front of a photograph of a woman flat on her back in limbo laid out in a flowing seventeenth-century gown, with candles at her head and feet.

"Who is that, for God's sake?"

"Dame Edith Sitwell."

151

"The anthropologist?"

"The poetess. John, did you really go to the University of Chicago?"

"I really did. Art history was my field. Not poetry. Vera, what are we doing here? Where is Peter? Where is Francie? What are we doing here being pushed and shoved and plied with bad champagne all to ogle Vincent's family album and comb his ego?"

"You have too much moral conviction. And a limited vision. Some of these are quite good. I am not suggesting you buy any—"

"Thank you."

"On the other hand you should enter into the spirit of the thing. *De gustibus non disputandum est.*"

"God! What is that?" The young man was staring at a huge egg yolk suspended in liquid.

"An egg yolk."

"An egg yolk?"

"Our darling Vincent sees beauty everywhere."

Peter entered the library with a nagging uncertainty as to his welcome. But the affection of Jamie's greeting reassured him.

"It's good to see you again, Peter."

They shook hands, and a glance with their old warmth passed between them. They'd grown up in the same world, gone to some of the same schools, many of the same parties, belonged to some of the same clubs. And though Jamie was eight years Peter's senior, as they grew older, the age difference ceased to matter.

"Come sit down. Can I offer you something? Francie is upstairs changing."

"Yes. La Ina. I think it may be a long drinking evening."

Peter took out a cigarette from a silver case, placed it in a cigarette holder, and then seated himself in the armchair opposite Jamie while Jamison made him a drink.

"Thank you for doing the honors tonight with Francie. I did not expect to be back in town this evening," said Jamie.

"Would you like to join us? There is always room for one more at an opening, you know. Especially for a bona fide collector."

"I don't collect photography. But thank you, no. I am in no mood for cigarette smoke, noise, and inane conversation with people I do and don't know. I regard your goodwill in escorting Francie as something akin to heroism."

"I suppose I mind it less because it's part of my business."

"Photography? What has that to do with antiques? Dagguerreotypes, maybe, but not photography."

"Well, there is always an overlap in clientele."

"I suppose that's true. There is a tribal resemblance among those who go to gallery openings and auctions and the Met showings and estate sales. I see that."

"Exactly. And now it's photography."

"Yes—the new game in town."

For some inexplicable reason, Peter had a distinct sense of expectancy. Jamie was making conversation until he was ready to say what was on his mind.

"And as a matter of fact I am quite grateful to you for having seen to Francie's amusement while I've been so preoccupied with work. She wrote to me how kind you've been. Thank you again."

"My pleasure. She is very easy to be with. Actually quite engaging." He continued to eye Jamison with fascination, waiting.

"How is her French coming?"

"She's at the Institute faithfully three times a week."

"She can be quite singleminded."

"You're really to be congratulated. She's a remarkable creation. Shaw himself would have been impressed. She's become literate, civilized—and more so everyday. Even the gourmet thing is developing. The other evening she gave me a lecture on claret. Her marshaling of facts was pure Jamison. Her mind is turning out to be quick and fastidious."

"Once in a lifetime every man should be allowed to play God."

"Not every man has the imagination. Or the foresight. I doubt that I would have seen as far as you saw; but now that Francie's been created, anyone can see her." He paused and looked inward as though at a memory. "Of course, she's not as happy as one would expect from a young woman as beautiful and with such great expectations. Sometimes I have the feeling she's elsewhere. Sleepwalking as it were. Dreaming."

153

Jamison gave him a quick look. "Then thank you for escorting my dreamer."

"I suspect she'd be less a dreamer if you were around more often in the audience to applaud or criticize her performance."

"I am in the audience. And I do applaud the performance. But at a safe distance." It was the first time Jamison showed Peter clearly the direction of his thoughts, and Peter decided to ignore it. What he saw was something he didn't like.

"Well, I know what you mean by 'safe distance.' We spent one Wednesday from nine in the morning to nine at night canvassing galleries. She has the energy of an electric clock—no rewinding necessary. I almost couldn't move the next day, my legs were so shot. I had to go to the Buell estate sale. Suddenly, fresh as a daisy, Francie appeared on my doorstep because she wanted to trot along and learn about cameos. Old Lavinia had a wonderful collection of Saulini pieces."

"Did she buy anything?"

"No. Everything she liked—and her taste was excellent—she thought would be too high. And they did fetch some fancy prices."

"She could have had anything." Jamison smiled in spite of himself. "But that's quite like her. She was not born to be a rich man's darling. I bought her a rope of pearls in Paris. Really quite splendid ones. She forgets to wear them. And it's not affectation. She forgets. But we picked up a rather delicate enameled miniature case—actually quite a nice eighteenth-century example, but nothing special—at a small shop in London, and that she wears almost constantly. Fortunately it hangs on a thin gold chain that seems impossible to snap. I've seen her wear it to bed."

"I've seen it too." Peter laughed awkwardly. "Of course, not in bed."

"It could have been in bed. I know my young lady."

Jamison said this without emphasis, yet the result was to make Peter stare at him in puzzlement. What was startling was how out-of-character this remark was for the man he knew Jamison Welsh to be. Jamison was never, to Peter's knowledge, one to speak loosely with exposed feelings and raw nerves showing. He was not given to the standard betrayals of himself or others by any of the approved methods of accusation, innuendo or confessional with which so many men give away their lives so cheaply.

But as he listened, Peter realized that Jamie knew exactly what he was doing. He even had a plan. Speaking in another vein entirely, his voice now businesslike and efficient, Jamie continued, "I am going to close the house for six months. Except for the servants' quarters. I'll be on the road during the time doing work for Jack. Talking to people; listening to opinions; helping to forumulate the thinking that will go into his economic policies. If, hopefully, he is elected. This country needs a tax cut very badly."

Peter, casting about him for the right thing to say, could only remark vaguely, "That's a big order."

"Yes, it is."

"But it's what you want, isn't it?"

"We'll see," Jamie said with such a drop in vigor, such fatigue and resignation, that Peter knew it was coming: "I won't be taking Franciejean with me, you know."

Peter had recognized for months that the situation between Francie and Jamison contained all the elements of an explosion; but in his personal experience, he had seen the same combination in other lives subside eventually into nothing. For the moment he did not say all he felt. "Then you'll leave her in New York?"

"Yes."

"But you said you were closing the house? Where will she live?" His concern was so naked and genuine that Jamie could not take offense.

"I had thought of leaving the house open for her. But it would be a mistake. She'd misunderstand."

"You mean you want her to stop hoping?"

"Yes."

Peter knew Jamison could be cruel—could even enjoy being cruel. But unlike others Peter had known, Jamie watched himself and guarded against his own sadistic streak. Yet, of all women, somehow Francie had invaded and then wounded him; and Peter was afraid of an involuntary reflex in Jamie's nature that might force him to hurt her deeply. For a moment his discretion deserted him, and he spoke with insistence: "But you care for her, don't you? I know she cares for you. How can you just leave her?"

"I know. But it's no use. There are reasons, and I am

sure you can guess why it's impossible that we marry. Why it's even advisable to end this affair now."

Peter considered this. "But you knew her history when you took her up." He said it almost critically.

"Of course. From the beginning."

"And yet you believed in her?"

"Yes, almost completely."

"In spite of what you knew?"

"Isn't that part of our myth? Love conquers all."

"In the movies. But for you?"

"Oh! I'm susceptible to our cultural myths. They have their virtues."

"They make the world go round."

"Our world at any rate."

"I've always thought of you as beyond illusions."

"I would hope not. After all, something did happen between us. Something real and rare. You call it illusion—and with an undertone of scorn, at that—because it didn't last. What has duration got to do with the depth of an experience?"

"You're more romantic than I realized."

"No, I'm more American. And I value our illusions. Isn't it equally possible that the disillusionments we meet are what is false? And it is our illusions, about ourselves, about each other, about the world, that give our lives motive and meaning?"

"I suppose I don't have your guts." Peter said this with something like resentment. "It's a bitch to discover how wrong one can be about something or someone."

Jamie gave him a sarcastic, affectionate grin. "A bitch. But that's an old price. And we have to pay it. Or what right do we have to dream?"

"Of course, Francie helped you to accept the illusion, to believe in her, believe she could be faithful."

"She believed it herself."

"She made you think it was possible."

"As I said, she herself thought it was possible. And my imagination did the rest."

"You lied to yourself?"

"Who could do it more effectively? But I can only do it for so long." In his hard, strong-willed way, Jamison had braced himself to meet this fact. But there was something in

156

his face that Peter had never seen before—an unconscious plea. "You see, I've caught a wild bird. I can't keep her in a cage. If I marry her, she'd think she was happy. She'd peck her seeds and sing in her cage. But then she'd die—or something worse. Because that's what being married to me would do to her. And if she didn't die, she'd ruin the both of us."

"But what can she do if she doesn't live in a cage? We all live in cages."

"I know. But there are other kinds. I would like her to find one to which she is more easily fitted. Where she can spend herself as extravagantly as her nature demands." He paused. "Otherwise, I don't know what to do."

The seconds were brief, but they lasted long enough to refresh Peter's sense of the unusual intimacy he was sharing. In the light of it, Peter's courtesies were thrown away. "But she depends on you. How will she live?"

Jamie looked at him with an expression of bewilderment. "Peter, remember, I love her. I don't intend to leave her penniless. I'll buy her an apartment. Something spacious, sunny, charming. The maintenance will be paid for at least two years. Longer if necessary. And of course, I would appreciate it if you would help her find something suitable. And keep an eye generally on her. But she'll by no means be homeless or destitute."

Peter did not believe in stripping wounds, but he could not help himself. "It isn't simply money, Jamie. She's starting to make money herself—big money. But she's a child. She needs a home. She's a waif."

Jamison could not deny to himself the truth of what Peter said, nor could he see any way to make use of this truth. "I agree, Peter," he said quietly, "but I cannot buy her a husband, a family. If I could, I believe I would."

Saying that, he rose from his chair to pour himself another scotch. Watching him reminded Peter who Jamie was, who he had always been in Peter's life. His brilliant, rich, eccentric friend who was Peter's benefactor too. For Jamie was a man who respected no conventions but his own; and with a mixture of practical sense and cynicism, he refused to be embarrassed by Peter's sexual "irregularities." It was Peter's life to handle as Peter saw fit. Jamie's friendship with him had always been casual, almost accidental, comradely; and during their younger and growing years, Peter had admired him greatly the way he would have admired an older, more gifted brother; one who could do what he couldn't do, be what Peter couldn't be.

He remembered a day years before when Jamie was playing in the Meadow Club tournament; the quarter finals against a very young Australian, one of the postwar prodigies. He remembered the fourth set and Jamie pounding across the court to try to reach a sharply angled volley. When he reached the ball, he hit a backhand that was so perfect, so flat, so hard that the ball was a blur until the chalk flew. And he remembered the young Australian standing there for several seconds staring; then leaning his racket against the net and applauding. Peter had been as proud of the shot as if he had made it himself. And he remembered later explaining impatiently to the mob of reporters when Jamie lost in the fifth set, six-one, that after all, Jamison was a turned-thirty banker who happened to play tennis. He should not be compared to a twenty-year-old kid who was destined to be a champion.

Then he remembered another Jamie on another weekend, when Peter and his friend Roger had been invited over to play on Jamie's private court. There he found Jamie playing in the briefest of shorts, a fifth of Beefeater gin standing at the net. He was playing a one-set match with Ginny Cartright, a young lady known for her great ground strokes and her equally exceptional sexual athleticism.

Ginny was wearing a classic tennis dress, minus the panties. Everytime she moved and the short skirt swirled, her body movements became more interesting than her strokes. For you could easily see her ass and her pubic hair. And when she bent over, either to pick up a ball or reach for a shot, you could see even more clearly her pink vagina.

The bet required that Jamie drink one ounce of gin after every game. If he won the set, Ginny was to be his slave for the weekend. If he lost, it was to cost him five thousand dollars. There were two high points in the match that Peter never forgot. The first was when Ginny hit a very short lob with Jamie at net. Just as Jamie was about to hit the ball, Ginny turned around, flipped up her dress, stuck out her ass and called, "Jamie, here!" pointing to her behind. Jamie roared with laughter, but he was able to tap a very gentle return that hit Ginny smack in the center of her behind. As the set wore on, Jamie was obviously having as much trouble adjusting to a very obvious erection as to the gin.

Near the end, Ginny pulled one more stunt. She put two fingers into her vagina and rubbed them on the tennis ball she was about to serve. She called out, "Jamie! Since spit balls are illegal, I thought I'd try a cream ball." Jamie laughed so hard he missed the serve completely. The match ended indecisively. Jamie was ahead. They were changing courts between games when Ginny whispered something to Jamie. They both put their rackets down on the bench, and Jamie turned to the group of watchers, saying, "Ciao, kiddies, enjoy the courts. See you in a couple of days."

And then there was the Jamie who invited the Budapest String Quartet to be his houseguests; and there were, for a few selected friends, three brilliant weekend evenings of the Beethoven Quartets, early, middle and late.

That was Jamison, an original, an enigmatic human mixture of flesh and blood and brain. Peter's friendship with him was unlike that which he had with any other man; and as it had been difficult for Peter in the past to look at Jamison with envy, so it was difficult now for him to look at him with pity. "I feel so totally useless. Is there anything that I could possibly do to help?"

The question held Jamie a moment and then he half smiled. "Find someone suitable to marry her." Then he seemed to let himself go. "There is something, though."

"There is?"

"It's nothing very original. But it presents a problem."

"I meant what I just said."

"I know." Jamie was forcing himself to continue. "Francie is pregnant. Did you know?"

Under the pressure of Jamie's eyes Peter tried to keep his face a blank. "No! She never mentioned it."

"That's surprising."

"Why surprising?"

"She has to talk to someone. And she likes you."

"Perhaps one of her girl friends?"

"She doesn't trust women. You know that."

Peter evaded and lied. "She said nothing to me."

"Then why don't you congratulate me?" Jamie asked caustically. The question was so bitter and self-mocking that it made Peter squirm.

"Because that would be a tasteless joke at this point."

"Thank you. I acknowledge your discretion. We won't pretend that it's my child." He said this with no reserve, as though it was a release finally to say it at all.

"I'm not so sure. How can you be certain it's not your child?"

"I'm not that certain."

"Then—?"

"But neither am I sure it is mine."

"You mean with Francie one can never be sure?"

"Never."

Peter sat for a moment and then saw—or thought he saw—Jamie bend his head. He had never seen the gesture before, and the startling image came to him that Jamie's head was on the block, as though submitting to a will far greater than his own. "You see, I can't change my own nature. I am a man of my tradition. And while I can share my women, I cannot share my wife."

"I know."

"Though I accept that many other men can, and do."

"That's true."

"I've asked too much of her." His tone was gentle and matter-of-fact. "She knows now how much I have asked, but she never seriously considered it in the beginning." He said this with resignation. "I am hardly monkish. Or an ascetic. Sex is my release. But with Francie the feeling runs too deep. And whatever my passions, should I ever decide to marry, I would undoubtedly be monogamous. And like Caesar's wife, my wife too must be above reproach. I could not risk the weakening that would happen otherwise."

"You would have been happier never to know her."

"I would have been different. Happiness is just one of our many necessary illusions. I prefer what I have."

The rages of jealousy, the rights of protest were not for Jamison; and it provoked Peter into an amused irony. "It's almost a pity she's not more mercenary."

"A fortune hunter."

"Who would keep hr skirts clean."

"At least until after the wedding day. She hasn't enough guile."

Peter knew how much pain was banked beneath Jamie's

160

lightness, and he regretted his teasing. "That's part of her real specialness."

"Yes! I don't think I shall ever find one like her again."

"One is enough in a lifetime."

Because Jamison was prouder than most men, he was also more vulnerable to shame; and now Peter saw him look at his own humiliation and then pass beyond it. "She'll need the best medical care. And someone to look after her to make sure she takes good care of herself. Since I won't be available, can I count on you to watch her? Naturally, I'll pick up the costs. The baby must be bouncing. The mother must be healthy."

Peter felt himself stopped at the sane, high intention he was dealing with. "Of course. Yes, of course. For a man my age I suspect I know very little about the human heart. What better place to begin my training than with the care of children?" He managed to say it good-naturedly, wanting desperately to preserve Jamie's good faith in him, in whatever shape Jamie wished.

Somewhere a telephone was ringing, and Jamison turned toward the sound. "That must be the advertising agency calling for Francie. She's slower than usual. Would you like another sherry?"

Francie, in a simple, white, silk satin shirt waist dress, that looked as expensive as it was, stood in front of her boudoir mirror trying on different sets of earrings. But she liked nothing. She then proceeded to search her jewel box frantically. There must be something that would do. Jamison had taught her all too well the lesson of understatement; and at the moment, everything looked bizarre. Finally, unwillingly, she picked up the telephone on her boudoir table. "Yes, I am coming, Matt."

"What the devil is taking you so long?"

"I am coming. I had to change and put on makeup."

"Well come! Half the champagne is gone. The press is here, drinking like fishes! How can we get pictures if they're blotto by the time you arrive?"

"I am looking for my pearl earring."

"Oh, for God's sake, screw the earrings! Francie, Lawrence Buckman is coming! Get here, please!"

"I will be right there. I am minutes away."

When Matt slammed down the receiver, Francie went back to scrambling among her earrings. She knew that she was running out of time, and she also knew with a fierce stubbornness that she had to have the right earrings. Jamie must be proud of her. This sent her on another frantic search through her jewel box. Still, she could only find one pearl of the only pair of pearl earrings that she felt were plain enough to go with the dress. She was continuously losing earrings, gloves, umbrellas, cuff links. It occurred to her to investigate Jamison's jewel box. Perhaps Agnas had put the earring there accidentally. Sometimes earrings looked like cuff links; and as a matter of fact, she would occasionally wear a pair of Jamie's clip-on cuff links as earrings. For good luck. Those somehow she never lost.

Actually, she loved any excuse to pry through his jewel box, caressing and studying and tirelessly memorizing every item in his vast store of studs, links, rings, tie pins.

Now, suiting her actions to her idea, she left her boudoir table and went to Jamie's dresser; opened the drawer containing his jewel box; and standing over the huge velvet rectangle, began methodically to ransack it. First day—studs, no earring. Second tray—more studs, cuff links. Third tray—beautiful dress cuff links—and Francie gasped. Tucked inside was a wafer-thin gold cigarette lighter, but Jamison never used cigarette lighters. It jolted her to think that it might be a gift from an old girl friend. Or far worse—and panic laced with jealousy ran through her—a new girl friend? She took out the lighter and gingerly examined it with distaste. The gleam of the gold seemed to burn her hand. It was when she turned it over in her palm that she saw the initials: MH. Then she remembered.

She stared at the thing numbly, knowing she was looking at her future. She had known something was coming; it had merely been a matter of when it would arrive. Now and then in the past few months, the veneer of life had shown such ominous cracks that her fear had gathered itself crouched and waiting to spring. Sometimes she had wondered what would give way first—her resolve or Jamie's. Now with a long fall of hope, she knew that there had never been a question. She had lost him long ago. The only surprise was that she had not recognized it sooner. But of course, how could she? He had smiled at her, been kind to her, he had kissed her; and she had needed to keep on hoping if she was to go on living as was expected.

Night after night she'd lain awake alone in the darkness wondering if he too were awake. And if he were awake wondering, was he thinking of her? Now when she could not sleep for thinking of him, she would know, even in his arms, how really far away from her he was.

The life she had longed for with Jamie, the love and happiness she had reached for—it had all seemed so possible. But at last she knew, once and for all, that try as she might, it was beyond her. It had slipped through her fingers.

She understood all too well that it was her own nature she'd been fighting; and that the fight was hopeless.

She stood there, absolutely still, thinking about her secret hope. Now that it was dead, she felt the exhausted relief that comes with an acceptance of failure. There was nothing more to do except bury the dead. She picked up her satin evening bag, dropped the lighter into it, reached for her white fox wrap, and left the bedroom.

Francie entered the library where Jamie and Peter sat talking, her cheeks flushed and her eyes shining with a peculiar nervous luster. "Well, who invited you?" she teased Peter.

"You did."

"That's right, I did. What is this world coming to?"

"You look feverish. And you sound it. Are you feeling well?" asked Peter.

"I believe I am coming down with a cold. The flu. Pneumonia. Or tuberculosis."

"Temperature?"

"Probably." She glanced at her watch. "We're late, late, late."

"Are you sure you want to go?"

"I have to go. Jamison insisted." For the first time since entering the room, she looked at him. "You did insist, didn't you? And do I really look terrible?"

"I did insist. And you look beautiful."

She gave a faint sigh of relief. "I trust your judgment,

dear. You are my best and severest critic." But still she took a small, jeweled compact out of her bag, opened it, studied her face, and patted her hair with her hand.

"Oh well! I'll do." She closed the compact and put it back in the bag, but continued to stare into the open purse. Then she looked up and, sounding offhand and sensible, remarked to Jamie, "By the way, dear thing. I thought I'd do a good deed while I was out."

"I am certainly for good deeds."

She nodded her head. "I know you are. You are a devoted doer of good deeds. I speak from experience." The slight tremor in her voice was the only sign of emotion she showed. "Anyway, one of our friends—I am sure you remember him—left his lighter here some months ago." Her tone had regained lightness. "Considering how long we've stored it for him, we ought to ask for storage charges." She rummaged in her evening bag and pulled out the lighter. "You remember, Jamie. Matt's lighter? I thought I'd return it to him tonight. A form of house cleaning. I'll explain how Agnas found it under the sofa only the other day. Although it does say something unfortunate about Agnas's talent for vacuuming. But I don't think he'll notice, he'll be so glad to have it back."

"That's an excellent idea."

"I think so too."

A change had come over Jamie's face as they spoke about the lighter, and Francie had a sudden perception of what he was thinking. Whatever despair he felt over her infidelities, however little he understood the compulsion that prompted them, her candid reaction to finding the lighter reaffirmed his faith in her. He was satisfied that she would not excuse herself or embarrass him by stooping to denials, recriminations, bluff.

And it was true that this sense in her of fine discriminations, of her own kind of honor that would not evade consequences, was a quality of character that always had for him the same appeal as her purity of feature. It made her for him, collector that he was of the rare and beautiful, a being impossible to match.

Peter had been watching and listening, but he had no idea what the talk was about. Yet he knew enough to know it was deadly serious and sugar-coated with good humor. Now he rose from his chair and walked toward Francie. "My dear, if you have good deeds to do, we had better get on with it. You did mention a moment ago that you were 'late, late, late.' And though it's fashionable to be late, there are limits."

Peter's reference to 'good deeds' made Francie anxious that she had said too much. And she did not want to appear either clumsy or foolish in Jamie's eyes. Nor did she want him for one moment to think that she might make Peter a confidant in this matter.

So she turned to Peter quickly, the concern wiped from her face like excess makeup. "Let us go then you and I, when the evening is spread out against the sky"—she reached for Peter's arm—"to the Battenberg Galleries." She waved her free hand at Jamie, as though in fact nothing more important than a discussion of household trivia had taken place between them. "If you stay awake and wait for me, I'll come home with a basketful of tales as fascinating as those of Scheherazade."

"That would certainly be an improvement over my dreams. They are all numbers."

Francie considered this. "No, I've changed my mind. You're a lousy night owl. Go to sleep, dear. You deserve a good night's rest. Scheherazade will hardly sound sexy if you're half asleep."

Watching them, Peter was moved by the total reality of their feeling for each other. It was all such a bloody shame.

10

The April evening was cool, and Francie shivered in the taxi under her fur stole. As she stepped out onto the sidewalk where people were still coming and going into the crowded Battenberg Galleries, she wished with all her heart that the evening were over.

"Extraordinary," said Vera. "Vincent is really a talent."

"For photography, it's exceptional," said John. "Does he use that new Japanese camera?"

"John, my dear, how would I know? He does his own developing, of course. Whatever that means. You know, she is extraordinary-looking. A real beauty."

"I was talking about the string beans."

"John, really!"

Vera and John were looking at a photograph of Franciejean judiciously spearing string beans from a dish laden with beans.

"I admit if I were a photography buff I'd be impressed. Those string beans are very convincing. The very spirit of string beans. Authentically vegetarian. I can tell. I grow them on my terrace."

"What do you think of Francie?"

"Very girllike. Indeed, as you said, Vincent can do anything."

As Francie and Peter entered the gallery, Vincent, a small man in evening clothes with an ugly, agreeable face, surrounded by an entourage of friends, admirers, detractors, and climbers, watched them enter. Since the *New York Times*

166

critic had not only put in an appearance but had even shown some enthusiasm, Vincent was feeling his oats. Now that the critic had left, Vincent felt less cramped, freer to indulge his quite sizable talent for selling; a talent usually overlooked in the successful artist. If photography, by some freak of fashion, should lose its profit margin, Vincent could make a handsome living selling used cars or used cans. Now he detached himself from the human zoo surrounding him and, with a face full of predatory high spirits, hurried to greet the newcomers. It was not simply by reason of their artistry that the La Petite photographs were being displayed.

"Peter, you old goat, you're late." He grasped Peter's hand warmly.

"Looks like a success, Vince. But you never were one for failure."

"You know your Vincent, don't you?" And then turning to Francie, his zero target, he murmured, "Darling, where is your illustrious friend, Jamison? Coming later I hope?" Saying this, he put his arm around Francie's waist and led them into the gallery. "Jamie must see you immortalized by my Nikon. Actually, the photograph should hang in the Modern. Or at the least in your boudoir."

"With all those string beans and green peas, I'd say they belong in the kitchen," laughed Peter, who knew exactly what Vincent was up to.

At that moment two hired photographers drifted over. "Hold it, Vincent," said one. "Let's have you and Miss Stewart together. The artist and his model. Get it?"

"Say *money*, Francie," said Peter.

"Money," said Francie.

There was a flash of bulbs; and out of nowhere, Bob Hale, Matt Harris, and Charles Kreiger materialized around the threesome.

"Hello, Francie," said Matt. "Glad you made it." Then he turned to the photographers, who were fading into the crowd. "Hey boys! Get one of Miss Stewart next to our photographs."

Francie looked at Matt with impatience and then at Peter, seeming to say how dreary this all was; but what could she do. She was a fly caught in a bottle. Then she left with Matt Harris, Charles Kreiger, Bob Hale, and the photographers while Vincent and Peter continued to enjoy the zoo together.

They knew each other well. Vincent sent Peter clients, and Peter would get Vincent Queen Anne pieces at a price.

"Let me get you a drink, Peter. Not that god-awful champagne."

Vincent spoke to a young man standing behind him. "Freddie, Pinch on the rocks. Right, Peter?"

Peter nodded as Freddie detached himself from the group and went toward the Battenberg private office. Freddie had no trouble persuading Anya Battenberg to lead him to her father's liquor supply.

"Peter, please come and sit for a portrait."

"You're too expensive Vince, and it's not deductible."

"My pleasure. On the house. Even the film. Your face has always reminded me of Verrochio's Lorenzo."

"I am not sure that's a compliment. Anyway, Francie's the beauty in our group. The rest of us are beasts."

"I am not sure that Jamison would like being characterized as a beast," Vincent laughed. "Yet, of course, someone has to be."

"I'd say we are all beasts. More or less. On different days."

"Philosophical as ever. Incidentally, is her great and good friend coming? He's one of the reasons I exhibited those La Petite photos. I was taking a chance. They really don't belong in this kind of thing. But they are quite good, and I thought I'd risk it. It might amuse Jamie to pick up the original negative of her. Of course at an acceptable price."

"Of course."

"Well! You know he can afford almost anything."

"Only if he wants to afford it. And he doesn't collect photography. Only paintings."

"This isn't ordinary photography. It's Franciejean. Old Battenberg tells me it really would add to my market value if, besides the Modern, I was seen in some important collection. And the Welsh collection would certainly do."

"Vincent, my friend, your gospel is correct, but you're in the wrong church. I don't believe Jamie would buy a photograph of the Christ child. It may be all that Eastman Kodak stock he owns has soured him."

"Eastman is an excellent stock."

"But it's money, not art, to Jamie. Snapshots are what

fathers take of babies, and young and old men take of their girls. With their legs spread. That's how he thinks of film."

"You have a dirty mind."

"A realistic one. I know my friend. Buckman is a far more plausible catch."

"Lawrence Buckman. Yes, I hear he's coming. But he doesn't have the Welsh reputation. Ah well, any collector in a storm."

The photographers had now finished taking their shots of Franciejean and the vegetables and were moving off into the crowd.

"Where do you think Buckman is?" Charlie Kreiger asked reverently.

"I don't know, Charlie. But I do think we'd better get over there before some idiot hands him a tray."

Kreiger did not smile. Instead he took a deep breath, squared his shoulders and, followed by a chastened Bob Hale, ruthlessly pushed through the crowd to the doorway, leaving Franciejean and Matt posted as an honor guard before the photographs.

"You're looking gorgeous, Francie," said Matt. "But a little piqued? Let me get you a drink."

"No, thank you."

"Not drinking?"

"Not thirsty."

"Hey! You don't have any earrings on?"

"I couldn't find the right ones."

Matt was lighting a cigarette. For a moment the little flame lit his coarse features, and Francie averted her eyes with a momentary feeling of self-disgust. But now was not a moment for soul searching; and with a slight embarrassment she began, "Incidentally, Matt"—she wanted to get this over quickly—"Agnas found your lighter."

"Agnas? My lighter?"

"Agnas, our housekeeper."

"Oh! My lighter! Good Lord! After all this time. I gave it up. The one I lost at your place, I mean. That one?"

"That one. It rolled under some furniture," Francie improvised casually. "I have it with me." She opened her bag to take out the lighter, when, chancing to look up, she noticed that Peter and Vincent were watching her from across the

169

room. With reflex fright her fingers dropped the lighter as though it were alive and instead drew out a compact. Not wanting any hint of her nervousness to reach Matt, she began to powder her nose saying, "Let's move out of this mob. I think I have it. It's somewhere in here. But these people are elbowing me so."

"Oh yes! Sure!" Matt sputtered. "Do you think you have it? Irene's never forgiven me for losing it. It wasn't even insured."

"I'm almost sure I brought it," she said as she steered him out of Peter's line of vision.

"Is that your husband with you? Did he think anything funny about the lighter?"

"Why should he think anything funny? Anyway we're now separated."

"You and Stewart?"

"Yes."

"Then that's not your husband?" He nodded toward Peter at the other side of the gallery.

"No."

"But you still live at the same place?"

"We're not that separated. Not yet."

"I really hope the lighter didn't have anything to do with it. You could have said I dropped by one day with the commercial script, and I forgot it. It didn't have to mean anything."

Francie felt suddenly defenseless. Matt's concerned, if tactless reference concealed so much smug boastfulness that she wanted to hit him. But she knew that was impossible, and her helplessness only served to renew her sense of shame at the blundering mess she'd made of her life. "No, Matt. Our separation is not due to your lighter. Neither you nor your lighter came up in discussion. Don't put on airs." It was hard to keep irritation out of her voice. "Marriage is not as simple as crossword puzzles."

"Don't I know it." He was all sympathy. "It's no bed of roses." He paused to consider this insight and would have continued in the same vein if he had not been suddenly galvanized into action. "Christ! There's Barnett and Kreiger at the door wigwagging us. Buckman must have arrived!"

"I suppose I have to meet him?"

"What a question! Come on!"

170

They edged their way slowly through the crowd to the agency group now huddled together in front of the La Petite photographs. Charlie Kreiger, upright and eager, stood at attention, while Abe Barnett and a thin man, a little taller and at least twenty pounds lighter than Barnett, chatted.

"W-W-We're glad y-y-you c-c-could make it, L-L-Larry."

"I wanted to, Abe. I wanted to see these photographs. I'm a camera bug myself."

"Would you like some champagne?" asked Bob Hale, arriving with two full glasses.

Barnett and Buckman both shook their heads.

"I'll stick to scotch," said Buckman. "Charlie, you take the champagne."

"Of course, sir. Delighted," said Charlie. "Incidentally, sir," he muttered between swallows, "I want to apologize for the goof."

"What goof?" asked Buckman.

"The photograph. It doesn't have the product name."

"What product name?"

"La Petite. Ours. The brand name."

"Ah, I see. How keen you are, Charlie."

Kreiger shrugged this off modestly and finished the champagne with a gulp.

"We did argue, Larry. We argued and argued with Vincent. He absolutely refused," said Bob Hale, finishing his champagne.

"Absolutely," said Kreiger.

"Undoubtedly," said Buckman.

"With the kind of money he's getting . . ." Kreiger ran on.

"He can afford to be independent."

"That's the trouble," said Hale.

"That's the wonder. Money usually makes men softer. And careless."

At this remark, Abe Barnett, who had studiously kept out of the discussion and was waving Matt and Francie onward through the crush, turned back to Buckman and grinned. "I'd h-h-have thought the s-s-same thing. W-W-Wonders w-w-will never cease."

"I don't follow you," said Bob Hale.

"He could sluff it off by just doing what we tell him.

Why take the trouble to argue? To think for yourself. When you don't have to make money, it's sometimes easier to simply be agreeable.''

Fast on his feet as always, Bob Hale turned on a dime. "Of course, I see what you mean, Larry. Vincent cares. He's an artist. And his art comes first."

"Yes, he's an artist. They're great photographs. When the time comes, they'll make great ads. But right now, it's photography as art. Not ads. And it doesn't need a logo."

"Oh well! Let's forget it," said Charlie. "I'm just a stickler for details."

"Don't worry, Charlie. Don't ever worry. Your enthusiasm for the product makes up for your obvious lack of taste."

"Thank you, sir," said Kreiger.

Buckman studied the photograph and Franciejean. "She is a beautiful girl."

"She'll be right over to meet you," said Bob Hale. "Ah! Here they come, and Vincent is with them." As the group approached, Lawrence Buckman watched them with a polite casualness that masked his concentrated reading of motive and character.

"Good evening, Mr. Buckman. I am delighted that you could come," said Vincent, who was now quite openly stalking him with all the skill reserved only for the biggest game. Vincent had decided that this might indeed be a man worth knowing. He had noted Buckman's great vitality, and confidence—the look of a man absolutely committed to his own vision. If such a man were to build a collection, it would be a good collection to be in.

"I am delighted to be here," said Buckman, shaking hands with Vincent and then looking at Franciejean.

"And this is Franciejean Stewart. The beauty of New York. The success of La Petite."

"How do you do, Miss Stewart? What all food needs is a beautiful woman to serve it. You add immeasurably to our product line." Her disinterest piqued him to an attempt at flattery.

"Thank you. I was telling Vincent that he is the Vermeer of photographers. It's the way he handles light. Isn't it a shame that Vermeer never painted food."

"Never?"

"I think not. Only women, maps and light."

"Beautiful women," said Buckman.

"Not always beautiful."

"You know you're right," Bob Hale cut in. "The photos do suggest Vermeer. If Vermeer had painted food, of course."

"Stop it. You'll turn my head. So much flattery is bad for my artistic sense and worse for my character. But Francie, if I remind you of Vermeer, don't you think this photography might be an idea for Jamison? He is very fond of Vermeer. And of you."

"And if Vermeer had painted me, I'm sure Jamie would buy it. But not a photograph."

"You know, of course, that Jamie is one of the world's few private owners of a Vermeer," Vincent added, his face sparkling with cunning as if everyone present knew Jamison intimately.

"Is that Jamison Welsh?" asked Buckman.

"Of course!" said Vincent, smiling.

"A friend of yours?"

"Of course. Of mine, of Francie's. A great and good friend, I might add, and a collector like yourself." Vincent went on spinning out his pitch.

"Now, Vincent. As a collector I am not in a class with Jamison Welsh. Let us say it is quite the same as comparing you to Vermeer."

Vincent laughed good-naturedly. "You're quite right." The sarcasm only increased his respect for the man. "On the other hand, let us say there is a small grain of truth in the comparison. A speck. Just enough to make one's eyes tear. Still, I did think Jamison might want this photograph—for sentimental as well as artistic reasons."

"I think not," said Buckman, perfectly aware that he was being baited. "We bought those photographs, and we'll keep them."

"Oh, but you don't own them. That's in my contract. Certain photographs are only for advertisements. I retain the rights to the negatives."

"Really?"

"Of course."

"Well, Miss Stewart, do you think I should purchase the negatives myself? For my collection? Let's say for artistic and business reasons?"

173

Francie felt unexpectedly a curious gaucheness, like an actress who has forgotten her lines. Actually, she didn't want him to buy the negatives, but she felt that to say "No!" would hardly be appreciated by anyone. "I don't really know. If you collect photography, it's certainly one of the best."

The lack of spontaneity in Francie's answer told Buckman all he cared to know. "Correct me if I'm wrong, Miss Stewart, but I have a sneaking suspicion that you'd rather I did not buy the negatives." He was speaking with intimacy, but intimacy coded in bantering good humor.

"No! Really. It's simply that I don't feel qualified as an artistic advisor."

"Very well. Why don't we discuss this over lunch? You and Vincent are my guests. I'll be in town all week, and I would like the benefit of your opinions on a number of purchases I am considering."

"Mr. Buckman, I have no insider knowledge about art collecting."

"Francie! Shhhh! I'll double for both of us."

"All right. Vincent will do the art seminar. And as for me, at least I am an authority on food. Lunches are one of my specialties. Let me check my appointment book at home, and I'll telephone you. Where do I reach you?"

"I'll give you my card." Buckman reached for his wallet. "And one for Vincent, too." He glanced at Vincent indulgently.

"Larry, we'll handle it." Bob Hale was always quick to respond to royal wishes. "Matt will call Miss Stewart and Vincent first thing tomorrow. He'll set up everything, and we'll be back to you."

"Fine." Buckman allowed himself to be helped.

"That's wonderful," said Francie. "And now, if you'll excuse me, I have to leave. I am not feeling well. Flu or pneumonia or the dreaded Mobus."

"What's that?" asked Kreiger.

"A fatal disease about to be discovered. Vincent, where is Peter?"

"But you just got here. Oh, all right! He's with Vera and John and Gian Carlo. Over there."

"Take care of yourself," said Buckman. "I don't want you to miss our lunch. Drink lots of hot tea."

"Gallons," Francie agreed as she and Vincent started to

move away. "How could I miss lunch? 'Feed a cold and starve a fever.' " She gave Buckman a smile. "I look forward to our first white wine together."

"Make mine a martini," said Vincent, taking Francie's arm.

"Models! They think they're artists," Bob Hale complained. "They have vapors."

"A girl that beautiful can have vapors." Buckman smiled. "Jamison Welsh has an eye for the whole world." He watched Francie as she moved through the crowd toward Peter and his group. "Is she with Borelli?"

"You mean the opera singer, Corelli?"

"No, I mean the opera singer, Borelli," said Buckman, looking at the man Peter was speaking to. "I heard him sing the Count in *The Barber of Seville*."

"Yes," Bob Hale replied.

"She's with the thin one," added Matt.

"How does she know Jamison Welsh?" asked Buckman.

"Who's he?" asked Matt.

"The f-f-f-financier. A-A-And a-a-art collector," Barnett stuttered.

"What I like about you, Abe, is that we subscribe to the same magazines."

Peter, Vera, John, and Borelli were standing in front of a photograph of Vera.

"So this is why you dragged me to this festival of clowns."

"Why else, John? Isn't it wonderful?" said Vera.

"Yes. Vincent has caught the essential you. The dissipated nun."

"Nun? I think you're right," said Gian Carlo.

"You know, Vincent says she'll be a top model," remarked Vera. "Besides being so photographic, she can invent new poses endlessly. Then hold the right one forever."

"Well, not quite forever. But who can?" Peter turned to greet Francie and Vincent.

"Well, I may have caught a big fish," Vincent crowed. "And thank you, darling, for cousin Vermeer."

"Be my guest," said Francie. "But in the future, let's have a little less about our great and good friend, Jamie."

"Ah, pet, it came up quite naturally."

"About as natural as the sun rising in the west. And now, Peter, could you take me home?"

"Children, we're having a shindig at my digs later. Come one, come all. I insist on your celebrating with me."

"Oh no, I can't, Vincent. I really am tired."

"Peter? After you tuck Francie in?"

"I think not. I'm a little beat myself."

"You know Henri will be there. He's looking forward to seeing you again."

"Henri?" Peter took this in slowly.

"Yes."

At that moment Matt Harris made a sudden, rambunctious appearance in the group. "Francie! Francie! I want to talk to you."

Recognizing his purpose, Francie called on all her remaining nerve to carry it off. "Oh yes! Your lighter." She opened her evening bag and rummaged around in it. "Here, Matt." She took out the gleaming gold lighter and handed it to him. "And thank you again for lending it to me."

"Oh yeah, sure. Thanks." And Matt dived back into the crowd.

"What are you doing with that strange man's lighter?" asked Vincent archly.

"I borrowed it on the set and forgot to return it."

"But you don't smoke."

"Vincent, there are things about me you will never know. I am a complete mystery, even to myself. A nest of Chinese boxes. Come, Peter. We have miles to go before we sleep."

"Will we see you later, Peter?" called Vincent.

"I don't know," said Peter. There was nothing specific in his apprehension; but he knew quite clearly that, for Francie's safety, he wanted to be with her that evening.

Francie and Peter stood side by side on the pavement staring out into the darkness around them. People were still pushing in and out of the gallery, while to their left and right the headlights of cars could be seen charging up and down Madison and Park Avenue. Standing there with the light from the lamp post and gallery shining on her, Francie might have been a completely strange young woman. There were dark shadows of exhaustion under her eyes, and the paleness of her skin accented the gleam of her hair, as though what was left of her vitality had centered itself there. She was still beautiful, but her beauty was a failure. At this moment her face was confused with pain, with the dreadful faraway look of an animal that is ill but cannot tell what is the matter.

"Take a deep breath, dear," said Peter almost protectively.

"Yes."

There was a long pause, neither knowing exactly what to say next, now that the noise and the courtesies of the performance were behind them. Then tears came unexpectedly to Francie's eyes, and a wry smile to her mouth. "Well, what now? What do I do now?"

"You don't want to go home?"

"I don't want to go home. I can't yet." Saying it made her know how true it was.

"What would you like to do, then?"

"Anything. Anything at all but go home."

"Are you sure you're all right?"

"I'm all right," she said. "It's bearable." She stood there with her head high, borne up by her own stubbornness.

"Make a suggestion. What would you think you might like?"

"Some peace and quiet." She slipped her hand into his like a good child. "Perhaps we could find some peace and quiet for a while?"

"Food too?"

"Peace more."

Peter stood thinking where he could take her. PJ's was too noisy and the Brussels would remind her of Jamie. He decided on a course that was not really in keeping with his usual behavior with Francie. It might bring him more than he bargained for. But if so, so be it. Perhaps she looked different to him? But then, neither did he understand himself tonight. "Francie, the most peaceful place I can think of at the moment is my place. There's food, too. And wine. And it's in walking distance."

"That's a wonderful idea. Wonderful." And Peter knew from her voice that she scarcely realized the unexpected shyness he'd been feeling.

As they strolled together hand and hand down Park Avenue, anyone looking at her casually could easily believe that she had cost a great deal of money to put together, and that she had always had everything she wanted. However, anyone watching with a more discerning eye would have noted the almost feverish brightness of her manner and would have sensed that she walked on the edge of a cliff; that each step she took was an insistence that the ground was not falling away under her.

Peter's apartment, in the lower east sixties in a remodeled Victorian brownstone, was as Francie remembered it from the few times she had been there; a place where she felt very much at home. It was a place she sometimes thought of as being done in planned disorder. For though Peter was an antique dealer—or maybe precisely because he was one—the apartment was dominated by no particular period of furniture. Instead, English, French and Italian pieces in walnut, cherry and mahogany were all mixed together; as were appointments like a Ming vase and an Aubusson tapestry. But such calculated carelessness, Jamison had once explained, was only possible because Peter knew exactly what he was doing. It was not recommended that Francie ever consider following his example, Jamie had noted, when he gave her a blank check to redo a small parlor room on the third floor for her own uses as a sitting room. Now she knew she would never do that room.

Dropping down on one of the sofas she sighed with genuine wonder. "You know, I've never had an apartment of my own. Not ever. From the first day I came to New York, I've lived with people. First the girls. Then Jamie. Do you think I might be happy if once I could furnish a home exactly as I felt? Even if it turned out to be awful?"

"Many people use decoration as therapy, so why not? Now what would you like to munch on? You need some food in you. And what to drink?"

"A ham and swiss. And a Coke."

"Franciejean, you are regressing to your childhood in Davenport. There is no ham, no swiss, no Coke in the house. On the other hand I do have a quiche in the icebox that was to be the opening course for a three-course dinner tomorrow night. But we could gorge ourselves on it tonight. And I have a fine bottle of Chablis cooling."

"Peter, I was never a child in Davenport. Or anyplace else."

He looked at her with kindness. "I suppose not. Now what can I get you? The quiche?"

"Nothing yet. Just stay with me a moment, please."

With quick sympathy Peter sat down on the couch beside her, and, seeing that she was shivering, asked, "Francie, is it too cold in here for you? I'll turn the air conditioning down."

Her body started to shake with sobs.

"What is it dear? What can I do?"

"Hold me, Peter. Hold me," she wept. "I'm so cold. I'm too cold to go home." Peter felt lost and useless, but he put his arms around her awkwardly.

"Is there something I can do? Francie, what is it?"

"There's nothing anyone can do. Jamie doesn't want me anymore."

Peter accepted her statement in silence. He did not believe that Jamie had told Francie his plans. And he did not feel free to mention them himself. Yet something had warned her, and he could not even guess what it was. But he must keep himself clear of the situation, and he tried to comfort her with absurdities. "Why do you say that? You know it's not true."

"Yes, it is." She was trying hard to control her sobs. "And what do I do now? I don't know what to do."

"Francie, you're a beautiful young woman. You have a whole life ahead. If it isn't Jamie, there'll be other men. Hoardes of them."

"No, no, no. I'm nothing. Nobody."

"That's not so." He said it softly, rocking her gently in his arms. "You have everything ahead of you. Everything. One day you will meet some nice young man from Harvard, Yale or Princeton and get married and live happily ever after."

Francie's sobs stopped for a moment and she lifted her head. "Peter, don't do that. Don't make fun of me. Please. Nobody will marry me. I'll be alone. That's it." She said the words despairingly as though she could see into the future and the loneliness to come.

"My darling, have you ever looked at yourself in the mirror? Really looked. They'll be banging down the door to get you!"

"No, they won't. You don't know."

179

"Yes, they will. I do know."

"You don't. Before Jamie, nobody ever noticed me. Except to want to lay me. Nobody cared if I lived or died. Only Jamie cared. Only he. He understood. And I spoiled it. I. Now he doesn't care either."

"Of course he cares. He cares very much. He loves you. He's not doing this because he wants to hurt you." Peter stopped in his tracks, realizing he'd said too much.

But Francie had heard him, heard him all too distinctly. She turned her face up to him, flushed and tearstained but suddenly calm. "He's talked to you, hasn't he?" Peter felt an acute sense of the complications he'd raised. He did not for the world want to betray Jamie's confidence in him, and for the moment he could think of nothing to say. But Francie filled in for his silence as though he had answered. "Everything I said to you is true. He's leaving me. He's told you so. He's talked to you, hasn't he?"

"Let it go, dear," Peter begged her. "I was only making an educated guess. Let it go."

After a minute she said, "I can't let it go. If it's so, I want to know it's so. What did Jamie tell you?"

"Nothing. Nothing that I'm sure you don't already know."

"You're not being honest, Peter. I thought you were my friend. I've counted on you."

Peter readied himself. "I am your friend."

"Then tell me the truth. Don't lie. I need to know the truth so I can tell where I am. I always felt I didn't have to pretend with you; to always be on guard with you. You know all about me. You know just about as much as Jamie."

"But this is between you and Jamie. I'm not involved. It has nothing to do with me."

"But if he talked to you, you're in it. You are involved. Don't you see?"

All her misery swept over him, making demands which he'd never known how to meet, invading him with her shame, with her appeal to his compassion, even as his mother had done when he was a boy. From somewhere he heard his own voice speaking. It sounded unlike him, thick and rough. "Give him up, Francie. Give him up. It's no use."

"No?" But she already knew it, and there was no dissent in her voice.

"No."

"He talked to you?"

"Yes."

"When?"

"Tonight."

"While I was dressing?"

"Yes."

She could see he was struggling with his emotions. He did not want to hurt her or be disloyal to Jamie, yet there was something he wanted to say. It touched her. And since she suspected what he was struggling with, she said, "Don't worry. I won't think it crude. What you're trying to tell me is that my great and good friend will provide handsomely for me?"

"Yes." He was relieved to have it said, and not by him. "I know it's none of my business, but you know he is one of the most generous men alive."

"No one knows it better than I." She said this slowly; and realizing that her remark carried an unfair edge of nastiness, she added, "It would be a good reason for my loving him if there weren't so many other ones."

"That I can believe."

Francie nodded her head gravely, guessing all the possibilities of embarrassment which any further close questioning of Peter could lead to. All she said was, "So, I guess that's it. There'll be no shortage of money." She faltered. "But how do I stand living with myself without him?"

"You will find others."

"Not like him."

"No. But they will do."

"Yes. For dinner and theater and sex. But that's not what I mean. I'll be alone again. That's what hell is—eternal solitude."

Watching her, there was a new feeling at work within him. Little by little, in Jamison's absence, he had grown more fond of her; fonder than he had ever been of anyone. Except perhaps one of two ex-lovers, and Jamie himself. Relationships between men and women, men and men, women and women—human relations in general—they were all bizarre. There was no understanding them unless you were in them, and then it was even more confusing. Searching for something reasonable to say, Peter got up and walked across the small room. Then he came back and sat down on a hassock facing Francie.

"Francie," he said, "I am very fond of you. In fact I am so fond of you that I am sick of your playing Miss Sad Sack of 1960. It's not chic. As we both know, you, and nobody else, for some asinine reason, got yourself pregnant. You, for some other stupid reason, made a hobby of sleeping around. And so you made it impossible for Jamie to consider marrying you. And there you sit, wailing like a banshee: Woe is me! Woe is me! Woe is me-e-e-e! As though you're the only person in the world who ever made a mess and lived to regret it. Francie, there are probably three components to happiness—money, love and sex, and health. I don't know a single person who has all three, though I admit I know quite a few who have none. I know some who have one out of three. Others who have two out of three. But at the moment, I don't know a soul who has all three; including me, you, Jamison, Vincent Richards, Lawrence Buckman, and millions of other homey folks out in TV land." He paused for breath.

"Now Papa is going to tell you a story about Papa. You said once I never tell you anything. Do you know anything about me except that I am a friend of Jamie's, a homosexual, and seem to get around a bit and know a lot about antiques?"

Francie had tensed at Peter's unexpected attack; but now she shook her head slowly, leaning forward to listen as Peter continued.

"See that picture over there?" He pointed to a small, gold-framed black-and-white photograph standing on an end table beside the couch Francie sat on. The photograph was one of a strikingly beautiful dark-haired woman; a tall, handsome blond man in riding pants, boots, a sport shirt; and young blond-haired boy about ten or eleven, standing between the woman and the man.

"The man in the photograph is my father," said Peter. "The woman, my mother. The fair-haired boy with cheek is me. I'll come back to that picture in a moment. My grandfather, Francie, was a banker, like Jamie's father and grandfather. But unlike Jamie's father, who along with Joe Kennedy, Bernie Baruch, and a few other of Wall Street's more sensible types, he didn't go liquid in 1928. Do you know what I mean by 'liquid'?"

"No."

" 'Liquid,' my dear, means cash. Not stocks, not bonds, not land, not real estate mortgages. Not a thing but cash. Coin of the realm. Pennies. Nickels, dimes, dollar bills. Ten thousand dollar bills. Most people think that the market went to hell in one day in 1929. It's called Black Tuesday. That's not strictly accurate. There was a small fall in prices, then a bigger drop over a couple of weeks period. My grandfather told Jamie's father, Francis Xavier, that if the market ever came back even fifty percent, he would sell. Well the market did come back over fifty percent—and sixty. And Francis Xavier, Bernie, and once even Joe pleaded with my grandfather to sell. But he wouldn't. It wasn't enough. And then the bottom fell out. And he couldn't sell. He was, as the saying goes, 'wiped out.' Do you know what 'wiped out' means?''

"Yes, I think I do," Francie said softly.

"Just so that you really know—it means broke. Flat broke. My grandfather jumped out of a window. There is a remarkable picture in the morgue of every major newspaper of the day—of my grandfather standing on the ledge, and a crowd yelling 'Jump! Jump you bastard!' They yelled, and he jumped. Unfortunately he missed those bastards and simply made a splash on the pavement.''

Francie flushed at the rage in Peter's voice and the picture in her mind of the jump.

"Francie, grit your teeth. Remember this all happened before I was born. The best is yet to come. When I said we were flat broke that wasn't precisely accurate. My father had had a direct inheritance from his mother, my grandmother, of some nine acres of land along Cross Roads and Apaquogue in the village of East Hampton. It was, my mother claimed, the largest single land-holding in East Hampton Village. Far larger than the Welsh holdings in the Hamptons. By this time my father was a young lawyer with one of the big downtown law firms. Cravath, Sullivan— I can never remember the name. Well, Francie, guess what? When that picture was taken, my father, for reasons that I now understand, decided to join the Lincoln Brigade—that was the Spanish Civil War. That picture was taken in 1936. Before 1936 ended he was dead.

"And that beautiful lady, my mother, spent her days of mourning, lying under, over, and in any inconceivable position she could think of, with anything that had a male sexual organ and would or would not move. If it would not move, she could move enough for both of them. By the time I was seventeen, my summer vacations were spent watching my mother fuck anything and anybody wherever the opportunity presented itself. At the Maidstone, she was known as the lady with the loose thighs.''

"I am absolutely delighted with you for telling me this story," Francie cut in in a fury, every instinct of pride and self-defense aroused. "But I fail to see any resemblance between myself and the lady with the loose thighs. Whatever I do is my own business and has never been anyone else's. I am nothing if not discreet. And I am sorry I ever said a word to you."

"Francie, stop personalizing. I am telling you a story for a reason. If you will bear with me you will come to see my reasons."

Francie hesitated a moment, and then said in a quieter tone, "Go on."

"Thank you. At any rate, while this mother of mine knew a lot about sexual movements she knew nothing about the movements of money. The idea of living off income was simply out of her ken. She could only live off principal. So bit by bit, half acre by half acre, which they don't permit today, she managed to sell off acres of land that today would be worth a considerable amount of money. And undoubtedly will be worth much more in years to come. When she died, what was left was the estate garage with three rooms over it, standing on a half acre of land on Cross Roads. That's what I still own; and where I now live in the summer in East Hampton."

In spite of the moderation of his tone, each word increased Francie's anger at him. From Peter she had expected sympathy, not a further awakening of her own fear. His air of sober righteousness turned her offended pride into resentment. The conviction grew within her that he was not to be trusted again; and she would never, by so much as a blink, admit him any further into her confidence. However frightened she might become, she would rather live in fear alone than share it with Peter.

"I don't know why," she said when he paused, "you imagine you have to tell me all this."

"Because I wish to," he persisted. "You'll see. Anyway, when I was seventeen, I stopped going home during summer vacation. The war was over, and I went with a friend to Fire Island—it was between Andover and Harvard. One night we went to Cherry Grove; and I met a man, Giusseppi Zucchini; Il Conte Giusseppi Zucchini. Incredibly beautiful, a count, and we called him Joey Squash. Well, he seduced me. He was my first, but by no means my last. At Harvard I was celebrated. As a friend once remarked, it was considered suspicious to be found in the locker room shower with me. Jamie is one of the few people in my life who has never felt the least compromised at being seen in my company. He could not have cared less what people thought or said.''

Here Peter stopped long enough to draw a deep breath. He had been speaking rapidly in an effort to avoid Francie's interruptions, and to make certain within himself that he actually finished. For Peter was not the kind of a man who talked about himself without a reason; and as he had hurried through his history, it had come to his groping mind exactly where he was headed. His talk was serving the same purpose as a magician's stage conversation—to keep the audience occupied while he prepares to pull something astonishing out of his sleeve.

For the dazzling perception had slowly dawned on him that what was not right for Jamison might be exactly right for him. He knew that he had always had a fear of the deepest kind of human relationship. Homosexual or heterosexual, he had never felt equal to it. They demanded too much, and he had seen how love destroyed. He'd been hurt too much, and his need to protect himself prevented him from allowing anyone to guess how personally wounded he was.

But now with Francie there was the possibility of a bearable intimacy. She would never expect more than he could give her. He would never expect more than she could give him. They both knew each other's limits. His mind stood still in wonder—why not? Why not marry Franciejean? It was a fine idea. Even if a little ridiculous. Though she was hardly the woman to be Mrs. Jamison Welsh, it seemed to him she would more than do as Mrs. Peter Devlin.

If she had not been certain before, she was now fully acquainted with some of his sexual behavior. In fact, she was undoubtedly acquainted with a whole range of eroticism considering her life with Jamison, though he strongly doubted that Jamie had ever taken her the orgy route—he cared far too much for her for that. Still, knowing Francie and her earlier years, she might have found her way on her own. And that at last was exactly the point—none of it mattered. Sexual fidelity was not what this was about. He would not make the same mistake his father made. Marriage was what this was about. And what made it all so eminently possible was how different, yet how alike, they were. Thanks to their peculiarities they could be the gold-star couple of the world.

"Well, dear, listen." His voice had grown lower, more a feeling than a sound. "I've been thinking about you."

"I bet you have." Francie was sitting up very straight, outraged with what she felt was the comparison with his mother.

"No. You misunderstood me completely."

"Well, if you think I'm like your mother—"

"Yes, you are. But you're not. You're alike but different. You're beautiful. So was she. You're highly sexual. So was she. You're smart. She was dumb. You came from nowhere and became a lady. She was born a lady and became a whore. And that's why we match. Do you understand?"

"No." Francie looked at him curiously. She'd been thoroughly surprised at his outburst of personal reminiscence; and in spite of herself, now she wondered what was coming next. "I don't know what you mean."

"I see I've offended you. I didn't mean to. I've been thinking that neither of us are very good at living too close with other human beings. But I believe we could do it with each other."

There was an implication in Peter's words that she could hardly believe, and she could only stare.

"Well, let me make the final point of my autobiography. We're both at the age of consent. You need a home. I need a home. And a hostess. So I am asking you to marry me."

"Marry you?" A quiver went through Francie, struck by the note of purpose in his look and tone.

"Marry me. I mean it." He kept his eyes fixed on hers. "What's wrong with the idea? Not a thing."

"How can I?" She was breathless and sounded faintly giddy.

"You said yourself no one else will ask you. How can

you not?'' He persisted cruelly, measuring the effect of his words on her nerves.

She had for a moment nothing to say. As a breathless fugitive pauses at the crossroads to consider alternatives and try sensibly to decide which turn to take, so Francie paused to consider Peter's offer. He had put her case as bluntly as she would have herself. And facing the plain truth, she looked down the full length of the road to its consequences. If he wasn't teasing her, if he was serious, she must pick her way carefully. Her future might hinge on the way she answered him. "I suppose it's certainly a possibility. And it's the nicest, if not the only proposal I've ever had.''

"Then accept it. Now. You won't get a better offer.''

"I know that.'' She said it and she meant it. Yet it all seemed so impossible. When she'd first learned that Peter was homosexual, she had thought, no matter how handsome he was, he wasn't normal. Coming from her background, the idea of homosexuality revolted her. It seemed almost nonhuman. So the thought of actually marrying Peter frightened her; even though, until he'd proposed, she only occasionally remembered that he was homosexual. He'd been so kind. They'd had so many good times together when Jamie was away. He was so smart—but marry him? "But I'm a woman.''

"So?''

"Well then, how would we make love?''

"You are being silly. I'm not half as narrow as you are. I've made love to women.''

"But you're gay. That's not normal.''

"What's normal? Let's say I'm uncommitted.'' He laughed. "I've never fully made up my mind. And I like it that way. The best of both worlds.''

"Or the worst.'' She felt a reluctant respect for his honesty. "You're AD-DC, then?''

"I'm, as you say, AC-DC.''

"Could you make love to me?''

Peter looked at her slender figure, graceful as a young boy; and he knew he'd always found her sexually exciting. "I'm sure I could manage it. Of course not as a steady diet. You don't want any man as a steady diet. Not even Jamison.''

Her mouth started to tremble. "I do want him.''

"Maybe you do. But not till death do you part. The

human heart is subject to strange convolutions. More than I can understand. But the fact is, want him or not, he won't have you. That is, as a wife. You can't be faithful.''

Francie felt as though he'd slapped her in the face. But there was nothing she could say.

"And he is a man who is quite adamant on that point. He requires fidelity.''

"Yes.''

"But I don't. Expect fidelity I mean. I believe, if you like, in the science of the possible.''

A light seemed to be breaking through the fog that had enveloped Francie for months. "You don't?''

"Of course not. First of all, I need my own freedom. And I would despise having to lie. I won't do it. But with you, I wouldn't have to lie. And why should I expect from you anything different from what I expect from myself. In fact, the idea of your fidelity does not interest me in the least.''

It was a standard of values so different from Francie's own that she had no idea how to respond to it. This was true even though she knew full well she could not maintain her own standard. "But I'd be your wife.''

"You'd also be my friend. As you have been. And I never interfere with the sex lives of my friends. I might have an occasional twinge of jealousy. But then, so might you. But that would be all. Like a passing toothache.''

Francie's astonishment was reaching the point of incredulity. It was too much for her to accept. "You won't be jealous?''

"I think not.''

"Then what kind of man are you?''

"I don't think sex in and of itself matters that much.''

There was a slight tone of ridicule in her laughter. "That's hardly a male attitude.''

He took no offense at this. "It's a point of view.''

"You certainly don't sound like any man I ever knew. If sex matters so little to you, why do you want to marry me?''

"I didn't say that sex does not matter. I question whether sexual fidelity matters. In any case, I've told you why I want to marry you.''

"Are you sure that's why? Maybe you're fooling yourself.''

"I do very little of that. I want a home. A hostess. A friend."

"You're over my head." People usually thought Francie younger than she was. For the moment she looked older.

"I agree. Now say 'yes.'"

From the way he said it, she knew she must make up her mind now. He would not wait; and if she said 'no,' he would never ask her again. She would have hurt him too deeply. Faced with the decisions, the fact of her loneliness returned with redoubled force; for she realized that to say 'yes' was to accept that what had been between her and Jamie was over. Finished. That was the nature of life. It wasn't television. You can't rerun it.

And there was a fate even worse—the sense of being rootless, belonging to no one and no place. That was the way she had grown up—alone, unwanted, having no meaning for herself or anyone else. Looking back, she realized that only with Jamie had she felt a real connection to life. Now that he was gone, she would be faced with nothingness again.

Turning, she saw Peter watching her intently and felt the constraint beginning to mask the openness in his manner. Such a situation could not go on much longer without embarrassment and then disintegration. She must decide now— she must—and so she did. In a wild anguish of tears, she laid her head on Peter's chest while he quietly stroked her hair. It was no use, and she knew it. So she would take what she could get.

"Yes," she said. "Yes, again. You know I always cry at weddings, so forgive me."

"It's all right. It's quite all right," he said. "Here's my handkerchief. And now we must take you home to tell Jamie."

"Tonight?"

"Tonight." It was as though he would not give her time to lose her courage. "Can you?"

"Yes," she said, acquiescing with the passiveness of the patient who can no longer postpone the surgeon's knife. "I'll tell him. Take me home."

11

By the time the cab pulled up in front of the Welsh home, Francie's strength was rapidly draining away. For once her body did not respond to her will; she sat leaning back in the cab, frozen.

Peter turned to her. "Are you all right?"

She nodded, making a desperate effort to compose herself. To gain time she said, "What do we do if he's gone to sleep?"

"We won't do anything. It's up to you. You decide what you want to do. I'm not coming in with you."

"No? You don't want to speak to him yourself?"

"Of course not."

Peter leaned forward and spoke to the cabby. "Hold your flag. I'll be getting in again. I just want to take the lady to the door."

He turned to Francie. "Come. Let me help you out." And taking her arm, he half forced, half lifted Francie out of the cab.

Standing on the steps, out of earshot of the driver, Peter continued. "Now look, my dear. I am not coming in. This is between you and Jamie. He's not your father. I am not here to ask his permission to marry you. He's your lover; or your ex-lover; or whatever way you choose to handle it."

"Don't you want me to come back to your place?"

"I want you to do what makes you happy. Those are the new rules. But there are rules. The first one being that you tell Jamie yourself that we plan to marry."

"Yes, that's first." She said it like a student learning a catechism. "But suppose he's asleep."

"It seems to me there's a light still on upstairs in the library. But if he is asleep then you either wake him up and tell him, or wait till the morning and tell him. Or come back to my house tonight and return here in the morning to tell him." He paused. "Or you cannot say anything at all and telephone me in the morning and call it all off."

"I won't do that."

"We'll see what you will and won't do. You're a big girl now, and you have to make big-girl decisions."

"But suppose he wants to make love—one last time?"

"Then you will make love. Or you won't make love. Francie, I told you, I am not your keeper. I do not expect you to become the Virgin Mary. You are what you are. I am what I am."

"But you were so angry at your mother for being what she was."

"You still don't understand me. Look, for the last time, it took the human race a few million years to climb down out of the trees, build houses, take baths, eat with knives and forks and napkins. And I have a slavish respect for that effort and for how much more comfortable it has made our lives. It is what is called 'civilization.' I respect civilization. But what you or I do sexually is our own business. Nobody else's. Except, of course, our lovers, whom I hope we will both choose with some circumspection. To the world, we are Mr. and Mrs. America. And why not? Some people have money problems. Some religion. Some color. We have ours, but they are our private matter. We render unto the bedroom that which is the bedroom's and to the dining room that which belongs there. We do not perform in Macy's window. That was the real error of my charming mother's way. She was totally uncivilized. She had a microphone attached to her ass. Her sex life was public property. Her movements were regularly reported over morning coffee. Do you understand now what I mean?"

"If you'd met me before I knew Jamie, you wouldn't have come near me with a ten-foot pole."

He hesitated an instant. "Well, you must admit that what went on in those 'dear dead days beyond recall' was a bit of a circus. But people forget if you let them forget. Since

191

you've lived with Jamie, you have changed." He thought this over. "You've learned many things. And I believe you have learned the value of keeping one's private life private. I know you very well, and I only know what you have chosen to tell me yourself. There's been no gossip."

She nodded bleakly, thinking about Warren and his possessive manner and how accurate Peter was. She decided she would not make a mistake like that again. "I see what you mean."

"Fine. Now in you go. And I'll see you later. Or tomorrow. And I hope you don't change your mind."

Francie shook her head, then turned and looked at the huge door with the large iron grate. She took two steps up to it, put her key in the latch, and then faced about to Peter with sudden gravity. "You are sure you want to marry me?"

"As long as you want to marry me."

"You're not afraid?"

"Of course I'm afraid. But it's worth the risk."

"It's a great risk." She came down the steps and kissed him on the cheek. "I'm not as neat as I should be. I leave things around. But I bathe regularly, and I eat with a knife and fork."

"You are also, at times, a terrible coward. Now go inside and do what must be done. This is good night. Or good-bye. Or see you later. Or whatever you wish." He leaned forward and kissed her on the nose. Then he drew a cigarette case from his pocket and slowly lit a cigarette. Francie waited until he'd exhaled, and her mouth trembled into a smile. "It's 'see you later'." She went back up the steps to the door, turned the key, and went inside.

Alone now, in the softly lit entrance hall, her mind was flooded with familiar associations. In the peace of the sober and splendid old house, she felt again a deep regret. In contrast to the unknown that lay ahead of her, the air of repose and stability in the very placement of the furniture spoke to her of how much she had thrown away. But she knew full well that this was no time for lingering memories, when the critical new work of reshaping her life lay ahead. She drew on this thought to keep her resolve firm as she walked slowly up the steps to the second floor. She arrived at the library almost on tiptoe and peered in at Jamie, seated at his desk, deep in concentration over a pile of papers. There

192

was almost no color in his face; and, unguarded as it was, he looked more worn and sad than she'd ever remembered seeing him. A stranger seeing him this way would have guessed he was as unhappy as she was.

When Francie knocked lightly on the doorpost, Jamie looked up in some surprise.

"Well, hello."

She had a fleeting sense of happiness, for his face seemed to come alive; even with all the hurt that lay between them, he could still be glad to see her.

"Aren't you home early?" he asked.

"No. Not home yet. I have to go out again. I'll tell you about it in a few moments. First I have to go upstairs and pick up some things."

"Of course. Go ahead."

"I'll stop in before I go out," she said, her voice was slightly unsteady. She hurried away, afraid that if she did not go quickly and do what she had to do immediately, she would lose the will to do it at all.

In her dressing room Francie set about thoughtfully packing a small suitcase, puzzling over every single article, wondering what to take and what to leave for after. She scarcely understood the nature of the life that lay ahead of her, but at the least she intended to have some kind of trousseau.

She knew better than to draw any false hopes from the pleasure she'd read on Jamison's face. The result was her immediate resolve to move out and spend the time until they were married at Peter's home. So she took dresses, lingerie, bags, shoes; and while she packed, she concentrated, refusing to allow her mind to wander to the man working in the library.

Finally she was finished, and there were only two things left to do in this house which had been home. Her first home since childhood. She must change out of her evening clothes into something more appropriate for her first appearance as a bride-to-be in Peter's house. She did not think she would call first. She would simply show up. Second, and last, she must go downstairs and say good-bye to Jamie. After that would come tomorrow. And tomorrow would take care of itself.

Standing silently in the doorway of the library, her suitcase beside her, wearing a light tweed suit, she tried to memorize forever the look of the room—the bookshelves, desk, chairs, shaded lamps, the globe, the slightly worn leather chair that Jamie always slouched in when he worked at home. And Jamie's face, the way it was. Every object, every color seemed strangely vivid, and she almost wanted to close her eyes against the brightness. But she kept them open, because she knew that she had to remember it all her life; just the way it looked this minute. Even if she saw the room again, she knew it would never look the same. Nothing would be the same. Not the room, not Jamie, not herself. So she stood there, still, waiting, taking it all in—every subtlety of color, every flavor of feeling. And while she gazed, she knew with comforting foresight how little of the scene she would lose in the years to come.

But something in the very quiet seemed to vibrate and become audible, so that Jamie raised his eyes from his work. "Francie?" he said in mild surprise.

"Hello."

"You've changed?"

"Yes."

"The suitcase? Are you going to an airport? At this hour? Where are you going?"

"Away."

"Now?"

"Now is as good a time as any."

Faced with her words, Jamison accepted that what she said was true. He also found now how much he resisted the fact, but it was true; a truth so final that it did not permit him the indulgence of pretense. Obviously, something had happened. "Has Peter spoken to you?"

Francie smiled at this unexpected question. Her net had drawn in more than she'd bargained for. "Is there something he should not have spoken to me about?"

"No. Not if he chose to."

"What is it then?"

It made him feel a little awkward, uncertain of how much or how little to say. "Only that I am closing the house for six months. Except for the servants' quarters. I'm going on the road for Jack. I planned to get you your own apartment before I left."

He rose and, giving in to an impulse he'd held in check, he went and placed his hands on her shoulders, drawing her close, holding her hard against him, shaking his head, as if in response to all the things he wished to say and could not. Francie leaned against him in relief, burying her face in anguish in his shoulder; and they clung together for uncounted moments, sharing their loss.

Then, looking up at him, and as though carefully extracting the hurt from the view of what his words implied, she said, "Thank you. For worrying about me."

"Of course I worry about you."

She continued in a lower tone. "But now you won't have to worry anymore. I won't be a burden."

"You were never a burden."

"I know what I was."

Jamison stood back and looked at her carefully, seeing in her face a reflection of things to come. "What has happened?"

"Can you guess?"

He shook his head, waiting, divided between curiosity and reluctance to listen.

"I wonder if you had anything to do with it?"

"To do with what?"

"With it. You're so—so—Machiavellian."

"I've never seen myself quite that way."

"You are sometimes. Well, it's simple enough. And though I can't tell you how I feel about it because I don't know yet, I think Momma would have been reasonably pleased. More or less. He is so good-looking. And social. And moderately well off. And even, if he is 'gay,' well half, he is very kind."

Never before had Jamie felt such a wish to postpone hearing more. But it must be heard. "Are you speaking of Peter?"

"Yes—Peter. He has asked me to marry him."

"Well?"

"Yes—well? Did you put him up to it?"

"I put him up to nothing."

"You didn't pay him to marry me?"

Jamie almost laughed. "No. Peter may be buyable. All men have a price. But not Peter when it comes to wives."

"You're sure?"

"I am positive." He knew how sure he was, remembering his earlier conversation and his own bewilderment. Well,

Peter indeed had found her a husband. "He must care for you a great deal. That's the only explanation."

"You think so? He likes me. I know that. I think he needs a wife."

"Rubbish."

"Well, he knows all about me. And he doesn't mind."

"And you know all about him. And you don't mind?"

"Should I?"

She was such a child. Only a child could ask of him such a question. But it was an extremity he was not to be spared. "I think not. I think together you will have a very workable life."

"So do I."

"Then you accepted him?"

"Yes."

Her "yes" gave him the sense that she was responding to her idea of how she thought he wanted her to behave. As shown by her very next question: "You do think it was a good idea?"

"Yes, I do."

It was settled then, and he knew he must take care. Extreme care was what was called for. He must not by any false note compromise the journey she and Peter were undertaking.

"I'm glad you think it's all right," she said in a soft voice. "If I had a mirror in which I could see myself without you in ten years, I wouldn't have the heart to look. This way there is a chance."

Jamie had a moment of intense release. So she'd seen it too.

"It's been coming through for a long time, but I didn't want to see it. Then I found Matt's lighter—" She took a deep swallow. "Well, that did it. Everything became dreadfully clear. I could see me with your eyes. See what I was doing. Now I know what to expect of myself."

In the face of her unsparing honesty, any effort at glibness was frivolous and futile. To be of service to her, he had to take his arms and his lips off her, to release her from his dreams, his bitterness, his judgments. He must give her her freedom. "What you can expect, dear, is a better life than many people know."

"Well, we'll see. I've still a long way to go."

"You do. A long full life ahead."

"I don't know. I don't see it the way you do—but I do see that I can't change myself. I suppose it will have its advantages." She said this with grim humor, and added casually, "I haven't told Peter about Momma, you know."

"Very wise. There isn't anything to tell."

"I hoped you'd say that. Being me is not that easy to be. It rules out so many things." She couldn't stop herself. "Things like you and me."

He did not say, "But not like you and Peter." He did not say anything. In his perplexity he felt ugly to himself; ugly for wanting to find excuses and make apologies for not being up to her needs. But his saying nothing told her even more than words.

She said with infinite gentleness, "You must believe I will always wish it might have been different. But it's not possible. I simply hope I'll make a passable wife."

"I know you will," he floundered. "I even expect you to enjoy it. To be happy."

She accepted his lie. "Ah, yes—happy. Yes, let it go at that. I am going to live happily ever after. And ever after or not, it's the best I can do. And you did the best you could do."

There had been moments in these past months when there was no relief or escape for Jamie from his feeling more abject and less honest than other men. Now, with her few words, he felt forgiven; and for his recovered sense of decency, that was enough. She had saved it for him intact, even while being unaware how she threatened him.

"I have to go now," she said. "I think he's expecting me."

"I think so, too. I'll have Patrick drive you."

"Oh, darling, don't. I told you. You don't have to worry about me anymore." She looked at him, and abruptly remorse and grief and guilt dropped away as though cleansed by the ordeal of parting. Now there was no time left for anything but acceptance. "Maybe I will take the car. It's hard to get a cab at this hour."

"Thank you."

He had always thought he would be prepared and ready, in possession of words that would tactfully gloss over this moment when it came. But here it was. It had come; and he found himself stopped short with nothing to say; like a man at his own door, fumbling for his house keys, who discovers that somehow he has lost them.

"I love you," she said.

"Don't test me, dear. It's hard enough."

"For you too?"

"Yes." Jamie was shaken by a furious resentment of how life had played with and caught them both. But with their minutes now so numbered, a deep dread that he had absolutely not wished to show Francie rose within him. It had been in his mind since she first gave him the news of her coming marriage: "Will you keep the baby then?"

Francie blinked. She was too intelligent not to grasp immediately the flicker of possibilities. "You mean Peter and I?" She saw the meaning of her words and she saw beyond them, too. "I don't think he would mind." But she was struck by Jamie's expression. "You'd hate the idea, wouldn't you?"

"Hate is a strong word. You're asking would I mind?"

"You would mind."

"Mind? What right have I to mind?"

"Because it just might be your baby."

"It just might be mine."

What it came down to, then, was that she "had" him, in a way that she had never intended to; and now she could see all too clearly the unspoken appeal in his eyes. But she was haunted by other realities. "You know it is my baby, Jamie."

"I know, dear."

"How can I give up my own baby? If now I really don't have to."

For the first time he realized how much she had wanted to keep the child; how, hidden away from even her own sight, she had clung with passion to the possibility.

"It's my baby," she continued. "Doesn't that make a difference?"

"Of course it does."

"And yet?"

He sensed, and it touched him, how much she wanted to do whatever would please him, even without quite seeing his reasons. But it left him still at a loss. "What do you want me to say?"

"I can't talk to anyone about this."

"Except me?"

"Except you. And if you won't tell me what you think—"

"Again, what can I say?" His question stood for all the things he must not go into.

"I feel so sorry for us."

"Please, dear."

"But I do." Oh, she understood him all too well—too proud for pity, too fiercely private to admit his fear. Compassion was the one thing she must now show. What she said then was her last effort to justify her need. "How can I give it up? Suppose Momma had given me up for adoption? Then where would I be?" Saying it like that, she heard the words and was stopped midway in her plea, confronted by an odd new thought. "Then there would have been no Uncle Paul."

"Uncle Paul?"

"I never told you about him?"

"No. Who is he?"

But Francie was lost in a scene from her past. The memory, the sorrow, the shadow of it absorbed and silenced her. Finally she said, "He was a bad dream." She hesitated. "Give me a minute to think. I feel very strange."

"If I am pressing you, I apologize."

"It's my mistake. I should never have asked you. I know what you think. What you want me to do."

"And you don't want to do it." He wondered unhappily what he could and could not say.

"I know you have your reasons for feeling as you do. Very good reasons they are, too. I don't need any details. I am sure I can guess them all." She stood there close to him, in her way trying to soothe him. "You want me, dear, to be sublimely unselfish."

For an instant Jamie looked away. "I suppose that's it. Though why in God's name I presume—"

"Why not? You know me better than anyone else." She made a quiet, resigned connection. "And you think I am hardly the stock of which ideal mothers are made."

So she spelled it out. "Well, I understand your feelings completely. I have never thought of myself as the motherly sort. Or really to wrap it up, of Peter as being meant for fatherhood." She shook her head vaguely. "Well, now I will have to think this over. And over. And over. But if you ever loved me, help me. Don't telephone John Drew."

Jamie frowned slightly. "Are you saying—"

"I'm saying, help me."

"But if you won't speak to John—"

"I won't speak to John. I don't want to listen, to be advised, or to be reasonable. I don't want to hear the pros and cons. I'll make this decision myself. Without anyone's help but yours."

Jamie heard this as if he'd been expecting it. "All right, dear, how can I help?"

"You're afraid to trust me to do the right thing. Not the awful one. Trust me. Forget everything you ever knew about me. Help me by trusting me—this once!"

They had an extraordinary moment, and then Jamison smiled. "I trust you, dear." He leaned forward and kissed her lightly on the forehead. There was only one thing more for him to say. "Now trust yourself."

PART TWO
The Pursuit of Happiness
1960–1971

Amercia can break your heart.

W.H.Auden

12

The telephone rang once. Then stopped. As though somebody had hung up. A minute went by. Then it rang again . . . again . . . again. Francie watched it with the alert eyes of a dog following a bouncing ball. Wary. Interested. She had decided she would do nothing. It was finished. Over. And it was time he got it through his head. Deliberately or not, he had caused her enough trouble. *Ring.*

While the telephone tugged at her nerves, she went back to buttoning up the pale yellow silk crepe de chine blouse she might wear to the ceremony. *Ring.* Then she stepped carefully into the matching pleated linen skirt and slipped on the nubby-textured jacket. There—not bad. She posed and twirled and smiled into the seventeenth-century Chinese mirror as though it were a photographer's lens.

But when was he going to hang up? *Ring . . . ring.* Or when would Peter's message service pick up? The telephone stopped suddenly, and silence flooded the room. It was like the sudden ending of a headache.

She looked around the smaller-than-it-seemed sunny room that served Peter as a combination studio and guest room. It conveyed intensely the sense of Peter, with souvenirs of the past: snapshots, a mask, post cards, a 1953 ballet program; combined with the current auction notices, museum showings, invitations, newspaper clips on V.I.P. arrivals. All were jammed together on the changing tapestry of a bulletin board over a leather-topped directoire mahogany writing table. Actually, the only other concessions to the twentieth century in the room were the drafting table and the large beige corduroy sofa that opened into two single beds for guests. Which Francie was not. It gave her some small pleasure that this room, now strewn with her clothes, was to be part of her "home." At least she had a home.

Peter had been out late last night, and she'd slept almost not at all while she busily put on and took off clothes, trying to decide what to take on their honeymoon. Shopping used to be her favorite pastime until Jamison's eyes taught her to question her taste. Now, without his quick headshake to guide her, she was not yet quite sure that the new things she'd bought to fill her honeymoon suitcase were up to snuff.

She had hinted once or twice to Peter about his helping her to select a trousseau that would please him. But he'd conscientiously ignored the hints and bought her just the one dress for the trip. Well, sooner or later, she knew she'd have to stand on her own judgment; and, like it or not, it was turning out to be sooner.

The telephone started to ring again. Once. Hang up. Then again, again. She gritted her teeth. Then made a face and stuck out her tongue. Doing that childish thing made her giggle and let go of the fear. Once in a while you get back your own. Truly it was a pleasure to stand there and watch the fool thing shriek. No, there was no point in answering it. Not when she knew who it was: Warren. That was his signal. Ring once, hang up, ring again. He'd stopped playing that idiot game when she was living with Jamie. Somehow he didn't dare. But now he was at it again. He did it to show how special he was. He was so certain that if she heard his signal, no matter what she was doing—on the toilet, or screwing, or anything—she'd leap to the phone to answer it. "Hello, Warren honey, hold on a minute, I'm having an orgasm. . . . ahhh— Now, what were you saying, honey?" She should've done that once. Wonder how he'd've liked that. The prick. That was the word, prick. Men knew what they meant when they said it. It didn't sound like a scratch. It sounded like a knife in the back. Deep.

She didn't suppose for one minute that he was calling to wish her well. Not that prick. He was hot on the wire because she'd been avoiding him ever since she'd moved in with Peter. That he hadn't expected. And now that Josie had told him she was actually getting married, no spit, he must really have his ass in a sling. He wanted to cover his bets;

make sure there was still room for little old Warren on the mattress. Well, he could fuck off! She'd like to tell it to him in person in front of Saks Fifth Avenue. But that would hardly be elegant. She didn't know if he'd ever actually said anything to Jamie, but she had a hunch. True, it was senseless to blame him for anything. It really was her own fault, and she knew it. But still, she hated him. The bastard! It was too bad how rotten people were to each other. Especially men and women.

Of course, it would be a small wedding. At City Hall. Just Peter's friend Bruce to be the best man. Bruce was a playwright even if nobody had ever produced anything he'd written. But still, everyone said he was extremely promising. And then Josie. She was the best matron of honor. And undoubtedly Warren. But not Momma—no, not Momma. Anyway, small was the way Peter wanted the wedding. And, given the circumstances, she had to agree.

Although, in a way, given the circumstances, she would have liked a big bash, to keep her from thinking. She knew that she must not think, must not recognize the awful splintering of things; a whole ripple of reactions must be blanked out of her mind, out of consciousness, if she wanted to keep her balance and sweetly say "I do." So to replace the reality of City Hall, she fantasized another wedding.

It was on a yacht or in an elegant town house. Or the Hampshire House. Or the Plaza. The kind of wedding people liked to read about. Jamie had even taken her to two: one in San Francisco on Nob Hill, one at Zermatt. At hers, she would have gallons of French champagne. And caviar. And an orchestra. And at least three hundred people. In fact, she didn't know ten in New York, let alone three hundred, well enough to invite to her wedding. But what difference did that make? The way she felt, it was the veil and the clowns and the music that mattered. And there were hundreds of people who would come just to be photographed. There was probably even a RENT-A-GUEST service in the yellow pages. Especially for weddings. Or funerals. Or Bar Mitzvahs. New York had everything. So you rented the guests. What a promotion! Only beautiful-looking people need apply. Distinguished, well-dressed people who laughed a lot. Talked a lot. Some in French or Italian. A little German here and there. Very classy. And everybody holding his liquor and behaving well because otherwise they would not get paid. Or called back. A bloody good idea. Because the family and friends stuff was old hat. As far as she could see, very few people in New York actually had family. Or friends. Jamison's type excluded, families were practically extinct. Either they were dead and it made no difference, or they were alive and you wished they weren't. Then why not hire strangers for a wedding? Strangers would have no hard feelings. They were not jealous. They did not remember old hurts. They just came and had a good time and went on to the next wedding.

She whirled around in a pale peach camisole with a matching skirt, every inch edged with a wisp of lace. She looked quite beautiful turning this way and that in the mirror, the $300.00 tag swinging in the breeze she created. But still she was unsure. Next she tried the Pucci; all geometry and a swishy flare—hmmm.

She tiptoed barefoot over to one of the closets and rummaged out a blue-and-green silk tunic and skirt with a watery print. It was soft and blouson but not too. Seeing herself in the mirror, she was sure no one would think she was pregnant. Jamie had always liked the dress, and she was sure Peter would like it, too. She would take it with her on her honeymoon. Plus the semi-sheer Italian sun dresses and the T-shirt top with billowy pajamas. And the oversized zip front white nylon Windbreaker to wear over shorts and bathing suits. Her legs were fine in spite of her condition. And the yards of chiffony things from Dior that Jamie had given her—it seemed years ago. And—and— In truth, almost all the clothes she was taking on her honeymoon were old ones that Jamie had selected. The new things she had bought on her own for her trousseau were good enough. But she didn't feel she'd struck quite the right note. She had never told Peter about the fears she had about her own judgment; she had enough difficulty chewing on the hard nails of the fact privately.

She squirmed carefully out of the Pucci and hung it up in the closet. That was that. To hell with the trousseau. She stood naked in front of the mirror, examining herself dispassionately. It was only quite recently that it had started to show. For six months pregnant, she was doing very well. She'd gained only four pounds. You couldn't tell a thing unless you saw her naked, or in a bikini. And then, you had to have a suspicious nature. But she was going to be married, and married women were famous for having babies. So what difference . . .

"Say, girlie, is this where they're making the dirty movie?" A voice like a barking seal filled the room.

Francie spun violently around to see a tall, laughing young woman leaning against the doorway, looking as if she had just left a circle of masseuses, chiropodists, manicurists and hairdressers. It was a trick Josie had—never to look half finished. "You!" Francie half screamed.

"What small boobs you have, girlie. Ain'cha heard about silicone?" barked Josie in the seal voice.

Francie made a face. She didn't like Josie when Josie made "dumb model" cracks. "You scared the hell out of me!"

"You left the front door open for visitors," Josie said in her normal tone.

"The front door? To the apartment? Damn. The lock didn't catch. It's been open all night."

"You could have been raped in your sleep. How relaxing."

Francie glanced at her impatiently, wrapping a flowered cotton robe around her naked body. "Have you ever been raped?"

"No. Have you?"

"Yes. It isn't relaxing." She said it with a murderous honesty. "Were you surprised about Peter and me?"

Josie started to say something teasing then stopped. A careful groping was going on behind the mask of the well made up face. Finally she said, "Not much. I had my money on you. When it didn't take with Jamison, I knew there would be someone else. Here's something borrowed. And something blue. A blue eyeliner. And my menses pills. Every girl menstruates on her honeymoon."

Francie accepted these small trophies of marriage, feeling throughly sorry for herself. This then was all she was to have of wedding-cake dreams. No champagne. No gown by St. Laurent. Just Josie's blue eyeliner. Josie's pills. And honeymoon clothes selected by Jamie. "Here comes the dumb bride. Thank you."

"Are you going to quit modeling?"

"I don't know." She uncapped the eyeliner and, staring into the mirror, applied the merest dot to her right lid for luck; then put it down, remembering Jamie did not think much of eye makeup.

"You're doing awfully well, you know. That La Petite assignment is impressive."

"Lots of money. It comes in handy." Someone had always taken care of Josie; it was an accidental kind of self-sufficiency that Francie envied. But Peter and Francie had agreed that she should continue modeling. The money would be helpful, and so would the glamour it bestowed. Other than the Jamison episode, she was not, it seemed, destined to be taken care of.

"I notice congratulations are in order. I'll take back my pills. Do you think it's a boy or a girl?"

"I don't think, but I accept your congratulations." Francie avoided Josie's eyes and headed for the master bedroom to dress, followed by Josie, her curiosity now more than showing.

"How many months?"

"Six."

Josie counted backward on her fingers. "This is May. Then there's May, April, March, February—that makes it December?"

"That's what the doctors say. December. Due in August."

"Thank heavens for December—it's not Warren's. We were in the Bahamas all through December."

For an instant Francie found it difficult to think. She had got hold of something sticky and unsavory. "Warren? Whatever gave you such a dumb idea?"

"Well, it has to be somebody's. If it were Jamie's, he would have married you. I know Jamie."

"It's Peter's."

"I don't believe it." Josie said this firmly. "He's gay."

"He's bisexual."

"I don't care if he's trisexual. No matter what, he wouldn't permit such nonsense. You'd have had an abortion. And no matter whose it is—it could be the Man in the Hathaway Shirt—you and Peter would be crazy to raise a child. You two are not exactly equipped to provide a stable family atmosphere. With bottles and diapers."

"Thank you for the sisterly advice."

"My pleasure. As long as it's not Warren's."

Francie glanced sideways at Josie. What was she up to? But Josie's face showed nothing. Her eyes were mesmerized by her fingernails as Francie slipped into her panties and chemise. "Are you out of your mind?"

"Well, fucking does lead to babies, Francie. They do not come via the stork, no matter what your mother told you."

"Josie, if Warren says I've slept with him, he's sick, sick, sick. He ought to see a shrink. You're my best friend. Warren is your husband. I'd never go near him. And with Jamie in my life until now, it makes even less sense. What's got into you?"

"My native intelligence."

Francie could see bad weather coming. Clearly Josie didn't realize what she owed her. She didn't see that if Francie hadn't taken care of Warren, somebody else would have. Some greedy bitch would have come along and sunk her hooks into him, tried to marry him for his money. Then where would Josie be? But how do you say that? Instead she said, "Are we going to have a fight?" Which was not at all what she'd meant to say.

"No. An understanding."

"About what?"

"About you and Warren. Your best friend's husband, Warren, is worried sick about you."

Again their eyes did not meet. Josie knew something. Or else she was fishing. Either way was not good. "Maybe he's concerned about my welfare. My life with Peter? Well, Peter and I have talked it all out. We're going to have a wonderful life together. It's a fresh start for both of us."

Josie gave a tense little laugh. "I don't think Warren's concerned about your welfare. It's his welfare he's thinking of. I think he thinks you don't want to see him anymore."

Francie decided to ignore the meaning. If not the words. "Of course I'll want to see him. You'll come to dinner. And we'll go out together. Like now. Except I'll have a husband. Peter."

"And everything will be the same?"

"I don't see what you mean."

"Yes, you do."

Francie liked Josie far better than Warren. Warren was just another Wall Street social type—the rich boy who made good. Good-looking, good in bed, good spender, nicer than many. But somehow dull, not that interesting. And he'd made trouble for her. Furthermore, since Jamie, Francie had learned to draw distinctions. She knew that by the cynical, hungry falcon standards of New York, Warren was not that rich. But that made no difference—Josie was in another league. She was old family, not merely money; she smelt of good schools, music lessons, French, dancing classes. Her father was a judge, her uncle an ambassador. She'd never done a day's work in her life, except for fun. But she seemed to understand other people's pain. Even though Francie was sure she'd never felt any pain herself. And she'd been nice to Francie. She'd given Francie her first close-up view of what it meant to be rich. Things like having a massage every day if you wanted it. Your hair done at Michel Kazan whenever necessary. Shopping for clothes on Fifty-seventh Street and in Madison Avenue boutiques. Or in Paris. Leaving New York when it became too cold. Or too hot. Or to watch the leaves turn. Or to ski at Davos. What Jamie had overlooked in her training, Josie had filled in. And in fact, if it hadn't been for Josie's party invitation, she'd never have met Jamison. Yes, she liked Josie. "Would you hand me the brush?" she said vaguely, hoping to derail the conversation. "I like your dress. Where'd you get it?"

"Xanadu. Francie, I want to say something."

"That's an interesting shop."

"Yes, it is. Now, let's have a heart-to-heart."

"You want to know what I want for a wedding present?"

"No. Tiffany is full of ideas. Listen to me."

Francie bent her head with false calm. Seeing her body, she realized with a start that she was still undressed. She began carefully and quickly to slip onto her garter belt and hose. Her lace panties. Her bra. "You sound so serious. Do we have to be serious today? It's my wedding day."

"A perfect time to be serious. For taking vows. I want to talk about Warren."

Francie danced a clumsy ballet putting on her Beth Levine pumps, her Chanel suit. It was not a proper wedding dress, but it was a Chanel. That ought to do something, even for a City Hall wedding. Once she was dressed she felt more secure. If there was going to be a yelling at least she'd look as respectable as Josie when the police arrived. "There's nothing to say about Warren. Nothing."

"You and Warren have been having an on-again off-again affair for years. That's not nothing."

Now that it was out it sounded ordinary as a weather report. And quite as unbelievable. Francie decided her tack was not to believe it. "It's ridiculous. I can't imagine where you got such a foolish idea. You're too young to be having a menopause breakdown."

"It's true enough."

"It's nonsense. With Jamie in my life? And, if I chose to, this city's full of gorgeous men. Why go near him when you're my best friend? He has a rugged kind of maleness, but he doesn't attract me."

"He doesn't have to. He gave you presents. Jewelry. Perfume. Things."

"Josie, do you think Jamie deprived me? I needed Warren's 'things'?"

"I don't think. And I don't care. I know Warren bought you gifts. And you took them. I watch our bank and charge accounts more carefully than he knows."

Francie thought about this. He did give her gifts, but so what. It wasn't the gifts that accounted for Warren in her life. In fact she had no idea what accounted for him. But there he was. She'd taken the gifts because it was nice to have someone give you presents. Like having a birthday party. She wondered if Josie wanted them back. She could have them all, with Francie's blessings!

"Gifts!" she finally said. "Did Warren tell you a dumb thing like that?" Francie sounded more indignant than she felt. What she felt was surprise at the calmness of the conversation. No screaming. No high drama. This was civilized New York. "If he told you that, he's lying. I don't know why."

"He's said nothing. But if he gave you nothing, you're a fool. He can afford gifts."

Josie's words were as shocking as a sudden street accident. "You mean you don't mind? I mean if it were true. Which it isn't."

"Of course I don't mind." Josie looked at her with

straight gray eyes, faintly amused. "I wouldn't marry a man who couldn't afford 'other women'—if need be."

She stood there quietly, giving off no scent of either anger or jealousy. Finally she said, "So, I'd like you to keep on seeing Warren."

It seemed to Francie that Josie was not speaking English.

"You look puzzled. I said I'd simply like you to continue sleeping with Warren. Keep him occupied."

"I thought you said that." Francie giggled helplessly, confused by a sense of the familiar with a twist. You never knew what to expect these days. "Josie, are you serious?"

"Very."

"Then you're a modern marvel. Like the pill. If Warren and I were for real, I think it's pure inspiration that you manage his extramarital sex life."

"Thank you. I've always thought I'd make a good executive."

"I would never have known. I am impressed. But I'm the wrong girl. Warren and I have never gone beyond the stage of playing kneesies under the table. We're like kissing cousins. Too inhibited."

"Francie, I wish you'd stop acting like a politician who's been caught with his hand in the contributions."

"You have no proof of anything you're implying."

"I have enough proof if I needed it. Let's say Warren talks in his sleep. But what do I want with proof? I'm not going to take you into court."

Francie knew she should change the subject; she was certain Josie had no proof. It was pure bluff. But her curiosity was too much. "I don't understand any of this. Aren't you jealous—that is, if it were true?"

"Why should I be? I want Warren to be happy."

"He's your husband."

"All the more reason for considering his well-being. And if I think you make him happy, you ought to be complimented."

"He's your husband."

"You said that before. Actually, you've helped our marriage. We haven't been making it in bed too well. Marriage can become boring for me with a man like Warren. My

212

heart isn't in it. So I don't put in the effort. You've kept him satisfied. And out of more predatory hands. All in all, he's easier to live with; and it's been a good arrangement for everyone.''

Those once had been Francie's thoughts. But how could Josie see what Francie had seen? It went against nature. Then it struck her. ''You have a lover!''

Josie laughed outright for the first time. ''Do you know how angry you sound?''

''That's why you don't mind about Warren and me!''

''Why does the idea upset you? You should be relieved.''

''I'm not.''

''Oh, come on. Be yourself.''

''You made friends with me because of Warren!''

''Well, I must admit that was my original reason.''

''I was a setup for him.''

''True. I picked you with great care. It's not easy to find an appropriate girl for Warren. He's more discriminating than you realize. And then I discovered how much I liked you, too. You're intelligent, even-tempered. Nice. Francie, I like you.'' She added good-humoredly, ''Even without Warren to hold us together.''

''I was your cover! My God!''

''Too true.'' Josie looked sheepish. ''Every time Jamie took you to Europe you've no idea how difficult life became.''

Francie had been wrestling with a sense of unreality; blundering, as though in the dark, against her traditional prejudices and clichéd opinions; and now abruptly she'd stumbled into light. She looked at Josie in a new way, felt the shock of utter familiarity mingled with utter surprise. Her general impression of what Josie was like was purely imaginary. It was not the real Josie at all. ''You're immoral.''

''What goes on inside your head?''

''You are *immoral*.'' She was still astonished.

''And you are full of contradictions.''

''I'm not married to anyone, yet.'' Slowly Francie became aware that Josie was bargaining with her.

''I'm married to the wrong man, that's all. It's not an uncommon affliction. You have your ways. I have mine. *Chacun à son shack*.''

"Does Warren know what you do?"

"Don't be silly. Look, I'll tell you this because I like you. Yes, I do have a lover. But he's married. And will stay married forever and ever. He was married when I met him." She paused, remembering. "Someday I am going to have to give him up. And for that day I want to keep my marriage intact. As long as you keep Warren occupied, he won't ask me questions. He won't want to notice. Because if he asks me questions, there is always the danger that I'll ask him. You can understand that."

Francie was struck by Josie's practicality.

"And he really is fairly decent in bed. If your heart isn't somewhere else. And you're in it just for larks. So why not?"

It was all too bad. Francie was surprised to find how much she cared about losing the old vision of Josie. She would miss it. Not a lot, but like a piece of cigarette paper stuck to the lip. It hurts at first when you pull it away. She took a deep breath. "Well, however it was, and I don't agree with your view, it's going to be different now. I'm getting married today. And I plan to stick to Peter like a postage stamp."

"No you won't! You don't know how to be faithful. You're a born free lance. And Peter wouldn't want you any other way. I know Peter." She continued with an air of boundless generosity that implied she could understand and accept anything. "No. It's too late to change. For either of you. You won't have one lover, Francie. You'll have hundreds. All I am asking is that you do not leave Warren out."

"I won't! I hate him! Anyway, none of this is true! How dare you talk to me this way!"

"Francie—I dare. It's me, Josie. Everyone, even Jamie, knew about your sexual appetites."

"Josie! It was you! It was you who told Jamie about me!" Francie felt a shrill low-keyed rage and a need to try to mask that rage.

"For heaven's sake, if I ever said anything—and I don't remember saying a word—it was purely accidental. If Jamie heard something, he could have heard it from anyone. Francie, your exploits were a minor legend. Your history preceded you. Even to Jamie's lofty ears."

In the presence of Josie's logic, Francie had nothing to say.

"Francie, what could I say that wasn't already common gossip?" She shook her head in compassion. "Don't be so upset. Look, your hands are shaking."

Francie looked at her hands. They were trembling. "I'm trying to keep myself from strangling you," she remarked calmly. "This whole Warren thing makes me so mad."

"Sorry."

"You should be."

"I'm just trying to be helpful. Even if you want to, he won't give up easily."

The telephone rang once. Then stopped. They both stared at the instrument as though it was alive.

"It must have been a wrong number." Francie poured a torrent of words into the silence. "I get that all the time. People call up, and then they remember they've dialed the wrong number. Another thing is sometimes the telephone circuitry gets out of whack, and it rings automatically with no one at the other end."

Her mind cleared, and she moved toward the telephone to lift the receiver. Then Warren would get a busy signal when he dialed the second time. But she was too late. The telephone rang again. Once. Twice. Francie had the look of a child who has been fed broken glass.

Josie did not stir. Only her gray eyes moved between the phone and Francie. "Warren used to do that to me too. In the beginning. Ring once. Hang up. Ring again. A kind of silly game he plays." She smiled at Francie, and the moment seemed to stretch out long and still. "I guess you dropped the candy in the sand."

It was no use. No use at all. Francie giggled in spite of herself. On a rare impulse of affection toward another woman, she threw her arms around Josie's neck and hugged her. "Well, stuck is stuck, my mother used to say." She shook her head, laughing harder. "You win."

"Why don't I answer?" Josie grinned and Francie nodded in hypnotized admiration. She had not had such crazy fun since high school when she and Angie once hid the helmets of the football team the night before the big game.

"This is the Devlin residence. Yes?" There was a pause, Josie turned to Francie. "Guess what? He hung up. On his own wife." At which the two young women collapsed into each other's arms laughing hysterically.

13

"Your idea, Jamison, is to put the principal in trust and let them spend the income," said Gardiner.

"For ten years. After that, if they decide they want to manage it themselves, Peter can do that."

"You want them gradually to grow accustomed to their affluence?"

"Something like that. Not that Peter needs training. You knew the Devlin family, Raymond. It's merely a precautionary measure."

"Still, it's sound. That's why it's called a 'Spendthrift Trust.'"

"Of course, neither of them is overly extravagant. And at a reasonable rate of return they'll still have a substantial income."

"The trust still has its advantages." Gardiner's tone was gentle but determined. "Jamison, are you sure you want to do this?"

Jamison was standing at the high-windowed wall running a full sixty feet along the side of the building and opening up onto a leveled terrace. Facing south, he had a clear view of the harbor, the Statue of Liberty, and perhaps eternity. It was this view from his office at Welsh Brothers that Jamie liked best. Seated at the oak conference table was Raymond Gardiner III, head of the London office. Together they had been reviewing the transfer of authority, during his leave of absence, from Jamison Welsh, managing director, to Raymond Gardiner III. In addition they were tying up the last details of what Gardiner privately described to himself as the "Franciejean dowry."

"You are sure you want to do this, Jamison?" Gardiner repeated.

Jamison cocked an eyebrow. "Quite sure."

"Then it's two million to Francie," Gardiner began, making notes.

"No, Raymond. Three million to each. Though I doubt it will happen—they are both too realistic—there is always the chance of divorce."

"I must admit I don't understand what you are doing."

"She doesn't know how to think about money. I simply want to make sure she'll always be protected."

It took Gardiner a long time to answer. In his curious way he had a deep affection for Jamie. The buried, unqualified affection of forty years of a formal relationship laced with family ties. "Well, we'll handle the Devlin portfolio, hopefully as well as you would. But that wasn't what I was referring to."

"I know, Raymond."

Jamison left the window to face the west wall of the huge office. The west wall was a map of early New York, copied from an original land map from the time of Peter Minuet. Very prominent on the map were the Welsh land grants which, even to the untutored eye, seemed to run, starting somewhere on Fourteenth Street, north and uptown endlessly. After a thoughtful moment he remarked, "I appreciate the effort you are making to do properly something you so thoroughly dislike."

"We will keep you regularly informed of what we do with the Devlin moneys."

Jamie glanced at Gardiner briefly and smiled with mild annoyance. "You don't have to, Raymond. I trust your judgment." He went on studying the map, and there was a time without sound. Then he resumed. "And purchase the main house of the Devlin family on Further Lane in the village of East Hampton. Including, of course, the guest house, tennis courts, pool, et cetera. Add to that the cost of maintaining it with two servants, a caretaker, and so on."

"In short, a good part of the original estate," said Gardiner.

"Yes. Dinny Donaldson, the IBM specialist, bought it

for a song. At first I thought we might purchase the entire original Devlin properties but there are too many owners today.''

"Jamison, property values have gone up out there. You know that. That's a three-acre establishment you are proposing to buy. And if Dinny smells that Welsh money is the buyer, he'll triple the price.''

"Let him. By the way, speaking of Dinny, a last suggestion to the firm. Look into taking and holding a substantial position in IBM. Tom has high hopes for the computer operation.''

"Dinny could ask half a million.''

"Pay it. It will be worth double to them in ten years. And I want them to have it. Put it in both their names. Francie and Peter Devlin. She'll always have a home.''

Gardiner shrugged with exasperation. "One is inevitably at sea. With the best will in the world, I sometimes have difficulty understanding you.''

"Unfortunately, I understand myself too well.''

"If you care so much to give her this kind of marriage settlement, why didn't you marry her yourself?''

"My dear friend, the great loss we suffer in understanding ourselves too well is to know what we can never do.''

"But you still seem to love her. And I believe she loves you. I've seen the two of you together.''

"What an odd line for you to pursue. You who were so against my marrying her.''

"I never raised an objection.''

"You were too polite.''

"My disapproval was never personal.'' His expression was sad and resigned. "She is not your equal.''

"Raymond, by the standards of our common world, you know she is quite suitable.'' Jamie gave him a wintry smile. "It seems to me you had her family history traced. Am I correct?''

"I was concerned.''

"And on her father's side the line is as old as mine. If not older.''

"Simply impoverished.''

"Raymond, sometimes you display the soul of a bank vice-president.'' He was pleased with his sarcasm. But he continued with effort. "From the standpoint that concerns you

219

most, our marriage would have been irreproachable." He summed it up for himself. "And what a creature she'd have been as a wife. What a genius she has for life! What a sense of the so-called 'possibilities.'" Jamie spoke as if the pain were too recent to feel; as if he did not know how much had happened to him. He was light-headed with loss and defeat. He finished up lamely, "It is hard, though, to lose her. It always will be."

Gardiner could only shake his head. "Then why did you let it happen?"

"There was nothing I could do."

Gardiner's attention rested for a moment on a reference to things unmentioned. Patient and weary, he wound up his thinking. "Well, at least financially, she will have realized her passion." Jamie winced, but Gardiner insisted: "She won't have loved you for nothing."

Jamie made no sign that he had heard; but when he spoke, his tone was preoccupied, weighed down with memory. "You completely misjudge her. She is not a fortune hunter. She is not that practical. I could almost wish she were." Then his thinking took a different turn, and he asked curiously, "Why are you so against my making this settlement?"

Raymond shook his head. "I don't really know that I am. Perhaps it's a middle-aged man's instinct for the proprieties. Or a friend's affection for a lifelong friend and dislike of the gossip that could occur. Or perhaps an average man's admiration for an extraordinary man—and an unwillingness to see you make a fool of yourself."

The two men exchanged a look of quiet understanding. "Raymond, it isn't that much money. Six or seven million is all it comes to."

Gardiner sighed, realizing that for him there were links still missing, that might always be missing, try as he would to make them out. "I realize it hardly makes a dent in the Welsh holdings—"

"Not a crack." Jamie's tone was sardonic. "At the last count I believe it was...Let me see. Allowing for daily fluctuations, the last audit said I was worth between 450 and 500 million. All things considered there is something faintly smacking of Hollywood in controlling that much money." He laughed at his own expense.

"Six or seven million may not make a dent in the Welsh fortune, but as a wedding gift, it could be a circus for the newspapers."

"It won't get into the newspapers."

"How can you be sure?"

"I know my people."

"And if there is publicity it would reflect on you. And on the firm."

Jamison listened with his imperturbable consistency. "Your delicacy, Raymond, is a scruple too much for me." He smiled with amusement. "If you persist in this attitude, I shall double it. It will be twelve million, not six."

The Devlin marriage was small and quiet and only moderately eventful. The room at City Hall that was available was being repainted, so the wedding formalities had to be conducted with dispatch in order to avoid everyone's being spattered with white paint. Unfortunately, the Justice of the Peace who married Peter and Francie had a face pulled slightly out of shape by a new set of dentures which were either poorly fitted or to which he had not grown accustomed. Whatever the reason, throughout the entire reading of the rites, he kept putting his finger in his mouth to adjust the dentures, and thus considerably slowed the pace of the ceremony. After it was over, Peter, Francie, Josie, Warren, and Bruce went to the Carlyle for a wedding breakfast with champagne and caviar.

It was of meager relief to Francie, some months later, when she learned that through unobtrusive uses of Welsh moneys, Peter found himself in a more comfortable financial position than he had ever before been in. The addition of a wife to his household added considerably to his net worth. Through the efficient management of Raymond Gardiner III, Franciejean had brought to her marriage a substantial dowry. If she'd wished it, she might never have done another day's work in her life. Like Josie, she was being taken care of.

About three months after their marriage, a seven pound, six ounce baby was born to Franciejean Devlin. After which, Monroe Perl, Mrs. Devlin's personal lawyer, was instructed to place the baby for adoption with a suitable family.

221

14

Whenever Francie and Monroe had one of their infrequent legal conferences, Monroe always enjoyed beginning with lunch at the Lawyer's Club on lower Broadway. Francie could be depended upon to cause a quiet sensation, and Monroe relished it as deeply as he did his Bock beer, which unfortunately Isabelle objected to as German. Francie too liked the admiration, if not the cuisine. It was middling roadside diner that she was offered at the Lawyer's Club. Half the reason she met Monroe there for lunch, instead of insisting he come uptown, was to please him. The other half was to please herself. For, from the moment she entered the beamed precincts, it was as though one hydra-headed man turned and stared at her in awed appreciation and then rose and applauded.

Some lawyers were rich, and some not so, some fat, some thin, some bald, some had hair, some were young, some old, but one and all wore dark suits, white shirts; and one and all they worshiped her as the very spirit of romance. When Francie passed, it was as though a different order of being had dropped into their mundane lives. To a middle-aged man, the managing partner of an impeccable firm, she brought to mind lines of poetry he had read somewhere long before he'd grown rich helping to dispose of surplus government war material: "A beautiful girl pacing with unforgettable ease down Michigan Boulevard one April morning—but this does not contain the facts . . . disconnect the telephone . . . cut the wires.'' Why, he wondered, had those particular words occurred to him the two times he had seen her, since he knew he was essentially a money-and-baseball fan and not much given to admiring high-sounding poetic phrases that he did not understand.

After lunch, and for the next few days, the returns would come into Monroe's office, and the ayes would certainly have it. Monroe would frequently receive as many as five or six telephone calls from fellow citizens and bar members on one pretext or another, but eventually they all came down to the hub of the matter. "Who was that blond you had lunch with the other day, you lucky bastard?" The calls were not all from bachelors or divorced men, and it served to give Monroe a jaundiced glimpse of the private lives of some of the city's most distinguished practitioners.

For his part, as chairman of the Franciejean Lunch Committee, he took the questions from the floor well in his stride. Leaving nothing to chance, he lied with great élan. She was a West Coast client here only for the day. When he acknowledged in his mind's eye that certain other eyes had a more determined look, he allowed himself to be pressed into revealing, in the strictest confidence of course, that she was the illegitimate daughter out of a San Francisco socialite by Moe Cohn of Las Vegas. At which he imagined the eyes had a disconcerted look; and the subject was diplomatically changed, despite the seemingly perfect opportunity for mixing lust with greed.

Although restrained by the fact that she was a client, the response to Francie's presence, as she passed through the corridors of Davis, Polk, echoed the homage she had felt at the Lawyer's Club. Francie herself gratefully acknowledged the silent admiration of senior partners, law clerks, and secretaries. To the secretaries in particular, she was kind because she, of all people, knew what a narrow escape she had had from a life far grimmer than theirs. And because she had no natural inclination either to snobbery or to malice, she pitied them the two sets of brassieres they all seemed to wear; the steel corsets that made of their buttocks a mound of flatness; their shut-in lives. These were the women who wore evening clothes in the subway. She'd seen them. She'd done it, too. And in return for what they thought of as her "niceness," they gave her the unenvied appreciation and attention that was the right of this dazzling creature from another world. Her ready smile and courtesy made each one of them her friend for life.

The first time she had come to Monroe's office to discuss tax matters and tax shelters for the Devlin family's now-quite-respectable income, Monroe had felt extremely uneasy, as if every partner could see projected on the wall a film of him and Francie in bed. But, by the second time, he realized that all the partners, even the most senior of seniors, those who had not felt the sap rise in their arteries in years, even they felt a mild pang of jealousy at the sight of Francie-jean. A beautiful young woman was grudgingly welcome even in this sacrosanct monastic temple devoted primarily to corporate interests. But a beautiful young woman who was also worthy of being a client—she deserved an ovation.

Monroe's office always looked to Francie like a well-furnished sublet. It was wood paneled, with a mahogany desk positioned at the far end in front of a window that provided a breathtaking view of the Hudson. Knowing Monroe, Francie suspected he was scarcely aware of the view. He probably never daydreamed over it, or prided himself on it. What he did was check it for the weather and the time of day. She was certain he would have been just as happy if the window faced a wall. Or if someone had done to it what Bart Howard, one of her photographer friends, had done to his bedroom window: papered it with a blowup photo of a masked and naked girl masturbating. Every time Bart and Francie had sex, she had to start by imitating the girl on the window. Absolutely crackers. But Monroe would never have noticed.

To the left and right of the window behind the desk were wall-to-ceiling bookshelves holding thick red and gray leather-bound volumes with very complicated titles. Francie could not make head or tail of the titles, but she noted that they all had the sacred word TAX printed in bold gold. A brown leather couch stood against one wall; a small round leather-topped conference table stood in front of the couch; and flanking the couch and facing the table was a leather club chair, while another club chair faced Monroe's desk. The walls were hung with maps of nineteenth-century New York City and lithographs of sea engagements of the American Revolution.

It was as though the original owner of the office had done it with thought, a sense of tradition and a feeling for an orderly world. While Monroe had overlaid the order with a fine film of mess. An umbrella stand with two broken umbrellas was clearly Monroe's contribution. Other contributions could be seen on the windowsill behind his desk; the couch was piled high with briefs, reports, black folders anointed with the holy word TAX in their titles, month-old *Wall Street Journals;* and, as a final disgrace, Monroe's tennis racket and tennis bag tossed wantonly on a chair instead of neatly stored in a closet. Everything about the room was mute proof not only of Monroe's systematic disorderliness, but also of his gifts as a lawyer. It was the chaos of his office that had originally reassured Francie that Monroe must be quite capable of handling any tax problems that might arise in the Devlin family. In fact, he must indeed be a brilliant lawyer. Nothing less could account for his 1) being Jewish and a partner in this firm in the first place, 2) having a corner office of this size, and 3) indifferently leaving its unpoliced anarchy to the open view of his partners.

Now, sitting in the chair facing Monroe at his desk signing the adoption papers, she thought of her presence as another testimony to the disorder of his office. What were she and he doing there together; playacting this Stella Dallas scene that had nothing to do with the word tax. The word tax was clean-cut and easy to grasp when compared with the word *adoption*.

Her face was smooth, her manner subdued and thoughtful; and she sincerely hoped she had powdered over her shame. She signed her name four, perhaps five times on different lines, different papers. And each time she signed, it became more difficult to remember the spelling—did Francie have an "i" or an "e" or both?—and to keep the hysteria from showing in the signature. Franciejean . . . Devlin. Not Stewart. Devlin.

When it was over, she looked up at Monroe with affectionate hatred. He was her partner in crime. But seeing his face she knew better. He had such a queer helpless look, like a fish that has been caught and laid on a dock; and she had to drop her eyes to avoid the hurt. You'd think it was his baby they were signing away. For a minute, she was quiet;

but then she asked humbly, "You are sure this couple is nice? I mean, they're responsible. You know—decent and kind and respectable. And they will love her?"

"I am positive."

"You haven't made a mistake? It's my baby. She's a beautiful baby."

He shook his head.

"Are they clients?"

"Francie, please." He tried to soothe her. "They're a very sweet, clean-cut, well-bred, warm young couple. Unfortunately, she cannot become pregnant."

"Catholic?"

"Catholic. And social."

"Why didn't you put her with a Jewish family? You're Jewish. You told me yourself that Jewish people are very family-oriented."

"But you're not Jewish. So I picked the kind of family I thought you would be pleased with."

"All right. All right. I'm pleased." She realized she was perspiring and shivering at the same time. "Monroe, how does she look?"

"She's a very beautiful baby."

She stood silent waiting for him to say more. When he said nothing, she asked uncertainly, "Does she still look like me? She did at birth."

"She's a beautiful baby. She looks like herself."

"I bet she looks like him," she said wistfully.

"Her father?" It was hard to keep the scorn out of his voice.

Francie knew he was judging her; and because she was afraid of the pity in his judgment, she said to him gently and gravely, "You're my lawyer, my personal lawyer. If I can't say what I think to you, whom can I talk to?"

"Of course."

Then, inconsistently, she gave him a cool smile. "Of course, he's hardly beautiful. Her father, I mean. But there are wonderful things in his face."

With women like Isabelle, demanding, manipulative, domineering, Monroe had learned soon after marriage how to be self-protective, when to be assertive. But Francie was a curious original; lovely, forlorn and misused as she might

226

seem to him, it was still out of the question to patronize her. He wanted to say that he believed the man had behaved like a bastard. But what he said was, "She is a beautiful baby."

"What does she weigh now?"

"About fifteen pounds."

"And she's grown?"

"I told you at lunch. Two inches."

"She's going to grow up to be beautiful. I know it." Then she examined her long, delicate fingers and asked, "I know your thoughts on the subject, but I've changed my mind. I'd like you to arrange for me to see her again. One last time."

"No."

"Monroe, I will never ask again. One quick look—"

"No, Francie. I told you that last week. No!"

Abruptly, Francie stood up and pushed the papers on the desk away from her. "Why can't I see her? She's my own flesh and blood. I saw her come out of my body." She laughed unsteadily. "And she came out so fast, you'd think she had a date."

"Francie, you're making it harder for yourself. And for me. You've signed the adoption papers. That ends your connection."

"But one last look. Looking at her can't deprive her new parents. People look at me all the time. I'm a model. I don't feel a thing. I get paid to be looked at. I'll pay her."

Francie was now trembling. "She won't see me looking—she probably can't see anything yet."

"Shhhh!" Monroe hurried around the desk and put his hands on her shoulders. "Quiet down!"

"I am quiet." She felt his fingers dig into her shoulders. She wanted to cry but she knew she mustn't. Her tears would punish her brutally. They would do more than spoil her makeup. "I'm very quiet," she said softly.

"You weren't. You were screaming," he said in a loud whisper.

"I was?" She dropped back into the chair, clasping her hands in her lap, recovering her composure. "Monroe, you are not a very good friend." She did not give up easily.

"It's impossible. The arrangement is that you are to give up contact completely with the baby from the day you

227

sign these papers. And her family is to have no contact with you. Nobody is to know anybody. This is not a picnic. This is an adoption. Do you want to call it off?''

Francie knew from his tone that it was no use arguing. She stared at Monroe, who looked sick and stern. ''Just one last thing. Monroe, would you give the couple this miniature case? It's only a small thing. And they don't have to give it to her until she's old enough. They don't even have to tell her whose pictures are in it. They can say they're long-lost cousins of their own.'' She rummaged in her purse and brought out a delicate blue enameled miniature case, attached to a thin, gold chain.

Monroe tried to concentrate on the floor. He felt drained and weary with the effort of making her accept the reality. It was like working on a brief in a foreign country, in a language he did not understand. ''Francie, listen to me. From this day forward, you're to have no contact with the baby. This is the end. Finished. Kaput. That's the arrangement.''

Monroe was thoroughly exasperated. The whole affair upset him. He assumed the father was some rich bastard and undoubtedly married. The fact that Francie had now married Peter Devlin was only mildly reassuring. He understood Peter's feelings about not wanting to have to raise another man's baby. He'd probably have felt the same. But still his soft heart ached. After all, it was a beautiful little baby. Knowing nothing of the sexual quirks of both Francie and Peter, he concluded that the whole sad business was simply the result of the narrow-mindedness of men like himself. And Peter. The fact that Francie continued to sleep with him, even after marriage, he considered simply an expression of affection between old friends. ''Let's get this thing over with. Now. Here's the money.'' He took an envelope out of his desk. ''The check's in the envelope,'' he said, not looking at Francie.

Francie stood up and took the envelope. Carefully, as though it were something poisonous, she took out the check. It was made out to her, Franciejean Devlin. For $10,000. Drawn on a special Davis, Polk checking account, and signed by Monroe Perl and some other name.

''What is this for?'' she asked, a panic spreading in her as though something had muddied the clear waters of a lake.

"It's the arrangement. You give up the baby. They give you ten thousand dollars."

"Oh my." A deep blush spread over her cheeks. "I forgot about the money. I don't want it."

Monroe realized with confused sympathy that she really didn't want it. "Well, go buy a hat then. Or something. Give it to charity."

"I don't need a hat. I don't have a charity. I don't want it." She started to hand the check back to him, and then a great, ecstatic light passed over her face. "Oh, Monroe—how wonderful. Would you open an account for the baby with it?"

Monroe stared at her, startled. He was a scrupulous, analytical, loyal servant of the facts. He knew he could do it. He could set up a blind trust for the baby. Lawyerlike, he was not given to making quick summaries of situations. But this time he knew with a certainty that he would not mention the trust to Francie. She would never give up the baby if she had any connection to hang on to.

"It's impossible, Francie. And I can't take the check back. Do something with it. Please."

"Can I tear it up?"

"No, Francie, if you tear it up, it will never clear the bank. And the transaction is unfinished. So don't tear it up. Cash it and spend it. Give it to a charity. The city is full of worthy causes."

Francie felt suddenly light-headed and giddy; as though an effervescence of bubbles from a soda bottle were rising within her. But it wasn't tears, it was laughter that was coming up. She started to giggle.

"Are you all right?" Monroe was concerned at this quick change of mood.

"I'm fine." She gave him a triumphant smile. "Super-special. I'm going to find a worthy cause. Where is the nearest place I can cash this check?"

"It's drawn on the Morgan. Go there. It's at 23 Wall. Ask for Ronald Kirk."

Francie went up the steps of the great, gray stone fortress at 23 Wall Street, pushed through the heavy iron doors and entered the marble rotunda of the Morgan Bank. Yes, this was the Morgan. With no identifying name on the front door.

According to Jamie, his grandfather had once said that old J. P. always insisted, "If you don't know where I'm at, I don't want to do business with you."

It was as she'd remembered it from the one time she had lunched there in the Partner's Dining Room with Jamison. Accustomed as she had become to noting everything he said, catching and storing every allusion to people, art, books, finance, politics, her ear had grown attuned to the occasional note of judicious seriousness that he reserved for those rare "lots" of the world's inventory that commanded his respect. Among them was the Morgan Bank.

A man in a dark business suit came forward to greet her. "Can I help you, madam?"

"I'd like to cash a check."

"You do not have an account with us?" He said it graciously but with confidence. Jamison had told her that he knew all the Morgan clients by sight.

"No, I don't."

"Well, madam, actually we only cash the checks of people who have accounts with us."

"I know." She surveyed her surroundings. To some extent the Morgan looked like a small, elegant concert hall. Or an important state building. But hardly like a bank, with only two tellers and its subdued hush and artistic interior. There were those fantastic panels lining the walls on either side, each one a mosaic of tiles showing wild life—deer, tigers, birds. The ceiling itself was a high dome with small, recessed ornamental panels of what looked like light and dark marble, here and there interrupted by squares that secreted a subdued and golden light.

Off to the right was a large carpeted area with rows of old-fashioned, roll-top desks. Behind some of the desks, men were seated, busily at work. A few of these men had stashed their hats on the top ledge of their desks. Francie knew that this area was the Partners' domain; and traditionally, only the partner who had put his hat on the desk ledge was technically "in" for callers. The others, with their hats on the chair beside them, even though in clear vision and at work, were technically "out"—not available for consultation. It was the Morgan manner.

The man who had greeted Francie was again repeating

courteously, "I am sorry, madam, but we only cash client checks—people who have accounts with us."

"I know. It is a check from one of your clients: Davis, Polk."

"I see. You'll have to speak to one of the managers, then."

"Yes," said Francie. "I was told to ask for Mr. Kirk. My name is Mrs. Peter Devlin."

"I see," said the attendant. "I have to see if Mr. Kirk is in." He led Francie to a small, comfortably furnished, glass-enclosed waiting room. Someone who looked like the Duke of Windsor was seated on one of the couches reading *Life* magazine.

"Is that the Duke of Windsor?" Francie spoke softly to the attendant.

"It is, madam."

He then went off to speak to a man seated behind a roll-top desk with no hat atop his desk. Francie presumed that was Mr. Kirk. And Mr. Kirk was not "in." She was right. When the attendant returned, he murmured politely to Francie, "Mr. Kirk is not in at the moment. As soon as he returns, I'll tell him you are here."

A half hour later, having finished reading *Time,* and still seated opposite the Duke of Windsor, Francie wondered if she should become impatient with Mr. Kirk. But the elegant, withered, public face of the Duke of Windsor was placid, for he was serenely dozing. Francie then decided that if the Duke of Windsor could doze, she too could doze patiently at the Morgan. She did not mind being patronized if that was the "community practice," as Monroe would say. And she settled more deeply into her chair, closing her eyes.

When Francie left the Morgan, the late afternoon sun was shining; and the stock, bond and commodity markets had closed for the day. Standing on the stone steps, it seemed as though the street sparkled and gleamed with energy and color. Now the turbulent, struggling, desiring world of Wall Street passed before her on its way into the summer evening. Over there was a runner, hurrying between two masters; there a group of secretaries going somewhere to celebrate something.

Down the street came stock or bond or commodity or ship brokers with their expensive brief cases, tennis satchels and rising blood pressure. Four priests hustled by, bent on secular business at a financial temple. The enticements of a hot dog vendor settled the dinner arrangements for some clerks, while a policeman stood passively admiring a Brink's armored car. A gang of construction workers headed into the subway— Boston could have landmarks; New York was on a continual spree of architectural rejuvenation—the Wall Street day was almost over.

Then Francie looked at the buildings with floor upon floor of desks and phones and ticker tapes; conduits for the business life of the country; and saw it, not as she had years ago when she had worked as a secretary at 112 Broadway and it seemed a vast maze of steel and concrete; but as Jamie had taught her to see it, as the financial beehive of America, a honeycomb of banking messiahs, commodity mystics, stock and bond visionaries and typical American dreamers like those tourists over there—that father and three boys coming from the New York Stock Exchange, clutching their pamphlets. She had done that, too.

Watching the people jostling each other, Francie felt a deep relief. She'd been in a war in which she did not know her adversary or what she was supposed to be fighting. But now the war was over; and the people drifting and milling around gave her a feeling of anticipation, the promise of adventure. She felt as though the whole city and all the people in it belonged to her. She no longer had her baby, but she did have the city, and the city had given her everything she now was.

Once there had been a desperate and lonely time. She'd come to the city for victory and had found unspeakable loneliness. She had come to the city of a million doors and found all of them closed. She had been a blinded stranger, dazzled by a million lights and unable to find her way. She'd been hopeful and eager, then homeless and wretched. There had been years of loneliness in the middle of mobs of people. There had been dingy rooms and empty refrigerators and no one to talk to. The city had then seemed to her like a huge orphanage where no one had a home or belonged to anyone.

And then the city, so cold and uncaring, had turned on a dime and adopted her. She had become a citizen of the city, and she understood its ways. There was violence, greed, fear, and the belief that everything had its price. But there was splendor that was free, and unbuyable beauty, inexplicable generosity, decency, good luck, and quiet bravery. And passion. And love. The city had given her Jamison. The night they met was the most vivid memory of her life. Their time together was now a bright incandescent blur, but it had been real once. The city had given that time to her. And had given her the baby. Now they were both gone, but she still had the city. It had given her a life far beyond anything Davenport could have imagined. The city was her home. Her only home.

She decided to look for a cab. She had a particular type in mind. A large Checker with a special kind of driver. She stood in front of Trinity Church and finally hailed a cab that seemed to her the right one.

"Where to, miss?" The driver looked like a young version of W. C. Fields. He sounded like him, too.

Francie leaned forward, "Are you George Tyler?" She'd seen the name posted on the interior of the cab.

"That is the name. Has been for thirty-five years. Give or take a few."

"Mr. Tyler, are you a family man?"

He turned and looked at her humorously. "Miss, I will no longer accept any indecent proposals. I've given up the high life."

"Then just answer the question."

"I am indeed a family man. With a wife—and two children eating us out of house and home."

"Girls, boys, or one of each?"

"One of each," he said, beginning to show impatience. "My dear young lady, pretty as you are, I am a working man. I'm accustomed at this moment to picking up the senior partner of Allen and Company, Mr. Charles Allen himself, who I understand, according to his secretary, who came downstairs specifically to inform me of the problem, is at home with a golf elbow. Therefore, you had the good fortune to procure me for your services. But this is not a coffee klatch. And I have hungry faces to feed. So whence are you bound?"

Francie studied him keenly. "A girl? When is your daughter's birthday?"

"What is this, a quiz show?"

233

"Yes. And the winner gets to star opposite Marilyn Monroe."

He looked at her for a moment. "April. A very likable month."

Francie sighed deeply and gave a short sharp laugh that was half sob. "Nice month. Begins with A. Mine was born in August."

The driver coughed nervously. He clearly mistrusted the atmosphere he felt building up in the cab, the pressure of an emotion that he did not understand. "O.K., August and April. Now, where to?"

Francie ignored his question. "If you were not a family man I'd have given you two dollars for the time spent taking my quiz and gotten out of your cab. I am looking for a family man. To drive uptown. There is a sizable tip involved."

This was an engrossing idea to the cabbie so he remarked with more kindness, "O.K., I am a family man. With a girl and a boy."

"How old is your daughter?"

"Eight. How old is yours?"

"One month. But I cannot give her a birthday present. So I am going to give you a big tip. So you can give your daughter a birthday present." She quivered slightly and fished in her purse for what the cab driver assumed was cigarettes. But she pulled out a bill. "I would like you to give your daughter a birthday present next April—from me. Use half of this." She handed him the bill.

After taking the bill and studying it, the cabby shook his head admiringly. "Well, you are a live one," he said it to nobody in particular.

"Yes, I would hope so."

"You're also nuts."

"Aren't you glad?" Francie's voice curved upward with elation.

"I don't know. It's scary. This ain't Monopoly money."

"Would I do that to you?"

"It isn't counterfeit, is it?"

"Honor bright. It's the United States Treasury's best."

"You do have an honest face," he said gravely.

"Thank you."

"But this is a thousand dollar bill."

"I know exactly what it is. It includes cab fare and the

234

rest is tip." Francie had an air of celebration about her. "Now, let's be on our way. I have things to do." The late afternoon sun had begun to distort the perspective of the street shadows and to reflect off the cab windows. "See this envelope?" Francie held forward almost under the cabbie's nose a pale manila number-eleven envelope that was stuffed fat with bills.

"Good God! That's a lot of money," said the driver, glimpsing a couple of hundred dollar bills.

"It is. And it's mine, all mine. I can do with it what I please."

"What are you going to do?" it was all beyond him, and he was full of irresolution.

"I am going to give away this money. To the city. The city is my favorite charity. So I'll drop it out the window as we go uptown."

"I'll be damned!" he exclaimed in an amazed whisper.

"No, you won't. And neither will I. Only you must not drive too fast or too slow. Just try to make all the lights. And go any way that pleases you. I don't want to attract the police. Or have the people who pick up the money catch us."

"They'd have you institutionalized. You're not for real." But he was awed by her romantic illogic.

Francie giggled. "How could they do anything? As you say, 'I'm not for real.' There's no such person as me. Now, let's move. And when I run out of money, you'll pick up speed and take me uptown. Drop me at Saks. And forget you ever met me. Forget forever. Except for your daughter's birthday present." Her eyes shone with mischievous delight. "You with me?"

"This city is full of nuts," he said with sublime resignation as he stepped on the gas.

Laughter began to pile up inside Francie, as the cab started. Then she lowered the window; and dipping her fingers into the envelope, she picked bills at random and started dropping them out of the moving cab. Sometimes she looked out the back of the cab at the faces of the people racing after the money. Some of them were laughing and shouting. Others had a look intent and lustful that was vaguely disgusting and made her mouth feel dry. She had not meant to set those kinds of emotions loose.

Francie ran out of money around Canal Street, and then the cab raced uptown. She sat back, drained of feeling as though she'd exhausted herself sexually. By an act of will she emptied her mind of everything that she had just done.

The driver pulled up to Saks. "Hope you enjoyed yourself, lady," he said, feeling as if he were dreaming.

"Very much. Don't forget your daughter's birthday present."

"I won't. You're okay. Good luck—you deserve it."

"Thank you. We all deserve it." She threw him a kiss as she entered Saks, thinking she would treat herself to a silk scarf. In blue. And then walk home.

When Francie arrived home, she found a note from Peter. He was having dinner with Wallace and would be home quite late. Francie had never met Wallace, Peter's current trick. She had a vague idea that he must be rough trade, probably "Wally" to his friends, or Peter would have brought him home for dinner or drinks.

She went to Peter's bedroom which he had turned over to her until they moved. He now slept regularly in his studio. She yawned and stretched with a kind of satisfied pleasure. She was glad Peter was out, she was glad she was alone; she didn't want to see anyone, she didn't want to talk. It had turned out, unexpectedly, into a high-sky day, full of sun and fun. She would take a bath, make herself some scrambled eggs, and go to bed early. She hoped Peter did not bring his friend home because his friend might be drunk and noisy. Peter was always quiet when he came in late, as she was herself; but one could not always count on the courtesy of his friends. Particularly the temporary ones. She would be glad when they moved into their new co-op, and she had her very own bedroom to sleep in, off its very own corridor.

Francie was sound asleep the first time the event came over CBS radio news:

WCBS time is 9:00 P.M. The seventh game of the World Series is scheduled for Yankee Stadium and it's a do-or-die situation between the Yanks and the Dodgers. . . . This is Ed Engles. . . . Now, here's some surprising news from Wall Street that does not include the Dow Jones Averages. It's *cherchez la*

236

femme, as the French say. A blond woman in a speeding yellow Checker cab distributed fifties, twenties, one hundred dollar bills, and some tens from the cab window on her way uptown, causing crowds of passersby to chase behind the cab and leaving traffic jams in the cab's wake. CBS man-on-the-street Don Walker says that between five and ten thousand dollars in tens, twenties, fifties, and hundreds were distributed starting on lower Wall Street and continuing past Trinity Church and up Broadway. WCBS will keep you appraised of any further news on the identity of the mysterious blond as the police continue their investigation. . . .

This is WCBS eleven o'clock news. . . . The temperature is seventy-five degrees and the humidity is seventy-six. The barometer is rising. . . . The excitement on Wall Street today had nothing to do with stocks and bonds but with the mysterious blond young woman who distributed thousands of dollars through the window of a speeding yellow Checker cab as she flew uptown. WCBS man-on-the-street Don Walker, who has been questioning the lucky pedestrians who picked up the money in an effort to discover the unknown blond's identity, has told us that at least three people have said she resembled the La Petite Girl who appears regularly on television for La Petite Gourmet Foods. One woman wondered if there might be money stashed away within frozen food boxes or cans of La Petite Foods. Could this be the start of an advertising promotion for La Petite Gourmet Foods? Costly though it is, it isn't as costly as television time. Well, we'll see. . . .

The next morning Francie, who had slept the sleep of the virtuous, awoke at seven-thirty. She showered and dressed slowly and, having no professional morning appointment, decided to do some early morning marketing. The pantry was bare of soda, peanuts, potato chips, paper toweling—all the necessities that had to be regularly replaced in order to keep giving the cocktail and dinner parties they so regularly gave. Leaving her room, she noted that the studio door was closed. Peter must have come home very late, because he rarely slept later than seven. She tiptoed to the kitchen and made herself a cup of instant black coffee, running the hot tap water over a spoonful of Medallio D'Oro. During the two years she'd lived with Jamie, she'd been accustomed to an entirely different household routine. Angelique had seen to the shopping for household supplies. Francie never saw the inside of a super-market, greengrocer, or butcher shop. But, as Peter's wife, she did the shopping; and no matter what he said about her having more valuable things to do with her time than haunt the supermarkets for penny savings when Gristedes was convenient, she still searched for bargains. It was a hang-over from her first years in New York and her semistarved life as a teenager.

Of course the A&P, Grand Union, Food Fair, et al. she knew were strictly for staples; the Maryland was their butcher and Angelo's was their greengrocer. But this was A&P morning; and after gulping her coffee, she left Peter a note saying, "Gone to the A&P for discounted Canada Dry." Then she picked up her small Paris purse, containing her keys, a comb, a twenty dollar bill, and stepped out the front door into the soft, warm morning; her face fresh, scrubbed, and free of makeup as a twelve-year-old.

It was 8:35 and, aside from the people going to work, there was not much movement on the streets. Francie felt young and strong as she sniffed the odor of the morning city, not yet heavy with gasoline fumes. She walked east on Sixty-third Street and then up Third to the A&P on Seventy-fifth. The fine, mysterious translucence of a late summer haze was over everything, and the elegant East-Side asphalt, sprinkled with mica, glittered responsively to the sun when the sun peered out from behind the summer mist. The air was still and cool, and Francie could tell by the half-dry streets and the green smell of wet leaves in the air that it had summer showered the night before. She thought she wouldn't mind living on Fifth Avenue opposite the Park, but then what a nuisance it would be going to Third Avenue for groceries. Of course, if you lived on Fifth Avenue, you had your house-keeper do those chores, the way Angelique ran Jamison's house. And she did her shopping on Madison. Still, Francie did not believe that she and Peter were ready for live-in help . . . those were thoughts for another day.

As she walked toward the A&P on Seventy-fifth and Third she passed a newsstand piled high with newspapers. But since Peter had the *New York Times* delivered daily, she didn't bother to pick up a newspaper. Or notice the headlines. Outside the A&P, a Schlitz beer truck had parked and two truckers were busy unloading beer cases. Francie recognized one of the truckers; she'd seen him once before unloading Schlitz beer at Grand Union. He was a very big guy, outsized really, with big shoulders and big muscles and a square jaw. And he looked like his name was Jake. Jake was always shouting and stomping and laughing loud enough to start dogs barking. What a commotion he made, and he didn't seem to give a fuck for the shocked looks on the faces of the proper men and women on their way to work. The other guy was smaller and sour. He lacked Jake's character and personality. Probably his name was Charlie. But it was a pleasure to watch Jake—he handled the beer cases as if they were weightless; and the first time Francie saw him, she stopped and stared. And he stopped and stared back. And grinned a big grin. This morning he said, ''Hi, kid!''

She gave him back a smile, uncontaminated by snobbery. '''Hi, kid' yourself,'' she said and it took her ten seconds to realize how much her smile said, and that this wasn't Davenport, and she no longer had room in her life for a Jake. ''Bye,'' she said, and turned a bit sadly into the A&P.

Francie felt at ease in the A&P. There were products all around which she'd done ads for—Scott Tissue, Pepsi, Ipana. Of course, none of them had been an entire campaign like La Petite; but they would certainly have helped pay the rent if there'd been no Jamie in recent years. No wonder she felt a personal kind of brand loyalty to ''her products.'' They were old friends.

Usually when she entered the supermarket, Lucy, one of the checkers, spotted her and waved. Lucy was an older sallow-faced woman who, in spite of far too much rouge, lipstick, and hair permanently curled, managed to look mousy. Lucy read fashion magazines the way Billie Graham read the Bible; and having once recognized Francie in *Vogue*, she decided Francie was ''somebody.'' After that she thumbed all the magazines for Franciejean advertisements; and whenever

Francie came in, she informed her immediately where and when one of her ads was appearing. And usually had a magazine handy for Francie to autograph the advertisement. Lucy had the makings of a dedicated Franciejean Fan Club President, and her presence at the A&P almost caused Francie to consider sticking to Gristedes, as Peter advised. But she disliked admitting to herself that Lucy's fawning admiration frightened her, and anyway, she did like the savings.

This morning when Francie entered the A&P Lucy was busy checking out a customer; and when she happened to glance Francie's way, she gave her only an unsmiling, blank stare. No wave. Unexpectedly, this gave Francie a chill that had nothing to do with the air conditioning. What difference did it make if Lucy smiled at her or not, and anyway she probably didn't see her. Francie decided she'd make sure to get on Lucy's line on her way out and say hello.

Picking a cart, Francie moved quickly down the beer and soft drinks aisle. She loaded up her cart with two six-packs and four quart bottles of soda water, plus plenty of tonic, ginger ale, and Pepsi for the soft drinkers. Then she reached for a six pack of Schlitz as a nod to the trucker, although she knew she and Elaine, their part-time maid, would probably be the only Schlitz drinkers. Peter and his guests drank things like Watney's Red that she couldn't buy at the A&P. When she finished in Aisle Five, she pushed toward Aisle Seven—Pet Foods, Nuts, Candy, Toiletries. Her cart rolled more slowly now, heavy as it was with liquids. As she walked against the traffic, the people she passed sometimes twitched or blinked or jerked when Francie's blond hair startled them awake. Then, trancelike, they resumed their checking of grocery lists, reading labels, talking to themselves. Though here and there a few turned and stared after her.

Turning into Aisle Seven, Francie noted it was fairly empty except for a huge mountain of quivering flesh, the fat lady from the circus, standing in front of the dog food, blocking the way to the peanuts.

"Excuse me, please," said Francie, hoping somehow to work her way around the mountain who was hypnotized by a newspaper she was reading. But the mountain never moved. The huge figure under its loose green wrapper that dropped almost to her ankles remained stock-still, looking like some alien plant growing up from the rubber-tiled floor of the A&P.

"Excuse me, please. I have to get to the peanuts," said Francie again, politely.

"I seen you on television last night," rasped a voice behind her. "You're the La Petite Girl, ain'cha?"

Francie colored a little as she turned. She thought only Lucy ever recognized her; but now she saw a shabby scarecrow of a man standing right behind her, his tongue moving endlessly around the edge of his dried lips.

"Yes, I am," she said uneasily, moving away from him and toward the fat lady.

At the sound of their voices, the huge figure, sloping out from triple chins into a rounded barrel of flesh, slowly raised her eyes from the newspaper to stare at Francie. After a pause she said in a basso voice, not as a question, but a statement of fact, "You're the La Petite Girl."

Francie nodded, sensing trouble in the air, and backing warily away from the fat lady. As she did, she collided with the scarecrow in baggy pants; and this time she got a whiff of his horrid breath.

"Miss, I need some money," he whined. "And I need it now. If you got all that money to give away, give me some!"

Blindly, Francie moved away from him again, toward the fat lady.

"Thief!" said the fat lady, spitting at Francie as she stared.

"What?" Francie ricocheted backward in surprise and fear.

"Thief! Where'd you get all the money?"

"What money?" Francie could feel the fat lady's rage as though it radiated out of her mountainous body.

"Bitch!" she squawked. "You stole that money! Nobody gives away money like that." The fat lady leaned across the cart and stuck the newspaper under Francie's nose. "See—see—see! That's you! Bitch!" And there it was, on the front page of the *Daily News,* a photograph of a speeding cab and a girl with sunglasses and blond hair blowing in the wind leaning out the cab window and with one hand dropping paper bills. It certainly was a photograph of her, though the face was a blur.

Francie put her hand to her chest, aware that she was out

241

of breath, fear knotting within her, the old fear, the paralyzing fear. Though she was free to run, somehow she could not move.

"Give me some money, please," the scarecrow repeated, following her closely; and then unexpectedly, his head lunged forward like the head of a jack-in-the-box, and he started to lick her bare arm.

"Get away from me!" she shrieked, trying to rid herself of the scarecrow's tongue.

But he was stronger than he looked, and he grabbed her arm and buried his mouth in her shoulder. "Give me the money."

"Give it to him, you bitch! Give it to him!" screamed the fat lady, reaching across Francie's cart and grabbing a fistful of Francie's long, silky hair, shaking her head from side to side. Then, with a violent yank of the hair, she slammed Francie against the shelves of dog food, scattering them to the floor.

Without knowing it, Francie started to scream. "Let me go! Let me go!" Her eyes were wild with terror.

"Hey, folks! Get a look at Miss Rich Bitch! The La Petite Girl who gives money away!" And the fat lady continued to yank Francie back and forth by the strength of her grip on her hair.

The customers who had been sleepily going through the aisles with their carts now started bumping into each other in their haste to get to Aisle Seven. Way over by the vegetable counter, people who didn't know what was happening were leaving their carts to go and see.

Delirium clouded over Francie's consciousness, and she no longer felt the pain in her head and body as the Fat Lady yanked her back and forth like a yo-yo, and the scarecrow tugged and bit at her arm. Then out of nowhere, an ugly young man appeared and hit the scarecrow hard in the face with his fist, forcing him to release Francie's arm and stumble backward out of the aisle. After that, the young man grabbed the fat lady's wrist. "Mattie, leave the pretty girl alone," he said. "Leave her alone. She's my meat." And the fat lady let Francie's hair go, and Francie staggered back against the peanuts. But the young man caught her before she fell and, holding her by the shoulders, forced her to stand. His white

242

nasty face came up close to hers; and he crooned in a low, smiling voice, "Come on, baby. Pretty baby—don't be afraid. I won't let that old fart eat you. I'm going to do that myself. But tell me first—where's the money?"

Francie shook her head, no longer able to understand.

"Where's the money?" screamed the fat lady, longing to attack again.

The shoppers were now huddled together, women with children, older women, middle-aged men. They were standing and staring at the scene taking place in Aisle Seven, their faces riveted, watching something they didn't want to see but could not help looking at.

"Where's the manager?" said a balding man in his fifties, wearing a white shirt and suit pants; his face shining with perspiration. He was standing at Lucy's check-out counter.

"In the men's room," said Lucy with a nasty grin. From where she stood at her register, she could see the ruckus; and she hoped it wouldn't end too quickly. That rich bitch model making believe she had to save money buying at the A&P.

"They'll kill her. They'll kill her!" said a housewife in curlers, looking back over her shoulder. Then she glared at the man in front of her. "Do something, can't you? You're a man!"

"You do something. I just got over an appendicitis operation. Where's the manager?"

"Coward!"

"Drop dead." And they both continued to stare at the disaster in Aisle Seven.

"The money. The money," the young man was saying. He made a sound like a snarl; and taking hold of Francie's arm, he twisted it until she cried with pain. "Tell me where the money is. In this?" He picked up and squeezed the small, flat purse that Francie had dropped to the floor. "Not much in here." He tucked the purse into his belt. "Is it in the cans? The boxes? Which ones?"

"Is it in the cans or the boxes?" screamed the fat lady.

Francie struggled to be free of him, but he struck her in the face, purposely and firmly, once, twice, three times. Then he looked around quickly to see who was watching. Everyone was watching, and he smiled. No one moved. He struck her

243

again and she fell to the floor. "Listen, you little bitch, I'll mop up this floor with you, I'll break you into little pieces. Where is the money?"

But Francie was gasping for breath; and though she saw his lips moving, she couldn't tell what he was saying. He pulled her purse from his belt, opened it, and dumped out the contents. He caught the twenty dollar bill that fluttered toward the floor, and then threw the purse against the shelves. "This is small change. Where's the real money? I heard it on the radio. It's in the La Petite cans or boxes, isn't it?"

"Yeah, yeah, which ones?" roared the fat lady. "It's a premium. It's for us."

"You better tell me where it is, sweetheart." He lifted Francie to her feet, but she couldn't stand because the floor beneath her was tilting like a trick ride at a carnival. "Tell me," he said, holding her under the arms, "or there won't be much of you left to go on television."

But all she could do was look at him stupidly. She denied his reality so he no longer could hurt her. Her mind cowered somewhere else, hidden out of his reach.

What happened next happened so fast that no witness would or could clearly describe it. But the young man was suddenly flying through the air, down Aisle Seven. He crashed into the freezer counter, where he may or may not have fractured his skull. For a moment Jake looked after him, slowly shaking his head while supporting Francie with his arm. Then he turned and looked down at her and spoke softly, "It's all right, little lady. It's all right. There are bastards like that in every group."

With his free hand, he picked up Francie's purse and keys from the supermarket floor; and half carrying her, he started toward the A&P exit, pushing Francie's cart out of the way. But the fat lady had planted herself firmly in front of him. She screamed and spat, "She's a thief! A thief!"

"Listen, Fatty," said Jake, "if you don't get out of my way, I'm going to do to you what you meant to do to this little kid here."

For one minute the fat lady stood her ground, bracing herself to charge the trucker. But Jake sighed deeply and continued matter-of-factly. "Fatty, if you don't get outta my way, you're gonna wake up in Bellevue after a very delicate operation when they remove my shoe from the inside of your ass. Or your stomach—depending on which way you're facin' when I kick.''

The fat lady stood stock-still another instant and then turned with surprising speed for her weight and shuffled down the aisle.

Francie, leaning helplessly against Jake, was sobbing now in a lower key and talking to herself. "Momma, Momma, I didn't mean it. I didn't mean to do it. He hurt me. He hurt me.''

"Honey, honey, it's all over," Jake whispered gently as he half carried her through the store. "Where do you live, honey? We gotta get you home.''

But Francie couldn't answer. She just went on sobbing and talking to herself. She could taste the blood in her mouth.

"She lives at 164 East Sixty-third Street," said Lucy as Jake passed her checkout counter. "You're a real hero, ain'cha, George?''

"Yeah," he said, looking at Lucy with disgust.

Outside on the street, the Schlitz truck was parked and Charlie was waiting. "We gotta stop off at 164 East Sixty-third Street," was all Jake said as he lifted Francie into the cab of the truck.

Peter was coming out of the house in slacks and an open shirt when the Schlitz truck drew to a stop. There in the cab sat Francie, her face red and swollen, her hair tangled, her mouth bleeding. She was crying bitterly and quietly, leaning against the shoulder of one of the men in the truck cabin, a giant of a man.

Peter walked slowly over to the truck. He knew he could never take either man, and he wished he had a gun. Had these men done this to Francie? Then the bigger of the two men said in a sad voice, "Do you know this kid?''

"Yes, she's my wife." Peter tried to keep his voice level. "What did you do to her?''

"I didn't do anything. I got her out of the A&P.''

"For God's sake—what happened?''

"Some damn fools thought she was that crazy broad who threw that money away yesterday. They were after her hide.''

"Jesus!" Suddenly Peter felt like throwing up. He walked around to the side of the cab while the big man lifted Francie down from the seat. "She's all right. More frightened than hurt. People can be swine. I understand it and you understand it. The average guys; they can be swine when it comes to money."

"Thank you for getting her out." Peter was embarrassed and nauseous with anger.

"It's nothing, buddy. She needs some rest. And probably a doctor should look at her. She got batted around a little before I got there."

He handed the dazed and sobbing Francie gently into Peter's arms. Francie clung to Peter, sobbing hysterically.

"Darling, darling, it's all right. It's over. You're safe now, you're home."

And as Francie slipped away into the oblivion and safety of Peter's arms, she had the odd notion that Peter was crying too. Why was he crying? It wasn't his mother who was angry.

15

It took Francie only a few days to recover physically from her body's aches and bruises. But walking down city streets, she felt as if she had gone through some long illness. Half awake, voices seemed to leap out at her from the buildings. A man said, "Hi, Francie. How are you?" and it took a minute to remember who he was. During this period she seemed to have lost the gift of fitting names to faces. Nor could she remember exactly what had happened. The entire A&P episode was invested with a kind of nightmare improbability that left her picking her way through a wreckage of unreason, searching for a clearing of sanity.

One morning at breakfast, she said to Peter, "You know it's impossible to have any privacy. Any at all." She was struggling with unrehearsed words in an unfamiliar scene.

"What are you talking about, dear?" He'd been worried about her, but he'd rather she didn't know it; and hoping to conceal his worry, he studied the butter knife, thinking that he did not like the design and that silver should be less ornate.

"I mean modeling. Your life becomes too public."

"Darling," Peter said, trying to keep every trace of irony out of his voice, "if you make a habit of throwing ten thousand dollars out of cab windows, you are not apt to have a private life. No matter what you do."

"It was nine thousand dollars. And how did the *Daily News* get my photograph?"

"I told you—an amateur photographer walking up Wall Street. From Iowa at that. He was taking pictures of New York City."

"In Davenport he'd be a Peeping Tom. Here the windows are too high. Did Matt Harris call?"

"Yes, indeed. And I denied everything."

"Why didn't you tell him I'd lapsed into a coma?"

"That's an admission of guilt. No, dear, we deny, deny, deny."

"I suppose." There was something in her manner that suggested a coloratura gathering her forces to take E flat over high C. "You know, Peter, when you work in television, people do know you. Yesterday, someone—a complete stranger—asked for my autograph in a restaurant."

"I know, darling. The martyrdom of celebrity."

"I don't like it. Suppose Momma had seen that *Daily News* picture. She would have been shocked."

"But Francie, she didn't. Momma is dead." So that was it.

"I know—but still." She paused and then took the E flat: "I want to quit modeling."

The honest stonework of her anxiety now showed. "Francie, I think you're overreacting to an unfortunate accident. You ran into the luntic fringe. You can have a completely private life and still be a model. It's really not the same as being Marilyn Monroe."

"I suppose. I guess I'm putting on airs, but modeling makes me feel like a sideshow freak."

"And what will you do if you quit modeling? How will you fill your time? Will you sit home and mend my socks? Or take up cooking? You'll never make a first-rate cook. And you do have to do something."

"It's not the money, Peter, is it? It can't be. Didn't Jamie make us rich, rich, rich?"

"Let's say affluent. No, it's not the money, darling. It's you."

She laughed wryly. "Do you think I'll take to drink? Or drugs? Or turn into some kind of nut if I don't work?"

"I think for some people work is as necessary as sex." Peter judiciously blew two smoke rings. "You're one of those people. I'm another."

"Jamie's a third. He explained to me once that work was not simply a matter of making money. Now I understand."

"You have the kind of vitality that has to become

248

professional. It can't use itself up in one person in private. You could take to drink.''

"Or shopping."

"Or shopping. But you're not the charity work type."

"In Davenport I once sold ribbon in the Five and Dime."

"This is not Davenport. And I don't think I want Mrs. Peter Devlin measuring out ribbon at the dime store—or even Macy's. So, until we think of something suitable, you'll have to continue modeling."

"No, I won't." She said this with finality. "I will not do modeling anymore."

"Well, my pet, we'll have to think about that. Especially since the other side of Matt's call was that they're planning the new La Petite cycle. He wants you next week in the agency at two on Tuesday."

"I don't want to be the La Petite girl anymore."

"I think you ought to discuss it with Matt. And I think we ought to think about it ourselves. Hard."

In the middle of the night, Peter awoke to the sound of running water. Getting out of bed, he put on a bathrobe and headed toward the sound in the kitchen. There was Francie, rinsing out a glass which had held milk.

"Can't you sleep, dear?"

"No. I keep thinking about my future. Maybe I could be a librarian?"

"Or do embroidery for wealthy ladies. Do you have to solve it this minute?"

"Maybe I could sell antiques—help you?"

"I do not believe in Mom-and-Pop stores." He said this with affectionate disdain.

"Sorry, sir. Maybe I could be a model's agent. I know the business. And have the contacts."

"That's a better-grade ribbon clerk. I insist that you can have a completely private life as a model. And you're so young, Francie. Modeling will give you time to look around and decide what you might want to do later. You'll even have the chance to go to school if necessary and prepare yourself for when life begins at thirty-five."

But she was only half listening. "That's a good idea.

School. I could go to school and then to college and study something. Do you think I could be a doctor? Or a vet? I like animals better than people, anyway." She was thumbing through options.

"Why don't you learn to play a flute?"

"Or glass blowing?"

"Or raise mushrooms? Go to bed. We'll draw fortunes in the morning."

In the elevator, Francie stared straight ahead, arguing silently with herself. Was this decision a mistake? Could she ever do anything besides model? For a little while a fire had blazed up within her. She could feel all kinds of ideas, schemes, plans glowing in her mind. But now she was uncertain, and every gleaming possibility seemed to fall to ashes. What could she really do after she bowed out of modeling? The very idea gave her a fright. She remembered Jamie's saying he'd never seen such a waste of a good mind. He'd said she was his second-best assistant after the Fulbright scholar. So she couldn't be that dumb. Jamie would never have stood for it. Still, it was a good thing she and Peter were married or she'd never be up to this ordeal. The mere thought of an empty day, with no one to talk to, or to see, and nothing to do that made you feel important, brought a hungry look to her eyes. She would be like those solitary people drifting through the city streets, crumbling into corners on benches, wandering like lost souls, trying to fill up their time. And then what would she say to Matt? How would she rationally explain breaking an important contract? Suppose someday she had to return to modeling?

"The Barnett Company." These were the first words to greet her when she stepped off the 17th floor. She now realized that it was not the executive floor. No, it was one of the creative department floors; in this case, television art, copy and production.

Directly below the name "Barnett" were swinging glass doors, and beyond the doors she could see the reception room; and sitting behind the curving beige wood desk with a bowl of apples in front of her sat Evie, the sexy seventeenth-floor receptionist, usually eating an apple. Apples were Evie's lunch. Sometimes her dinner too. Apples were frequently the lunch of Barnett employees; especially the Evies who spent their entire week's salary on clothes.

Apples at Barnett were a company perk and a company legend. The myth had it that years ago, when Abe Barnett discussed leaving his job at Irwin Wasey to open his own shop, an old friend advised him, "Abe, you are nuts. You'll be selling apples on the street in six months."

That decided Abe, who was never known to take any advice but his own. He quit Wasey, leased a floor of office space in the London Guarantee Building in Chicago, and put out a bowl of apples on the reception desk. Later, the agency grew like the beanstalk it was, with the Green Giant sitting smugly on top of it; there were more and more floors appearing with more and more reception rooms, and more and more bowls of Delicious or MacIntosh or Baldwin red apples to feed employees, clients, space reps, typewriter repairmen, job seekers—anyone and everyone who was hungry. And for free. Far better than selling them, Abe said.

But today, small, dark, sexy Evie was not sitting eating an apple behind the reception desk. She was out on a coffee break, or out sick, or romancing, or she'd quit. Francie sincerely hoped not. Evie was not a Francie fan—she was more like a distant cousin. To Evie, Francie was Franciejean, not the glamorous model but the girl who gave Evie clothes, who once, when Evie was behind in rent, lent Evie money. And Evie had to force her to accept repayment. Today she missed Evie's "kinship" badly. She needed it for courage.

The girl seated behind the reception desk was clearly not interested in clothes. Or in Francie. She was small, dry, narrow-shouldered, and broad-hipped. She wore rimless glasses and had beige-colored hair that blended with the wood of the desk and the wall paneling; and with her pointed chin and thin nose, she looked as if someday she might age into someone's peppery maiden aunt. Her fingernails were broken; and she looked unkempt, with a deliberate sloppiness that was as studied as good grooming.

Being a receptionist clearly did not interest her. One got the message that she was doing the company a favor by sitting there. She was buried in a book that did interest her, something about torts and contracts. It looked to Francie like a school text, and this somewhat reassured her. Here was someone else studying for a different career. But the girl did not look up when Francie entered.

This lack of response made Francie uneasy. It reminded her of the first time she'd arrived at the Barnett Company for the La Petite auditions and how frightened she'd been. And here, with this strange cold girl, it all came back. It wasn't really a memory. It was a true reliving of the feeling of being an outsider in the world.

"Excuse me," Francie said, and the girl finally looked up.

"What is it?"

Francie, with her inveterate watchfulness, recognized that this girl's rudeness was impersonal. She would have been the same with anyone. She disliked having her reading interrupted. "I'd like to see Matt Harris."

"Do you have an appointment?"

"No."

The girl looked her up and down candidly. "You're a model?"

"I'm a model."

"Mr. Harris is not seeing any models today. We've no 'cattle call' out. Sorry." And she went back to her reading. The girl's bad manners made Francie feel better, made her feel like laughing. Or fighting with the young woman. Maybe hitting her. "I do think he'll see me. I'm Franciejean Stewart."

"I doubt it," she said without looking up. "Why don't you call for an appointment?"

This futile dialogue with the receptionist gave Francie the feeling of shaking hands with a glove from which the hand has been withdrawn. She had to do something. "Is a tort like a Sachertorte?" she asked.

This time the girl looked up and grinned. "No, I wish it was. I love Sachertorte. But it's very fattening. This tort is like any wrong private or civil act or omission for which a suit can be brought, but not including breach of contract."

"You're studying torts? What's that?"

"Law. I go to NYU Law School at night. And tonight I have an exam." She made a sour face. "It's not that I am unsympathetic with your predicament. Modeling is a very tough business. It's hard on the feet and the heart. It's tough to break into, and I do sympathize with you. But you should have an appointment."

"Well, why don't you just tell Mary Ann that I'm here? I'm sure she'll see me."

"I know. You're Franciejean Stewart. The La Petite Girl."

"That's right."

"Well, I do admire your chutzpah, but I'd admire you more if you told the truth."

"I am telling the truth. Don't I look like the La Petite Girl?"

"How would I know? I never watch television. I'm always studying. And when I'm not studying or in school, I'm reading science fiction."

"Oh."

"But Franciejean Stewart, our new star recently born, is now in Acapulco. Or Monte Carlo, Mary Ann thinks." Nevertheless, she dialed the interoffice number for Mary Ann. "Well, both lines are busy. That's because Matt is on the telephone, probably talking to Franciejean in Monte Carlo. And Mary is on the telephone talking to her boyfriend."

Francie sat down in a chair. "I'll wait."

"Be my guest. But you're wasting your time. I'll dial again in three minutes. If they pick up, please give me your real name. They won't admire your brass the way I do. They'll be mad."

In Matt Harris's office, Matt was seated behind a massive desk strewn with production quotes, photostats of TV commercial storyboards, staff travel schedules, three ashtrays piled high with cigarette stubs. Matt, his shirt collar unbuttoned and tie unknotted, was holding a telephone to his ear, finger poised midair, ready to dial, but doing nothing. He had a tired, helpless expression on his face. "Now God damn it, who do I call next? Where is she? Eileen Ford doesn't know. I can't reach her husband. The maid speaks French. Maybe I should call the Missing Persons Bureau."

"Who has she been shacking up with most recently? Besides you, that is. Call him," remarked Lillian Morris.

"Lillian, my darling, you can bad-mouth me all you want; but you are still my own true love."

"She probably screwed your ass off for the job."

"Ahhh, cut it out. You're hurting my feelings. Though

why you should deny a man the simple pleasures of life in a business that eats him alive is beyond me." He shrugged his shoulders in fake humility. "But lest you forget, my darling, it was you who discovered our jewel. She's your very own Kohinoor. You brought in those Richard Avedon shots. I never knew who Avedon was. In this group I'm the crude boy from Queens. I sweat. I changed my name from O'Hara. Or was it Goldberg? I practically never read *Vogue* or *Bazaar*. My wrist isn't limp enough. She's your doing, honey chile."

"I make mistakes too."

"It certainly warms the cockles of my heart to know you are human, Lillian. May I kiss the hem of your Pauline Trigère? But sweetheart, Grayson thinks that she's a sensation. And Grayson thinks that because Osgood thinks that. And Osgood thinks whatever he thinks because, as the saying goes, he's wired to Buckman's ass. So that's what Buckman thinks."

"I sold Lawrence on Franciejean Stewart, and I will simply have to unsell him. I have no desire to be difficult, but I am particularly interested in the La Petite campaign. For, as we all know, the advertising concept was my very own idea."

"Darling, no one would dare deny your contribution."

"Fuck contribution, Matt Harris. The whole idea of doing a tony campaign was mine. Mine alone. And I fought for it tooth and nail to get you peasants to buy it. So I do not intend to see it go down the drain because a greedy little model pulls a cheap publicity stunt. She probably hasn't had any movie offers yet, so she's out drumming up more PR."

"I have to take my hat off to you, Lillian. You sure do dredge up the angles." Matt nodded his head respectfully. "But movie offers or not, according to Osgood, the publicity is selling La Petite like crazy in the New York area. Furthermore, we have a contract with the young lady that was drawn up by some damn wise-ass lawyer that isn't going to be easy to break."

"We'll break it. Or buy her out. There are ways. The La Petite Girl does not go around throwing away money. It makes her seem like a mindless rich bitch. Or high on pot, pills, or the hard stuff. And once the excitement dies down, decent people will wonder about her. And think twice about her. And worry. And their worry will rub off on the product. No! She has to go."

Watching Lillian hold forth, Matt thought, what that woman needs is a good fuck. Or a drink. "Look, sweetheart, your reasoning is reasonable, but not irrefutable. First, in another week or two, people will have forgotten all about her largesse. There's too much else happening. Second, her husband absolutely denied that it was Franciejean who pulled this Lady Bountiful act. And there is absolutely no way we can prove otherwise. Which does not give us a great handle for breaking the contract without buying her out. And that's a sizable buy."

There was a detestable realism in Matt's logic, but Lillian would not give up. "Well, I believe we can find a way if we present a united front. I don't want her in the next La Petite series; and if you stand with me, we can convince Abe. Or I can always do it alone." Lillian had presence, she was accomplished, she judged; she was too thin and too tall, with long, strong, swordlike legs and a surprising sensuality. Men treated her as she seemed to demand; with respect, with lust, but rarely with tenderness. Nor would she have expected otherwise; a man who lay with her sensed the threat that he might not rise again. Her sexuality implied struggle. It was closer to murder than to pleasure. What she searched for in a man was good looks, power, intelligence, and sensibility. To the kind of man she chose, the experience was at first exhilarating and sometimes worth the cost. But not for long. Soon they grew weary of the implicit conflict and the explicit demands. And they bowed out. But Lillian was not sentimental; she had long ago resigned herself to satisfying her need for intimacy among men friends who were homosexual and seldom available for passion. "What about it, Norman? What do you think?"

She turned now to look at a mock-robust man, with thinning hair, a thick mustache, and glasses, seated beside her on the couch, wearing an expensive well-cut business suit that somehow suggested a costume. He had been quietly listening to the rat-a-tat-tat between Lillian and Matt. "I rather like this Franciejean, myself. I don't object to our continuing use of her. I think this hoopla with the money is silly. And irrelevant."

Specks swam before Lillian's eyes. Her voice grew higher, fanatical. "She's contaminating the campaign. I would think you at least would see what I see. Actually, I feel so strongly about it, I wish we could call back all the ads we've run using her."

"Are you suggesting a burning of the ads?" Norman took Lillian's hand into his and stroked it gently. "Maybe we could build a bonfire of the print ads and the TV reels and set fire to them on Park Avenue."

"Norman, really, you are a true bastard." She pulled her hand away from his.

"Now, Lillian, that's no way to talk to an old friend. How can we have a warm meaningful friendship if you insist that I agree with you on everything. Because I have an opinion that differs from yours, you grow angry. That shows a narrow-minded disposition hardly worthy of the Lillian I know and admire."

Lillian felt her face grow hot. She wanted to get up and leave, and she did stand. But then she experienced that unique sensation in the knees and ankles that is best described as nonsupport. For a minute she wished she could kill him. Instead she sat down. "Thank you, darling, for bringing me back to my senses. You are a real human being." If she could have, she would have liked to torture Norman to death. "You bastard. Here I telephone Abe and ask him to send you to New York; a free trip on the agency to Sodom and Gomorrah to participate in this meeting and cast your vote as the art director on the La Petite account. I didn't need you. I could have done this alone. But what do you do, you louse? You fuck me. Well, thank you, and fuck you!"

"Land's sake, Lillian, watch your language," chided Norman, in a Southern dialect. "You wouldn't carry on like that back in ole St. Louis. The very idea—at your age. Why, back there you never walked with a man after sunset. Even your ex-husband."

The coffee cart had pulled in front of the office and Mary Ann was buying coffee. "Cream, anyone? Sugar? Brandy?" she called. In a minute Mary Ann entered with three black coffees balanced on a tray. She put one on Matt's desk; and two on the coffee table in front of the couch on which Norman was seated and Lillian slouched, her elegant long legs flamboyantly crossed while her dress hugged her thighs.

"Careful, folks," Mary Ann remarked demurely. "It's very hot and very wet. But it will clear your heads." She did a deep knee curtsy and left.

"What's the matter with her?" asked Norman.

"She's only that way for company," said Matt.

"Quaint, I suppose."

"Fire her," said Lillian peevishly.

"You're trigger-happy, girl," said Matt. "She's a super-secretary. She does not want to be a model. Or a producer. Only a production assistant. She has her little games. She thinks she's a natural stand-up comedienne. Don't fight it."

Norman leaned toward Lillian, holding his cup of coffee gingerly in one hand. "Lillian, my duck, we are having our first spat. It's a landmark event. After all these years." He chucked her playfully under the chin with his free hand. "Look at us, fighting like cannibals over the missionary's leg."

But Lillian was having no part of his play. With a violent and unexpected shove, she pushed Norman back on the couch; and as she did, his cup of coffee splashed on her beige dress. Lillian jumped up with a scream as the steaming coffee soaked through her dress and ran down her leg. "Norman! You lout!"

"Sorry," said Norman contritely, moving rapidly out of the way of Lillian's clenched fist. He carefully put the remains of the coffee down on the table and reached for a paper napkin. "Oh dear." He was ready to help Lillian mop up the coffee stain, but Lillian, stung into action, was already at the door. "Damn you, Norman, this dress cost me two hundred dollars. The Barnett Company will have to pay for the cleaning. At Deniham. Or a new dress if necessary. You scalded me, you clod. I hope I'm not scarred for life."

"Lillian, don't dramatize. Think of it as a good excuse not to use the missionary position." When Lillian glared back at him, mouthing soundless obscenities, Norman smiled compassionately. "Be sure to bundle up when you go out, dear. You don't want to catch your death of cold."

After Lillian vanished, Norman turned to Matt, a sly smile on his face. "I must say I did that well."

Matt sighed deeply. "Very neat."

"I thought so. She was beginning to pall."

"I don't know how your nerves stand her. She drives me crazy."

"I have my ways. A little coffee here; a little pot there." Norman smiled to himself. "Unfortunately, one cannot hit a woman. Even a woman like Lillian. Not that I have socked anyone since I was twelve and punched my sister for locking me out. I'm not sure I still know how to do it. A punch is not like a serve in tennis which is overhand. Or a crawl stroke. It is a straight arm motion.''

"You old bastard. You enjoyed the whole number.''

"Well, action does have its virtues. An artist is always looking at things. But action is red-blooded. It's pleasant occasionally to give up voyeurism.'' Then with a buttery friendliness he probed. "What is this bee in her bonnet, really? Why all the fuss about a model?''

"Buckman is now seeing Francie. At least he was until she got married. Now I don't know.''

"Ah! So our little flower is seething with jealousy.''

"Seething. She thought she'd hooked him. You know, two born killers finding each other. But he unhooked.''

"Lillian always was a spoilsport.''

"I don't know how Abe stands her.''

"She's quite useful. That old biddie is not always wrong. She's the kind who stumbles into a pile of garbage and comes up with a diamond bracelet in her mouth. That's the damn trouble with her. She's not a fool, and she has very good instincts. What she says about the danger to the product and the agency's masterly effort is not all a can of corn. Pardon the pun.''

"You think there's something in it?''

"Publicity can cut two ways. After listening to her caterwauling, I must admit I am of a split mind. I don't really know whether we should ride it out, or buy out Franciejean.''

"But if we buy her out and she takes a job with General Mills? And becomes Miss Wheaties, the Mother Of Us All—what happens? Buckman yells. He doesn't want her working for another food company. Not after launching La Petite. And that's in the contract.'' Matt sighed nostalgically. "Also, he was sleeping with the little lady.''

"Abe assumed that. Lillian thinks I'm here on her invitation. I'm here on a special mission for Abe. To help make this decision.''

"Our absentminded Führer. He doesn't miss a trick.''

"It will be jingle bells in July, as they say, when he does.''

There was a gentle tap on the door, and Mary Ann

entered, clapping her hands gleefully. "Fair sir, guess who found who?"

Matt leaped to his feet. "Where is she, damn it?"

"Entrez, s'il vous plaît." Mary Ann turned to Francie, motioned for her to enter, and turned back to Matt. "Would you believe? She's been waiting for half an hour in the reception room."

Matt shook his head in exasperation. "I'll kill Evie."

"Evie has gone to the great reception room at Y&R. Martha was on the desk. She was subbing for Arlene Mann, who was at the dentist, who was subbing for our new seventeenth-floor receptionist who has not yet been hired. Evie did not give notice," said Mary Ann, curtsying out.

"Well, why the hell didn't Martha call us?"

"She did not believe I was Franciejean Stewart," said Francie, laughing. "And she never watches television if she can help it."

"Those damn copywriters. They're so snooty and live on such a high plane of intellectualism that you wonder how they ever lower themselves to sit on the toilet. And Martha's the worst."

He sat down and turned to Norman. "Norman, this is Franciejean Stewart, the hub of the matter we've been discussing." He turned to Francie. "Francie, this is Norman Hook, the art director who oversees the entire La Petite account. Print and television."

Norman stared at Francie from behind his thick glasses, his small, porpoiselike eyes spying on every item of body and clothing as though he were taking a private inventory for resale. At last he made his pronouncement. "You look even better off camera. I am impressed."

Francie smiled as she spoke. "It's my diet. Coconut milk, raw fruit and nuts."

Norman nodded; his mustache beamed approval. At least this one did not think of herself as an enchanted princess. Then his face took on a wondering look. He stared at Francie, thinking, deciding, trying to remember—ahhh, he had it. "Franciejean! There cannot be two beautiful models named Franciejean in this one city. No, not even in New York." He started to smile and his smile became increasingly intimate. "Are you any relation to Franciejean Devlin?"

Francie felt an inward start. "Yes, we're very close. That's my married name. How did you know?"

"I didn't. I put two and two together and came up with twenty-two. I know Peter Devlin. He speaks very highly of Franciejean Devlin."

It was oddly pleasant hearing her married name on the lips of this stranger. She could feel her tension relaxing, sensing that here she had a friend. Seating herself on the couch, facing the ruddy-cheeked art director, she became charming. "I'm sure Peter has mentioned you. I forget names lately."

"Maybe not. I'm not in New York that often. However, I am a substantial client. In fact, I've just purchased an unreasonably expensive eighteenth-century commode from your husband."

"Peter has beautiful things."

"I have extravagant tastes."

"I don't think antiques are an extravagance. I think of them as an investment."

"You're well tutored." Norman was looking at her with lazy good humor. "Do you know I'm having dinner this evening with you and Peter?"

It was a moment for tact and Francie responded perfectly to the friendly familiarity of his tone. "Wonderful! You're the client Peter mentioned at breakfast. Now I remember."

"At breakfast? Amazing. He only knew I was in town at lunch. An absolute demonstration of clairvoyance."

Francie gave him a shrewd, steady look. So he'd caught her out. She saluted him with a nod, smiling. "It must be that—seeing the future. Precognition, isn't it?"

Matt, sounding grumpy and feeling left out, interrupted. "Look, I'm glad you two are so cozy. But Norman, we have business to discuss with Francie. The new La Petite series. Remember who pays our social security?"

Norman looked at Matt with mild impatience. "Matt, let us not be crassly commercial. We all know that business is best conducted over a bottle of wine. Francie and I will have a nice quiet chat tonight. I'll fill you in tomorrow on every clause."

Matt slowly reddened. He gave a nervous twist to his tie, shifted in his seat, and sullenly accepted that Norman had pulled rank. Norman was a vice-president in charge of the entire Barnett Company art department, and Matt was simply head of television production for the New York office. Running his eyes over Francie and Norman, he said, "Well, now that you put it to me in laymen's terms, I pass."

Francie gave Norman a puzzled look when he said with a proprietary air, "You and I will have a heart-to-heart tonight, ducky. On the enigma of La Petite. The new series."

Francie suddenly realized that the unpleasant need to make decisions about her modeling career was temporarily postponed. The sense of freedom and safety caused her spirits to rise. She stood up quickly and, with a bright wave to Matt, moved to the door. "See you tonight, Norman. If you see the future, you'll know I'll be wearing an orchid behind my left ear."

Francie telephoned Peter at the shop to tell him she had just met Norman Hook, his client, who was also a big mucky-muck at Barnett. "Why didn't you tell me he worked for Barnett?"

"I didn't know it. He never mentioned the name of the agency. I only knew he was in advertising."

Francie thought about this. "Peter, what does he know about us?" There was only a touch of caution in her voice.

"Not much, darling." He understood her all too well. "Though he and I have met over the years. In bars."

"He's gay?"

"Oh yes." His face at the other end of the telephone showed the calm indifference of one accustomed to false positions. "He may assume I've now gone the straight and narrow."

Francie gave the receiver an unbelieving if sympathetic smile. "He said he was coming to dinner tonight."

"Did he now? I invited him, and he said he was otherwise taken. Ah! You charmed him."

"Charmed that one? Fat chance. What did you tell him about me?"

"That my wife was a beautiful woman who did modeling but was thinking of giving up modeling. And did he have any ideas about advertising?"

"Then he's plotting something. Secret agent six and seven eighths."

*   *   *

After dinner, they retired to the living room to sip Courvoisier and chat. Norman spoke slowly, deliberately, and a little fuzzily—he had quite a bit of the Pouilly-Fuissé preceded by several Jack Daniel's—of Francie's future as a model; her rousing success as the La Petite Girl. Playfully he offered to read her palm, and artfully she accepted. "I see a beautiful, fearless young witch climbing the heights. The world at her feet. Her shopping cart runneth over with pear-shaped diamonds, pearl pill boxes. Fourteen-carat gold sink faucets. A villa in Estaril. A tan out of season. A Merce. A sable—"

"Enough! Enough!"

"Yes, quite enough. Now I see you pausing at a cross-road?" He looked up at her impudently. "Are you pausing at a crossroad?" He took off his glasses to wipe them; and in spite of his mustache and thinning hair, he looked like a plump Puck. His eyes were wide, blurred, and full of wonder at a world he'd never really seen.

Francie watched him, holding back her smile. She liked him enough, though she knew he had come with a plan. A plan she might or might not like. "It seems you are taking an intelligent interest in my career."

"I am indeed. I am giving it my undivided attention. Your husband has included me in a family confidence."

"Husbands do that. They give away household secrets."

Looking at her, Peter thought, as he often did, how beautiful she was. How quick. How curious it was that this exquisite thing that was his wife was so often so passionately sad.

Francie was listening, but not listening to Norman as he spoke with his odd, roughish intimacy. "Now why, with so much to gain, are you pausing at the crossroads? Modeling as we know, for the lucky ones, can be insanely lucrative. Particularly television modeling. Hundreds of thousands of dollars change hands. In addition you are a public figure."

Francie and Peter smiled at each other with a wordless understanding. "Let's just say her handwriting is poor, and it embarrasses her to sign autographs," said Peter.

Norman nodded as though he understood, but he didn't. If he had been a woman he would have wanted to look like Francie. He usually fell in love with beautiful women who had something strange about them. "Well, I admire your

262

spiritual vision," he said sipping his brandy. "But I do have difficulty understanding anyone who lacks a sordid craving for money. For fame. For adulation."

Francie giggled. "Well try this scenario. Two ex-models meet on the street and reminisce about old times." She mimicked two graty voiced women from Jersey.

"Gee! Do you remember Franciejean?"

"Oh sure. Wasn't she somethin'? Whatever became of her?"

"You'll never believe it. I heard on the radio this morning she was named the fattest woman in the world!"

"In the world?"

"The world!"

"Gosh, I always knew she was going places."

Francie's wide eyes shone with pleasant horror, the way a child's will when it scares itself.

Norman shrugged. "You have your nightmares, I have mine. Enough of this cat-and-mouse business. Painful though it is, I have to tell you the truth. Because if I don't, your lawyer will. We at Barnett have a contract with you. If either party chooses to break said contract, said party is liable to damages."

"Are you thinking of suing me?"

"I certainly am not. What kind of wretch do you take me for? After drinking your Jack Daniel's. And your Pouille-Fuissé. And eating that superb trout. Lawyers sue. Clients get drunk together. No, I am only an unofficial advisor. Here to exchange a hosannah over your decision."

"You like it?"

"I like it."

This time she had caught him out. "And you want to make sure I'll stick to my guns."

Norman stared at her in open admiration. "What gave you that impression?"

"I take an intelligent interest in your intelligent interest in my career."

"You are a 'wunderkind.' That is exactly what I do."

"So we can have an amicable divorce. Not a sloppy one." It had dawned on her almost immediately that this was one of the reasons for Norman's presence at dinner.

"As amicable as possible."

"Otherwise I might sue you?" she said, smiling faintly.

"What are you two talking about?" asked Peter.

"Darling Peter. Norman does not want me to sue the Barnett Company."

"Why would you do that?"

Francie had been very well schooled by some very bright men. She owed her present insight to Monroe. "Breach of contract is the term, I believe."

"Ahhhh."

"Yes," said Norman. "As your astute wife has surmised, we are thinking of dispensing with her services as the La Petite Girl."

"Are you?" said Peter, struck. "Why would you want to stop using Francie? She's so perfect?"

"The Lady Bountiful bit, I think," said Francie.

Norman nodded. "Very unkosher."

"Yes, but it wasn't Francie."

"Deny, deny. Of course it wasn't. But it rubbed off," said Norman. "That's the trouble with good deeds. Anyone's good deeds. They always come back to haunt us. Every one."

"You can put your mind at rest, Norman. At the moment I have no intention of suing Barnett and Company."

"But there will be other moments. And how about your constitutional rights?"

Francie lifted her eyebrows quizzically.

"Like freedom of speech. The right to be a pitch girl for another food product. Let's say HONEY BUN—HONEY BREAD. Lawrence Buckman would not like that."

"I think you're right. He wouldn't like it."

"Therefore, as I understand from your spouse, you are looking for something superior to do." There was a serrated edge in his voice. "Let's get down to brass tacks, luvey. What do you want to do?"

"Could I do something worthwhile?"

"Oh, for God's sake! Like giving measles shots? Or blood?" Norman was exasperated. "Don't let's waste our time. Clearly, you don't need money. And every idiot who doesn't need money wants to do something worthwhile for humanity. That's why humanity is so fucked up. Only the fools work for them."

"Then you don't think the world is improving?"

"Nothing's improving. Especially the world. Don't be silly. You are far too smart. The instant anyone runs out of money they revert to type. They act just like the nobility did in the Hundred Years War. Nobles formed outlaw brigades and clumped around in rusty armor massacring peasants and each other, because the king's privy purse had run out of silver ducats to pay them. Now what can you do that isn't worthwhile? Put yourself on a platter. You're a roast pig with an apple in your mouth." He was studying her, his expression alert and inquisitive. "It's my idea to keep you under lock and key. Where I can see to it that you develop properly. It would be sinful to allow so much talent to bloom unseen."

"It's one way to make certain she doesn't sue Barnett." Peter grinned at him.

"And no tomfoolery with Larry baby, either," added Francie, laughing. "How are you proposing to buy me off, Mr. Hook?"

"I am proposing a career with the Barnett Company. I think you will find that the advertising business may be the place in the world that suits you best. Of course, the salary will be paltry."

"Like a ribbon clerk's?"

"Some ribbon clerks are unionized. Less. But I gather you are independently poor. So I've worked it out in my mind." He burst out laughing. "You'll go to work for Lillian Morris, née Moskowitz, our fashion director. As her assistant. The lady primarily responsible for the beginning and the end of your career on La Petite."

"The lady primarily responsible is myself."

"That's hair splitting." Norman's eyes had an angry twinkle. "Of course, she'll hate you." He paused cryptically. "But she'll give you the job."

Francie and Norman eyed each other. "Why, if she hates me?"

Norman looked at Francie more confidentially, a subtle malice in his expression. "You'll work for her, be her assistant, and tell me anything she says or does that concerns the art department. Or myself in particular."

"You want me to be your stoolie?"

"Darling, you show amazing perspicacity."

"Oh Norman! How low!" Francie laughed.

265

He continued softly. "You will lie for me and defend me on all counts. Against all charges, direct and indirect. She hates me too."

Francie mused. "She hates a lot of people. Are you afraid of her?"

"Some days I want her head on a silver sword," he answered. "Other days simple blackmail would do."

"And when does the job start?" Peter asked.

"If Francie does not hear from me tomorrow, she is to be in Lillian's office Monday at eleven o'clock. She's on the fifteenth floor. The executive floor. The bitch."

Peter was thoroughly amused. "Francie you're getting yourself into a life of office politics."

"All life is office politics," said Norman, standing up. Readying himself to leave, he turned to Francie. "It will make a man of you, my dear. You'll take it, won't you?"

"I'll take it."

"Good. You'll have a brave life."

Lillian adored Twenty One. She adored the noise, the crush, the people she recognized, the people who recognized her. She adored the Krindler brothers who owned it, and Lota Krindler, who had married it, and certainly Chuck Anderson who never failed to greet her warmly and give her one of the important, visible tables downstairs in what she described to herself as the Boy's Club Room. She adored going to her table, followed by some "important man" whom she hoped Chuck had had the sense to recognize. He usually did, but he had been known to flub, when the "important man" came from out of town and was not particularly flamboyant in his life-style.

Lillian never missed a week when she did not have dinner at least once at Twenty One. This week, since she and Lawrence Buckman had finally ripped at their seams, she decided to settle for Norman. Not that they were again buddies. She still longed to murder him. But he was showing signs of giving in on La Petite. And then too, he'd promised to bring along a door prize; and he had indeed.

The door prize's name was Christian Monet, a magnificently muscled photographer with the perfectly chiseled features of a Greek athlete. He had the kind of blond good looks

266

that, if there had been no California, they would have had to invent it for him. After her third martini Lillian leaned over and stroked Christian's forehead. Delicately her fingers outlined his eyebrows, and then slid down his nose. His skin beneath her touch felt smooth and fresh and she wanted him. He was so young and beautiful and strong with life.

"You know you have a very interesting face and body, Christian?" she murmured lightly into Christian's ear.

"But could you ever care for someone who is not your intellectual equal?" asked the young man archly.

"I'm afraid I could. There are no rules in affairs of the heart," sighed Lillian as she rose to go to the powder room. "Excuse me, Christian, nature calls. It's all those martinis and no food. And Norman pet, before I fall passionately in love with this man, we must talk seriously about our lack of shoulder-to-shoulder on the La Petite Girl."

Norman nodded amiably. "Lillian I will speak as seriously as you wish. But remember, no shin kicks or rabbit punches."

Lillian's eyes glittered dangerously. "You still don't know me, do you, darling? You overlooked a morals charge."

"What did I do to deserve such deathless devotion?" But by now she was out of earshot. Norman turned to Christian. "Now Crystal sweetie, she's all yours."

"I do my best," said the young man sulking.

"Yes, you do your best. And your reward will come long before heaven. We are doing a sun-and-surf Vitalis commercial I hear, and you are the beach boy par excellence."

"Yeah, but when do I get to use the camera? I want to be on the other side of the lens."

"Patience, patience. The sheer poetry of your natural beauty will carry you further than your lens."

"Not far enough. She looks like the Queen of the Cat People."

"She is. And she is yours for tonight. We'll order her another martini—four really makes her mischievous. Then I will go to the men's room and out the front door, leaving the two of you to find each other."

"Cash please."

"When do you not think of money?"

"Never."

"All right." Norman sighed, taking three hundred dollar bills out of his wallet. "Here's three. In case you have to do an encore. I don't want you to stint our little flower."

"I'm a steal at five hundred. Make it five."

"Where's your fun-loving spirit?" He took another two hundred dollars from his wallet. "Now that is all. Blow out your candles, Crystal. And so good-bye."

16

Since Lillian Morris's office was located in a thoroughly modern building, along a corridor of offices furnished in a completely modern manner, entering her office gave one something of a time shock. One stepped into another world. None of the furnishings except the telephone and the electricity suggested the twentieth century. No fluorescent lighting. Only two elegant Chinese lamps and a desk lamp softly illuminated the room. A Sheraton-styled sofa stood against the far wall, strewn with small swatches of fabric. The floor, carpeted in a muted, dark brown, was a grudging concession to the cost of large, authentic, antique Orientals; but discreetly covering the carpeting, as though it were an eye sore, was a medium-sized, antique Bokhara rug.

Lillian was seated stiff-backed in a copy of a Louis XV armchair behind an Empire mahogany and ormolu desk; firmly clear of the usual functional desk accessories, and displaying instead snuff boxes, paper weights, a Chinese mineral tree, objects de vertu and a nineteenth-century English woman's work box, open and stuffed with lipsticks and jewelry. A Rococo bread basket worked with a coat of arms—Francie wondered if Lillian claimed they belonged to her family—was piled high with interoffice memos. The disharmonies of the furnishings would have given Peter a headache.

Over the desk hung a romantic oil painting of a small girl in a large pale blue plumed hat, done in the style of Mary Cassatt. It was not a very good copy.

Following Francie's gaze, Lillian smiled. "Do you like it?"

Francie thought about her answer. Tell the truth. Or lie. She decided on a half-lie. "It's a very good copy."

Lillian studied Francie more carefully. "It is a copy. Most of the philistines who come into this office think it's the real thing. Can you imagine—an authentic Mary Cassatt?" She shook her head. "I'm a Sunday painter."

"You're talented," Francie said smoothly, feeling that insincerities were the order of the day. Seated across the desk from Lillian, Francie thought that the woman looked like an intelligent, black-haired snake poised to strike. An insolent snake. With poisonous fangs.

"You're Franciejean Devlin?"

"Yes."

"I thought your name was Franciejean Stewart."

"Devlin is my married name."

Seated as she was behind her Empire mahogany desk, Lillian might have been a hostess in conversation over tea with a guest, rather than the twentieth-century career-driven workhorse she was and always had been. "I have a note on my desk from Greta, my secretary, that tells me Norman Hook called from Chicago at nine. He knows, of course, that I am never in before ten. The note says that Franciejean Devlin would be here at eleven to take the job."

"Yes."

"What job?"

"Mr. Hook told me you'd work it out." Francie said this with a guileless confidence in her voice that only deepened Lillian's suspicions.

"He did, did he?" Lillian's tone changed. "Do you iron blouses well? Or make watercress sandwiches? What is your specialty?"

"I can type and take shorthand. I learn quickly."

"I don't mean to sound uncharitable," said the hostess, "but I do not need a typist. Or a stenographer. Now, if you can lay kitchen tiles? Decent workmen are at a premium. Or know anything about housekeeping—cleaning silver, crystal, mop work, serving dinner? My housekeeper just went home to France. Well, then, I believe I do have a job for you."

Francie ignored the sarcasm. "I'm sorry. I don't have a knack with either tiles or mops. So I don't know what Mr.

Hook had in mind. He may have thought you were looking for a new assistant. I think he mentioned that."

"Did he indeed? Well, I have a call in to Norman at this moment. He is in a meeting, but I want to ask him exactly what is going on. I am neither unworldly nor good-natured, and I do not like practical jokes. You are the La Petite Girl. Am I to understand you've agreed to become a private citizen?"

"Yes. Didn't you know?"

Lillian shook her head. "Like the wife in the soap operas, I seem to be the last to know." At that moment Greta tapped on the door to tell Lillian to pick up on 5056. It was Mr. Hook calling from Chicago.

"Would you mind sitting outside for a moment?" Lillian nodded to Francie.

"Of course." Francie rose and slipped out as Greta closed the door behind her.

When Francie left the office, Lillian sat still, rigid with rage, thinking of Norman. Norman, the senior art director, head of the art department of the Barnett Company. Norman the rat, scab, louse! What had he gotten her into? Art Director! Art! Ha! She would like to slice off his ear. Both ears! Then she prepared her voice to show just the right amount of edge. "Norman, darling. I can't let you out of my sight. You are a seething caldron of ideas. Imagine, finding me a new assistant."

"Lillian pet, your teeth are showing. What is the matter? This was your idea, not mine. I thought you'd be thrilled."

"My idea? Norman what are you talking about?"

"Your idea, dear heart. You know yourself I was hardly enthusiastic about dumping this Franciejean. Personally I think she is fabulous. As far as I was concerned, I'd rather gamble on the whole thing blowing over than risk a law suit from her. And an explosion from the beloved chairman, Lawrence Buckman. Let me remind you, little flower, Lawrence Buckman is sweet on that little chit."

Lillian stared at the telephone receiver. It was a Jesuitical needle, done so deftly she could almost disregard it. But not quite. The feeling of shame, like hives, spread over her body. She felt that he had somehow accused her of being old and unlovable. But it wasn't true. She was smart. She was stylish. She was sexual. But yet, she could not hold a man.

Some indefinable superiority, some unspoken intolerance eventually put them off. A wave of self-pity swept over Lillian. She wondered how often Lawrence saw Franciejean. "All right. All that is true." Her voice was flat. "But I do not believe I ever suggested that I would hire her."

"My pal, you did indeed. And I must say you were brilliant. Brilliant. On Wednesday night in the pub room of Twenty One you told me that you would offer her a job as your assistant, if she would give up the La Petite assignment."

"I don't remember saying anything like that."

"You said it." This was slippery ice. "I must say I did think it an original ploy. Original. But I also admit I was dubious. It was Christian who convinced me. He agreed with you completely."

"This is crazy."

"That's precisely what I thought. I didn't see why she would even consider the job. Six thousand a year is hardly $25,000. And that's only one campaign. It's just the beginning of what she can make this year as a model. And after that, the sky's the limit. All six figures of it. But you were stubborn. Persistent. You laid out the logic—A.B.C. You said that I should point out to her that fashion is a far bigger field than modeling. That she must realize that a model's career is a short one. Five years at best. A modeling career is about as long as that of a child star. Who has heard of Shirley Temple since *The Good Ship Lollipop?* While fashion girls go on forever. Witness youself. You were offering her the opportunity of a lifetime."

"I don't remember a word of this conversation."

"Well, we had it. I said I didn't think this Franciejean had a brain in her head. And she wouldn't have the sense to make plans for the future. You know how stupid models are. But you begged me to try because I knew her husband Peter. And Christian agreed with you. He thought you were being splendidly generous."

"Christian heard this blather?" Her head felt fuzzy.

"Every word. He sided with you one hundred percent. I assume he remembers the conversation vividly. In fact he thought it was a stroke of a genius on your part. Pure genius. So I said I'd give it the old college try. And I did. Well by God, she's not so stupid. She adores you."

"She's a les?"

272

"No, no. Not like Hortense. She admires you. The way she would a personage. Lady Astor, for instance. She'd rather work for you and make six thousand a year than do modeling and make fifty thousand."

"She's bananas."

"It does make one wonder about her I.Q., at that." Norman seemed to consider this deeply. "I put it down to your charisma. Lillian, you do have charisma."

"Well, I am chairman of Fashion Group."

"That's what I mean—charisma."

"Oh God, Norman! Shut up! I don't believe any of this bullshit! It's too insane."

"Lillian, the world is insane."

"None of this ever happened. You are lying to me, Norman. You always lie to me."

"I am not lying. If you don't believe me, ask Christian. He'll remember your exact words. He suffers from total recall. Of course, if you don't really remember, it's my suggestion to you that you go on the wagon. Now. Today. At lunch. You know what blackouts are. You know your mother's history. That's what the agency really needs, an alcoholic Miss Moscowitz."

"Shut up, Norman! Shut up!" She would have liked to step on him like some ugly crawling bug.

"Listen my little black-haired Brünnhilde, who is it who tells you when the gray in your roots show? I do. And I do not want to see you in ten years with holes in your shoes, totally gray, wrinkles in your cheeks because you cannot afford a decent face job, sprawled in an empty doorway with a bottle of Muscatel lying beside you as you snore. It would break my heart."

Other than being afraid, Lillian felt she was the butt of some comic absurdity that was out of her control. Norman was making a fool of her, and she did not know how to stop him. She brooded for an instant, then recklessly gave in. "What else did I say in my Utopian mood?"

Norman had won. "Well, your point was that you were doing it for the good of the Barnett Company. It would keep the wench off the streets and not working for another food company. We won't get a peep out of Buckman either. After all, the girl has the right of free choice of work. And she won't be selling any other product. She'll still be exclusively

Buckman's. At least where work is concerned. Actually you can put her on the La Petite account. And in about a year, you fire her. They'll be finished by then. You can stand her for a year, darling. And I'm sure Abe will show his gratitude with a sizable bonus."

"He agrees with me?"

"Let us say, he follows your thinking."

"A raise is what I want. Regular income."

"A raise and a bonus."

"Did the old bastard say so?"

"Lillian, darling, we all respect your intuitive knowledge of Abe. You know him better than I do. You know how generous he is. But if you like, I shall do what I can to help it along. A suggestion here. A small envelope there. I'm your best friend, darling."

After she hung up it took several moments for Lillian to collect her thoughts. She sat and glared at the telephone, wondering if she was turning into an alcoholic. Or if that S.O.B. Norman was terrorizing her for his own vile, sly reasons. She knew what gay boys could be like. She'd worked with them long enough. She knew what a devil Norman could be. Still he was absolutely right about the raise. And the bonus. Abe owed it to her. And once she made it clear to him that he had a moral obligation. Yes, a moral obligation. She might as well make some money on the blond bitch. The fight she and Larry had over Francie's continuing as the La Petite Girl almost made headlines. It was a lulu— even by Lillian's high standards. Buckman would have pulled the account out of Barnett if that letter hadn't come from the mayor's office, suggesting that New York could do without that kind of publicity stunt. That was a close one. But it was all so nutsy. Imagine Lawrence Buckman, the wheeler dealer— *Fortune* called him "Buckman the Buccaneer"—acting like an ass over a model. A dumb fool model. Who shacked up with TV commercial producers? Actors. Grips. Where were his brains? Everybody knew what models were—faces for make-up, bodies on which you hung clothes, with voices you usually had to lip sync. Of course, to give the devil her due, this one was beautiful. And could speak general American English. But still a model. She wasn't even an actress. She might as well have been an airline stewardess. God, what made people tick? Who ever knew? Did God? Probably not. She doubted if Francie knew what a big fish she'd hooked. Lillian had watched her at that landmark lunch with Larry, and Francie had not batted an eyelash. She did not give an inch. Not even her telephone number on a napkin. Maybe that's what turned him on so—the challenge. He'd certainly gotten the number later. Idiot! She buzzed Greta and told her to send Francie into her office.

"Can you type?" Lillian asked when Francie seated herself opposite her desk.

"Yes."

"Hunt and peck?"

Francie decided again on a half-lie. "Something like that. Maybe a little better."

Lillian sighed. "I suppose one can't have everything. Beauty and typing skills. Do you know what *Women's Wear* is?"

"The newspaper?"

"Fancy that! You can read. Well, I am giving a speech at the Coty Award dinner honoring Rudi Gernreich. It was mentioned in *Women's Wear,* and I would like you to transcribe the speech from my notes." She fumbled around her desk and came up with notes, some poorly typed, some handwritten. She handed the sheets of paper to Francie. "Try to have it by tomorrow. I'd like a chance to look over a clean copy and make necessary changes. Greta can type the final." The two women stared at each other, assessing each other's strengths. Lillian wondered what Francie knew that she didn't, and loathed her for being alive. Francie felt something akin to gratitude for the fact of the job. But no more. Neither of them referred to the salary, and Francie, accepting the sheaf of dog-eared papers, paused only to ask where she would work.

"Tell Greta to find you an office on the copy department floor. They always have empty offices—if it isn't the turnover, it's vacation time." Francie nodded, and Lillian watched her briefly as she walked from the office. She noted the line of her dress. It looked like a Rentner. Well, she'd have less spending money working for Barnett.

She could, of course, have had Greta type the speech. Or given it to the typing pool. But she gave it to Francie in the fervent hope that it would keep her at the typewriter until

3:00 A.M. Perhaps, when the building was quiet and empty, the girl would be raped and murdered by one of the cleaning men. Lillian believed in positive thinking.

In the office Greta found for her, Francie went to work immediately. She quickly saw that her first task was to make sense out of the hodgepodge of pages that comprised Lillian's speech, and to translate the illegible passages. Secondly, she had to organize them properly in their place in the speech. Finally, she decided that she ought to type slowly until she discovered if Greta was the watchdog type who'd make a practice of dropping in to see how she was doing. Greta wasn't. Francie never saw her again that day. So by 4:30 she decided, with all the notes sorted, to shift to her natural tempo of 80 words a minute. As a result, she was out of the building by 6:00, home by 6:30, dressed for a dinner party at 7:30. She left the speech neatly typed and stapled on Lillian's desk with seven carefully selected misspellings.

The next day Francie showed up in a simple little Balenciaga suit that took Lillian's breath away. With the speech on her desk and the suit on Francie's back. Lillian grew quite uncomfortable about the kind of bird she had let Norman flummox her into hiring. For $6,000 a year. "I hope you didn't stay too late typing the speech?" She was angry at herself, at Norman, at Francie.

"I didn't mind," said Francie. "I love the job. And I like to work late. It makes me feel I'm accomplishing something."

Lillian chewed on this high ideal and it soured her stomach. It came too close to home. She was an obsessional worker herself, and she often worked at home until dawn. Dr. Nathan, her psychoanalyst at forty-five dollars a visit, three times a week, explained to her that her work-drive was a reaction-formation against Electra longings. She wondered if Francie too suffered an Electra reaction. But typing was sewage work. How could you be incestuous about a Smith-Corona?

Lillian than decided that rather than jam up the typing pool as she usually did, she would give Francie the Brown Shoe Company hundred page fashion report to transcribe, composed in her inimitable combination of typing with hand-scrawled inserts. A week later, when the report was finished, Lillian told Francie she would feed her, as she finished them, the fashion reports for all the agency clients who required them. These reports concerned current and coming trends in colors, textures, skirts, hems, waists, and bodice lines. It also concerned hairstyles and cosmetics.

Francie quickly saw the use these reports had for products like Brown Shoe, Max Factor, Modess, Ban. But why Ford? And then she realized, as she read, that cars come in colors and designs, that women have preferences formed by fashion, and that women vote in the car-buying decision. Francie learned about business, advertising, and Lillian's surprising acuity from these reports. Lillian worked like a stevedore; each report emphasized those aspects of fashion relating to the particular client, plus an evaluation of what the competition was or wasn't doing about the new trends. Lillian knew her business.

Each day that Francie made her way to her cubicle, the men in copy reacted as though they'd received a brain shock. Her swinging blond hair, her profile, awoke frail lost dreams. One had his shoes shined for the first time in months. Another took to wearing a fresh shirt daily. All kinds of intimacies were imagined. Desire was munched in the corridors like peanuts. They would ask Francie for lunch. And as they took to working later, they would ask her to dinner. The office was a jungle of thorny, delightful, guilty impulses.

Even Martha asked her how she got her hair that color. And Francie repaid Martha's original welcome to the agency by suggesting a Clairol mix that she guessed would turn Martha's hair orange. It did. One morning Martha burst into Francie's office with orange hair and fury. Instantly she and Francie were shouting at each other like fishmongers, their eyes full of tears. Afterward, a chastened Francie—the orange was worse than she'd expected—went home with Martha to expertly dye her hair a glowing nut brown. She and Martha were now almost friends.

But Martha aside, Francie was the undisputed pet of the department. What the male writers gave her was more than blatant admiration—it was worship; and since she wanted to know about the advertising business, and after a few conversations could not imagine a better source than talkative, paranoid, insecure copywriters, she told Peter that for a while she might not be home regularly for dinner. She would have dinner with co-workers and do her typing afterward.

Peter quite understood. He was already familiar with her capacity for subtle calculation, observing again the healthy cunning of the animal raised in scarcity. But since their marriage he had grown gradually aware of sudden, inexplicable silences, of mood swings between black depression and exhilarating pleasure in just being alive. Perhaps it was her longing to escape the depressions that brought on the explosion of animal high spirits. Whatever it was, Peter discreetly refrained from probing. When they first married, he realized that her temperament might be unstable. But he didn't care; he wanted to look after her. Now he wondered whether someone with her temperament would have the will to commit herself fully to the necessary hard work, inconvenience, stress—to everything required to succeed.

One evening, Norman telephoned, on his semiregular checkup, asking for a report on Lillian's activities and the state of campaigns in the New York creative department. Francie was precise, accurate, unemphatic. Listening to her, it fascinated Peter to perceive again the hard-headed, businesslike quality of her mind that so contradicted the volatility of her emotions.

When she hung up, his look confused her. "Why are you smiling at me, Peter? Did I say something dumb? Or funny?"

"No, darling. You said everything right. I was admiring your sound business judgment. It's amazing how much you do see. And hear. And interpret. Who makes the decisions. Who ducks. Who's an enemy and why. Who might be a friend. Who goofs off and is talented. Who works hard and is a dud. Who's after whose hide. You have a natural instinct for the game. It's called a business sense."

She thought this over. "So do you."

"In my field, yes. But it took me years to develop. You were born with it."

She shook her head. "No. If you're an orphan you learn fast. Or they may find you someday behind the garage. In splinters."

She said this matter-of-factly. But it prompted Peter to go to her and clasp her hands. She gave him a wry smile, putting her head on his shoulder. "Forgive me, I don't usually do that."

"Do what?"

"Put on 'poor little match girl' airs. Feel sorry for myself." She put her head on his shoulder. "But you're such a pushover."

"I'm glad," he said, stroking her hair.

"So am I," she said. "So am I."

Francie was completely even-handed in her interest in her copy department admirers, giving the same wrapt attention to one and all. At lunch and dinner or coffee breaks she played no favorites; her manners with each were equally courteous, equally shyly seductive yet reticent; meanwhile prompting them, probing, drawing each out in turn on his thoughts on the agency business. In this way she gained a great deal of valuable knowledge on the workings of the advertising business. She quickly digested the mechanics: like billings, media costs, new business presentation costs, servicing costs. Why radio was right for one product, TV for another, print for still another. Her capacity for learning was formidable. On weekends she read advertising books and marketing reports lent her by the copy chief, Hibbard Murray. She called him "Hibbard," not "Mr. Murray"; and when he permitted himself to look up from his desk and glance at her, he stared with a startled, hopeless longing.

Francie had awakened every morning since her marriage to Peter with a goal: not to think of Jamison. She was like an alcoholic who knew she must not take one drink or she would be off on a downhill slide. She took a bleak satisfaction in the pain of the abstinence, because at least the pain connected her to him. They had not seen each other alone since her marriage. It was too dangerous for both of them. But one Wednesday in April, Jamie telephoned Francie as she was preparing to leave the office early and meet Peter at a cocktail party. Jamie told her he was leaving for an indefinite period; and within the month, Patrick, Agnas and Angelique would follow him to Brussels. He'd called to say good-bye.

There were devils inside Francie as she listened. She knew she should say good-bye then and there. But it was useless. She could not help herself, her need was too great. To see him anywhere, on the street, at the airport, alone or with others. She had no choice.

"Well, well," she said, forcing a lightness into her tone.

"You're leaving Doggy Dew Canyon. Where are you now?"

"At home. We're leaving for Idlewild in about fifteen minutes."

"Easy come, easy go. Well, darling, you brought it on yourself. It's your superb good manners. I have never stood on ceremony. I frequently invite myself. You do recall our history? So I'll meet you at the house. In a jiffy. The idea of your going to the airport without me is absurd."

"Francie, I have often gone to airports without you. I am quite capable."

"Darling, who knows that better than I?"

"You do not have to disrupt your evening to come along."

"Of course I do not have to. I want to. I'll be at your place in five, maybe ten minutes."

"Don't you have any evening plans?" He seemed to be laughing.

"Nothing that I can't telephone and change if I have a terrible head-splitting toothache. Are you laughing at me?"

"At myself."

"You knew this would happen?"

"Of course."

When Francie hung up the telephone, she realized it had been almost one year since her life with Jamie had ended, and that nothing had happened to her since. Her experience of life had gone from primary colors to pastel, and people moved from close-ups to long shots. She had not stopped to ask herself what she felt, because she felt very little.

Without Jamie, there was always an incompleteness at the core of her life; and sometimes she felt herself lost in a bewildering flood of inexplicable events and meaningless people. Beyond the pressure and release of her sexual hungers, or the sudden senseless fear that Momma would find her, Francie's life seemed to have stopped. I have died, she would think to herself.

No, you haven't, her body would answer with the confident healthiness of her twenty-five years. When she thought of her new job, the thought seemed distant and unimportant. Yet it astonished her that she thought about it at all; and she acknowledged that it meant more to her than she realized.

They rode to Idlewild with Patrick behind the wheel. Francie sat straight and still as if all her muscles were drawn against pain, while, with her eyes half-closed, she felt the warmth of his fingers interlaced with hers. But there was little they could talk about—there were so many subjects she felt she must not raise. It was one of the reasons they never saw each other alone. And it was proof of her anxiety that in searching for a neutral topic she selected the most sensitive. "You were so delighted to be working for Kennedy. Why are you going to Brussels now?"

Jamison visibly winced at the question. Yet it gave him something to share with her without feeling placed in an untenable position. In her effort to be tactful, she had touched that fact in his life which was most disquieting. She was asking, he understood, only to know the barest facts; for that matter, only to hear him say anything. He could have lied; he could have given a makeshift reason; he could say he was on a government mission, a confidential study. He could say anything at all. But there was something in her face, so absolute in its trust, that made lying awkward. "I'm going Francie," he said, "because I've been a failure in Washington."

"You a failure?" She had to swallow the intensity of her astonishment. "That's impossible. How could you be a failure?"

"You mean I'm so rich? Is that it?"

"Yes—rich. But that's not it. I'm smarter now." She dismissed his idea almost with disdain. "Rich men can fail when they want more than money. But they're not you." She meant it. She'd seen exactly what he'd feared; but she had saved his self-respect, as at another time, by not knowing it was menaced. "It's not that you're rich, it's that you're you. You can't fail."

"Thank you, dear, for your confidence. I hope I prove out."

"Whatever happened?"

He had hoped they could drop the subject, but she wouldn't. And perhaps not to profit by her trust would, in the end, deprive them both of a needed resource. After a moment he found what he wanted to say. "You know, dear, I inherited a major position on the Street. And maybe I thought there would be a carry-over. Maybe it isn't all Kennedy. Maybe I

281

expected too much. But whatever it was, I felt that what I believed and what I stood for wasn't being taken very seriously and wasn't being listened to."

"Our touch football playboy wouldn't listen to you? You know more than anybody. More than he does—about everything!"

He had clumsily brought it on himself, and now she was defending him. "Maybe I do. Maybe I don't. It is true that Jack is not his father's son. That, of course, cuts both ways. I'd hate to see the old man as President even though he helped create the SEC after profiting magnificently from the lack of just such a commission." He stopped short for a moment, then spoke with impatience. "Jack is not interested nor does he understand economic planning. And that's what's going to have to be done in the future to avoid what I see coming—a runaway stock market boom. And then bust. And a very nasty inflation." The anger in his voice was reflected in Francie's face. "I'm sorry. I'm an awful bore on this subject. It's my pet hobbyhorse. And Jack does disturb me. His major interest seems to be power. For power's sake."

"And women! How can he find time for economics? That takes work. I've tried reading about it—it's tough." Her voice dropped. "You know all he thinks about is girls. Every hairdresser in New York has a client on his list. I know two sisters, actresses. He invited them to Washington. Dinner à trois. He didn't even miss me." She started to giggle, but the look on Jamie's face made her realize her mistake.

"You too?"

She cast about in a sudden fright for a way of making reparations. "I'm sorry, darling. That was my foot in my mouth. But you know he is a terrible chaser. And I have a reporter friend who wanted to set it up."

"Did you go?"

"Oh, for Christ's sake, no! It was too crazy! It's like being part of a circus act. Anyway he's not my type. And he is the President," Francie wound up with a kind of nervous inconsequence. "Furthermore, suppose I'd bumped into you."

"He is the President. And that is the problem." The image she'd evoked in him loomed still larger. "He's missed conferences, briefings, even cabinet meetings for a girl." He had a long pause, and they might have been thinking of the

282

same thing. "You were the only woman who ever came between me and my work. And I am not the President."

"I love you." She smiled, her eyes misting over. "Anyway, suppose he was off screwing a girl when the hot line rang. And they couldn't find him. Imagine being responsible for the explosion of the world."

Her speaking as she did was an extravagant and kind humor, and he turned from the pain within himself to give her as straight an answer as he could. "Well, there was all that—the lack of economic thinking, the girls. And I suppose for me the final break came when he added the 20,000 'advisors' in Vietnam."

"What is Vietnam?"

"It's a place, darling, in Southeast Asia, that the Chinese tried for two thousand years to conquer and couldn't. And the French, who were the most vicious of all the colonial governments, tried to rule and couldn't. And now we, the Boy Scouts of the Western World, just might be going to take a crack at it. And we'll be slaughtered."

"You can't stop them?"

"I have no power."

"I understand. You're worried about that," she said flatly.

"I am worried."

"You think you'll be too old before you can get in there and be counted?"

She'd recognized so much from his partial confession that there was no point in evading. "Yes. That's it. I am forty-three. For what I want to do and be, it's now or never."

"But that's not true. You'll never be too old. You're not that kind of man."

"Well, we'll see. Anyway, that's why I'm going abroad. I have to build my own public position so that if I come back to Washington, I'll come back with a public reputation. Not a private one. A nice spot opened up at the EEC and I'm taking it. It's not number one, but it's high enough up that I can use it as a beginning." Their eyes met and he saw with a sober acuteness how she never judged him. She had come as far as she dared in order to show her complete acceptance, her love. "Thank you, Francie, for listening to me."

"Thank you my love, for telling me."

At the airport Jamie put his arm around her shoulders knowing what she felt, but unable to find words for his own feelings, so ambiguous and so absolute. He realized quite clearly that though he still loved her, he could resign himself, if necessary, to never seeing her again. This knowledge, defined so sharply in his own mind, gave him an advantage over her. For she was a blur of ambivalence, choking on feelings of rejection, mingled with passionate yearnings and self-abasement.

"I guess this is it then," she said.

"Whatever 'it' is. At any rate you do look splendid."

"I weather well. There are no broken bones. Though naturally I've thought of suicide."

"Naturally."

"But my vanity prevents it. I have such a marvelous profile. And even a good job."

"Exactly. An embarrassment of riches." He knew she had her own idea of herself to deal with now, and it was this private recognition that troubled and tied her. He wanted to help her, but that was no longer possible.

Sensing his concern, Francie tried directly to salve his anxiety. "Don't worry a bit about me. I've already planned our relationship for years to come."

"Very sensible. We'll grow old and mellow together."

"Something like that." She pressed her cheek against his shoulder. "I've more plans than you think, now that I have this new job." She felt that unless she was careful now she would lose him forever. "I won't flap around like a loose sail. I am going to have a real career. Not just a face in an ad for smiles. You watch and you'll see my name in lights. On memo pads anyway."

Then it was time to board the plane. He turned and waved to her from the top of the steps; and she waved back, tears he could not see now filling her eyes. The plane taxied down the runway; soon it was a spot in the sky that Francie could barely make out. Francie and Jamison were not to see each other again for several years.

That evening Francie returned home very late after hours spent wandering the city; not because she wanted to, but because she had nowhere else to go. Nowhere else where she belonged. And she had to belong somewhere. That was an absolute necessity. When she opened the door of the dimly lit apartment, she assumed that Peter was out. She went to her own bedroom, and stood at the window, gazing blindly out at the starry night sky and the lights of the city. But she saw nothing. What she was seeing was beyond the skyscrapers of the city, beyond the East River, the low factory buildings and five-story apartment houses of Queens; beyond Queens and Nassau, beyond Northern State Parkway—where was the place, what would the map say? Was it Quogue or Southampton or East where the wind moved almost without sound among leaves, and rustling fingers of sun reached tentatively through trees. . . . She saw a land she had wandered with him where a rabbit dashed out of the woods, chased by a barking dog, chased by a yelling boy waving a butterfly net. And the dog and the boy danced around them and vanished into the woods again. . . . And she saw how they both laughed and put their arms around each other and kissed. Then he gave her a child asleep on a leaf. . . . Will I ever find that road again? . . . "I never pass a road but that the whole world calls to me." Does the rabbit still live? Does the dog? Does the boy? Is the child still asleep? Can love restore ghosts? She was staring, straining, seeing the barns and the potato fields and the gray shingled houses and "the shore beating its slow code, and low lighted towns seeming to tell me to stay." Here is a map of the area. This line runs along Montauk 27A, that blue patch to the right is the Atlantic and the arrow is the Montauk lighthouse. And beyond that is the ocean, the great ocean and the wide sky where a plane is flying eastward. . . . She could almost see it.

She was shaking with fever, and she thought, Dear God, how can I sleep tonight? There should be a lock to put on my brain.

When she turned at the sound of a footstep, she saw Peter standing silently behind her, looking concerned. "Are you all right, Francie?"

"I was thinking of quitting my job."

"Why?" Peter stared at her puzzled. "Has Lillian become too much?"

Yes—why? Why, she asked herself, and the answer was not acceptable. The answer was she was tied to Jamie, as he

285

was not tied to her. She was letting her grief change the course of her life. Much to her dismay she could feel hot tears in her eyes.

"It's just a joke, Peter. A form of the bends."

He fell silent. Then he said, "You saw Jamie off tonight?"

"Maria gave you the message?"

"Yes." He was searching for some way to reassure her. "Did you have any dinner?"

"Do you mind?"

"Your seeing Jamie?" Just for an instant his courage left him as he thought of the danger of minding. "Of course not."

She smiled at him under wet lashes. "You're so good. You never ask of me more than I can do."

"Nor do you of me," he said in a low even voice. "We are neither of us the masters of our fate. So we make the necessary concessions."

"I know—you've taught me that." She leaned toward him and put her hands on his shoulders. Her just touching him made everything more simple, and he took her in his arms and kissed her. She felt a spasm of protest—and desire, giving him back his kiss in full. She must go where she was invited or she would always be alone.

They lay in bed eye to eye, their naked bodies hardly touching. Francie thought of a long time ago, of the first boy she'd been to bed with, of the fiftieth, of Jamison—all those men. All those beds. Suppose she had lived her life differently. But could she? Do we own our own bodies? Make our own destinies? She closed her eyes and let her trembling fingers move slowly over Peter's body, shutting out the past.

"It's been a long time."

She smiled gently. "You have your amusements."

"I do. So do you. But still . . ." He felt his body stirring with pleasure as her tongue licked and caressed him with the delicacy of a cat. He discovered that he was angry at her, at her teasing; and it fueled his passion. "Let's do it this way for a change." His knees, his thighs drove her legs apart.

She gave him a dazed, lustful look. "That's so well bred," she murmured, but there was no resistance in her. Now he was like some stranger who had fallen upon her and was forcing something into her. She was furious; but with her fury, her passion rose; and though she wanted to tear at him, she could only gasp for air. Then he took her by the shoulders and turned her over on her stomach and whispered an obscenity into her ear.

"That's dreadful," she said, pretending shock; but the crazy mix of obscenities and caresses confused and disoriented her. At first she struggled like a fish on land, but soon she forgot her objections and sank deeper into the moment. She hoped she would be tight enough for him. She then gave up thinking, her face growing quiet, chloroformed by his love-making.

Later she woke with a start and heard the regular breathing of someone beside her. She turned and stared at the naked man lying with his back to her. Who was he? What was she doing in bed with him? He was making noises in his sleep. Talking. She wanted to shake him and say, "Wake up! Who are you? Get out!" But she was afraid to touch the man. She thought she would like to kill him—but with what? How? Her body felt stiff and aching and tense with fear. She was bathed in sweat. She had to get away. Run. Then the man turned over on his side, and she saw his face. It was Peter, dear Peter. Her terror started to ebb.

Peter wouldn't hurt her. He never had. He was her anchor of safety in a world that buzzed and swirled with fear. She wanted to ask his forgiveness for her murderous intentions. She could remember now how they had made love. But the memory seemed to belong to another woman. Who? Still, a special danger for her had passed. Her breathing became slower. She drifted off to sleep again.

20

One by one Francie would complete the typing of a fashion report for this or that client and turn it in to Lillian. After Lillian had made the few sparse corrections, she would call Francie in; and fixing her with glittering, suspicious eyes, hand her another report to type. Francie always accepted the papers with a neutral smile that revealed neither pleasure nor distaste.

"Aren't you bored sick typing these things?" Lillian finally asked Francie when she'd finished the Ban report.

"No. I learn about advertising and business from them."

This answer caused a tightness in Lillian's chest. The idea that Francie might profit from Lillian's perspiring labors was enough to make Lillian vomit. Lillian said to herself that she was basically a good person, and she did not deserve to be saddled with a succubus like this girl. Her paranoid spite clearly saw Francie as a threat to herself. How or when or why she did not know, but the threat was there. As Francie left, Lillian stared after her with grieved eyes, wondering what she could possibly do with her that would not aid in the hateful girl's success. The result was that while typing the Brown Shoe report, Francie was called to the fifteenth floor and told the typing would be rerouted to the typing pool. Francie was now to do research for Lillian in the fashion market. Plus being her Girl Friday.

Actually it was dog work on Seventh Avenue that she did, picking up fabric samples and color swatches for Lillian's fall fashion presentation to the Brown Shoe Company. Secretly, Lillian prayed that a manufacturer would get the "hots" for the girl and offer her a job with a huge salary. Out of the goodness of his heart—ha! Francie might just be dumb enough to take the job. Please the Lord. And since Seventh Avenue and Madison Avenue were two separate continents, Lillian might never see Franciejean Devlin again.

Aside from their value as soothing daydreams, Lillian did not place much hope in her fantasies. She no longer subscribed to her theory of Francie's stupidity. Though the girl seemed unaware of any potential rivalry between them, Lillian had an almost tangible apprehension that another day would come. And she wasn't sure she'd be the victor.

So it was that Francie came to do the dirty work of the fashion office of the Barnett Company. She called model agencies and sifted through composites but never sat in to vote on final choices. She fetched and carried and searched and sweated and dug for props, for print shots and TV filmings till she found exactly the Basset hound or picnic basket or candlestick or cape or cage that Lillian wanted for shootings that Francie never attended. She made lists of locations and alternatives, with weather reports and flight reservations for filmings she never saw.

Anyone else who looked like Francie, had Francie's private income, and lived Francie's private life would have quit. Lillian wanted her to quit. Francie knew this and it increased her stubbornness. Her life with Jamie and now with Peter had made her neither soft nor self-indulgent. She kept her mouth shut and her eyes open and followed the tack Norman had set for her. She kept him informed weekly of the art department storms.

And storms there were. For the flare-up and fury of art directors when Lillian butted in on locations, on model selections, even on type faces, were a weekly entertainment. But the A.D.'s suffered a handicap. They were afraid of Lillian. No one really believed that Abe would side with her against a better idea from an art director. There was no historical evidence this had ever happened. Yet it was tacitly understood that long ago and far away she and Abe had had a "thing." And people went to shameful extremes to prove their loyalty to Lillian, while discreetly trying to feed her to the fishes. The worst was that Lillian had good ideas as well as bad. But since she could not distinguish between them; since she could argue longer and louder than anyone at

Barnett; since she telephoned Abe promptly when anyone opposed a pet project, she was roundly mistrusted, even hated, by art directors. She might attack at any moment from an unexpected direction. The best one could do was be prepared. Which was exactly what Norman was doing.

Francie had been working at Barnett for almost two years, leading a near schizophrenic life. In the evening at art openings, previews, opera, theater, dinner parties, charity balls, auctions, she met and mingled with the multimillionaire major stockholders, or the descendants of founding fathers of the industries which comprised the life blood of the advertising business. During the day, she was Lillian's fashion assistant slavey. When Lillian sneezed, Francie handed her a Kleenex.

One evening, exhausted after two weeks of nonstop activity, Francie collapsed into bed at 9:00 P.M., only to be awakened at 3:00 A.M. by the telephone ringing. In her sleep Francie grimaced, dreaming she had turned off the telephone. Whenever possible, she tried to be in bed and asleep by 9:00 to make up for the nights when she had better things to do with her time than sleep.

For it had become her practice, whether she had a solid eight hours sleep or only three behind her, to be in the agency at 8:15. Lillian arrived at 10:00, while the rest of the agency straggled in around 9:30. So at 8:15 the corridors were sunlit and silent, and Francie could drift through the copy department, reading the hottest copy still in the typewriter or strewn on the desk. There was Shelly's yahoo Kellogg's Bran ad nailed to his wall board. It had won the Barnett prize for Most Potent Ad of the Month. It was a drawing of Queen Elizabeth in full, ball dress seated on a toilet holding a scepter. The headline read: "Hi there, I'm Queen Elizabeth, and Kellogg's Bran Flakes keeps me regular. I use it. Winnie uses it. Phillip uses it." Francie giggled. It was a good thing the Kellogg people never saw it or Abe would have some hard explaining to do. Such lack of respect—my, my.

Then there was Martha's travel copy for St. Croix: "Get to the difficult islands before Hilton does." That wasn't half bad. Hibbard said Martha was a "natural." Too bad she was studying at night to be a lawyer.

When Francie finished poking around the copy department, she would walk upstairs to the seventeenth floor and wander around the print and TV art departments, studying layouts and storyboards for different campaigns, deciding which she liked, and which she didn't.

Later, Francie would check her choices against what Abe himself accepted. For it was universally accepted at Barnett that what the client bought or didn't buy was a secondary consideration. It was Abe's opinion that mattered. Not because he was boss, but because he was Abe. In Francie's mind she called Abe, "the Giver of Anxiety." That plumpish, unbeautiful, little man with the stutter could make high-paid creative directors perspire when he criticized their thinking. Top-drawer art directors paled when he pouted, as though their layouts were an insult to the public's intelligence. No one ever explained to Francie why Abe's opinion was so important. He couldn't design an ad, and he wasn't a very good copywriter, either in print or television. Still his was the one vote that counted with his staff.

It took Francie years to understand that what made him so good was that he knew what was good. It was then that she renamed him the "Giver of Truth and Anxiety." For Abe loved good advertising the way some men love women or money. And his love made him brave. He was not afraid of clients; not afraid to lose an account over a campaign; not afraid to disagree with the board chairman of a billion-dollar corporation. Abe stood pat on his opinion, unless the opposition could give him a very sound creative/marketing reason why it should be changed. He had been known to resign accounts because he did not believe they would accept good advertising. If he approved the work and the account remained dissatisfied, then damn the torpedoes; and no one was fired.

Abe's staff knew this. They knew that the beginning and the end of what he cared about in them was their creative competence. Nothing else. He rarely smiled at any of them. He often didn't recognize them on the street. He did not have lunch with them except to discuss a campaign. He did not care about their family life, religion, their politics or sex life, color or their drinking habits. He cared only about their creative abilities. There were no excuses. No alternatives, no clever politicking could substitute for lack of ability. But if you had the ability, if you could create good ads or commercials, you needed nothing else to win Abe's gratitude. Then Abe gave silent applause for the pleasure he took in your accomplishment. He could not have been more pleased if he'd created the advertising himself.

And this recognition gave to those who won it a feeling of self-respect that no one else's approval could match. Knowing his total commitment to good work, his staff went out on a limb for Abe. They stretched, they reached, they risked, they invented the wheel. They made blue carrots for Campbell's advertising that the public never saw; a Joy that made "dishwashing almost nice" until dishwashers made hand-washed dishes almost obsolete. They created a Marlboro Man that nobody forgot and that changed the face of a cigarette—as well as of advertising.

After the telephone rang five times Francie picked it up in a daze.

"Francie?"

"Mmmm, yes. Who is it?"

"This is 'God,' doll—"

"Oh, Norman. I'm sleeping. It's three in the morning. Where are you?"

"Chicago."

"I thought you were putting out a fire in L.A."

"I was. I just got off the plane, and I made the horrid mistake of stopping at the office to see if the Marlboro contacts had come in."

"They should be there."

"They are. And they're hideous. Diseased. I can't trust anyone to follow instructions. Not even you. If I'm not there, alive and beating my brains out, terrible things happen."

"Norman, listen. I went over everything you told me— twice with Gil. We even had him to dinner; and the three of us, Peter too, looked at the composites—"

"Well, darling, it adds up to zilch."

"But they're gorgeous. I saw them Monday when they came into the agency. They're the sexiest male shots I've ever seen."

"Sexy! Christ, have you had a change of life! The contacts on my drawing board are of some kind of Raphael castrati."

"Oh, the choir boys. I saw them. There's more. Those were Lillian's idea."

"I can believe it. Also some crude blond beach boy

292

numbers. Another of Lillian's grotesque ideas, I'm sure. She adores young men who count on their fingers and move their lips when they read.''

"Temper, temper. Love is something you can't control. Look at you. Look at Crystal.''

"Crystal is my own private obsession. But I would not foist Crystal on the mothers and fathers and other chain-smoking straights of America. He's not for them. I believe in sexual as well as religious freedom. What is on my drawing board is not what I told Gil to shoot. I wanted male men. Straight arrow.''

"Gil took those. Those are the models Peter and I helped Gil pick. Lillian only let me go to one shooting. But I saw all the contacts when they came in. Didn't you see the shots of the gentlemen jocks?''

"I do not have any gentlemen jocks. Or any teamster jocks, either. I told you what I have. I've been sitting here for one hour brooding.''

"And drinking. You don't have the bull with the tattoo?''

"What tattoo?''

"On his hand? The eagle.''

"What a splendid idea.''

"You like it? I drew it. But I'm no expert.''

"Where'd you learn to do tattoos?''

"Oh, it's not a real tattoo. It's washable ink. I can only do a few things. Eagles. Roses. Don't you remember what a rage it was at the Pines last summer? Tattoos?''

"At the Grove too.''

"Exactly. You remember the party that Violet Battenberg came to with her crotch shaved and around it tattooed the pincers of a crab. It blazed out red when she got excited.''

"Didn't it? Violet—my own dear, darling, little sadist.''

"Full of sweet girlish dreams. But some men go for sadism. And it was funny. So I decided to learn how to draw a few things. In ink. Washable. I did a rose for myself on my thigh. That's why I sketched the eagle on the model's hand. I thought you'd think it was funny.''

"I'm convulsed.''

"Then laugh.''

"I will when I see the contact.''

"It should be on your drawing board. It should have been in the package of contacts that was sent to you.''

There was a long silence on the telephone. "Norman—Norman, are you there?"

"I am here," he said in a choked voice. "I am trying not to have a heart attack. Nothing is here. Not a thing! Junk! I want those contacts—every single last one of them. I do not want Lillian's selections. That's just what's happened! She's terrorized Gil into sending her choices! I won't stand for it! I will make my own selections! Lillian has the soul and sensibilities of a topless waitress, and I will not have her dirty little paws meddling with my work."

"Norman, if I could get you an Alka Seltzer, I would."

"What I need is Librium. Or a hit man. With a heavy, blunt instrument. Francie, I want you to get all the contacts for me. All of them! If you have to pull out every single hair on her head! And her cunt too! And I want them sent to me air-express tomorrow morning!"

"Just how do you propose I get those contacts? And stay alive? Will you give me a blood transfusion when I need it? What do I do—pull a gun and say, 'Lillian baby, the jig's up. Hand over the haul or there'll be nothing left but your bridgework!' You're drunk, Norman. Falling-down drunk. This isn't the movies."

"Darling, I leave it up to your unscrupulous woman's intuition. You are a true female of the species, and that is exactly why I got you the job. I knew the time would come, and it has. This is a major campaign. I will not have that sex-starved, she-wolf sabotaging my genius with her infantile eroticism. Do it, Francie, and God will protect you."

"Amen."

The Marlboro cigarette campaign was Norman Hook's private fiefdom; he planned to use it as the launching pad for winning the Art Director's Club Medal. Properly handled it would make his name an advertising legend. And over and beyond useful financial benefits, it would undoubtedly give him considerable cachet with the more attractive younger "tricks" in the business. It might even save him substantial sums of money in trick pay-outs. Tricks loved celebrities. Sometimes for a celebrity they would do it for free.

But much to his disgust, Norman had not been able to attend the New York shooting of Marlboro because of a conflict with a previously scheduled West Coast assignment on Kellogg's. The Kellogg people would have felt very touchy about being snubbed for the Marlboro people, who were after all a nouveau account. And in point of hard fact, the advertising dollar Kellogg currently spent was quite a bit more sizable than that of Marlboro. So Norman had no doubt as to where duty, if not celebrity, lay.

As a consequence, the responsibility for executing Norman's instructions on the Marlboro campaign fell to Gilbert Schmertz, head of the New York art department, and unfortunately a man who lived in quivering fear of Lillian. The fact that Gil, and not Norman himself, was shooting the Marlboro campaign was sufficient cause for his exasperation. If the results had been exactly to his order, he would have found fault. As it was, he was livid.

The next morning Francie arrived at the agency at 7:30 A.M.

This time she scoured the art department, going from one A.D.'s office to another's, searching for the missing contacts. Then she ransacked the bull pen with the instincts of an FBI agent. Nothing. Finally, she went over Gil Schmertz's office like an SEC investigator reviewing Louis Wolfson's stock registration filings. Nothing. The contacts were nowhere.

Reluctantly she descended the two flights to the fifteenth floor, and, hurrying through silent corridors, headed for Lillian's anachronistic suite. Once inside, she realized why she so disliked entering it. It was not simply Lillian's presence. It was her perfume. Tabac Blanc. Though every drop was ultimately as expensive as seed pearls, when combined with Lillian's personal essence, the odor was that of decaying gardenias. Knowing that Lillian, unlike the art directors, had a vulture's eye for the exact placement of the objects in her office—be it the tilt of a picture on the wall, papers on her desk, a pencil, a paperweight, anything, Francie proceeded with exceeding care. Lillian would know to the centimeter if something had been moved. Months before Francie had discovered that the Queen Anne bachelor's chest (a reproduction of course) on the side wall away from the door was where Lillian kept things of special interest—reports, composites, contacts, newspaper clippings, memos, desiderata. The original piece had come without locks; and Lillian, unwilling to tamper with the authentic look, had never had locks put on. As a routine matter, Francie had made a study of where what was kept; and now with unerring instinct, she beelined for the middle bottom drawer. And since Lillian was nothing if not orderly, neatly stashed beneath a pile of Max Factor photographs were the missing Marlboro cigarette contacts.

Lillian did not speak one word to Francie the rest of that week, though the following week she exuded an exquisite mildness which made Francie think she bore her guilt with admirable bravery. She'd pictured Lillian's wretchedness on discovering the contacts missing and her treachery revealed. Now she assumed Lillian was following a line of pride marked out for herself to hide her strain, and Francie felt a compassionate urge to tell her she was safe. She, Francie, would intercede for her with Norman. After all, Lillian had hired her.

On Saturday, Norman called from Chicago and told Francie what a smasheroo he'd made. The Marlboro Man was acclaimed by all. All being Abe first, the Creative Plans Board second. The tattoo was regarded as sheer genius. Norman was a hero.

Francie was delighted. It never occurred to her that she deserved a bit of applause, too. The idea of a male Marlboro Man, a nonmodel type, was Norman's. The tattoo was only a joke. If it worked, she was glad. She expected no more than Norman's thank-you for services rendered. Pleased with his success, she took the opportunity to suggest he be generous with Lillian; not mention her chicanery to Abe. This idea convulsed Norman with laughter. "Ducky, you are young. Power politics is new to you. Dear heart, you underestimate our little vampire. Lillian lives by treachery. Abe knows that. It's part of her virtuosity. Of course when it misfires, blood can flow. But usually not Lillian's."

A chill of fear passed over Francie like the remembered gleam of a knife in the dark. "But what she did was wrong?"

"There is no right or wrong. Only good ads. If Abe had hated my campaign, she might have been 'right.' Ducky, get sick this week. Hide in a closet."

Lillian's reaction was as predicted.

"B-B-But who is F-F-Franciejean?" asked Abe in Chicago.

"A junior in the fashion department. Lillian is going to fire her."

"W-Why? And w-what is it our b-business w-what h-happens in her d-department?"

Norman sighed. He loathed chivalry. And he hated giving credit away, but he had no choice. Anyway, he might need Francie again. "Abe, the tattoo on the Marlboro Man. It was Franciejean's idea."

"N-N-Not yours?"

"No. The idea of using a nonmodel male type was mine. But she did the tattoo. I know her. She meant it as a joke."

"Mmmm. I s-s-see."

"A lucky idea."

"V-Very l-l-lucky. You s-say she's in the f-f-fashion d-d-department?"

"Well, she won't be much longer. Lillian telephoned me this morning. She plans to fire her."

"Why?"

"Abe, Lillian is a natural paranoid personality. It's part of her great gift."

"I d-d-don't want this F-F-Franciejean f-fired. If s-she has m-more than one j-j-jokey idea of that cal-caliber, the cr-creative de-department c-can use her s-s-services."

"Well, you'd better telephone Lillian and stay the execution."

Abe thought about that. "I'm g-going to N-New York t-tonight. I h-h-have a m-meeting tomorrow morning w-with C-C-Cullman on M-M-Marlboro. I-I'll s-see L-Lillian afterward."

The following morning Lillian called Francie into her office. "Of course you know about the new Marlboro Man campaign?"

Francie had been waiting for this and had been planning a vamp till ready. "No. I know the contacts were wonderful. I saw them just before Gil sent them out. They were fantastic."

297

"There were some marvelous ones in the batch. And there were some repulsive shots. I found that sweaty longshoreman-type repulsive."

"Oh, you did?"

"Yes, I did. That was Norman's idea entirely. Depend on a gay boy to pick something like that. He thinks that type has a bigger prick."

"I don't know. I thought those pictures were rather—uh—sexy. But, of course, I don't know too much about it."

"Of course you don't. I tried to save Norman from his own deficiencies by sending him distinguished-looking gentlemen. Marlboro men."

"I know. The blond ones. They were wonderful, too."

"I thought so. Distinguished. Very English. Very Marlboro. Gentlemen. Exactly the right tone for the cigarette."

"I thought so, too."

"Very astute. You manage to agree with everybody."

"Uh yes," said Francie, stumbling. "I can see there's more than one point of view here."

"There certainly is. That's why I kept the contacts of the meatballs from going out to Chicago. I did not want to cater to Norman's crude sexual appetites."

"Oh—you didn't send them?"

"No, I did not send them. Nor did Gil."

"Oh—I see."

"You sent them!"

Francie was properly flabbergasted. "Me? Send contacts to Chicago? Why would I do that?"

"Because you are a treacherous, contemptible little slut under the diabolical influence of that fiend, Norman Hook. I told him what I think! I am furious! Now the Marlboro Man is going to be a sweaty offensive brute! Just because of your stupid meddling!"

Francie stood there dumbly, trying to think what to say.

"Franciejean, I am not a complete fool. Just a partial one. I should never have hired you. But once having hired you, I should have kept everything of importance under lock and key. It simply never occurred to me that besides being a slut, you are a thief."

"I am not a thief!" Francie's pale skin grew paler; she was torn between fright and anger.

"You are a thief. What do you think it is when you take someone's personal property out of her office?"

Francie's temper went out of control. "It was not your property," she said in a furious outburst. "It's agency property."

"There," said Lillian with a malevolent smile. "You admit it. You stole it! You thief!"

"I did not steal anything," said Francie fiercely but her mouth was beginning to tremble. "It was agency property. And Norman wanted it."

"Yes you did. You stole it." Lillian was beginning to scream. "And when I put it to Gil—I explained to him that his job was on the line unless he told me the truth—well, he told me everything. Also about that damn fool tattoo you invented. All about it. How you painted it on that sweaty meatball's hand. It must have given you an orgasm."

"I didn't do anything. It was a joke." Francie's anger had gone; and bewildered and terrified, she was beginning to cry.

"Yes you did, don't tell me! You even would like to have my job. I know your type—greedy, grasping slut!"

"No! No! No!"

"Yes! Yes! Yes!" Lillian was beside herself with indignation. "Go to your office and think about your sins. And at the end of the day you pack up and leave. You are fired. *Fired!*"

Francie stumbled backward and found her way to her old office through the blinding tears streaming down her cheeks. She had never thought this would happen. She had never really thought at all about the consequences of doing what Norman had asked her to do. She never wanted to lose her job. She even liked Lillian in an odd way. This job was like home. It was even more home than her life with Peter. It was her first home since that other home with Jamie. And now it too would be lost. It had given her a place to go in the morning. And things to think about. And talk about. It had given her a sense of belonging. Of importance. And when people asked her what she did, she wasn't just a dumb model, a good-looking piece of tail. She was a lady. She worked in the fashion office of the Barnett Company. Even the actors and stockbrokers and social men she slept with respected her job. She was somebody. She had a career. What could she do? What could she do to live now? She might as well be dead. She put her face into her hands and wept heartbrokenly. Where would she go? What would she do? Who would she be? The idea that she had money of her own, a private life, Peter, never occurred to her. It all swept over her. The ancient terror of being adrift in the world with no anchor, no one who cared, the prey of every passing stranger. Momma would find out, and Momma would never forgive her, would never love her again.

She was crying so hard she did not see the plump little man standing in the doorway, red with embarrassment and shaking his head. "Th-there th-there, y-y-young l-l-lady. D-d-don't cry, d-d-don't cry," he was saying.

But she didn't hear him, and she went on weeping her heart away. So finally the little man, very carefully and very uneasily, stepped over to the desk where she was sitting hunched over in tears and stiffly patted her on the shoulder. He wasn't very good at soothing emotions; and the clumsiness of his gesture showed his lack of practice, as well as the great effort he was making. At first Francie felt nothing; but when she did, she almost jumped out of her seat in fright.

"Momma!" she screamed. "Momma, I'm sorry! I'm sorry! It wasn't my fault."

The little man stood there beet red and shaking his head. "I-I'm n-n-not your M-M-Momma, and I know it w-w-wasn't y-y-your f-f-fault."

Somehow Francie recovered her senses and slowly came back into the daytime world. "Oh— Oh— Mr. Barnett. Mr. Barnett, I'm sorry. I'm sorry." In spite of herself she started to sob again.

For now there was Lillian standing at the door and glaring at her. Seeing her standing there like the Furies, Francie shuddered and wept even more violently. "I didn't mean any harm. I didn't—" Her voice trailed away in sobs.

"We-we know y-y-you didn't, m-m-my d-d-dear. P-please st-stop crying, w-won't you?"

Francie tried very hard to get hold of herself.

"L-L-Look. L-Lillian has ch-changed her mi-mi-mind. Y-y-you are n-n-not f-f-fired." Francie kept on shaking so Abe continued. "Y-you're n-not f-f-fired. I-I-I s-say so." He smiled suddenly. "I am trans-trans-transferring y-you t-t-to the copy department. Y-y-you b-b-belong in c-copy. N-Not in fash-fashion." Then he turned to Lillian and said with a tone as close to anger as he ever came. "D-Did you t-tell Martha t-to come down-downstairs im-im-immediately and t-take this g-g-girl up-upstairs to her n-new office?"

"Abe, you know how I feel—"

"And you know h-how I feel, L-Lillian. D-Did you tel-telephone M-Martha? If y-you didn't, then I will."

Lillian left abruptly, and Abe Barnett continued quietly standing there watching Francie and shaking his head. "N-N-No j-job is th-that im-important, y-young lady," he said. "Y-You sh-shouldn't l-let yourself g-get so up-upset. Y-You c-c-could always f-find another j-job."

"No, no—I have no place else to go. No place." Francie said this between sobs. "I want to stay here. I don't want another job."

"W-Well, y-y-you w-will. We-We-We're k-keeping y-you. Y-You g-get an-anymore s-such g-g-good ideas as that t-t-tattoo, and y-y-you'll be-be a v-v-vice-pres-president."

At that moment Martha walked in, glasses on, her new nut brown hair gleaming and braided in short pigtails. She saw Francie sitting there hugging herself in misery; and having once sheltered, loved and raised a very young sister, when their adored mother died, she felt a sudden return of her mothering instinct. This wasn't just the prettiest girl Martha had ever seen. This was a scared kid like any other scared kid. She went over to Francie and put her arm around her saying, "Come on, Francie. Don't let that old battle-ax, Lillian, get to you. Come on, it's all right. We'll go upstairs to where the classy people are."

Abe gave Martha a rare approving smile that Martha didn't see. "Y-Y-You t-t-take care of h-her. G-Get her c-coffee."

"Yes, Mr. Barnett," said Martha who had not looked at Abe once since entering. "I'll take care of her now."

And she did.

18

Francie and Martha went up to the sixteenth floor, and Martha helped Francie settle into her new office. It was clean and empty, except for a desk, a chair, a typewriter, and an umbrella stand left behind by the previous copywriter who'd gone home to New Zealand. Martha helped Francie stock up with reams of yellow, white, and carbon paper, manila folders, pencils, ball-point pens, paper clips, stapler, and so on.

"You can bring in your own things, you know," she told Francie. "To make the place more personal. Maybe you have prints you'd like to hang on the walls? Or a plant for your desk? Or for the floor? Or a family heirloom? Nan Ehrlich once brought in a spinning wheel. Dan O'Brian keeps his grandfather's false teeth in a leather box. It's on his bookshelf. But nothing live—like gold fish or canaries. Hib had a fit when Gordie bought in a coop of chicks. I'll order you a file cabinet. And try the typewriter. We may need to call a repair man to fix it."

Francie obeyed, seating herself at the typewriter and inserting a sheet of yellow paper in the Smith-Corona. She typed: "Once upon a time...Once upon a time...Once upon—"

"Enough, it works. And you could get a job as a typist." Francie folded her hands in her lap; and as she did, Martha noticed that they shook. "Are you all right?" she asked. "You really mustn't let a harpie like Lillian get to you."

Martha's concern pulled Francie up short. "I do feel a

302

little queasy. Getting fired is hard work. It'll pass. Don't worry about me."

Martha fixed her with deep eyes. "I don't. You're okay." But what had come up for her suddenly and checked further questions was the sense that Francie's "okayness" was a subject it might not be wise to delve into. So she contented herself with suggesting, "You deserve AWOL time. Go home. Or to a movie."

Francie hesitated and then disagreed. "I'd rather stay and work."

"But I give you permission. I'm your boss. Abe said you're to be my assistant. And I want you to use what's left of today to recharge. Go shopping. Have some fun. Don't you want to?"

Francie sat for a moment quietly thinking, feeling a longing, shy but deep, to put her case to Martha—but also not knowing exactly what her case was. In the end, unwilling to reveal the extent of her anxiety, she answered lightly, "I could use a chocolate soda."

"So could I. But I don't dare. *Vaya con dios.*"

"Well, if you don't mind." Francie had realized that to take advantage of the time off was to strike the more natural note; to prove with a smile that there was nothing the matter that a lark couldn't cure. "Thank you. I'll see you tomorrow."

When Francie left the building, she started walking slowly west, then north, up Fifth Avenue. Something, a fierce shrinking from observation and sympathy, had built up inside her; and she could not yet go home. She was glad to be alone as she walked, alone with the human race at large; intimate and impersonal. They wouldn't care that she had failed. They wouldn't know she could be fired. Had been fired. But she knew her probation had ended as it had ended once before when she lost Jamie; and her small sense of safety was gone again. It was the loss of a precious, hard-won illusion, like the giving up of some cherished piece of jewelry when the jeweler's glass tells you it's only paste.

Without thinking, she knew where she was going. To Central Park. To the zoo. With the Crackerjacks and the man with the balloons and the children. Yes, the children with their mothers. Usually she avoided that part of the Park. She never wanted to see the children. Especially the little ones. And she didn't want the mothers to feel sorry for her. Although she knew that was a stupid idea because why should they feel sorry for her? They didn't know her—she was a stranger. Walking, she dreamed, wondering what it was like to be a mother. To raise a child. Thinking about this, she thought about her baby; and the anger broke through. She should have kept the baby. It was hers. It was the one and only thing in the world that was hers. She should have kept it. Why had she let it go?

She felt a quick sting of loneliness and a sense of injustice that, in truth, she knew was out of place. It was foolish to be angry. She knew why she'd given up her daughter. She knew exactly why. She'd wanted her to have the time to store up security, the kind of security that comes from the long golden celebration of a safe childhood. And a girlhood such as Francie never had. One filled with summers and winters of unquestioned certainties, and no fear at night. Night being only a time of stars and coming home to love and sleep. She wanted her child to have it all—faith in tomorrow and the strength faith could bring for facing the infinite risks of womanhood.

Little by little her anger subsided. By the time she reached the bench where she decided to sit and rest, she could think about her baby calmly. Sensibly. She could watch another young woman rocking her own baby to sleep and let the past come back to her. She remembered when they'd brought her her daughter, how little she was; the eyes unfocused, rolling and unstable; the hands waving slowly and aimlessly like plants underwater. And she remembered with a rush how she had felt then—not tender but savage and committed. Nothing bad should happen to her baby. Yes, she would have a different life from her mother's. Francie would see to that.

"Hello," said a small voice.

A little girl was standing in front of her. A small girl with dark, silky hair, humming to herself in wrapt concentration. "What's your name?" the child asked.

"Francie."

"I'm Jill."

"That's a lovely name, Jill."

"Where's your child?"

"I don't have one."

"You're not a momma?"

The sly innocence of the question caught Francie off guard and brought her hand out unconsciously to touch the little girl's cheek. Francie shook her head.

Silence. Then, "Don't you like kids?"

"I like kids very much."

The little girl hummed some more, considering this and then, as if she'd just thought of it, said, "Would you buy me an ice cream?"

Francie smiled delightedly. "I'd love to buy you an ice cream. Where do we go?" She rose from the bench.

"I'll show you," said Jill slipping her hand into Francie's and leading her along.

"Jill, where are you going with that lady?" A voice followed them, shrill with surprise and vexation.

"Come. Ice cream." The little girl started to run pulling Francie's hand to make her hurry.

"Jill! Young woman, you let her go!" Now the voice tugged at Francie; but she only half heard it, helplessly letting the little girl lead her. Then Jill turned around and continued skipping backward, holding Francie's hand tightly and staring at the voice chasing them.

Without looking around, Francie could see in her mind the figure of a panting young woman. She could feel the thumping of the mother's heart, and she felt in her own body the woman's sensation of terror. "Is that your mother, Jill?" she asked.

"She won't buy me ice cream."

Francie stopped and turned around as a dark-haired young woman, out of breath, her face tense and flushed, caught up with them. She grabbed the little girl, who immediately started to squirm and cry. "Where were you going with her?" She accused Francie.

"For ice cream. She wanted ice cream." The old ache was somewhere in her body—she was going to lose something again.

"Honestly! She's had two. But she never talks to strangers. I've warned her and warned her." The two women stared at each other, both drained of emotion.

"I'm sorry I frightened you," Francie apologized, her eyes filling with useless tears. "I like children."

"You must. Jill likes you. She doesn't talk to strangers.

Stay still," she said to the little girl. "Do you have kids of your own?" Her eyes on Francie were sharp and cautious.

"No." Francie's body sagged with weariness. She longed to be rid of the young woman.

"Kids can make you nutsy if you let them." She put the child down, but held her hand firmly. "Sometimes I want to give her away."

"I'm sure you don't mean that." Francie gave Jill a kind, protective smile. "You give her, I'll take her."

"Yes—yes—yes. Ice cream," said Jill, pulling toward Francie.

The young woman's eyes dropped to her daughter's face. She was tired, and felt guilty at her own words. Love to her meant responsibility and abruptly she knew she wanted no release. "I guess I don't mean it. She looks so much like me I'll have to keep her." Then her eyes shone with sudden teasing and she looked at Francie appraisingly. "You're pretty enough to be married and have your own. Stop wasting time."

With that, she turned and, holding firmly to her small daughter's hand, led the way back to the group of children with whom Jill had been playing. Jill looked back once to wave and then ran ahead of her mother.

Francie nodded. It was the best she could do. Somehow she had retreated back to that other time, and she could think of nothing but her lost baby. She felt alone, abject and helpless. She had to blot out the memory.

Eventually, she found herself at a Broadway movie house. She hadn't looked at the marquee, and the picture was one she'd seen with Peter at a preview. She sat down alone in the dark, staring unseeing at the screen. She never knew afterward exactly how long she sat there or what she thought about while she sat, but it seemed to her later that she saw the movie twice. Maybe more? When she came out, the night had come down on the city, the moon was out, and the street lamps lit. She wondered what time it was and where she had lost her watch. Whatever the hour, it was time to go home. She could do that now. Peter had not been sure if he'd be in early or late this evening. Now she hoped he was home.

When she entered the apartment, the glow of a shaded lamp cast a soft glow over the foyer, exuding warmth and intimacy. Peter was home. Knowing Francie's fear of entering

306

a dark house, he always left the small lamp on, for those nights when he came in first and went to sleep before she arrived.

Taking off her shoes, Francie tiptoed slowly down the corridor to her own bedroom. As she passed Peter's closed door, she stared silently, wondering how sound asleep he was. She felt cold and weary and alone in her heart, alone in some place that felt like world's end. In the cab coming home, a tower clock told her it was one o'clock. It would be hours until morning, hours that she must spend alone, shivering and sleepless in her bed. What she longed for was the comfort of human closeness, the silence that is not solitude, but sharing. Maybe Peter wouldn't mind if this once—just this once—she slid into bed beside him. For warmth alone, human warmth. She felt she was freezing to death.

She hurried into her bedroom, breathing unevenly as though after a race, and turning on a lamp, stepped carefully out of her clothes, putting each item where it belonged with a studied precision. Then, stripped down, she slipped into a nightgown—she usually slept in the nude—and giggled in spite of herself, hoping Peter would recognize her cue, that her intentions were strictly honorable. She would try not to wake him. She would crawl into his bed and fall asleep beside his warm body. Barefoot now, she tiptoed down the corridor to his room and carefully opened the door.

Within was a muted gleam of light, and the sight that met her eyes froze her in place. Two bodies were entwined on the bed in what seemed a slow incoherent dance. It was Peter and a young man, their penises erect as each one feverishly sucked the other's flesh. Watching with a terrified fascination, it seemed to Francie they were engaged in some clumsy obscene experiment whose meaning shot like lightning across her mind with a horrid attraction of its own.

Then she closed the door as softly as she opened it. "It's a mistake!" she wanted to scream, "a mistake!" But she pressed her lips tightly together so she would not cry out and hurried back down the corridor. Inside her bedroom her eyes traveled despairingly around the room, staring at the furniture. "I can't breathe, I can't breathe," she moaned, closing her eyes, trying to shut out all memory. Once in that other life with Jamie, she had read about the Eumenides, the Furies, and now she knew how real they were. They were all around her, and her ears were filled with the noise of their wings. She opened her eyes and stared about. Where was she? Was this her room? Was that her bed? What right had she to be here? What would happen to her with that strange boy in Peter's bed?

Afterward, she never knew how long afterward, she left her bedroom and went down the corridor as quietly as she'd come. She went through the living room, through the dining room, to the cabinet that served as a liquor bar. There she took out a bottle of scotch and poured herself a tumbler full. Unaccustomed to serious drinking, she was dizzy after taking three swallows. After two more gulps, she left the almost empty glass standing on the bar; and on swaying feet found her way back to her room. She sank down on the bed that might or might not be hers and forced herself to close her eyes, to let herself dream her terrible dreams.

It was a game. She had had too much wine and was feeling giddy. Then he started to tickle her, and this made her giggle hysterically. He told her she must stop giggling or he would have to spank her. "Naughty girl. Cruel, naughty girl."

But she couldn't stop giggling so he said he must punish her for being disobedient. Uncle Paul must teach her manners. Then he lifted her up and laid her across his knees, pulled down her new, lace-trimmed panties and spanked her smartly on the buttocks.

Momma was seated there on a pink velvet cushion, wearing her beautiful wedding dress and weeping. "Obey! Obey!" she cried. This only made the little girl shriek and squirm, and now his spanking changed to slow patting and caresses.

This frightened her badly and she tried wriggling off his knees; but he caught her fast and she felt his piggy hand around her waist as he lifted her up with her legs kicking, her arms flailing, her mouth screaming.

"Oh, Momma, help me! Momma, help!" But Momma had flowers and combs in her hair; and she rose up, up, up to the ceiling like a great, hungry serpent and fixed the little girl with a glare, while Uncle Paul unbuttoned her dress. He smiled slyly. "Now, you act like a little lady. Even though we

all know what you are. We'll have ice cream and cake later, little lady, if you're good."

And while he talked his hands were undressing her and tickling and caressing her small, budding breasts. She was screaming with laughter and terror, her skin shivering, her feelings shifting rapidly between fear and pleasure. And the warring of sexual excitement and terror made it harder for her to scream and squirm away from him.

When she was naked and gasping for breath, he bent his immense wet, red mouth to kiss her; and she hit him hard on his lips. This made him laugh even as his mouth bled. "My little tiger," he crooned, throwing her onto the huge bed; the biggest bed she'd ever seen, with furs all over like a wild animal. She struggled and wriggled on the ocean of fur, feeling the hairs against her skin, smelling the fur and fighting him off with her teeth and nails and knees. But he was an animal without fur, his weight pinning her in place, while she felt his fingers searching for the soft spot between her legs. She tried to scratch and wriggle and squirm away, but he pushed her legs apart with his knees; and suddenly she felt something hard against her softness. She screamed at the top of her lungs: "Momma, Momma! Help!" She knew she was being ripped apart by this terrible animal with the burning knife inside her. Then suddenly she exploded in one wild, blind burst of violence and with her fist struck something soft in his lower body. He screamed with pain and rolled off her as she sprang from the bed to race for the door. But standing up straight she saw it—the blood streaming down her legs and soaking the fur.

Then Momma waltzed toward her across the tightrope, brandishing her parasol furiously. "Leave my daughter alone, you beast! You animal! Leave her alone! I will not permit it!" After that Momma started to sing softly and sweetly:

"Lullabye and good night, with roses delight.
All tied up with bows, slip under the clothes.
When the morning shall break,
Please the Lord, thou wilt wake.
When the morning shall break,
Please the Lord, thou shalt wake."

On the bed Uncle Paul grew smaller and smaller until he was an insect crawling across the huge bed. It was then

Francie broke into heaving sobs. She was so ashamed at still being alive. "Momma, Momma, he hurt me! It's awful!"

But Momma said, "Stop fidgeting child. Of course he hurt you. Now you know what hell is about. So let's talk of something pleasant. When you grow up, you'll have it all your way. You're beautiful, you see. They'll give you everything you want."

Francie slowly opened her eyes and looked warily down at her white nightgown. It was still filmy and fresh with no sign of blood. Yes, she'd had another of those damn dreams! Damn rotten dreams! Then she saw Peter in his navy bathrobe; he was gently shaking her while a golden morning light poured in the window. For a moment her heart beat wildly; and she turned her face in revulsion from his, shrinking back from the memory of the scene in his bedroom.

"Francie, wake up," he was saying in a strained voice. "You've been having a nightmare, dear. You've been screaming."

Hearing her name, she faced him again, her eyes clinging to his desperately. "I had no place to go," she said, the tears starting to come. "I was so cold and so tired. I had to come here."

He was genuinely puzzled. "Darling, what is it? What are you talking about? Where else should you go? This is your home."

"Is it, Peter? Is it?"

"Of course it is. What a foolish question." He carefully released her to lie back on the bed, while adjusting the pillow under her head. Then he sat down again and took her hands gently but firmly between his. "You've had a hard night. I see you drank a bit of scotch. Scotch never agrees with you."

"It wasn't the scotch. It was the boy in your room."

Peter, after a moment, made the best of this. "I see."

"He was in your bedroom. Is he still there?"

"Of course not." Peter sat there in a deep and grave amazement that seemed to hold both their lives in suspension. "Yes, he was in my bedroom. But Francie, I never lied to you. You know what I am."

"I know. But I didn't know. Not that clearly."

Peter reddened, and it would have been difficult for him

to look more disarmed and defenseless. "But you know this is not the first time I've brought home, let's say, a 'guest.'"

He had to wait a little for his answer. "I guess I tried not to notice."

Listening to her words only added to his sense of wonder. What had they been doing through three years of marriage? How little they knew after all of each other. He could only sit there helplessly brooding on the mystery of the remoteness and the intimacy between them. "Well, it won't happen again," he said finally, his face haggard and perplexed. "I won't bring my friends home. It is a breach of our relationship."

Francie was visibly touched and surprised. "Oh, Peter—no! That wasn't my point." She pulled one hand free of his clasp and slowly caressed his cheek. "I'm making matters worse when I only meant to explain what happened." She drew together troubled brows. "I didn't mean to pry, to look into your room. I was cold and frightened. And the idea of being alone in my bed was horrid. I just wanted to sleep next to you. No sex. Just sleep. Comfort."

After a perceptible pause, Peter replied, "Whatever your reasons, it won't happen again. Without realizing it, I've been acting like my mother. Not as flagrantly, but still—our home is our home. You've never insulted it by bringing home a lover. I can take a lesson from your natural good taste."

This time it was Francie's turn to blush, and for a moment she felt she dared not speak or even breathe. The words were like some rare and exquisite butterfly that the slightest motion might startle into flight. Then she spoke with a sudden decision. "You do as you wish; but you must understand, I'm not criticizing you." She said this with quiet insistence. "I—of all people. I haven't the right."

"Who has more right? You're my wife. We have a life together. And in this matter I'm the best judge. I criticize myself. It's settled." Peter knew the passion that feeds on body lust, but his passion for Francie was like his breath and not superficially satisfied. His one fear was of doing something that might put distance between them, and he was thinking now what to do to prevent it. This thought prompted in him an impulse to ask, "But why were you so frightened last night? What happened?"

311

For a moment Francie said nothing, surrendering to a feeling both humble and stoic. At last she answered, "I was fired yesterday."

"Oh?" Though he could not understand it, Peter did not mistake the sincerity of her anguish. "I know. Norman telephoned me. He said Lillian fired you, and Abe rehired you."

Francie gave a sharp intake of breath—so he knew. But now she knew, too, to her own surprise, that she didn't dislike it—this being found out. In fact, it was truly what she wanted if he truly didn't mind. For now, it gave her a firmer ground to stand on. "Who told Norman?"

"Lillian. She telephoned him and screamed bloody murder. He telephoned me about ten, dying of laughter."

"It wasn't funny, Peter."

"I understand that now." A sudden restlessness possessed him; and letting go her hand, he rose and paced the room. "But Francie, I thought you'd be well rid of that job. You'd learned all you could from it."

"I might have learned more."

"How could you? You were Lillian's bondage and discipline victim. Doing dog work. Nothing creative to grow on."

Francie's lips trembled. "But I was happy working there."

Seeing her withdrawn face and disarrayed hair, Peter felt he was shouting across an endless distance. Still, he must try to make contact. "But Francie, there are other jobs to be had. Even if Abe hadn't rehired you. You would never have lasted two days with Lillian—let alone as long as you did—if you weren't highly competent."

She knew Peter was probing for answers almost as hard as she was trying not to give them. "But I was doing a good job. Really I was. And nobody likes job hunting. You know that."

"Some people regard it as a challenge. People leave or lose jobs for all kinds of reasons. And then they get new ones. I've the impression you think this reflects on your abilities." He stopped. Her face had grown excessively pale, making her brilliant hair seem almost artificial. Her eyes, now half-filled with tears, warned him of some hidden wound he had too roughly touched.

312

"Advertising jobs aren't that easy to come by. It's a very tight market."

She mystified him enough; but now as she gave successive cues, he was affected by a sudden vision of having pushed too far. He had never seen her look so stricken, and he had never cared for her quite as much. "Oh, let's forget the whole thing. Norman says you have a much better job with this Martha in copy. So there's nothing to worry you now."

Francie detected, she could always detect—in precisely the way of the suspicious, the suspected, the condemned—when she was being hunted. Now she saw Peter give up the chase, and the result of this perception was singular. She would never consent to being pushed; but in their brief exchange, she sensed that he wasn't there to judge her. He was rather there, so far as he dared, to comfort. As a consequence, if she'd been afraid of him before, her fear now dropped away; and all that remained was a deep wanting to make up to him for mentioning his friend. She wanted, too, to prove to herself that she didn't blame him for his ways. And what better proof could there be than to tell him her fear, to sacrifice her secret to his comfort. "It's hard to explain, but I guess I went 'nuts,' you might say. Out of sync. Being fired made me feel like an orphan again. I was that kid being handed around from one family to another. For anyone to abuse in any horrid way they chose. I was alone. Momma was gone. There was no place to hide. No place where I was safe."

It was this at last that made Peter think. "But Francie, your job is only your job. The Barnett Company isn't your home. Your home is here with me. Don't you know that?"

"I do. But I don't. Not quite yet." For a second their eyes met and his pain echoed within her, pain she hadn't intended.

"But you're my wife."

"I know, Peter. But it didn't help." She couldn't stop now. She was saying things she had never said to him before, quite as much for her own relief as for his knowledge. "You see, Momma would be so pleased with my job at Barnett. Pleased and proud. Working in the fashion department I was somebody. I had status. Momma loved fashion."

"But you're Mrs. Peter Devlin. Doesn't that have meaning?"

"To me. But not to Momma."

It was at these words that Peter's attention flickered highest, and he met them as he would have the revealed truth. "But your mother's been dead for years. Why should her opinion matter now?" The pieces were slowly fitting together.

"It doesn't always matter. But sometimes I have the feeling she's watching me. Judging." She let herself go, in irony, in extravagance. "Should I have told you sooner? We have a live-in ghost." She had been feeling for a while on firmer ground, and it was odd indeed if her safety depended now on his accepting that, in her way, she felt menaced.

"Well, one thing you can say for ghosts, they do not require guest rooms." He came back to where she was now sitting up in bed, and took her hands again awkwardly in his. "I'm glad you told me. What are Momma's visiting hours?" He saw the relief she took from his keeping the tone light and afterward felt a great gladness in not having failed. Out of all the possible choices, he had selected exactly the right note.

"She's not around a lot. Only when I'm very frightened." She drew her hands from his, and pulled her hair back from her face, in a way she had when she was thinking something through. "If I can keep my job with Martha, I'll be fine. If I'm smart enough."

"Good Lord! You're smart enough. You lasted with Lillian—actually you lasted too long. But this explains why you didn't walk out on her a month after she hired you." He spoke flatly in an effort to overcome his eagerness. "I've known for a while that something's been frightening you. But not what. There must be a way to persuade your mother to move out. Wouldn't you agree?"

"If you're thinking of a psychiatrist—no."

"I was thinking of Kirby."

"Did he 'cure' you?"

"I live with myself more easily than before treatment."

"When psychiatry works—if it works at all—the patient has to want it. I don't. I have to do this myself." She faltered. "With your help, if you will. I mean with our marriage. Our life together. If you'll help me?" If she wanted to show Peter she trusted him, how could she show it better than by asking his help.

He rose and took another turn around the bedroom and came to stand before her. "Will my help be enough?"

"I think so."

He had asked how he could help, and she was telling him. It might turn out to be more than he'd bargained for. But there was only one answer to her appeal. "If you think I'm up to it, I'll do my best to prove you right." He knew now of what he was most afraid—that he might fail her. "All right, my first assignment begins now. Let's get you up. You're starting a new job today. With a big future. It's almost eight-thirty. This is no day to be late."

"I know. And I feel so rotten."

"You're hung over." Peter moved to the bed, reached down and lifted Francie up bodily, standing her on feet. Then he let go and stepped back. "Can you stand and walk?"

She swayed and lurched. "I've done better."

"Right." He swooped her up and carried her to her bathroom.

"Peter, what are you doing?"

"Darling, sooner or later, we must all pay for our pleasures." They looked at each other and started to laugh. In the bathroom, he put Francie down. Supporting her with one hand that gripped her arm, with his free hand he turned on the shower. The cold water. "Now, dearest, here goes. Under you go. I'll hold you."

"Peter, my nightgown! My hair will be soaked!"

"Silk is washable and your hair's wash and wear."

"Please! Why not coffee, aspirin, Alka Seltzer?"

"Francie—under!" And lifting her up, he stood her under the shower while she screamed and the water splashed over both of them. The ice coldness of the water took only seconds to revive her. "Peter, my lips are turning blue!" Suddenly she shivered and stood up straight, pulling away from Peter's support. "I know I'm building character," she said, stepping out of the tub.

"Good show. A real class act." He handed her a bath towel. "Get out of that nightgown and dry yourself. I'll be back in a minute."

By the time he returned she'd rubbed herself down and

315

was in panties and a bra. "Drink this." He handed her a glass of murky brown liquid.

"What is it? It looks yucky."

"Hair of the hound that bit you. Brandy and raw egg."

She closed her eyes and swallowed it. "If I don't throw up, I'll live. What about my hair?"

"Dry it and pull it back into a ponytail. And forget all makeup but mascara. Your color's coming back. Your skin is smooth as a baby's behind. You're going to the office today as Plain Jane. All business. Get dressed, and I'll call down for a cab."

Peter left Francie's bedroom as she sat down in front of her boudoir mirror to arrange her hair. She was barely dressed when he returned.

"We got lucky. Marty tells me 5A just came home from a late night. Marty's holding the cab. Move your ass, darling. You're not going to be late on your first day with Martha."

"Wish me luck, Peter," Francie said grabbing her bag.

"Always luck." He leaned over and kissed her lightly on the cheek. "Did anyone ever tell you you're beautiful?"

"Yes. It seems to be my major symptom." She returned his kiss lightly. "Whatever would I do without you?"

Peter felt suddenly shaken by a passionate sense of her nature, her fate. "You'll never have to find out, darling."

For an instant Francie could not find her voice, then an expression of tranquility passed over her face. She turned her eyes full on Peter. There was no longer room in the moment for anything but understanding. "Thank you, Peter," she said. "You know, it may work. You can quote me on that." She hurried for the elevator.

19

The years that followed were like a fresh dawn for Francie. Even before Women's Lib forced locked doors to open, Franciejean Devlin started moving upward in the Barnett Company.

When Martha English had taken her on as an assistant, she had not recognized Francie's natural talent for advertising. Martha thought she was doing a good deed. But her good deed turned to good luck as Francie's ability worked for both Martha's and her swift advancement.

Then, in time, after Martha passed the Bar Exams and left the company—her real goal having always been to be a lawyer— she left Francie in undisputed possession of her title as Copy Supervisor and of her accounts, including Ban, Modess, Ipana, and Brown Shoe.

Quixotic as life can be, Francie and Peter's marriage was evolving into a surprising success, a happy convenience and comfort to both of them. They had much in common in the way of interests and friends; and at social and business gatherings, they presented an affectionate and unified front.

Watching them together, people would envy how much they enjoyed each other's company; and in truth, they did.

There were those, of course, who resented them for seeming to have so much. Certain women in particular resented Francie. They saw her beauty and gaiety and success as evidence that she had the best of all possible worlds. Which was, Peter realized, exactly what Francie wanted.

No one was ever to suspect what spells of blackness she held at bay. As time went on, Peter became aware that a door had been silently closed even to him; and she'd shut away from his eyes her sharpest fears. No questions were to be asked, no sympathy given. Part of the reason, he thought, could be protective of him; to spare him her suffering.

But another, perhaps deeper motive was an intensity of pride—and of hope. As long as she need not deal with his compassion, his pity, as long as she need not confess to self-despair, then she might be steadier in her purpose, in the struggle with herself, against herself, to be well.

When Peter considered her partying, her lovers, how she flung herself into the social life their careers demanded, it seemed remarkable that Francie had traveled so far so fast. But it was no conjuring trick, as Peter well knew; for he had seen her come home exhausted in the early hours just before dawn and recover completely over breakfast to be in the office by 8:30.

One evening, to celebrate Peter's new career, they dined out together at Lutèce. Peter had bought a brownstone on the corner of Sixty-third Street and Third Avenue with the proceeds from investments he had made from their joint incomes and was now extending his business in antiques by opening an interior design office.

Watching Francie across the table, Peter felt that perhaps at last she had begun to feel her life was her own, that her success marked the end of the obsessions that preyed upon her so long.

She spoke easily of her plans for her future at Barnett. Of Abe and his genius. Of her immediate boss, Hibbard Murray, who had become a friend of the family. While Peter was acutely aware that Hibbard was very attracted to Francie, he was equally certain that nothing sexual had occurred between them. Francie had learned well from her experience with Warren. She would never risk the publicity; she would never consider "fishing off the company dock." Nor, for that matter, was Hibbard the kind of man who would have an affair with the wife of a friend.

However, he couldn't blame Hibbard for his feelings. Franciejean had developed into an extraordinary woman. She was beautiful, intelligent, a complete professional in her field; as well informed and astute as the best in the business. And watching her as she spoke, he saw that her eyes had the dreamy stare one sees on the face of a woman talking compulsively about a lover. Which Peter knew was exactly what Francie was doing. In its way, her work was now her lover; and when they talked about it, they were discussing her love affair.

But if Francie's work was a drug, a kind of charm against the dark, her actual success meant less to her than the act of work itself. But with Peter she felt otherwise. She wanted his success.

"You are pleased with your move, aren't you?" She was almost insisting he be pleased.

And he was. "I've been aiming at it for years. But I was short of confidence."

She gave him a glance edged with fellow feeling. "Whoever has enough confidence? Still, you are a single-minded creature."

"Like you, my darling." He was relaxed and lit his cigarette as though it were a pleasure to be thoroughly enjoyed. "But I am happy about this. I've found a work where I belong."

Francie was pleased that he was happy. By the nature of their marriage, she might have done him harm; brought him misery. But they'd been luckier than she had a right to expect. Proving that good can happen as well as bad. People could run into a little luck. "I believe you'll be an overnight success," she said.

"A ten-year overnight success, probably. But we did get two inquiries today."

"And there'll be more. Many more. And the more you succeed, the more I shall bask in your reflection."

So they were allies. Their marriage had changed them both. They relied more and more on each other, depended upon each other for imaginative sympathy and consideration. And if a final depth of intimacy was lacking, still their life together required less masquerade than many marriages arranged along more conventional lines.

Francie picked up her wineglass. "To you, Mr. Devlin. To your success and the pleasure it gives me."

Peter picked up his own glass and smiled. "Funny what some people see in each other."

"Isn't it!" Francie laughed. "Who else would think as highly of us as we do?"

Then one morning in May, 1964, scanning the *Wall Street Journal*, a habit she'd adopted for reasons she refused to admit to herself, Francie read that Jamison Welsh would be among those attending an international monetary conference in Bermuda. She reread the item thoughtfully, her face taking on an expression of guarded hope. After finishing her coffee, she slipped on her camel's hair coat and left for the office.

Later in the day, Francie went to see Hibbard Murray. Finding the outer office empty, she gave a ceremonious knock on the door. Hibbard was at his desk in his shirt sleeves scribbling notes on a yellow pad. When he looked up, she saw he was tired, angry and glad to see her.

"Hello, Beautiful!"

"Hello, Handsome," she answered, seating herself opposite him. "I hear Abe has been leaning on you about Vitalis."

"Word does get around."

Francie nodded. "Hib, what's the matter? Why is it getting so hard? You're a very talented man."

"Was a very talented man."

"Are!"

"Francie, I swear I'd like to chuck this whole business."

"And do what? Run off to the South Seas like Gauguin? You're forty-five. With a wife. Two boys. You've built a reputation in advertising. What is this—midlife crisis?"

"I'm sick of it. It bores me!"

"That's like jumping out of a lifeboat because the conversation is dull."

"I just don't care about advertising anymore."

"What do you care about?"

"You." Francie made a childish face. "And, I guess, government. I want to feel I've done something before I die. That my life has made a little difference."

She had known for a long time that something was preoccupying him, and now she knew what it was. He sat silently, lost in his own dreams. Finally she asked, "What else? What's the full plan? The plot?" She gazed at him with sadness and affection.

"I'm going to ask Abe for a leave of absence."

"I should have guessed that."

"I want to work for Senator Goldwater. Do his advertising. That kind of advertising matters to me. It's important. I despise Johnson and I don't trust him."

"I don't like Johnson much, either. But I think you're making a bad decision." Then she went on with a rush. "I seem to be suffering from *déjà vu*. Another man I knew rather well made the same mistake."

"What difference can that make to me?"

"You might profit from his experience." She spoke with warmth and force. "He was, and is, a much more important man than you are, Hibbard. With far greater stature in his field than you have in advertising." She said it cruelly and intended to be cruel. "He went to work for the Kennedy campaign at about the same time you are going to work for Goldwater. But once Kennedy was elected, Washington ground him up into sawdust. He was ignored because he had a great private reputation but not a public one. And no political base. You're in the same kind of bind."

"And, as you say, with 'far less stature.' I'm flattered that you let me share his failure." Like it or not, he knew that her words made sense; and it was simply her hard-headed pragmatism that made him ask, "And what, my dear, do you suggest I do?"

Out of a desire to make amends for her cruelty, Francie accepted his dream. "Okay! Do it. Just make sure your authority is spelled out—A, B, C—beforehand." She paused for a moment, thinking. Hibbard didn't have enough courage to deal with a second career setback, and she wanted to try to prepare him for the possibility. "And don't burn your lifeboats. Be careful with Abe."

He had to check his laughter. Francie always had a canny instinct for the main chance. "Yeah, there's the kicker. I will not be leaving in a cloud of glory. My Vitalis campaign did not, let us say, 'sing.' And if I leave Abe with a sour taste?"

"You may not be welcome back. If that ever becomes necessary."

Neither of them said anything for a minute. Then, with his head bent looking at his pad, Hibbard said, "I am worried. But I have to risk it."

Francie stood up, and he could feel her warm fragrance hovering over him. "Hib, all I wanted was to be sure that you knew the risks." She said this with resignation. "So, listen. I've got an idea for Vitalis. I got it Sunday afternoon watching Jack Nickolas. You know—the fat kid they call the 'Golden Bear.' Peter tells me he's a great golfer and going to be greater, but he looks terrible. His beautiful, golden blond hair was all slicked back—grease, I suppose. Anyway, you're using sports figures in the video—right?"

Hibbard studied her. With Franciejean anything was possible. "Right. Skiers. Racing car drivers. What's your idea?"

"Fine. Take a skier. Long shot. Christying down the Chute at Mad River. Followed by three other skiers as back up. Cut to your star. In the locker room. Showered. One of the other skiers who followed him down the trail pours some stuff on his hair, too. Your sports star looks at him and asks, 'Say, are you still using that greasy kid stuff?' Kid looks embarrassed. Picks up Vitalis. Tries it. Likes it. End of pitch." She caught her breath and wound up. "That's your theme line: 'Are you still using that greasy kid stuff?' "

Seeing her standing there, Hibbard was reminded of her extravagant heart. "You know, Francie, with you around, I don't have to think for myself."

"It'll work," she said.

"Oh, will it ever work!" He had a feeling of unbelieving relief.

"I'll give you the rationale before I leave tonight." She hesitated for a moment. "I'd like my first vacation week starting tonight. Okay?"

"Tonight!" He was astonished. "I don't want to hog all the credit. Come to Chicago with me. We'll take the bows together."

"No. You take them. Let's just say I have a marker on you. Also, I need a vacation now. A rest. Wish me *bon voyage*."

"Very *bon!* Where to?" His tone had become briskly conversational.

"Bermuda."

"Bermuda! That's for honeymooners."

Francie smiled. "Maybe that's why I'm going. I like to be reminded what it's like. Young love." She threw him a kiss and moved quickly to the door. "Have a *bon voyage* in Chicago." When she reached the door, she made the V for Victory sign.

Alone in her office, she dialed slowly. When she made her connection, she asked for Mr. Raymond Gardiner. Eventually she reached his private secretary.

"Mrs. Austin, this is Mrs. Devlin." Her voice stayed even. "May I speak to Mr. Gardiner?"

"Mrs. Devlin. How nice to speak to you. Mr. Gardiner isn't in town this week."

"He isn't?"

"Perhaps I can be of help?"

Francie had not thought ahead. In fact, she had not thought at all about what she was planning, and she found herself groping for words. "I suppose you can. I would like to contact Mr. Welsh. An item in the *Wall Street Journal* made me think he might be in his home in Bermuda."

"He is. That's where Mr. Gardiner is staying."

Mrs. Austin's tone was such that it gave Francie a cue; and it was this cue, intelligently and gracefully accepted, that set Francie inwardly wondering if she'd made a mistake. Unexpectedly, she felt uncertain of her welcome; but there was no going back. "Do you know, Mrs. Austin, if Mr. Welsh has a full house? Or is there room for another guest? Me?"

For a space Mrs. Austin gave no reply. Then she said, "Why don't I telephone him in Bermuda and find out?"

"Fine. I'm at my office. I'll be working late. My night line is PL 3-0501. And you have my home number. I would appreciate hearing from you as soon as you contact Mr. Welsh."

"Of course." And it passed between that good lady and Francie that something quite exceptional was happening. Francie had the feeling that Mrs. Austin was taking pity on

323

her. And the strain of this kindness on Francie's nerves was evident when, after hanging up, she again picked up the telephone, holding it ready to dial. And then slowly replaced it in its cradle. She had had an impulse to call Mrs. Austin back and cancel her request; but that would be making too much of too little and truly investing the whole incident with an absurd importance. And yet, as she said this again and again to comfort herself, she still had to confess the peril in what she had done. She knew, beyond a doubt what she was most afraid of, and why she had not thought ahead. It had taken its time to arrive; but once before her, the reason was obvious, telling her all too bluntly what might happen. And what might happen was what she particularly dreaded. It was the tactful excuse, the reasonable explanation, the tender apology involving work or guests or whatever, as to why she had best not come. Never before had she admitted to herself a fear of testing him, of desiring, of needing to see what he would do in this kind of situation; the situation being that she again submit to his judgment, always aware that these days she was powerless to effect his response.

For the reality was that their separation, his and hers, was of course, perfectly plausible; but plausible only on the basis of the sternest of reasons. Well, she had given him the very sternest of reasons; and all those years ago he had accepted it as a practical finality. That was why she had learned to wait—days, weeks, months, years—with a fair, indeed an excessive, imitation of serenity. But the moment had come when her sense of caution snapped, and she felt she must see him; if he would see her. And it was this fact, this old, unyielding necessity, that told her there was nothing more now for her to do but wait. To wait and work and wait. She might have hours before her, she realized, of feeling abjectly linked to him by the rule of the telephone.

It was 8:30 when she looked at her watch again. Mrs. Austin had not yet called back. Of course she would. Or she'd call at home. Or in the morning. But the waiting was terrible. It stood for the failure of her life—and yet was it such a failure? She had had a daughter, and her daughter was safe. The love she felt for her child made all other failures unimportant. It filled her mind so completely that, as always, it drove away the shadows. Her daughter had been her master stroke. Once she'd thought she couldn't bear to live without her baby. Instead, she found that thinking about her, alive and laughing somewhere in the world, often made life much easier. She loved the unknown little girl and she loved herself in her. It was only when thinking of her child that it ever occurred to Francie to love herself.

She wondered what she was like, now that she was no longer a baby but a little girl. She wondered what she looked like? Dark hair, light hair? Light blue eyes, dark brown ones? Arching eyebrows, thick straight ones? Whatever she looked like, Francie was sure she was lovely. And she would be smart for her age too. Smart and ask lots of questions. Thousands of questions. She would be quick and curious. And even though young, her manner would be gentle; but she would not be afraid. She would probably not be afraid of anything. Francie had read somewhere that children whose parents had been very much in love have a fearlessness toward life that children born out of cooler matings never know. The primal forces of life having been present at their birth, when they meet them again as adults they know how to deal with them. It comforted Francie to think this. Then the telephone rang.

The Bermuda afternoon was bright and soft; and the warm, fragrant air drifted in through the windowed wall that opened from Jamison's study upon a vivid, luxuriant garden.

"Jamison! Annabelle arrives tomorrow."

"I know." Jamison had risen from his desk and was pacing up and down the room, lost in thought. Listening to Gardiner give him the news of Mrs. Austin's telephone call, Jamie had been thinking, weighing, deciding; and he found he was prepared. In fact he was amazed at the extent of his preparation.

"They can't both be here, not at the same time. Not Annabelle and Mrs. Devlin." Gardiner was firm.

Jamison said nothing. But he knew more and more with every passing minute what he would do.

Gardiner went on: "You'll simply have to tell Mrs. Devlin it's not possible right now."

"I'm deciding what to tell her, Raymond." His answer was easy, but it cost him an effort that was almost physically

325

painful. "You see," he said, "I've wondered for years what I would do when this situation arose. And now that it's here I'm making up my mind."

"For years?" Taking this in, it occurred to Gardiner that he must act with the utmost diplomacy, must reckon with something he had not even remotely considered. "But what have you been thinking? I suppose I am dense, but I've always assumed that Franciejean Devlin was no longer a live issue."

"Originally, I assumed the same. Emotions, however, are not that easily manageable." Jamie found relief in giving an account of himself. An account of himself was one of the things he had long been in the habit of doing privately, never sparing himself when judging either motive or behavior. But so much of him now was in turmoil that he felt a reliable account could only be given to someone else; someone he trusted. "Raymond, I find I do think about her. More than I expected to."

"Jamison, she's Mrs. Peter Devlin. A married woman."

"I'm very well aware."

"The whole thing is too absurd—the idea of her coming here. Why does she want to come? Why now? These years later?" Gardiner was thinking as he spoke, watching Jamison carefully. What, in the name of heaven, was Franciejean up to? And what effects would a visit from Franciejean Devlin have on Jamison?

The jolt of this thought brought Gardiner up against the real question. "I gather she has reasons of her own for wanting to see you again. What troubles me is what do you want?"

"I believe I want to see her."

"But that's impossible."

"Why impossible?"

"Because Annabelle is coming." Gardiner had his reserve and timidities, but still he took off after each hesitation with a further, stronger leap. "Jamison, you can't still care for that girl?"

"I can. I do. What I don't know is how deeply."

He said it simply, and its effect on Gardiner was prodigious. Raymond Gardiner knew all he cared to know about life, which he regarded as essentially occupied with financial arrangements. The emotional scrapes and predicaments of other men neither surprised nor shocked him. They scarcely even amused him, which may have been his greatest loss. He took them for granted without moralizing, classified them and calculated their consequences. But he suffered a failure of understanding when dealing with such a lapse in Jamison. He had consistently found it impossible to swallow, to fit the influence of Franciejean in with his view of his friend. She was, to Gardiner, Jamison's sole, major aberration; and the idea of her forced him to show a rare impatience. "Truly, Jamie, I can't think why you permit yourself even to think of her. To let her waste your time. She's past history. Over. It was my impression that you and Annabelle were planning to announce your engagement."

"It has been discussed."

"I would hope so. I, for one, think it's high time you married."

"To make you feel more comfortable?"

"Well, it will. But there are other reasons. And Annabelle's eminently suitable."

"A charming young woman."

"The daughter of a highly respected ambassador. A distinguished family. Born and bred to the political world. In tune with every nuance. And, Jamison, a beauty. The ideal wife for you." Gardiner's words gave so fully his meaning that Jamison could only stare for a moment as he listened.

"I am thoroughly complimented by her interest in me," he said dryly.

For reasons then not quite clear to himself, Gardiner was moved to caution. "Jamison, I wouldn't mind a bit your inviting Mr. and Mrs. Devlin down. Or Franciejean alone if you and Annabelle were married. Then it would be quite appropriate. It's her turning up this way—before. It's pure perversity."

"No, it's pure accident. She doesn't consciously intend me the least complication. The hairshirt is my own invention."

Gardiner took the measure of these words. His passionate prudence played over their implications, reading betrayals of his hopes into everything he heard, for he had not for an instant lost sight of what he wanted. "I believe what we had best do is call Mrs. Austin and tell her to contact Mrs. Devlin. She will explain quite tactfully that another time would be more convenient for a visit. The next time you and Annabelle are in Bermuda you can have both of them visit.''

Jamison sat down at his desk, his whole body stretched out and relaxed, pretending to listen. Now that she was real again, he accepted that he'd never gotten her out of his imagination. "Ahh yes, I can have them both in the future." He said it with a musing smile that fully appreciated Gardiner's anxiety and felt it deserving of courtesy. "Raymond," he humorously inquired, "have you never been in love?"

An unexpected amusement suddenly aided Gardiner, and he met Jamie's eyes with a certain accommodation. "Well, I admit that if by love you mean a relation that would cause me considerable inconvenience—then, no, I've never been in love." To which he added, "Does she know how you feel?"

"I don't know how I feel." He paused. "I don't know how she feels."

It was at these words that the loyal, fond, frustrated man sounded his strongest protest. "Well, she certainly knows how you felt. Yes, she knows that very well. You made her a wealthy young woman."

"Raymond, you are a cynic. It limits your view. There are people, my dear friend—haven't you suspected it?—who are not primarily motivated by money. Who can more or less ignore it when they put their values on the scale."

For this Gardiner had a harsh, grim laugh. "I think it would take considerable effort to ignore a few million dollars."

"Oh, of course she likes money—or what money buys. But, as I indicated once before, not with the usual zest. I believe, though I shall never have the chance to test my hypothesis, that if I had been a poorer man, she would still have been the same for me. We would have done what we could. If there had been a way. But there wasn't. And she understood that too." He stopped to think a moment; and it was strange for him that when it came to Francie, Gardiner's probing only made him more sure; yet when it came to Francie, what in the world wasn't strange? Nothing, for instance, was so odd as his past and present behavior. Yet he was only saying and doing what he must. "She doesn't have to have money. She's not selfish enough, God forgive her.

She doesn't miss things. I mean she is not petty—she doesn't bookkeep. She overlooks when she loves.''

"Overlooks?"

"What you might do for her and don't do. It's not for you, it's of herself that she demands heroism—of herself she asks everything. She is not one to be easily, if at all, spoiled.''

In Gardiner's face there were many questions, but the one he eventually put was, "If you felt so deeply, I ask again, why in heaven's name didn't you marry her when you could?"

Something rose within Jamison that made it quite definite that he had no answers for Gardiner. "Why? Because after looking the facts in the face, I knew our little romance was our little tragedy. We had no future. Have no future. Plus today she is married to an old friend. We would probably have been happier with each other than either of us can be with anyone else. But it isn't possible. Nothing has changed. Except that perhaps the doors between us now are double bolted.''

Gardiner had given Jamie his quietest attention; but Jamison could see that so far as hearing the real story, his old friend was divided between the desire and the reluctance to know. Finally letting it all go, Gardiner simply said, "So there is no possibility—''

"None.''

"And Peter Devlin? He won't mind her coming here alone?''

"He won't mind.'' Jamison gave him no aid, letting him work it out whatever way he would for himself.

"Well, it is sad.'' This statement marked the waiving of Gardiner's resistance.

"Do you mean for me?''

"For you.'' Gardiner felt a sudden pity for his extraordinary friend, and a prescient, painful wisdom. "You may find you can't marry anyone else, either.''

For a moment Jamison was lost in thought, remembering it all, piecing it together, living it over, the life Francie and he had shared. "It is a risk. I agree. But you think of nothing that I haven't; and in this connection, I think of things you never will.''

Gardiner was one of those men in the world least equipped for pretense; and in this prolonged afternoon of his good faith, he could not help stating the case. "I think of children."

"So do I. Of sons and daughters. Of the Welsh name." Jamie stated it as he might have quoted from a column, after adding up the figures. "I have, as they say, been a fool. But there's no help for it anymore. I must see it through. I must live in it and with it."

Gardiner's patience did justice to Jamison's confession of despair. And to his own. "Well, if I must, I give up something, too." He sighed deeply. "I saw your sons in the bank. I saw your sons helping mine. Working together. Building. So you see what I give up." He blinked hard to keep the grief from his eyes. "What do we do now—how do we handle it?"

Jamison had not yet been so glad that he trusted his old friend; and it drew from him, for so proud a man, an almost touchingly grateful "Thank you."

But Gardiner shrugged. "Please. Don't. It is as it is. We are each what we are. We live our lives as best we can. Tell me what you want me to do."

It took Jamison a time to answer, occupied as he was in making up his mind, in measuring the distance between choices, in considering the consequences. "I think," he said at last, "that you telephone Mrs. Austin and tell her Mrs. Devlin is welcome. I will telephone Annabelle and make new arrangements."

For this Gardiner had a humbugging laugh. "So we sacrifice Annabelle—"

"Let's not use words like *sacrifice*."

20

When Francie stepped out of the airline terminal in Bermuda, she recognized Jamie's 1938 MG-TC waiting for her with a driver who she did not recognize; and no Jamison. Nor was he at the house when she arrived. On her arrival at the graceful beige stucco house, set several hundred yards back from the ocean, the disinterested housekeeper showed her to a pink and lavender guest room. The realization that she was not to share Jamie's bedroom came to Francie as a small shock. But she changed quickly into a white nothing of a bikini and decided to sun herself by the ocean-fed pool. Much later, Jamie, coming home from a meeting, found her curled up on a beach towel asleep on the sand at the side of the pool, wrapped in his terry-cloth robe. Looking at her sleeping figure, he recognized the defiant intimacy in the gesture of using his robe.

When he woke her, she was embarrassed and explained that she'd borrowed the robe because she'd forgotten her own and was cold. Making polite, meaningless talk she asked, "Where's Raymond? Mrs. Austin said he was visiting, too."

"He had an unexpected business call from New York. He had to hurry back. But he leaves you his best wishes."

His answer lingered in the air between them as they exchanged looks. Then Francie smiled lightly. "I don't mean to sound ungracious, but I hope my arrival didn't drive him away? Though I do accept his best wishes."

Jamie gave a slow head shake. "Do you think he secretly telephoned Mrs. Austin and had her arrange an emergency?"

After an instant Francie showed how she could always meet him halfway. "It's true. I forget. Raymond has no talent for intrigue."

"Or lying."

"Yes. I've always admired that shortcoming." It was by now a matter of good taste that they drop Raymond. "Anyway, it doesn't matter since you had no unexpected emergencies." She faced him in all her desire to please him. "I am very glad of that." She repeated her expression of pleasure as they entered the house and parted to go to their separate bedrooms and change for dinner.

When Francie entered the library, she looked fresh and composed in something soothing and silken and blue. She went toward Jamie smiling with affection and holding out her hands. He took them and clasped them close to his body, and they gazed at each other in silence. Both of them had come under new influences, and the faces they turned to each other were subtly changed.

"I've so much to tell you." She said it hopefully, but what on earth had she to say to him now that he was standing before her. He seemed to have an air of preoccupation and remoteness, and she could not decide how to break through his reserve. She raised her hand and put it on his cheek. "It's like old times," she stammered uncertainly. "Or better than old times. New times." She found herself searching for the word or phrase that would unite them. But it was uphill work, and he did not seem to want to help.

By the time they went into the dining room, a constraint had fallen upon them; and they ate, in near silence, a delicious dinner. Francie did her very best to keep the conversation going, and never afterward could she remember if what she said was significant or foolish. She had the sensation of being a puppet figure planted for the evening in a chair, and she could not really move until he pulled the strings.

When dinner was over, they rose from the table and walked out onto the terrace overlooking the ocean. The evening sky was cloudless but a faint and penetrating rolling of thunder sounded in the distance. The ocean before them was dancing in glory beneath a full moon, and for a moment all constraint seemed to vanish in the splendor of the scene. Almost forgotten memories and moments out of the past arose intact to beguile them. They were able at last to talk, more or less, unfolding to each other by curious implications and evasions, their feelings and unintended hints of the nature of their more recent past.

"Darling Jamie," she said finally, hesitantly, almost to herself. "But how are you really? How am I? How is the world?"

He smiled at her patiently. "I can't answer for the world. Not even for myself." He looked at her steadily. "It's been a long time."

"A lifetime. Or two."

A quiet seemed to envelop them; and then moving like a sleepwalker in bemused rapture, Francie slipped her hands around his neck. "Oh, my dear love—how I've missed you."

Jamie heard himself give a dry sob disguised as a cough as he accepted her into his arms. "It's late," he said at last. "I must be out early tomorrow. Let's go in now." And he led the way to her bedroom.

They lay in bed, in the guest room, coupled as though in a trance, trying to re-create a single one of those afternoons or evenings of kisses and caresses which had once held for them both the sum of the meaning of life. But though they made love, they seemed to be separated by infinite distance. And afterward, hearing her even breathing as though asleep, Jamie rose and went to his own room.

One half hour ticked away before Francie changed position to lie on her back and stare blindly into the darkness. She was half awake and had been when Jamie left her side. Now between sleep and waking, she felt the tug of memory. Was this what she had come for? Had they never existed for each other? Had they never inspired in each other the passion and pain of her memories? Had the water closed over that enchanted time forever? Silence lay all about the room; over the elegant, unfamiliar, impersonal furniture and vaguely oppressive ceiling that disappeared into almost invisible walls.

Francie shut her eyes, hoping to shut out the hurt, but it was useless. She felt as though some heavy weight were pressing on her breast; she thought if she could only weep, the weight would evaporate. But the tears wouldn't come, and the weight remained.

With a start of restless energy, she sat upright, turning her body so that her feet touched the floor. The restlessness moved along her legs, her arms, rising within her till she felt she must move, must run, must do something to get away from the weight. In some way she felt she was going to pieces; and she decided to go out into the calm night air, to feel the swish of warm sand beneath her bare feet, to feel the warm ocean water on her naked body. She would swim in the pool.

She stepped out of her bedroom and listened. Down at the far end of the corridor was Jamie's bedroom. The door was closed, and no light shone beneath the door crack. There was no sound upstairs or downstairs. Without bothering to slip on a dressing gown, Francie pattered down the hall, down the steps on tiptoe, through the winding corridor to the side door that led to the terrace. She opened the terrace door carefully and slipped out quietly. Her body gleamed white and luminous as she moved across the terrace and down the path between the high hedges of bougainvillea that led to the pool. As she walked toward the water, her eyes scanned the small shining wavelets; her right hand strayed between her pubic hair, searching for her clitoris to play with and comfort herself. With Francie this was an ancient and time-honored custom when anxiety grew too great and there was no man to caress her. By the time she reached the pool she was trembling with sexual excitement brought on by her own fingers. But rather than reach a climax standing there on the sand, she slid into the water, deciding to swim to the raft to complete her pleasure, stark naked beneath the full moon.

Since she had learned to swim all those long years ago, swimming was her favorite sport. Now she swam a slow, expert crawl, making as little sound as possible, thinking of the pleasure to come on the raft. The water in the pool felt warm and silken and sensuous. Swimming in the nude always made Francie feel that the water was male and was stroking her body. As she moved, she was like a warm white flame. Her legs, as she kicked, looked slender, round and promising; and the moonlight sparkled on her wet, ripe buttocks, giving off a sense of their richness.

Then, as she swam, she felt herself caught by a sudden rush of water pressure running around her legs and thighs and causing a heightening of erotic sensation. Thoroughly aroused, she paused and faced the pressure, realizing it was caused by the ocean stream feeding the pool through an underground channel. Unable to resist, she turned on her back to float, closed her eyes, and opened her legs wide to welcome the onrushing water. As she drifted closer to the outlet, the force of the water grew stronger, and desire rose in her. She felt the water lick her vagina with a gentle tongue, felt the water change in fantasy to a man stroking her loins as a man would, longing to enter her as a man would. And her body opened in response as the water caressed her, bringing to a pitch the fire within. With her eyes closed and her face pale, she looked like someone mysteriously drowned and submitted to fate. She was being made love to by the force of the water, by the thrust of the onrushing stream. And half opening her eyes, she gave a low moan of frenzied delight as her whole body was shaken by the spasm of orgasm.

When she opened her eyes fully, she saw Jamie standing at the side of the pool, watching her, his face very still. And seeing him standing there, it awoke again the odd and irresistible wonder of loving him. He looked so alive and proud in the moonlight—moonlight that gleamed on his strong, naked body, on his thighs and flat belly and his penis, quivering and starting to rise from the dark hair around it. She could never tell him how beautiful he was to her. But he was. She stared wide eyed, excited again by the sight of his body, of his rigid sex.

"What are you doing my love? Masturbating?" His voice was half bitter, half amused. "Evidently the evening's entertainment was not fully satisfactory?"

"It was enough—or would have been if you'd really been there." As she floated on her back, one hand played again with her clitoris while the other caressed her breasts. Her insinuating movements were deliberately intended to arouse him.

He stood silently watching her performance while his penis grew thicker and more rigid.

She caught her lower lip with her teeth to stop its trembling. She wanted to swim over to him, crawl on her knees out of the water, and put her arms around his loins. She wanted to hold him fast against her breasts, let her tongue taste the tip of his erect penis. But controlling herself, with the intuitive knowledge she now had of him, she turned suddenly; and, with a little teasing laugh, started to swim swiftly toward the raft. After about ten yards she looked back and saw Jamie was in the water racing after her. She had nearly reached the raft when she felt his hand grasp her ankle; she shrieked and splashed and squirmed, trying to break his hold. But he was too strong; she'd forgotten how strong; and still treading water, he grasped her other ankle with his other hand, pulling her soft, yielding, naked body to him. He spread her legs apart and circled them like a belt around his waist. As her body closed against his, she let herself go, locking her hands behind his neck in a swoonlike embrace. He had won, and she was glad. Feeling him gather her buttocks, one in each hand, and tilt her back, her head grazed the water. But all she knew was that her vagina demanded to be penetrated, to engulf his penis. Then suddenly he was plunging within her, entering further and further, even as the walls of her body, pulsing with suction, tried to draw him still deeper. "My God!" He shuddered feeling her contractions; and for a moment he was so filled with excruciating pleasure that he forgot to tread water. All tangled together, they sank below the surface of the pool. When they came up sputtering, panting and laughing, they were both throbbing with desire. "Swim to the side!" he said. "Quickly—we have only moments!"

Not understanding his words but obeying the urgency of his tone, Francie followed him to the edge of the pool.

Once there, he lay back on the sand, and she saw the surging rise of his penis again. As she stumbled toward him, her mouth was open, gasping for breath even as her whole self was open and hungering for his closeness. "Periscope up!" she said half sobbing, half laughing. He put his hands under her armpits, and first lifting her up, he then settled her down on his sex. As he entered her, her body fell forward on his, curling and undulating over his, pleasure running over their skin like the water, waves of ecstasy washing over their bellies and hips, running up and down their legs and spine. He thought he could never possess her enough, he must bury himself more and more deeply within her. And now it seemed to Francie she was like the ocean itself. Nothing but waves rising and falling. While deep within her, with each violent thrust she felt her orgasm climb higher and higher. Finally it mingled with Jamie's great shout of furious enjoyment.

It was a mere minute later that they heard the thunder in their ears, and lightning struck the nearby ocean. "So lovely, so lovely," moaned Francie. But Jamie pulled the dazed girl to her feet and away from the peril of the pool water as the rainstorm hit. Because she was groggy, weaving and stumbling, Jamie lifted her up and carried her into the house, kissing her throat and breasts as he walked. Between kisses he murmured, "I don't know if it's more dangerous to be struck by lightning—or by you."

He carried her up the stairs and into his bedroom, tossing her lightly onto the bed. Then he went into the bathroom, came out with a huge towel and rubbed her down, the way he used to when they came out of the ocean at East Hampton.

"Now get into bed," he said, once she was dry.

"Here?" she asked.

"Here," he said, smiling. Francie climbed with relief under the sheets of Jamie's huge bed. When he came into bed after her, she felt a curious shiver of changing consciousness and relaxation going through her. She knew they would make love again.

Afterward, having completely exhausted each other, they slept, Francie nestled into the curve of his body, feeling safe and completed—home.

In the morning they talked over breakfast as they had not done the night before. Something unexpected had happened. It was as if they'd not been apart for a day; as if nothing had ever happened to make them mistrust each other. No doubts, no second thoughts, no misgivings. Francie felt the instant rightness and a great relief. She breathed again; and whatever happened next, she knew it would not change this. And for the next week, everything went right. When Jamie came in from his conferences, they swam and they ate and they talked. Her very manner of talking to him was a way of making love. And she could make love, when it came to it, far better than that. They had long conversations into the night, sharing deep and intimate awarenesses; laughing at the same absurdities; thinking the same things admirable and the same things foolish. What they possessed in common were many ideas about the nature of life, the consequences of action, the uses of judgment. They were both different and similar, but with odd quirks of mind and outlook that made them essentially companionable. She was quite clearly a rare and special product, more his equal now than in years before.

What he had originally missed in her mind chiefly was education. Now there was much more concrete knowledge and the talent to use it. For in Francie, her intelligence in these days had become a value in itself. And almost a mystery. Nothing in her history could explain her mystifying grasp of complex ideas, and her sheer ability to conceptualize. He remembered how he had been struck by her native keenness, and been exasperated by her almost childlike lack of interest. Now all that had changed, and her own explanation only added to the mystery. She had had to learn facts, she had had to learn to think, she had had to learn fast, she said, in order to keep her job, in order to keep her life with Peter in running order. Such explanations made some sense, but they did not prevent Jamie from thinking that generations back, some highly developed mind had made itself ineradicably felt in her blood, in her heredity. Francie had no knowledge of such an ancestor, but she accepted his theory gratefully, as a compliment from him to be stored up against their time of separation.

Francie stayed with Jamie in his home in Bermuda; and when the conference was over, he decided to remain an extra week. So Francie called Hib and asked for an extension of her vacation time.

"Beautiful, you're entitled. I—you—*we* received a standing ovation."

"I'm so glad, Hib."

"But I've put you in charge of creative on the account. You write the TV commercials, Dean can do the print ads, get the commercials storyboarded and see to it that Matt doesn't louse up the production. I leave for Goldwater's headquarters on the seventh."

"Oh, Hib—you are going."

Jamie heard the catch of her breath and raised his eyebrows quizzically.

"I sure am." He sounded half depressed, half boastful.

"I'll be back before you leave."

After she hung up, she gave a wistful sigh. "It's a repeat performance. My boss, Hibbard Murray. He's been bitten by the Washington bug. He's leaving to work for Goldwater. The way you did for Kennedy."

"He has no better way to waste his time?"

"He's committed to the idea of a heroic destiny. Weren't you?"

For a second Jamie's face was cool. Then he broke into noiseless laughter as though sharing a family joke. "Yes. But at least I was practical. I backed a winner. Goldwater will lose."

"He will?"

"Of course." Now Jamie's face hardened; and knowing him as she did, Francie could sense his cold outrage. "I'll grant you that between the two men, I far prefer Goldwater as a person. Johnson is vicious, greedy, preoccupied with power and the manipulation of people."

Though Francie shared Jamie's opinions, it surprised her to hear him speak with such absolute harshness. "He's not exactly your cup of tea, I gather." She reached for his hand and put her lips against the palm.

"Not exactly." He leaned down to kiss her cheek lightly. "You remember our conversation years ago about Kennedy and Vietnam. Well, I may have been wrong. I don't know it for a fact, but the usual 'informed' sources hold that Bobby tried to pull us out of that swamp." He was speaking to her simply and naturally as he had when her life had been a part of his. "But Johnson—he'll get us in all the way."

"Why? Why do a damn fool thing like that?"

"Darling, I have no idea." She clung to the word *darling*. They were close again, safe and together; and she must not miss a word or a thought. "But he's campaigning as a man of peace opposed to Goldwater, the man of war. When in reality he's sending more and more advisors. Goldwater's stupidity in talking about bombing North Vietnam makes Johnson seem like St. Francis."

"The New York press makes Goldwater out to be a fool."

"He is not a fool. He plays with electric trains. Gadgets. Thousands of men do that. As vices go, it's one that would hardly attract blackmail. He's an honest, decent man. But his advisors are ideologic fools. Troglodytes. They've pushed him to the point where the only votes he'll attract are the right of right. Even if your Hibbard gains Goldwater's confidence, he's wasting his time. They will lose."

For the next week they did not leave each other's side. It

was strange enough for Jamison; his old sense of possessing her was combined with an altogether new sense—the recognition that he must choose, in a way that he had never done before. He saw more and more distinctly that what Francie's nearness meant, as his very blood warned him, was that if he did not give her up, he might be forced to live in a state of war. If they were to become again more constant lovers, any marriage would become decidedly uphill work, a daily effort on behalf of a woman for whom he felt so much less.

Francie had for him an unfailing magic; and though he could offer no explanation, she had but to lay her head on his shoulder for all the wonder in the world to blossom forth. She awakened in him another self, a buried, more passionate self. She gave him intimations of an earlier, sunlit life from which, without her, he was inexplicably cut off.

Taking everything as it came, he decided that he would do nothing. Wait. For they had to part shortly; and he wanted to see what Francie would say. By saying nothing, he left her free. It would be up to her to suggest any future meeting. But he could not deny how intensely he hoped.

So it was, inevitably, that a recognition took place. Francie became aware of a growing impersonal pitch between them, of a cultivated lack of possessiveness on Jamie's part. When she was younger she'd had no insight. But by now she had learned. She still had ardor and nerve and hope of the blood; but she was aware that something was failing, and her sense of propriety, especially alert, told her this episode must end soon. So on the Saturday of their second week, while Jamie stood silently smoking and watching, she began packing to go. It was in the middle of packing that she paused to ask almost offhandedly, "Do we have to wait another three years to see each other again?"

Jamison's heart beat more quickly; the unspoken had come up. "It has been quite a while."

"A very long while." She said it bravely enough. "It was to see you again . . . and to arrange to see you more often, if possible—that's why I came to Bermuda, you know."

"You mean you didn't come for a free vacation?" Jamison smiled.

"I came for you." She stopped pretending to pack and faced him directly. "I wanted to see you once more and be with you once more, as we used to be. Even if it turned out to be the last time." Her voice trembled slightly, but there was no failure in her logic. "For, of course, I knew you might not want to see me. I thought it quite possible that you wouldn't. I think it quite possible that you may not wish to see me again. Ever. If you don't, I understand that."

"Do you really?"

His tone made her for a moment consider, and she gave him a tenderly critical look. "Of course I do. There are so many demands on your life, on your time: your work; people; women. I do understand."

She struck him as curiously conscientious; and it affected him deeply, on the whole with admiration. "Do you know, Francie, you have the instincts of an English gentleman."

"I take that as a compliment." And with that gentle answer, so as not to appear too much to teach him about honor, she went on. "I can bear whatever you decide. Because now I've had this. And it's what I'll always have. I would have missed it all—if you'd chosen not to let me come. But you didn't do that. You are as I remember." She paused for a moment without moving, as if to let her words sink into her own ears. "It's what I wanted to find out—was it true what I remembered. It is and I wanted to tell you that. You're all I ever hoped for, and for me nothing has changed. I want you to know that. Or perhaps just hear it. It's enough that I know. I don't ask anything of you now—even that you think well of me." She spoke with a sudden flare of pride. "I have what I came for. I've been here with you—as we were, as we are. We had this time together. And you'll remember it, you'll never quite be done with it. Or rid of me. I know that now, too. But you owe me nothing. I give you my love— myself I give you. But it's quite for free. I simply want you to have it."

In reality, her small recital had taken place, it seemed to him, almost at the level of a high court decision—in the cool upper air of fine discriminations, of the larger philosophy. What she asked was so little compared to what she gave. And again she had let him off, if he so chose to take it, without even the need for an explanation.

"But I gather you would prefer that we see each other again?"

"Only if you would like that, too. Not otherwise."

His conviction was complete, filled to the brim. She would, if he wished it, renounce everything—without resentment, without even the teasing plea of a post card to remind him she existed. And so without intent, she'd set a trap for his spirit; as his vision of alternatives other than Francie fell away entirely with the almost tangible truth of her feelings. Of course, what she didn't, what she couldn't foresee, was what he himself might renounce by keeping her close. It could be precious indeed—quite like a last jewel sewn into the coat lining of a pressed and fleeing exile, to be bartered someday in the marketplace of misery. But all this was something only he could judge; only he would know the immensity of his gain—or loss. Sounding his secret unrest, he confessed at last fully to where he was. "And if someday I want to see you again?"

"Because you want to—or to comfort me?"

He passed a strange moment then, seeing the future in a blur of light. "To please and comfort us both," he said almost humbly.

Holding his eyes as she drew a long breath of rich relief, Francie put her hand on his shoulder and nodded. She smiled. Speech had failed because there was so much to say.

"Then if you wish it, I wish it too. We'll work it out as we go."

Francie left Saturday afternoon, Jamie stayed on until Wednesday and then flew to London.

When Francie arrived at her office at 8:00 A.M., she found Hal Wilson, the TV art director of Vitalis, seated behind her desk. He was sketching on his storyboard.

"Ta-ta-ta-taaaa!" he said without looking up.

"Would you like to say a few words before I ask for my chair back?"

Wilson sighed. "Just keepin' it warm for you, boss lady. It's how I get my jollies." He grinned lasciviously. "Old Hib has deserted us for Goldwater. He leaves Friday, and as you must know, you're in charge. Now we have a lot of lunatic work. I can draw pictures of sporting figures. But we're into talkies. I need words. Dramatic, licentious, peppy, and so on. Words. But no *War and Peace*, please. Maybe fifty. Hib give you the theme?"

"Something about 'greasy kid stuff.'"

"A real grabber. Gets you where you live." He got up to go. "Find the words, boss; and bring them to me."

During lunchtime, with the copy department silent, Hibbard appeared at Francie's door. She was typing while eating a sandwich and drinking coffee.

"Hello, Beautiful," he said softly.

"Oh, Hib." She turned to him with a face full of welcome. "Glad to see you before you become legendary."

"Likewise, I'm sure. Let's go over to my office."

"Yes, sir," she said, getting up from behind her desk and following him. When they entered his office, she sat herself in the chair opposite his desk. "I hear you leave Friday?"

"Yea! Goldwater is delighted to have me."

"And Abe?"

"Thanks to you, Abe will be delighted to have me back."

"Then you know?"

"Oh, yes! I'll be back. Barry won't win." Hibbard was standing behind his desk studying the fingers of his hands, spread like a starfish. "I've had a few hard facts to face in the last two weeks."

"And you still want to go?"

After a barely perceptible hesitation, he said, "And I still want to go." He had learned something; and in learning it, had lost his high spirits. Something new had happened and now he knew he was not immortal. He was like everybody else. He would grow old. He would die. The recognition gave him a more authentic courage. "Everything clusters together, you know," he said. "Funny the way you go on for years with very little change on the surface of your life. And then one day it's *boom! boom!* The world turns upside down. Things happen like crazy."

"What happened like crazy?"

"Hazel happened."

In an instant Francie understood. "Hazel? She's leaving you?"

"Friday. It's a mildly historic day." It would have been difficult for him to look more vulnerable. "She goes to Reno."

"But why?"

"Why? She found herself our dentist, that's why. Dr.

343

Arthur Bohn. A very nice guy. Widowed. You never know what people see in each other. He thinks she's wonderful, and she thinks he's wonderful." He made a wry grimace. "Possibly once, a long time ago, in another world, Hazel thought I was wonderful. And I thought the same of her."

"I'm sorry, Hib."

"Don't be. I've postponed and postponed asking for a divorce. Our marriage hasn't worked for years." He reddened slightly and dropped into his chair. "What shames me is that she had more courage than I did. Said all the sane sensible things I would have said if I hadn't been such a coward. How we have only one life. How it's more damaging for kids to live in a loveless home than to deal with the honesty of divorce. Et cetera and so on. Quite an experience."

Francie gazed at him in anguish. For there was something in his face that warned her what was coming.

"Francie, now that I'm about to be divorced, a free man, I want you to know that I am—that I have always been—very interested in you. Attracted to you." He was fumbling for words. "What I mean is I would like to get to know you better, and I'd like you to get to know me better. And if it works out—"

"Oh, Hibbard."

"Please listen. If it works out, and I'll do my damnedest to make it work out, I would like to marry you."

For a second Francie could not trust herself to speak or look at Hibbard. When she did, all she said was, "Hib—I can't."

"Why can't you?" he asked in a muffled voice. "Because of Peter? Peter's a lovely guy, but I know you don't love him."

Francie sat motionless with lowered lids. "I do love Peter."

"You care about him, you're friends. But you don't love him. Not the way a woman loves a man. I've watched the two of you together. You don't feel passion for Peter."

"There are many kinds of passion. But that's not the reason." Francie folded her hands in her lap. "It has nothing to do with love. Or passion. Hibbard, I'd make a terrible wife."

"Wouldn't I be the best judge of that?"

"No! You're no judge at all or you'd never ask."

He was a big, energetic man; and women, seeing him, found him virile and attractive. Yet, sexually, he was a genuinely humble man; and now his confidence was badly shaken. "I don't understand you."

"I know you don't."

His imagination spun around grasping at straws. "There must be someone else."

"It isn't that simple."

"What's simple? But that's the reason. Isn't it?"

"No! It isn't."

Her tone was so natural that he felt more at a loss than ever. "It has to be that."

But she wasn't listening. "Let me tell you, dear, something else about passion." She paused, and then, seeming to think out loud, said, "There is something—I don't know what else to call it—there is a passion of the soul."

"You were that deeply in love with someone?" he asked in stony misery.

"Yes."

"And it's over?"

She looked at him with quiet solemnity as though in the presence of some final mystery. "Are such things ever over?" Then she added, almost indifferently, "But that isn't the reason we should never marry."

In the silence that passed between them, he understood at last that she had told him the plain truth. He had tried to understand her in conventional terms because he was a conventional man. Now he saw how little he knew about her. Only what she had permitted him to see. Her beauty. Her intelligence. Her life with Peter. But there were huge gaps.

He had never known her, and now he never would.

There was a tentative tap on the door, and Francie turned. She saw a short young man peering perplexedly into the office.

"Excuse me, Hibbard," he said. "I'm looking for Franciejean Devlin. Her phone doesn't answer, and Bob Hale sent me upstairs to leave a note on her desk. Where's her office? We have a Vitalis meeting at two. As the new creative supervisor, we'd like her there."

"Andy, this is Mrs. Devlin. Franciejean Devlin." Hibbard turned to her. "Francie, this is Andy Anderson, Bob Hale's new assistant."

345

Francie smiled at the young man. "I'll see you later, Hib," she said, walking toward the door.

"Much later?" he asked humbly.

"Late enough to warrant a bottle of champagne. We have to celebrate your new lease on life. I'll tell Peter to put a magnum on ice."

"Fine," he said, grateful for any crumb of her life she was still willing to share with him.

Then, just before Francie disappeared through the door, Hibbard called after her. "Incidentally, Francie, that's a really great headline idea: Passions of the Soul. Only what would the product be?"

For a moment Francie stood in the doorway without moving or looking back. Then she answered. "Dante's Inferno."

21

Through the next few years Francie and Jamie would meet in Paris, Rome, Copenhagen, Washington, New York. They would have a brief and passionate encounter and both be off again. There was no permanence in any of these episodes of the flesh, which were inevitably compromised by the pressures and the demands of their own rising careers. But their connection was further strengthened by Francie, who had prepared in advance the creation of a new relationship. She kept pace with Jamison's growth with long, well-written, intelligent letters on all the subjects of Jamison's world that had now become relevant to hers. The delight he took in her business success led her to stretch her mind continually. She took courses in finance, government, economics, politics, adding these disciplines to her already considerable store of knowledge on advertising, marketing, design, painting, music, movies, antiques. She began by informing herself to be informed for him, and ended by becoming genuinely interested in these topics. She called on all she knew both to amuse and advise him. She was compassionate and devoted and thus became for Jamison, beyond everything else, something like his closest friend. And though she was deeply attached to Peter, touched beyond expression by his unselfish kindness to her, it in no way counted beside her love for Jamie.

It was a measure of the trust that slowly grew between them that as time passed he would on occasion confide in her, without reserve, details of the passing personal histories that occupied him: his affair with a diplomat's wife, which barely escaped newspaper coverage; his passion for a brilliant young soprano, which almost exposed him to the dramatics and gun play of the soprano's husband.

If Francie felt pangs, she concealed them behind advice, consolation and the sympathy of apparent detachment. They were quite frank with each other; and, in fact, if it had not been for Jamie, the variety of her own affairs would have completely diluted Francie's personality. For Francie, like Jamison, was a born solitary, with large, unfilled areas of the heart like the early maps of the world. And except for Peter, and a few people she partially trusted, she lived surrounded by the greedy, the competitive, the lustfully ambitious who taught her only how to outmaneuver their stratagems without any deepening of human intimacy.

As the years passed, the whole drift of the wealthy and fashionable life of the city moved more and more around Francie and Peter. For Peter's business had prospered; he became one of the most sought-after interior designers for private homes, yachts, palaces, and pieds-à-terre.

After the Goldwater disaster, Hibbard returned for a brief three years to Barnett and then bowed out permanently to work for the Nixon campaign, politics being more to his taste than product advertising. But before leaving, he persuaded Abe to make Francie copy chief of the New York office, explaining how much she had contributed to the "greasy kid stuff" slogan for Vitalis and the "closer you shave" theme for Noxema Shaving Creme; to say nothing of how successfully she handled her own account assignments. He was enthusiastically seconded by Norman Hook and Bob Hale, with Lillian casting an uninvited dissenting vote. So Francie became the first woman vice-president at Barnett, and one of the few women copy chiefs in New York. This added considerably to her status in the advertising community. For unlike most agencies, where, in lieu of money, almost everyone above the mail room was named a vice-president, at Barnett the title meant authority, and the entire industry knew it.

With a sense of irony learned from Jamison, Francie noted the new value people placed on her now that, along with beauty, she might also flaunt brains. Now there were more huge dull business dinner parties to go to; more celebrity-hunting charity parties to drink at. More people asked her and Peter to fill their box at the tennis matches, the opera, or horse show; there were more invitations to concerts to hear poorly played Mozart. At theater and museum and gallery openings, more people knew or wanted to know them. Cynically, Francie saw her powers of attraction increasing. And cynically, she knew too that it was no longer her beauty that was the great drawing card. Yes, she was still stunning. Her face had lasted well into her thirties—without cosmetic surgery. The essential structure was there. But there was no escape, she was older. Not that her magnetism had gone; but in the old sexual sense, she was not as confident of her power as she had once been. She felt a subtle change in the way men treated her. She had influence with them, she was a power in her own world; but she could feel their careful stock-taking eyes upon her, telling her she was no longer quite as sexually desirable.

The hurried, crowded years moved steadily onward, and by virtue of brilliance, hard work and concentration, Jamison climbed smoothly and faultlessly up the ladder toward the anteroom of power. The success which he sought when he started his career had not come quite as quickly as a man of his originality and brilliance might expect. But now honors were suddenly heaped upon him. He wrote several books on world monetary matters, one of which became a generally accepted school text. He invented the concept of the GNP dollar and he became economic advisor to the outer four of the EEC. He left the administration of the family bank almost totally in the able hands of Raymond Gardiner.

Now in a world so impressed with wealth, so susceptible to unexpected politeness, so respectful of hard-headed intelligence, Jamie was becoming an international figure. And by the judicious use of foresight, courtesy and wit, he won the unusual distinction of being an economic thinker with real press popularity. He was interviewed with regularity, and news shots of himself continuously stared out of the financial pages of newspapers and magazines. He was undeniably distinguished with his graying temples and strong face; but sometimes looking at these photographs he would think, with wry amusement, that "it takes all kinds of people to unmake a world." His reputation was almost as high as he had ever wanted it to be.

As his life became more public, he came to value even

more highly judgment, coolness, and reserve. His sexual experiences had taught him the hardest lesson of all—a long Jesuitical training in the hopeful deception of others. Since he was surrounded constantly by beautiful and eligible young women, by distinguished and elegant older women, he had several times considered marriage. But suppose he became bored? What would an indignant wife do? It was then that he thought of Francie. Of her sensuality, her beauty, her power to absorb his mind and his senses. And the extraordinary happiness of that first year together would come back to him with a bygone melody, a certain scent. People and places would melt together, almost indistinguishably, to feed his sense of the beauty of that time. And strange indeed was his present perception of himself. For even in their new here-and-now relation, she possessed over him some spellbinding advantage. And when he distilled the fullness of their nights and days, of their wandering and resting and dreaming in one final essence, the strongest feeling it brought him was of being made one with life, of not being alone, of loving and being loved.

Then came the hour inevitably when he had to accept again the reason for their separation. If he could not afford to trust her all those years ago when their passions were at their high-water mark, now with what the years had taught them both about each other, it was utterly beyond question. So marriage, if it happened at all, would not be to Francie.

Once, with a show of bravado, Francie herself had teased him about not marrying. "You know you are simply the best man I've ever known," she declared with a flourish. "So how come some *jeune fille* or *grande dame* hasn't led you to the altar?"

Jamison weighed her question almost as if it were new to him. "Marriage, my dear, is a solemn matter."

"But everyone does it. The world goes two by two."

"Then whom do you suggest I marry?"

"Why, some beautiful, charming woman." She appeared to be disinterested. For, after all, was she not also a beautiful, charming woman, one who had very definitely a life of her own, and was therefore free to ask persumptuous questions?

"Well, I do my best. I consider everyone. But somehow it never comes off." His detached tone—half humorous, half serious to show his willingness to accommodate—made her laugh lightly and pass from the general to the particular. "I see quite a bit in the papers about you and Cecily Atwater."

"Charming girl. Very interesting."

Francie accepted his estimate with a remark that seemed incongruous. "I'm older now. I'm a better judge. I see more in you than I've ever seen. You deserve the very best."

"You do or don't think Cecily is the very best?"

"I don't know. But if I'm to lose you, I would want it to be to the very best." She went on with more emotion imperfectly smothered, "I mean I don't want to see you wasted."

Jamie went to her and put his arms around her, drawing her head to his chest where she let it lay. "Don't worry, dearest. I won't be wasted."

She remained for some minutes resting against him and then pulled back to look up at him earnestly. "You know I often think"—she quickly smiled and looked away—"that you might be afraid to marry." She had meant to say, "I often think you should have children. Heirs." In the beginning it had not struck her as singular that she and Jamison could live at once so separately and yet keep their lives so intimately connected. But somehow, recently, she felt herself in a false position. Jamison was so profoundly a man who should be married, with children.

"I suppose I am afraid of marriage. I stand to lose so much."

"You wouldn't lose me."

"We'd be platonic friends?"

"I have thought of that." So their small talk came at last to its climax, and they ceased to cheat each other with tact. "Your wife would object." Then unable to keep it back she added, "And so would you."

His silence held them, warning her away from things he left unsaid, but fear had its own seduction and she couldn't help asking, "Does it trouble you much—that you're not married?"

He thought of all the answers he might give. Then, still adjusting his manner, he smiled. "No more than it should trouble you."

She could not let the thing rest. "But you must not—you must not be wasted."

Jamison shook his head. He knew what she meant. "My darling, how can I be? I work. I do. I'm far from wasted."

The immediate effect of his quiet words was to act as a sudden reminder of all he had done, of who he was, above and beyond her lover. She could see him all at once with the eyes of the world—the brilliant, the original, the splendid American; a high authority on economic and financial matters, a Nobel Laureate to be. These qualities struck her, as almost never before, as ones to be taken into account. She knew with a deep and proud relief that his life was hardly a failure, could never be wasted; and it purged their predicament of every sordidness.

So if marriage happened at all, it would have to wait. Jamison's sexual life remained a buried stream, flowing underground, never emerging into the world of affairs in which he moved. Was he unhappy? The question to him was irrelevant. He was first and last the born innovator, to whom the awareness of a great adversary sufficed. And if the demands of life, as he chose to live it, often included loneliness, well, so be it. He accepted the hazard and lived with his solitude.

22

What for many of us gives to life its uneasy party smile is our awareness of life's glib unpredictability. The very moment when we feel most "on top", "making it", "in the cat bird seat", is the moment that the bomb casually explodes.

On a cool evening in August 1971, the telephone rang in the Devlin apartment. Francie and Peter were on their way out to a tennis appointment at the East Side Club. Maria, the maid, was off for the evening; and Peter had closed the door. When they heard the telephone ring, he groaned in irritation. They were already late. The phone continued to ring. Francie watched Peter for a cue; and Peter, a victim of his own politeness, opened the foor, while Francie hurried to pick up the phone. "Hello?"

"Hello? This is Monroe," said the voice at the other end.

"Monroe! This is telepathy. I was going to call you tomorrow."

"I want to talk to Peter."

"Monroe, stop ducking! Her birthday's Thursday. How is she?"

"Jim dandy. Is Peter there?"

"Yes, I bet she's beautiful. She's twelve now. Monroe, could I possibly send her a present? From an unknown admirer?"

"We go over this every year. No! No! Where's Peter?"

"You can talk to Peter after you answer me why—"

Peter, who'd been listening impatiently, now gently but

firmly took the telephone out of her hand. "How are you, Monroe?"

"Fine, Peter. Sorry to interrupt your evening, but I need your professional advice. It's been a bloody nuisance figuring out what to do. I almost gave up. Then I thought of you."

"Monroe, could we talk tomorrow? We're late for a tennis date."

"I'm in Washington tomorrow. If you can't help, that's it. But if you can, just a tip, we'll talk at your convenience. Say Friday?"

"All right. But fast, please."

"Did you ever hear of Rubens?"

"The restaurant? Or the Yippie?"

"Neither. The painter. Peter Paul Rubens."

Peter sighed. "Yes, I've heard of him. But, Monroe, my expertise is not Flemish paintings. It's furniture, antiques, interior design. When I need help on paintings, I go to professionals in the period that interests me."

"Well, offhand, do you know if this Peter Paul Rubens painter has any value?"

Peter's face at the other end of the telephone was a study. "Yes, some value. If it's authentic. And of museum quality."

"How much would it be worth?"

"Hmm. It could go as high as a million dollars."

"A million dollars! Good God!"

"Monroe, I fully appreciate your respect for art values; but I have a game waiting. What is this all about?"

"Isabelle's Uncle Ben. On her father's side. Old. Very, very old. And very, very rich. Eccentric. Over the past ten years he has been giving away to museums, piecemeal, his art collection. He's owned this Rubens for forty years. Now he wants to give it to a museum. It's called 'The Garden of Love.' "

"My God! 'The Garden of Love'! If it is authentic, that's worth a million. Maybe more."

"He knows that. He doesn't care. He's worth a hundred million. He wants to give it to a museum. For the tax write-off. His original contact, a man named O'Toole, who did this sort of thing for him, has retired to Ireland. Do you think you could place it for him?"

"No, I could not. Placing paintings with museums is a business unto itself."

"But, Peter, I just can't call the Metropolitan and ask T. Hoving if he happens to be in the market for a Rubens."

"No, that's not quite how it's done." Peter studied his watch. "Okay, Monroe, grab a pencil. Call Vera Busch. Her number is RE 4-6753. It's unlisted—don't lose it. She deals in Old Masters. Use my name. Uncle Ben will like her. She'll know what to do."

"Oh! That Busch woman is just who Ben wanted. He mentioned her!"

"Good. Glad I could help. Now I must go." He hung up and turned to Francie with affectionate impatience. "Darling, you must stop badgering Monroe about the child."

"But she's mine."

"She's not. She belongs to the people who adopted her."

Francie took a deep breath. "Peter, I've been fine these last years. I almost never think of Momma. Let's adopt a baby."

Peter gave her a rueful smile. "You're prepared to leave Barnett and raise a baby?"

"We could hire a nurse."

"True. But even with nurses, babies make demands. Can you give up your life as you live it for a baby? To say nothing of how my life as I live it might affect a child. Darling, are we that unfeeling that we'd raise a baby within our kind of life-style, which, except for the consideration we give each other, is quite self-centered?"

"It is, isn't it?"

"We are what we are."

"And all choices have consequences. And some exclude children."

Peter was dismayed at his clumsy opening of a wound he could not heal. "Yes. Discussion closed. We're late, my little realist. Move your ass." He gave her an affectionate goose, totally forgetting Monroe and the Rubens. Years later, reading the past in the light of what was then the present, he wished that he had never answered the phone.

Monroe leaned back in his chair in the office and thought about Isabelle's Uncle Ben. On and off through the years, he

355

had heard about Uncle Ben, Isabelle's father's much older brother; and always there was an almost religious reverence when his name was mentioned. Monroe had met Uncle Ben three times: once prior to the wedding, once at the wedding, and then last week at a luncheon set up by the old man's surprising telephone call. The old man had made a lasting impression on Monroe. It was a source of distinct relief to Isabelle, he had observed, that Uncle Ben had seemed to like him. Monroe now understood her relief. Uncle Ben was the true family patriarch.

Over the years Monroe had put together bits and pieces of the story, and he knew now that Uncle Ben was the essential reason for Isabelle's family's wealth. For her father, for her other uncles on both sides, for all the myriad of relatives, Uncle Ben, like the Nile, was the source from which all largesse flowed. He was self-made and Byzantinely rich. Eccentric, secretive, he had never married.

Monroe recalled him now from their luncheon as small, bony, and softly sardonic, in complete possession of faculties that Monroe suspected might be younger and sharper than his own. Though very old, he gave the impression of a precocious, prematurely aged boy. In their short meeting, Monroe could feel beneath his agreeable courtesy a kind of dangerous waiting, like that of some fine, sharp blade, carefully sheathed and put away, but ready should the occasion arise. That Uncle Ben would telephone Monroe to request a favor was as mystifying and flattering to Monroe as it was inconceivable and offensive to Isabelle. Why had he not asked her for help? Or her father?

That evening, Monroe walked into his apartment at Seventy-first Street and Park Avenue feeling very pleased with himself. They were going to a benefit that evening. Though he had to get into a black tie and dinner jacket, and though he'd left on his desk some newly proposed government tax legislation that he far preferred reading to attending a benefit performance of *No, No, Nanette,* he was still pleased with himself and the evening ahead. Isabelle would be impressed. Her father, whom they were meeting at the theater, would be impressed. The whole family would be impressed. And if Uncle Ben himself was less impressed, he would at least accept Monroe's coup with his own peculiar brand of cynical good humor.

Entering their sumptuous bedroom which had always seemed to Monroe, in certain disloyal, furtive moments, to be overheated, overupholstered and underlighted, it occurred to him, for the first time, that his judgment of the room was correct. The bedroom had been done in Rococo to include a complete set of eighteenth-century painted and lacquered Venetian furniture, with a ceiling that was also Venetian. The silk upholstery of the furniture and bedhangings of the canopied four-poster bed suggested to Monroe the boudoir and exotic delights of a well-setup whore he had once known. What Isabelle lacked in honest sensuality she made up for in rampant femininity. Monroe then had the pure and startling recognition that though Uncle Ben had never been to their home, let alone seen their bedroom, he knew what the furnishings would be like, down to each sparkling crystal sconce in the dining room; and based on this knowledge, he selected Monroe rather than Isabelle or her father to negotiate for him in the art world. Based on this same knowledge he preferred to give away his paintings as a tax write-off rather than bequeath them to the unseeing eyes of his relatives. The old man was an aesthete in the purest sense; and as such, he preferred Monroe's pragmatic primitivism to the tasteless pretensions of Isabelle and her father.

Isabelle was fussing with her evening dress when Monroe entered; but when she raised her head to greet him, something in his manner struck her with interest and curiosity. "Zip me up, please," she said, shaking her shoulders and putting her fingertips on her shimmering hips. As he proceeded to zip her up, Monroe was aware of the question in her eyes; but it amused him to ignore it.

Monroe's illusions about Isabelle had long gone. His feelings for her having died, chilled by the constant effort required to win any concession of passion, he now accepted her as his wife, in a society that preferred married couples by two. What had surprised him even more than the dwindling of their sexual appetites, was that, given her intelligence, she showed a complete absence of imagination. There was something hard and dull about her, yet she was far from stupid.

When he had completed zipping and hooking her dress,

he started to turn away, but she put her hands on his shoulders, fixed her eyes on his, and asked with real interest, "Did you get your preliminary okay from the Treasury Department on your movie deals?"

Monroe watched her guardedly. "It's coming along. Slowly. The usual red tape." He moved out of her grasp, sat down and started to pull off his shoes.

"Is the sale of the G.E. computer division closed?" She was fishing.

"Just about."

"You like your new secretary?"

"She's hardly new after three months. Yes, I like her."

"Sorry. Temporary dysfunction in the memory banks." Isabelle shrugged. "Rockefeller has offered you a judge-ship?"

Monroe looked at this wife with good-natured forebearance. "I must admit that I am constantly warmed by your enthusiasm for my career." He added judiciously, "How with so much else to occupy your mind—our houses, your father, our daughter, your charities—you still manage to keep up on my cases."

"I am 'up,' as you say, on anything that affects my life. And you are my husband, and you affect my life." She continued conversationally, "And so I congratulate you. Now that I know what I am doing it for. You pulled it off. It's written all over your face. You worked it for Uncle Ben, didn't you?"

He stared at her in wonder. "You are your uncle's niece."

"Of course I am. You found someone for him, didn't you?"

Isabelle was a woman quite unaware of the feelings of anyone but herself, and Monroe was momentarily shaken by her quick perception. But, of course, it followed. She'd just said it herself. She was "up" on anything affecting her. And this certainly did. She'd had a short, sharp struggle with her pride because Uncle Ben had chosen Monroe, not herself, to represent him. But once the game was up, she intended to take credit.

"Who did you find? Tell me."

"Well, I do have my own sources," he answered

imperturbably, wanting to maintain his superiority as long as possible.

"Monroe Perl, what did you do?" Isabelle's splendid brows were drawn together, and she raised her hands as though to shake him.

Monroe made a burlesque feint of ducking a blow. "I'm about to put Uncle Ben in touch with the proper fence."

"I know. But who?"

A subterranean chuckle rose within him. "As I said, I have my contacts—"

"I will kill you."

"Then you will never know. And poor Uncle Ben will miss his chance. You will be disinherited." It was the most fun he'd had with her in years.

"Monroe! Tell me what happened this minute!" She tossed her head and stamped her foot with impatient arrogance. "Who did you find for him?"

"Vera Busch."

"Oh my." She was suitably affected. "She's the only one Uncle Ben wanted. I've asked all my friends, but nobody seems to know her." She said this with a tinge of reluctance. "I don't suppose they're really art collectors, the way Ben is, or they would."

"No, they are not in his class."

"Well, Rosalie did pay $25,000 for a Rauschenberg."

"I believe Vera Busch deals only in Old Masters." Monroe allowed himself a further play of humor. "Twenty-five thousand might buy a corner of a Botticelli. An angel maybe."

"Oh, Monroe! Now the art mavin! Come off it! How did you find her?"

"Through Peter Devlin."

"Peter Devlin?" Isabelle's eyes darkened. "How do you know him? I've been trying to engage him for months. He's booked solid all year. I want him to help me redo this apartment. And the house in Southampton."

Monroe made no reply. He took off his jacket, placed it on a hangar in the closet and started unbuttoning his shirt. "Uhm—well, I've known him for years."

"You have? You never told me!"

"What's to tell? I never knew you wanted to reach him." He made a gesture dismissing the subject.

"Want to reach him? Of course I want to reach him!" Indignation almost suffocated her. "All I ever get is his secretary. And his next free moment is five months from now. He's worse than a psychiatrist!"

"That's too bad." He said this with some effort, and now in his shorts, he stepped into the bathroom to take a shower.

"How do you know him?" Isabelle called after him.

He turned on the shower and called back, "I can't hear you." But how would he answer her when the water was turned off? What would he say? Monroe thought about this. He thought too that the drab years had taught him that it did not matter much to him if his marriage had become a dull duty. As long as Isabelle provided him with a stable, practical private life. He had numbed himself to living with her by staying in his office as late and as long as possible. If it were not for their daughter Lisa, he might long ago have left her. Or confronted her with the fact that they might as well not be married, considering how frequently she went away skiing or sunning, while he worked his ass off in the sleet and rain of a Wall Street winter. But when it came right down to it, he didn't care. He rather liked their arrangement. He preferred his work to her company. And then there were his occasional peccadillos with young women lawyers, or the wives of friends; which, if Isabelle scented, she gave no indication. As to what she herself did for sex, his suspicions faded before the reality. It was not passion Isabelle wanted, but the admiration of her family.

And because of family standards, she had her values for him. When she was in town, she was an amiable, able business hostess. He knew he was a personally disorderly, thoroughly monomaniacal man; absentminded, bored with small talk, social amenities, the arts. He was given to falling asleep, sometimes even snoring, at the theater, at the opera, at the ballet. With Isabelle to run his private life, he could depend on well-organized dinner parties, the right people sitting next to the right people, eating well-prepared food, drinking decent wine. His suits and ties were cleaned and pressed and regularly replaced by Isabelle when replacement was necessary. His shoes were heeled and soled as required. His lost umbrellas, torn tennis shirts, worn brief cases were never missed. New, more stylish versions appeared.

And when Isabelle was in Sun Valley or St. Thomas with a cousin or an aunt, he was still provided with well-cooked, if solitary, dinners, when he came home late from the office. Isabelle had been expertly trained by a mother who knew the intricate niceties of selecting and holding able servants; a facility that is today almost a lost art. So with or without her presence in the house, Monroe's life flowed smoothly and evenly. What more could one ask of a wife? Perhaps she was not a prize, but neither was he. He wanted tomorrow to be the same as today. His work was hard enough. He wanted peace and quiet and no needless fusses. Therefore what would he say?

"How do you know Peter Devlin?" Isabelle repeated with her diamond bracelet now shining and her eyes shooting more sparks than her diamonds.

"He's a client."

"You never told me. What do you do for him?"

"Handle the tax problems of his wife's estate." He was not accustomed to her cross-questioning, or to having to lie.

"His wife? I didn't know he was married. Who is his wife?"

"Mrs. Peter Devlin, naturally."

"Mrs. Peter Devlin. How do you know her? Peter Devlin is very social. She must be, too. What was her maiden name?"

"I don't know. She's a client of the firm," said Monroe, concentrating on getting a shoe horn into his patent leather evening pumps. "God, these are tight."

"Well, what's her first name?"

"Really, Isabelle, the way you go on about society, you'd think there still was such an animal."

"Maybe there isn't. But there is a Maidstone Country Club. And there is the Meadow. As well as the National. And I don't believe we've been invited to join any of them."

"You're still on that kick!" He was thoroughly exasperated; as much with himself for the hole he was in, as with her.

"Yes, I am still on that kick. What's her first name? Maybe I can place her."

"Mmmmm. There, now I have them on. But I ought to have them stretched."

"Monroe, what is Mrs. Devlin's first name?" She said

this with the pained air of a teacher dealing with a particularly dense student. "For all I know, I may know someone who knows her. And between your knowing him, and my knowing a friend of hers, I'm sure I can get him to move up my appointment from May or April or whatever it is." Life seemed full of promises. "Who knows? She and I might even become friends."

At that remark Monroe sank into a deep gloom. He found himself floundering, groping for evasions. "I don't know her name—it's Jean, I think. Or Francis. Something like that."

"Well, it's either Francis or Jean. It can't be both of them. Would Hiram Crawford know? I can call him at your office tomorrow."

Even in his confusion Monroe was impressed by the cold competence of her voice. No, she must not call Crawford. "I am fairly sure the name is Francis Jean. Francis Jean Devlin."

Isabelle stood quietly for a moment in a state of happy self-absorption while a dim idea slowly took shape and color in her mind. Suddenly she gasped, "Why, it's Franciejean Devlin! That's who she is."

But she sounded so pleased with herself that Monroe was at a loss for what to think.

"Isn't she the Franciejean Devlin who is always in the newspapers and women's magazines as the gorgeous, glamorous advertising genius?"

The pause between Isabelle and Monroe prolonged and deepened until Monroe broke it with a grim laugh. "Yep—that's the one."

"Now, why do I kow that name—Franciejean," Isabelle continued in her bright, animated tone, "Somehow I must have met her at a luncheon or a cocktail party or—" There was a long stretch of dead air; and then, bending her head to Monroe, she said slowly and distinctly, "Monroe Perl, does Franciejean Devlin bear any relationship to Elloweise Schmerhorn?"

Monroe experienced a slight skip of heart as he shrugged his shoulders.

Isabelle grew paler even than her very powdered face, and drawing herself up to her full five feet four, she glared up at Monroe. Suddenly, a scream burst from her. "You disgusting cad! You liar!'' She picked up an ivory handled hairbrush from her dressing table and hurled it at Monroe's head.

"Isabelle, please! There has been nothing between Franciejean and myself in years.'' He dived for her hands trying to keep her from throwing the bottle of perfume she now had in her fingers. In their struggle the Baccarat perfume bottle flew open and two hundred dollars of Joy splashed over them.

"I don't believe you! I don't believe you!'' She was beside herself with rage. "You've been seeing her regularly behind my back! When you say you're working late you're fucking that disgusting bitch!''

Now they were struggling together in earnest, Monroe trying to calm her by holding her arms pinioned to her sides.

"You beast! Don't come near me! I hate you!''

"Isabelle, for God's sake, listen. I am not seeing her. I have talked to her on the telephone once in the last six months.''

"If you're not seeing her, why do you talk to her at all!''

"Because she calls me about twice a year to find out how her child is doing.''

"Her child?'' Isabelle stared, incredulous.

"Yes. Her child.'' Watching her, Monroe felt himself break out in perspiration. "Years ago I gave her baby out for adoption.''

Standing in the middle of her bedroom doused in too much perfume, her hair disarrayed and flying, Isabelle went limp with a mingling of outrage and fear. "Is her baby your baby?''

"Of course not. It's her baby. Illegitimately. I don't know who the father is. And it happened almost twelve years ago.''

"After we were married?''

"Yes. After we were married. The same year that Lisa was born.''

Isabelle was still very pale and her lower lip trembled queerly, but something was changing. "It might not be your child.'' Even in her distress, a hundred qualifying reasons were rushing to aid her belief in him. "You wouldn't give up your own child for adoption, would you?''

There was a curious baffled quality in her voice that

reminded Monroe of another year. "No, I would not give up my own child for adoption. I'm glad you have the sense to know that."

"Even if it caused me to divorce you?"

"That's quite right." His will hardened slowly as he sensed her retreat. "I would not give up my child. Even for you."

She stood irresolute, tormented, struggling with a dim feeling of revulsion yet unable to act. How could she forgive such treachery?

"You're sure it isn't Peter Devlin's child?"

"I am positive. Why should a man give up his own child?"

"But he married her anyway? Peter Devlin married that—that—slut." She was struggling with a problem beyond her experience to grasp. "I don't understand these people."

"You don't and don't try." He said the words with a certain satisfaction.

"You don't understand them either," she lashed out suddenly.

"I don't have your aspirations."

She looked for a moment abashed, then asked in a low voice, "Where did you place the baby?"

"That is none of your business." He had the upper hand and he meant to keep it. "Now let's drop the subject."

"It is my business," she flared. "It could be yours, no matter what you say!"

He looked at her as if she'd grown small and insignificant. "I told you. She's not!"

Isabelle pounced on the word: "It's a girl!"

"Yes." He regretted his temper.

"Who has her?"

"I won't tell you."

"Then it must be your child."

Monroe felt a tinge of disgust for Isabelle's personality, and satisfaction that he again had the power to wound her. "It is not my child, and I don't want to discuss it any further. I want to take another shower and get rid of this damn perfume smell."

It was the first time in their married life that Monroe had flatly opposed her, and the humiliation she felt was merged with her loathing of Franciejean Devlin. She felt a defiant desire to get at her somehow. And the only way to do this was to know where the child was. Now she leaned toward Monroe somberly, her eyes wide and trusting. "All right. I believe you. It isn't your child. Why then can't I know where you placed her?" She knew she had blundered in her original handling of him; and it strengthened her determination. "If it isn't your child, why can't I know?" She hesitated. "Unless of course she looks like you. Or someone in your family. Your Aunt Elsie perhaps?"

"She does not look like me! Or anyone in my family!"

"So?" She knew she had scored, but every alert nerve told her to move lightly.

He began without knowing what he meant to say. "I don't want you interfering with her life. She's happy."

"How do you know?"

"I know."

"You keep in touch, then." She was becoming shrill again. "She is yours! She is!"

"She is not! I don't keep in touch!"

"Then how do you know? With strangers?"

"They're not strangers." The instant he said it, he knew she'd outsmarted him. Their eyes met through minutes of speechless communion. "Now let's forget it," he said hoarsely.

"So we know them. We know the child's parents."

"Yes. And it's still none of your business." He was straining to regain his lost power.

"Are they a Jewish or Christian family? That's the last thing I'll ever ask."

"What difference does it make?" Monroe did not know where she was going.

"If they're Christian, then I know it's not your child."

"They are Christian."

"Well then, I believe you. I know you. If you were the father, even though the mother is Christian, you'd have put the child with a Jewish family. And if I know Elloweise, she wouldn't have given a damn." She said it triumphantly. "Now who do we know who is Christian and has a twelve-year-old daughter like Lise. Could even be a friend of Lise's—"

"Isabelle, please—"

"Let's see. It has to be one of Lise's Southampton friends, I think. It could be Maureen—no, it's not Maureen. Barbara? Mm, no."

"Isabelle, stop it!"

"I can't think of them." She was pulling on her hair. "Pat . . . Jenny . . . Cassie . . . My God! I'll bet my life it's Jenny. Jennifer Farrell. Even without that blond hair. It's Jennifer, isn't it?"

"Isabelle!"

"Yes, it is. It is! It isn't her looks—no, it's the way she moves. It's something that says to me Elloweise Schmerhorn!"

Monroe lunged for her and she dashed away laughing hysterically. "Now, isn't that an odd coincidence? Isn't it, though!"

"Isabelle, shut up! Shut up! Shut up!"

23

"Okay. What else did our delicate flower say?"

"The answer to that, dear Mrs. D., is what didn't she say. She told them what she thought of them."

"How courageous."

"Courageous," said Bob Hale wiping his forehead with his handkerchief. "She told them what she thought of their flair. Mind you, *flair* was her precise word. She insisted it had the *je ne sais quoi* that she meant, their flare for fashion—it was zilch."

"Grand." Francie let out a deep breath. "She was drunk?"

"Lillian drunk or Lillian sober is our Lillian. But please, let me share this experience with you. Every single tingle. She told them they were as 'corny as Kansas in August.' She hummed a few bars. I thought she might do a buck and wing. She told them they knew everything when it came to chrome-plated flat-line wrenches, twelve-volt electric winches—not wrenches, or wenches, but winches."

"Who invited our jewel to the Sears presentation, anyway?"

"She invited herself. To stop her I would have to know judo."

"Yes, she can be irresistible. A life force."

"Precisely. A pain in the ass. She also applauded their expertise in two-speed six-cycle washers—"

"With self-cleaning lint filters, and fabric dryers."

"Be quiet. I never saw such a performance in my life. She eulogized their food waste disposers with half-horse power motors, two swivel impellers with stainless-steel grinding chamber.''

"Bob, you're a natural homemaker."

"Francie, let me tell it like it was. It's a catharsis." He closed his eyes. "But when it comes to girls' dressy polyester blouses with open-pointed collars, button-front closing, and long sleeves shirred at the bottom, she said they had taste in their mouth.''

"She's capable of more originality."

"True. And she began to say, if I am permitted to read her mind, that they could take their account and stick it. But Norman fortunately, seated at her right, spilt his coffee on her.''

"Very resourceful. I've heard of that tic." Francie looked out the office window at the wintry streets, thirty-nine stories below her office in the GM building, where streetlights splashed their yellow gleam on dirty snow. "The Fashion Division of the Sears, Roebuck advertising budget was to be our opening wedge. The entire Sears budget, including hard as well as soft goods, amounts to some few hundred million dollars. I gather we've lost our wedge. Sears threw you out. More or less.''

"Wrong. What we both failed to grasp was Lillian's higher inspiration. She knew they could not conceive of her insulting them. So she buttered them on buzz saws and creamed them on fashion. Their lack of understanding of fashion psychology. Trends. Price points. And while they might make more money on the sale of a saw with a Sears Specific Warranty, they blew their profits on that warranty. Whereas a fashiony split cowhide bucket bag with smooth cowhide handle carries no warranty. Once the sale's made, it stays made. With pure profit and no guarantees. Women do not expect fashions to last. If anything, they'd hate it. They like spending money on themselves. She did a small number on ego narcissism that went over their heads, but I think Hansen wanted to kiss her. We now have the account.''

Francie was almost sorry. With Lillian bowing in as the Winged Victory, it would make it almost impossible to control her. Over the years, Lillian's lurking delusions of grandeur had intensified. Her high-handed meddling with both client and staff business had grown more unmanageable. Now she would fanatically believe that it was she alone who was responsible for the addition of Sears to the Barnett client list. The Barnett reputation for superb creative work, the months of preliminary talks between top Sears management and the Barnett creative team headed by Francie and Norman—of none of this did Lillian know or knowing would she have cared. It was, she thought, her show and hers alone. If Francie had been subject to migraines, she would have had one then and there.

"You should have been with us, Francie."

"I've not yet acquired the art of binary fission. Amoebas, as Mark Feinstein who writes the Cyclamate account tells me, can split when they want company. I can't, and the one me I own had to be at a Polaroid meeting on Route 128, Electronics Row, outside Boston."

"Dr. Land was presiding? Well, better you than me. He's an odd one."

"Odd and incredibly intelligent. An entrepreneur with the unique ability to run a major corporation. He can also think for himself. A talent hard to come by even at Harvard's Business School. It's easier if you're born with it. I like working for Land. He's like Abe. When he gives an okay, he means it."

"You made a bundle on your Polaroid stock, didn't you?"

"I told you to buy it."

"Is that what paid for your East Hampton acres? That little twenty-room cottage on Further Lane, for instance?"

"No, dear. Those acres and that cottage have been in Peter's family for generations."

"Ah—the rich and mighty. Your family owned property there, too?"

Francie smiled at Hale's tacit assumption of her background, her heritage. People had been making those assumptions for years. But she'd traveled so long with a false passport that she half believed it herself. She also knew that, given a choice, people preferred the fiction they'd manufactured about her to the far less sunny truth. "Yes. In a way I grew up there. It has memories for me."

The telephone rang; Nancy, Francie's secretary buzzed her. "Ah, Warren. You called earlier. How are you? I thought you were in London." She listened for a minute, then said, "I'm in a meeting now. Let me call you back." She hung up and turned back to Bob Hale. "You catch the 4:45 to Westport. *Vaya con dios*. Let's talk Sears first thing tomorrow. Who does what. We've a lot of pieces to put in place. Account man. Copywriter. Art director." Francie looked at Hale. "Let's make it eight?"

"Eight it is. Breakfast meeting. The Brasserie?"

"No, I'll have something sent up from downstairs. Eggs and bacon? And English and black coffee?"

"You do know my diet."

When Hale left the office, Francie sat quietly thinking about Warren and Josie for the first time in a long time; about time and change; about friendship and love and loss. She and Peter had not seen the Van Nesses in over a year. She tried to reconstruct from grudging memories that had become faded and fragmented her remembered affection for Josie, her attraction once to Warren.

For one thing, Josie's experiments had all fizzled out—one in a disastrous heart-hurting affair—and she had finally decided to settle for Warren. And children. She now had two. A boy and a girl of whom their parents were as proud as any other cliché of parenthood. Josie herself lived to smile again if not to dream of love in the same way; and though she was passingly occupied with other men, she held Warren on a shortened leash. He was now the father of her children and, as such, the first man in her life. But somewhere deep within her, there rankled a sense of injustice, and her attitude toward love itself now had a faintly jaundiced edge. But if they failed each other in one of life's more important experiences, it made no difference. It was not a total failure. When they were together, though you felt their incompleteness, you knew they would last; cemented as they were by a common heritage, pride in their children, good manners as well as the will to make the best of a less-than-perfect bargain. That they no longer saw much of Francie and Peter was due not only to a loosening of the ties that originally bound them but also to the fact that the Van Nesses had moved to Rye, joined Winged Foot and become a complete suburban couple out of the city orbit of the Devlin life.

Francie's secretary interrupted the flow of memories to announce that Warren was again on the telephone. Francie picked it up. "Hello, Warren." She was overly cordial. "You

370

do sound very chipper. And how are Josie and the kiddies?"

"The Van Ness ménage is thriving. And the Devlins?"

"Shipshape. What can I do for you, Warren Van Ness?"

"Well, life does take strange turns." He felt suddenly awkward having to explain himself to Francie. "Yes, indeed. Take business—business is life. Do you know the oldest writing in the world inscribed on clay tablets is not love poetry or prayers but the price of goats?"

"I know," said Francie. "So let's get down to goats. Why have you called?"

"I've had a brilliant idea for the Barnett Company. Or to be precise, I picked it up from a young woman lawyer I met at a closing. Very bright. She used to work for Barnett, Martha English. Remember her?"

"Very well." Francie was suddenly alert, her pencil dangling precariously between her fingers. "Your voice is full of portents."

"Portents mean prophecies. Well, yes—and no. Not portents—cash flow projections. I would like to take the Barnett Company public."

Francie leaned back in her chair, dropped the pencil onto the pad and stared at the ceiling. "Martha's idea."

"SEC law is her specialty. She suggested you personally introduce me to Abe."

"So you could charm him down to Wall Street?"

He could not decide if she was teasing or not. "Are you as unenthusiastic as you sound?"

"I am unenthusiastic."

"Francie, you and the other principal stockholders stand to make millions. Even minor-league stock-owning talent will have orgasms each time the stock rises."

"Unless, of course, the stock drops. And the 'principals,' as you call us, do not need millions. The 'principals' are doing very well now."

Irritated, Warren asked with deliberate crudeness, "Did Jamie give you so much money that money is now meaningless?"

"What was that meant for, Warren? Shock value?"

"Just a question. It always puzzled me how much."

"How much is much?"

"Millions."

"Well, rest easy. I've enough."

"My compliments. Forgive the vulgarity, but there are others in the agency who do not have your fortunate history."

"Then this is a humanitarian effort? It's not the money your firm would make taking Barnett public that appeals to you. It's your sense of public spiritedness."

Francie's sarcasm forced Warren's anger into the open. "You've always underestimated me. You never thought I compared with Jamison. And now you're underestimating this idea because it comes through me."

"That's absurd. I simply see no gain in Barnett going public. Did Wells Rich do better work after they went public? Has Ted Bates done poorer work because they stayed private?"

"It's not a matter of work quality, it's a matter of business. It gives the company money for expansion. As well as negotiable stock for deserving employees."

"Our deserving employees do very well."

"You might want to diversify."

"Into what? Swimming pools? Bird seed? Buy a newspaper?"

He breathed hard and then said it: "You won't introduce me to Barnett, then?"

"To recommend this idea? Absolutely not."

"For God's sake, Francie. Why not?"

"What's the gain? Abe will have to answer to public stockholders. To a public board of directors. They won't understand what a genius Abe is. Because he doesn't act like a genius. Or look like one. Central casting would never call him. He's too plump. Too short. He wears thick glasses. He tries his slogans out on the cleaning women. And you may or may not know it, but he stutters when he becomes vehement. And he's vehement all the time. Suppose the board won't understand or listen to him?" Francie paused because for a moment she wasn't sure she could trust her voice. "He's been decent to me and to a lot of people. I'd hate to see a bunch of amateurs telling Abe how to run his agency. Or his campaigns. Or his clients."

"My God, Francie, you sound like you love him."

She suddenly smiled. "I believe I do. He's a remarkable man. But you have to work with him to know it. Abe consults with God. And the cleaning women. And they understand him. Stutter and all.'' Then she went on thoughtfully, ''War-ren, you want us to go public. Let me give you some of the reasons why you think we should. One—money.''

''Obviously. Outside of you, who are already rich through family connections, all the principal stockholders will make a bundle.''

''As noted, even without my own fortunate history, our principal stockholders all live very high on the hog. Right now. So much for money. Now, two—going public, you believe, is a good source of cash for expansion.''

''The best. You could, if you wanted to, buy—if not swimming pools—other agencies.''

''True. But if we want to expand, we don't need OPM—other peoples' money. We have our own. We run a tight ship. We're cash rich.''

''Sure, sure. But there is rich, and then there is *rich*. If you wanted to buy other agencies, the Barnett Company simply could not have that much free green stuff floating around.''

''We have that much free green stuff.''

For a moment Warren seemed nonplussed. But stubbornly he picked up the chips of his argument and continued. ''Well, it's just possible that your major stockholder himself would like to diversify his holdings.''

''You mean Abe, of course. Our major stockholder. And Abe would as soon diversify as buy the Bronx Zoo. He lives, breathes and will, in the mellowness of time, die with advertising slogans on his lips; chanting as his soul rises to Nirvana, 'Joy makes dishwashing almost nice!' ''

''Okay, that's your story. But suppose you're giving me a song and dance. And in case you're not doing as well as you're saying, going public is a good way for the principals to make a killing. That, my dear, is you too—before the company does a deep six.''

''You mean that if the Barnett Company is a promotion, this is a very good way to get out and let the devil keep the ass end.''

''Francie, I always admired your direct approach to life.''

''Okay, Warren, admire some more. The Barnett Com-pany is not a promotion. If anything, it's an explosion. We can generate all the cash we need for anything—including a company Lear Jet, which idea Abe despises. And buying a substantial amount of acreage between Dallas and Fort Worth, which Abe happened to consider a singularly snappy investment. We generate all the cash we need internally. Hard as it is for a Wall Streeter to believe. We happen, all of us principals, to be tycoons-in-training. Abe has that effect on people."

"Will you tell Barnett how negative you feel?"

"Of course."

"Why do you dislike me so much?" He sounded young and peevish.

"I don't dislike you. I simply don't agree with you."

"Jamie has overeducated you," he said sourly. "Francie, we are old friends. We know a lot about each other." He spoke now softly, menacingly.

"But nothing that's usable as blackmail."

Warren realized he'd gone too far. "What a thing to say."

"I'm a mind reader."

"A man could learn to hate a woman like you." He said it with conviction but more to himself. "All right, you might as well know. I've already contacted Abe. Martha wrote an introductory letter. I counted on you to help change his mind. He said no."

"I told you he was a genius."

"Francie, what do you think of me these days?"

"I don't think of you these days, Warren."

Susan Ellis was twenty-five, a twenty-five that Franciejean had never been. She was born in Omaha, Nebraska, one of five children; and Francie saw her as heaven-sent for Sears. Because Susan's entire family had actually ordered coats and sweaters and dresses and pants and pruning shears from the Sears Catalogue. Susan admired and respected Sears; and when Francie assigned her as copywriter to the account, she felt a fantastic pride. It was Susan's first big project, and it was Sears, to boot. Now she sat beside Francie at Francie's long boardroom-type desk with her shoulders straight, eagerly reading every word of the Sears marketing reports as though they were the Sermon on the Mount. Both Francie and Susan were deep in note-taking when Nancy buzzed Francie. It was Matt Harris in a manic state.

"Francie, where's the Jolly Green Giant?"

"Norman? At E.U.E. with Steve, shooting the new Polaroid series."

"Then he's using an impenetrable disguise. Steve never saw him. He was supposed to check the set. The model, that Pam Winters kid. Check the little boy. The doodads and doohickeys for the thirty-third, or is it the thirty-fourth time? Remember, Francie, the TV production department is not responsible for the clothes, the furnishings, the props, et cetera. We have opinions about choices of actors and models. What they should look and sound like. But ours is a voice in the wind. Ours is not the final vote. Yours is. Norman's is. And Norman was not there."

"Matt, what are you telling me? My God! You called in Lillian?"

"Would you rather I hung myself? As I said, TV production takes no responsibility for what is not its responsibility."

"Why didn't you call me?"

"I did. You were meeting with his honor, Bob Hale, and not to be disturbed. Steve, who is sweating this opus, could wait no longer. It was eight-thirty, and studio time, as we both know, is one ounce of gold per minute."

"Where was Al Gerhardt? He's TV art director on Polaroid."

"Al baby was right there. But he has no clout, and you know it. So lacking the Chicago imprimatur, we substituted Lillian. Though at eight-thirty—we woke her up—her mouth should be washed with Clorox."

"She hated everything?"

"She howled like a cat making love. Bitched, then bitched some more."

"How well you put it."

"She's out for blood. Yours. She especially hated the model."

"I know. She wanted Dina Devereux. Perfect for selling hashish."

"Mrs. Devlin, I suggest you find our lover boy and get him to E.U.E. double quick. Steve will be shooting all day. Lillian will be telephoning Abe tomorrow when he returns from L.A. to tell him the commercial stinks. Norman should fly back tonight and be in Abe's office, singing our praises, before Lillian dials. She'll be doing her situps at 7:30 Chicago time. That gives Norman a short lead.''

At that moment Francie looked up to see Norman, elegantly coated, hatted and gloved, standing in the doorway and swaying like a leaf in the wind. His addiction to alcohol was a well-kept agency secret, but she had never seen him smashed during the day. Now he was waving wildly, partially supported and restrained by Nancy, flushed with embarrassment. Under his arm he carried a manila envelope that Francie hoped contained the ektachromes for the coming Sears magazine campaign.

"Young lady, let me be," he said in a voice of slurred formality. "You're hanging on to me as if I were a long-lost husband. Let me go. I am an Englishman on my mother's side, and I won't have it!" Then he collapsed against the girl, exhausted by his own words.

"Matt, I'll call you back. Something just came up," Francie said, hanging up the phone. "Nancy, help him to that chair. And get me five cups of black coffee.''

Nancy led Norman to the indicated chair and hurried out, dismayed by the downfall of an agency myth figure.

Susan, who had been sitting quietly through it all, trying to concentrate on the Sears report, now stole a sidelong glance. Norman shook his finger peevishly. "You, young woman, should never pick your nose!''

Susan gave him a small, shocked stare. "I never pick my nose!''

"This is Norman Hook, Susan," said Francie. "Our senior vice-president in charge of art. Usually he is not three sheets to the wind. Norman, this is Susan Ellis. She'll be the writer on Sears.''

"I am delighted that you never pick your nose. Excellent. I am merely alerting you to the temptation." He smiled at her. "Now about your feet? No doubt tucked neatly under your chair? Do you have your shoes on? Or are they comfortably off while you rub your stockinged toes together? In fact, do you take your shoes off under restaurant tables?''

"No. And I have both my shoes on right this minute.''

"Well, little lady, in that case you may stand up and let me see them.''

Susan was struggling with an unfamiliar mixture of astonishment and hilarity. She looked to Francie for help; but

Francie, her head in her hands, was laughing too hard. "Norman, you're hopeless!" So Susan stood up very straight.

"Ahhh, little lady, you did not fumble furtively. Truth will out. Your shoes are on. Superb. Now you can leave this office in perfect dignity instead of slumping out like a shoeless trollop in your stocking feet."

Susan turned to Francie in confusion. "Shall I go, Francie?"

"Yes. Take these reports and continue reviewing. I'll have Nancy call you later, and we'll get back to work."

After Susan left, Francie looked at Norman reproachfully. "Where have you been, my alcoholic rabbi?"

"I've been to market, my pretty maid. Romping around the city. Drowning myself in crowds. You know how I hate to be alone." Norman drew a long bitter sigh of vexation. "You haven't heard of my grief? I thought bad news traveled with the speed of eagles. Hasn't Peter told you?"

"Peter has told me nothing."

"I fell in love. I, who have always laughed at such self-importance, fell in love for the first time like a boy with wet dreams. I beg you—don't smile. It's no laughing matter. My choice for worship, of course, was a ballet dancer. It could have been a truck driver. He's illiterate. Unintelligent. Not even a good dancer. But he is so beautiful. He looks like David. But don't they always? Yet he is stupid, petty, venal, and greedy. That is my Eugene. The David of the pickpockets. I gave him thousands in cash. He's run up tens of thousands on my charge accounts. I got him credit cards. Would you believe I am in debt beyond belief?"

"You sound like a parody of a summer romance at Cherry Grove. 'Now that you've sucked me in the summer, will you see me in the winter?'" Francie hoped the crudity would shake him out of his self-pity.

"Anything you say I've already said to myself. Every morning I looked in the mirror and spat at myself while I shaved." He spat on Francie's desk top. "Like that."

"Stop it! I don't need a demonstration!"

"Sorry." He mopped up the spittle with his handkerchief. "I just wanted you to understand how I hated myself." He turned his face to the window and made a spitting noise: "Pfffah!"

"Norman, please! Enough!"

377

"I knew what Eugene was, the minute I met him. But how could I fight it? The gonads on the march. Worse, I couldn't fight my own jealousy. Eugene was inventive beyond belief. Dense but devious. He originated tortures that would have cheered the Inquisition. I lived in terror that he'd leave me. I thought of suicide. I toyed with murder."

"How long has this been going on?"

"Months. All winter. It's been a winter in hell."

"Norman, why didn't you tell me?" She remembered conversations they had had during the years, lasting sometimes far into the night, in which they had shared not only ideas on work, but their most private thoughts on the nature of love, life and death. She was hurt now that he had shut her out like a stranger. "I might have helped," she said.

"I thought of it." He cast a miserable look at the floor, then back at Francie. In a way, Norman's devotion to particular women throughout his life was one of the more peculiar things about him. He idolized them, romanticized them until a profound, devouring friendship crystallized. That Lillian had once been enshrined as a deity left one to wonder on what basis he made his choices. But in the last ten years, Francie was his ideal.

"I was too ashamed to tell you," he said with a sob. His eyes filled with childlike tears. "Anyway, one night I knelt down at my bedside and prayed. I haven't prayed since I was twelve." Norman got out of the chair and slid to the floor, taking a kneeling position and clasping his hands together in prayer. "I said, 'Our father who art in heaven, save me!'" He gave Francie an exalted look.

"Will you please stop behaving like an Actor's Studio reject?"

Norman rose from his knees, brushed off his trousers, and returned to the chair. "But my prayer worked. It was a miracle. I was saved."

"What happened?"

"Abe happened. You know how that old devil prowls around; how canny he is behind that absentminded, foggy stutter. What happened was I was working on a new Pillsbury box design. With all the other cake mix brands lined up around the office. But I'd become self-conscious. I couldn't get the design right. You can't imagine what I did."

Francie couldn't help laughing. "General Mills will love it."

"I'm a genius. The perfect Betty Crocker design." He crumpled some paper up into a ball and tossed it over his shoulder.

"Stop polluting the office with Betty Crocker."

"Abe saw it on my drawing board." Francie closed her eyes. "Yes, he did. What prompted his visit was an eye-catching layout I'd done the day before. He'd seen it when he was padding around the bull pen. That monster, Lollini, showed him how they were revising it. I had quite unwittingly designed a Green Giant ad with a shocking pink giant."

"Norman, you camp!"

"It was not camp. It was real life. Lollini said I was over the hill, or drunk. So Abe came to my office to talk to me and there on the board was my Betty Crocker design. I didn't realize it was Betty until I saw him staring at it. He then said I was overworked. I needed a vacation. Lollini would take over in my absence. The swine." Norman shuddered at the memory. "That did it. For the first time I knew what to do. It was as if Eugene's invisible hand was always there, pulling at my wrist, whispering torments, distracting my thoughts, my designs. There is no sense suffering like a dumb animal. And also losing face, rank and salary. It was me versus Eugene and Betty Crocker. I won. Eugene had to leave town. Leave my thoughts. So I called Morton at the New York City Ballet. Morton will think of something. He'll look divine in a tutu. And I called Lillian and told her to find him an apartment here."

"Lillian! Why didn't you ask me for God's sake!"

"I told you. I was too ashamed." He was in a fury at himself. "She found him an East Fifties apartment, near two gay bars. I was there this morning. Paid a year's rent. Ordered furniture from Bloomies'. Gave him a settlement. And we're divorced."

Francie sorted out her thoughts, while Norman shut his eyes in resigned humiliation. "And the Sears contacts?"

"In here." He indicated the manila envelope. "They'll do for what we want. The model looks like the cheerleader for Walla Walla High. Pam Winston, the Polaroid Girl, yes? My mind is chicken soup."

"That's who we picked. Leave the contacts with me. You head home. Sleep hard tonight. You must see Abe first thing tomorrow."

"I should be at E.U.E. To see what muck Steve is making."

"Not in your condition. I'll check the studio and report in. Go home. While you were furnishing Eugene's nest, Matt replaced your expertise with Lillian's. She hated everything. She's telephoning Abe in the morning to tell him that for the sake of the agency's integrity, the commercial should be junked."

"If only Lillian could be found dead in an alley."

"So you must be there before she reaches him. With a few uplifting phrases to assure him it's all pure magic. Pray it's pure magic."

"Ah, Lillian. Some people drink. Some take dope. She knifes."

"Yet you let her find Junior an apartment."

"Pfah! So she tells Abe. He wouldn't care if I screwed a sheep if it inspired me."

"Agreed. But Eugene inspired the pink giant."

Norman gave Francie an almost comical look of alarm. "You're right." He'd almost completely forgotten his recent fall from grace. "I must be losing my marbles. I'm too young to be senile."

"Take Abe's suggestion. A vacation. Then come back and be glorious. Abe will be delighted at being right. Merely overworked. Could happen to anyone. Except, of course, himself. He never takes vacations."

At that point Nancy came in carrying a tray with five cups of black coffee which she put down on Francie's desk and left.

"Drink up, Norman. Two cups and you'll stand straighter." She buzzed for Nancy.

"Yes, Mother." He gulped down two cups, then rose; he swayed out of the office, passing Nancy as she entered with memo pad and pencil. "Good-bye, you angel of mercy," he said. "Just remember, none of us are perfect."

"Nancy, this is a memo to Mr. Barnett. RE: Going Public," said Francie starting to dictate. "I understand that Warren Van Ness has been doing his utmost to persuade you to consider a public offering. I am delighted to learn that you stood fast. Should any similar pressure arise in the future, let me make the following points to help you solidify your position. In the event that you have not considered the effect of going public on your own control of the agency . . . ."

Norman took a four-week vacation and returned a new man. Francie did not hear a word from Abe about her memo. This mysteriousness was out of character. Abe always enjoyed healthy discussions. She decided he'd have to raise the subject first. She wouldn't.

Then one morning she came into her office to find Abe seated behind her desk writing a note. " 'Somebody is sitting in my chair,' said Momma Bear." Francie stood in front of Abe laughing.

"I was l-leaving you a n-note. I thought I should t-tell you wh-what I've b-been thinking."

"Your answer to my memo?"

"My a-answer. We c-came t-to the s-same con-conclusions, b-but you g-gave m-me something to th-think about."

"Did I now? I gave you an idea?"

"A v-very good idea." He was quite pleased with himself, laughing in a curious, internal happy way. "I've l-landed on m-my f-feet again."

"You've always been on your feet."

"N-No. I had to be p-pushed to d-do the s-somers-sault. And I'm in m-my s-s-sixties." He smiled his rare smile. "I've finally m-managed t-to g-grow up." He hardly looked fifty. There was no gray at his temples, and his voice was eager, rich and young. "I am g-going to admit that I am m-mortal."

"I object."

"D-Don't. I'd rather be. It's a g-great b-burden, im-immortality. B-Being responsible f-for the w-world for the n-next th-thousand years. F-Founding a dynasty a-allows for more l-leisure t-time."

"Abe, what are you talking about?"

"L-Listen. When a s-stranger from W-Wall Street comes n-nosing around and offers m-me this and th-that—which a-amounts to m-millions and m-millions—for a m-mere twenty p-percent of m-my company. A-And then y-you s-suggest it c-could ha-happen again, well then, I've n-no longer got a o-one-m-man band. And if that's s-so, it's t-time I-I founded

381

a d-dynasty. Th-That m-means broadening the m-manage-m-ment b-base. In other words, I am not i-immortal. I n-need heirs."

"Oh, Abe, you'll live forever."

"I hope not. I won't. I-It might g-get v-very boring. And y-you won't, e-either. Given th-that. Y-You my d-dear Fr-Francie are d-due for a promotion."

"Me?"

"Y-You. Next month. In Chi-Chicago. Chic-cago. Where I know a man who d-danced w-with his w-wife. Me!"

24

One morning Francie was reviewing Sears copy themes when Nancy buzzed her to say Bob Hale was on his way into her office. When he arrived, Hale sat down in a chair facing Francie, stretched out his long legs, folded his hands in his lap, and stared at the ceiling. He had a peculiar look on his face.

"What's up, Bob?" Francie asked without looking up.

"I can wait."

Francie looked up. "No, I don't think so." Without anything said, Francie knew his mood; knew with certainty that something was wrong. "You look funny. As if you'd seen Hamlet's ghost. And he bit you."

"I did. And he did." He looked at her hopefully as though needing help to climb out of a swamp.

"Which account is giving you gastroenteritis?"

"Polaroid. What a business. A thrill a minute."

She understood more than he told her. "It's not entirely an account staff gaff. Or you wouldn't be here. It's a creative screw-up?"

"Yes and no. Actually, if there's a hanging party at Black Rock, we shall all hang together. Bruce Blanchard, the incomparable brand manager, telephoned ten minutes ago." Francie said nothing. "He'd just come from a meeting with Michael Flemming."

"Vice-president in charge of advertising."

"Aha! I knew you'd rise to that one. Mike thought Bruce ought to alert us." He paused. "Beg me to tell you why."

"Nothing could stop you."

He sighed. "Too true. Is the name Pam Winston familiar?"

"The model we use in Polaroid commercials?"

"Sweet child." Hale started to laugh in spite of himself. "I believe Creative, Account, and Bruce himself voted for her."

"What's with Pamela?"

Hale gave an exasperated shrug. "She has no business sense. Let me tell you the gory details. Bruce, in his less corporate moments, joined the Club of Eros. As such, he's entitled to monthly specials. In this month's batch of specials, arriving in a plain brown wrapper, Bruce discovered that Pamela has many talents other than simply being a TV pitch girl for Polaroid."

"Dirty movies?"

"Oh, you sophisticated New York women." He raised an eyebrow solemnly. "Dirty stills. Photographs. In full color." But he couldn't control his laughter. "Instead of watching a jolly, dirty movie in a jam-packed movie house, eating popcorn with friends and relatives and feeling each other up, Bruce is a 'dirty still' man. I believe it takes a special brand of decadence to look at dirty stills. Alone, and locked in one's bathroom. Doing God knows what!" He pursed his lips in mock prudishness. "Don't you?" His tone showed how thoroughly he enjoyed his mental picture of Bruce.

The questions and tone made Francie smile. "What is this world coming to? Of course, our Pam stars in these stills?"

"Of course. Showing a decided lack of taste. And financial sense. That work pays peanuts, no matter how much she likes it. So there she was doing all those obscene, erotic things that young virgins, who use Polaroid cameras to take pictures of their babies, which incidentally they conceive via immaculate conception, should never know how to do. Dirty pictures taken by a Rollei."

"Not a Polaroid? No wonder Bruce was shaken. Didn't you show me a confidential report that claimed that Polaroid had a corner on the dirty family album market? The favorite of married and unmarried licentiously bent on taking pictures of themselves in ludicrous positions."

"Forget you saw that report. The sexual act, you have to

admit, in all its glorious variations has none of the grace of a grand jeté. Even an adequate plié." He sighed. "What do we do?"

Francie and Bob had been so intent that neither had heard Lillian enter the office, sit down, and listen. Now Lillian said, "Francie, I never wanted to use that girl." Her tone carried a warning like an animal baring its teeth. "Now we're going to lose Polaroid because our model is a well-publicized whore. Who enjoys her work."

"You wanted Denise Devereux. Suppose she were interviewed in an opium den?"

"Denise is the mother of two beautiful children."

"The unmarried mother. By that I do not mean divorced. Dear heart, I too stay in touch with the grapevine."

"There are alternative life-styles these days."

"Of course. But not in advertising. Bob, will you tell Abe before Dr. Land does?"

"I've a meeting this afternoon with Sears. Francie, I suggest this situation requires your incomparable tact. Go home, pack an overnight bag. Abe will need you tomorrow when they lower the boom."

"We also use Pamela in Sears Junior Bazaar ads. Our back-to-school type," said Lillian innocently.

"Oh, Christ! We'll have to reshoot immediately."

"And that headline Susan showed me, 'Pants That Fit.' It's vile!"

"Lillian, would you like 'pants that don't fit'? Damn Pamela! Who would believe that one of nature's clumsier inventions, the sexual act, in its acrobatic glory, could cause such tsorus!"

"I would," said Francie. "And so would you."

When Lillian returned to her office, she telephoned Tom Wolff, advertising manager of the Sears New York office. She persuaded Wolff to see her for a short meeting at eleven. But since Bob Hale and the entire copy and art team assigned to the Sears fashion account was due at three for a full-dress presentation, Tom was mystified by Lillian's insistence on a private meeting. The idea of being alone with her made him uncomfortable.

When Lillian arrived at Sears, she had her usual sense of surprise that a company with the resources and reputation of

Sears should house its New York offices in a reconverted loft building. Compared with the dash of the J.C. Penney headquarters, the Sears building gave the impression of a company on its last legs instead of what it was—the gigantic, successful, largest mass retailer in the country. My God, she thought, they could buy Radio City, if they wanted it.

Tom Wolff, a genial heavyset man in his thirties, was unaccustomed to having ladies from the great world of advertising sweep into his office. He knew he was the client, and he knew the power of the Sears name, and he loved the Company, even as he loved his own family. But Lillian Morris intimidated him. He was impressed with himself that she'd asked for a private meeting, but he was also scared stiff.

"How are you, Mrs. Morris?" he asked, coming forward to greet her.

"Now that we're co-workers, call me Lillian." She sat in the chair indicated while he returned to the safety of his desk. "My reason, Tom, for visiting you this morning is to make certain that Sears has the most effective fashion advertising possible. And in order to do this, I must have your complete confidence."

"You all do," said Tom squirming inwardly. "You and Mrs. Devlin and Mr. Hale. Sears has a lot of respect for the Barnett Company."

"That's quite right. But where Sears is concerned, I, more than anyone at Barnett, have the Sears interest at heart."

"Oh," said Tom, not knowing what to make of such total lack of the team spirit Sears prized so highly.

"Not Mrs. Devlin. Not Mr. Hale. Or anyone else. Only Lillian Morris knows what is and isn't good for Sears. Mrs. Devlin, our creative director, has already blundered seriously."

Tom wasn't sure he should listen to this kind of disloyal talk, but his ears pricked up instinctively. It was no accident that, coming from the shipyards of Boston and starting out as a clerk in retail, he was now New York advertising manager. "What kind of blunder?"

"Well, for one thing that new headline for the pants series. It's 'Pants That Fit'."

"Really? Pants That Fit! Why, that's wonderful. I like that!"

"That shows how much you have to learn. Now if you called them Pretty Girl Pull-ons or Tramp Around Trousers—"

"I do like Pants That Fit."

"Skip it. It takes time to catch the rhythms of fashion copy. But with me to teach you, you will. Now I must tell you another of Mrs. Devlin's blunders that is far more serious. The model for Sears Junior Bazaar ads. Back-to-school merchandise."

"That's a pretty girl. Looks like Laurie, my wife's kid sister."

"Whatever she looks like, Pamela Winston is not the kind of kid sister a self-respecting family would care to claim. I did not choose her. Mrs. Devlin did. So, in the future, I think it would be wise if you insist that I make all model selections. Plus auditing all advertising meetings so that the proper tone is maintained—in clothes selection, copy, art, models—"

"I understand, Lillian." Tom Wolff's eyes were wary. "But what were you saying about the model for the Junior Bazaar ads?"

Lillian lowered her voice. "Have you ever heard of Eros?"

"No," said Tom, lowering his voice too.

"Then allow me to be vulgar for a moment. The Club of Eros, with a few hundred thousand members, is an organization that distributes to its members still photographs of men and women in erotic poses—obscenely erotic poses."

"Naked?" Wolff felt suddenly short of breath.

Lillian smiled at him tenderly. "Naked. In the nude. How else could one do sexually erotic poses?"

"Oh, I see." A slow comprehension was dawning on his face.

"Yes. And Pamela Winston, soon to be seen in Sears Back-to-School advertisements, has done a series of modeling jobs for the Club of Eros."

"Oh." Tom could feel that his palms were sweating.

"Now you see why I should have authority to pass on everything suggested for Sears advertising. Do you know I was not invited to this afternoon's meeting?" He shook his head because he was having difficulty speaking. "Will you please see that I am invited?"

"Yes," he heard himself saying. His mouth was tight and his stomach queasy. "Now if you'll excuse me, Mrs. Morris."

"Lillian, please—"

"Excuse me, Lillian. I have to call Chicago." He was having difficulty getting the words out of his mouth.

"Of course," said Lillian, rising. "I'll see you this afternoon." And she wafted out, trailing clouds of Tabac Blanc.

Francie and Peter flew to Chicago together. He had clients to see, including Norman; and she was full of gratitude for the luck of having him seated beside her. Talking to Peter was like thinking out loud. Only better. It had not always been so; but the passing years had taught them to exchange their strengths; the granite they had mined out of the deep stony quarries of self-knowledge and experience. In their marriage she had shared what might not have been possible if she had been more passionately linked; for the deepest feelings too often, and paradoxically, isolate people from each other more completely than they bind them. Now, Peter's familiar presence beside her rescued her from a failure of nerve. What she did not know was how quickly Peter had read her need. And though there were concrete reasons for his going to Chicago, beneath them all lay the gentle, enduring, and obstinate determination to go on rescuing her whenever it was required.

Arriving at Abe's office at eight the next morning, Francie knew immediately that he had already heard of the Polaroid imbroglio. For, though Abe was nowhere to be seen, Norman was seated in a chair, ashen and apathetic.

Francie seated herself in a chair facing him. "I gather you heard the headlines?"

"Loud and clear. Abe telephoned me last night at home to give me every happy detail."

"How did he find out? I'm here to tell him."

Norman gave Francie a slightly sick smile. "Lillian telephoned him. He telephoned me."

"Ahhh, Lillian. How that name leaves a bad taste in the mouth. How could I have forgotten her."

"Because you're not naturally vicious. It's a flaw in your survival drive. Lillian suggested that Abe fire you and me and Bob Hale and countless others in nonalphabetical order. She also reminded him of my Betty Crocker caper. She said my sex life was a public disgrace and the cause of my work slippage."

"What did Abe say?"

"I asked h-her if sh-she was. drunk," said Abe, who walked back into the office, having gone to the coffee machine. "Now, d-do I c-call Flemming or w-wait for h-him to c-call me? By the w-way, h-how did this h-happen?"

"We don't keep an FBI file on our models," said Francie.

Abe sat down at his desk. "That's what I plan to s-say. A-And w-we're p-pulling all the commericals to-today. W-We'll p-pay for the t-time and c-cost of re-reshooting."

"Even if we lose the account?" Norman asked with some effort. His mouth was dry from last night's drinking; and inventorying his body, he knew he had the inevitable hangover.

Abe nodded and sipped his coffee. He drummed his fingers on the desk and then buzzed Anita. Anita who always knew everything. "Get m-me Dr. L-Land. Or-Or M-Michael Flemming."

While they waited, Abe sipped his coffee; and Norman put his hand on his chest, comforted by the thump of his heart. He was still alive. "Francie, if I ordered up a Bloody Mary would you like one?"

"Norman, stop it."

"I hate executions. I could never finish *A Tale of Two Cities*."

Abe said nothing, slouching in his chair. Only once did he glance at Francie. She sat there actually too poised for comfort. But she looked straight at him, not past him, or inwardly at some thought of her own. He realized that she usually looked straight at him like that. If she had bitten her lip or clenched her fist, he would have understood. But she did not allow herself the relief of a physical gesture. He respected that.

Then Anita entered the office. "Dr. Land and Mr. Flemming are in a meeting."

The telephone rang. All four listened, superficially indifferent.

"It could be Flemming," said Norman finally.

"No," said Francie. "Nor Dr. Land either."

"How do you know?"

"T-Too soon," said Abe.

By now Anita had reached her office and picked up. After a moment she came back. "It's Mr. Garson of Sears. Will you talk to him?"

"I might as w-well. W-We have other accounts th-that n-need a-attention."

Abe picked up the phone. "H-Hello, Joel. H-How are you?" Francie watched; and as the minutes passed, she saw his shoulders give an imperceptible sag. After a time he said, "I don't s-suppose there is anything I could say to change y-your mind?" Francie was surprised at the sober, sad sound of his voice. Freer than usual of its stutter. "Well, thank you for telling m-me yourself, Joel. Yes."

Abe put the phone down and stared at them. "We just lost Sears."

"Sears! Why Sears?" Norman could not contain his shock.

"It was a b-big opportunity." He was helpless before a fact he could not alter.

"What happened?" asked Francie.

"Pam-Pamela Winston. In J-Junior B-Bazaar."

"Who told them? We killed those ads yesterday before I left. We're reshooting today and tomorrow. And eating the cost. Pamela Winston would never have appeared in any magazine." Watching, Francie saw the effort Abe made not to show his hurt pride.

"It's t-too bad. We w-were d-doing a g-good job for them. Lil-Lillian t-told T-Tom Wolff. She was m-making sure she was p-put in ch-charge of Sears." He buzzed Anita. "C-Call Mrs. Morris and t-tell her t-to be in my office tomorrow at eight. Sh-Sharp." Then he looked hard at Francie. "Sears and Polaroid. That's close to f-forty million."

"Unfortunately, yes." Francie never knew until that moment how much she loved that old man and how sorry she was. And she knew then it was now or never. "Abe, Lillian's become pure melodrama. We can't afford her."

"I know. B-But she w-was a g-great a-asset once. And a

gr-great lady." Francie heard no resentment, no apology in his voice. "S-She's just gr-grown t-t-too old t-t-too s-soon."

Twilight had only begun, but they had been drinking steadily for an hour. It was Lillian's treat, and Norman wished he liked champagne. It would have struck the perfect note of celebration to order a bottle of Dom Perignon. Why not? She was even canny enough to say nothing of what it would cost her. But since he couldn't abide champagne, he had to stick to Jack Daniel's. Norman knew he was getting smashed, but he didn't care. It was too much fun to be sitting at his favorite gin mill, "The Top of the Rock" in the Prudential Building, and watch Lillian squirm. He had no feeling of the sixty stories below him. The city, like the blue of the sky and the denser blue of Lake Michigan, was a spectacle, absorbed as he was in a more human theatrical: the sight of Lillian on the rack. Just to further provoke her, because he knew how it irritated her, he kept up a running conversation with Peter on the proposed sale of some of his furniture.

"Well then, how much for the Flemish chandelier? Or the Louis XV console? Peter, you have to admit that it is practically of museum quality."

"We'll talk after dinner. After I have a chance to study the pieces. I know the quality of what I sold you; but I can't judge your European exuberances until I actually see them."

"Wait till you see the seventeenth-century Antwerp bed. It's a prize."

"Norman, if you and Peter don't stop haggling, I shall scream. I did not invite the two of you to drink up my bank account just to hear this twaddle."

"Lillian, my pet, Peter is here at my request because I am in straitened circumstances. Going to the dogs as they say. I married the wrong man—or is it woman? The alimony was outrageous. I am in debt. I need money. Peter set this date a month ago. Since I gave up reading goat entrails, I had no way of knowing you would grace this crude outpost with your presence this evening."

Her voice had a petulant whine. "But why does Abe want to see me?"

"Maybe he misses you."

"Bastard."

"Honestly, Lillian, you don't look your age."

"Happy birthday to you, too. You son of a bitch!"

"Now, that does it. I will not have you talk about Millicent, my very own mom, that way."

"Oh, shut up!"

When Lillian had telephoned Norman from O'Hare that afternoon, he had been tempted not to take the call. But then it occurred to him that though he had a prior appointment with Peter, it might be entertaining to let Lillian take them for a few pre-dinner drinks and watch her wiggle like a cockroach on its back.

But now, two hours later, sitting next to her, he felt mainly disgust. Though he had learned through the years never to trust her, he had fought essentially a defensive battle aimed at protecting himself and the agency, not destroying her. Norman, for all his personal quirks, was a courtly man. What he had misjudged in Lillian was the progressive viciousness which now matched the artistry of a screaming queen. He knew she had made at least one sincere effort to have him fired. She'd probably made others that Abe had politely refrained from mentioning.

"He's up to something." She was thinking of the message on her desk that morning. "Anita called at nine-thirty. Abe knows I don't spit before ten. 'Be in my office tomorrow morning, eight o'clock Chicago time.' Why couldn't he talk to me on the telephone? Why am I being presented at the Court of St. James? I called back three times before I left for La Guardia. He was always in a meeting. That's suspicious."

"Lillian, what you need is a Family Bible. Religion. Or Emma Peal's survival kit. It fosters self-reliance."

"Abe is probably going to give you some sort of special assignment."

"You shut up, Peter Devlin," she abruptly screamed. "You keep out of this. I'm not here to talk to you."

"Lillian, you must learn to curb your temper or you won't have a friend in the world."

"Peter is not my friend. He married that vampire; the worst thing that ever happened in my life." The waiter brought another round of drinks while Lillian went on raving. "Why did you desert me, Norman—for that slut? Why? You left me for her. You went over to her side. We were such

392

friends. We had such times. What did she do to turn you against me?''

It astonished Norman that she believed her own words. Here she was obstinately insisting on an identity in his life that she had long ago forfeited. She could not conceive that it was far too late in the day to arouse his compassion by calling on memories they had once shared. He who was so steeped in her most recent betrayals.

She leaned back to breathe, whistling through her long Roman nose. "Abe, too. That she-wolf has you both hypnotized.''

"Lillian, your mind is a sewage system of self-pity and delusions.''

At his words her face broke. Her shoulders started to shake, and at first he thought she would sob. Instead she laughed in a harsh, drunken croak as though at some stupid obscene joke. "You take her part! And she has ruined me. You think you're ruined? It's only money. For me, it's my life. Abe would have made me a vice-president. I know. I know." She drew an inward hissing breath. "And Hale eats out of her hand like a trained seal. Her bargain basement mind rules the agency. Imagine, Pants That Fit.'' She stopped. A sudden rational connection had come into her mind, and she wondered how much the trip was due to Sears.

Peter had been sitting quietly, stony-faced, listening to Lillian's outburst against Francie. This was a pity, he thought. To see someone at such a pass. He felt disgust and fear too; recognizing on a deep level that he was sitting face to face with a victim of a personal catastrophe that, in one way or another, could happen to anyone. The futile record of her failed life seemed to rise up and shriek at him. Now he judged he had had enough. He pushed back his chair and stood up. "Norman, I think it's time we went. I'm going to the men's room, and when I get back, let's go.''

"Have a pleasant pickup,'' Lillian said as Peter left.

"Lillian, try to behave like a lady. It's difficult enough knowing you were once my pet disease. You have a devastating, self-consuming egotism that is worse than a male model's.''

"What did that bitch do? Why did Abe tell me to come out?'' Lillian was obsessive and unlistening; her voice gradually ran down like a timepiece that needs winding. "What does he want?"

"You'll die laughing when you find out."

"I have no sense of humor."

"That's quite true. You have become a tiresome, hysterical old crone. With no redeeming social value." In Peter's absence, Norman's speech grew more slurred. "Franciejean did nothing to you. You managed it all by yourself. You know what you are? You're *meis*. That's what you are."

"What's *meis?*"

"Some Jewish lady you! Not to know that."

"I'm not Jewish."

"Well, my German-Jewish grandmother was. And *meis* means—in Yiddish, not German—not exactly ugly. But in a free translation it means that you are a 'poor thing.' You've become a 'poor thing.'"

There was an instant of silence. Then Lillian suddenly gathered her strength, reached across the table and, as Norman swallowed his Jack Daniel's, she slapped him hard across the face, almost knocking him off his chair. Norman coughed, choked, sputtered, and turned red, the design of Lillian's hand on his face. "Faggot! Pansy! Don't you dare talk to me like that. You goddamn cocksucking freak!"

"Sheer poetry, Lillian. Sheer poetry." Norman rubbed his cheek as he regained his balance and coughed his throat clear. "The beauty of your body is equaled only by the beauty of your spirit. With a little bit of luck, Abe might just fire you tomorrow. That's what you're here for, Baby Jane."

"I'll kill you," Lillian screamed reaching toward him, but this time Norman caught her arm.

"No, you won't, you bloodthirsty cartoon of a woman. I may have a limp wrist, but I have a very strong grip. I might just break your arm."

"Norman," said Peter joining them, "let go of Lillian. Let's move on."

"Yes. Of course," said Norman, dropping Lillian's wrist as if it were hot. "Let's blow this joint. Pardon the pun. Lillian, with her usual good taste, has managed to bore me." Norman got up unsteadily from his chair. "As I was saying about the Antwerp bed . . ."

Lillian rose as well, swaying a little. "I think it's time I

394

returned to my hotel.'' She hailed the waiter, who came at a trot, having seen the fight and glad to be rid of them. Instead of a credit card, she handed the waiter two twenty-dollar bills. ''Keep the change. Come along, Norman. Let bygones be bygones. We all have our falling outs. Get me a cab. You can drop me at the Drake on your way home.'' She looked at Peter with contempt. ''You come too, wifey.''

Downstairs in front of the Prudential it was difficult to find a cab. Lillian, Norman and Peter moved toward Michigan Boulevard. Traffic was heavy. Cabs were scarce, and it seemed as though hundreds of people were waiting for them. They decided that the best idea was for Peter to take the west side of Michigan and Norman the east. Lillian waited on the corner of Prudential Plaza, her eyes cold and empty as she watched Norman walk unsteadily up toward Wacker Drive. He was wildly waving his hands. An empty cab did appear, turning out of the Regency Hyatt Hotel, but it speeded by, ignoring Norman; as did a second which picked up a red-headed girl standing a few feet south of him. He seemed to miss everything. He looked a little dizzy.

''Over there, Norman. Over there!'' Lillian shrieked. But the cab passed him before he could attract it.

''There's one. There's one.'' But Norman missed that too; he couldn't react fast enough. Lillian's face was savage and red. There were rage lines running from her nose to the edge of her mouth. She was breathing hard and screaming. ''Get a cab, damn you. I can't stand here forever.''

Peter called suddenly to Lillian from his side of Michigan Boulevard. ''Lillian, come on over. Here! I have a cab.'' There was a cab waiting.

She gave Peter a venomous stare. Then she looked down the block where Norman was recklessly and uselessly trying to intercept a cab. She looked beyond Norman to where one of the Michigan Avenue buses was barreling over the bridge toward Wacker Drive. Without turning her head, she called to Peter, ''Thank you for the fucking cab.'' Then she shouted, ''Norman, here. Peter has a cab. Across the street.''

Hearing her voice, Norman, who had only dimly focused on the bus, turned toward Lillian and watched her wave wildly to him to cross the street. She was crossing Michigan herself and urging him on, clapping her hands as though he was a dog who she wanted to do tricks. He looked over at

Peter. Peter was shouting something. It sounded like "Stay there!" How could he stay here and still get to the cab? Did Peter think the cab would turn and pick him up—in this traffic? Ha! This was one of those rare occasions when Lillian was right. In his alcoholic haze, Norman couldn't help laughing as he stepped between the parked cars to cross Michigan Boulevard. The bus driver barely had time to slam on the brakes. Norman never knew what hit him.

It was a warm, green spring morning with the sun moving in and out of thin clouds. The air was calm and the landscape, with its trees and clear lakes, looked more like a forest park where the people of St. Louis might picnic than a place where they buried their dead.

"Into your hands, oh merciful Saviour, we commend your servant, Norman Hook. Acknowledge, we humbly beseech you, a sheep of your own fold, a lamb of your own flock, a sinner of your own redeeming. Receive him into the arms of your mercy, into the blessed rest of everlasting peace and into the glorious company of the saints of light."

The congregation said, "Amen."

The pastor raised his head. "Let us go forth in peace."

As the coffin was slowly lowered into the Hook family plot, Francie heard people sobbing softly. Only Lillian's tears were high and wild as though she had carried a heavy load of sorrow a long way.

Francie did not cry. In her mind she was remembering Peter's terrible words, "Francie, I saw it happen. He never would have stepped off the curb if Lillian hadn't signaled him to cross."

When the ceremony was over and people slowly filed back along the paths, Francie could still hear Lillian's wails.

Then suddenly Lillian was standing beside her, yanking at her, speaking in a hoarse, accusing tone. "Franciejean! What did you do?! How did this ghastly thing happen to my Norman!"

An awful dread of what she might do to this woman swept over Francie. The next moment she struck out, a direct punch to Lillian's mouth. The pain and taste of blood in her mouth took Lillian by surprise. Before she had time to react, Peter had a restraining arm around Francie's shoulders and forcibly steered her down the path and away.

396

It seemed dark in the early spring sunlight, and now the tears that she would never permit herself came hot and fast through her half-closed eyes. For a second she felt beside her, real as Peter, and yet not real enough to subdue her grief, the presence of her old friend, impudent and arrogant, his breath smelling of bourbon, telling her as he did in the beginning, all those long years ago, "You will have a brave life, Franciejean." Well, maybe this was what he meant after all. She hoped he was proud of her. Leaning against Peter, she smiled and she wept. She would never again find someone like him.

The morning after the funeral Abe was at his desk at 6:30 A.M. At 7:30 Anita arrived, bringing with her his usual sizable breakfast on a tray sent down from the Top of the Rock restaurant. While he ate breakfast, Abe dictated a memorandum to the copy group on Marlboro, and two letters to clients. At 8:00 Anita buzzed to say that Mrs. Lillian Morris was waiting to see him in the outer office. Abe grunted. He'd known from the beginning that he had had only two choices in this situation. One was to have Bob Hale do the dirty work and keep out of it entirely. The other was to do it himself and try his best, knowing all the time it was impossible, to come out feeling as clean as possible. But in the end he knew Lillian was his job. So here she was.

"All right. C-Come in and t-take the tray. A-Afterward s-send Mrs. Morris in. H-Hold all c-calls un-until she leaves."

Sitting in the reception room waiting for Abe, Lillian tried to concentrate on *Business Week*. But she could not see the words clearly. It seemed to be saying something about Arthur Burns and the economy. Her head was lowered in concentration but her knees were trembling. And though she'd put on her complete makeup, she was afraid her lips had turned bluish under the lipstick. That happened when she was frightened. And her heart was pounding dangerously. God damn it! she thought, sickened by her own cowardice. Son of a bitch! Bastard! Shit! She must make her mind empty. Make everything seep out of it. She must not think of . . . would not think of . . . To keep the panic down she said to herself her own name—Lillian Morris, Lillian Morris, Lillian. It was an incantation to keep her mind free of the other names—Franciejean, Norman, Norman, Francie—

397

"Mrs. Morris, excuse me."

Lillian looked up startled. She had not heard Anita's approach. "Yes, Anita?"

"Mr. Barnett will see you now."

"Oh? Yes." Lillian jumped up and let the magazine slide to the floor. Without stopping to pick it up or looking around, as if escaping from the flames of an advancing fire, she hurried past Anita toward Abe's office.

Her words were abrupt and reckless as she entered, "Abe, my dear. Abe! What a marvelous tête-à-tête. Wonderful. Like old times, isn't it? When the Barnett Company was just a small suite of offices and mine was two doors away from yours? Remember?" She heard her own voice say those words as if she were outside herself. She could almost see the shape of her mouth as she pronounced the words coquettishly. "Oh, how we used to talk over every problem. I must have been in and out of your office ten times a day." Sitting in the chair facing Abe, she felt an urgency, half fear, half acquiescence—like love, it was something like love. But it was also like hate.

"I remember." Abe was quiet for a long moment. He had enough of his own thoughts to occupy him. "It is s-some t-time since we've had a s-serious t-talk about an-anything. I should l-like to m-make it clear th-that y-you have l-long been an asset t-to the c-c-company."

Lillian raised her eyebrows and there were sudden deep lines in her forehead. Her face, which once had been so striking, was wearing out. "I think so. You and the company have had the best years of my life! The best of the bargain!"

Polite, patient, judicious, Abe showed neither encouragement nor discouragement as he listened.

"And I've put in my time when I was dog-tired. Beat. When I've been ill. Even when you promoted that preposterous Franciejean over my head."

"L-Let's leave Francie out of th-this."

"Leave her out? My God! She's a dirty little bitch! I will never understand men—making such fools of yourselves over a face."

It was a long time since Abe let his temper run loose. "Lil-Lillian, l-leave Francie out of th-this!"

"Leave her out! I certainly will not! Do you dare deny that I haven't done more for Barnett than she has? Do you?"

"Y-You've made a con-contribution th-that c-can't even be measured."

"Who was it who helped you get Max Factor! Brown Shoe! La Petite—my God! What a mistake that was! Who taught you to see fashion in cars? In bathrooms? In food? Who taught you about design? And photographers? Who?"

"L-Lillian y-you've b-been of e-enormous h-help."

"Then show it! Why have you brought me out here? I hope at least to make me a vice-president!" The look in her eyes was not now malicious. If anything, it was pleading. She had no self-control. She would always be strident. This was the only way she knew; to beg him to be as he used to be to her. Except that she was no longer the woman she used to be. Their relationship had changed long ago, and now she was like a woman suddenly struck blind, blundering about, lost, frightened, trying to find again her vanished world.

"Li-Lillian, I am not going to make you a vice-president."

Her face puckered. "Well, at least a second lieutenant."

"N-No. N-Not that either." For the first time Abe's tone showed pain, and he paused. "I-I am g-going to ask for y-your resignation."

"Oh noooo!" It was a wail so jarring it made Abe's flesh creep. "You can't! You can't. I won't!"

"I have t-to. It's t-time. Y-You can take early re-retirement. The c-company is prepared to buy b-back your stock at t-top d-dollar. P-Plus your profit sh-sharing. Plus a y-year's severance pay. You'll b-be a w-wealthy w-woman."

"How dare you! How dare you! After all I've done for the Barnett Company! For you!"

"Y-Yes. Y-You have l-long b-been an asset."

Lillian's existence rarely gave her sufficient opportunity for fury. Now she could give her heart up to the rapture of rage. Her lust for anger was the highest form of her sensuality; and if society and life would have permitted it, she would ask nothing better than the capacity to kill and be killed once a day. "It's that disgusting little tramp, Franciejean. She's the one who put you up to this."

"N-No one p-put m-me up to it. Y-You've gone t-too far. Lil-Lillian, we l-lost the S-Sears a-account because of y-you."

"Because of me! Your darling little tramp lost you the

399

Sears account. Imagine! 'Pants That Fit.' What a damn fool slogan!'' Her only chance was to match will against will.

"Sears l-liked the s-slogan very m-much. Lil-Lillian, you l-lost it. Y-You t-told Tom W-Wolff about P-Pamela Win-Winston. That w-was tot-tally ir-irresponsible.'' His tone had a curious formality.

"Pamela Winston! The model?''

"Y-Yes.''

"They should have invited me to the meetings. I brought that account in. And I voted against that trollop. She was your darling Francie's choice.'' Lillian's blood seemed to have leaped into her brain. "I'm only sorry I didn't kill her, too—that's all I regret. She should have been holding hands with Norman when he crossed the street.''

"What are y-you t-talking about?'' Abe spoke the words in sheer despair knowing all too well the answer.

Lillian gave a savage, croaking laugh. "Naturally, Norman. Why do you think he crossed in front of the bus? I waved at him. I saw it coming. He didn't, the idiot.''

Abe heard the words clearly but it took minutes for him to accept the meaning. The shock was so great that for once he lost his stutter. "Lillian, I wish you had not told me that!''

"Oh hell!'' she cried out. "Oh hell!'' She reached out her arms to him, trembling with panic, leaning forward across the desk. Was it for this that she'd given her whole life?

But Abe's face had grown gray with the strain of the meeting. "Let's forget you ever said it. There's nothing now to be done about it. But leave now! Leave the Barnett Company!'' He shook his head trying to clear it. "Don't go back to the New York office. Your personal belongings will be sent to you. As for your stock—sell it or don't. I refuse to think about you anymore!''

She meant to go on speaking but she felt the pressure of fear on her chest. Her mouth opened and shut twice without sound. At last she could only whisper, "Don't do it, Abe. Don't.''

"Get out now! Please!''

Lillian stared at him silently and then nodded, drawing herself up slightly. Abe was a blur before her eyes as she slowly stood up. No, there was nothing more to say or do. And though she knew she did not stand a chance, yet her whole being still longed for his approval. "I loved you once," she said, rubbing her fingers across her forehead. "And it wasn't all in vain." Then she turned and walked out of Abe's life forever.

Abe sat quietly as the door closed after her. From where he sat he could see the towers of Chicago, soaring, glittering, exultant in the sunlight. But this morning he saw nothing. A gauze of pain, of restless bitterness misted his eyes. His whole being rose up in disgust at what she had done. But he knew too that if she'd kept her nerve, said nothing, fought as she could fight, he might never have had the will to force her out. Her claim on him was too real. They had once shared too much. The human bond was deeper than his anger. He knew he'd miss her. Even her hysterics. Anita buzzed and life began again.

Seated around the mahogany table in the conference room reserved for the Board of Directors were ten directors. The table was laden with filled ashtrays, empty coffee cups, pads with crisscross opinions. The room was full of smoke and optimism. Among those present were Abe Barnett, former President of Barnett, now newly elected Chairman of the Board of Barnett; Bob Hale, newly elected President of the parent company; Franciejean Devlin, newly elected President of the New York office, and a variety of other Barnett executives with new titles and authorities.

It was the end of the first meeting with the new corporate management; a reflection of the company growth and the need for a broader-based management group. Abe was speaking: "I am gratified b-by your v-vote of confidence re-regarding our m-managem-ment changes."

"It's from here to the stars!" said Hale. "So we lose Sears. I have a date with Penney next week."

"I'm glad we held Polaroid," said Strother Cooper. "Those ads win all kinds of awards. And attention."

"Land wasn't going to pull Polaroid," said Hale. "He knew we were doing great work for him. That model muck-up could have happened at any agency."

"Personally I think we were just lucky," said Cooper. "Land was just too taken up with his problems with the SX-70. That camera's been trouble enough to keep his left and right brain occupied. He had no time to consider switching agencies."

"I disagree," said Francie. "I think Land knew the problem and wasn't concerned. The difference between Polaroid and Sears is that Land *is* Polaroid. Even though it's a publicly owned company, Land is the last word. Sears is managed by committee. With committee management, no man is indispensable. And criticism can make any man expendable. But Land believes he *is* indispensable. If he receives critical letters, he'll have his secretary answer them politely, then dump them into the circular file."

"Well, Sears didn't leave us empty-handed. I saw 'Pants That Fit' in *Glamour* last week," someone added.

"So did Lillian," said Hale. "My wife bumped into her at a fashion showing, and she screamed like a maniac about it. Falling-down drunk but still full of the same old Lillian brand of poison."

"Speak kindly of souls in torment," Francie said. "Lillian without a job here is Lillian burning in hell."

"Even with all the money she took out of the company?" said Strother. "But I think you're right. In a way I feel sorry for her."

"S-So d-do I," said Abe. "B-But it h-had to b-be d-done."

"Even with everything, she's all alone," said Francie. "You know what will happen to her."

"She'll d-drink. A-And d-drink m-more."

"She'll drink herself to death," said Hale.

"E-Enough of L-Lillian. W-We all have w-work to d-do." He started to smile. "We w-will d-do this b-by the b-book. D-Do I he-hear a m-move to ad-adjourn?"

"I so move."

"S-Second?"

"Second!"

"A-All in f-favor?"

There was a chorus of ayes.

"O-Opposed?" Silence. "The m-meeting is ad-adjourned."

The group pushed back their chairs, rose and, still talking enthusiastically, left the conference room. Only Francie signaled Abe to wait, and the two remained seated alone at the huge table. At last Francie spoke, "May I make a suggestion?"

"A-About what?"

"Lillian."

Abe's face changed and he seemed to look older and more worn than before. He folded his hands on the conference room table. "G-Go ahead," he said, evading her glance.

"For years Lillian's walked a very fine line between sanity and madness. Now I think she's crossed it. If she's not put in a sanitarium, she'll drink herself to death. Or wind up one night in bits and pieces in Central Park."

"I know." The idea frightened Abe, for he still had it in him to be frightened for Lillian. "But there are th-things y-you d-don't know a-about h-her."

"I know them all." Francie's voice was hushed. "Remember, Peter was there."

Abe lifted his eyes slowly to meet Francie's. A great weight seemed to have been removed; the relief for him being in the fact that someone else knew. "A-And you s-still w-want to h-help her?"

"She did a lot for the Barnett Company. I want to help her enough to keep her in one piece. Her life, at its very best, will be punishment enough for her."

"W-What are you s-suggesting?"

"That, through intermediaries, you suggest—she'll do anything you suggest—that she enter a sanitarium. I'll make the arrangements."

Abe thought this over for a little while. Then he said, "I'm l-lucky I n-never fired you w-when I had that g-golden opportunity." His voice was filled with affection and sadness. "Funny, and s-so is Lil-Lillian."

"Thank you, Abe. So am I."

When Francie left late that afternoon, she took a cab to O'Hare and, on the spur of the moment, telephoned Peter.

"Peter, I'm elected."

"President?" He was exuberant.

"President of the New York office. You can salute now or later." She was groping for an appropriate lie, not even sure why she was lying. "Abe wants me to stay over and discuss business plans."

"Ahhh—I've Taitinger in the fridge and caviar."

A pang went through her, hearing the disappointment in his tone. "We'll celebrate tomorrow night."

"Yes, of course. Tomorrow night. I'll leave the champagne in the refrigerator."

She could feel his disappointment, bereft of that first flush of shared victory; and she felt ashamed at her own hypocrisy. "I've so much to tell you. I'll call in the morning."

"Good. Congratulations, dear."

"Congratulate yourself. It would never have happened without you."

"Enough. You'll turn my head."

"Wait till I get home. I will." She hung up, staring unseeingly at the telephone. But through all her confusion of mind, she held fast to her purpose. She wanted to see Jamie and then let events shape themselves as they would. She knew he was in Washington on a semipermanent basis, and she decided to risk an unexpected visit. In the early years of her marriage, she had postponed thinking about its permanence, in the unstated hope that Jamie and she might someday marry. But as the years passed she had come to accept, with absolute finality, the hopelessness of her dream; rather, she felt that they were like people on separate icebergs steadily drifting apart. But still she wanted to tell him of her coup. He would be so proud. After all, the Barnett Company was not a little boutique shop. Their billings had peaked this year at five hundred million, making it one of the five largest advertising agencies in the world. And she was President of the New York office, and a member of the Board of Directors and the Executive Committee. Her pride would be his pride—she owed him so much.

She took a cab from the airport to the small town house Jamie owned in Georgetown. She arrived just in time to meet Jamie on his way to the White House.

"Francie, darling. Why didn't you phone?"

"It only became official today." She told him of her new title.

Jamison looked at her with deep pleasure. "What a wonderful surprise!" His face was full of admiration.

"I wanted to tell you in person. It will be in the business news tomorrow. There aren't that many women presidents."

"It's wonderful. Really wonderful." He looked at his watch. "Look—I have to go to another insane White House conference. Nixon is going to announce something or other. The Krauts won't tell anybody what it is. In any case, I'll be back by eleven. Then we'll have champagne and celebrate.

Tell Patrick to put some on ice. And there's Beluga from the Russian Embassy. What a pleasure.'' He kissed her hard on the mouth and then started moving toward the foyer door. Abruptly he turned with an afterthought. ''You know, Francie, it just occurred to me. We could fly up together to New York tomorrow. Raymond's first grandson is being christened at eleven. I have to put in an appearance.''

''A grandson?'' She shook her head in wonderment. ''Are we that old?''

''You're not. I am.''

''Oh you—you'll never be old.''

''I accept all flattery.'' He gave her a long, quiet look. ''We'll celebrate everything when I return.'' And he left the house.

Francie sat down in front of the fireplace to wait. Their brief meeting had left her with the strangest of impressions—a feeling forced upon her, as had never happened before, that he did look unexpectedly older than she remembered. His face was not one to take lines easily, but his eyes looked weary, as though something that used to be right with his life had somehow gone wrong. Yes, he was having a big career, but that was all. And she had then a fine flicker of vision as the truth widened before her. He should have his great career—he should also have grandchildren. It had never occurred to her so clearly and absolutely that for a man such as he, on the strictly human side of the ledger, his life had been very lonely. Lonelier than even her own, because she had Peter. That he had millions and worldwide celebrity had nothing to do with it—or to be absolutely precise, it had everything. She was sure that Jamison would have preferred to have married, to have had children. Grandchildren. Then, why hadn't he? The one time they had dealt with the subject he had had an air of detachment and discretion. He had explained nothing, denied nothing; he had kept his manner absolutely neutral, as though he had made a vow with himself to abide by whatever she should decide.

She paused then in her thinking with the recognition that there were things she did not yet want to put names to. She watched herself in the act of mentally ducking and dodging, and the more she avoided, the more vividly she knew what she feared; why it was from the first she had not wanted to see what she was doing. But at any rate she was seeing now.

She found herself compelled, minute by minute, to come to terms with an alarming idea.

For at last she was facing the truth. Yes, she had had her value, no doubt about it. But then, and she held her breath for the surprise of it, the truth seemed to be that her mere presence in his life had somehow worked to make marriage—and thus children—impossible. And though nothing had passed between them this evening, with the word *grandchild,* everything had passed. It told her that if she were to be of value to him in the future it would be better if her life touched at no point on his; if she gave up seeing him at all.

If Jamie were here with her now, he might have made some sign—she hardly knew what—that would save her from having to act. Out of kindness and caring he might say something to indicate that the sacrifice she was proposing to make was more than he required. But he wasn't here; and in the next moment, looking quietly around the softly lit room, she felt like some poor lost woman who has stumbled accidentally into a great and beautiful home, and the sole dignity left to her is to look at least as if she isn't ashamed, isn't afraid. And then leave.

The next shuttle was at 8:30 and if she moved quickly, she might still make it. It was then she thought of Peter, and she felt a sudden hunger to see him. Their marriage had been a continuous blessing, a voyage on a calm sea through fair weather. She went to the telephone and dialed New York. While she listened to the phone ring, she felt her heart stop beating. "Did I wake you?" she asked when Peter answered.

"No, dear, I was reading."

The sound of his voice sent a warmth through her numbness. "We've finished early. Get out the champagne. I'm coming home."

"When will you get in?"

"About an hour. I couldn't get a through flight. I'm in Pittsburgh now. I wanted to surprise you."

"Better for my blood pressure that you didn't. Come home. Your husband needs you."

"I am. I am. Your wife needs you." And she hung up the telephone. Now that it was done, she found that the decision to call had been unexpectedly easy. She felt her heart starting to beat again; and looking around the living room, the family furniture had already grown strange, and she knew she had one thing still to do. She had to say good-bye to Jamison. She rummaged in her purse for her calendar and opened to the date. September 14th. She pulled the page from the book and wrote, *"Couldn't wait. Remember Feste's song from* Twelfth Night. *'A great while ago the world began, with a hay, ho, the wind and the rain. But that's all one, our play is done. For the rain it raineth every day.' My version—not William's. But it's true, darling. There is a kind of rain that raineth every day. Not just occasionally, but every day. It's time I faced that fact. I love you, but our play is done. Good-bye. F."*

Looking at the page folded beneath the empty champagne glasses on the table, she knew he would take it exactly as she expected; soberly, sadly, with no dispute.

On the plane back to New York she remembered one of Jamie's favorite poems, and she wished she'd written that instead. "This is the way the world ends, this is the way the world ends, this is the way the world ends, not with a bang, but a whimper."

PART THREE
Was It Enough?
1977–1978

*"It was enough," he said
"It was enough,
And it was all there was."*

—Edward Arlington Robinson

25

The first time Franciejean heard the singing, she was seated in a screening room next to Matt Harris, reviewing a Star Bird test commercial for GM. For once she had to work to achieve her air of imperturbability. The shock of the song mingling with the announcer's voice and blotting out his smooth delivery was registered only by the blink of her eyes:

Somewhere west of Tau Ceti
There's a bronco-busting, steer-roping girl
who knows what I'm talking about.
The truth is that Star Bird was built for her,
for the girl whose face is brown with the sun
when the day is done of revel and romp and race.
She loves the cross of the wild and tame . . .
> Lullabye and good night
> With roses delight
> All tied up in bows,
> Slip under the clothes . . .
There's a savor of links about that car,
of laughter and light, a hint of old loves,
and saddle and quirt and rocket power.
It's a brawny thing for the sweep of the stars . . .
> When the morning shall break,
> Please the Lord, thou wilt wake.
> When the morning shall break,
> Please the Lord, thou wilt wake . . .
Step into the Star Bird when the hour grows dull
with things gone dead and stale . . .

Guten Abend gut Nacht,
von Englein bewacht,
die zeigen im Traum
dir Christkindleins Baum.
Then start for the planet of real living
with the spirit of the lass who drives lean and rangey
into the red horizon of a Tau Ceti twilight.

When her nerves had quieted, Francis wondered which creative genius had thought that mixing the sound track with the Brahms *Lullabye* would be funny? Or was it a commentary on women as sex objects—mothers for instance. Had Angie's psychiatrist suggested she liberate herself from writing commercials and take up singing? Was this Meg's fantasy? Or was Matt going through an early second childhood? Whoever was the guiding light was going to have his parade rained on—hard!

10 9 8 7 6. . . . The track ended.

The light went on. People yawned and stretched and watched her expectantly. Her people, long trained in following her moods and mind, sat silently alert, waiting for a cue. But Francie was cueless. Immobile and furious at Matt—or Angie's psychiatrist. Or Meg? Whoever it was, she decided to let them tangle on their own with the tender mercies of Tommy Dominico who hated the whole Star Bird concept to start with.

She usually tried to protect her people, to get their best ideas sold, and applauded with appropriate raises. But to have someone pull a stunt like this!

A deadly calm filled the room. Finally Hank Grayson sputtered, "I thought you said she was pretty."

Even through her haze of irritation, Francie felt sorry for him, Tommy's most recent acquisition from Stanford. Cleancut, dumb, eager; Tommy's lieutenant. He should know Tommy well enough to know he'd hate the sound track. Advertising was not fun and games. It was big business. Not simply a matter of pretty models. Or was Tommy in on this romp? Did he think for one minute she'd let him kill Star Bird because of somebody's clowning?

Since Hank couldn't keep his feet out of his mouth and wait for his betters to speak, Meg Dodge decided she'd have to take a position. "Personally I find the face very appealing. Evocative."

Francie gazed at Meg—was she responsible? But why spoil her own presentation with that sound track? She had found the girl.

Then for a moment Francie forgot her irritation at the conspiracy of silence. She remembered instead her own surprise at the fine, charming ambiguity of the young girl's face and manner. She had seen the youngster first seated in Meg's office being interviewed, and she was caught by something in the tilt of the profile. It was not a face she recognized. Or a particularly beautiful one. Actually it was a face that, owing to too much forehead and too little conventional line and color, was curiously irregular. And yet Francie felt a pleasure in looking at her. "Let me see your composites," she asked with unusual gentleness.

"She has none," explained Meg briskly. "Jennifer did not come through standard channels. Not Whilhemina. Or Ford. She just walked in. Jenny, this is Franciejean Devlin, head of creative services in the agency. Mrs Devlin, this is Jenny Farrell."

"How do you do, Miss Devlin," said the girl politely.

"Mrs. Devlin," said Francie. "How do you do, Jennifer. You know you'll need composites if you plan to do modeling seriously. Even my assistant, Miss Dodge, cannot suggest you for commercial or print ads if you don't have composites."

"I understand that now. But how do I get composites?"

"You go to a photographer . . ." Francie thought about this and then stopped; blocked by the total ignorance in the young girl's eyes of the simple mechanics of the business. It awakened in her memory of another young girl long ago who didn't know where to go or even where to ask. "Do you have any money?" she asked sympathetically.

"Well, some. How much do I need?"

Francie stared at the girl in some puzzlement. Then she did one of her magic tricks, characteristic yet irritating to both her subordinates and rivals who took pleasure in cataloguing her every strength and weakness. Suddenly she was somebody else. Someone out of keeping with her public image and highly prized reputation for hard-headed business acumen.

413

She suggested that Meg contact Bob Weitzman, head of the art department, and have Bob make an appointment with Edek to give Jennifer a sitting and prepare her composites. Francie would personally pick up the tab for the photographs.

Having made these arrangements, Francie touched Jennifer lightly on the shoulder and murmured with a smile, "Good luck. Very good luck." Then, turning to Meg, she remarked speculatively as she left the office, "Maybe we can use her—I was thinking of Star Bird."

Francie did not know that Meg had stared after her in dazed bewilderment. There was an extravagant quality about the episode. It reminded Meg of her dear, departed, pickled-in-alcohol grandfather, who used to tell her tall tales about the golden boys in the legendary days of advertising. Young men came out of the cornfields to write ads. They did no research, no market testing, they flew blind by the seat of their pants. And built American business—automobiles, drugs, food. Advertising was not their job. It was their way of life.

But Francie was this year's breed. The research fiend. The bottom line addict, the marketing genius. She studied Nielson ratings, meditated on Burke scores. But when she did things like this, a halo of the old adventurousness circled her decisions. When you felt confident that you had her pegged, she would come up with one bright bit of real risk and make it shine as she turned it over in her fingers. Take this Star Bird campaign—that was not a safe play. That was a thirty-million-dollar risk, at least. And then to suggest this young, unknown, unpretty, untried child as the Star Bird. Had she Margaret Adams Dodge, heard Francie properly? Or was Francie balmy?

Meg squinted at Jennifer. Clearly the young girl had no idea she'd caught lightning in a bottle. Feeling giddy, Meg dialed Bob Weitzman. She was thinking then that Francie did not know what everyone else knew—that Edek Pilansky, one of the most expensive photographers in the city, would never, but never, charge Franciejean Devlin for a favor. Not that Polish count.

"Well, it is an interesting face," agreed Tommy. "That is the appropriate word—interesting. I'd even go further. I'd say it was unique. *Sui generis.*" He laughed the laugh of a

414

confident man. "Wonderful phrase—*sui generis*. I learned it in Latin. At Brooklyn College. You thought I only studied double-entry bookkeeping."

Tommy, in his mid-thirties, was lean and graceful. If one took him at face value, he seemed almost boyishly spirited and agreeable.

"Yes, I congratulate you, Francie. A highly creative commercial." He smiled a waggish little smile. "We could run it in the Lincoln Center film festival. It would win a prize. But will it sell cars?"

Matt was the elder statesman in the group, and he deeply resented the way Tommy studiously ignored his experience, title, and long years of successful TV campaigns. "It will sell cars. I know it."

"I have great faith in Francie's judgment," said Tommy, looking at Matt. "But I've never been able to muster any faith in yours."

In the uncomfortable silence that followed Francie felt a scorn for Matt's dense male pride. It never let him admit he was no match for Tommy. So there was no help for it. She had to take over the meeting before Matt's ego and Tommy's arrogance made a shambles of their work.

"Incidentally, Tommy," she said in a voice gone unexpectedly dry, "some idiots in the lab were fooling around and attached the wrong audio to the right video. Sorry about the sound track." The first thing she must do was disassociate that bizarre sound track from any connection with the campaign.

But Tommy was indifferent. "I really didn't listen to the claims. I know the copy needs more work. But the whole theme worries me."

Suddenly Francie realized that something was not right. "Matt, have Rudy rack up that rough cut again," she said.

"Not for me," protested Tommy. "I know what I saw and heard—"

"Not for you. For me. I want to be sure."

The lights went off. On the screen Jennifer Farrell appeared again in the Star Bird test commercial.

The lights went on in the screening room and Francie looked around. There had been no voice singing the lullabye.

Just the predictable sound track. People sat waiting and puzzled. Controlling a wave of nausea, she said to Tommy, "You see, it does work."

"Francie, this time I paid attention to the copy. You'll never get away with it."

"Why not?"

"It's pure plagiarism."

Francie had to suppress an impulse to laugh hysterically when she realized what Tommy was objecting to. "You mean the theme? The swipe from 'Somewhere West of Laramie'? That's public domain."

"It's plagiarism."

"It was written for the Jordan Motor Car," insisted Tommy. "Did you think I wouldn't know it?"

"But there is no Jordan Motor Car anymore," said Matt. "Remember—that ad was written over fifty years ago."

"And sold cars like crazy," said Meg. "Fantastically memorable."

"The point is we're combining the past with the future. Nostalgia for the old West. Visions of the future—sky travel. And the headline is not 'Somewhere West of Laramie.' It's 'Somewhere West of Tau Ceti.' That's the future," said Francie.

"And who's the girl, Francie? I've never seen her before."

"Now you want to play casting director too?" Matt all but shouted in his demand for recognition. "She has no credits. She's a TV virgin."

"Well, I'm always interested in virgins. Now that they're in such short supply." For a moment he seemed to take delight in the whole notion. "A true virgin bride for the TV monster." Then, returning to his original concern, he gave Francie a hard look. "All right, the model aside, and the Laramie swipe aside, I'm not convinced this whole sci-fi concept will sell cars."

"I am sorry, Tommy," said Francie, her face dead still, "but this is what we're recommending. Star Bird the car name. Star Bird the advertising theme and concept."

"And if I disagree with you?"

"I suggest you don't. Your job is business—ours creative." They were obviously, as everyone in the room could see, at war with each other. Since he had been hired last year, he had supervised the GM account. Given their natures, the feud was inevitable, and watching their sword play, even the keenest observer of office warfare would have been pressed to know on whom to place his money. Francie rose quietly. "I would dislike having to go ahead without your support." She said it offhandedly. "But of course if you give me no choice—"

Leaving the screening room, she had to stop herself from laughing. What a macabre joke on herself. But she was, at least, completely confident that no one but she, certainly not Tommy, had heard that incredible singing on the sound track.

The morning had been an absolute bitch. Millions of drudge details that demanded full-focus attention. And today her concentration, which for her was as natural as seeing, took an act of strenuous, almost muscular will. Francie's mind kept spinning down strange alleys and byways, musing, meandering, thinking the impossible, asking questions, then suggesting answers that brought more questions and fewer answers.

Ever since that extraordinary day in the screening room when she'd first heard the song, her tendency had become to listen. Today the impulse was all but overwhelming. What created the stress was not the reality of the voice—she never doubted its reality for herself—but the feeling of sadness it had given her, separating her from other people.

At first she had an impulse to avoid all screenings, but the idea of a haunted screening room struck her as something by Woody Allen rather than H.P. Lovecraft. And the sequel would be "The Kellogg Corn Flake Horror." Or "How Love Came to Mr. Kleen." No, she'd have to face the demons of the screening room, if demons there were. She did; and the demons, as usual, slyly bowed out.

Yet, as the weeks passed and meetings followed dinner parties followed screenings followed opening nights followed client visits; and friends and lovers and enemies and her husband, her hairdresser, her masseuse, her secretary, her assistant, her co-workers whirled around in her brain at ever-increasing speed, she came to know that the air surrounding her, though crammed with activity and the heat of human bodies, was growing increasingly cold. In the middle of the great rush of business and personal events, compounded as they were by the shifting, incessant tug-of-war of the city, she knew that she was totally alone.

There was no one in the world with whom to share her thoughts. No one close enough to enter the rarefied zone where she found herself living. Her senses were so heightened that the smallest things—a man's tie, the lipstick on a woman, the disorder of a desk, the expression on a waiter's face—could set her mind vibrating with infinite possibilities. Her perceptions had never been so keen, too keen for anything like comfort. For comfort, if comfort it was, all she had was the human race at large; pushing, crowding, impersonal, all around and everywhere.

So on this fine Wednesday in September, she was propelled by that singular inner excitement that today caused her to pause unexpectedly in the street—she did it more often than she knew—listening, listening. Was there a singing in the air around her head? Did she hear a faint, far off girlish voice? A heartbroken sob? She shook her head—no, nothing, nothing, only the noise of traffic, the bird calls of the city. She looked over her shoulder to see if someone was following her. But there was no one, and she continued her blind, headlong rush; hoping to escape; hoping she wouldn't.

She arrived at the restaurant fifteen minutes late, looking elegant and faintly flushed. Charles, the maitre d' and co-owner, saw her and nodded with cordiality. "Mr. Barnett has not yet arrived," he said.

It was one of the things she had noticed lately—that her habitual consciousness of success, of being a kind of minor celebrity in the city in general, with headwaiters in particular, had somehow lost its savor. She had left that satisfaction behind in the screening room. For, from sadness, she had descended to meet her fear; that fear that as long as she could remember had been her closest intimate, lapping at the periphery of her consciousness, sometimes barely perceptible, sometimes so paralyzing that she dared not think or talk or move. When she was younger, there had been long stretches of calm, and the visitations had been briefer. But as the years passed, it seemed to grow in aggressiveness and frequency. It might suddenly leap out at her from nowhere—in the middle of a meeting she would start to perspire; after theater or during a telephone conversation her heart would unexpectedly pound. It was that kind of fear, jealous of the sunlight of ordinary life. It would spoil things for no apparent reason. Once in a restaurant she caught herself drawing a picture of her fear on the tablecloth. "What's that?" Peter had asked. "You'll never guess," she said.

And now there seemed to be an all-out offensive. Fear laid siege to her consciousness day after day, showing the familiar camaraderie of an unwelcome houseguest, come to stay for breakfast, lunch and dinner. She smiled at the thought—the Fear That Came to Dinner. Well, it truly did. The only time she felt safe was drugged with passion in some man's arms. It flashed on her then that sex might be her one escape hatch. Could that be what all that infinity of beds was about? She could see them down the years like a series of stop action photos, and the idea filled her with a sinking numbness. What a tasteless joke on herself. But if so, so what? She would still have to sift through the dregs of her own personality. If only she could think of a practical reason for the new intensity of fear. Was she afraid of growing old? There was always cosmetic surgery. Was it overwork? She might need a vacation. Business stress? Too much of Tommy? A little psychotherapy might do. But the truth was, she and her fear had passed the honeymoon stage where easy answers were in order. It served no practical purpose to lie to herself. A showdown of some sort was coming, and it demanded she keep her hand steady. It would not become her before God, or anyone else she had failed, to start now behaving like a child. Then, too, there was no place to hide.

As she paused with Charles, waiting for him to lead her to her table, she noticed a small, rumpled man seated near the door who suggested a moderately overweight, gray-haired troll. This small, eye-glassed troll was absorbed in reading the *Wall Street Journal* in the dim light of the restaurant, oblivious of the forced geniality of the men and women talking and laughing only inches away.

Looking at him, Francie shook her head in wonder. He was such a contradiction of the things she had so painstakingly trained herself to appreciate. Despite his fine intelligence, he was uncultivated, educated but illiterate, caring very little for art or music or food or wine or the amenities of civilization—and yet he was not uncivilized. He often unexpectedly showed a far-reaching subtlety of mind that could put one's own values

419

to shame. Yet, he was somehow indifferent. That was it—indifferent to everything in the world but his work. That was how he was, and that was who he was, and perhaps that was what accounted for his genius.

"Charles," she said, patiently turning back to the maitre d', "are you sure Mr. Barnett hasn't arrived yet?"

"Quite sure," said Charles. "I'd have recognized him immediately."

"Indeed. When did you see him last?"

"Last week. His picture was in *Advertising Age*. They showed the chairmen of the ten largest advertising agencies in America. Barnett and Company was number eight." Charles smiled respectfully. "He's certainly a dynamic man. You understand what I mean—forceful-looking."

"Yes, forceful. And speaking of forceful types, I see Bob Hale is here."

"Yes. With Mr. Klinger. From P&G."

"Incidentally, Charles, tell me about that little man over there squeezed against the wall behind all those high-powered executives. Do you happen to see him?"

Charles squinted in the direction of the small troll. "Yes. He came in about fifteen minutes ago. He said he was early, so I suggested he wait over there."

"You didn't suggest he wait at the bar?"

"Well, it's so crowded today. All our regular customers—"

"And you didn't ask who he was looking for and then perhaps seat him?"

"No. It was very crowded, and then your Mr. Hale came in with Mr. Klinger. And you know how much attention Mr. Hale requires."

"He certainly does. It's his forcefulness."

"And you see he was with your client—"

"I do indeed see."

"And I had to seat them quickly."

"So Mr. Hale never noticed that tourist over there?"

"No, I believe not."

"And the tourist never noticed him?"

"I can't say."

By now Charles was staring with uneasy fascination at the little man seated against the wall reading. With the kind of practical prescience that had enabled him to climb from his beginnings as a dishwasher in the Automat to the co-

420

ownership of one of New York's most prestigious restaurants, he knew that he had pulled a boner. He faced Francie squarely and sighed wearily at his own indiscretion. "That, of course, is Mr. Barnett," he said to Francie with something like self-disgust.

"Of course."

"He does not resemble his picture," said Charles with an attempt at apology. "I am sorry."

"It's quite all right."

"Shall I go and tell him you are here?"

"Yes. And for God's sake don't apologize for not seating him. He doesn't notice things like that."

Eventually Francie and Abe were led to their table, one of the state tables in the restaurant, while those in the room who recognized Francie but not Abe tried to decide who he was that Franciejean Devlin should treat this rumpled little man with such respect. When Bob Hale and George Klinger rose from their table to go over and shake the gentleman's hand enthusiastically, the curiosity level rose higher and higher and the chattering increased. No, he was not an impressive-looking man, not at least by the standards of the restaurant. Yet he was certainly a solid fact, indelibly real; a man who, though rumpled and undistinguished, affected the more astute onlooker as someone to take into account. For a moment the whole restaurant seemed poised and ready to hear him speak.

Francie took a crumpled package of Gaulois from her purse and offered one to Abe. He shook his head impatiently.

"That's the wr-wrong brand. And you know it. If you're in-interested in c-cancer, show a little b-brandy loyalty." Whenever he was distressed his stutter grew more pronounced.

"I had a French grandmother. And we won't tell them in Louisville, will we?" She poked him teasingly. "Abe, you must admit I'm showing some kind of moral courage. Freedom of choice of cancer."

"Cr-crap. Why don't you wo-worry about the mor-morality of making cigarette a-ads at all?"

"I believe the litany runs that we don't believe in government scare statistics. If one went along with all the scare statistics, we'd never have had penicillin. Or ever get out of bed. Occasionally I do feel that way."

"L-l-life causes cancer. It can also le-le-lead to death."

"Thank you, John Leonard." She smiled soothingly. "Would you feel better if I put Gaulois in my Marlboro pack?"

"No, I would n-not."

"All right, all right, Abe. Whenever we have lunch I'll chew gum." She patted his arm. "You *are* a loyalist. However, you do look well. Italy agreed with you—whatever you smoked."

"Well, it certainly isn't Ch-Chicago," he noted petulantly. "I should have gone sooner."

"I've told you that for years."

"I'm st-stubborn. Isn't that the ru-rumor? You look well too, Francie."

And she did, very much a lady, turned out and elegant in darkest brown, which contrasted evenly with her golden hair and luminous face. When she was younger, years ago, it was easier for Abe to read her face and judge her motives. But today her warm smile, her candid eyes, her neutral tone revealed only a diplomatic reasonableness.

"We b-bought some statuary," he said. "For the garden. Hildie likes that sort of th-thing. And T-Tommy encouraged her. Very old s-stuff."

Francie had a moment of surprise, as ever so many things fell into place at the mention of Tommy's name. "I didn't know Hildie and Tommy were so chummy."

"It's a re-recent infatuation. She feels you ad-ad-advise m-me, so he advises her."

"I thought I helped her too." By then Francie realized she had said too much, and now it was important to say less. "Where did you buy the pieces?"

"In a mon-mon-monastery on the Gourdon. We b-bought an altar piece too. For the g-grotto. T-Tommy's idea."

Francie could not help smiling appreciatively at the idea of Tommy Dominico playing the Bernard Berenson of Italian art.

"D-don't you think it was a g-good idea?"

"Splendid." An altar piece for the grotto. From a monastery on the Gourdon. How wonderful. Too bad, she thought. Abe did not deserve the fakes. But he was out of his depth.

"I probably paid too much." He watched her for clues—

422

then suddenly he pounced; "Do you think they're ph-phonies?"

Caught off guard, Francie turned on a dime and replied with sympathetic deceit. "Of course not, Abe. You have an excellent eye. I trust your judgment."

"You d-do? Well, I don't." His eyes were fixed on her with his typical pouting irritation. "But I read up on all those antiques before we w-went. R-remember—you g-gave me the books." Full of perversities, he couldn't resist the temptation to prod her further. "That's what g-got Hildie s-started w-w-with T-Tommy."

"Why? I believe I sent the books to both of you."

"H-H-Hildy didn't see it th-that way. She's j-j-jealous. So she t-t-teleph-phoned Tommy and in-invited him to dinner in Ch-Chicago and asked f-for advice. I t-t-told her it was damn f-f-oolishness. But she pointed out that a-a-after all Tommy is a b-b-onafide Italian so he ought to know s-s-something."

"He's a bona fide Sicilian. He probably knows the black hand better than art." As she said it, she knew she was not successfully hiding the impatience she felt.

Abe took it in, took in everything in her tone that she least wanted him to grasp. But still she could not stop herself. "Did you say Hildie was jealous?"

Abe did justice to her question with a smile. "Th-that's what I s-said."

"After all these years. For heaven's sake, why?" Francie tried to be amused so as not—it was too ridiculous—to be angry.

"Of you and m-me." He relished his own impudence.

"Abe, have you been feeding her imagination?"

Abe decided at this point that he'd overdone the whole thing. He'd never been one to fish off the company dock. Especially his own company. Years before when Francie had been more accessible and he more inclined, he'd half considered making an offer. But in the end the idea struck him as too ordinary. A cliché come true. And he hated clichés; in advertising and in life. It was also bad business, so he dropped it. Now he had to stroke Francie's feathers. "Well, it's hard for a woman like H-Hildie whose whole life has been spent r-raising children and b-being a wife—of course, she does other things. She w-works with the handicapped and

423

r-reads to the old; and she's the m-major fund raiser for the Art Institute. But it's h-hard for her n-not to be jealous of a woman like you whose-whose-whose whole life has been d-devoted to her work—d-doing what she wants to do."

"Hildie's life has been devoted to her own work. It's just a different kind of work."

"She d-doesn't see it that w-way. It s-seems to her th-that you've d-done what you wanted to all your life. It's n-not r-really you and m-me she's j-jealous of. It's y-y-you yourself."

"Because I've done everything I wanted to all my life. It's all been so glamorous." It wasn't the first time she had accepted with smothered disdain other people's view of her life. "Well, so it is—glamorous." She considered the word as if it had taken on a grotesque reality.

"I kn-know it's a n-na-naive position, b-but that's the way she sees it. She's b-been to a number of women's con-con-consciousness r-raising sessions," he explained.

Francie looked at him briefly and then went on with her performance. "Did you go to Paestum?"

"N-no. Where is it?"

"I sent you maps. Don't you remember?"

"I-it must have b-been lost in the mails. I n-n-never saw them."

The possibility of this happening occurred to both of them as being rather improbable, so Francie decided to hurry past the embarrassment. "Ah, too bad. You missed it. The only perfect Greek temple in the area. And it is perfect. That's why I sent you the map."

"We stayed mostly in R-Rome. And a-around Rome."

"You didn't go to Assisi and do the Lombard climb to the castle with the St. Francis's tomb? You didn't see those marvelous, mystic underground arches?"

"No, I suppose we missed a lot." The thought for him dangled in the air.

"You didn't go to Sienna? There's that jewel of an opera house." Franciejean raced on and on with undue talkativeness as if to postpone a little what she knew was coming.

"We were at the Ex-Excelsior. I I-liked the V-V-Via Veneto at night. We s-saw St. P-Peters. And the S-Sistine Chapel."

"Well worth seeing."

With luncheon they had white wine. "We should like to know what you think of it, sir?" Charles asked Abe respectfully, politely including Franciejean in his question.

Abe tasted it thoughtfully, "I'm sure it's f-fine. Re-remarkable d-dry. Is-isn't that w-what it's su-supposed to b-be?"

"Yes—yes, of course. Very dry," said Charles, perplexed by the stutter.

Francie smiled at Charles. Francie, not as young as when Jamison first introduced them, yet still a woman to turn people's heads. Her once-flaxen hair had darkened to a burnished gold. Her face had matured—but exquisitely, intensifying the remarkable cheekbones and the eyes. It was a face that would last well into old age too. The bones were fine. But inescapably, she, like Charles, was older. And yet, as she sat there, wafting Nina Ricci, holding her Gaulois lightly in hand, the tilt of her head, the tone of her voice were memories to Charles of a sunnier time, so he presumed on their long acquaintance to exchange a small gossip.

"Mr. Welsh was in yesterday," he remarked not without some mild self-importance.

Francie did not answer at once. She went on quietly smoking. Only her blue eyes were wary. "How is he?" she asked.

Charles bent his head as though imparting a highly prized intimacy. "In good spirits. Our pastry chef is most pleased. Mr. Welsh appreciates a light crust."

"F-Francie," said Abe, frankly interested. "That's J-J-Jami-s-son Welsh?"

It occurred to Charles he had made a mistake and he retired discreetly. Francie nodded and continued to smoke.

"What is he really l-l-like? He always st-struck m-me as something d-d-different from most p-people. A genius of s-sorts."

Francie stared at Abe for a moment without seeing him at all. Then shrugged. "He is different."

Abe paused in detachment and then, as if the thought had just struck him, he turned to Francie and asked, "H-how d-deeply are you committed to S-S-Star Bird?"

Francie realized now why he'd invited her to lunch. Why he'd come in from Chicago. "Completely," was all she said. "Y-y-you know how T-Tommy feels about it."

"Indeed I do. I didn't know you knew."

"Of c-course I knew."

"Of course."

"You kn-know that we c-can-cannot a-afford a-a-another mistake with GM."

"Clearly."

"Or we l-lose them."

"Y-yes."

"Th-that's forty million do-doll-dollars."

"I know."

"W-w-what m-m-makes you think Star Bird will work?"

It was at that precise moment that she heard the voice, young, soft, and low, begin singing the lullabye in German.

Francie waited an instant to see if Abe had heard what she heard. But his face showed nothing. "I know it will work," she said carefully.

Through the distraction of the singing she heard Abe say, "W-What would you s-say if I t-told you I was a-a-against St-St-Star Bird?"

Francie managed to say, "Abe, I'd do my best to convince you." But she could no longer hear Abe or the noise of the restaurant. It was as though a glass wall surrounded her. She might as well have been in a soundproof booth with the sound mike turned off. She could hear nothing. Only the voice singing. *"Guten Abend gut Nacht, von Englein bewacht."*

Francie could tell by the motion of Abe's lips that he was saying something, but the voice kept filling her ears: *"die zeigen in Traum dir Christkindleins Baum."*

With what amounted to a superhuman effort, Francie did what she had never done before. She asked, trying to keep her voice steady, to be excused. "Could we discuss this Star Bird problem in your office tomorrow? I'll call Anita for an appointment. You'll still be in town, won't you?"

As suddenly as the song came, it was silenced. She heard Abe say, "F-Francie, what's the matter?"

"I don't know."

"Do you feel s-sick?"

"Uhm . . . sick isn't the word."

"You l-look p-p-peculiar."

"I feel very peculiar."

"I s-s-said, Francie, that the Star Bird idea was b-b-brilliant."

"You did?" She felt drained.

"Yes."

"Oh, Abe. I'm so glad."

"T-T-Tommy is wrong."

"I know."

"I'll t-tell him th-this afternoon."

"Abe, let me handle him." Abe seldom smiled, but when he did, it was as surprising and quixotic as if a gargoyle had smiled; and suddenly you knew the world was full of unexpected wonders.

That night the air was still and bright, and the coolness lay on Francie's shoulders like a caress as she drifted slowly up Park Avenue. She was no longer as frightened by the fact of the voice. Actually she almost welcomed its coming. Now she could feel its presence under the skies, in the air around her, almost visible. She fought with a constant impulse to look behind her, to stare up into the air, to reveal even to an empty street the degree of her expectancy. She walked slowly, holding her breath, waiting, listening, spellbound by the possibilities.

At East Seventy-fourth Street and Park Avenue, she stopped and stood at the corner. A most familiar corner; but once there, she was not sure what she wanted to do. She crossed to the opposite side of the street and walked halfway down the block to stare fixedly at the graceful, well-kept limestone and brick mansion. She was both relieved and disappointed that there were no lights anywhere in the house, except for a small gleam coming from the depths of the servants' quarters. More or less the house looked as it had always looked. Austere rather than beautiful . . . quietly rich. Almost ascetic in its lack of pretension.

In the marble foyer there would be no bells giving buzzer entrance to chic, small apartments that helped the owners of such fashionable East Side establishments to have a posh address and the facsimile of the gracious life, while paying off the mortgage. Here, the marble foyer led only to a wrought-iron door that would be opened by Patrick into the small anteroom of the huge living room of the whole house in which Jamison lived when he was in town; as his family before him had done for generations.

Francie continued to stare, then abruptly turned and

walked briefly around the block feeling the foolishness of an adolescent. But she came to stand in front of the building again. Exquisite in her fine clothes she was yet swayed and driven as an animal. The need to behave in this fashion was inexorable. She was compelled to walk there and stand there just as other women in other times have been compelled to stand with offerings before temple altars. So Francie too was paying homage to needs unanswered, unsolved, unextinguished.

It was then that it came to her, from somewhere in the air around her, slipping into her ears like the fated poison of Hamlet's father. She heard the young girl's voice singing sweetly, sadly—oh, who would have believed that poison could be so sweet and sad ... or that memory could be so bitter:

> Guten Abend gut Nacht,
> von Englein bewacht,
> die zeigen in Traum
> dir Christkindleins Baum.
> Schlaf' num selig und suss,
> schlaf' im Traum's Paradies
> Schlaf' num selig und suss,
> schlaf' im Traum's Paradies.

26

After that troubled time the voice was stilled. Weeks passed in silence, a silence for which she was no longer prepared. Sometimes Francie half wondered if she'd actually heard the singing. But only half wondered—her deep self knew it would come again; and knowing this, she grew impatient to see Jamie.

Often, along city streets, she found herself searching for his solid, big-boned figure; once someone's profile struck a chord; once with beating heart she thought she recognized his old Rolls moving down Fifth. So she passed her days in indecision, treading water as it were, waiting for some inner signal.

Then, late one afternoon, she wound up a telephone conversation with a writer who wanted to interview her for *Business Week* and told Meg she was going to leave early, in order to bathe and dress at a leisurely pace for the big evening ahead. There was nothing on her calendar that could not be postponed, and at the moment the agency was calm—no one had pressed the panic button. And tonight was the preview of the New Frontiers For Women series, commissioned by *Esquire* and painted by Sparafucile. Peter and Francie were going down to a champagne party at the painter's Soho loft to celebrate the event, since Francie was one of the subjects of the series. Meg was more excited by the whole affair than Francie and kept reminding her that she ought to go home and get ready. Finally Francie agreed.

She left the building quickly and started walking briskly uptown. Then turned east at the same hurried pace. Then north, then east again. Then west. All with the same stubborn self-pretense that she was going home.

But the signal had come. For the first time she felt the full weight of a decision that had been forming inside her, grain by grain through the last weeks.

In an effort to distract herself with meaningless activity, she stopped into Halston's where everyone made their usual fuss over her, and she felt for the first time an embarrassment that she could never remember anyone's name. From Halston's she went to Phoebe's Whamburger and there, shivering like someone in a high fever, ordered a cup of soup that she left steaming and untouched while she chain-smoked three cigarettes. After the third she sat absolutely still, allowing no thoughts to shape in her mind. She stayed like this till she could stand it no longer, then rose, paid the check, and left. Outside, the wind was blowing and the temperature forty; but Francie perspired freely.

She crossed the street to the Carlyle, found an empty telephone booth in the lobby and dialed Vera Busch. Vera's housekeeper, Frieda, said Miss Busch was expected home momentarily. Francie thanked her and said that she would be over shortly. After she hung up the receiver, she stood a long time staring at the telephone. It was as if the whole city had changed beneath her. She started down Madison Avenue feeling like the sole survivor after an earthquake, surprised to find how quickly the familiar world can become unfamiliar.

Not wanting to arrive too soon, she entered the Madison Avenue branch of her bank, and asked for the balance in her personal checking account. The respect in the clerk's eyes when she gave her the balance only increased her feeling of despair. She left the bank, an old impatience settling over her, and walked swiftly down the Avenue to Sixty-fifth. There she turned left and walked slow steps toward a modest but distinguished apartment house off Park Avenue. As she approached the building, she might have been a gambler who has exhaustedly decided to "stake everything on zero, hoping so to gain cool air, light pockets and his solitude."

The doorman nodded a welcome, and the elevator man smiled and took her without question to the duplex on the tenth floor.

Standing in the foyer, she was again conscious of unwilling admiration at the opulence of the small room. She realized anew that the glowing fourteenth-century tapestries hanging on the wall were worth a fortune. That the seventeenth-century gilded console nestling beneath them was museum quality. Having, as she now had, a keenly developed taste for the beautiful and the rare, it left her feeling uncomfortably humbled, knowing that her bank balance could neither bring life to the negotiating table, nor even afford this caliber of possession. But her face was smooth and unimpressed when she rang the bell.

"Hello, Vera Busch, friend and mentor," she said with stiff lightness when Vera opened the door herself. "You never change."

"Neither do you. Not a day older."

"Well, a few days."

"How I've missed you!"

"And I you." Francie took careful stock of her old friend. She had blue white hair, kind eyes, and a smile that made her seem very young. She was still a pleasant woman to look at.

Francie followed her into the huge high-ceilinged living room, filled with the opaque quietness of a floor twice hushed—once with wall-to-wall carpeting, and again by Oriental rugs flung with a lavish hand over the carpeting. Francie placed her brief case on an exquisite tulipwood marquetry table, the long-ago delight of a blond-haired queen, and stared around her reverently.

Here the sunlight would always be muffled by heavy damask curtains; because sunlight can bruise old paintings, old furniture, old tapestries, and the usually older people who buy these precious items. Here the only light came from lamps and from the carefully lit paintings of hundreds of years ago. Again Francie's avid eyes took a tour of the room with the solemn respect she reserved for only the best of the world's plunder. Jamison had taught her almost too well.

There was still that marvelous secretary with the heavy patina of time, signed by the master of London; there the small inlaid jewel chest, once filled with jewels, the gift of a king to his queen to bind a marriage. And everywhere on the walls, the awesome and visionary paintings of the prime of God.

Vera had learned well her lessons of taste. Her hearty St. Louis provincialism had been sanded down by the tutelage of fifty years of seeing and judging and longing after beauty. The room, a lesson in history and vanity, was filled with the loot and pride of Europe's proudest years.

Francie cast about for what to say. The beautiful room had stirred old memories, some pleasing, some harsh; an old wound began to throb.

"I've been away too long." Her eyes, for a moment clear as a child's, asked for sympathy.

"Yes, you have," said Vera. "And thank you for sending me Abe."

"Of course."

"No, not of course. I haven't been in touch."

"City life. We are all too busy."

"We shouldn't be for friends. I know you hate my saying it, but you must be the kindest person in the city."

"But in this city that is saying very little. The old devil never told me he finally called you. What did he want?"

"A panel from a tryptch. Fourteen inches by sixteen inches."

"Bully for Abe. A hundred and fifty?"

"Two hundred and ten. What he really wanted was a Caravaggio."

"Oh, no. He didn't. My God! Are there still private people who own Caravaggios?"

"I do know of one in a private collection. But even if it were available—which it isn't—that's a bit too rich for Abe, really."

"Yes, I would think so. The art business is flourishing."

"Flourishing."

"There is no shortage of nouveaux riches?"

"Or oldveau riche. There's only a shortage of Perugino. And Martini. Sometimes I hate to sell a painting."

"Pity you don't like modern work. There's always plenty of that."

"It's not what my eyes were trained for."

"And there's less money to be made."

"You are an authentic, Franciejean."

"Let's say a graduate of the school of hard knocks—the survival of the greediest or something like that."

"I'd rather say the fittest. Would you like something to drink?"

"I could do with a brandy."

"Would you mind getting it yourself? I am weary."

"Of course. Can I get you something?"

Vera shook her head, and Francie went to a paneled cupboard that incongruously held, not imperial manuscripts on bleached vellum, but Vera's liquor supply and glasses. As she poured herself a brandy, she was aware that Vera was watching her with a curious look on her face; a face that longed to ask a question, that had whole piles of questions stacked inside it, lying unused. Catching Francie's glance, Vera looked away, hoping to spare her friend her gentle, pitiless appraisal. But even though she wished to, how could she respect that privacy? Vera knew Franciejean too well.

Finally Francie said it, "We've run out of small talk."

"That can happen with old friends."

"Your face says everything."

"You are oversensitive."

"I must have a generous nature. I do not hold it against you for having been so disgustingly right."

Vera laughed. "Exactly how old is he?"

"Twenty-five, I believe."

"Fragile age." Vera was very good at drawing people out.

"Too fragile. We all make mistakes." Francie knew that Vera never judged her, for Vera's detachment sprang from the conditions of her own withdrawal. As long as the game of sex went on with the proper style, Vera would accept and approve any version. So now, as always, Francie accepted the fiction that they shared the same detachment. "But I won't repeat the same one twice."

The buzzer rang and Vera went to answer it. "You know you haven't told me a single thing. I mean about you. Yourself."

"Isn't it more fun to guess?" Francie started to rise, feeling disappointed. "I didn't realize you were expecting anyone. I'll be going along."

"Don't be absurd. It's only Jamie."

"Jamie?"

"Yes. You didn't know?"

"No."

"I thought that was why you were here."

"No. I mean yes. But no."

They were both stricken. Vera made no show of taking

this in her stride, yet she kept herself in hand. "I wish I'd realized you didn't know. But I can't hide you in a closet."

"And I won't leave by the servants' entrance." Francie did her best to keep up the pretense that they could treat the situation like a French farce.

"Forgive me. I simply assumed when I received your message that for some reason you'd both arranged to meet here."

"Very practical assumption."

"I'm nothing if not practical. Have you seen each other at all?"

"Not recently." Francie watched Vera raise her eyebrows. "You're waiting. I can hear your brain tick. Which way will the frog jump?"

"I haven't said a word." Vera sounded offended. The triumph of tact, the warmth of patience. This was Vera. And at the moment Francie hated it. But it was better than nothing. "Well, the truth is I would like to see him. That's why I did come. I thought you'd be in touch. So now is as good a time—"

"I wish I'd realized—" Then thinking to herself that there must be some virtue in being seventy and out of it, Vera remarked, "Will you let an old friend ask a question?"

"Ask. It's the privilege of old friends. The thing is to have sycophants."

"Are you still in love with him?"

Francie laughed, covering her irritation with pleasant, official manners. "That sounds like a religious question."

"I suppose. And those are always impolite."

"Always." She shrank from further comment. She felt caught; brought by the unpredictable sequence of events to the brink of change; felt a threat in saying anything; yet felt she must not stay silent. So, when the doorbell rang, she felt positive relief. The reality was less painful than all this artificial candor.

Jamie Welsh entered quietly. He looked almost exactly as she remembered, not even a day older. And for all his large bulk, his clothes fitted his body perfectly—in fact they were so free of wrinkles and bulges that, given his age, one might suspect he wore a girdle. But as many a woman and his friends in the locker room at the Racket Club could testify, he did not. His eyes still looked into other eyes unerringly, insight, dead plumb into character and motive.

"Jamie—how nice." Vera said.

"Sorry to be late. Conferences. You know the way they go on. Everybody makes their point. Then they make it again." He paced the room with easy, absentminded animation. But he must have felt the force of Francie's recognition passing on him, for he suddenly straightened and turned. "Francie! How pleasant."

"Hello, Jamie."

For a moment they were both silent, then Jamie said, "I'm so glad to see you again."

"I had no idea you were coming." Francie had a sensation of shyness, and an acute unwillingness to have Jamie think this meeting planned.

"But you don't mind?"

"Of course not."

"Then I am pleased."

Their eyes brushed. Francie drew a deep breath and stood staring at Jamie. The two smiled warmly at each other, then Jamie said with a low laugh, "I am quite real."

"Yes, you are."

"So let's sit down." Jamie seated himself opposite Francie. "I debated calling you when I arrived. I do it everytime I arrive."

"I heard you were in town again."

"How convenient gossip is. We don't have to tell each other a thing."

"How was London?" asked Vera, goaded by the need to keep the conversation intact.

"Pleasant. Sometimes it's like living in a painting by David Hockney."

"Have you saved the pound sterling?" asked Vera.

"I do what I can."

"The winters are not nearly as cold as here."

"Not nearly," said Francie, but she was hardly listening. Jamie's appearance had worked as a drink on her, throwing a flush into her brain.

"The English are the best balanced people in the world."

"My English are not."

"But at the least they don't talk air pollution constantly," said Vera.

"Mine do."

Frieda came into the living room. "Hello, Mr. Welsh."

"Hello, Frieda. It's good to see you again."

"We are glad to have you back, sir. There's a telephone call for you."

Jamie excused himself and went into the library to take the call. Vera said with an air of resolution, "He's looking well, isn't he?"

"Yes." Francie did not say more. She did not dare.

"You and he visiting. It could be old times."

"Hardly, Vera."

"You're right. History does not repeat itself." She gave a short, dry laugh. "It merely contradicts itself." There was benevolence behind Vera's words, benevolence and compassion. All unwillingly, she had glimpsed the anguish behind Francie's formal friendliness. "Things have not been happy for you lately?"

"Who is happy lately?"

By the time Jamie came back into the room, they were exchanging courteous pleasantries, neutral conversation; safest for both.

"Michelle will pick me up here, Vera. All right?"

"Of course. How is Michelle?"

"She's on a holiday in the New York environment. And interacting strenuously. With Michelle everything is a crisis. Buying a pair of shoes is a crisis. Going to the toilet is a crisis. Her anxiety is genuine but it always smells of grease paint."

Francie felt a sparkling of jealousy at the mention of the name. "Is that Michelle Colbert?"

"You know her?" Jamie's smile was unexpected, as though revealing a good private joke.

"What's she doing here now? Louis is making a movie in Africa?"

"No. Louis goes next month. But it's no matter. Michelle and Louis have agreed to disagree. For now, anyway. Michelle is staying with me. For a while."

In spite of herself Francie said, "Good Lord, Jamie! The world is larger than Michelle Colbert."

Jamie smiled. "You're not my spiritual advisor, Francie. And Michelle is amusing."

Francie could not contain her malice. "You always said she was a fool."

"She is."

"Then why—?"

"We are somewhat alike. She is merciless in the pursuit of pleasure."

"The marriage of two minds."

"Not exactly minds." Jamie enjoyed Francie's discomfort. He had the air of a man in complete agreement with himself.

Vera said tactfully, "I liked her last picture. She was quite believable. The teenagers are mad for her. My nephew writes her letters constantly."

"Like myself," remarked Francie. "She has one great talent. Sheer hypocrisy."

Jamie laughed. "It's unlike you, Francie, to take such a high moral tone."

"Can I get you something, Jamie?" asked Vera, relying on the social amenities to keep peace. "Scotch?"

"A spritzer?"

"I may be out of soda. Frieda hasn't marketed yet."

"White wine will do."

Vera rose quickly with barely disguised relief, glad of any excuse to be out of the scene that was being enacted, a scene whose meaning she grasped too fully.

Then Francie rose, too, shook herself and stretched. Her body was still trembling with overreaction. "You should have telephoned," she said.

"I felt it might be inopportune. A complication. I never know how much you might have changed. Or haven't changed. There is no way of judging since we agreed not to write. Or to telephone. Or in any way to make contact. And six years is a long while."

"That was a childish notion of mine. One of my typical mistakes."

Jamie took a deep breath. It seemed to him that somewhere a window had opened and fresh air was pouring into a room that had been closed and tightly locked for a long time. "Then you should have written to me."

"Yes, I should have."

"I thought about you." It was the first time he allowed himself to reveal the emotion he was feeling.

"I've thought about you, too." Francie turned away, her mind dizzy with the recognition of how much she still loved him.

"That's exactly how it is. We never realize how much room we occupy in another's life."

"Have I changed much?"

"Not at all."

"Of course I have. Everyone changes."

"Well, if you have changed, it's for the better. You look very well."

"You sound surprised." Francie pretended indignation. "Did you hear that I'd gone through a process of disintegration?"

"No. And you haven't."

"Well, it shows how wrong you can be. I have."

"Have what?"

"Gone, I believe, through a process of disintegration."

He gave her a long, appraising look. "I don't believe it. You may seem to others to be made of porcelain but I know you have the constitution of an ox."

"I do, don't I?" She laughed. "There are other forms of distintegration."

He accepted this new idea. "You never really cared for alcohol?"

"There are other dooms available."

"I can't picture you as a bondage-and-discipline convert."

"Guess again."

"You are too vain I believe to waste your body on drugs."

"You're right. I'm really not crude. You educated me too well."

Jamison said nothing. He only waited, letting her talk.

Sensing his openness she made an effort. "Well, actually—it's quite awesome." She hesitated. "Even beautiful . . . sometimes."

"I believe it is."

His manner told her that he had fully accepted that something indeed rare had happened.

So they sat and talked; or rather, Jamie sat and Francie talked, moving about restlessly as she spoke. "The fact is,

Jamison—I'm haunted." She said it with a whimsical flourish.

Seeing Jamie's face, another person present might have wondered with which private vision of her he was squaring this speech. But all he said was, "Yes, haunted. But haunted by what? I'm prepared for the worst. The depths of hell. Or the choirs of heaven?"

Francie considered the options and left the choice with him, saying after a moment, half shyly, "I'm haunted by a voice singing a song. Sometimes in English. Sometimes German. Sometimes a mix. I may hear the singing in a studio, on the street, in a restaurant. Anytime. The same voice. The same song."

Jamie nodded, taking his amusement where he could. "Male or female? Not your mother by any chance?"

It gave her an inward start, this reminder of her ancient obsession. He knew her so well; and for a moment she could not speak. She felt too sharply, a mingling of relief and humiliation. Then the long habit of self-control asserted itself and both feelings showed themselves in the straightness of her reply. "Momma, you'll be glad to know, hasn't been around for years. At least not consciously."

"Forgive me, Francie. I am sorry that I brought her up."

"Please. It's done no harm. She's our old family ghost." She smiled and took a breath, gathering strength. Even under the most difficult circumstances, the sight of Jamie affected her as it always had. He quieted the distress of her spirit; and his very allusion to the past, by reason of its offhand, matter-of-fact intimacy, seemed to place the whole subject on a more reasonable basis. "No. I don't know if I'd even recognize Momma's voice anymore. Anyway, this is a young voice. A young girl. I suppose my mother was young—but was she ever that young?"

Having said this she felt less strange, but the passing exhilaration she had enjoyed at being able to share her secret had gradually faded to misery. Putting it into words did away with her panic. But it also did away with something else. She felt she was left empty-handed. She had given up a unique part of herself. A secret wonder of life had shown itself to her, had proved its existence; and now it was as if, by speaking about it, she denied its reality. She reduced to a shared ordinariness, like the weather or a menu, what had been for her a lonely splendor.

"What does the voice sing?"

Francie looked at him startled, as though he had awakened her from a dream. "The Brahms Lullabye." She felt a sudden irrational resentment of this man—who was he? She rubbed her forehead. He looked so familiar. He looked to her fancy like a defrocked priest. Or her lover. But who? She could not at the moment think of his name. And if she could not think of his name, what right did he have to ask such intimate questions?

"You think I'm mad?"

"Yes, of course. But so am I. Isn't everybody?" And there passed between them a flicker that together they knew the truth.

"Well, I am not mad. I am not a freak of nature. I am not on show. I have nothing more to say."

"You claim diplomatic immunity?"

She sighed gratefully. "That's what I claim."

"You can depend on me to respect your rights."

"I should never have mentioned it. I only make the biggest mistakes," she said forlornly.

"Only the biggest are commendable."

It touched her the way he controlled his impatience with her and she yielded to an impulse to be further indulged. "I don't believe I'm insane. Or at least no more than the rest of the world. You have a few eccentricities yourself—if I could just remember them."

"I have quite a few." He took it pleasantly, for what it was worth. "You and I are quite a pair. Side by side, two perfectly matched white mice, scurrying around our cage."

The caustic words and the smile made everything seem freer. But her relief was patent when Vera came back into the room carrying a spritzer; and it came to her suddenly that this man was Jamison, actually Jamison.

"We had soda after all," Vera said to Jamie.

"Thank you, my dear."

Francie stood up abruptly and spoke quickly as if to dispose of a disagreeable subject. "I must be going. We're going to a party tonight."

"We've had no gossip," said Vera. "How is Peter?"

Francie rose to the amenities. "Looking years younger

han he is. Not much cholesterol. Doing well, very well. And
my neurosis made to measure." She turned to Jamison. "This
was nice."

"Yes. Wonderful. Let's repeat it—lunch?"

It was the first time he struck her as unsure. "Yes. Why
not?"

"I'll call you at the office. I should be in New York at
least a month."

Knowing him, she knew how great a concession he had
made in asking her to lunch. That, more than anything he had
said or left unsaid, caused her an acute uneasiness.

At the doorway Francie kissed Vera apologetically on the
cheek. "I won't stay away so long this time."

"Let's try," Vera said affectionately as Francie stepped
into the foyer and rang for the elevator. "But let's not swear
in blood. Let's just try."

Afterward Vera turned back into the apartment, softly
closing the door. "Well?" she asked the air. "What is it?"

"I'm not at all sure."

"She looked well enough."

"Didn't she—"

"Is it some peculiar illness? Or money? Or what?"

Jamie seemed on the point of saying something, changed
his mind and said with a slow headshake, "I am not an
authority on Franciejean. Only a friend, and one-time lover."

Vera sighed, reminding herself that both of them—both
Jamie and Francie—had never been easy to know. One saw
them often or seldom—it depended on the tides of city
life—but to know them was another matter. She decided to
talk about art.

Francie walked out into the twilight immensity of the
city, and now she knew why she had wanted to see Jamison.
No one in the world except Jamie could have entered into her
state of mind with such soundless facility. He had treated her
exactly as she wished—with a strange mixture of candor and
tact. He had behaved as if she were completely sound in mind
and body. There had been no intake of breath, no veiled
alarm in his eyes, not the merest hint of doctors, of hospitals,
of "help." Yet, that was the damning fact; and it brought her
to a stop, standing stock-still amid the rush of people on
Madison Avenue. If she was such a tower of strength, why

was he so tactful? Why, given his probing mind, his unwillingness to evade the facts, did he let her off so lightly? Why had he let her drop the subject so quixotically? It was also out of character. Jamison looked at the world straight totally unsentimental. He kept his self-deceits only for the highest uses.

What came over her then, with her new, lonely acuteness was that what she might have been witnessing was a generous, benevolent dishonesty. And if that was true, the reason was compassion; an emotion he rarely permitted himself to waste. And if there was compassion, was there not also pity? Well, if he pitied her, there must be good reasons. She understood his mercy all too well. It told her exactly what she had not wanted to know—that indeed she was damned. It was as good a word as any.

"Are you all right? Can I help you?" A pretty fuzzy-haired young girl in jeans stood beside Francie, concern on her face.

Francie looked at her startled. "Oh, thank you. I'm fine." She smiled. It was then that she realized her cheeks were wet; tears had been streaming down her face; people were passing and staring. "I weep all the time," she said. "In the oddest places. It's unrequited love."

The young girl nodded sagely. "I know the feeling. A good cry is better than Valium. What this city needs is decent public transportation and lots of wailing walls. Free—for everyone. It's cheaper than psychiatry." And she turned and walked on up the Avenue.

For once Francie did not mind making a fool of herself in public. It was such a relief to go on leaning against the wall and sobbing.

27

Through three cups of black coffee swallowed slowly and five cigarettes that burnt her fingers while she forgot to smoke, she sat at Leo's counter on Madison Avenue musing, meditating, dreaming. Staring unseeing into space, she thought about Peter with a feeling of wonder, as though seeing him for the first time. Early in their marriage, she had thought about him constantly, almost obsessively. But not with love. No, that was hardly the word; rather with the sense of a hunter tracking his prey. Her attention for years was secretive and relatively scientific. Looking back, she saw herself laying traps for him like a spy, applying tests, searching for clues to his truth, to prove his worthlessness.

Or how else could he have married her? He would never have done it if he'd been straight. Any man worth having, the kind of man her mother had yearned for, would never have married her. Not what she was then, a poor lost thing and a Jamie-discard to boot. No, such a man would have seen her as a mistress—archaic word—or a girl friend; but a wife? Hardly.

In the beginning she had been frightened by the knowledge that Peter was AC-DC. She had forced herself to marry him, but she was afraid. After all, he wasn't a real man. She couldn't have been more wrong. His bisexuality had nothing to do with his essential masculinity of spirit. And it rarely touched their life together. Sometimes an awkward situation would occur. Like the evening she found him in his room with a young student. Well, she had no business peering into his bedroom like that, and once he knew what had happened, he never brought a guest home again. But he had never tried to fool her; and without being crude about it, she'd gotten her money's worth. He may never have been her ideal, but he had arts and intuitions that were a daily grace if you lived with him. Their marriage had its problems but all marriages had problems. She remembered Peter's words all those years ago—"money, religion, infidelity etc." At least with them, infidelty was given. There were no obligatory lies.

Yes, it served her right long ago to have thought him not good enough; and then to have found, to her dismay, that perhaps it was she who was not good enough for him. Peter was strikingly handsome, educated, an authority on antiques, an important interior designer, the son of a dyed-in-the-blood social family; and though gay, quite acceptable in their most intimate world. And what was she when he married her? Nothing but beautiful. The beaches were full of beautiful girls. And some were even literate. Her best recommendation was Jamie.

Abruptly she rose from her seat at the counter, paid her check and walked the short and long blocks down and crosstown to their apartment house. The uniformed doorman as usual was delighted to see her; it was Sean, whom she always made a point of tipping when he found her a cab, because he reminded her of a probably dead uncle who had looked equally grand in his World War I uniform. The elevator man, Tony, was an Italian who once had operatic aspirations and, when she was the sole passenger and her face permitted it, serenaded her on her way to the fifteenth floor with snatches from *Traviata* or *Pagliacci*. He had a wavering tenor that pleased his vanity more than her ear.

When they reached fifteen, Francie stepped out into a small foyer and smiled involuntarily with pleasure at the glowing Steuben swan floating on the shining surface of a Regency table. Perhaps the furnishings were not of the caliber of Vera's, but they would do.

She opened the door, and there was Maria, in her standard white uniform, rearranging a bowl of flowers in the entrance; an eighteenth-century mix with a Danish gilt mirror, an English blue lacquer clock and a rare Bessarabian area rug whose geometric pattern was quixotically suggestive of a modern painting laid out on the floor. Maria threw a quick smile at Francie and in her usual mixture of Spanish and English said, *"Buenas noches,* madam," then turned quickly back to something she was doing in the dining room.

Before going on to her bedroom Francie asked if Mr. Devlin was home yet.

"Senor is *en la cocina."*

Franciejean nodded. Now what was he doing? She went first to her bedroom to drop her briefcase beside her desk and her purse on her dressing table. She hung up her jacket in the closet and then, fluffing out her hair with her fingers, went toward the kitchen.

There was Peter, holding between his fingers a long, amber cigarette holder containing an unlit cigarette, peering interestingly at something in the refrigerator. In his late forties, Peter had an agreeable, sensitive, intelligent face that somehow justified his look of casual but foppish elegance. He wore gray flannel trousers, Gucci moccasins, a well-cut jacket of brown velvet with a white silk shirt open at the throat—all carefully protected from flying foodstuffs by a huge professional-looking kitchen apron that covered him from the neck down. His whole manner exuded good cheer and high spirits. When he saw Francie, he smiled delightedly and went to her, kissing her lightly upon the cheek. "Darling, you look wonderful. But a little piqued. Did they nibble on your heart today?"

"Well, this time they anesthesized me first. What are you up to in the kitchen tonight?"

"Pre-party snacks. You know very well that La Spada won't serve until eleven. It'll be champange et al. until we're swinging from the mobiles. So I thought for those among us like you and me who need our protein to keep above sea level, a few fresh Belon oysters on the half shell. Steak tartare—made by my very own chubby fingers. French bread by the French at Bloomie's—"

"Spada will have hors d'oeuvres."

"Champagne and Italian 'horse devers' give me indigestion."

"I thought you had a business appointment tonight? I didn't know I was being escorted."

"I changed my mind at the last minute. Do you mind?"

"Of course not. I'm delighted."

"Don't worry about my amusing myself. You know I'm never at loose ends. And Monroe will be there, too. Now fill me in again. If I'm not asked to rethink someone's outhouse, I never remember names. Who will be there?"

"Let's see. There's Electra O'Toole *en famille*. Stella and Lionel Coleman—"

"Ahhh! Electra! The activist actress who refused to marry the father of her child. Now what New Frontier of Womanhood does *she* symbolize? Aren't unmarried mothers a bit old hat these days?"

"You miss the point. Electra stands for the legitimacy of illegitimacy. The conscientiously unwed mother. She's the standard bearer of the unwed family."

"Fascinating. Electra reduces the divorce rate, while Stella raises it. I read somewhere Stella has eighteen husbands."

"Love nests all over the world. They interviewed a sheikh in Morocco. She's a member of his harem. And she has an Eskimo husband. An Aukland husband. It does add up."

"While the government must grin and bear it since Lionel doesn't sue for bigamy, trigamy et al."

"Not him. They make a mint on her method of studying family relations she marries in. Her books really sell. They're drenched with foundation grants. I wonder what he does for sex while she wifes it around the world?"

"Masturbates. Reads in bed. Maybe he likes boys."

"Or girls." Francie rolled eyes in her best high-class whore put-on. "There are other freethinkers besides you, darling."

He leaned over and caressed her breast. "And what does Mrs. Coleman symbolize?"

"Fresh," she said, smiling and kissing his hand. "The obsolescence of the monogamous family. Couples like us— one husband, one wife, one hundred percent cliché." She made a flamboyant gesture.

"Stereotypes at last." But Peter was watching Francie with thoughtful calculation. "You're pretty wound-up. Are you all right?"

"Of course. How could I not be splendid? I am beautiful, successful, and obsoletely married"—she grinned teasingly—"to a handsome, urbane, international authority on interior design." There was an abrupt drop in her voice like a reflex to a general fatigue. "Peter, do I look green?"

"You look golden. In fact, a little feverish. What is it?"

"Stop looking around corners. I'm fine."

To avoid any deeper sounding, he resumed the party topic. "Enough of the guest list. And you symbolize the new careerist?"

Francie stretched herself, rose from the kitchen stool where she'd been perched and started to emote. "That's me—a force. A lioness of industry. In sum, a working wife. Written up in *Time*. On the cover of *Forbes*. The idol of every female business schooler. Wait till you see La Spada's painting. À la Picasso's cubist period. He did two Franciejeans, facing two ways. Francie the lioness facing one way, Francie, the wife, the helpmate, facing the other way. There is an inner tension holding the two Francies together." She gave Peter a mischievous smile. "He said it. I didn't. And he isn't all wrong."

Peter leaned over, and she felt his breath on her cheek as she raised her lips. It was a long, searching kiss. Then he stood back, surveying her with enjoyment. "The homey lioness. Underneath all that drive is pure Pillsbury cake mix." He put his hands on her shoulders. "Come—cat got your tongue? What'd you think of my creation?"

She was genuinely puzzled. "What creation?"

"It's over your bed."

"My bed? My mind wanders. What is over my bed?"

"Come along, self-absorbed lioness." Peter took off his apron, flung it on the kitchen counter; and taking Francie by the hand drew her after him into her bedroom suite. "There! How could you miss it?" And he pointed with a flourish toward the wall over Francie's bed. Yes, she'd missed it totally. Slightly to the left of center above the brass headboard and framed in antique gold leaf was a reproduction of that scandalous masterpiece, "The Naked Maja" by Goya. After a moment Francie's cool gave way and a slight blush rose in her cheeks. "Darling! You stole it from the Prado—just for me. Were you trying to tell me something?" She looked sheepish.

"I thought it would make the perfect companion portrait for 'The Naked Franciejean.'"

"Monroe told you, didn't he? Monroe—the rat with

447

women. Why do I trust him? I wanted to surprise you. He was the one who persuaded me to pose.''

''I don't think it took much persuading.''

''La Spada begged me. Pleaded. He prayed. He said he'd give me the painting free when it was finished. He considered it such a privilege to paint me.'' She giggled in spite of herself.

Peter shook his head in comic exasperation. ''I understand the business point of that other silly painting for the magazine series. But to pose for La Spada, nude. That's pure, unbridled vanity. Plus a childish indulgence of other licentious activities that undoubtedly occurred.''

Francie lifted her brows in mock superiority. ''An artist of La Spada's caliber does not see a woman as flesh and blood. He sees only color and design. He considers it a matter of honor to steel himself against personal feelings.'' But she could no longer contain her laughter. ''Peter, you're jealous. And a prig.''

''I am not jealous. And I am a prig. You could have had your hanky-panky without posing naked as a jaybird.''

''It would have lacked dash. And admit it: I'm in a great tradition. If the Duchess of Alba could make a fool of herself, I can too. Although La Spada is hardly Goya.'' Francie's face was full of fun. ''And even allowing for historical exaggeration, he's not Goya in bed either.''

At that moment the telephone rang. ''That's Meg. She's called before.'' Peter's face was now grave. ''Word of mouth travels faster than telex. The 'Living' section of the *New York Times* wants to interview you on the pros and cons of personal portraits in the nude. As a marketing pro, is this the new, trendy thing?''

''Oh, my God! La Spada blabbed. He swore on his mother's soul—''

''He has no mother. He has hatched from a snake egg. Also *New York* and *People* would like a photo of the painting. With or without the interview. They can always make one up.''

Maria tapped on the bedroom door. ''*Scusa*, madam. Telephone.''

''Tell her to hang on.'' Francie waved Maria away. ''Peter, he'd never show the painting?''

"I agree. But why do we call him La Spada? The Knife. His real name is Nick Fornese. But he looks like Sparafucile, the assassin in *Rigoletto*. And he is an assassin who doesn't take lives. He takes personalities, using them to build his own celebrity. He has an instinct for hitting the right perversity in the press." His tone held a certain amount of respect. "Imagine—doing you nude."

"Oh, Lord! I can see them on their knees begging for a look-see."

"And if no look-see, think of the salacious tidbits they'll write."

Francie picked up the telephone. "Meg, Peter just told me all. It's nonsense. I'll talk to La Spada tonight. He'll make a public retraction. What? No, I'm not part of a chic, new trend!" Francie hung up and turned to Peter with a look of enjoyment. "The word is out. It's not only me the sharks want. He did Trisha Nixon in her engagement dress. And dozens more. The question is has he done a nude Jackie O?"

Peter was now dead serious. "Francie, La Spada must not make a public retraction. He must shut up. The less talk the better. Got it?" Francie nodded her head humbly. "I told Monroe to pick up the painting this afternoon and take it home with him."

"Monroe! And let the charming Mrs. Perl have a private viewing? Peter, you've lost your marbles."

"The charming Mrs. Perl is in Paris. When she returns, La Spada is doing her portrait. So Monroe is persona grata with Spada."

"La Spada is doing Isabelle's portrait. Ahhhh, me. Since the Perls became art mavins, there isn't a loft in Soho where they don't stop by to water the plants."

"Enough of your girlish malice," Peter sighed. "I only wish he'd call. I want no evidence lying around on which an investigative reporter can make a name. The idea of the assassin playing horse thief with your reputation truly irritates me. What a way to waste one's precious private time. I had to cancel Jamison tonight."

"You were seeing Jamie tonight?"

It struck Peter she was too sharp. "Yes, he's in town so I telephoned."

"And made a dinner date?"

"Of course. We often get together when he's in town."

Francie's mind filled with blurred pictures and mixed echoes. "You should have asked me first."

"Why?" He breathed deeply waiting for her to speak.

"No reason. Sorry."

"Francie! He's an old friend. A client. He wrote to me that he wanted to redo the guest rooms in the Bermuda house. We've discussed it on and off for a year. So of course I'd telephone him when he's in town. Sometimes he calls me."

"Of course."

"It never occurred to me, Francie, that you'd mind anymore." Peter's eyes were fixed on his fingers. "I've been dense. I wouldn't hurt you for the world."

How like Peter's genius to know what she was feeling; but not put more words to it than was absolutely necessary.

"I know. You dear thing—you wouldn't." Francie touched his cheek with genuine tenderness. "You're wonderful."

"No—no, it's you. God knows where I'd have been without you."

"Or I without you."

"Never were a married couple on such excellent terms." She thought once he would be easy to manage. He was so easy it seemed unbelievable. And it was unbelievable. For she knew now, all these years later, how it only seemed so easy because of his extraordinary stamina, his ability to endure her, his infinite tact which she had recently come to believe was the special gift of the meek who indeed inherit the earth. She leaned over and kissed him lightly, almost antagonistically, on the mouth. He returned her kiss with enthusiasm and surprise.

"You are wonderful," he murmured.

"That's why I torment you so." She laughed a jeering, uneven laugh like someone recovering from a bad fright.

He held her to him, caressing the lobes of her ear, the nape of her neck, caressing her breasts gently, lingering over the nipples, feeling them rise like blades of grass under the silk shirt. "It's been a long time," he whispered into her ear. "We have the time."

Francie nodded. "I want a brandy first."

"Do you have to get drunk to make love with me?"

"No, darling. I get drunk to celebrate. Get me a small one while I slip into something more comfortable."

By the time Peter returned to the bedroom, Francie was almost nude. "See? 'The Naked Franciejean,' " she giggled.

"Yes, love. Here." He handed her a small glass of brandy. "Your bed, I gather," he said, closing the bedroom door.

"Mine," she said. "My mattress is harder."

"Your mattress is a rock."

The living area of La Spada's three-story studio loft was high and spacious and elegantly uncluttered by the more untidy elements involved in the creation of a painting. He had bought the entire building before the price of Soho lofts skyrocketed, and now he lived like a pasha where once the ILGWU had fought tooth and nail for chastity and survival ("If you don't come in Sunday don't come in Monday.").

Stepping out of the small suede-lined elevator always produced in Francie the effect of a fanfare. The vastness of the living and dining room instantly impressed one with the sensual theatricality of the owner. The luxury and lavish scale of the area was a tour de force, even by Manhattan standards.

La Spada became a portrait painter of women when long years ago he sketched, for a glass of vino, a portrait of Sophia Loren as Aida. The then-unknown actress gave the sketch by the unknown artist to a new friend as a birthday present. The new friend helped the young actress to get the part of Aida. And so two unknowns were launched.

As Sophia's fame increased, so did La Spada's; and through the years, his clients came to include Maria Callas, Margot Fonteyn, Princess Grace and her daughter, Jackie O and daughter, et al.

That "serious" artists and orthodox art critics regarded his work as planned mediocrity did not gray a single strand in La Spada's shock of black hair and beard that tonight matched the black velvet suit he was wearing. They were jealous; he was rich; that was that. And now that realistic painters of all types were creeping out of the woodwork and exhibiting everywhere there was an available wall, it grew more difficult to argue with his success.

La Spada even had his defenders. One critic maintained that he painted quite shamelessly. If you looked at his portraits carefully—not too quickly—you would find they were not at all sentimentalized. You would see what he saw.

Only it was done on the sly, by ironic indirection. Almost flirtatiously. Merely a suggestion.

That evening, when Francie and Peter arrived, the other guests invited to the preview were already present. Decked in their party finery, snorting, sniffing, oohing and aahing, up on their hind legs, purring approval, they sipped champagne and swallowed Italian salami, pickled carrots, sardines, and wandered around giving and receiving cozy intimate words, gazing at one another blissfully, or at the works of the New Frontier series. The paintings were hung on a section of the far left wall. The wall was temporarily cleared of Winslow Homer, two Cézannes and a Master of Moulins. La Spada was both eclectic and knowledgeable. Now, he was holding forth on his favorite subjects: La Spada, La Spada's paintings, La Spada's philosophy of painting . . .

"My effort, as you can see from my comments on the painting of Electra and of Franciejean, was not simply to do the sitters in a way that would be easy to recognize. I follow the great Leonardo's principle, to 'paint the face in such a way that it will be easy to understand what is going on in the mind.' Some say I idealize my subjects—I do. But I do it by suggesting their fine psychological characteristics. I never serve mere vanity. I serve truth. . . ."

"A man with the courage of his convictions," murmured Peter.

"And his bank account," said Monroe, joining them.

"Monroe—did you get the painting?"

"No. I spent all afternoon upstairs in his studio drinking myself blind. And massaging his ego until I have a tennis elbow, and in thirty years I've never had elbow trouble. It's a matter of stroking, not snapping. In any case, he wouldn't talk about it or show it."

"I will not soil myself by doing propaganda portraits," La Spada was saying. "It is not enough that a woman be famous. Beautiful. The heroine in her field . . ."

"In fact," Monroe continued, "when he came down here to interview Billie Jean King, who has never had a tennis elbow, I ransacked the entire studio. No Franciejean. Nude or Saran-wrapped."

"Where's Tommy?" Francie asked.

"With that nymphette. And Electra." Peter nodded toward the far end of the immense room. There stood a long refectory table set with Chinese export porcelain and surrounded by a mix of Queen Anne chairs, Hepplewhite mahogany chairs and two from seventeenth-century China. Above the table, a Waterford crystal chandelier struck flashes of light from the Venetian glass and Irish silver. Behind the table a late eighteenth-century Chinese screen created an exotic background for the centerpiece, a Chinese red-lacquered pewter pagoda. To Peter, La Spada's place always seemed a riot of decorative excess. Looking round, he remarked wryly, "La Spada may be a freethinking painter, but this is not a place one takes off one's shoes to relax."

"Who's the girl with Tommy?" Francie asked.

"Who knows? He brought her. And why in the name of all you hold dear—namely the Abe Barnett Company—did you invite him?"

"He invited himself. He'd heard about the preview and asked if he could come. How was I to know the Naked Me was about to become famous?"

"Since knowing our dear Lillian, though I lay no claim to clairvoyance, my nose has grown more acute. It twitches when I smell murder in the air." Peter was watching Tommy. "And the idea of a nude painting of Franciejean Devlin, President of the New York office of the Barnett Company, hanging somewhere within sighting distance of our friendly barracuda." He shook his head. "Let's get him out of here with due dispatch."

"Seconded," said Monroe.

Francie was gazing fixedly at Tommy. "And how do we invite him to go without alerting his radar?" she asked.

La Spada was now in front of Stella Coleman's painting. "Of course one cannot paint two subjects with the same method. I often have stage fright before starting a new portrait. For example, you cannot always do full face. Or a profile. Or finish the head before going on to the body. Rules guarantee failure. . . ."

"Francie, go talk to La Spada. Say a few choice words. We want that nude. Then go to Tommy," said Peter. "I'll be by shortly to help. I want to case this place. We must have the painting tonight. Wrapped in the thirty-six gallon Hefty garbage bag in my briefcase."

"You think of everything, Peter. But what is Spada up to? He's a promoter. Not a blackmailer."

"The types overlap," said Monroe. "I speak from grimy experience." And he followed Francie as she moved off toward La Spada.

"What makes a Gainsborough so remarkable is not planning. It's the sudden bold stroke of insight—"

"Spada, we must talk," Francie murmured, standing beside him.

"Later, *cara*, later. So in my own work, my greatest successes are the result of the inspiration of the moment. . . ."

Peter stared around the room searching for an answer. There was Electra OToole looking pale and talking to her non-husband, the heir to a shipping fortune who funded anticapitalist causes.

"For Stella Coleman, I took my cue from Titian. As a student of worldwide marriage rites, I did her as the Goddess of Chastity. The new chastity. The universal woman, continuously recreating her virginity in the purity of her response to each new mating situation. . . ."

Listening to La Spada's twaddle and looking at the painting of the lushly curved Stella in a gossamer night shift, Peter was suddenly aware that the New Goddess of Chastity had advanced upon him like some seductive bird of prey. Controlling an impulse to laugh, he stood feet apart, solidly planted, waiting for her attack.

"You're Peter Devlin," Franciejean's husband," she said, looking up into his eyes. "She's very beautiful," she continued flatly, while Peter decided that Stella wasn't. But she was handsome, sturdy in build, of medium height. Her throat was solid and strong, her arms solid and tan, her brown eyes now full of serious provocation. "You both are beautiful," Stella went on. "But I find Franciejean too hairless. Smooth as a plucked chicken."

Peter studied her interestedly, noting the outline of her full breasts and hips, unbraed and uncorseted under the thin silk caftan. "You object to hairlessness in women?"

"It's unsexual. La Spada says I have a genuinely sensual body—the finest he ever painted. And I'm quite hairy."

"La Spada is certainly a judge."

"I have hair on my thighs. Between my breasts. Ringlets

of pubic hair. I never shave or use depilatories. I have never found a man in any culture who objected. All truly sensual women are hairy."

Peter thought about this. "You do have long lovely lashes."

"I am magnificent." She leaned closer in anticipation. "But I am one of those women who look better without clothes than with them." She drew herself up, and Peter thought she might disrobe then and there. "I want to see you again. But of course you want to see what you're getting."

"I am completely enchanted with what I see before me."

"You are not." She said it half stubborn, half pleading. "So I will insist that La Spada show you my portrait."

"I can see it from here. It's splendid."

"Oh, that. No, that's publicity. I mean the nude painting."

Peter stared at her incredulous. "La Spada painted you nude?"

"He begged me. He was beside himself, poor man. We're taking it home tonight. But I'll have him show it to you privately first. Then I will give you my telephone number."

"Yes, I would like to see the painting."

"Good. I whetted your appetite."

Peter looked at La Spada explaining another portrait: Dallas Klein, the journeying spirit in search of identity. On the way downtown, Francie had explained that Dallas had left her husband and two children, to become an identity seeker. First she was a cab driver. Then a "kept" lesbian, a poetess, remarried, redivorced, then opened a yogurt health-food restaurant. Now she was running for councilwoman from her restaurant's district. The world was Dallas's frontier.

"You see I have painted her in the manner of Rousseau's 'Sleeping Gypsy.' Exhausted, she too sleeps, wrapped in a towel, on the beach. A rapist wanders by. The equivalent of Rousseau's lion sniffing the gypsy. But does he rape Dallas? No. As we would say of Rousseau's gypsy, Dallas's incorruptible purity of heart always protects her from the evil surrounding us. . . ."

"Peter asked Stella, "Did he do Dallas in the nude, too?"

Stella became totally indignant. "Now why would La Spada want to paint that scarecrow nude? She's a bag of bones. And hairless. She certainly does need an identity."

"As for Rachel Speers, better known as Bunny, I painted her in the Surrealist manner; those who plunge downward seeking life's ultimate meaning in the unconscious world that replaces the objective one. . . ."

"Did La Spada paint Bunny nude?" asked Peter.

"Why would anyone want to paint her nude? She probable has flabby thighs, sagging breasts, and a pimply behind." Stella was angry.

Peter repressed a smile. "Do you think she has hair?"

"Of course. Bristles. From shaving. A bearded body."

Realizing this was not the time to get La Spada's attention, Francie drifted, seemingly aimlessly, toward Tommy. The girl with him was staring around in an ecstatic trance, and Francie could study her unobserved. There was about her a total look, her black hair dropping to her shoulders, framing an angular, striking face, her slender body in a loose, light wool, half leaning possessively against Tommy.

"Hello, Francie," said Tommy as she joined them, a cautious welcome in his tone. "I'd like you to meet Edwina Keyes. My fiancée."

"Fiancée! How wonderful." Francie's voice was only mildly surprised. "How nice to meet you, Miss Keyes, soon to be Mrs. Dominico." Anyone seeking Francie and Edwina standing together would feel that, on principle, they could never exist side by side. Anyone with sense would try to keep them apart. Now Francie smiled at Edwina. "Tommy is the most eligible bachelor in the advertising industry."

"My father is thumbs down on advertising as a profession for my husband. He wants Tommy to go into corporate finance."

"I gather that's your father's field."

"My father is Douglas Keyes, Vice-Chairman of First Cambridge Corporation. Investment bankers. My great-grandfather founded it." Then her eyes canvassed Francie. "I was dying to meet you, Mrs. Devlin. I know it's improper to ask intimate questions, but I am curious. Have you and Tommy been sleeping together a long time?"

Francie had a split-second jolt, then started to laugh. "Do you mean do we take naps together? No."

456

"No, I mean do you fuck together?"

"Eddie, I didn't agree to bring you here to insult Francie. I'd be embarrassed if it became necessary to forcibly evict you."

"It's all right, Tommy," said Francie. "She believes she's being outrageous. Instead of silly." She must really want him, thought Francie. Probably a case of strong chemistry, mixed with strenuous parental objections. The Brahmin Keyes were not the kind who took well to lads from the wrong side of the tracks. Even with Tommy's success; even in these seemingly trackless years.

"I am not silly!" Edwina raised her voice. "I have an instinct for the possible. It runs in the family." She glared at Tommy. "Keep out of this. You didn't agree to bring me. If I hadn't seen a blurb in the *Times* 'Arts' section about this whoop-de-doo preview, I'd never have known about it." She gave Francie a fierce look. "When I wheedled it out of Tommy that he had to put in an official appearance, strictly business and such junk, I said 'balls' and held a gun to his head. I wanted to meet you, Franciejean Devlin. At least you're beautiful. I'd be very concerned if Tommy was hitting the sack with some dowdy type. That's too ambitious. It smacks of a low I.Q. and gigoloism. But you'll do." She spoke rapidly in a disjointed manner. "I am also impressed at how young you are to be Tommy's boss. You must be good. A formidable competitor. I like that." She breathed. "I don't give a fig what you two did before he met me. I passed a few ships in the night myself. But I want it clear there will be no more bed hopping once the banns are posted. I never want to sniff some stranger's perfume on my sweetheart's prick. Or find somebody else's pill wheel in his vest pocket. I want no social diseases. Just a good old-fashioned marriage. Like my mother and father have. With two or three children."

The look of pain on Tommy's face would have been funny to Francie if she didn't feel sorry for him. He'd spent his life climbing out of his gutter; angling, plotting, scheming, working for success. But no ordinary college or finishing-school girl for our hero. He must have a thoroughbred. A swift, assured, purebred young lady. From one of the right families. And at last he'd found her; a true-blue pedigreed hellion with the panache of a drunken sailor. "I think a solid family is the basis of lasting happiness." Francie felt she sounded like the first copy draft for a life insurance ad

"And a family that prays together stays together," said Edwina. "Family life is what made America great. That and a sawed-off shotgun."

Tommy cut across in exasperation. "We're getting married on Christmas Eve day." He said it neither romantically nor gallantly but to change the subject. "Eddie doesn't believe in long engagements."

"And when will you start your family?" Francie asked wondering how to get rid of them.

"Soon enough." Edwina was thinking of something else. "I was just talking to Electra O'Toole. She thinks a woman is the most beautiful when she's pregnant. And La Spada agreed. So he painted her in her seventh month. Naked. With her big belly. A symbol of female fertility. I wish he'd do me—one before, one during."

Francie stood perfectly still. "La Spada painted Electra as a madonna. It's there on the wall."

"That's for the Frontier series. But for herself, he did her naked. She said she'd have him show it later. Would you mind if he painted me nude, Tommy?"

Tommy looked at his bride-to-be with a faint distaste. "Why not get paid for it? Call up *Playboy* or *Penthouse*." With Edwina there was rarely a middle ground. They had bitter quarrels. And explosive sexual reconciliations. He believed in marriage deeply, and at thirty-five it was time he married. So he had chosen Edwina—Boston, rich, social. Plus good-looking, intelligent, sexual. He told himself he was in love. But often the illusion was difficult to maintain. Those things he had once wanted to say from the heart to another girl, he now said to Edwina, using his best marketing skills to persuade himself as much as her. But listening to his own words, he could hear the lie in the love words. For, by now, he knew himself far too well. He had learned, too, how rare it was to meet true emotion—in oneself or another.

But he was as much a pragmatist as Edwina's own kin. He would marry her; and if it failed, he'd bow out. By then he'd know her friends. And there might be something in switching to investment banking.

La Spada was winding up his spiel on Bunny. "So we have our Bunny drawing inspiration from her unconscious.

She dislikes dusting, cooking, child care, while John loves it. So Bunny works, and John, the natural homemaker, keeps house. So, in this canvas, vibrating with love, you see Bunny, our new traditionalist, feeding her paycheck into John's vacuum cleaner.''

Francie shook her head impatiently as she watched Edwina walk back. Then in a half-commanding tone she said, ''Tommy, I invited you. Now I suggest you two leave. This is no place for Edwina Keyes.''

''Agreed. But when she gets stubborn, she hisses. Draws blood.''

Out of nowhere Peter appeared. ''Tommy, is that girl Edwina Keyes?''

''That girl is my fiancée. Yes.''

''Then, what do you mean bringing that brat into contact with this group? She's more trouble to her family than a cat in heat. A throwback to her great-grandmother. I just recognized her. Her father and I are cousins. If Douglas Keyes ever hears of this escapade—''

The import of Peter's words winded Tommy, but he made a quick recovery. ''If you're related, you throw her out. I'm not her husband yet. Only her fiancée. And she'll bite. Kick. Scream. To get her own way. Right now, her own way is to stay.''

Just then a shriek came from the spot where La Spada stood facing Stella, Electra and Rachel.

''You bastard! You did Electra O'Toole!''

''Stella, darling. Calm yourself!''

''But you begged me. You plagued, nagged, pestered me. You said I was the one woman you'd longed to paint all your life. A true woman.''

''He wrote that to me too. In a letter,'' said Electra.

''He even wept!'' said Stella.

''He wept for me too,'' said Bunny.

Rising clear and bell-like above the voices of female indignation came Edwina's ''La Spada, you don't have to beg me. I'd love to have you paint me nude. I think it's super.''

''Edwina—you come with me!'' Peter suddenly had his arm around her waist and was dragging her toward the elevator. He deftly moved his head in the nick of time to avoid the full slam of her clenched fist. Then she saw his face. "Peter—angel!" she screamed eagerly and stopped flailing around. "Another black sheep of our family—like me! What are you doing here?"

"I'm with my wife, Franciejean Devlin."

"That Franciejean is married to you? I'll be horn-swaggled."

"Yes. And I want you out of here. Now!"

"I won't budge!" she said, starting to struggle again. "I want an appointment. To be painted nude."

"Eddie, you listen to me! Your father and I are not as close as we were years ago. But we are cousins, and we both respect the family. And if you don't leave here now, I will call Douglas and tell him your plans. Then let's see what happens to your independent income. And your inheritance when grandmother hears about it. And your marriage to Thomas Dominico when the family realizes he brought you here—you, a gently reared young lady."

Listening to Peter, Edwina knew he meant it, and that the consequences were as he described them. Mortified that she could not stop him, she gave a low moan. "Peter, don't be a killjoy. I was having such a great time."

"Edwina—out!"

At Peter's word, Tommy appeared in his top coat, carrying Edwina's sheepskin coat which he put over her squirming shoulders while Peter held her in place.

From the center of the room Stella was screaming, "You do not realize what an offense to my sensibility this has become!"

"You think you're the only one attractive enough to be painted nude?" shrilled Electra.

Monroe had rung for the elevator while Peter and Tommy, one on each side of Edwina, firmly gripped her arms, waiting for its arrival. When the elevator came, Peter shoved Edwina gently but resolutely into it, and Tommy held her in a fireman's grip. "Please—please let me stay!" wailed Edwina as the door closed.

"Good-bye, you wild, lovely, fairy creature," said Monroe.

"Yeeee!" came an anguished scream from Bunny Speer's husband, John. "You mean this bastard painted you naked!" The new traditionalist was seething.

"John Speer, I earn the money! If I want to pose nude, I pose!"

"It's hard to tell the new from the old traditionalists," giggled Francie, standing between Peter and Monroe, watching the four ladies snake-dance in fury around La Spada. Only Dallas was enjoying it, throwing off her clothes as she shimmied and shook.

"Peter, he painted us all nude, swearing each was his grand passion."

"La Spada restores my faith in the depravity of human nature. I can say nothing finer about him."

"Dear ladies, please! Let us not have secrets from each other. Let's cleanse and open our hearts." La Spada was speaking in a basso profundo. "I cannot stand here in front of you and lie. It is beneath the true artist. Yes, I painted you all—nude."

"Beast! You said the sight of my body hallowed your life!"

"Stella, I'll explain—"

"You said I aroused your higher nature!" shouted Bunny. "Me—me!"

"But you did! You all did! Ladies, listen to me! Please."

"You said seeing my body—mine—soothed your soul!"

"It did, Electra. Ladies, listen! Do you know how I have longed to let my id go wild! Unleash my baser nature to run amok? And sometimes it has. My life has been corrupted by passion. Wild, orgiastic sensuality could become the dominant note of my existence. If I did not do hand-to-hand battle with my own lower nature and hurl it to the wall. The wall."

"Does he remind you a little of Saint Augustine?" murmured Peter.

"But you five ladies, you frontier women, awakened by higher self. You exerted a purifying influence."

"Ahhhh—"

"Ooooooh—a purifying influence."

"Yes, a purifying influence," said La Spada.

"Hmmm," said Stella.

"Hogwash," whispered Francie to Peter.

"At last I could dwell in the realm of the greatest painters. For a nature with my emotional intensity must be constantly policed. And now I have won. The test succeeded. In painting you trail-blazing women, I saw the possibilities of the human spirit. I could do what Titian did. Rubens, Raphael, Goya, Matisse. I could rise above the beast within and paint nude women in their glory. Arch upon arch opened, I had the vision of something beyond the body, beyond mere sexuality."

"Okay. I want to see them," said John Speer, "these purified nudes."

"So do I," said Harley Matson.

"Ah, but these paintings are sacred," said La Spada. "Holy paintings. Not for public viewing. Each lady will see hers privately. I will set up appointments for next week."

"Bullshit!" said Stella. "I want to see me now!"

"So do I!" said Electra.

"Me too," agreed Dallas, who up till then had said nothing.

"Ladies, it is unwise to view such paintings in a group. Instead of seeing yourself in your splendor, as I saw you, what you will do is make comparisons with each other. Absurd comparisons since no two bodies are comparable."

"I don't care. I want to see me now!"

The men agreed with the women.

La Spada sighed. "Perhaps this is the best way. Roland come here." Roland, La Spada's houseboy, who had been serving champagne, went to La Spada, his face concerned, having observed the temper of the women. La Spada whispered something. Roland nodded, turned and left for the studio upstairs. "While we wait for Roland to return with the canvases, let me tell you about these paintings. Of you Dallas. Electra. Francie. Bunny. Stella. As we all know, the world's greatest masters have done nudes. And in Rome, many years ago, as a student, I studied those masters of the body. But I wearied of flesh tones, hair textures, the sensuality of arms, legs, breasts. Having gorged myself on the passions latent in the body, I decided that optical illusion of a nude woman interfered with seeing the reality of her spirit. It was then, living in poverty on the Via Margutta, that I created a radical school of nude painting. A school in advance of anything at the time. But it was so advanced that I failed. I had to give up nude painting entirely. My portraits, till now, have been fully clothed."

Francie knew how cunning La Spada was, and she'd have far preferred the private showings. She hoped the other women would have the sense never to discuss these paintings publicly. She, for one, would take her painting home; and if necessary, burn it. If questioned, she'd deny its reality. She watched Roland return and set up easels, each with a covered canvas, next to what she supposed was its sister painting of the frontier woman. Francie next to Francie. Stella next to Stella.

"But times change. Today there is Ad Reinhardt with black on black. Franz Kline's magnificent line slashes. And for me too, a new and radiant creative impulse has dawned. It crystallized while doing the frontier series. Then I realized it was time to revive the ideals of youth. Ideals whose time had come. For the frontier series I used many styles. For my nudes, I used my own discovery. My own school of painting called 'Suppressionism.' To be a Suppressionist, one needs, of course, proper light, a huge palette, an infinite number of brushes of varying sizes and textures—but above all, one needs women of noble spirit to pose willingly, revealing not merely their glorious bodies, but their glowing souls."

Roland had finished setting up the covered canvases.

"Stella stand next to your painting. You too, Electra. Dallas. Francie. Bunny."

The ladies did as they were told, Francie feeling like a fool.

"Notice ladies, that each canvas is carefully covered," said La Spada. "For I want you to see them in all their splendor, simultaneously. And remember, I painted your spirit, not your body. That is the essence of Suppressionism. It requires subtlety and intellect to grasp my accomplishment; but I am confident that you frontier women will see what I have achieved. Even Matisse's 'Joie de Vivre' has lascivious overtones that will not be found in my work. Now, ladies, adjust your vision to the logic of the soul. Remove the cloth from the canvas!"

There was ten seconds of suspense, pure silence in every heart, and then the ladies did as told. For at least three minutes nothing was said. Not a word. Not a breath. You could have heard a pin drop. A feather.

Then Bunny said meekly, "But I don't see anything."

"I don't either," said Dallas.

"Of course you do," said La Spada. "Ladies, this is Suppressionism. To be a Suppressionist painter you must have a steady hand, great technique, and unceasing control. Understand that the idea of Suppressionism is to paint the soul. Therefore, *you must paint as close to the canvas as possible without touching it*. It is an idea beyond Titian, beyond Renoir, beyond Matisse, Picasso, de Kooning."

"It is *nothing on nothing!*" muttered Monroe.

"I don't get it."

"I don't see anything," complained John Speer.

"It's a blank canvas."

"Try. Try to see the radiance of your spirits."

Harley Matson walked up to the empty canvas, theoretically containing Electra's soul, and pressed his nose up against it. Then he picked it up and turned it upside down to see if he could see something that way. Doing this, it slipped from his fingers and fell with a startling crash to the floor. At that moment La Spada's control went. Peel upon peel of deep, helpless laughter came over him.

"Oh my God!" shrieked Stella. "You damned stallion! You made believe you were painting us nude so you could fuck us!" And even as La Spada laughed, she picked up her canvas and crashed it down on his head. It broke the canvas, but not his bull-like neck.

"He fucked you too?!" screamed Electra.

"He fucked us all," said Dallas.

"I'll kill him!" said Harley, shooting a soft punch at La Spada, who picked him up and hurled him across the room. And then doubled over again with his hands on his knees and laughed and laughed.

At that point Bunny Speer took off her belt and, swinging it in the air, gave La Spada a sharp blow in the face with the buckle.

That hurt, and a welt of blood appeared. "Ladies! Now, let's not be enemies. We all enjoyed ourselves, didn't we?"

Suddenly, with cat like swiftness Electra hurried to where the dining table stood and picking up two plates, hurled them at his head. One caught La Spada on the side of the ear, staggered him backward, dizzying him for a moment. After that, Electra, joined by Dallas, continued throwing whatever was on the table.

La Spada had stopped laughing and his eyes were alive with fear as well as fury, as he tried to duck the flying objects. Meanwhile, aroused and ready, Stella and Bunny circled him, their eyes glittering, their hair flying. La Spada crouched like some huge animal held at bay.

Only Francie kept her distance, quietly watching.

"Say, La Spada!" shrilled Stella. "Who was the best fuck? Who?"

He hesitated a moment. "You were all superb, ladies. All. Now, stop behaving like children and come to your senses." He tried to speak with authority, but was too frightened. He knew their blood was up and he was their meat. Then Stella and Bunny hurled themselves at him like two wild, crazy creatures, ripping at his clothes. Bunny grabbed his scarf from behind in an effort to strangle him. He was struggling now in a frantic madness of rage and terror.

"Peter! Monroe! Help! Get these harpies off me!" But nobody moved. The men stood still and watched, while the women mauled, kicked, and bit as though to tear him to pieces; clenching their fists and socking him; and by yanking the scarf harder, Bunny kept his hands at his throat, preventing him from defending himself. Finally, striking with all their might, they knocked him down, their blows growing more intense, their expressions more grotesque. Then Electra and Stella started to pull at his pants to get them off.

"We'll castrate him! Castrate him! We will!" screamed Stella.

"Do it," said John Speer primly. "He seduced my wife."

"And the mother of my child."

La Spada lay there with his face bleeding, his body squirming as best he could, as they tugged at his pants. Suddenly he saw Francie standing apart and out of it, and he shouted, "Francie, help me! Help!"

But she winced away from his words and eyes. Then started to giggle crazily. "Help you Uncle Paul? Help you? Are you crazy?" She spoke in a low, deadly tone. "You know what you did to me. You know." There was a Samurai sword hanging on the nearby wall; and she reached for it quickly, pulling it from its scabbard. She moved as though in a trance, toward the writhing mass of bodies. "It's your turn," she said in cold triumph, "to bleed and bleed and bleed."

"Francie, put that thing down!" yelled Peter, racing after her. He reached her just in time, as she stood with sword raised over La Spada. In one swift, strong gesture, he wrenched it from her grip and tossed the sword to the far end of the room. Then, taking Francie by the shoulders, he pulled her close against him. Her face was trembling with a kind of agony and suddenly she was sobbing wildly, "Help me, Momma! Help me! Get him away!"

Her sobs and screams brought all the furious activity on the floor to a stop. The other women turned to stare at her shaking figure.

"Okay, ladies! Stop it!" said Peter. "You've had your fun. That's enough."

"He's right," said Dallas, getting up. "I don't want to castrate him."

"I don't either," said Electra. "Though he replaces King Kong as my favorite male hero." She rose. "Come on, everybody. Up!"

"He is absolute proof that virtue is its own reward."

La Spada rose slowly, a dazed, ragged creature. "Please, everybody, go home."

"John, take me home," said Bunny. "I need a bath."

"Monroe, get Francie's coat. I have to hold her."

"Right," said Monroe. Then, pausing for a moment, he remarked sadly, "And dear ladies, while you bathe or shower to wash away the shame of this evening, please remember it was written, 'It takes two to tango.' If your antics tonight were meant to save La Spada's soul, you might think seriously about your own chances for salvation."

When Peter and Francie arrived home, she collapsed in her bedroom in her favorite club chair by the window. Her eyes were red from weeping. "What happened to me, Peter? What happened?"

"I don't know. Would you like to talk about it?" he asked hesitantly with the cautious tenderness that always possessed him when facing the inner truth of his wife. Lately there had been questions in the air; questions in the way she looked at him, in her voice, in everything about her. And yet, there was also their historic discretion with each other, that they not ask any questions. And of all the people in the world whom Peter would care to please, he most cared about pleasing Francie. But tonight she not only permitted his interest, she positively invited it. "No, I wouldn't mind talking."

"I don't know what happened, Francie," he said, feeling his way as he seated himself in the opposite chair.

"There are some things I'd like to talk about," she said. "If I weren't so afraid."

"Something serious is the matter, isn't it?"

"The matter? What gives you such a notion? My theatrics tonight?" She said it sardonically.

"Other things. I assumed when you were ready you'd talk about it."

"Have I been acting queerly? Eccentrically? Nuts?"

"This isn't criticism."

"I know, I know." They were near the window where she could see the lights of the Queensboro Bridge. But Francie closed her eyes to the view and dropped her face in her hands. The long silence that followed was her answer. When she looked at him again, she could see the worry in his face. His fine composure had dropped. "Peter, I don't really know what's the matter. I think I'm haunted. Something peculiar is happening to me." It was a relief to tell him, and it struck her sharply that, when it came right down to it, he was probably the only proper sympathizer. He was her husband.

"Haunted—you?" He fixed her with deep eyes. "Haunted by what?"

"Perhaps it's only my vivid imagination."

Her voice was steady, but the undercurrent of terror made him wince. "You're really having a bad time?"

"How bad is bad?" she asked with apology, almost shame. "Poor Peter, why did you ever, ever marry me? I'm such a trial. I mean really—why?"

Peter looked back at her thinking that if he answered truthfully he might cause her more pain.

Catching his guarded expression, she prodded him gently. "Whatever it is, I won't mind." She remembered the scene so long ago. "You said once you wanted a home? A hostess? Was that it? Did I prove out?"

It struck him then that this subject had never since that first time arisen between them. From the beginning, she had accepted everything at face value. How odd to spell things out all these years later. "You won't believe me."

"I'll believe anything tonight." They had lived in a state of polite intimacy. They had not named names, or labeled actions. There were subjects they avoided, out of tact, even in their closest moments.

467

"I married you for quite an ordinary reason. I love you." There was an awkward, adolescent ring to the speech, but he went on anyway. "I always have. Do you mind awfully?"

His truth given to her full in the face was absurdly embarrassing. "You love me?"

"I love you. Didn't the possibility ever occur to you?"

"No, never."

"I thought that. That's why I never mentioned it."

"But didn't you love Jasper? And Roger?"

"Yes."

"Well?"

"My loving you didn't preclude my loving others. Francie, I do not wish to discuss at this time the pros and cons of the medical or moral basis of my personality. Because I enjoy a man, does not mean for me, that I can't enjoy a woman sexually. You, for instance. Yes, I loved Jasper. And Roger. Ecstatically. Despairingly. And I would never have survived them had I not known I had you. You were stuck with me. You couldn't leave. And I loved you."

"Jamison wasn't stuck with me."

"No, he wasn't. But I was. As you were with me. And since it was clear that you didn't marry me for love—"

"It was clear, wasn't it?"

"Totally. So why burden you with my feelings. But now that we're opening graves, let's be honest. Let's say that originally you tolerated me. Because you desperately wanted a husband. To be respectable."

"So did you."

"Not with quite the same virulence. Remember, I grew up in a tradition of outsiders—but outsiders for which my group had established a place. But what did you have? At twenty-two? Where could you go?"

She would have been ashamed at this late date to have him catch her flinching. "Nowhere. Except down."

"Well, that didn't happen."

"Thank you."

"Thank yourself. I only bet on a dark horse. Women are different than men. Heterosexual or homosexual. I don't know all the differences beyond anatomical ones. But I do know one major difference. That has to do with stamina. When one is a man, no matter how he satisfies his sexual appetites, he must endure what he must endure. If he runs away, then he's a damn fool. And it costs more in the end. Not enough women know this. They let themselves off the hook too easily. They're self-indulgent. They complain. Make excuses. You don't. I wasn't wrong in loving you. You'll do. You're quite a woman.''

It was before her now, and she had not much more to ask. It was her own insensitivity and fear that had left her blind. She could barely see him because there was a mist of tears before her eyes. "I wish you'd told me sooner."

"No you don't."

"Come to bed."

"Darling, contrary to Jacqueline Suzanne, once is enough for now. We're not going to live happily ever after on your big rock candy mountain. We're not a nice, normal couple—if such couples exist. And we mustn't waste our energies tinkering with a false front."

Nothing was so odd for Francie, nor could she have measured it, as how impressed she was with her husband. In a way he was an honor to human nature. Given what psychologists might have called the worst conditions, they'd made a good life. She had her troubles with herself, as he did with himself. But they buoyed each other up, and there was mutual respect. "It's been a good marriage."

But Peter was thinking of something else. "Francie, what do I do to help?"

"Stay with me. Bear with me. Do as you say men do—endure." It amounted to a surrender, a confession of weakness.

"I'm staying. I'm here for keeps." A great wave of feeling swept over him. "In sickness, in health. In everything."

They were silent for a moment. Then she said lightly, "I do try your patience, don't I?"

"Yes, but I manage." Despite his effort, his face was now wide open with concern. "Besides what went on tonight what are the symptoms? What is the form?"

She faced him with the remnants of her strength. "I'd rather not discuss specifics now. But if I'm not haunted, I'm crazy."

"Then, we have to do something. See a doctor."

"Or a priest. Or a witch doctor." She wanted him to

know she trusted him, and what better proof than to accept his help. "I'll do anything you say."

"All right. Go to bed. Tomorrow you'll call Dr. Ornstein."

"I suppose I am running out of time." She said it then, acknowledging her menace; feeling she must make the best of everything, of Peter's caring, of his kindness, of his compassionate strength.

Her words carried such a note of truth that Peter gave up all hesitation. "Lean on me, please," he begged.

"Oh, I will, I will. This has only begun."

28

One afternoon about two weeks later, Francie arrived at her office around three o'clock, having been with a client all morning and through lunch. Her office was one of her favorite places in the world, giving her a view of the park, the city, the river, and the westward horizon of America. It was a view she never tired of, but this afternoon she saw nothing—not the view, not the walls hung with photographs and TV clips from her various famous campaigns, not the perfectly proportioned Hans Knoll furniture, not the mementoes and tributes to her personal achievements—nothing.

She sat down wearily behind the long slab of gleaming plastic that served as her workbench desk and gave herself up to exhaustion. Her consistent method of suppressing anxiety by keeping feverishly busy was stretched a little thin, and it had come to her that her experience of life these days was one of suspense. She was waiting—that was the long and short of it.

She told Betsy to put through no calls. She wanted ten minutes of quiet. Then she found she could barely sit still for three without growing inwardly frantic. Exhausted or not, the state of her nerves required her to keep moving, so she buzzed for Betsy to come and take notes for the Marlboro campaign.

Betsy entered with a stack of messages and the information that a gentleman was waiting to see Ms. Devlin on the thirtieth-floor reception room.

"A gentleman?"

"He didn't have an appointment, but he said you'd see him. I told him you might be out all afternoon, but he said he'd chance it. He's been waiting quite a while."

"What's the gentleman's name?"

"Here—I wrote it down. Jamison Welsh. I don't remember him ever being on your appointment book." Betsy was young and Betsy was nosy. So she permitted herself liberties. "But he did say he was an old friend . . . and he really wasn't the kind of man one throws out. He's so distinguished-looking."

If it wasn't that Betsy was a crackerjack at steno, details, reports, filing and general mop-up work, Francie would have had her transferred months ago. But she was that good. "He is distinguished. And he is an old friend."

Betsy sighed with self-approval. "I'm glad I guessed right. Somehow I thought you really knew him."

Francie nodded and went on riffling blindly through the messages. Everything could wait. She was aware at this moment that she would not be in even for a call from Abe Barnett. "Tell the receptionist to send Mr. Welsh up. And hold any calls until I tell you otherwise."

Betsy was triumphant. This was part of the fun of working for Franciejean. She wasn't like any other woman boss. Betsy loathed women bosses. But Francie was something else—nutty and brilliant and beautiful. She never minded the length of Betsy's lunches, the office flirtations. She never tried to marry Betsy to her desk work —as long as the work was done well, she let Betsy live her life.

And you could count on Francie for a little everyday fireworks. Sometimes there would be a copywriter's explosion. Sometimes a TV star would visit. Or a guru. For a commercial. Or a chat. God knows she knew everybody. And here was Jamison Welsh. She'd seen the story on him in *Time* magazine. He was very rich and some kind of an economist. He had lunch at the White House. And he was Francie's old friend. Probably an ex-lover, if she knew Francie. She sighed with dreams of glory.

Betsy went to call the receptionist while Francie sat quietly staring out the window. She had a feeling of clinging the view, hanging on to it as though this view, this office, this desk, this place was her refuge; her ark in the flood.

Jamison had waited—oh, unmistakenly he had waited, and her first flare of eagerness to see him momentarily canceled her fright at what might have brought him to her so unexpectedly. For it was so out of character, it could be regarded as outlandish. With his commitments, his conferences, his scheduled seconds, how could he possibly waste a half hour; or, for all she knew, an hour, sitting and waiting in a reception room for Francijean Devlin. She started to laugh. She was not even an OPEC minister's girl friend.

Her eyes fixed on the legendary city around her and she remembered afresh the poet's words: "Some think they're strong, some think they're smart. Like butterflies they're pulled apart, America can break your heart." Then a faint current of air told her that Jamison had entered. Turning and seeing his large, quiet presence, she realized that his was the help she had been wanting and waiting for without knowing it. She rose quickly from her chair and went toward him, grasping his hands happily.

" 'You don't know all, sir, you don't know all.' "

Quoting poetry at each other was a private pleasure from long ago, and he answered her in kind. " 'In the streets of New York I was young and swell, I rode the market, the market fell. One morning I woke and found myself in hell. . . . I know all, ma'am, I know all!' "

Then they both laughed, and it soothed Francie's nerves to remember him reading Auden to her in the days before the earth turned over. Face to face, there with Jamie, she enjoyed for a moment a quiet lift of feeling she had not known in months. It came to her with pain how sad it was, and how hard that we cannot always choose to love what is good for us. Thinking this, she let go of Jamie's hands. "I'm so glad you stopped by. I feel as if I'd been waiting for you."

But Jamie retreated abruptly from the intimacy aroused by the poetry. His response was offhand. "You were at a meeting?"

"Yes, a meeting."

"And solved many advertising problems?"

"Other problems. That will be solved." She said th[is] wearily, almost serenely. "And to what do I owe the ra[re] pleasure of this visit on a hectic autumn morning with t[he] gnomes of Zurich awaiting your dictums? And Presiden[t] too."

For a moment Jamison knew as little about what to sa[y] as he had ever known in his life. Casting about for a dece[nt] reply he settled on the superficial. "I've been called [to] Geneva. I must leave tomorrow morning."

It came to her then, the dreary and obvious fact that h[e] had come at last, probably against his rational judgment, [to] keep himself straight with his conscience; to dot his *i*'s an[d] cross his *t*'s. It was his cross that he knew her secret, that h[e] knew she loved him still. "I suppose you wanted to sa[y] good-bye?" As she said it she hoped she was giving him h[is] out.

"Yes, I wanted to see you before I left."

"That was thoughtful of you. This time let's write."

He seemed to realize immediately that small talk an[d] platitudes would not be possible. "I came because I've bee[n] concerned about your health."

"You mean my sanity?"

"Call it what you will."

"You weren't tempted to throw away the key and wal[k] away?" It might have sounded like resentment if she hadn[']known her man so well; known his capacity for accepting th[e] truth without a tremor. That she read him well was proven b[y] the matter-of-factness of his reply.

"It wasn't a possible alternative. Nothing between u[s] has ever been simple. I wanted to insist on your contactin[g] me if you felt you needed my assistance."

"Well, give thanks, give thanks. I flourish. I gro[w] younger and younger. I need not a thing."

He knew he had brought it all on himself. Still, it had t[o] be done. "I would like you to keep me informed."

"Of my coming breakdown?" She gave him a grave[,] quiet look that made him wince at his clumsiness. "But I tol[d] you I am fine."

"I am glad."

"Sometimes when I see myself in the mirror I full[y] believe I am my own best friend."

He had only wanted to be kind, and now he felt crudely superficial. But he did not want to sweeten Francie's hopes. She must not think him more committed than he was. "Look, Francie, I came here to make a point. I think you ought to see a professional."

"A psychiatrist? A priest? A witch doctor?"

"Start with the psychiatrist."

"I have an appointment."

"Good. That tells me you'll be fine. You're still taking care of yourself."

She was forced to smile. "No, I won't be a public nuisance, or a burden on you. I do have Peter, thank you."

He had no answer for this. He knew full well how niggardly he'd been with emotional support. Two weeks had passed and he'd found no time to telephone. Only his presence here today, the hour he spent waiting in the reception room, stood for an apology and concern. "Tell me about the doctor? Who is he?"

"He is a she."

"What else?"

"My first visit is next month. But she sounded definitely interested. In the brief sketch I supplied." She played her little tune out to the end. "Time will tell. Time will undoubtedly tell us far too much."

"What's the doctor's name?"

"Do you really care?"

"What is her name?"

"Elizabeth C. Ornstein."

"I believe I've heard of her. I'll check."

"Thank you, but I already have, and so has Peter. She's very good. And expensive."

"I will find out." He was speaking now with his old deliberateness and directness.

"If not, I'll ask for my money back."

Jamison took a turn around the office and then stood staring out the window at the view she so regularly dreamed over. Francie stared at his familiar back and shoulders, and they seemed to tell her of connections that she would never understand. In a careful hand-to-mouth way, she asked, "I have the impression, my dear, that you are worried about me."

"Yes, I am concerned." He accepted then that exactl
what he had feared was happening—he was being drawn i
deeper and deeper. "I am very concerned."

"So am I," she said softly. There. Now it was all out i
the open, with no time for postponements. "Jamison, did yo
ever really love me?"

For a moment he was at a loss. "What do you thin
I'm doing here? With all the gnomes of Zurich at m
heels?"

She gave him a mechanical smile. "Pity. Friendship
Auld lang syne. A sense of responsibility. I can think of te
reasons." She held herself hard. Once and for all the thin
had to be said. "It would all be so much easier if it was onl
a matter of love."

"If my being here doesn't strike you as meaning some
thing, I've singularly wasted my time."

"But you hate it so."

"Yes, I do. But that makes no difference. I am here."
His great scruple, doggedly maintained at such merciles
cost, over so many years, had finallly dropped; he accepte
her deep reliance on him. The truth was that, like it or not, h
would always be involved with her fate. He could no longe
deny that her passion was wasted.

"Why has it always been so hard for us?" she asked hal
wistfully.

"Maybe Iago was right. *Credo in un Dio crudele ch
m'ha creato.* Maybe God is cruel. Maybe someone has t
suffer."

"But why us?"

"Why not us? What do people say who lose children
Or each other. Or their lives. Why us? Why me? I don'
know. I am not a religious man. I only know it has nothing t
do with wealth. Or virtue. Or intelligence. Or decency. O
indecency. Some people have happy lives. Many peopl
don't. All men are not created equal. I told you years ago
'Some are more unequal than others.' It's a fact of nature
Even in the United States of America. Even though it flatly
contradicts the American dream. I have no idea why it is so
but it is so. I don't pretend to understand anything more tha
a portion of the monetary system."

"You minded so much about the baby?"

476

"Yes. But I was younger then. And prouder."

"Would you be different now?"

"I don't know. And it makes no difference now."

For a moment they stared at each other, across the ruins of time, remembering what they had lost.

"I've driven you to the wall, haven't I? I'm sorry," she said.

"I am not drivable. You know that. Anyway, I've been satisfactorily punished."

"You, punished? Good Lord—" She said it almost for her own amusement.

"You thought it was only you who could suffer?"

"Yes. I've had the longest adolescence in the history of the world. And adolescents think only they can suffer."

"Well, you've always been my favorite child."

"And you've always been my favorite adult." She smiled at him almost without pain, and with a new confidence. More than anyone else—anyone in the world. I've always believed in you."

He drew a long breath, letting her light the way for him.

"More than anyone—anyone at all." She knew how true the words were. "Why, without you I might never have existed."

Jamison smiled as he could always smile. "Francie, you always have been extravagant."

"No, no. It's a fact! and you know it, too." The truth of what she said hung in the air; and as her eyes met his, she found herself able to take a further risk. "And that is the tie that binds us. That you saved me. I've heard the Chinese believe that if you save someone's life, you are responsible for them forever." She said it as it came to her; she was unable not to, even though as she heard herself, she felt like a fool. But what was the difference? She loved him.

But he accepted the full weight of her verdict. "I have the impression you might be right."

She knew then that she had not failed. That he had loved her, too; always loved her. Well, she asked for nothing more. It was all she'd ever wanted. "So we really are a perfect pair." Everything had been said now. She had nothing more to say.

He walked toward her and kissed her briefly, lightly on the lips; then stood back to look at her, seeming to see the the futility and weariness of many things. Meeting his eyes, Francie was conscious that never before had he looked at her so deeply or seen her so completely. brought an unwilling anxiety. Quite unaware of what she was doing, she took his hand. "I'm so glad you could stop in."

"So am I. I'll call you when I'm settled."

She took it as a promise. They walked toward the door. "I'll be shipshape when you come back. You'll be so proud of me."

Jamie's face was wonderful. "I'm proud of you now."

But Francie had this last new effort to make, the effort of letting him go; and doing it after everything that had passed between them in the preceding minutes. She still clung to his hand, struck by a strange intuition of things coming to an end. The external facts of where they were and who they now were seemed to have vanished completely; and for a rare moment, she was with Jamie in a more sunlit time and place before the mists had gathered. The radiance of the memory shone in her face when she said half shyly, "We had so little time together, Jamie. So little time."

He stroked her cheek gently.

"If I had one last wish," she said, "I would wish that there had been more time—more time to remember."

Her words were a reminder of the waste, the pain, the useless knowledge of all they had lost. And it prompted him to end their meeting as she had begun it, with lines from their shared past. "Francie, remember what Tristam said, 'Whatever it is that fills life up, and fills it full, it is not time. Years are not life.'"

She felt her eyes blue and dim, knowing what he was remembering. "'Then it was enough?'" she asked, keeping to the lines of the poetry.

"'It was enough. And it was all there was.'"

He stroked her cheek again gently, very gently, as a father, baffled and loving, might touch a hurt child. Then he walked out the door, passed Betsy, and disappeared around the corner.

The result of the conversation for Francie was the consciousness of a blessed calm after a great storm, as though she'd been on her knees to a priest, had confessed and been absolved.

29

In the russet, cool afternoon of November 1977, Elvis
Presley was still alive. So was Bing Crosby. But Chou En Lai
and Mao t'se-tung had dropped off the planet. *Star Wars* had
not yet been replaced by *Close Encounters*. Nureyev, if not at
the height of his powers, was still dancing brilliantly. And as
Pan Am's flight 74 passed over the 60 degree longitude into
the sudden starry darkness of the Atlantic time zone, at about
2:30 P.M. New York time, 7:30 London time, Jamison Welsh,
up front in the top cabin, paused in the study of the Zaire
financial report showing their incredible debt, and stared
ahead at nothing. Against his will he thought to himself,
Francie, Francie, Francie—saying it as if the deepest meaning
of all the years of his life were expressed in the name. Of
what use had been all her beauty, all her strength? He
shrugged his shoulders helplessly, finding no answer. Perhaps
its ultimate use was to keep at arm's length her misery and
madness.

Out of the darkness his memory tossed up a picture of
East Hampton long ago, of the waters lapping on the pond,
and Francie's exultation over the swans, of her tanned legs
moving around the boat, and the hot sun and the golden flash
of her hair in the sunlight. And her moist mouth and her
clinging body and her freshness like the morning itself. The
past was more real to him now than the present could ever be;
and he had a sudden fear of losing it forever. These wonders
had once existed, and now there was nothing. It seemed
impossible, but they were gone. For the first time since his

hildhood, Jamie's eyes were wet. And the tears were for imself too. He had gone away once, and now he knew he ould never go back. There was no place to go to, and she vas no longer there waiting. For the gates had closed forever, he sun had set; and the joy he'd felt so long ago was left behind in the country of the past, of dreams, where once, for a brief time, all the richness of life had flourished for him. amison Welsh shook his head to clear it and returned to the inancial report of Zaire. He sipped his Courvoisier and made a grimace of disgust, perhaps at the financial report, perhaps at himself—and died. He had no warnings. No visions. Death vas quite as his finely tuned, acutely rational mind would ave expected. Nothing.

In Franciejean's bedroom she turned to look at Peter vho had just entered. "Something very strange has happened."

Peter had tapped on Francie's door for a late night chat and found her sitting at her desk, pen in hand, glasses on, taring out the window with a confused expression.

"What strange thing has happened?"

Lately Peter had found himself watching her constantly or cues to her state of mind. But there had been no unexpectedly ed eyes, no pained features, no neglected items of appearance or clothing to warn him. She had been, as always, his beautiful, quicksilver wife. There was nothing telling him more now. Except her voice.

"It's the radio. The eleven o'clock news. Either the announcer is lying, or it's me. And if it's me, I am really off ny rocker."

"What did the radio say?" Peter looked at the desk radio with a kind of foolish apprehension.

"How could it be? He was in my office just yesterday afternoon."

"Who, dear?"

"Jamison—he stopped by. He stopped by to apologize." She held her breath every few seconds, as if to prove she could control her agitation. "He was called back to Geneva unexpectedly."

"That happens," he said soothingly.

"Oh, I know that. But he wanted to be kind. That's why he stopped in. He was worried about me and my voice."

"The voice you hear? Jamison knows about all that?"

"Of course. He was the first one I told."

"Of course. He wanted to make sure I was going to a good psychiatrist. If he didn't love me, I'm sure I would bore him silly. He's so eminently sane."

"Yes, he is. Did the radio say something unpleasant about him?"

Francie looked at him and, rising from her desk, roved around the room. When she faced him again, it was as if she'd not heard him at all. "How could they say such nonsense about Jamie? How could they?"

Peter stared at the small radio as if by staring he could squeeze out of it the information it had given Francie and thus spare him the effort of asking her what she had heard. Or not heard. "Well, the news media will do anything for news."

"I love him, you know."

"Of course."

"He loves me."

"It would be hard not to."

"You really think he does? You never said so before."

"What would be the point of digging into a past that was better off solidly buried? It had no use in our life."

She went to Peter then as she had never intentionally gone to him before, and buried her face in his shoulder.

"Do you think he could be dead?"

"Is that what the voice said?"

"Yes—on the radio. Or in my head." She pressed herself against him. Seeing now everything in all its dread, there was nothing more to add. She was asking him to help her help herself, if it was still possible.

Peter waited for more. He wanted her to talk, to say something. He wanted to ask her questions, but her manner stilled him to a quiet acceptance of her anguish. Finally he thought, at least they might turn on the radio.

"Francie, let's turn on the radio."

"Now?"

"Now. Then we'll know what the facts are." He reached over and turned the switch. CBS had been discussing the rate of inflation, and then there was a cut in from Heathrow Airport outside of London. "The ambulances are waiting; but

s far as can be ascertained, Mr. Jamison Welsh is dead . . . has
been dead for hours. The reports are heart attack." Peter shut
off the radio.

"Darling, it wasn't in your head. It was on the radio.
Jamie is dead."

She was sobbing into his shoulder. Holding her close, he
felt depth upon depth of her grief flowing over him; and he
breathed the cold air she breathed. With the intensity of his
compassion, he could feel her groping blindly in a gray mist,
this way and that, asking herself where she could rest.

Poor darling, he thought, hang on to me. This will
pass, it will pass.

But even as he thought it, the truth hushed him, for he
now knew it would never pass.

On page one of the *New York Times* the headline ran:

JAMISON WELSH DEAD
SPONSOR OF THE GNP DOLLAR HAS
HEART ATTACK ON FLIGHT TO GENEVA

Jamison Francie Xavier Welsh, world famous economist, sponsor of the Gross National Product Dollar, and international financier, died today aboard
Pan Am flight 74 bound for London, at the age of
fifty-eight. Mr. Welsh was on his way from his
home in New York City to an emergency meeting in
Geneva of the International Monetary Fund of which
he was a director.
He is survived by a cousin, Anthony Conway, who
lives in Nassau.
The funeral will be held Tuesday, at 10:00 A.M. in
St. Patrick's Cathedral. Burial at Pine Tree Farm,
Vermont, will be private, the representative of the
estate, Mr. Douglas Reynolds of the law firm of
Sullivan & Reynolds announced. . . .

After describing the most recent feats of Jamison Welsh,
the *Times* went on to discuss his past; noting that "for twelve
years prior to entering the world of international economics,
he was senior partner of Welsh Brothers, Gardiner, the

483

private banking house founded by his great grandfather, Michael Welsh, with offices in New York, London and Geneva. As the scion of a huge fortune stemming from mining, real estate, railroad, and oil interests, Jamison Welsh was the establishment personified. Yet he was in the vanguard of the new economic thinking that may well reshape the monetary systems of the future along more socialistic lines. . . ."

For its part, *Time* magazine noted regretfully:

LOSS OF THE VISION

The world may be certainly poorer, literally as well as figuratively, with the sudden death of Jamison Welsh, international financier and freebooting economic theorist. One of the wealthiest men in the country, "Jamie" Welsh, was undoubtedly the most original economic thinker since Maynard Keynes. His famous project that originally seemed quite radical, resulted in the formation of the International Monetary Fund. It will take many years before we can fully assess his achievements but it is a measure of the stature of the man that those at the memorial service included men of such divergent opinions as Gerald Ford, Henry Kissinger, Arthur Burns, Walter Wriston, John Kenneth Galbraith, George Meany . . .

The impact of his death will be felt not only in financial and political circles, but in the world of the arts. In 1959, he personally took over the financing of the Salzburg Musical Festival. Since 1965, he was subsidized the Robb Royson Ballet. His European tapestries are rivaled by only one museum. His collection of Chinese coins is the finest in the world. His European art spans five centuries in drawings, paintings, and sculpture; his Islamic art includes ceramic and tiles. The breadth of vision and the standard of quality of the art assembled by Welsh make his one of the finest collections in the world . . ."

Whenever Francie remembered this day, she saw Jamie's limousine, the beautiful old family Rolls, with Patrick waiting in front of the house for them. The limousine was not rented, the chauffeur was not rented, the entourage being one of the many seldom-used, taken-for-granted luxuries of Jamie's life. Francie felt outguessed. As though by dying Jamie had anticipated her. And yet she had the automatic, visceral wish to talk it over with him.

But there was nothing to be done. Slender in her dark clothes, she turned and entered the living room, looking exquisite and weary. Peter, who had been ready for a half hour, rose quickly from the couch and went to her.

"I suppose there will be a big crowd."

Francie nodded. She was standing looking out the window at the cold Tuesday morning, and the waiting limousine. Peter touched her sleeve.

"Don't, please," she said.

Peter moved a few feet away and waited uneasily.

"Do I look presentable?" Francie asked him finally.

Peter scanned her briefly. "A-plus." Their eyes met. "Don't look so sad," he pleaded. "It's none of their business."

"I will probably break down and sob." All moments were the same to her now. "What difference what they think now?"

For years Francie had not been able to guess what would happen at the end. And now some kind of end had come, with a minimum of drama. And nothing was settled. But all she said was, "Let's have juice and coffee. Funerals make me hungry."

The ride to the church was less than a mile, but it seemed longer.

30

Days had passed, weeks had passed. Francie lost track of time as she searched for some escape from herself. She had made with herself a pact to pretend that Jamison was not dead. He had simply left on one of his countless trips to Europe. This, in its turn, imposed a need to blank him out of consciousness. For if she were conscious of him, she would have to remember he was dead, he was nowhere, he was not coming back; and she was not yet ready to deal with this vacuum. But shutting her eyes to reality was not easy, and her plan went forward with neither marked success nor consistency.

Each day in itself was not unpleasant. The golden autumn had turned into a dry, brisk winter with cold sunlight and gray blue skies and people hurrying along the streets, the women in boots, the men in overcoats; everyone going somewhere in the city. For Francie, work went on as usual; and in the evening there were art openings or parties, or theater with clients or friends or strangers. But somehow nothing made sense now. Food had no taste, music no melody, laughter no pleasure. Her sessions with the doctor seemed blank—she had not heard the young voice in weeks—maybe it was all a bad dream. She found herself missing the song. At least it was something she and Jamie had shared. It would have meant that once she was alive. Instead it was as though the entire world was silent, frozen, waiting. But for what? Another ordeal? Hadn't she had ordeals enough? It seemed not. She was waiting; and she knew it, for some final experience that might be, for the pain of it, even more unbearable.

It was in this mood that she stopped by to watch the shooting of the final test commercial for Star Bird. The studio where the filming was taking place was cavernous—so large it looked empty of people. Actually, it was a swarming beehive of activity. Besides Meg Dodge, Matt Harris and his second man, Don Wells, there was the account contingent from the agency, including Tommy Dominico and his waterboy, Hank, Jim Daniels from GM, and the sizable technical crew of cameramen, lightmen, grips, propmen, and whoever else might be needed for the shooting of a test commercial that was budgeted at $100,000. Mounds of equipment lay all around the floors, and in the set where the main filming was to be done stood an elegant silver streak of a car—the Star Bird.

While Matt and Don discussed the shot as though it were a decision about open-heart surgery, Nick Gardiner, the cameraman-director, fussed with the lighting. After one solid hour the car was not yet lit to everyone's satisfaction.

"Joe, hit the 750 on camera right. And gimme a cone. I wanna fill in here."

Another light flickered on from the grid above and hit the car, making it sparkle. Matt walked up to the camera and studied the result through the lens. He shook his head. "Damn it! We're still getting a shadow, Nick, on the side mirror."

Hours of shooting had made tempers short. The cameraman had a collection of five tea cartons stacked by the camera. The ashtrays overflowed. Aside from the production team, most agency members were only halfheartedly focused on the set. But Francie, standing off to the side, watched intently, as though there was nothing else of interest anywhere.

On the set, Jenny was sitting in the car, pretending to drive. But by now Matt too was beat, and the girl's face was pale with fatigue.

"Okay, I've had it," Matt called. "Kill the lights. Let's take a break." He turned from the camera and shambled toward Jennifer seated behind the wheel. "Kid, you're starting to look frazzled." Jennifer nodded silently.

"I think we'll call it a day for you. We can't have a collapsed star. We'll do upholstery shots and so forth. You head home and hit the sack. We've a full session tomorrow, and I want you daisy-fresh."

Then, unexpectedly gallant, he opened the car door. When the girl slid out, saying "Thank you," Matt had the odd feeling he'd been promoted. Jennifer started quickly for the dressing room and as Matt watched her, he could not help admiring the lightness of her movements and wondering if she came from a family of dancers.

At that moment a peculiar image occurred to Francie. She saw herself at the age of five, standing before the house she had lived in as a child, holding the hand of a woman who had straight, golden hair like her own, but pulled back in a tight bun. It must be my mother, she thought, as the two figures grew smaller and smaller, receding into the distance of time.

Moved by an impulse to shake off the vision, Francie went to the coffee machine to get herself a cup. Standing beside the machine, woolgathering among memories, irrelevantly it occurred to her that Jennifer might like a cup of coffee too. On a guess she added milk and sugar and then walked slowly toward the dressing room. On the way she met Amy carrying the expensive Star Bird costume off to be cleaned and pressed for the shooting next day.

"Didn't she look straight of Frank Herbert?" laughed Amy, the TV stylist.

"Or Lester Del Rey. Or Gordon Dickson. Or Marion Zimmer Bradley."

"Bradley? She's a Bradley nut, too. Christ, I didn't know this place was swarming with sci-fi buffs. You too?"

"Not really. I track trends not starships."

When Francie entered the dressing room, she found Jennifer already in her shirt and levis, sitting on a chair, pulling hard on a boot. The young girl looked up at Francie, giving her a tired, kind attention, as if Jennifer were some kind of star, and Francie had come to ask for her autograph.

When Francie offered her the cup of coffee, Jennifer accepted it with a polite "Thank you." Disconcerted by the young woman's effect on her, Francie tried making casual conversation, instead of simply complimenting her on her

488

work and leaving. "You're very welcome," she said. "You must be very tired. These sessions can be killing."

This was the first time since their original meeting in Meg's office that she could study Jennifer at close hand; and she felt as if they were two people who knew each other very well, meeting after a long separation.

Jennifer took a large swallow of the coffee and asked with a half smile, "Do you sleep on silk sheets?"

It was an odd kind of question, but because she was so young, Francie decided to humor her. "Of course. Silk-satin to be precise. And they are changed every day."

"Do you bathe in perfume?"

"Chanel Number 19. Occasionally Nina Ricci. Sometimes Joy."

"The most expensive perfume in the world."

"So they say. I never look at bills."

"What about Chloe?"

"No, no. My secretary bathes in Chloe."

"Doesn't the perfume burn your vagina?"

The young girl was so impertinent that Francie started to laugh in spite of herself. "Of course. But beauty has its price. You must use it yourself, or how do you know it burns?"

"I use Jean Naté cologne. I always wondered if the expensive stuff burned too."

"Oh, yes. Probably more. That's half the fun—the higher content of sadism per ounce."

"Do you believe in Women's Lib?"

An aching dizziness had come over Francie, and she sat down in the empty chair. "If this is a quiz show, that's a dull question. Why don't you ask me if I believe in motherhood and apple pie? That's more original these days."

"Do you?"

"I believe in everything that works."

"I believe in dreams."

"So do psychiatrists."

"And I believe in you."

Francie's dizziness increased, and she found she had to put down her cup on the dressing table and hold on to the seat of the chair to keep from swaying.

Jennifer stood up, faced the mirror, and began to comb

her hair, all the while singing to herself, in a kind of low, perpetual hum of concentration. After a minute, she spoke to Francie's reflection in the mirror. "Do you know who you are?"

"I've always thought I did."

"No—I mean, let's consider other incarnations."

Francie found this kind of remark tiresome, but Jennifer was, after all, only a child, and perhaps children played these games.

"All right, let me think. I was never Eleanor of Aquitaine. Or Betsy Ross. Or—hmm—St. Theresa de Avila."

"You were also not Thomas Aquinas, Juste-Aurele Meissonier, or Stephen Foster."

The name Meissonier struck Francie as odd. "How do you know Meissonier?"

"I love silver. Your husband does too. You love glass. But you were never Renée Lalique."

"Well, you do know a bit about me." Francie was starting to see Jennifer in an altered light, and it occurred to her that this might be a wise time to end the conversation. But something in the young girl's smile made her decision founder. "All right, now that we have established that I was not a historical personage, let's simply agree on who I am today. And while we do that, how do you come to know so much about me?"

"I know because I've made an in-depth study of you. You are Franciejean Devlin. We met at Barnett last September."

"Your memory is in good working order. In Meg Dodge's office."

"Yes. But you are still somebody else."

"You mean my name is only a label concealing the real me?"

"I don't think there is one real you. Or a real me. Or a real anybody. We're all a lot of people in one body. You are also, for instance, Franciejean Stewart."

The more the conversation went on, the more Francie became aware of how, by a conscious art on Jennifer's part, she was being led in a particular direction. But what was the direction? Where were they going? "I gather you read *Time* Magazine."

"Occasionally. You were also orphaned when you were quite young."

Now Francie had a sense of danger in understanding this girl too well. What made her stay was the dawning recognition that this danger could not be avoided. "You really have done a study of me."

"Yes, you are my favorite subject. You have been for years. You have another name, too. But that's a title of honor. Or dishonor. It depends on how it's used. And by whom."

"A title? Well, I am not the Queen of the May."

"No, you can do better than that." The gaiety had faded from Jennifer's face. When she spoke again, she sounded as though she were out of the habit of speaking. "Do you ever dream of me?"

"Of you? No—never. Why should I?" Francie picked up her coffee cup from the dressing table and sippled slowly, aware of the bizarre turn the conversation was taking.

"Well, I dream a lot. In dreams the world forms around me. I lie there with my eyes closed, and a whole universe happens. In some of my dreams the world is full of horrors. Big, dark monsters are waiting to eat me, and I wake up sweaty and scared. Other times my dreams are full of wonderful color and warmth and happiness—feelings I only have rarely in the real world—and I hate waking up and losing all that happiness. Sometimes you are in those dreams."

"I am?"

"Sometimes."

Francie knew that this was the last stop. If this conversation continued, it would carry her from the daylight of her life into a region of unknown darkness. She felt a sudden wish to see how far Jennifer would go. So she asked, "How long have you been dreaming about me?"

"Seven years. Seven lean years."

Francie couldn't help asking. "What started you dreaming?"

"It happened in the summer. We were sailing all day—that day Lise asked me. Seven years ago."

"Asked you what?"

"About you. About me."

In spite of all her efforts at denial, she knew everything now; knew it only too well. "Who is Lise?" she asked.

"Lise Perl. My friend."

"Is that Monroe Perl's daughter?"

"Yes."

"Did Monroe talk to Lise—about you? About me?"

"No. Her mother did. She told Lise to be very tactful and see what she could find out without coming right out and asking. But Lise's my friend. So she just came right out and asked if it was true."

"What did you say?"

"I guess I said a lot of things. Mostly I said I didn't know. Then I went home and asked Mom."

"And she told you."

"She told me."

Francie felt a sudden violent desire to seize this girl and strangle her; this strange, young creature whose very existence was somehow, she felt, responsible for all the misery of her life. At the same time she shuddered at the mere idea of touching her.

"What do you want?"

"Nothing that you can't give."

"But what could I give you?"

"Myself." Francie met Jennifer's eyes with a recognition that she could no longer suppress. "I haven't felt real since I found out about you." Jennifer was speaking slowly, as if she wanted to choose precisely the right words. "I put if off for years and years. But eventually I had to come and talk to you. In spite of everything. Because of who you are. And who I am."

Their eyes met, and Francie did not disgrace herself by looking away. "All right—you're real. Quite real. Do you hate me?"

"Not anymore. I did in the beginning. But the more I learned about you, the more I understood."

"What did you understand?"

"I can't really explain it. But after I met you, I was sure."

"Of what?"

"Of your having no choice. You had to do what you did with me." Jennifer reached out a strong, expressive hand and with gentle fingers lightly traced the outline of Francie's face—her forehead, cheek and chin, doing it as a sculptor might, to learn the exact shape. And though it was hardly easy, Francie let her; though a slight shiver ran through her body.

"I have your forehead," said Jennifer. "And your chin."

492

Then she gave a short, clear sob and hung her head. "I'm so glad we know each other at last." She said it as if she had lived for many years in expectation of this meeting. "You are my 'mother of memories, mystery of mysteries . . .' "

Automatically, in the same manner that Jamie had so often corrected her misquotes, Francie started to correct Jennifer; but the young girl shook her head, knowing what was coming: "No, my version suits me. You will always be my mystery."

Francie stood up, and she and Jennifer stared at each other for a moment in silence. Francie wondered if Jennifer might say something more, might make a sign that would spare her from being the one to pay all. But either the girl would not or could not understand the costs.

"Well," Francie surrendered. "I am sure you want to know about your father." Little drops of perspiration had come out on her upper lip.

"Please tell me."

"I know now why the sight of your face pleased me so much. You resemble him. In a way. You take after your father's family—more than mine."

"Is he wonderful?"

"Quite wonderful."

"Did you love him very much?"

"With all my heart."

"But he isn't your husband?"

"No, he isn't my husband."

"Ah—I thought so. Who is he? Where do I find him?"

For a moment it hung by a hair—what Francie might say. Then, as though warned by the look in Francie's eyes that she'd gone too far, Jennifer dismissed the question. "Never mind. I don't have to have everything." She breathed deeply. "This is enough. I know who I am. Jennifer Farrell, adopted daughter of Lawrence and Barbara Farrell. Also a nameless love-child, illegitimate?—what a wonderful paradox, how could love be illegitimate?—of Franciejean Stewart Devlin and the man she loves."

Francie ran her tongue over her dry lips. "That's who you are. And that's enough to be."

Jennifer leaned forward and kissed Francie lightly on the cheek. "I have one last thing to ask."

"Only one?"

"One will do," Jennifer said. "If you will do it."

"I will if I can."

"I want you to believe this. I am no longer angry. I don't hate you. I may one day love you. Not yet. But one day. And should you see my father, tell him, please, I will love him too. Not yet. But one day. Whoever he is."

Francie stood still; the blank, blurred surface of her mind struggling with this final challenge. It was as though she'd been sitting at some high gaming table, risking huge stakes, and now she knew she'd won.

"I'll tell him," she said softly.

"Thank you," said Jennifer. "After all I owe you both my life." Saying that, she picked up her jacket and pouch and left the dressing room.

Watching her go, Francie knew that she had at last run out of pretenses. Her doom was there before her, hard and clear. But after staring at it with wide open eyes, she welcomed it into her heart. Now she knew who the young girl was. Now she knew, too, that she could not know who the young girl was. Finally, bereft of courage after all the years, she simply refused to know; even though she realized that in order not to know she would have to pay. What she would pay would be costly and her own wretched business.

When Matt Harris came hurrying into the dressing room, he was too impatient to more than glance at Francie. "What the devil do you think you're doing here? I've been looking all over for you. We're winding up the shooting for the day. Come and see. Come on, Francie."

"Hello," said Francie in a barely audible hoarse voice. "I knew I knew you. Your name has two syllables. Matt Harris. Well, three. I was close."

"We're winding up the shooting. Don't you want to look at what's happening?" Then the oddness of Francie's words and the lax way she was seated in the chair brought Matt to a dead stop. With rare sympathy Matt asked, "Francie, are you all right? What's the matter, honey? You sound funny."

Her eyes met his, and the sadness in them made him look away. She sang quietly as though to a baby: *"Guten Abend gut Nacht, von Englein bewacht, die zeigen in Traum, dir Christkindleins Baum."*

Few things that had ever happened to Matt frightened him

as deeply as did Francie's singing. He wanted to reach out and touch her but was afraid of disturbing her further. "Honey, what is it?"

"Schlaf num selig and suss, schau' im Traum's Paradies.
"Schlaf num selig and suss, schau' im Traum's Paradies."

Matt began to shiver violently. That Francie, who to him was a rock, a safety, should act in such a way made these few seconds feel like the first seconds of a great blast. He left the dressing room hurriedly, leaving Francie murmuring to herself. When he returned he had with him Meg Dodge.

"Look at her. Listen to her," he said brokenly to Meg.

Francie's eyes held Meg, and she said, "What time is it? The same time as usual. They said they had things to do. They said they had places to go."

"What's the matter with her, Matt?"

"God knows."

"Guten Abend, gut' nacht, mit Rosen bedacht . . . mit Naglein bestekt, Schlumpf unter die Deck."

"Matt, I'm scared."

"So am I."

Tommy Dominico was standing silently in the doorway with Hank Grayson. Tommy was studying Francie with a detached sadness, but Hank was shaking.

"God—she's crazy," he said.

Tommy looked at him with disgust. "Stop blithering, Hank. It's only a breakdown. Overwork. Go find Daniels and get him out of the studio. This is agency business."

"What'll I say to him?"

Tommy gave Hank a look of such scorn that it made the hairs on Hank's scalp rise. For the first time, he was genuinely afraid of Tommy; and he knew why Tommy was his boss, and he would never be Tommy's.

"I'll think of something," he mumbled and hurried out.

Francie was still singing softly to herself.

"Oh, God. I never saw anything like this." Meg was sobbing quietly into a tissue.

The room was hushed as an empty church, except for the sound of Francie's voice, almost young, singing softly, now in English. *"Lullabye and goodnight, with roses delight. All tied up in bows, slip under the clothes."*

Matt, brimming with terror and what little he knew of

love, tiptoed over to Francie and whispered in a very low tone, "Darling, come. You should go home." Like a trusting child, Francie rose to her feet, nodded and smiled.

"*When the morning shall break, Please the Lord, thou wilt wake. When the morning shall break, Please the Lord thou wilt wake.*"

31

Jamison Welsh had had many wills. The most recent one, signed in October 1965, was straightforward enough, except for one codicil. To Jamie, the necessity for a will, and for the will to express his current wishes, was simply a matter of rational thinking. To Francie, with her perspective as survivor of the death of Jamie, the idea of his will seemed shocking, and even heartbreaking.

"I never thought he would die."

"Everyone does," said Peter. He'd visited Francie everyday that he was permitted to since she'd first been admitted, some five weeks ago, to the Payne Whitney Clinic. Those times he had stayed away were when the attending psychiatrist had suggested he not come. Now Francie was dressing to leave, slipping on the straight-falling cashmere sweater dress, in which she looked far younger and fresher than her forty-two years, as if the film of the last months had been run backward and her breakdown had never happened. It was all unlived and sponged out. Peter had brought over the dress, the boots, the fur-lined storm coat in preparation for the for-once accurate snow warning.

"I don't look forward to any of this," she said as she belted her dress.

"You don't have to go, you know." He felt a smothered soreness at the mistake he'd made in telling her anything at all about the reading of the will.

"Yes, I do."

"You still need rest. And I'll come straight back from the reading and tell you which paintings he left you."

"Peter, I have to go. It's my last connection to him. But I don't have to like it."

Peter was at a loss. He should have been relieved and comforted by how well she had pulled together, but some inner monitor warned him to go cautiously. "Well, if you must go to the reading, I wish you'd do only that and then go home and rest. Why must you go to the office your first day out?"

Sitting in a chair and pulling on her boot, she considered his question. "Because I'm fine now. On the royal road to mental health. Am I not fine and dandy and spick and spruce, Peter, darling?"

"Fine and dandy. Crackerjack."

"There you are. And I want to go back to work. Even Dr. Ornstein believes work is good medicine. The more of it the better. I've been out for almost five weeks. That's enough. It took me a very short time, years ago, to learn that no one was standing on a rooftop scanning the sidewalks with binoculars, searching for me, my talent, my know-how. Now that I've been discovered, I want to stay discovered." She looked at him hard, and pity for his concern touched her. "Peter, meet me at the office and we'll go to lunch. Then we can go downtown together. After, if it makes you happy, I'll go home and read Tolstoy. Or watch TV."

"All right. So it's back to the salt mines for you." But while he surrendered, he still struggled. "Only promise me one thing."

"I promise," she said, pulling on the other boot.

"How can you promise? I haven't told you what it is."

She knew what he wanted, and a pulse began to throb in her temple. "You want me to alert you if I feel an urge coming on to foam at the mouth again."

Peter took the words like a blow, and there was quiet for a while. Then Francie turned her head away in shame. "I'm sorry I said that, Peter. It was rotten."

He shook his head because he was having difficulty speaking. "I was going to ask you to promise to keep on seeing Dr. Ornstein. Not cancel any sessions because you're well." He breathed deeply. "I want you to stay well—that's all."

"I know. Forgive me." She wanted to shake herself for using Peter's love against him. "Darling, don't worry. I've

498

d a breakdown. A psychotic depression as they call it. I as tired, overworked. Now I'm fine. But yes, I will keep eeing the good doctor. Repairing breakdowns takes time, I now that." She put her hand on Peter's arm. "But I'm m-dandy now. Truly."

"You are. And we're both jumpy. It's to be expected."

"Under the circumstances." She went to him, and he eld her in an embrace in which things were said that went r beyond words. They clung together, two children con-oling each other against an unnameable woe. "I'm sor-v," she said again. "In my own way, I love you, too." She ad never said this before; and now she knew the words night have no use, coming as so many things do, always too te; which was just one more weary lesson to learn.

Peter thought about Francie and Jamie and the nature of •ve. And what sweet sound had Jamison heard, that, like Ilysses, he longed to give his life to follow it? And perhaps at was what Jamie had done. Peter could think this now ecause it no longer mattered. Francie had been and would lways be enough for him. And yet, he was not enough for er. For what she gave him was not love, but the pale wine of ratitude.

She released herself from his arms and looked at him. Darling, to have a rich, full life every woman should own a air of red shoes. And have a breakdown. Now I've had both. 've been plied with lithium. Thorazien. Drug therapy galore. 've had inspiring sessions of psychotherapy. If there'd been a wimming pool, tennis courts, foreign movies, and a better hef, I'd say it was a two-star resort. There is not a screw ose anywhere now, not a nut—block that pun—or a bolt. m fine." She had known, she now realized, for years that here was something gravely wrong. Something behind Mom-na's voice and that ancient blind fear and the recent inability know what was happening and who she was. Now she had limpsed that other Franciejean; a Franciejean wrapped in a ine cloud, who melted in and out of sight. She had asked erself repeatedly if she were prepared to know that stranger. hen, perhaps, there might still be a chance to put Humpty Dumpty together again. She stared around the room, suddenly fraid. "Peter, did Dr. Ornstein tell you something she didn't ell me?"

Peter caught her in his arms, kissed her, and felt the

sting of frightened tears on his lips. "She believes as I do th
you're sound as a dollar."

"That's not too reassuring these days."

Having let drop her barrier of optimism, she recognize
what a burden she had placed on him; how he was strugglin
not to show fear. Longing to make amends, she wondere
how she might relieve and support him. She settled for
practical cheerfulness. "Never mind. With lithium and th
daily wonders of science, I'm a new woman. Though I d
wish, that the wonders of science could invent me anothe
childhood." The effect of her own words on Francie were tha
she held Peter's face and gazed at it wonderingly as if sh
were someone coming out of a darkness and his was the firs
face she saw. "You could have hurt me so often, Peter; an
you never did." For a moment her look was luminous. "I'v
lived so long in the company of shadows. I don't ask to
much of life anymore. Just the calm of a few sunny days
And maybe a few more laughs and kisses." But she broke o
abruptly. "Though I don't think I was ever meant to live ver
long. What would you do if I were to die?" The last word
had fallen like coins dropped accidentally on the sidewalk.

"I'd wish I'd died instead," he said quietly.

She realized too late that she'd taken unfair advantage o
him again. "Oh, darling, forgive my melodrama. I've alway
preferred myself as a tragic heroine to Ophelia. Don't die
Live with me and be my love."

"How can I, unless you live with me?"

"I promise, I promise." And her smile came so peace
fully, he could ask for no more.

Before leaving Payne Whitney, Peter saw Dr. E. C
Ornstein. The doctor, busily making notes, did not look lik
the highly respected, highly recommended, and highly expen
sive psychiatrist she was; someone devoted to the repair o
damaged human psyches. She looked, if anything, like somebody's pleasant, overweight wife and mother of two children
But perhaps it was the wife and mother aspect that accountec
for the lack of humbug and no-nonsense pragmatism Pete
admired in her manner.

The doctor, in turn, studied Peter. From what he hac
already told her of his and Francie's marriage, his life was nc

ess unconventional that his wife's. But still Peter struck her
us quite sane. Someone who could accept the heavy prices of
reality as well as its joys. Unfortunately, his wife could not.
Why, she wondered? Was it genetics? Was it environment?
Virulence versus resistance? What? It was their third conversation.

"She's going back to work?"

The doctor nodded. "It's good for her. She's made
remarkable progress."

"You do think she's well?"

"She has pulled together." Her eyes did not falter but
she frowned slightly. "Tell me. In the years of your married
life, other than the crack-up at the party, was there nothing to
warn you that she was ill?"

Peter shot a glance at the doctor, in an odd way his
tormentor for she aimed her questions so accurately. There
were no easy answers to those early vague suspicions. "I
wasn't a good judge. Yes, there was her promiscuity. But
many creative types are promiscuous and perfectly sane. And
for me to object would be the pot name-calling the kettle.
Otherwise, I suppose I thought, when she acted oddly, it was
nerves. The nerves of an intense, gifted human being. With a
vivid imagination."

"By 'acted oddly' you mean her ambivalence about her
mother?"

He nodded. "When we first met, she was haunted by a
recurring fear of her mother, who'd been dead since Francie
was a child. It would come up in situations of stress. Then
she'd sob and beg her mother not to punish her." He tried to
keep his voice even. "But she always snapped out of it very
fast. And in the last eight or ten years the symptom seemed to
have vanished entirely." The doctor could see how deeply he
was suffering behind his cool facade. "But the party episode
was bizarre; and then this last time— That was eerie. She
shifted back and forth between herself as a terrified child and
herself as her mother singing to her a lullabye." He stopped
and stared at the doctor with a mixture of guilt and incredulity. "Oh, the mistakes I've made. Not insisting on treatment
sooner—all those years ago."

"Self-reproach and recriminations will do no one any
good now."

"But I don't want to excuse myself. I can see you wondering, with a marriage such as ours, how could she ever maintain sanity."

"I am thinking no such thing." There was exasperation not condescension, in her tone.

"If you were, it wouldn't surprise me. But it wouldn't be accurate either. We do have an unconventional marriage. But there's a lot of mutual trust, good will and even love between us. Actually, it has worked better than many traditional arrangements I've seen."

"Believe me, Mr. Devlin, I do not think your marriage created your wife's condition." The kindly mother-figure put her view in a nutshell. "Yours was not a marriage made in hell. The human spirit is inventive enough to accommodate more than one kind of mating."

He knew he was in danger of sounding apologetic, but he wanted to put their case properly. "Truly, these last years she's been fine. There's been no external strain. Plenty of money. She's physically healthy, you know. I'm successful. And she's tops at her own job." He was trying to understand what had happened; threading his way through the recent chaos of their life. What was he leaving out? At first, it had been only a nagging perception, a mute recognition that something was out of kilter. "You know, I did start noticing something a few months ago that made me uneasy. Call it a wandering of her attention, a lapsing out of focus. And insomnia—that was new."

"This happened after the death of Jamison Welsh?"

"No. That was November. I know his death was a blow. But she seemed to come out of it, I thought. Maybe hoped. What I refer to started five or six months ago. Something happened. Something that triggered everything that may have been dormant for years. Just a feeling." He sighed. "No evidence."

"You think we've missed something?" She was following his line.

He had then one of the strangest impressions, that was at the same time an alarm. "I'm sure of it. And I think we'd better find it quickly."

Facing him, the doctor wondered what he sensed, what vision he groped for. She was ready to follow his lead but he

…d nothing to offer. "You may be right. But let's discuss …hat we do know. Did your wife ever mention Uncle …ul?"

Peter felt relieved to talk about it. "Not until the party …rack-up. You know her mother was widowed when Francie …as quite young. I think he was one of her mother's suitors." …e spat out the word. The encouragement in her face allowed …m to speak openly. "I believe Uncle Paul raped Francie …hen she was a child."

"I agree. But her memories are blurred. Though I've …eard her scream 'Go way, Uncle Paul! Help!'" The doctor …poke slowly and distinctly. "Then she'd shriek of something …uge and terrible forcing its way into her body and ripping …er to pieces. Of horrible, burning pain and how she was …urdered." Her voice was calm, compassionate. "Franciejean, …e little girl with that awful pain and blood streaming …ut—she died. Years ago—with her mother."

"What are you telling me?"

This time the doctor sidestepped. "This Jamison stood …or something in your wife's unconscious. Perhaps her father. …erhaps a symbol of safety. Something. With his death certain …ssential moorings were cut."

He asked humbly, "Then is she really well?"

The doctor considered him carefully. "I speak off the …ecord. Tell anything to your wife and you may hasten a …ossible disaster. She's well now. She'll stay well only if she …hooses."

"Why wouldn't she choose to stay well?"

"Mental health requires a real desire on the part of the …atient. It is hard, hard work for those who have lost it."

"You mean she hasn't decided that sanity is worth the …ight?"

"Precisely. There are aspects of her madness, Uncle Paul …side, that she far perfers to the hurt and hardship of the sane, …aily world. She has not had an easy life. Internally, that is. …nd since part of her feels she is already dead, death holds no …errors. She jokes about the high art of dying beautifully." …he paused. "It's never cut and dried, but I feel she stands at …a crossroad."

"Then my job is to roadblock the wrong turn." He was …n his feet. "Thank you, doctor, for your honesty." He knew the ordeal was beginning. "If we only knew what the trigger was—"

"Mr. Devlin, we are not gods, only doctors. If there is trigger, let us hope we find it in time."

32

At noon Peter returned to their apartment house to pick
up some sketches for a late afternoon meeting with Arthur
Thompson, who wanted his home in the Bahamas redone. He
would be meeting Thompson after the reading of Jamison's
will. When he reached the lobby, the doorman told him a lady
had been waiting for him for three hours, and nodded toward
a slender dark-haired woman in her early forties, seated on a
bench and bundled up in an opossum fur coat. The lady, in
turn, recognized from the tilt of the doorman's head in her
direction that this must be the man she was waiting for.
Seeming then to gather up her courage, she rose from her seat
and walked toward Peter.

"You're Mr. Devlin," she said.

"Yes, I am. And you are—?"

"Barbie Farrell. Mrs. Lawrence Farrell." She extended
her hand to shake his in a shy, awkward way. Obviously she
was unsure of how welcome her visit would be. But shy or
not, she was confident enough within herself of what she
planned to do. "I know you. But you don't know me." She
smiled.

"I see," said Peter, forcing a congeniality he did not
feel. "You're a friend of a friend. Or a friend of a client, and
you saw the way I did someone's penthouse—"

"No—please."

"We went to school together?" He was trying to be
kind, but he was pressed.

"No, I don't believe we went to school together. Could
we go somewhere and have a quiet conversation? Please."

There was an urgency in her presence that pulled him up short. He looked at her hard, and for a moment neither would speak. In the end, it was Peter's silent coercion that broke the impasse. "It's about your wife. Mrs. Devlin," Barbie Farrell said.

Peter didn't budge, and they stood on the polished tile estimating each other. Then he gave in to the inevitable "Come upstairs with me, Mrs. Farrell," he said. "I'll give you a cup of tea. Or a scotch if you need it."

Upstairs in his study, Barbie Farrell explained her mission.

"My name, I know, means nothing to you. Mrs. Lawrence Farrell. But I'm the mother—or let's say the other mother—of your wife's daughter."

"The baby?" He blinked.

"The baby. We adopted her. She's not a baby anymore. She's a young woman. A beautiful, happy, healthy young woman. I think you might see a resemblance to Mrs. Devlin in her cheekbones. And perhaps the chin. But that's it. There the resemblance stops, I hope."

Hearing her words, Peter felt a sharp stab of fear. "Does this young woman know about Franciejean?"

"Oh yes, that's why I'm here. I told her years ago. Seven to be exact."

"Was that necessary?"

"Yes. It would take too long to explain why now. Perhaps someday, if we have another chance to talk— Although maybe I've mishandled the whole thing. Maybe I should have told Jenny when she was even younger." Then, yielding to her own deeper need, she added, "But we couldn't love her more, if she were our own flesh and blood."

"I'm sure you've been excellent parents."

"Yes, we were all so happy until this happened—"

"What happened?"

"You see, I'm so worried now."

"Why are you worried?" He was frankly mystified. "What's the matter?" He studied Barbie Farrell and saw she was contending with unexplained dangers.

Then she made a heroic effort. "I've been frightened for weeks. And of course I can't say a word to Jennifer. I don't even want to discuss it with Larry, my husband."

"Frightened about what?" Peter tensed himself.

"About Mrs. Devlin." She paused as if waiting for his permission to continue and as he only let her wait, she said at last, "Well, if Mrs. Devlin's out of her mind—insane—"

He felt the pressure of her need for truth. Having heard about Francie's breakdown, all the high melodrama of insanity, bedlam, the menace of tainted blood passed along to the offspring, had kept her wakeful through endless nights. Science, she knew, had taken other positions. Insanity need not be inherited. But her honest terror was fortified by generations of superstitious fear. "Could this happen to my Jenny too?" she asked.

Peter felt by this time he could face anything. Even such questions. "Look—Francie's not insane. Not schizophrenic. The medical term for what happened is 'psychotic depression.' She's had a breakdown. It's not a matter of genetics. It seems to be the result of events that took place in Francie's childhood."

"You mean it doesn't have to happen to Jenny?"

"No, it certainly doesn't. In fact, as I understand it, if Jennifer were to be schizophrenic, it would have shown up by now. The symptoms appear very early. Jennifer is not a bad seed." He felt himself on firmer ground. "In fact, Francie's coming out of the hospital today. She's practically good as new." His face did not reveal the apprehension in his lie.

"She's been discharged?"

"Well, in a manner."

She heard what she wanted to hear, glossing over his hesitation. "Oh, I'm so glad."

This woman, by trusting him, had unwittingly caught him; and listening to her fears had forced into his awareness a new idea. "Mrs. Farrell, how do you know so much about Franciejean's condition?"

"Because I told her." At that moment Maria came in with the tray of teacups and tea, followed by a very young woman in suede pants and a fur parka who looked frozen and frightened.

"Mom, I'm sorry, I couldn't wait any longer downstairs. I had to talk to Mr. Devlin myself." She turned to Peter with an urgency that implied a positive claim. "How is she? Mrs. Devlin. Is she getting well?"

Staring at the girl, Peter's heart turned over in a kind of

507

final surrender to fate. He understood exactly who she was. A sudden golden light was breaking through the haze of the past, and he was back again in the early years of his life; in that brief and magical time when he was like other boys with a father and a mother, when he'd lived in joyful hunger for every new day. In the afterglow of that sunlit memory, he saw Jamison's mother coming one afternoon to find him, hiding in misery behind their guest house, putting her arms around him, holding him tight for comfort; while he sobbed out his heart in agony because his mother had mentioned casually at breakfast that his father was dead. He remembered, as though it were yesterday, the rich vitality of the woman, her grace and generosity whenever he needed it; and then, all inexplicable to a child, she, with such a rare talent for life, had died shortly after his father.

Looking now at Jennifer, who looked so little like Francie, he saw again Jamie's mother, even Jamie himself, and this realization brought him face to face with the new necessity for keeping Francie's contact with Jennifer to minimum.

Peter Devlin considered himself a man of the world. But Jamison was one of the very few true aristocrats he had ever known. And Jennifer, his daughter, was clearly the same breed. Though she might not know it, hers was a New York ancestry, with a history of wealth, influence, and, what was even more rare, true distinction of mind. What a pity, he thought, that she would never benefit from the knowledge of her own extraordinary bloodlines. But she did have the Farrells, and they had obviously been decent parents. It was clear now that he had only one more thing to ask. "Jennifer Franciejean is doing very well. Do you mind telling me how you know about her? Know about her breakdown?"

"I work for her. Of course I'd know."

"You work for her?"

"Yes, one day I decided I wanted at last to meet her. So I went to the Barnett Company to get a job. And she hired me. I'm the model in the Star Bird campaign."

Peter gave a jerk. It was almost as if a lash had touched his shoulders. "Francie hired you!"

"Well, it took five months actually for the assignment to be finalized. In that time we knew each other only casually. But the day they did the test commercial, we finally had a hance to talk," she said in a rush. "I mean about her and me. About out being related. I told her I was so glad that we finally knew each other." She hesitated under the weight of her next words. "That was the day she got sick."

The more simply she spoke, the more ironic it sounded to Peter. "Of course." What was there to say. There are some mistakes of chance that only the worst fumblings in the dark could have arranged so well. The child was the accidental innocent trigger. She'd meant Francie no harm. None whatsoever. He tried, out of kindness, to bury the burden of his knowledge; but his young visitor, watching, seemed to guess at his effort. What she herself made of it caused her to break into sobs. "Don't mind, please. I can't help it. It keeps coming over me like this." She was telling him sharply enough of what she was most afraid. "Do you suppose that meeting me . . . somehow caused her breakdown?" Her tears were the eloquent proof of the truth she suspected.

Watching Jennifer sob and the way Barbie Farrell's instinctive tact prohibited her from intrusion, he realized how much he liked both of these women. But Peter knew he had nothing more to say to them. Make-believe politeness was now impossible and straight talk was more impossible still. So he treated Jenny's question as though it needed no answer, and pursued only what he could not avoid asking.

"Jenny, have you tried to see Francie since her breakdown?"

She recognized the significance of his question as plainly as he measured the cost of her answer. "No, not personally. They told me at the office that she was at Payne Whitney. So some days I've waited in the lobby to see if she was being discharged. Other times I'd sit on one of the benches in the Rockefeller Institute Garden where I can see the exit and watch. The doorman in the building here knows me. Because I'd check with him first thing everyday to find out if she was home yet. I said I was her niece."

"How long have you been doing this?"

"Every day for almost six weeks. Even Christmas. Even New Year's." Barbie Farrell offered this fact as though it were a bit too warm and could be held only briefly with the tips of one's fingers.

"In this weather? This snow?" Peter gave the girl an incredulous stare.

"I didn't notice the weather." The effect of her reply was to make Peter see an abyss. All the Jennifers in Christendom were not worth to him the chance of causing Francie one iota of anxiety. He had a sense of negative relief because he knew exactly what he must do. "Jennifer, where do you live?"

"Since I came to New York, I've been staying with a friend in the West Village. Charlton Street."

"Where's your home?"

"We live on Toylesome Lane in Southampton," said Barbie Farrell, who had been taking in Peter's questions and seeing around corners.

"Do you think, Jennifer, that for a while, I could persuade you, for Francie's sake, to return to Southampton? So that for a while there would be no chance of you two meeting unexpectedly."

This was exactly what she'd been afraid of. "I understand," she said.

"Do you think," Barbie Farrell began, "that Jenny—"

"I don't think," said Peter. "I am taking precautions "

It struck Barbie Farrell then that it was a strange world indeed that the Devlins lived in, where precautions had to be taken against someone like Jenny. But she decided it was not her place to say so. What she did say was "Jennifer can live at home for a while if she wants to. We'd love it."

"That sounds very sensible."

"I'll go anywhere in the world if you like. If it will help Francie feel better."

This extravagance prompted in Peter a brief amusement. "Don't go anywhere. Just stay quietly for a while in Southampton, as your mother suggests. Or at any rate stay out of the city. I'll keep in touch and tell you when the quarantine is lifted." He was trying to sound light, the situation demanding that a normal pitch be kept.

"I will then. I'll go back to Southampton tonight. We'll drive back with Dad. Okay, Mom?"

"Yes, darling. Right after the will is read we'll go home."

"You're going to a will reading today?"

"It's something to do with one of my husband's clients. Do you know where 20 Broad Street is?"

It was then that Peter realized what Peter, given his instincts, should have realized much sooner. "You're going to the reading of the Jamison Welsh will?"

"How did you know?"

"There are not that many readings per day of wills in New York. Even with our overpopulation. And certainly not at 20 Broad Street. We've been invited, too."

"Oh! Did you know Mr. Welsh?"

"One of my oldest friends."

"Ah, well, we don't really know him. Socially I mean. I believe I've met him twice. My husband is in real estate in the Hamptons. He's bought large tracts of land for the Welsh bank. Larry thinks perhaps Mr. Welsh left him a few acres. He could be—uhm—well, eccentric, Larry says."

"Unique is more my word." Peter thought of how well Jamie protected his own. From Lawrence Farrell the Welsh bank bought land tracts. Undoubtedly at huge commissions. For the Devlins, the Welsh bank made investments that always multiplied in value.

"Unique. I think that is the right word," Barbie Farrell agreed. "He was unique. Different. And very nice. When he met Jenny he said that if he'd ever married and had a daughter, he would want her to look exactly like Jennifer."

Peter realized that it should have been clear enough years ago, but for his own stupidity, that on the chance that Francie had told the truth, Jamie would have found the baby, would have had continuing progress reports. And once having met her himself, he would have seen what Peter had seen. He'd have known he had a daughter. "Did Mr. Welsh see Jennifer often?"

"No. Twice, I think. Once when she was about five. And then some years ago. He was on his way to his home in East Hampton, and he stopped with us for lunch."

Peter knew his questions might have caused Barbie to guess what he was thinking, tactful as she was, she would hide that guess from him. For once he had to take himself in hand, do violence to his own feelings, to his irrational jealousy of all that Francie and Jamie had shared. It was as though the fact of Jennifer was, to take the vulgar view, a

511

confession of his own liabilities as a husband. His handicap.

"If you're going to the reading and you're concerned about your wife and Jenny meeting, Jenny could wait for u at her father's office in New York." Barbie Farrell had a rich impulse of sympathy. "We'll do whatever you think is bes for Mrs. Devlin."

Peter and Barbie now had a mute exchange, each having something in mind that eventually made a lie of Peter's "handicap." It gave Peter an answer, and he held it close. I explained and vindicated. For after all, was not his very handicap the gift that helped to make their marriage a kind o flawed miracle? Francie was never one meant to be a mother The baby had to be adopted. Jamison had known it. Barbie now guessed it. There had been only one reasonable and decent way to treat someone who had lived in the state Francie lived, and he had treated her in such a way. Jennifer no longer made any difference. Jamie, by his death, was ou of it; as much as Peter was in it. He was alive, and he loved her. It all came down to what he could do for Francie, and this made him remember how intensely she had insisted or going to the reading of the will. He thought of her reasons, but he no longer cared for her reasons. The life they had now was what mattered, and he had no taste for allowing her, ou of indulgence and his own timidity, to bring the house down on her head.

"Mrs. Farrell, you and Jenny go to the reading. I'm meeting Francie in about fifteen minutes at the agency for lunch. We have things to discuss." He saw the look of surprise on the face of both women. "No, we won't be there, dear. It isn't necessary." He got up in his impatience to get on with it. "There's just one thing you can do," he said, looking at Jennifer's frightened young face. "You must not make any contact with Francie. None. Until you hear from me." Then with his instinct for politeness he caught himself and added, "Pardon my sternness, Jenny. I want to be sure we understand each other."

She turned on him the shy, wise regard of a forest creature. "There won't be a peep out of me."

"Good girl."

"I am," she said it with beautiful authority, "A sociological phenomenon. My professors would say so. A prime example of the twenty-first-century extended family. I

ave extraordinary parents. Mothers and fathers galore. And
n extraordinary bloodline. And all class A.''

When Meg arrived at Francie's office, she found that
rancie still had not come in from Kenneth's where she had
opped to have her hair done. But Betsy, Meg's assistant,
as standing at Francie's desk, studying something in an
legant teakwood frame.

"Betsy, what have you there?" Meg asked.

"It's a reproduction of a BBD&O house ad that Mr.
arnett had Bob Hale bring in with him from Chicago. Mr.
ale has a meeting here on Marlboro. I'm to hang it upon
ne of the walls before Francie gets in."

"Why would Abe send Francie a framed BBD&O house
d?" Meg walked the long length of the office to stand beside
etsy. "I never heard of such a thing."

"Well, read it. It's called 'Brown's job.' ''

Meg began to read the ad.

BROWN'S JOB
By Robley Feland

*F.R. Robley Feland, treasurer of BBD&O from 1930 to 1962,
wrote "Brown's Job" in 1920, when he was a copywriter.
"Brown's Job" was printed in The Batten Company house
organ; then called "The Wedge" or "Batten's Wedge"—one of
the oldest house organs in the country, with a broad distribution
outside the agency. It was later reprinted in The New York Times
as a BBD&O corporate advertisement. Both the Wedge and
Times appearances created widespread interest, editorial praise
and requests for reprints. Over the years, "Brown's Job" has
appeared several times as a BBD&O ad. In 1919 it was included
in "The One Hundred Greatest Advertisements."*

Brown is gone, and many men in the trade are wondering who
is going to get Brown's job.

There has been considerable speculation about this. Brown's
job was reputed to be a good job. Brown's former employers,
wise, gray-eyed men, have had to sit still and repress amazement
as they listened to bright, ambitious young men and dignified old
ones seriously apply for Brown's job.

Brown had a big chair and a wide, flat-topped desk covered
with a sheet of glass. Under the glass was a map of the United

States. Brown had a salary of thirty thousand dollars a year. And twice a year Brown made a "trip to the coast" and called on every one of the firm's distributors.

He never tried to sell anything. Brown wasn't exactly in the sales department. He visited with the distributors, called on a few dealers, once in a while made a little talk to a bunch of salesmen. Back at the office he answered most of the important complaints, although Brown's job wasn't to handle complaints.

Brown wasn't in the credit department either, but vital questions of credit usually got to Brown, somehow or other, and Brown would smoke and talk and tell a joke, and untwist his telephone cord and tell the credit manager what to do.

Whenever Mr. Wythe, the impulsive little president, working like a beaver, would pick up a bunch of papers and peer into a particularly messy subject, he had a way of saying, "What does Brown say? What does Brown say? What the hell does Brown say?—Well, why don't you do it, then?"

And that was disposed.

Or when there was a difficulty that required quick action and lots of it, together with tact and lots of that, Mr. Wythe would say, "Brown, you handle that."

And then, one day, the directors met unofficially and decided to fire the superintendent of No. 2 Mill. Brown didn't hear of this until the day after the letter had gone. "What do you think of it, Brown?" asked Mr. Wythe. Brown said, "That's all right. The letter won't be delivered until tomorrow morning, and I'll get him on the wire and have him start east tonight. Then I'll have his stenographer send the letter back here and I'll destroy it before he sees it."

The others agreed, "That's the thing to do."

Brown knew the business he was in. He knew the men he worked with. He had a whole lot of sense, which he apparently used without consciously summoning his judgment to his assistance. He seemed to think good sense.

Brown is gone, and men are now applying for Brown's job. Others are asking who is going to get Brown's job—bright, ambitious young men, dignified older men.

Men who are not the son of Brown's mother, nor the husband of Brown's wife, nor the product of Brown's childhood—men who never suffered Brown's sorrows nor felt his joys, men who never loved the things that Brown loved nor feared the things he feared—are asking for Brown's job.

Don't they know that Brown's chair and his desk, with the map under the glass top, and his pay envelope, are not Brown's job? Don't they know that they might as well apply to the Methodist Church for John Wesley's job?

Brown's former employers know it. Brown's job is where Brown is.

"Oh my!" Meg's voice was shaky.

"Yes," said Betsy, for once subdued. "And Mr. Barnett sent this note with it. Here—"

Meg took the note which was scribbled in Abe Barnett's inimitable, unreadable handwriting on memo pad paper. It read, "Brown—please come back. We can't fill your job."

"Isn't he something?" said Betsy.

"Isn't he."

Francie finally arrived at the agency at lunchtime, and people were straggling out in dribs and drabs despite the blizzard outside. Amanda, the receptionist, greeted her with what looked like eighteen-carat gladness; but still Francie felt awkward when people passing out the doors said "Hi" or "Hello, Francie." It had gone out, of course, that she would be back in the agency that day; and questions about her would inevitably have been passed back and forth like baseball scores in the office pool. She had an instant of private speculation as to the fables and fantasies concerning her that had been circulated. But she had prepared herself for this particular stint, and she said "Hi" and "Hello" back as if the question was "What time is it?"

For they meant no harm. She knew that. And they had also been prepared for this encounter, carefully schooled to make no fuss, take no notice. You'd think she'd been out shooting a commercial in Mexico, or on a vacation in Morocco—not hanging out with psychiatric types on York Avenue. Of course, here and there, one of her favorites would glance at her with shy, lingering warmth and the tip of the iceberg would show in a flicker of concern. The lingering eyes would look her over, seeming to ask in confessed worry "Say—are you okay? Are you?" She had an impulse to reassure them and say, "Hi, Ginny. Smile! I am not Mr. Rochester." Or "Hello, Sam. It's no worse than your hepatitis." But she wasn't quite sure that she was fitting the right name to the right face. So she settled instead for a simple "Hi there." And "Hello."

Approaching her office, she saw the ever vigilant, nosy, incredibly competent Betsy, leaning against the doorsill guarding the entrance. When Betsy spotted Francie, she suddenly turned into a wind-up doll with all parts moving, and rushed toward Francie to hug her in a thoroughly unbusinesslike manner.

"Boy, am I ever glad to see you!"

"I'm glad to be back, too." Francie patted Betsy gently as she extricated herself from the hug. This was why Francie couldn't help liking the brash young conniver. For Betsy knew office etiquette very well. She knew her behavior was out of line. Secretaries do not hug their bosses. Especially when the boss was the President of the New York office of the Barnett Company. And Betsy's major claim to fame was that she was Francie's second assistant. But at the moment Betsy didn't care for protocol. She had reacted out of a simple, spontaneous, human concern; and it was warming to see it in action.

Meg came out of Francie's office where she'd been waiting and gave Betsy a warning look. But Betsy wasn't having any. "I don't trust psychiatrists. My cousin pays a fortune to one and lives in a closet because he can't afford room with a bath. A raincoat. A girl. A goldfish. Anything! Just his shrink. Joining a monastery would be cheaper."

Betsy's tirade made Francie laugh. It was what she needed now: Betsy's hard-nosed view of psychiatry as a purely practical matter, without any note of depths of darkness and fear. Betsy could have been talking about cooking schools. And the cost of cooking lessons.

"Betsy, Francie is delighted that you're delighted," said Meg. "But now we have work to talk about, so why don't you check on traffic schedules? Are we making our deadlines—

hen type me a report." And she moved into Francie's office with Francie, leaving Betsy only temporarily quashed.

"I can't help it—sometimes I would like to take her out and shoot her," Meg said with elaborate casualness. "I did not arrange a welcoming committee, though of course everyone is doing handsprings. But I thought you could use a little reacclimation period."

There was an affection between Meg and Francie that had weathered years of agency politics and hard work, and now Meg was speaking quite sincerely. "I may not wear my heart on my sleeve the way Betsy does, but it's wonderful to have you with us again, Mrs. D. The place hasn't been the same without you."

"No one is indispensable, Meg. Even genius. And fortunately I never set out to be a genius. Competence is hard enough." Francie seated herself at her desk, as if to get the feel of the office again.

"You are indispensable!" shouted Betsy from the door. "Meg, show Francie what Mr. Barnett sent her."

"Betsy's right. I almost forgot. Some people, Mrs. D., are less dispensable than others. Look what Abe sent you." And she pointed to the framed advertisement on the wall that she and Betsy had hung next to one of Francie's TV commercial awards.

"Brown's Job." Francie recognized the advertisement. "What a wonderful piece that is."

"That's what Abe thinks of you. And here's the note he sent with it."

Francie read the note and her eyes misted over.

"See what I mean?" said Meg. "Listen—there've been clashes, conflicts, skirmishes, scuffles and struggles, infighting and out-fighting, dog-fighting on everything that comes up from Schlitz to Revlon to GM. Tempers are lost. Language is strong. There was a brief interchange of blows between Hank Grayson and Art Dubinsky. Decisions are ducked. The buck has nowhere to stop. Tommy is on a rampage, driving people—" She caught herself. "Your country needs you, Franciejean. Tommy already sees himself as your natural successor."

"I have always enjoyed the art of making necessary enemies. How is the Star Bird campaign coming?"

"Two commercials ready to run, but Mr. Dominico has not agreed to buy time. And the print ads aren't finished. You're going to be out this afternoon. But first thing tomorrow we'll do a rundown." Meg was so relieved at Francie's return that she hurried on, forgetting that she'd promised Peter not to tire her. "I have the Star Bird contacts. Phil Roth was the photographer. Want to take a quick peek before Peter comes for you and lunch?"

"Yes, why not?" It was simple enough to say, but the consequence for Francie was that she felt as soon as the words were out that she had put herself in jeopardy.

Meg went to one of the files and took out one of the Star Bird folders. She spread the contacts on the desk for Francie to see.

The world stopped turning then for Franciejean. Space, time, heat, cold, gravity, and the comfort of the five senses lost all meaning. She seemed to be enduring in some gray and empty limbo while a voice came to her from a great way off. A voice singing, but she could not make out the words or the music.

Then slowly she returned to the noontime of this world, and her heart resumed its beating, her blood flowed again through her veins. But she'd completely forgotten the young girl in the contacts. Who was she? For the first few moments she found herself looking at the mysterious young face through a stream of tears. Perhaps it was the blurring that made the face seem so strange, the oddly irregular features; but the chiseled lips, the high forehead, the eyes so familiar—a face exquisite both for silence and laughter. A face she knew intimately—but whose? The question frightened her.

"Francie, are you all right?" Meg was asking.

"Yes, I'm fine. It's the excitement. I'm not quite myself."

"I am sorry. I should have waited until tomorrow."

But Francie didn't understand. Staring at Meg, Francie asked herself, once only, if Meg could conceivably have set a trap for her; and the question was answered on the instant: no. She knew too, in fact, why she and Meg Dodge had always worked so well together and with so much pseudo-intimacy. Because Meg was practically the last person in the world to have any idea of how much Francie was taken up with the unspoken. Meg would never know how Francie felt

518

about anything. And not from a lack of compassion or goodwill, but from a failure of common terms. She was a young woman of health, sanity and strength. She would never in her life be ill as Francie was ill.

"Don't worry about me, Meg. It's just reentry wooziness. But what an eloquent face."

"I like it. It certainly is not the typical model's look. But as I said, Tommy is kicking and screaming all the way about our using her. Though in private soul-searching moments he told me that frankly he finds her beautiful. Can you imagine that? From our Tommy?" Meg thought it quite funny. "But he feels her face is too classy for the masses."

But Francie wasn't listening to Meg. She was listening to a singing within herself, and Meg mistook it for a concentration on the contacts. Now Francie understood the words.

"Lullabye and goodnight with roses delight . . . all tied up with bows, slip under the clothes."

"I'm very glad you showed me the contacts," Francie said matter-of-factly, trying not to reveal her absorption with the singing. "Do you see a resemblance?"

"To whom?"

"I don't know. To somebody." Francie knew as much as she ever would and shook her head thoughtfully, still studying the contacts. "But the likeness is so great."

"She reminds you of somebody?"

"I think so." She heard Meg's questions as a counterpoint to the singing within.

"When the morning shall break, Please the Lord, thou wilt wake. When the morning shall break, Please the Lord, thou wilt wake." The singing stopped. Now there was silence. But Francie's face registered nothing of what had been happening; and she struggled to make contact, to span the distance between herself and Meg. "'Will you do something for me, Meg?"

"Anything, Francie. Ask." Her face lit up for an instant because she had a sense of having somehow failed Francie, and she wanted to make up for it.

"You must lie for me. To Peter. A little lie."

"I'm at your disposal. Big or little lies," said Meg, laughing. "Intrigue is what I was born for. The court of a Louis or a Henry."

"Peter will be here shortly to take me to lunch. Tell him

I've gone to Bergdorf to pick up warmer gloves. He'll squirm and be unsettled, but have him sit down and wait. Then, in about a half hour, when he's really beside himself, come back and tell him I telephoned in; and because I wasn't sure whether he was still waiting, I'd decided to skip lunch and go straight down to 20 Broad. I'll meet him there. He'll understand.'' Meg listened to Francie with affectionate indulgence. "Francie, what are you up to?''

"I am proving to Peter that I am finished with Payne Whitney.''

"I should hope so.'' Meg sounded almost impatient, as if finally she could say what she thought. "What could possibly be wrong with you that isn't wrong with everybody else?'' Meg said it as though it were a challenge. "I lock myself out of my house at least twice a month. I'm insomniac before every important meeting. I forget to take my pill, and I forget the name of the man I'm sleeping with. I even pile up two months of paychecks, and owe the cleaners, the cleaning lady, the laundry, Bendel's, and then they call me from Chicago and say I'm lousing up their bookkeeping, and then I have to deposit all my checks and I feel as if I'd had an abortion. And I'm not the least bit nuts.'' She stumbled over the word *nuts*. "Simply disorganized. Confused. Disoriented. Like you and the world we live in.''

"That's certainly one view.'' Francie seemed to be going over Meg's words in her mind, considering their validity, as one would test a piece of machinery. Then she added with caution, "Less philosophy with Peter, please. And just remember to tell him exactly what I've told you.''

"Word for word. And I promise to give him no maxims to live by.'' Then like a woman handling unfamiliar terms: "You are fine, aren't you?''

"Fine. Just aging too fast.'' Francie looked straight at Meg. "But, Meg, reality—sanity—is the essence of the game. And that brings with it disenchantments. Now if you had a choice, would you not rather have enchantments—be crazy in a world of gorgeous color, than sound as a Swiss franc in a world gone gray?''

"But that's not your choice. With all the color you have in your life?''

"What you see is just ritual war paint.''

"I'll settle. It's a four-color spectacular, coast to coast

520

prime time. You're President of the New York office of
Barnett. And God knows, you might one day be president of
the whole shooting match. And you have this incredibly
gorgeous husband who is also, by the way, rather a household
lord himself, when it comes to households. And he's nuts
about you. Why, good heavens, there's nothing you can't
have.''

Francie reached for and squeezed Meg's hand with
warmth. The younger woman's generous reassurance was
something Francie could lean on for a moment. Then rising
from her chair and picking up her coat, she said quietly, ''All
right, now, remember. Let Peter wait a half hour. Then come
back and tell him I called you, and I've gone downtown to
see the Statue of Liberty. From an office with a great view of
He'll understand. Love and kisses, Meg. Remember me
—to—'' She almost said ''life'' but changed it to ''Tommy.''

It was a particularly cold, bright-break afternoon when
Francie turned onto the Long Island Expressway. A powdery
film of loose snow traveled in wavy lines, pushed by the
wind, filling the air with a fine particled mist. There was no
sky overhead, only a vast ocean of white that was in reality a
mighty army of advancing snowflakes; and over it all, chilling
away the comfort from the lighted windows in houses one
would dimly see through the flakes and muffling the sound of
the few cars on the highway, was the interminable howling of
the northeaster.

But inwardly Franciejean applauded—it was magnificent, fantastic, the greatest show on earth; the world offering
itself up like a sacrifice to the pagan God of the Snows. And
she, Franciejean, was going home at last! To East Hampton,
to Jamie.

It had all been enough. Perhaps too much. She had had
all the things she'd wanted when she was very young. All the
things Momma insisted she have—the gold pendants set with
rubies and sweet water pearls, crystal chandeliers, rock crystal water glasses, a sable—my God! The things she'd had; a
surfeit of splendid doodads. All the thing-a-lings Norman said
she would have—whoever Norman was. And more men than
she could ever count. Or remember. Surely a few would have
married Momma. Not disappeared the way that bastard—

what was his name? Except, of course, for Jamie. Jamie w
hers. Hers alone—not a bit for Momma.

A thousand thoughts and ideas bubbled up inside h
which she wanted to express simultaneously. She was
expert driver; and while she drove, she talked out loud a
laughed. "Seriously," she said to an imaginary listene
"Life is a wonderful madhouse. An asylum run by th
inmates. But not all the inmates know they are inmates.
Then, as if to emphasize her statement, she burst into expl
sive laughter. "Every closet has its very own private skel
ton. But the joke is, all the skeletons are more or less th
same."

The image of Jamie rose before her eyes, and all at on
their separation became unendurable. The necessary slownes
of her driving was a torment, but she knew she must not b
careless. Perhaps she should have telephoned first to tell hi
she was on her way, but that would have spoiled the surprise
And the truth was she was a little shy. Afraid. Not certain y
of her welcome. Would he forgive her? That was the frightenin
question. Would he forgive her after all these years of he
being a fool? Now she could give him a million excuses. An
reasons. The doctors had explained to her how badly she'
been treated as a child. How she'd been raped and abused an
so on and so forth. And that was why she was as she was
But the fact was she was as she was—or had been—an
would he forgive her? The thought that he might not plunge
her, for a moment, into despair.

"Please, darling," she said, "forgive me. I love you."

She was silent now, seeing a still, clear Septembe
afternoon with the wind-tossed equinox ocean, the wild gull
flying and the nesting, old-fashioned mansions on the sea
She saw a young Francie and a far younger Jamie wander
ing barefoot on the beaches, looking for exotic shells an
slipping behind the dunes to make love. 'Take me back
darling," she murmured. "Now I can do it. I'm a complete
human being at last."

The reading of Jamison Welsh's will took place in one o
the smaller conference rooms of the firm. There were only
five people present, including Mr. and Mrs. Farrell, Jennife
Farrell, Vera Busch, Andrew Conway. Only Mr. and Mrs
Peter Devlin were missing. Considering the vast amount o

onies involved, the reading was relatively short, and the tention announced in it concerning Franciejean Devlin and nnifer Farrell was terse, legal, pointed but had something r the spiritual ear that could be heard as a far, faint, ironic ughter.

"I direct that a trust of $50,000,000 be created for the nefit of my friend, Franciejean Devlin. The income of said ust is to be distributed to the beneficiary during her lifetime d the remainder of the principal is to revert to my estate at r death.

"I direct that the balance of my gross estate, presently valuated at $585,000,000 is hereby bequeathed to my daugh- r, Jennifer Farrell, including those moneys currently invested Welsh Brothers, Gardner, on the condition that she ave those monies within said institution as long as Raymond ardiner III, or a direct descendant of same, remains a rincipal partner of the firm.

"I direct that the beneficiary of this bequest, Jennifer arrell, accumulate one half of the income that is distributable nnually and that this portion, plus the principal, be reserved rought her lifetime and distributed at her death to her issue, y grandchild or grandchildren per capita, or their issue. hould Jennifer Farrell die with no issue, this accumulated ncome is to revert to Welsh Brothers, Gardner. It is my rther wish that should Jennifer Farrell contemplate finance s a career, I direct that Raymond Gardiner III shall immedi- tely undertake to employ said Jennifer Farrell in a position ith the Company that will provide her with the necessary aining to enable her to eventually assume a position at the anagement level of the Company."

Where was she? It was 3:30 and there was no sign of er anywhere. Peter stood in the lobby of 20 Broad Street atching the snow grow heavier. He was bearing his nervousness s best he could by chain-smoking—something he disliked in thers and almost never did himself. Jennifer Farrell and her arents had arrived a half hour before. By now the will eading must be over.

Perhaps she was stuck in traffic. Or had gone back to the gency. Perhaps she was still at Bergdorf's. He thought of elephoning the agency and seeing if she'd returned. But he id not want to leave his post in the lobby, lonely sentinel that he was, watching for a beloved stranger. It was odd for him as he stood there with people coming and going, that I sensed that the thing he had most wanted to avoid, "the shock," had in some form come. Yes, something untoward had taken place. Something he had not planned on. He fe again the force of the veto laid on him; that Francie not me Jennifer. But Jennifer was upstairs—and Francie was where

When he had first telephoned Gardiner's office to ask they'd heard from Mrs. Devlin, Lorraine Austin, the execu tive secretary, had told him with a positive inhumanity of politeness that "No, Mrs. Devlin has not arrived and has no telephoned." That was two hours ago, an hour before the reading was scheduled. He'd been in the lobby since. Watching waiting. Where was she?

Walking around the lobby, he tried to domesticate h fear. She was stuck in traffic—the snow—the streets? He sai it over and over. But it was soon no use. His stomach was turning over and his throat stopping up. He could go on waiting there forever on the chance of catching her if sh came; and stopping her too, which would be in itself a prett stiff business. But the fact was, it was no use. This morning when he had received Dr. Ornstein's news, he could still p a face on it; make a pretense at hope, a pretense that ther still might be something to be done. But now he was runnin out of choices—he felt nothing but a sense of failure, los and misery. He was almost ready to accept the fact that sh wasn't coming, would never come.

It was then that he saw her, the slim, gray-haired austere woman in a navy dress, stepping out of the elevator The instant he saw her he knew she had come to find him and he stood still, seeing her survey the lobby. When she sav him, without a beat of hesitation she approached him.

"Hello, Mr. Devlin," she said.

"Hello, Mrs. Austin."

She nodded. "I was sent down to tell you that Mrs Devlin never telephoned."

Peter knew then that this was the verdict, his fate. Fo the rest of his life he was going to be alone. How little, h thought, we know of each other after all. How we let th precious moments slip away. Standing there before him, Mrs Austin gave him a queer, compassionate look, as though sh could read his mind and understood.

"The reading of the will is over," she said as if to waken him. "It will be in the papers tomorrow." Peter stood here, still lost in thought, asking nothing. "Your wife has inherited a great deal of money."

"Has she?" Since he continued to look at Mrs. Austin with a dazed exhaustion, that lady did something quite uncharacteristic. She told him the terms of the will. "Your wife will inherit fifty million dollars."

They stood there looking thoughtfully, even watchfully, at each other, before Peter answered. "That much? Indeed. What a nuisance she'll have trying to spend it."

"She will?" There was a note of chagrin in her voice.

"Of course. But it's impossible to arrange to have full justice for everyone. Meanwhile, should Mrs. Devlin telephone or arrive, please tell her to call me at home. Or better, come home. Thank you, Mrs. Austin, and good night."

When Peter reached home, the bright dusk of the late afternoon was beginning to deepen into evening. The glittering snow on the sidewalks, roofs, and car tops made the February evening brighter than it would normally be. The first thing he did was to go to his study and start telephoning. First he called Francie's office; and when Betsy said in a scared, puzzled voice that she hadn't seen or heard from Francie all afternoon, Peter had her switch him to Meg. Meg said, in an equally frightened tone, the same thing, and then asked hopefully, "What can I do to help?"

"Nothing. But thank you. Now I must make other calls. Good-bye, Meg." He hung up.

The next call was to Payne Whitney. By luck—he was these days scrounging for luck—he caught Dr. Ornstein in her office. "Dr. Ornstein?"

"Something has happened, Mr. Devlin?"

"Francie is missing." He was struggling to keep his composure. "And I know why. Remember my hunch about the trigger. Well, the trigger was waiting for me when I returned to my apartment. The trigger is Jennifer Farrell. Francie's daughter."

"She has a daughter?"

"She never mentioned it?"

"Not a word."

"She had a baby—not mine—years ago. For reasons

525

that must now be obvious to you, she gave the baby up for adoption. To make sure she was provided with, let us say, a more traditional home life."

"Remarkably farsighted."

"Francie is a remarkable woman." Peter's voice was unsteady. "Anyway, this baby, who's been out of our lives for almost twenty years, reappeared about six months ago in Francie's life. Just about the time I started to notice odd behavior in Francie." The words had for him meanings that he had not bargained for. "Francie's had no contact with the child except through her lawyer, who originally gave the baby out for adoption. She'd check him regularly to make sure the baby was fine. She especially wanted to send birthday presents. But still, in her own mind, I know that the baby was always her baby. Not somebody else's growing child. Then, through a series of coincidences that I'm not yet quite clear about, the eighteen-year-old baby found out who her mother was and went looking for Francie. And found her."

"What happened when they met?"

"Nothing. Francie liked her looks. That's a story in itself. And hired her as a model for a TV commercial series. Then in the studio the day Francie collapsed, the baby, now a young woman, told Francie who she was. Her daughter." He paused. "After Jennifer left the studio, Francie cracked up." The facts showed him sharply of what he was most afraid. "This morning, in the agency, I believed something happened that reminded her of Jennifer."

"And she went to flight."

"I think so." He was struggling to keep his composure. "Isn't it a pity that the idea of finding her daughter does not give Francie a reason for staying well?" He hoped the doctor would contradict him.

But she agreed. "It is a pity. But her daughter, as you seem to have correctly guessed, triggered Mrs. Devlin's breakdown. Her existence, I believe, stands in your wife's mind for the failure of her life." He had wanted to understand, and what he was now understanding was no small matter. "What are you doing to find your wife?"

"I called her office. I'll call friends. The police. A private detective."

"I suggest the police and the detective first. I know you

re distressed. You have reason to be." She was keeping her medical detachment, but she was genuinely sorry for the man. "You have to find her quickly. My experience tells me you don't have much time."

"You mean to save her?"

He put the question with such odd simplicity that she answered him as gently as one can answer such things. "I mean to save her. In her state she can no longer be responsible for her own welfare."

"She's taken the wrong turn at the crossroad."

"She's in flight. And that can lead anywhere to anything."

"You sound much less optimistic than this morning."
This morning was years ago.

"I am. I did not realize she was hiding so much anguish."

"Will she ever be able to face the idea of Jennifer?"

"It's too soon to say. But if she can't, she will go from one breakdown to another." So she had led him onto the battlefield. "And they could get progressively worse."

"Isn't there a cure—a drug? I'll spend anything!"

"It's not money that's needed. But time. Hard work. And—" She knew this man longed for his wife's health and would loathe the truth. "And most of all, a deep desire on her part to recover. As of now she seems to have chosen, as you say, 'the wrong turn.' The other road."

"To madness?" He longed for deafness and ignorance.

"Call it what you will. The heart of her life is like a sunken continent. I don't know if she can bear to have it rise." Now she spoke with firmness. "Call the police. Find her. Then, if anything can be done, we'll do it."

"Yes," Peter said and hung up. Then he dropped into his chair, in the soft, dim void of his study; and sitting there thinking, his eye came to rest on a piece of Francie's beige stationery stuck to his cork memo board. It was a note in a mix of Francie's handwriting and something she'd typed on her own typewriter. He knew precisely the look of her typewritten work, where certain letters were lighter than others. To his eyes it was almost as beautiful as her handwriting. He knew, too, without touching or reading the note, what it said. Then he rose, reached out his hand for the paper, sat down again and read:

"Time is not life. For many and many more
Living is mostly for a time not dying
But not for me. . . .
Years are not life
And I have not come so far to learn. . .
What years are for I know. Years are not life,
Years are the empty shells of life,
When they hold only days and days and days . . ."

And then in her own handwriting:

Peter—
Goodbye, my Fancy
Farewell, dear mate, dear love.
I'm going away. I know not where
Or to what fortune, or
Whether I may ever see you again . . .
So goodbye, my Fancy.

Peter was still staring at the note when he heard the doorbell ringing; and in a few minutes Jennifer, pale and grave, came in and sat down. "I didn't telephone, I just came. Where is she? What's happened?"

"I don't know."

"I know I'm being rude," she said, "but she is my mother. My other mother. Anyway Mom and Dad are staying tonight at the Plaza. The road to Southampton is no longer safe to drive. It's the snow. So they said I could come over here and keep you company until we found Francie." She said the words assumptively and calmly, to show him that, though she was not going to pieces, she was deeply concerned and had a right to be.

He rose and put Francie's note in a drawer of his desk. "It's so odd, knowing what's happening—you might as well know we may lose her—to see you sitting here in this place."

Jennifer remained perfectly still. Then she said, "Did I do it?"

"No dear, nobody did it. She's been on the verge for years probably. Let's not play the game of who's to blame."

"Do you wish I hadn't come?"

"Of course. But don't simplify. I am very grateful. Besides me, who else on earth cares as much as you do?" He

ent further still. "Who besides you and me has as much to
se?"

"Have you any idea—"

"What to do? No. I have no idea. I haven't a clue except
call the police. And a detective agency."

Jennifer remained patient and still, but she was thinking
hat else might they do. Peter watched her a moment then
cked up the telephone. "Excuse me while I check the
arage."

When he finished with the garage, he spoke clearly
nough. "Well, she's taken the car and gone somewhere."
o he dialed the police and told them his wife was missing
nd to look for a dark green XJS Jag. When they asked where
look, he considered for a second: "On the Jersey Turnpike
Washington. And around Georgetown." After the police he
lled the detective agency and left a message with his
lephone number.

"Where can she drive to in this weather?" Jenny
emanded. "Dad used to drive racing cars, and he and Mom
re holed up at the Plaza." Then she raised her imagination to
e reach of his own. "But with her, I suppose anything is
ossible."

"Anything—absolutely anything."

"I know it's not new to you, but to me she really is
omething." She meant it. Francie was the biggest impression
f her young life and she hardly knew what to do with it. So
he sat there waiting for Peter to tell her what to do, but he
as lost in his own maze.

With his hands in his pockets, he kept turning to scout
e room and stare out the window at the still-falling snow
nd the peace everywhere that was too heavy a burden for
im who would find peace never again in his life. "Where is
he?"

"What can I do. Please, what can I do?" The words
ame from Jennifer as though from a street beggar, and he
ad to turn and see her to remember she was still there and
leading.

She had her own grief to contend with, and her grief had
ts own laws. "I have to do something to help. Anything."
he visibly perspired at the thought of sitting still and doing
othing. "I have to! And I've a right!"

Peter understood. But he had begun to feel a strange reserve, born out of his talk with Dr. Ornstein, and recognition of the realities in Francie's case. He knew to much now, and there was no going back. What he had to do was abroad on the winds of the world. But he needed to but it out of sight for now, this sinister apple of knowledge. An certainly he must keep it out of Jennifer's sight. So he contented her with irrelevancies.

"All right. Go to 10 East Seventy-fourth Street, the big gray town house near the corner of Fifth, and patrol. Franc might just show up there."

"East Seventy-fourth? Isn't that where my father— mean my other father lived?"

"Yes. I believe the house is closed now. Wait outside But walk up and down. It's cold and snowing. If you start t freeze, go to the Carlyle and order a brandy. Have you money?"

"Oh, sure. I'm an heiress, I was in his will. I've go three dollars."

"Great! What an heiress. Here's twenty. Don't ge drunk."

She left with such a faith, a trust in his goodwill, that he found himself embarrassed at his duplicity. But once she had left he felt a relief. He could sit now with his ciga rette and count the consequences of his own logic. He considered himself a realist; and in many senses he was, for he knew exactly the implications of what the doctor had said But at the core of his nature he knew he hoped too often an too much. In business, he practiced an efficient control; bu where love, where Francie was concerned, it wasn't easy to give up hope for one's love.

He knew the wisdom of those who say cut your losses How often he advised others just that. Don't hope. Don' dream. Come to terms. What if you die a little? Be sane, b calm. There will be other loves. As if words meant anythin to the heart.

But there was no escape. Judging from her disappear ance, her mind refused reality. And should they bring he back, the prognosis was hardly optimistic. It was only matter of time until . . . So, obeying what he saw as he wishes, he had sent the police on a wild-goose chase. Jennife too. And the detective next. He was doing what he had ofte

530

vised others to do, in those days when he had never
pected that his turn would come. But it had come. And he
as cutting both their losses. They'd never find her in time.
d he would go through life with a ghost for company.

He would not die when the news finally came. He had
ed so often already. He knew they would find her where she
d to be—on some road to East Hampton. He had never
lly expected her to find a good enough reason for living
en it meant living in a world without Jamie.

So he sat watching the snow fall, wondering what it was
at Francie saw as she drove. What phantom house or boat or
rden against what phantom sky. He wondered if she'd
ught of him, if she remembered all the years they'd
ared. Anything at all. Perhaps something. Good-bye, my
ncy. . . .

Francie drove slowly and steadily on the white road,
most the only car to be seen for miles, though often enough
e passed empty, stalled and abandoned vehicles. It had
ken her four hours to get as far as Watermill, what with
inding around the back roads, taking detours, and crossing
Northern State when the drifts on the Expressway were too
gh. Even Horse Block Road was preferable to the Express-
ay because the wooded treeline seemed to shelter it from a
leup of snow. Still, the drive had been anything but easy.
ow, glancing in the rearview mirror, she saw the sky behind
r a glittering gray, and the trees lining the road, heavy with
ow on the branches, looking unreal and exquisite. Like
hristmas-card trees. The whole world seemed frozen and
undless, and she wondered if there were still human voices
ywhere in the world to be heard.

It was when she drove past the sign on the right that read
OU ARE ENTERING THE VILLAGE OF EAST HAMPTON, that slowly and
eadily it happened—the landscape began to change. Not the
ad. The road remained covered with snow; but the trees
ong the road, with a gradual insistence, seemed to be
sponding to other laws than those of the calendar of earth.
he winter sky too was turning to a brilliant twilight blue; and
a slow, oncoming way, spreading out from around the car.
came over Francie that the whole world around her was
rning to summer. She had a sense of awe—joy and fear. It
as the quixotic Montauk high that Jamie used to tease her

531

about—the high-pressure wall of air that was his explanati[on]
for why the sun kept on shining in East Hampton wh[en]
it was raining in Quogue, in Fire Island, West Hampto[n]
and New York City. Jamie insisted that East Hampton w[as]
like Avalon, where King Arthur slept, the Isle of the Blesse[d.]
It was a special place with other rules and climates. [Or]
perhaps, and it gave her pain to admit this, this was the Ea[st]
Hampton of once-upon-a-time, the ancient kingdom of h[er]
early years with Jamie; when every action, small or large—
digging for clams, guessing the weather, sailing a boa[t,]
listening to Debussy, going to sleep—was at once optimist[ic]
and forever. With the sound of the sea in their ears, gree[n]
lawns and woodlands about them, they were entirely unawa[re]
of a ruthless fate, of a sadness at the back of life, of their ow[n]
standing in the shadow.

By the time she passed the traffic light and turned in[to]
East Hampton, there were flowers and leaves and summ[er]
everywhere. Except on the road itself, and she knew why th[at]
was. The town council had all gone off to play golf in Pal[m]
Beach, and they could not see what she could see—th[at]
whatever it was anywhere else, it was summer in Ea[st]
Hampton. When she turned off Dunmere to Highway Beyon[d]
the Pond, to follow the road up and around and down th[e]
private dirt road to Jamie's house, she didn't really care wha[t]
was happening. Whatever it was, she didn't have to d[o]
anything about it. It made her happy just to see it, and sh[e]
didn't even care if it was a symptom of something tha[t]
someone said she had.

She drew the car up slowly in front of the house—he[r]
home, the home of Jamison Welsh. Looking at it now, he[r]
eyes glistening with tears, she was relieved to see it wa[s]
unchanged, exactly the same as she remembered it from thos[e]
long years ago. The glow of the setting summer sun washe[d]
the house in a pink and gold, and the shadows here an[d]
there only intensified the colors. She turned the ignition o[ff]
and leaned her head back on the headrest. The cold began t[o]
creep into the car but she ignored it. It had been a long an[d]
arduous drive and she was tired. Very tired. She could see [a]
light on in Jamie's study, and she thought how surprised he'[d]
be to see her. She felt only the immense silence around her, [a]
vague and unusual drowsiness. She thought, in a minute [I]
must get up and get out of the car and knock on the door. Bu[t]

...e needed that minute to collect her thoughts. So she sat ...with eyes half closed, half dreaming. I must go to ...nfession, she thought to herself, in infinite precaution. God ...nows everything already, but I ought to go and spell it out ...xactly. Make a clean breast and so forth. She was breathing ...rough her mouth and her breath was visible. But seeing it ...rough her half-closed eyes, she thought it looked like a ...retty mist; she was so relieved to be home again—home. ...hank God it's done, she thought. I do not have to start my ...fe over again.

A long, single file of minutes went by; and with a great ...eariness, she felt her eyes closing entirely. Then someone ...eemed to sit down next to her and take her hand. She turned ...o the person gratefully, "Why, Momma," she murmured ...oftly. "Have you truly come to see me at last, Momma?" It ...ally was Momma with her bright, gold hair pulled back in a ...not the way Daddy liked to have her wear it, and her face ...orcelain pale and free of cosmetics. "Momma, let's not fight ...nymore," said Francie, half pleading.

"We won't, Francie. Never again. That's what I came to ...ay. To tell you—" And Momma began to cry, and it made a ...arsh and bitter sound. "To tell you, if it helps you to know ..., I carry your hell with me. It's my hell, too."

"Well, it's over now. It's been over for years. Don't cry, ...Momma. In this kind of summer your tears could freeze and ...tick to your cheeks."

"He was a beast—and I knew it."

"You committed a war crime. We were a country under ...iege. Someone had to be sacrificed."

"I threw you to the beasts. To be torn to pieces. Why ...idn't I throw myself!"

"He wouldn't have you, Momma. You certainly tried. I ...on't think you hated me. Did you?" She said this in a quiet, ...nemphatic way that seemed to carry no reproach.

"I did the best I could. I cared for you. But it's not ...nough to care. It doesn't necessarily stop you from hurting ...our children."

"Can daughters hate mothers?"

"Mothers like me—yes."

"I'll think about that." The reign of ruin and disaster ...vhich had seemed so complete now magically allowed for ...ome patches of understanding. "But I guess I don't hate you, I simply don't forgive you. You must have been very frightened. And young."

"Twenty-nine on my last birthday."

"There you are. And I'm forty-two now. Older than you ever were."

"You look about twenty-five, Franciejean. I hope you've had some happiness."

"More than some. Less than others. I've been a victim and a victor." Her next words were wired like a booby trap. "I had a baby, too, Momma. And I decided to spare her my misery. I wanted her to have a chance. So I gave her away."

"You mean I was jealous. I didn't want you to have a chance?"

"It's a complicated subject," she sighed. "Momma, I don't hate you. But I don't forgive you. I have nothing to do with such liberal policies. But you don't have to burn in hell for me. Forgiveness is God's business. And your own. Not mine." She closed her eyes and tears streamed down her cheeks. When her mind cleared and she opened her eyes, Momma had vanished; Jennifer was seated where Momma had been.

"Please come home, Francie, please."

"I am home, dear. This is home."

"Here?"

"Here. I can't come with you, Jenny, because I don't want to. That life is over."

"He's here—Mr. Welsh—Jamie?"

"Of course. Jenny dear. To go back with you, I have to want something. And there's nothing in the world that I want anymore."

"Don't you want to come back for me?"

"Not one bit. And not that I don't love you."

"I know. And I love you. And him." The young girl held up her love, quivering with pain and hope, for Francie to see that it was real and whole. "I don't care anymore that you gave me away—you both had reasons." She understood everything, things Francie would not have credited her with guessing.

"We wanted you to have a future. Whether or not you sang our praises later."

"Now you're giving me away again?"

"Yes, but to your own life. You don't need me."

...as working hard to blink back tears. "Francie— ...e a picture of you and Jamie?"

"There are dozens of him in back issues of *Time*, *wsweek* and so on. And some of me too."

"I mean family pictures."

"Hmmm. There aren't many. But there's a pair you'll like a blue enameled miniature case. In the secret compartment my jewel box. Peter knows where. Peter knows everything. ive him my love." She sighed. "It's where I keep the welry your father gave me. Take it all. It's yours."

"All I want is the miniature case."

"Take everything. I'd like knowing you'll wear it. There e some wonderful pearls. The pictures in the case are very mall. One of Jamie. One of me. A long time ago. But they'll ."

"Thank you."

"You're welcome."

"I love you."

"It's mutual. Say good-bye now. I'm tired. I feel I could eep a week."

So Jennifer swallowed hard to keep her courage up, aned over, kissed Francie on the cheek. "Bye," she said d vanished.

Francie thought she would sit in the car and drowse a w more minutes before going inside to surprise Jamie. She idn't feel a bit cold. Somehow she wasn't afraid anymore of ot being welcome. She remembered the line: "Home is here when you have to go there they have to take you in." he was home. In the last moment of her vision, before she ank into her last sleep, she knew Jamie was waiting to "take er in."

CODA

It was well past midnight and snowing heavily when the bell rang at the Devlin apartment. Maria, who was still wide-awake and anxious, hurried eagerly to the door hoping to see Francie. But it was Jennifer, frozen and bleak-faced. Maria and she exchanged helpless glances, then Maria took Jennifer's parka and nodded in the direction of Peter's study.

Entering the study, it seemed to Jennifer that Peter had not moved from the armchair he'd been sitting in when she left hours ago. He was staring out into the snowy night, staring over the East River, over Queens, looking at something far away.

Jennifer had a moment of mute detachment. She had almost reached twenty, and her most general sense was that the world was different, whether for better or for worse, than her original estimate. It gave her a feeling of wasted time. If she'd known sooner she might have prepared herself to meet it. She spoke softly but with great effort. "Peter?"

He turned and it took him a little while to answer. "Thank you for checking in regularly."

"I didn't want you to worry about me too."

"Thank you."

She said nothing for a moment, occupied as she was with what she must tell him. Finally she said, "I've been wandering around the city weeping."

"It's all right, Jenny. I think you have something to tell me?" He stated it matter-of-factly.

"I've talked with Francie," she said.

Peter took this in slowly. "But not in person?"

"Not in person. But it might as well have been. It was very strange."

"What happened?"

"I was sitting on the steps of Mr. Welsh's—my father's house, waiting in case she might come there, and I guess I started dreaming. With my eyes wide open—dreaming."

"Dreaming what?"

"That Francie and I were talking. Do I sound crazy?"

For this remark Peter had a queer, strained smile. "No, not crazy—poetic. I wish it had happened to me. What did you talk about?"

Her eyes met the inquiry in his, and his pain made her flush. "I begged her to come back with me."

"But she wouldn't."

"No, she wouldn't."

Peter's face held no hope, so Jennifer went on. "She said she was home at last. With my father."

"I understand."

Jennifer took a deep breath, and then continued having to unburden herself completely. "She said I could have the miniature case—the blue enameled one with their pictures in"

This time Peter turned toward Jennifer and looked at her hard. "The blue enameled case?"

"She said it was in her jewelry box. You'd give it to me." The more simply she spoke, the stranger it sounded.

"You dreamed that?"

"I dreamed that. The case is in the secret compartment."

Peter looked away from Jenny and stared out the window. It was then that Peter knew, knew now once and for all, that Francie was dead. He knew she had died as she had lived, in her own way.

"There is such a jewelry box, isn't there?"

"There is."

"It has a secret compartment?"

"It does."

Suddenly Jennifer was weeping with tears as fresh as the first time. "What happened to me, Peter? What was it? Where is she?"

"I don't know what happened, I don't know. The secret compartment contains all the jewelry Jamie gave her. She never wore it again, after we married." His face was draw and unguarded. "But she had many other fine pieces. S had everything she wanted." When he spoke, he saw aga what he had lost. "I'll give you the miniature case. And a the rest."

"I only want the blue case." She had stopped sobbin and a kind of serenity filled her. "Is she gone, Peter?"

"I think so."

"I really want the blue case most of all. Could I have now?"

"I will have everything sent over to you at your parent suite at the Plaza first thing tomorrow morning."

Jennifer took this in and the way he said it told h everything. "I'm so sorry for both of us."

"So am I."

"I'm sorry you don't want to see me anymore."

Peter knew that Jennifer was intelligent. Intelligent enoug not to need indulgence. "If it were simply a question c wanting—it isn't that clear-cut. But I think for now, for bo our sakes—" So Peter acknowledged that it was imperativ that a friendship with Jennifer not develop. "When th official news comes, from wherever it comes, I will telephon you. You can handle it."

"Of course. Don't worry about me."

"I don't. You're her daughter. You're brave enough."

"It must be a family curse."

"It is. There never was anyone like her."

"Like her. Or like him."

"Or like him." For the first time in Peter's life h measured up to his own idea of himself. He said wit unstinted generosity, "You have an extraordinary heritage."

"Thank you."

"And thank you for sharing your dream."

Jennifer took this as he meant it, as a recognition of thei ending. "She meant me to. To share it with you. She sai you understood everything." She turned to go. "She love you, you know." And over her shoulder she said, "Th doorman can get me a cab."

The telephone rang about 9:10 the following morning Peter had been up all night. When he picked up the telephon he knew this was the call he'd been waiting for. "Hello?"

A heavy, brusque voice came over the line. "I'd like to speak to Mr. Peter Devlin."

"This is Peter Devlin."

"This is Sergeant Harris of East Hampton Police. Mr. Devlin, do you own a dark green Jaguar with a license D 7?"

"I do."

"Mr. Devlin, there was an all-point bulletin last night that you reported your wife as missing. Is she still missing?"

"She's still missing."

There was a short silence on the other end of the telephone, then Peter heard the sergeant clear his throat. "Mr. Devlin, we've been clearing the road in East Hampton. This morning one of our snowplows came across your car packed in a private road off Highway Beyond the Pond." The officer paused again.

"Go ahead—please."

The officer swallowed. "I have some sad news to report to you, sir."

"How shall we measure and weigh these lives of ours?
You said once that whatever it is that fills
Life up, and fills it full, it is not time.
You told my story when you said that to me.
But what of yours? Was it enough, Tristam?"
But he only smiled
And pressed her asking hands. "It was enough,"
He said, "and I may tell you more than that,
Perhaps when I am God making new stars
To shine for you to see . . .
It was enough,
And it was all there was."

"Tristam"
—*Edward Arlington Robinson*

THE BEST OF BESTSELLERS FROM WARNER BOOKS

CALIFORNIA GENERATION
by Jacqueline Briskin   (A95-146, $2.75)
They're the CALIFORNIA GENERATION: the kids who go to L.A.'s California High, where the stars come out at night to see and be seen, where life imitates art, where everyone's planning to ride off into the sunset and make every dream come true.

PALOVERDE
by Jacqueline Briskin   (A83-845, $2.95)
The love story of Amelie— the sensitive, ardent, young girl whose uncompromising code of honor leads her to choices that will reverberate for generations, plus the chronicle of a unique city, Los Angeles, wrestling with the power of railroads, discovery of oil, and growing into the fabulous capital of filmdom, makes this one of the most talked about novels of the year.

DAZZLE
by Elinor Klein & Dora Landey   (A93-476, $2.95)
Only one man can make every fantasy come true—entertainers, industrialists, politicians, and society leaders all need Costigan. Costigan, the man with the power of PR, whose past is a mystery, whose present is hidden in hype, and whose future may be out of his own hands. In a few hours, a marriage will end, a love affair begin, a new star will be created, and an old score settled. And Costigan will know whether or not he has won or lost in the gamble of his life.